COURT OF BLOOD AND BINDING

BOOK 1-4

MAGGIE ALABASTER

Cover by Covers by Christian

Interior art by Crooked Sixpence

Edited by Lily Luchesi

Proofread by Nora Hogan

SONG OF SCENT AND MAGIC

COURT OF BLOOD AND BINDING
BOOK 1

D awn came hard and fast.

Too fast. It always does on nights you wish would last forever.

"This is bullshit," I signed to Tyla. All right, not precisely that. The Silent Maiden's hand language didn't include a word for shit. Or bull, really. The literal translation was, 'male cattle feces.' Close enough.

Tyla grinned and signed back her agreement; gestures that loosely meant morning could go and fuck itself.

I started to laugh, but choked it back as one of the priestesses slid past the door on nearly soundless feet.

Geralda stopped to scowl at us. Her disapproving gaze lingered longer on me before she moved on.

When I first arrived in the Temple of the Goddess Breia, in Ebonfalls, I was terrified of her. We all were. For the first year.

After that, we realised her default facial expression was 'recently sucked lemon' and we learned to— Not ignore her, but we weren't as intimidated. Not of her glare anyway. She was quick to use the strap on any maiden if she caught us doing something she disapproved of.

Yes, I felt the sting of the leather often enough.

I pulled a face at Tyla and straightened my white, cotton dress. Not wanting to crumble the fabric by sitting down on my bed, I slipped my feet into white leather sandals and crouched carefully to tighten the straps.

"Do you think they'll let us wear another colour?" Tyla signed. "Once we leave here, I mean."

I straightened my slender silver choker, settling the amethyst pendant which dangled from the front of it, at my throat. The purple gem was the only colour we were allowed. We were never permitted to take it off. *Couldn't* take it off. There was no clasp. No beginning or end. The choker was wide enough to comfortably fit around my neck, but not over my head.

Some of the maidens referred to them as a collar. Others called it a noose.

I looked into the tiny mirror on the wall as I touched my choker with my fingertips. The amethyst winked at me in the light of the candle which burned on top of the dresser.

I turned back to Tyla. Like me, she was dressed from head to toe in white, her own choker around her slender throat. Where I had wheat-gold hair and blue eyes, she had dark hair and brown eyes like melted chocolate. Where my hair was straight, hers curled in soft waves.

"You want to dress all in purple?" I signed teasingly. "Or black?"

She shuddered. "Do I look like a Fae to you?"

I tilted my head this way and that and grinned before I was forced to dance away a couple of steps to avoid her swinging arm, aimed at me.

"You might," I signed. I grinned and held up my hands to ward her off.

"If Geralda knew you said that, she'd make you walk all the way to Haven-moor. After she straps your ass so hard you cry." She picked up a brush and started to tug it through her hair.

I scoffed. I never cried from being strapped. Not even the time she did it in front of the whole temple, including my sister maidens. I didn't want to admit to myself that I enjoyed the way it felt. The pain made me feel alive, aroused. In the hands of one of the priests, one of the younger, handsome ones, the strap was far from a punishment.

Of course, I didn't dare to mention that to anyone, not even Tyla. I didn't want to know what the punishment would be for having those kinds of fucked up thoughts. It was wrong, but I kept it to myself. My personal shame.

"What colour do you want to wear then?" I picked up my own brush and attacked my tangles as best I could.

"I don't know," she admitted. "Something not white and something not black."

Signing awkwardly, with one hand curled around my hairbrush, I replied. "Grey?"

She responded with what I referred to as the maidens' laugh. Soft, low and restrained. That was all the laughter we could manage, as loud as any of us could get. We could cry, but we couldn't cry *out*. Couldn't shout, couldn't scream.

I eyed the amethyst again. I could do those things before the priestesses and a visiting Fae slipped the choker around my neck when I was eight years old. I barely remembered the ceremony, just the years that lurched along following that.

Chosen, they called us. Silent. I couldn't even shout out to my mother that I didn't want to be chosen anymore. I'd cried, but no words came. I had to learn to speak again, but this time with my hands. So I learned, but I chafed against this pretty cage that held us. I pushed all the limits as far as they might go, even if it meant wearing red weals on the backs of my thighs, the palms of my hands, my ass.

I wasn't the only one who wondered if they chose wrong when they picked me.

Tyla snorted. That was a sound we could make, but the priestesses hated when we did it. Apparently it was unbecoming of the chosen, Silent Maidens.

I glanced towards the door, in case Geralda or one of the other priestesses happened past.

"You'd be walking to Havenmoor after having your ass strapped," I signed to Tyla. I pulled my hair into a ponytail and fastened it in place with a leather strap.

"Only if someone heard," she retorted. She carefully braided her hair and tied it up. Her plait was so long, it almost fell to her waist. She tucked a strand of loose hair behind her ear and regarded her reflection. "I think I'd wear blue. It would match the sky."

I turned to the door as a handful of my sister maidens walked past, movements smooth and quiet.

"We'll find out soon enough."

Too soon. I would have liked another few days. Another week. Another year.

"We'll be fine," Tyla signed. "Come on. If we don't hurry up, we'll miss breakfast."

She looked unworried, and in spite of her words, unhurried. She offered me her arm. We stepped out of the room we shared together and followed the other women down the corridor.

The breakfast room was large, but half empty. Several of the younger maidens moved around placing plates of food, crockery and cutlery on the tables. We were all assigned this job once a day for one of the meals. Sometimes we joked we were *chosen* to be servants of the priestesses, because none of them ever had serving duty, or kitchen duty. We couldn't talk, so we couldn't complain.

The truth was, none of us really minded. It gave us something to do between lessons, cleaning the altars and changing the candles. Not to mention kitchen duty was a good opportunity for a prank or two. Most of us had changed out the sugar for salt at least once in our time here. The strapping for that was particularly harsh, but didn't stop any of us from doing it anyway. It was a rite of passage for my sisters and I. Most of us.

We stepped over to the table we shared with six of our sister maidens. The eight of us were chosen, and chokered on the same day. All of us born within months of each other.

"You're late," sharp faced Hycanthe signed. She sat beside Jezalyn, the only one of our sisters who seemed to tolerate her. The gods only knew why. Jezalyn was sweet, if somewhat serious.

Tyla and I exchanged glances and matching rolls of our eyes. Just because we arrived on the same day didn't mean the eight of us were friends. Hycanthe spent the last ten years trying to find ways of getting Tyla and I into trouble. As if we needed help.

"We're not late, you're early," Tyla told her before Hycanthe could report us to one of the priestesses.

To punctuate her words, the breakfast gong rang out once, twice.

Tyla shot Hycanthe a triumphant glance. She would have stuck out her tongue if we weren't in a place where she'd easily be seen.

Hycanthe looked as though she wanted to slap the expression off her face. She wouldn't have, even if we were alone. Hycanthe never put one of her pretty little toes out of line. Not in public, and not so it could be traced back to her.

A couple of younger girls scurried to slip into seats before anyone noticed. Their eyes were wide. I recognised both as new arrivals. Initiates. After breakfast and after the morning's ceremony, they'd be busy with lessons in hand language with the older maidens. That was a job which fell to my group of eight, until today.

Until the girls learned to sign, they'd be as lost and confused as I was in the early days, stumbling through, trying to make sense of it all. Crying themselves to sleep at night and praying to Breia to let them return home. If Breia heard, she didn't give a shit. No maidens were ever sent home. Not alive.

We ate like we did everything else, in silence. The only sounds in the room were the clinking of cutlery and the rattle of plates, and those were brief. No one wanted to be singled out for being noisy.

Hycanthe gave me a dirty look when I snagged the last piece of toast on the plate in front of us. The upside to not being able to talk was not having to hear her bitch about it. If we were alone, she'd respond with a rude gesture. She couldn't do that here and we both knew it. Usually that meant payback later, like her pouring water into my bed. I'd have to keep my eye on her. Today of all days, I didn't need her fucking with me.

The gong sounded once more. We hurried to finish our mouthfuls and wash them down with sweet tea. Only the priestesses were allowed coffee.

I swallowed just before the second gong sounded. Anything not eaten by then, remained uneaten. The priestesses were suckers for a tight routine. They gave not even a centimetre of slack.

On the third gong, we stood, chairs scraping lightly against the worn stone floor.

I caught the eye of Zared, one of the temple's younger priests. He gave me a wink before brushing some of his long brown hair back off his handsome face.

I lost count of the amount of times I teasingly told him to have it cut. I even offered to cut it for him, but for some reason he didn't like the idea. Was it because of my suggestion to use a kitchen knife to do it? The gods only knew why he didn't think that was the perfect solution. My knife skills weren't that bad. Mostly.

6

I cut him a smirk, then looked away and stood nicely, my hands folded in front of me.

Eventually, the priestesses filed out the door. That was our cue to step away from the table and follow. The younger sisters hurried behind us.

The priests were allowed to walk wherever they liked. Probably something about being men and having cocks. If my hair was ever in my face, the priestesses would have shaved it off.

Zared hurried to walk beside me, earning him a nasty look from Hycanthe. I suspected she had a thing for the muscular man, but he'd made it clear he didn't reciprocate. Everyone knew it but her.

"Guess what?" He leaned to speak low near my ear.

I responded with a questioning look. Boys became priests by training with the Temple guards. Or if they were more daring, with the armies of the Fae, who held the land to the east of Fraxius. None of them were subjected to a decade of not being able to talk. It didn't seem fair their fate was chosen by them, not *for* them. Although, plenty of priestesses weren't Silent Maidens before they joined the temple. Only a select few of us were subjected to that.

"I'm coming with you to Havenmoor," he said. He grinned at my slight eye roll at his no doubt deliberate innuendo.

"Why?" I signed.

No priest or priestess was required to learn the Silent Maidens' hand language, but most had at least a passing understanding of it. Zared learnt enough that he could interpret even my more vulgar gestures. Many of which he was only happy to sign back. His particular favourite was, 'fuck you too.'

Needless to say, Geralda wouldn't be impressed if she saw it. While she couldn't have one of the priests strapped, she could inflict some other nasty punishment on him. The toilets always seemed to be in need of cleaning. At worst, she could recommend he be shipped off for more training.

Although, knowing Zared, he'd weasel his way out of anything more than a light reprimand. His pretty hazel eyes, broad chest and biceps that looked ready to burst the seams of his pale, cotton shirt, seemed to be all he needed to keep him out of trouble.

"Because I'd hate for anything bad to happen to you. Trouble likes to find you whenever you're out of my sight."

That earned him a bigger eye roll. If anyone knew where to find trouble, it was him. I knew, because he was only too happy to take me along with him. Always with some excuse like the gods needed me for something. Sometimes I didn't think he took the gods seriously. All right, most of the time.

Truthfully, I wasn't sure I did either. For one thing, I could never work out why Breia needed us to be quiet. It made the temple peaceful, I supposed, but none of the priestesses ever gave us the answer to that question when we inevitably asked. They gave us a cagey as fuck answer about Breia's will and refused to speak about it any further.

Sometimes, in the depths of night, I tried to talk, to hear my own voice. Tried to shout so loud even the choker couldn't stop me.

I never managed a peep. Whatever the goddess' reason was, she was as stubborn as the priestesses.

"You're only going because you're bored," I signed. "You're hoping for some adventure. You should have become a soldier or a guard instead of a priest."

He grinned. "Sorry, I didn't get all of that. Something about me being ridiculously good-looking." We both knew he understood every word I signed. Asshole. He also knew I would have punched him in the arm if we were alone. I might do that the first chance I got.

I grimaced at him and focused on the short walk ahead.

TWO

KHALA

The Temple of Breia in Ebonfalls was old, well over a thousand years. The stone walls, once stark white, were worn smooth and stained various shades of yellow and brown. Inside, the ceilings were so high light from the sconces which hung on the walls didn't reach the top corners, leaving them in shadow.

The Temple itself was enormous. Built for several times the amount of people who occupied it now.

According to one of the older priestesses, the Fae built the structure and some of the surrounding town before they moved out of these lands and left it to us humans. The land to the west was apparently the land of plenty. The Fae milked the east for what it was worth and abandoned it when they were done. Abandoned their cities and temples too.

We stepped from the corridor into the vast inner chamber. Before I could make my way over to stand in the centre of the round room, Zared put a hand on my arm.

"You'll be fine," he whispered. "You're stronger than you know."

I managed a half smile and nod, before he stepped away to join the other dozen or so priests on the stone benches at the back of the room.

The younger maidens sat in front of them, legs tucked neatly under themselves. More than one fingered the choker around her neck, even those who'd worn them for several years.

I wanted to tell them they'd get used to it someday, but I never had. Not completely. I was always aware of its presence against my throat, cutting off words I wanted to speak. It was a prison of sorts, but a comfort at the same time. It joined me to my sisters in a way nothing else ever could.

In front of them, the eight new initiates sat. Every one of them looked terrified and overwhelmed. Tears ran down the cheeks of a couple, but none sobbed out loud. They had more self control than I did at their age.

Geralda and three of the elder priestesses took the centre of the circle. On a signal from Nidua, the oldest amongst them, my sisters and I sank to our knees, as we'd rehearsed a dozen times before. This time, we did it without giggling, or making gestures like we were down there sucking cock. If anything would get us strapped until we bled, it would be doing that on a somber day like this. Breia wouldn't be amused, apparently. Was it our fault the goddess had no sense of humour?

We knelt on the cold stone for what felt like ages, while a handful of newcomers were shown into the inner chamber. We were supposed to keep our gazes on the floor, but I couldn't help glancing up. My breath caught in my throat.

Four men and one woman stood with the senior priestesses. The men all had long hair, tied back off their faces, and swords strapped to their backs. All four were muscular, without being huge, with bodies that looked graceful and powerful.

It was the woman with them who drew my eye.

She was taller than most of the priests. Her petite face was framed with straight, dark blonde hair. Her eyes were shaped like those of a cat, with a predatory look in them. Or was it curiosity?

She was dressed completely in black, a stark contrast to the white of the maidens, or the brown of the priestesses. She tilted her slender, angular chin to sweep her gaze across the room. Her glance settled on me for a moment. She nodded, then turned away.

Her hair covered her ears, but I knew if they didn't, I'd see the tips come to a point.

Fae.

They rarely came here, but they always made me tremble. I vaguely remembered stories my mother used to tell me, before I was chosen for the Temple. They were always along the lines of, 'if you don't behave, the Fae will get you.'

"Are they ready?" The Fae woman's voice was like music, soothing, melodic. A voice to draw in the unwary, to take them to their doom. Fae, according to everyone who dared talk about them, couldn't be trusted. They were only here now, out of necessity.

"They are." Geralda seemed even less pleased to see the Fae than she did to see the rest of us. Was there anyone or anything she did have a high opinion of? Outside the gods, I suspected not.

"Then have them step forward." The Fae woman looked irritated, bordering on bored. Evidently human ceremonies weren't exciting enough for her. Maybe she didn't want to be here, amongst us. Fae rarely bothered, and when they did it was only for occasions like this.

I glanced at Tyla. She wore Geralda's default expression on her face when she looked at the Fae, but in addition to disgust, hers was laced with fear. Fear, I suspected, that ran deeper than her wariness for the Fae.

Geralda glowered like we should have leapt forward immediately, even though she hadn't yet told us to. We practised this ceremony a dozen times. She strenuously and repeatedly impressed upon us that none of us were to move until she gave us the order.

She would never be pleased, no matter what we did.

As we'd rehearsed, Hycanthe rose and moved forward first. Slowly, reluctantly. Her eyes conveyed her nerves, but then she stepped in front of me and all I saw was the back of her head.

I dug my nails into my palms to resist the urge to flinch when the Fae woman stepped around to stand behind her. She was an arm span away from me. Close enough that I could smell her scent. Citrus and honey. Sweet, but slightly cloying at the same time.

I was expecting something malevolent like ash or death.

She turned her face and gave me the barest hint of a glance. Indulgent like a parent. Like someone with the long lifespan of the Fae, looking at someone who was little more than a child in her eyes.

I swallowed and forced myself not to lean away from her.

She looked amused before turning away and placing a hand on the back of Hycanthe's choker. I squinted, but couldn't see her do anything. When she lowered her hand, the choker fell away from Hycanthe's throat.

I squinted harder. What the hells?

Hycanthe caught it in trembling fingers and handed it to one of the priestesses.

Geralda gave Hycanthe a nod. "What is your name, child?"

The Fae woman moved away in time for me to see Hycanthe glance around uncertainly.

She cleared her throat. "Hy... Hycanthe." She seemed surprised at the sound of her own voice.

Geralda nodded again. "You may step aside."

Hycanthe did, her face pale, eyes blinking rapidly. She smelled of anxiety and peonies. One scent sweet, the other contagious.

At a nod from Nidua, I rose and hurried to step into Hycathe's place.

I inhaled the scent of the Fae woman again. Most of the people I knew smelled of everyday things, like strawberries and grass. Zared smelt of leather and sandalwood. Tyla a combination of lavender and rose.

No one else ever smelled like honey. Maybe it was a trap like night flowers. They smelled like perfume, but snapped closed around your fingers if you touched them. Their pollen burned like the hells. Zared dared me to touch one once. I shouldn't have, but the combination of the dare and my own curiosity made me do it anyway. Not even his pretty hazel eyes stopped him from getting into trouble with one of the other priests that day. He'd spent the next month mucking out stables. I spent it wincing every time I sat down. Evidently suffering with a painful finger wasn't punishment enough.

I didn't realise the Fae woman was behind me until her fingers brushed the back of my neck. Her touch felt like a silkfly, its long, furred feet reaching out, deciding where to burrow.

I narrowly managed to avoid jumping out of my skin and dislodging her hand.

Judging by the way she laughed, feather light and low, she noticed.

I swallowed down my slightly tarnished pride and stayed still, my eyes half closed.

The back of my neck tingled slightly. Where she touched me, my skin became warm, almost to the point of discomfort. I wanted to jerk away, but I forced myself to keep still.

The warmth grew to a heat that should have been unpleasant, but the pain actually sent a pulse of arousal right to my pussy. Thank the gods I didn't have a cock. If I did, it would iron hard right now.

Right before I moaned, I felt a click on the back of my neck. The choker dropped open and fell into my hand.

Whatever I was expecting to feel when I was finally free of the silver collar, it wasn't this. A sudden rush of sensation, like a mist cleared from my mind and body. Everything seemed sharper, intense, more in focus.

It lasted for the blink of an eye, before everything went back to normal. The whole world was dull again in comparison. Mundane.

I struggled to keep my hands steady as I handed the choker to Geralda. I took a long, shallow breath and waited for her to ask the same question she'd asked Hycanthe.

"My name is Khala Firneal," I said clearly.

Left tit of Breia, it felt strange to talk after so long. Did I really sound like that?

As I stepped aside to join Hycanthe, I caught Zared's eye. He was grinning as though hearing me talk was somehow hilarious.

I smirked at him. For some reason, that made him grin even more.

Tyla followed right behind me, standing where I just stood. Her lips were pressed in a tight line, so tight, her lips were white. Her eyes tracked the Fae woman as she moved around beside her.

For a solid half a minute, I thought she'd refuse to let the woman touch her. What would happen if she did? She couldn't remain a Silent Maiden forever, and the only way to remove the choker was with Fae magic. That was why they'd come all the way here. To free us from the collars that bound our voices.

Why was another question the priestesses wouldn't answer with anything beyond, "It's the will of Breia."

The goddess was fucked up, if you asked me.

I touched my throat lightly with my fingertips. It felt bare without the choker, naked. Most humans didn't encounter magic in their lifetimes and I had already encountered it twice. Once when the choker was put on there by a different Fae, a man that time, and once today. Was that what caused that flash of clarity? Some kind of residual effect from being touched by magic? If that was the case, I'd never experience a moment like it again. That felt like punishment in itself. To feel something like that and then to know I'd never feel it again.

For a moment so fleeting, it was strangely compelling. Addicting. Like I knew how it felt to be alive, only to have it slip away a moment later.

I blinked in time to see Geralda give Tyla a harsh look. The Fae woman placed her hands on my friend's neck.

This time I saw it. A flash of... Something. Not quite light, heat or mist, but somehow all of those things at once. It was both of no colour and every colour. Like the gods poured a palette of paint into the world and let every shade swirl together.

There was more. A scent of something I couldn't put a name to. Sweeter than flowers or honey, but not cloying. Like a perfume you couldn't bottle, because it was too perfect to sell or even to share.

All of that I got, and more, in one heartbeat. And then it was gone and Tyla was handing her choker to one of the priestesses and stepping over to stand beside me.

I hadn't even heard her speak her name, I was so lost in that moment, that flash of magic.

I watched the other five of my sisters have their chokers removed, each stating their name in turn. Then the chokers were placed around the necks of the newest maidens. Each one looked too big for their eight year old throats. They'd grow into them, eventually.

Not once did I see another flash of magic. Even the smell of the Fae woman seemed to have dulled. I was swamped by the usual smells of the temple: candles, incense and humans. The light was dimmer than usual, the Temple more tired and worn. Every movement seemed slower, monotonous as though time itself had slowed.

Maybe what I saw was nothing more than an illusion, or a daydream. Whatever it was, I wanted to hold onto it. Cling to it, to light a world that seemed darker than it had.

In the corner of my eye, I caught Tyla staring at the Fae woman. The expression on her face was different now. Not fear. She looked lost, bereft. Confused. A mirror image of my own emotions. A quick scan of the faces around us suggested none of my sisters felt what I felt, but somehow Tyla had.

I had no idea what the fuck it meant.

CHAPTER
THREE

KHALA

"This is strange," Tyla whispered.

Her voice started me out of my thoughts. My hand hovered over my leather bag, my fingers curled around the heel of a boot. I dropped it inside and reached for its pair. I placed it carefully beside the first and started to sign a response.

After a moment, I lowered my hands to the top of the bag and sighed.

"Yes." It was strangely uncomfortable to speak out loud. At the ceremony, it seemed easy. Easier. Now it was difficult to put more than one syllable together. Unnecessary, because we could say whatever we wanted to say with our hands.

It was too long between spoken words. Ten years. More than half our lives so far.

She started to say something before she too dropped her hands in frustration.

"It's all right," I signed. Then out loud, "We don't have to...to talk."

She nodded. "We should though. To...practice." She looked like she wanted to say more, to communicate more, but couldn't put her thoughts into spoken words.

My own thoughts were a jumble of confusion. Questions with no answers. With no one we could ask, unless the Fae woman and her contingent were still in the Temple. If they were, what would I say anyway? Would she give me any answers? If she did, what would the price for those answers be? Fae were notorious for not doing anything for free. Hells, so were humans. What price would she put on my curiosity?

"I trust you're ready to depart?" Geralda's voice travelled up the corridor, addressing all eight of us with her brisk tone.

She shattered the moment like newly formed ice. Tyla and I both jumped and hurried to grab the last of our belongings. Like mealtimes, whatever we didn't have ready when the time came to leave would remain behind. Fortunately, our possessions were few, and what we were permitted to take with us, lesser still.

Any dresses still in good condition, we folded and placed inside the dresser drawers. Sandals were left neatly beside it. In return, we were given cream-coloured blouses and dark brown skirts made of thick cotton. Thin socks and leather shoes completed our new outfits. Everything was suitable— Geralda's favourite word—for travel and sent the message that we were no longer Silent Maidens. We weren't priestesses yet either. In Havenmoor, they'd train us. If we were found suitable, we would take our vows with the temple there.

If not... No one ever mentioned what would happen if we weren't found suitable.

We'd discussed, imagined and discarded a thousand theories, but settled on none of them. Some were as simple as the temple handing us over to a suitable husband. Others involved feeding us to mythical creatures, such as dragons, to have as a snack. The reality is, they'd probably put us to work in the kitchen.

"At least it's not white," Tyla signed and tugged on the hem of her blouse. She curled her lip at the dull brown.

I laughed softly and smiled. "You wanted some colour," I said out loud. I cleared my throat. The words felt caught there. I cleared my throat. It would get easier, but for now it was a strain.

Tyla snorted, then clapped a hand over her nose and mouth. She looked toward the door with wide eyes.

If Geralda heard, she ignored it. What time she took to punish Tyla would make us late in our departure. That would be a bigger crime in the priestess' eyes than a mere snort.

I shook my head at Tyla and gripped the leather straps, pulling them to close my bag. I tied them neatly, making sure each end was the same length as the other, and each loop of the bow were equal size. Geralda would take the minute or two extra to make me fix it if it wasn't perfect.

No doubt there was a priestess in the temple at Havenmoor just as particular as Geralda, if not worse. I certainly wouldn't miss her. Some of the older priestesses, who were more moderate in their dealings with us, I might miss. Billia and Lalys, for example. I suspected they wouldn't feel the same way. Tyla and I had a way of, as Zared put it, finding trouble. We weren't the worst for it, but we gave the priestesses a grey hair or two in our decade here.

"Time to go." I took a long, last look around the tiny room we'd shared for so long. It was nothing more than four smooth walls, a small window and a doorway with no door. The only decoration was a triptych of paintings depicting a scene of a place neither of us knew. Trees, a mountain and a lake, with a castle on the far right. Like the temple, it looked Fae made, but it might have been born from the painter's imagination.

I'd asked one of the priestesses about it once, but she had no more answers than I did. Just that the paintings decorated the wall long before she arrived. They would continue to decorate the walls long after we were gone.

"Are you sad?" Tyla's expression was as wistful as mine.

I shrugged and settled the bag higher up my shoulder. "Somewhat." During my first three years here, I'd expected that, when I left, I'd go back to my family. To my mother and father, three older siblings and two younger. I dreamt of the day they'd come for me, and tell me I belonged with them and not with the Temple.

But they never came for me. Not once. I wrote some letters in my basic, childish writing. They never wrote back.

At some point in my fourth year, I stopped waiting and hoping. I don't know when I knew I would never go home, but it happened and that was that.

At some level, this was my final acceptance. I'd go to Havenmoor and take my vows in the temple there. I'd serve the gods by helping to keep the temple clean, and accepting offerings from people wanting more children or better crops, or whatever. If I was lucky, I'd find some ridiculously handsome men, like Zared, that I could fuck in my spare time. Maybe I'd have a baby or two. Fortunately, the temple welcomed that kind of thing. 'More people to serve the gods', or something along those lines.

As if he sensed I was thinking about him, Zared appeared in the doorway. He looked us both up and down and grinned.

"You don't look maidenly any more."

I gave him a rude gesture with my middle finger. "I don't think maidenly is a word."

He put a hand on his chest and reeled backwards mockingly. "She speaks."

I smirked. His powers of observation were on point, as usual.

He stepped inside the room and took hold of the handle of my bag. He pulled me to him and whispered in my ear, a purr in his voice, "I don't know whether or not maidenly is a word, but it hasn't applied to you for quite some time." He slid the strap down my arm, his eyes on mine, like he was undressing me, and stepped back.

With some amusement, I said words I'd never spoken out loud. "No shit."

He laughed at that. "And yet, I can't tempt you." His pretty hazel eyes lingered on mine with more than a hint of irritation.

He could definitely tempt me. That was half the problem.

"We're friends," I reminded him, signing again out of habit. "I don't want to ruin that."

"It may not ruin anything." The sides of his mouth drew back, frustrated with my stubbornness. I didn't need a seer to tell what he was thinking. At a word from me, he'd hike up my skirt, push me against the wall and slam his cock into me.

And then, everything would change. Whether he agreed with that or not, it would. He'd want more than a fuck. He'd want a relationship and I wasn't ready to have that. Not with him, or anyone else. Until now I'd been careful not to screw anyone who wasn't just in it for fun. I wasn't going to change that now. Not for him.

"There's always Hycanthe," I teased.

He grimaced, clearly not wanting to show too many signs he was pissed off. "I have some pride left. Not much, but enough."

I patted his arm, walked past him and out the door. His heated gaze and the scent of warm leather followed me. The three of us moved quickly down the corridor toward the front of the temple, my footsteps hurried by both the desire not to be late and the need to change the subject. I was sympathetic to Zared's damaged ego, but too much sympathy was a dangerous thing. Enough of it and I'd give in to him, against my better judgement. As it was, I spent enough of my time daydreaming about how it would feel if I did. His hands, his mouth, his cock.

Yes, I was tempted all right, but that was as far as it could go.

We stepped out to the front terrace of the temple and down the stairs in the unseasonably warm, autumn afternoon. A chill should linger in the air by now. Crackling fires and crisp apples. Not humidity, sticky air and sweat. I overheard the priestesses whispering about it once, but no one had any answers to that either. None they'd share with us maidens anyway. Now we weren't even that, we were less likely to get any answers if there were any.

"The Fae," Tyla whispered. Her brown eyed gaze was locked across the courtyard on a wide carriage. Black with gold accents around the doors and windows, and on the wheels. Four black horses were harnessed in front of it, each waiting patiently in spite of the sun.

The Fae woman stood in front of the carriage, talking to one of her entourage. As tall as she was, he was taller still, as imposing as the sword strapped to his back. He stepped over to open the door of the carriage for the woman, his movements lithe like a cat. A large cat.

She nodded her thanks and took the two steps up into the carriage. Before she slipped inside, she turned. Her eyes met mine. Something passed between us, I had no idea what. She was trying to tell me something, perhaps. Whether it was a warning or an acknowledgment, I couldn't tell.

She nodded slightly then disappeared inside.

I realised both Zared and Tyla were staring at me, and I managed to tear my gaze away from the carriage.

They didn't ask, which was just as well because I had no answers for them. No explanation for her interest in me. It could be nothing more than curiosity on her part. She might not see humans often, and I stared every time I saw her. Or maybe she smelled the fear of her on me, the way I smelled the scent of her.

Either way, I wasn't disappointed when the other Fae climbed into the carriage, and one at the front to grab the reins. On some unseen signal, the horses started to trot out of the courtyard and away from the Temple.

CHAPTER

FOUR

KHALA

"I felt like they should have flown or something," Zared said thoughtfully. "Maybe ridden on the back of a dragon. Horses are so mundane."

"If you think horses are mundane, then you are welcome to walk to Havenmoor," Geralda said as she slid past. She gave him an accusing look over her shoulder before making her way to our, much more average looking carriages.

"Horses are amazing," he called out after her back.

I choked down a laugh at the expression on his face.

"Maybe you shouldn't antagonise her," I signed.

"But antagonising her is so much fun." He grinned.

"I hear walking is good for you," I said out loud.

"I'll walk if you walk with me." He gave me a meaningful look like somehow he could get me to change my mind while we walked. Or better yet, talk me into sneaking off into the bushes on the side of the road so he could bury himself balls deep in my pussy.

"I'm not walking. Go ahead if you want to," I said tersely before grabbing my bag from him and making my way to the second carriage.

"She's been talking for an hour and she's already mastered the art of snark." He caught up to me and gave another one of the priests a dirty look, as though pissed off he was too close to me.

I gave him a dirty look of my own. We were friends, there was no need for him to be possessive. If he was going to start that bullshit, he could stay the fuck away from me. If I told him that, he'd keep away for half a day at most. He was nothing if not determined.

Because I knew it would piss him off, I smiled at that same priest and accepted his hand to help me up into the carriage. I smiled as Zared growled in annoyance behind me.

My smile faded when I realised Hycanthe was already inside the carriage. Her and Jezalyn.

Hycanthe looked as happy to see me as I was to see her. Jezalyn offered a small, awkward smile. Clearly she had no desire to get caught in the middle of anything between Hycanthe and me.

I slipped into the seat opposite them. Tyla slipped in beside me.

Zared climbed up behind her and stood, obviously trying to decide if he should sit beside Tyla or Jezalyn. With a grunt, he flopped down next to Jezalyn, but his eyes were on me.

Hycanthe whispered something to Jezalyn, who shook her head. Judging by the venomous look Hycanthe gave her friend, Jezalyn refused to swap seats so Hycanthe could sit beside Zared.

They reminded me of a pair of eight-year-old maidens.

I exchanged glances and eye rolls with Tyla. Evidently she was thinking the same thing. We were all grown women. It was past time to act like it. Not to mention the simple fact that if we wanted to take vows as priestesses, we were expected to behave like the voices of the gods, not children.

Although, from what we learned in class, many of the gods didn't behave much better than children anyway. Even the oldest legends were full of pranks pulled on one god by another.

The story of Haldor and Jyrisse was a particular favourite of mine. Apparently Haldor was in love with Jyrisse, but she didn't reciprocate. The goddess of fertility, fell in love with a river god. Haldor, as the god of earth and farming, built a dam across the river, so Jyrisse couldn't reach her lover. Jyrisse, pregnant with the river god's child, was desperate to get back to him.

She made her worshippers build a temple to Haldor. When he stepped inside, there was no floor, just a deep, deep pit. When he fell into it, Jyrisse and her followers collapsed the temple and the walls of the pit on top of him.

By the time he got himself out, she'd made her way across the river to her lover and they got married. Not even an infatuated god would get in the way of their love.

Of course, Haldor being a possessive, vengeful asshole, sent an earthquake to try to swallow them both, but the river god made the river rise high enough that they could get on a boat and ride out the tremors. Thousands of people drowned, or were killed in the quake.

The moral of the story, don't piss off the gods. According to the priestesses, that very quake created a lake between Ebonfalls and Havenmoor. We'd likely pass it on the way.

I peered out the window as the carriage started to roll through the courtyard and out under the stone arches.

Like everything else here, the archway was twice the size necessary for us to comfortably pass underneath it. Made of some kind of white stone that seemed to absorb light, rather than reflect it, every centimetre had leaves and vines carved into it. It was easily the most ornate part of the temple.

Anyone arriving got a good, if incorrect, impression of the place. When they left, they'd remember how drab the temple really was. More drab now clouds had rolled in above us, threatening an afternoon rain shower. Those were more common lately too. Almost daily. The persistent heat would have turned everything brown, but the rain kept it green.

"Well, isn't this exciting?" Hycanthe said, her tone much drier than the air. "Released from our duties as maidens, finally ready for our next step into the world. For those of us who are *truly* ready."

I turned my face to look at her. Her voice was exactly as I imagined. Clipped and imperious as Geralda.

"Yes, it's huge," I said simply. It was, but I could think of nothing else to say.

Before I could look away she sniffed and said, "If you're going to be that way the whole time—"

"I'll be however I want," I signed, once again falling back on the habit. "If you don't like it, there's the door." I gestured towards it. As if to punctuate my words, a peal of thunder rumbled outside.

I lifted my chin in challenge.

She sniffed and turned away.

Predictably, Zared grinned. He looked as though he might say something to Hycanthe, but for once, he didn't. The journey would be long enough without everyone snarking at each other. With any luck, we could swap carriages in the morning.

I turned to Tyla, whose eyes were on the window, her face paler than usual. "You okay?" I whispered.

She blinked as though surprised to have anyone speak to her.

"I suppose so," she agreed. "Just..."

"It's a big deal," I said softly. I ignored a huff of annoyance from the other side of the carriage. Speaking in whispers, it was the first time in years we could communicate in front of other people and not have them know what we were saying. I'd have to remind myself to talk more often. Whatever was said between Tyla and I should stay between us. It was no business of anyone else.

"The temple was home for ten years."

"And now it's not," Tyla said.

"No it's not, and it can't be. They need to make room for more maidens." That much was made clear to us from the beginning. The temple existed for the training of the Silent Maidens. To ready us for further training as priestesses. Someday, maybe, we'd be sent back, but not today. Today, it wasn't our home anymore.

"I know," Tyla said sadly. "Like you said this morning, this is bullshit. But we'll be all right."

I smiled at her choice of words. "Yes we will, because we're going together."

"With me," Zared said. Evidently he'd been listening in, but now felt left out of the conversation.

"Why *are* you coming?" Hycanthe asked him.

He raised an eyebrow at her turn of phrase, but she simply looked back at him as though expecting a sensible answer. She clearly didn't know him very well if that was her expectation. Sometimes he gave sensible answers, often not. He liked to remind everyone his favourite god was the god of jokesters.

"I'm *coming*," he said, deliberately emphasising the word, "because I don't want Khala to *come* without me. After all, where's the fun in that?"

Hycanthe looked disgusted.

I smiled sweetly and signed, "It's lots of fun. And a good way to stop being uptight." That last was clearly for Hycanthe.

She gave me a condescending look. "You know, you have to learn to talk properly. In Havenmoor, no one will understand your hand talk."

"Except all the priestesses and priestesses in training who were Silent Maidens before us," I signed. Out loud, I said, "I'm reasonably sure most people understand this." I made a rude gesture at her with two fingers.

"You're so revolting," she snarled. "There's no way you'll ever be a priestess. If they could have kicked you out of the temple before today, they would have. Do you think the priestesses didn't notice you sneaking around, spreading your legs for all the priests and guards you could find?"

"Not all of them," Zared said, his good humour gone.

Hycanthe rolled her eyes at him. "I would suggest you're the only discerning man left, but I've seen your calf eyes at her. No doubt your turn will come soon enough." She clearly meant that as an insult.

In typical Zared fashion, he chose not to take it that way. He let out a gusty sigh. "A man can hope."

If the look she gave him a moment earlier was disgusted, it was nothing to the one she gave him now. This was nothing short of revolted. With an unhealthy dose of disappointment and a dash of horror.

I steepled my fingers and put them to my lips. "I liked her better when she couldn't talk."

Both Zared and Tyla choked on laughs. Even Jezalyn looked amused, maybe even apologetic for her friend.

As for Hycanthe, she looked like she was ready to scratch my eyes out. For someone who seemed to think slut shaming was acceptable, she had thin skin. If she kept that up, she wasn't going to make herself any friends in Havenmoor.

I leaned forward towards her. "I don't know what your problem with me is exactly, and honestly, I don't care. There's nothing wrong with what I choose to do in my private time. I suggest you use yours to do something other than gossip or spy on me."

I narrowed my eyes at her. The inability to talk meant we'd had to create a new arsenal to communicate with. That included a whole lot of meaningful, cold or irritated facial expressions. She got the full brunt of all three right now.

She spluttered at the suggestion she might have watched me with any of the men I'd fucked, but she fell quiet. That was fortunate, because I was about done with talking out loud for a while. My throat was dry after only a bit of it. How people talked all day, I didn't know.

I lowered my hands to my lap. Tyla placed one of hers over them and squeezed lightly.

I gave her a soft smile. I saw my tired, anxious face reflected in her eyes. Evidently I hadn't covered it as well as I thought I had. On the other hand, no one knew me better than she did. And no one knew her better than me. No one but us would ever know the way we'd huddled together on one of our beds, comforting each other after a nightmare, or a particularly bad bout of home-sickness. Eight-year-old Khala and Tyla had no one but each other. I thanked the gods every day for her. I barely remembered my actual siblings, so she was the closest thing I had to a sister. To family.

I dreaded the day the temple would finally separate us and send us to different places. I knew that day would come, but I would never, ever be ready for it. Especially if the gods were particularly cruel and sent me to the same place as Hycanthe.

I shouldn't think that too loudly, I never knew when the god of jokesters was listening, waiting for an opportunity to screw with one of us. He was known for having a particularly wicked, sometimes cruel sense of humour. I did my best to stay the hells out of his path.

Thunder rolled again. A flash of lightning bolted across the sky. The rain started slowly but quickly turned heavy, drumming hard on the roof of the carriage.

It was so loud, I almost missed the sound of the first shout.

CHAPTER
FIVE
RYZE

I dashed the rain off my face with a sweep of my hand. Each movement slow and deliberate, I stepped forward through the trees. Senses all open, on alert.

The downpour slowed our progress, but did the same for those we hunted.

"Fucking rain," Vayne growled. "This idea was bullshit."

"It's necessary." I glanced back over my shoulder to see Tavian, his face tilted back, mouth open trying to catch raindrops.

Vayne gave him a dirty look, but he saved the dirtiest for me.

"Your objection is noted, now shut up or I'll put an arrow in you myself." I made no move towards my bow. On some level, Vayne was right. This whole venture might ultimately prove fruitless. Still, it was necessary. Vital.

"We should have gone straight to the Temple," Vayne grumbled.

He fell silent when I shot him another look. I'd make good on my threat if I had to. I wouldn't let anyone jeopardise this.

Tavian stepped carefully over the slick leaf matter that made up the forest floor. He put a hand on my arm and spoke only loud enough to be heard over the rain.

"We both support you in this. We know what's at stake. But if you need to put an arrow in Vayne, can I do it?"

"You first," Vayne growled. He slid past us through the trees and toward the road.

I shook my head at Tavian and followed Vayne. We were close, I could smell it. Horses, and people. Fear and blood. None of it was spilled, not yet.

I stepped past Vayne and moved silently until the trees thinned. I dropped to a crouch.

Keeping low, I moved forward, winding through the trees like a snake. Eyes always forward, but flicking this way and that.

Finally, I spotted the road, the carriages.

I sat back on my haunches, watching and assessing.

The carriages were simple, but the smell of humans from inside was strong. So strong I almost missed it. Almost rose and stepped out from amongst the trees. At the last second, I caught the flicker of movement, the scent of something different. Citrus and honey.

Dalyth slid out of the trees on the other side of the road, her usual escort on her heels. Then a dozen more. All Fae. All armed to the teeth.

She put up a hand to stop the lead carriage. The sound of drawn swords and bows was louder than the rain.

"We're too fucking late," Vayne snarled in my ear.

"Not yet." I reached for the hilt of the knife I kept in my boot, but didn't pull it.

One of the priests who travelled in the first caravan stepped out onto the muddy road. In moments, his clothes were wet through, dark brown becoming almost black, slick with water.

"What do you want?" he called out. "We have nothing of value. We're merely a caravan of humans travelling to Havenmoor."

Dalyth walked towards him, a smile on her lips. In spite of the mud, her movements were graceful, feline, predatory. She might have been walking across the tiled floor in the palace of the Court of Summer.

"You very much have something of value to us. The former Silent Maidens. I've decided your escort isn't adequate. We'll be taking them from here."

The priest looked disbelieving. Fearful but defiant.

"The hells you are. It's my responsibility to get them—" He took half a step toward Dalyth.

She nodded.

Without hesitation, one of her Fae raised his bow. The arrow struck the priest in the eye. He fell to the road with a squelch of mud and a spray of brown water that quickly turned red.

The remaining half-dozen priests pulled their own swords and bows. They arrayed themselves around the carriages. One of them shouted for the women to stay inside. The second arrow caught him in the throat.

One of the women screamed.

Vayne grunted at the sound.

I struggled to hold back my own wince. Why did human women have to be so shrill? Personally, I would have preferred them with their chokers still on. All of them, not just the Silent Maidens. The men too. Humans rarely had much of interest to say anyway.

One of the priests had the nerve to take aim at Dalyth, but he got an arrow through the forehead for his troubles.

Evidently she was done being patient. She waved them forward, then stood with her arms crossed, watching as the Fae men slaughtered the human priests.

Movement to the west caught my eye. The second carriage had stopped somewhat behind the first.

The door opened slowly and a priest slipped out. The gesture he made was clear. Stay here. He made it three or four steps before a woman followed him out.

Her straight, blonde hair plastered to her face within a moment or two. Her light coloured blouse clung to her, almost transparent over her curves and breasts. Her nipples hardened into points, which made me stare in spite of myself.

She's a fucking human, I reminded myself.

Even in the rain, the scent of her was so much more than that. The scent of several of the women, the former Silent Maidens, was more than just human, but this one most of all.

She gestured something to the priest with hand language too quick for me to follow. The gist was clear enough. *Let's get the hells out of here.*

He glanced into the carriage, then gestured for those still inside to follow.

One of Dalyth's men spotted them and gave a shout.

The priest grabbed the woman's hand and dragged her toward the trees.

"Tyla!" She cried out, but Dalyth's Fae hacked through the last of the priests standing in front of them and started toward the second carriage at a run.

"Come on, Khala." The priest pulled her harder, eyes wide and frantic.

Their pursuers slowed. One took aim at the priest.

Against my better judgement, I pulled my own bow and landed an arrow in the side of the Fae's head. His companion looked towards me and got one right between the eyes.

"And that's why you should practice shooting while you run," Tavian said to their corpses.

"What the fuck did you do that for?" Vayne growled at me.

"Shits and giggles." I put my bow back and pulled out my knife in time to throw it at a third Fae. It struck him in the chest.

Vayne grumbled something and pulled out his sword.

I rose as the priest and the woman disappeared into the trees maybe twenty metres from us. "Let's go."

Vayne scowled. "You're going to leave the rest of them?" He jerked his head towards the carriages and the remaining sisters.

"We're outnumbered," I pointed out. "We'll go after that one. We might not need more than her."

Without waiting to see if they followed my orders, I turned and stepped back into the trees.

"Be on alert for pursuit," I said to Tavian. "If you see anyone who isn't a former maiden, kill them."

"Anyone who isn't us too," Vayne said with a grunt.

Tavian flashed a grin at him as though he really needed the clarification.

I left them to glare at each other and opened my senses to the scent of honeysuckle. It was up ahead, moving rapidly through the trees, accompanied by the scent of leather and wet human. Conflicting odours at best.

A shout behind us was cut short. I didn't need to look back to know Tavian dealt with them. He was odd at best, but he followed the orders he liked, and he liked this one. Killing. Especially Fae from a rival court. It was what made him such a good Master of Assassins. And an assassin himself, when the mood took him.

"They have to be close," Vayne said. "The stink of human is strong. The woman too."

For some inexplicable reason, I was glad he added that. She wasn't just a human. She might be the key we needed...

I forced the thought away. Right now, my focus had to be on finding her and getting her away from here before Dalyth found her. The sense of her was strong. Dalyth would want her, beyond all doubt. She'd want all of them.

Too fucking bad, she wasn't getting this one. Not until I knew.

I slowed and gestured for Vayne and Tavian to do the same. I searched with eyes and ears. They were near. Very near. The canopy here was so thick the sun wouldn't have penetrated if it was shining. In the rain, it was all shadows and gloom. The downpour washed away scents soon after they were captured by the air. The heavier the rain, the harder it was to pin them down.

There.

Movement at the base of a large fern. A plant that couldn't, shouldn't grow here. The rain and the heat was encouraging things to appear in the wrong places. The groundcover should be thin, the trees bare of leaves. The air should be dry. If things were normal, we would have found them in moments.

Nothing was normal. It hadn't been for a long, long time.

"I know you're there." I forced myself to sound bored. I was anything but. If we didn't get out of here soon, Dalyth would find us. She wouldn't hesitate to kill any of us. Wouldn't care who I was.

I wasn't surprised to see it was the priest who rose, half his body obscured by the fern. He held out a sword like he knew how to use it. He was a head, perhaps a head and a half shorter than me. His reach was less than mine. If we fought with swords, he'd be lucky to last a minute or two. And I had a bow.

"What do you want?" Neither his hands nor his voice trembled.

I gave him credit for facing us down. Three Fae men, considerably bigger and better trained than him.

"Can I kill him, Ryze?" Tavian asked eagerly.

"Not yet, Tave," I said over my shoulder. To the priest I said, "What's your name?"

He hesitated. "If I tell you my name, you might use it against me."

Vayne snorted derisively. "Are they still spreading that shit about us?"

"So it would seem," I said. "We're not going to use anything against you.

We want to know how to address you. I'm Ryze. This is Vayne and Tavian. We call him Tave."

"Zared," the priest said eventually, reluctantly. He glanced down.

If I hadn't already guessed the maiden was there, the glance gave her away. When Zared looked back up, he realised his mistake. His face paled.

"What do you want?" he asked again.

"We want to get the two of you away from Dalyth," I said simply. There was no point continuing to pretend. We'd wasted enough time as it was.

"Khala." Was that what Zared called her? "Khala, you can come out. If you don't, I'm coming in after you."

"You can't have her," Zared snarled. "Stay down."

She stood, a vision of plastered cotton and hair, curves and hardened nipples. And defiance.

My treacherous cock twitched in response to her.

She's a human, I reminded myself again. A fucking gorgeous one, Haldor help me.

She raised her hands to sign but stopped, her hands out in front of her. "That Fae woman is Dalyth?"

"The one and only," I said wryly.

"What does she want with my sisters?" Her eyes flicked back the way we'd all come, towards the road.

"It's a long story." I shook my head. "We don't have time."

"What did she want?" Khala insisted. "My sisters are supposed to go to Havenmoor."

Figured that not only was she a human, she was a particularly stubborn specimen.

"Dalyth won't be taking them to Havenmoor," I said simply. "And you won't be going either. For your safety. We can protect you, but you have to come with us."

"One of my sisters, Tyla—"

I shook my head again. "There's nothing we can do for her now."

"But I can't just—" she started to argue.

"We're outnumbered," I said coldly. "If we go after them now, we're all dead. We need to plan and gather more of my men. Dalyth has no intention of killing them." What she did might be far worse than that.

I was done arguing. "Let's go." I nodded in a westerly direction.

"You're not taking her." Zared stepped out from behind the fern, the sword still firmly held in his grip.

"I can assure you, we're doing exactly that," I told him coldly. "I strongly advise you against trying to stop us." If he thought we'd hesitate to kill him, he'd have to think again. We needed her, not him. It might be better if we dispensed with him and got it over with. I suspected that would make Khala more difficult to handle. With humans, you had to tread carefully.

28

"I'll go," she said quickly. "But only if you promise not to kill him. And that as soon as we can, we'll go after Tyla."

"This is not a negotiation, human," Vayne growled.

I raised my hand to silence him.

"Deal, on the condition you do what I say, when I say. If you don't, you'll end up dead, and I can't guarantee it will be Dalyth doing the killing."

In the corner of my eye, I saw Tavian rubbing his hands together. Subtle, very subtle.

Khala lifted her chin. "Fine. Are we going to stand here all day?"

Tavian laughed.

I ignored him, along with her suggestion that we were the ones causing the delay. I gave her an ironic bow and gestured in the direction I needed her to go.

"After you, my lady." I smiled sarcastically.

She narrowed her eyes at me, but finally started moving the way I'd gestured. Thank the gods. I was just about to throw her over my shoulder and carry her. It would serve her right if I did.

Zared hesitated for a moment longer, then put away his sword and hurried to walk beside her. His hand found her back in a gesture that was as possessive as it was pointless.

If he thought he could stop us from taking her, he'd find himself feeding beetles on the forest floor.

CHAPTER
SIX
RYZE

"Since when do Fae fight other Fae?" Khala asked after I caught up. She didn't seem scared of me, just nervous. That alone made her different from other humans. Most of them were terrified of the sight of me and my men. As they should be. So why wasn't she scared?

"You don't know much about us, do you?" I asked flatly. "Allow me to dispel a myth or two. We have no use for your names, outside being cordial. We don't sacrifice humans to the gods. And we don't eat humans." After a moment I added, "Without their consent."

That earned me a look of surprise and appraisal. Yes, she was definitely not scared of me. I was going to have to work harder at that.

"So fighting other Fae is normal for you?" Her words were dangerously close to an accusation.

"It's not something I prefer to do," I said. "But if the situation calls for it, I'll do whatever is necessary. Currently, the situation calls for us to be quiet." Dalyth had probably recalled her men by now, and readied the carriages to move on, away from Havenmoor. It didn't hurt to put a bit of fear in Khala and Zared, if only to ensure their obedience.

I got that for a few minutes at least, until Khala broke it.

"Where are we going? Back to Ebonfalls?"

"Definitely not," I said. "It's not safe there for you."

She seemed to be thinking about that for a moment. "Is it safe for any of my sisters? The younger ones, who are still Silent Maidens."

"For now." I managed to sound reassuring even though it was a flat out lie. There was nothing I could do for the rest of them. Not today. As it was, we'd only come this far east for information. Once we learned the Temple was moving the maidens today, we had to act. If there was anything I hated, it was being taken by surprise. Clearly the information that they wouldn't be moved for another month was spurious. When I found out who passed that on, their head would adorn my city gates. It was too long since any decorated them.

"Where are you taking us?" Zared asked insistently. He looked very much like if he didn't like the answer, he'd refuse to go.

I silently dared him to try. He was more than welcome to return to the caravan. Dalyth might even let him explain who he was before she had him executed. She did like playing with her toys.

"Somewhere safe," was all I said.

He looked like he might argue, but Khala signed something to him with her hands. It must have been a request for him to keep the peace, because he became silent after that. Thank the gods. Another word out of his mouth and I might have reminded him we didn't need him to have a tongue.

I dropped back to where Tavian scouted behind us. "Any sign of anyone following?"

"There is one, maybe two," he said after a moment. "They're doing a crap job of keeping quiet."

I regarded him for a moment, then sighed.

"Everyone stop," I ordered wearily. "Get into the bushes."

Khala looked confused and, for the first time, scared. Miraculously, she didn't stop to argue when Vayne pulled back branches and waved her forwards. She and Zared ducked down. Vayne followed.

Tavian and I both dropped to a crouch, knives in hand.

There, I could smell them. Up ahead. They must have gotten around us while we were talking. If I could smell them, then they could smell us. Them and the two behind. They were moving through the trees like a flock of drunk griffins.

Two against four, those were fair odds. None of us had surprise on our side, but our opponents were split up. They were trying to herd us into a pincer, to catch all of us between them. I doubted they had orders to bring Khala back alive and kill the rest of us. That gave us an advantage. They wouldn't shoot blindly if they were armed with bows.

In theory.

They could kill us all and go back to Dalyth with some story about us killing Khala. That wouldn't end well if she figured out they were lying. And she would. Or she'd kill them, just in case. As far as I was aware, the woman didn't know the meaning of the words 'moral compass,' much less possessed one.

I nodded to Tavian and pointed back the way we came. I gestured to myself and pointed forward.

He nodded, rose and disappeared amongst the bushes and trees.

"I'm going with you." Zared crawled out from under the bushes. He looked like a half drowned mouse the palace cat dragged in.

"The hells you are," I told him. What was it with these humans? I thought I was stubborn and difficult.

"I can fight," he snarled. "I won't let them take Khala, even if I have to die to stop that from happening."

"That's noble of you," I said sarcastically, "and that's exactly what will happen. You're staying here."

"I—"

A blur rushed past his head, narrowly missing him before the arrow embedded itself in the tree behind him. Eyes wide, he ducked.

"Or they could come to us," I said with a sigh. I pulled out my bow and aimed where the smell of Fae was the strongest. I let the arrow fly before quickly nocking another and firing it.

A grunt said I hit at least one of my targets. I ducked before another arrow found itself embedded in my brain. That would be objectionable for so many reasons. Including marring my good looks.

I straightened back up and loosed a third and fourth.

I forgot about Zared until I heard a shout, and saw him jump out of the trees up ahead, sword slashing.

So much for knowing how to use it.

Keeping down low, I headed in that direction at a run. I stopped and slipped behind the thick trunk of a tree. The kind that looked as though it had seen a thousand years, and would stand for at least a thousand more.

Steel clashed on steel. Two figures appeared out of the driving rain. Zared, and a Fae man a head taller than him, were slashing at each other, each keeping the other just out of reach. A dead Fae lay on the ground, an arrow through his chest.

Good shot, I silently applauded. Sometimes I even impressed myself.

Reclining against a tree, I watched the two opponents parry for a minute or two before I decided to put Zared out of his misery. The Fae man didn't even know I was there until the arrow slammed into his right eye.

Zared paused mid-parry and glared at me. "Took you fucking long enough."

"What?" I said with mock innocence. "You were waiting for me? I thought you had everything under control."

I ignored the mumble that sounded like, 'Fae asshole,' which came from approximately his direction, and turned to locate Tavian.

It didn't take long. I followed the smell of blood and the sound of swearing.

I found them in a small clearing. One man was gripping the stumps where his feet used to be, groaning.

"He didn't step high enough," Tavian said. He was sitting beside a puddle, both hands and most of his weight pressed down on the head of another man. The puddle was just deep enough that the man's face was submerged. He kicked and fought, but Tavian didn't move.

I put my bow away and crossed my arms. "That's unorthodox, even for you."

"I thought I'd try something different," he said lightly.

"So I see." I cocked my head at him. "I think he's dead." His legs stopped twitching and he didn't seem to be fighting back anymore.

"Really?" Tavian looked down in disappointment. "That was too quick."

"On the contrary, I think it was just the right amount of time," I said. "Seeing we have no time to waste."

I pulled out my knife, walked over to the groaning man and jammed it into his throat. I could have left him to die slowly and painfully, but I wasn't a complete asshole.

"Come on, we should catch up with the others before Vayne gets tired of being in the company of humans and decides to eat them after all." I cleaned my knife on the man's shirt and put it away in my boot.

"If anyone is going to eat humans, it will be Vayne," Tavian agreed. He washed his sword and pushed it back into its scabbard.

"He might not even cook them first," I said. The truth was, I was going to have to be careful around Khala, because I very much wanted to eat her. The gods knew there were many, many conversations we needed to have before anyone ate anyone.

Gods, now I was picturing her mouth around my cock.

She's a human. A human, human, human.

But if I was right...

I couldn't be thinking any of this now. We had a long way to go before we reached our destination, and Fae like Dalyth were the least of my troubles.

I trudged through the continuing rain, cursing the gods and hoping like fuck it let up before too much longer. And knowing there was no point in cursing the gods, because this time, they weren't the ones creating the trouble.

They sure as hells weren't the ones who were going to get us out of it.

CHAPTER
SEVEN
KHALA

"What do you think they want with us?" I whispered. Talking was coming easier now, but I would have signed if not for the darkness, so we weren't overheard.

I squinted over to where two of the three Fae men seemed to be asleep. The third, Tavian, prowled around in the trees, on watch.

The rain ended a couple of hours ago, but it was too wet for a fire. The Fae shared bread and cheese, and fruit from their packs with Zared and I.

I gobbled mine down before I remembered there was no one going to hurry me. That was another habit I'd have to work at breaking.

"I don't think they want us," Zared said. "It's you they want."

I wasn't sure who he was accusing, me or them. I waited until my breath became even again after my sharp intake of annoyance. He was the last person I should be irritated with. If it wasn't for him, I'd be alone with them. Or in Dalyth's hands.

"I have no idea why," I said, defensive in spite of my resolve not to be. "Do you think Tyla is all right?" I was more scared for her than I was for myself. Whatever Ryze wanted me for, he didn't want me dead. He and his men defended us against Dalyth and the other Fae.

I didn't know what she wanted me for either, but killing priests wasn't a sign of good intentions.

"Tyla will be fine," Zared assured me. "We'll get to her before anything bad can happen." He didn't sound completely confident, but I clung to his words like a lifeline. She had to be all right, or I'd never forgive myself for leaving her in that carriage. When Zared and I fled, she'd frozen. I should have pulled her with me, but she'd insisted on staying inside like the other priests told us all to. If I'd tried a little harder...

34

I shifted and looked up at the few stars that were visible through the thick canopy. I only made out a handful here or there, their light twinkling like winking gods.

"Sooner if we leave now." His voice was barely louder than the whisper of a breeze. "We could be back at the road by morning. By the time those three wake up—"

"We would stop you before you take a step," Ryze said without so much as moving.

Zared's exhale was an irritated huff.

Mine was a sigh of acceptance. Of course at least one of them was awake, alert. Or they heard us talking. Didn't Fae have particularly good hearing? Hells, for all I knew, he could read our thoughts.

Ryze rolled over. His cat shaped eyes regarded me in the gloom. "I know you have questions. I promise, you'll get your answers."

"Why don't you go and give them to us now?" Zared sat up.

"Because right now, you should be asleep," Ryze said evenly. "We have a long way to go tomorrow."

"If we keep travelling with you," Zared said.

Ryze spoke like an annoyed father, having to explain something to his child for the billionth time.

"If you want to help your friend, staying with us is your best way to do that. In spite of what you may think, you don't want to end up in Dalyth's hands." His tone softened when he directed his gaze at me. "I know all of this is troubling. Trusting each other is difficult. But we need each other. Believe me on that."

"You need her," Zared said pointedly. "What do you need her for?"

"You're right," Ryze said without taking his eyes off me. "We need her." Then his gaze swivelled to Zared. "We don't need you. How many times have you almost gotten yourself killed since we met? Will you be unsatisfied until you get her killed too?"

His voice was so deep, so gravelly, that even when he was threatening Zared, he sounded compelling. I caught him watching me a couple of times before the sun set. I recognised the predatory look in a man's eyes, but I never thought I'd see it on a Fae.

He was tall, all three of them were. And, like Dalyth, dressed almost entirely in black. Ryze wore a white shirt under his black jacket, but he left it unbuttoned almost to the flat planes of his stomach. He looked as though he was almost entirely made of muscle. The only delicate thing about him, as far as I could tell, were the pointed tips of his ears. Even his chin, which also tended toward a point, was hard.

No one would ever mistake him for a human.

I was wary of him. Any sensible person, human or Fae, would be. He held himself like someone used to giving orders and having them followed. Not like Geralda, who wanted people under her thumb, just because she could. His was more effortless somehow, like people followed him because they wanted to.

"I'm not going to get her killed," Zared argued.

"No, you're not." Ryze propped himself up on one elbow. "Because I won't let you. You can get yourself killed as much as you want, but Khala is under my protection."

"She doesn't belong to you," Zared snarled.

I might have blanched at his tone, but Ryze was undeterred.

"I suspect you're labouring under the misconception she belongs to *you*," he said evenly. "You might find you're mistaken."

I found my breath in my throat. I didn't think what he was trying to say was that I didn't belong to anyone. It sounded like he was implying I belonged to him.

"Can you shut the fuck up?" Vayne growled. "Some of us are actually trying to sleep."

"Apologies." Ryze lay back down, but he didn't sound sorry at all. "I suggest we all get some rest. Like I said, tomorrow will be a long day."

I sensed Zared wanted to argue, but he flopped down heavily instead.

"It will be all right," I whispered, in spite of presuming we were being overheard.

He grunted. "What if we're not? What if you're not?"

I had no answer for that. All I had was Ryze's reassurance that Havenmoor wasn't safe. That Ebonfalls wasn't safe. And the evidence of my own eyes— seeing Dalyth attack the caravan. We weren't safe with her either. Was I really going to risk both of our lives based on an assurance from a Fae, just because he spoke pretty words, in a honey-smooth voice that threatened to make me wet between my thighs?

If he was one of the gods, he'd be one people should never turn their backs on. One people should never trust. One minute you'd be drowning in his eyes and the next he'd be flaying you alive.

"You don't know do you?" Zared's accusing tone was back, definitely aimed at me this time.

And this time, I didn't bother to hold back my own irritation from him. "Like Ryze said, they don't need you. I'm sure he'd be more than happy to let you leave anytime you want to go."

My throat hurt from all those words. My heart too, because I didn't want to fight with him.

He moved over and cupped his hands around my ear. When he spoke again it was softer than ever. "I'm not leaving you, because in spite of what he might say, you do belong to me. Even if you never feel the same way." Before I could respond, he rolled over to face the other way and settled into the damp leaves under him.

I screwed my eyes shut for a moment and grimaced to myself. When I opened them again, Ryze still watched me, the light from the stars enough to make his eyes glitter.

That was all he did, watch, but there was something in his gaze that was heavier than that. Like the weight of the sky rested on him somehow. On something he needed to do or be, and he wasn't sure whether or not he could pull it off.

I felt like I was intruding on a private moment. Maybe it was deliberate. He let his guard down enough for me to see behind the bravado. To make me understand there was more at stake than the friendship between Zared and me. More than the lives of two mere humans.

I wasn't sure if I should be offended or terrified. If this was beyond his ability, then whatever was going on, what chance did I have?

I felt as if that same sky pressed down on me.

He smiled, and the moment was over. The Fae male bravado was back, cocky as ever.

I rolled my eyes at him, then turned and tried to sleep.

CHAPTER
EIGHT

KHALA

I woke, cold and stiff, my clothes still damp from the previous day's rain. The early morning sun barely penetrated a canopy heavily shrouded in mist.

I sat up and brushed leaves off my skirt. My fingers snagged on a tear a couple of hands up from the hem. The gods only knew when I tore it and how. Pants like Zared's would have been so much more practical, or the leather ones worn by the Fae. I bet those didn't get torn on anything, and the way they clung to their muscular thighs...

I shook my head slightly. Best not let my mind wander off in that direction.

"Here." Ryze pulled a knife out of his boot and offered it to me, hilt first.

I stared at the blade, then at him.

"You might as well make it shorter. A skirt that long will do nothing but slow us down."

I hesitated for a moment before I took the knife and sliced at the fabric around the tear. It was thick, but the knife was sharp. It slid through the cotton like it was butter.

"Do you want me to do the back?" he offered. "Wouldn't want it to be uneven."

I glanced up from my cutting. He looked amused for some reason.

"I suppose so." I handed the knife back, stood and turned around. I waited to feel the blade slide between my shoulderblades.

He merely crouched down behind me and carefully sliced away the back of my skirt. His fingers brushed against the back of my knee.

Warmth surged all the way through me. My heart started to race.

He ran the back of his knuckles up the inside of my leg, halfway up my thigh, pushing my skirt up higher.

I struggled to contain my trembling. It was no more than the slightest touch, but it sent waves of scalding heat through my body. Flames crackled through me, threatening to set all of me on fire, to consume me down to ash and bones.

When he finally lowered his hand away and cut the rest of the cotton I felt bereft, empty. As if he burned a path through me before leaving the ground cold without a footstep treading there.

I felt desire before, but that was nothing like this. This threatened to swallow me whole.

When he rose, I turned but couldn't meet his eye. Had he felt what I felt?

Gods, I told myself, *he's Fae.*

"Did it take you long?" he asked as he put his knife back into its sheath on his boot. He glanced up at me sideways. "To learn hand language? I imagine it takes some time."

I nodded, then spoke and signed at the same time. "Yes."

He signed back, the same gesture. "This is yes?"

I nodded again, then signed something else. "This is no."

"Is there a sign for fuck off?" Vayne asked.

Ryze smirked at him. "In case you're curious, yes, he's always so cheerful."

I smiled and stuck my middle finger up at Vayne.

He grunted and did it back to me. "That's the same in Fae. More or less."

"Some things are universal," Ryze said. "Except sticking up your little finger at a griffin. Don't do that, they get really offended."

Vayne shook his head at him. "The great Ryzellius, the only Fae I know who knows a way to offend a griffin."

Ryze bowed. "Go ahead and mock me, until you meet a griffin and stick your little finger up at it. Then I'll be the one laughing."

"What happens?" I couldn't help asking, in spite of the fact I suspected it was all bullshit.

"They spit in your face," Ryze said. "Trust me, you do not want griffin spit on your skin. It burns like a bitch."

"It's probably harmless," Zared said. He shot a brace of daggers at Ryze with his eyes.

"I volunteer him for trying it." Vayne nodded toward Zared.

Zared gave him a dark look before turning away.

"Is he your lover?" Ryze asked me.

I signed, "No," while keeping my eyes on Zared. I didn't want to antagonise him any more than he already was. If I thought he'd listen, I'd tell him to go back to Ebonfalls. He'd be safe there. Or in Havenmoor. It wasn't him Dalyth wanted. He could go back to living his life. But I knew him too well to think he'd walk away, even if I insisted.

Ryze nodded thoughtfully. He watched Tavian pack up the last of his belongings, then nodded to all of us.

"Let's move. We have at least two hours of walking ahead of us."

Zared turned around. "Until what?"

"Until we reach the place we need to go," Ryze said reasonably, as if that was any kind of answer at all.

Of course it wasn't enough for Zared. "Which is where and why?"

Ryze sighed. "Riverrest. From there, we'll travel on."

Since he clearly wasn't saying any more than that, I asked, "Do you know where they took Tyla and the others?"

He seemed reluctant to respond to that too, but finally he inclined his head. "I have a fair idea, yes. It's going to take some planning to get them out."

"We could send an army of griffin after them," Tavian suggested.

Apparently that was something funny, because Ryze grinned and even Vayne barked a short laugh.

"I'd rather send an army of you after them," Ryze said to Tavian. "But things would get messy. Very messy."

Tavian swung his bag onto his back. "Messy is good though." He gave me a wink, which for some reason made me blush.

Predictably, Zared scowled at him. Did he really think I was any happier about this than he was? If he did, then he needed to think again.

CHAPTER
NINE

KHALA

Ryze gestured for Tavian to lead the way through the trees. How he had any idea where he was going, I didn't know. All the trees and plants looked the same. Green, damp and competing for sunlight.

The sun itself was barely high enough to offer much illumination. The mist still hung low and thick. It hadn't thinned at all.

The air was warm, sticky and humid. It smelled like decaying plants and dirt that never dried out entirely. That was overlaid with the scent of the three Fae, and Zared. Leather, wood smoke, cinnamon, apples, pine, walnut and cedar. They all mashed together until I wasn't completely sure which scent belonged to who.

We walked in silence, which left me with my thoughts. I'd heard of River-rest, but I hadn't been out of Ebonfalls since my parents left me at the temple.

I had vague recollections of fields of corn and a small cottage beside a stream. The farm I was born on. The only place I knew until a stranger came. I remembered tense conversation between them and my parents, then we were leaving for the temple.

I had recollections of other things here and there, but most of my life before the temple was a blur. For the longest time, I clung to the memories of my parents' faces and their voices, but those faded a long time ago. If I met them now, I doubted I'd recognise them.

"I know you're thinking this is all kinds of fucked up." It was Tavian who came to walk beside me.

I gave him a sideways look, but didn't disagree.

"It's weird for us too," he said. "We're not used to humans. Is it true you eat eggs boiled in the urine of virgin boys?" He seemed both curious and serious.

I stared at him for a few moments before I shook my head. "No."

"You don't, or humans in general don't?"

"I've never heard of it." It was lucky my stomach was more or less empty, because the idea was disgusting.

"I see." He seemed disappointed. "What about the urine of virgin girls?"

I grimaced. "Just water. Regular, well water."

"I had well water once. It tasted similar to piss." He frowned, thinking about that for a few steps before he shrugged. "Our water comes out of rivers and streams before it goes into the tap."

"Tap?" Wasn't that something people did with their hands? Usually to get the attention of other people.

"Yes, tap. Faucet? Don't know that either?"

I shook my head.

"Do you have toilets?" He'd started to look slightly alarmed.

I raised my hands to sign, then said out loud, "Yes. We have those."

"I don't mind if you use hand language," he said. "I learnt it a long time ago. I'm a little rusty, but if it's easier for you, go ahead."

"I should practice talking," I signed, relieved to fall back on something more familiar. "Where did you learn?"

"A small town on the border," he signed back. His gestures were awkward and stiff, but clear. "I spent some time at a temple there. One of the priestesses used to be a Silent Maiden. She taught me hand language and I taught her... other stuff." His cheeks turned slightly pink.

I made a gesture and they turned redder.

He cleared his throat. "Something like that, yes."

"I didn't know Fae could blush." I smiled slyly. I could easily forget he actually was Fae. He seemed sweet and warm. Friendly. For all I knew, most Fae were like him and not like Ryze and Vayne. And Dalyth.

"We can do all sorts of things," he said with a smile. "Can you sing?"

I was about to sign no, I couldn't, but I stopped. "I don't know," I signed instead. "I couldn't even hum until yesterday. Can you?"

I was more eager to talk about him than myself. He had to be a lot more interesting than I was.

"A little," he said out loud.

He took a breath and started to sing in a soft, but deep tone.

"In the land of the Fae queen,
    Amidst the mist and clover,
    A love was born, the bond a dream,
    Two hearts entwined, forever.

My love, my Fae so bright,
    Here with you, our love is made,

I ache for you, both day and night,
My love for you will never fade.

THROUGH THE GRASS, we dance and cry,
    Under moonlight, dip and sway,
    Our love, a flame that will not die,
    A bond that neither would betray.

MY LOVE, my Fae so bright,
    Here with you, our love is made,
    I ache for you, both day and night,
    My love for you will never fade.

FROM THE FAE realm we stray,
    Our love, a dream awakened,
    Through centuries, it will stay,
    And the mist will be forsaken.

MY LOVE, my Fae so bright,
    Here with you, our love is made,
    I ache for you, both day and night,
    My love for you will never fade.

IN THE LAND of the Fae queen,
    Our love, a bond, a moonlit spark,
    May it shine, the brightest beam,
    To guide the way out from our dark."

HE HELD the last note before he let it die away.

I clapped my hands with sincere appreciation. "That was beautiful."

He smiled modestly. "I'm surprised I remembered the words. I haven't sung that for at least a hundred years."

I blinked. "Right. How old are you?" Maybe I shouldn't have asked that. He might think it rude. The last thing I needed was an offended Fae who was armed and seemed to know how to use the weapons he carried.

He didn't look offended. He shrugged and signed, "Two hundred and twenty-three." Out loud he added, " I'm just a youngster compared to those two." He nodded towards Ryze and Vayne and grinned.

Vayne swung his face around toward Tavian. "I'm not that much older than you," he grunted.

"Only a hundred years," Tavian said.

"Ninety-eight, asshole," Vayne said. "Younger than Ryze."

Ryze shrugged. "With age comes wisdom." His eyes on me like a caress he said, "Age doesn't mean as much amongst the Fae as it does amongst humans. When you live as long as we do, and see as much as we have, you tend to forget about things like that."

I took that to mean he wasn't going to tell me how old he was. Clearly, he was a lot older than me, although he didn't look it. If I had to guess, I'd think all three were in their mid-twenties. Certainly no more than that. I knew Fae were long-lived, but I hadn't realised how long-lived they were. They all must have seen things I could only imagine.

"Did dragons exist when you were young?" Zared asked.

I couldn't tell if he was asking from curiosity, sarcasm or even accusation.

Ryze chuckled. "Do you think we contributed to the extinction of dragons?" He grinned broadly. "Dragons don't exist. They have never existed. They're a myth, like sea goats, tangie—"

"And humans that aren't as irritating as shit?" Vayne asked.

I gave him the gesture for fuck off.

He sneered in response.

"I might be cranky too if I was as old as him," I signed to Tavian.

He laughed. "I would be too," he said out loud. "On the other hand, he's been as cranky as that since I met him."

"What does that tell you?" Vayne asked. "I was all sunshine and rainbows before I met you. Everything went downhill after that."

"I'm starting to think Dalyth might be a better option," Zared said.

Tavian actually looked offended. "You think death would be better than walking through a forest with us?"

Zared gave him a, 'what do you think,' look, with no attempt to hide his disgust.

"We can arrange that," Ryze said.

"Can I, please?" Vayne asked.

Ryze hesitated.

"No, you can *not*," I said firmly. "Can't you just be nice to each other?" All of this arguing and animosity was becoming exhausting. The last day had been tiring enough. "We must be nearly at Riverrest?"

Ryze tilted his head back and looked up at the thinning canopy.

"Yes we are. In fact, this is close enough."

"Close enough for what? Zared asked. He raised his hands to either side and turned around in a circle slowly. "We're still in the middle of the forest."

"Perfect." Ryze swung his pack of his back and hand to Vayne. "There's no one here to see us."

My heart skipped. Was this where the Fae disposed of us and left our bodies to become part of the forest?

"The river is nearby," Ryze continued. "I needed that to do this."

He raised his hands out in front of him, palms forward. His eyes half closed.

"What—" I started.

Tavian put a hand on my arm. "Just watch."

The air was suddenly chill, like a blast of ice. This skin on my arms pebbled. Thankfully my clothes were dry now, because they might have froze to my body.

A white line appeared in the air in front of us. It hovered just above the ground before it started to open like two doors joined in the centre. In a moment or two, I made out a passage beyond the doors. Floor, ceiling and walls were all white, glistening.

The wider the doors opened, the colder the air that came from inside.

"Is that—" I frowned.

"Ice," Tavian agreed. "It's a portal home."

CHAPTER
TEN
KHALA

"What the hells?" I gaped.

This—what did Tavian call it—a portal? This was unlike anything I'd ever seen before. Like nothing I'd read about.

"Not hells, home." There wasn't a hint of mockery in Tavian's voice, just excitement. He wanted to go home.

"It's dry there," Ryze said wryly. "If you'd hurry up, this takes a lot of energy to keep open." If that was the case, he hid it well. He didn't look like he was exerting any more energy than he would if he was holding up a feather.

"You can't be serious?" Zared shook his head and stepped back from the portal. The scent of him was bitter with fear. Bordering on sour.

I wrinkled my nose, but it was a good question. Was Ryze serious?

"It would take weeks to travel on foot," Vayne said. "Stay here if you want, I'm going." He walked towards the portal without hesitation and stepped straight inside. He stomped along the white corridor for a metre or two before he disappeared out of sight.

"Come on." Tavian grabbed my hand and tugged me towards the portal.

Zared lunged to grab my other hand. "She's not going. You fucking Fae are out of your minds if you think you can take her with you. Especially through that... Whatever the hells, godsforsaken thing that is."

"It's just a doorway," Ryze said easily. "You might have encountered them before. I hear even human buildings have them." He smirked at Zared.

Zared looked torn between dragging me away from the portal and letting me go so he could punch Ryze in the face.

Before he could decide, I pulled him towards me.

"I'm going," I said firmly. I locked my eyes on his pretty hazel ones, so he

46

knew I was serious. "I told you before, you don't have to come with me. It's my choice to go with them. It doesn't have to be your choice."

His expression changed from furious to pleading in a blink.

"Kay, listen to me. They're Fae. When have they ever been friends to humans? You have no idea where they want to take you or why. If you step through that thing, you may never come out the other side. And if you do, they may never let you come back. You could be stuck there forever. Please, stay here with me. We'll find somewhere safe. We can be together, just you and me. You know that's what we want, what we *need*." He looked at me like a poor, lost puppy who wanted the last bite of food on my plate.

I pulled my hands away from both guys so I could sign to Zared.

"I know it's what you want." I kept my eyes on his face, hoping to make him understand. "I care about you, but I need to get away from here." I closed my eyes for a moment. "I don't want to be a part of a temple who does what they do to women." I nodded down towards my hands before I lowered them to my sides. I had to stop letting them influence me, and use the voice the gods gave me.

"I didn't ask to be chosen, to be kept silent. If I stay, I'm only going to end up back at the Temple and keep doing what they tell me to do. I'll be helping them do the same to other girls. You can't want that for me."

His expression wavered. "So instead, you're going to go with them and do what *they* tell you to do?" he said bitterly. "You don't even know what that is."

"I'm not going to stay here and wait for Dalyth to find me." I remembered the way she looked at me. "She'd kill you if she saw you with me. Come with us. You'll be safer than you will be on your own."

He didn't try to hide how conflicted he was. "You trust these Fae?" He clearly didn't.

"Yes, I do," I said firmly. "They saved our lives, remember? They saved your life. The answer to everything is through that portal and I'm going because I need to know. I think, deep down, you need to know too."

I lifted my chin challengingly.

He sighed. "Fine, I'll go, but only to keep you safe from them. And so I'll be there when you realise we belong together."

"Did I mention hurry up?" Ryze seemed less amused than usual. He raised an eyebrow at us and jerked his head towards the portal.

"It won't hurt," Tavian assured us, his words clearly meant for us both.

I turned to him and frowned. I hadn't thought of it hurting until he said that. "It's ice. Won't we freeze in there?" I eyed the portal doubtfully.

"Only if you don't hurry the fuck up." Ryze was obviously at the end of his patience.

Tavian grinned. "It's warm in there. I promise. As warm as your—" He signed the word, "Pussy."

Zared growled, but that made Tavian grin even wider.

"He's very possessive for a human, isn't he?" Tavian gripped my hand again and pulled me to the threshold of the portal. He stepped inside and kept pulling until half my arm was through the doorway.

"It is warm in there." I marvelled at exactly how warm it was. It wasn't like the sticky heat of the forest. It was more like the warmth of a blanket and a pile of pillows. Like an embrace. "How?"

"Magic," Tavian said easily. "It's blood warm in here." Obviously for Zared's benefit he added, "Just as warm as I bet your ass—"

Zared growled again.

Tavian winked at me and tugged me in deeper.

Inside the portal, the walls weren't so blindingly white. Rather, it was like stepping into an ice cave. I ran a hand down the side. It was hard, and surprisingly cool.

"It really is ice," Tavian said. "It's pulled from the river and frozen to let us through."

"And it's going to get really fucking cold in a moment," Ryze said. He herded Zared ahead of him with a gesture and stepped into the portal himself. It closed behind him, blocking off the view of the forest.

Zared's throat bobbed up and down as he swallowed, but he followed Tavian and I deeper into the portal. All the way to another doorway.

On the other side was what looked like nothing more than an ordinary sitting room.

Shoving down my nerves, I stepped out of the portal and onto plush carpet woven in deep shades of red, blue and green.

The walls of the sitting room were covered with ornately carved wooden panels. Above our heads, a light hung from a ceiling rose which was decorated with flowers and vines, and painted the same shade of green as the one in the carpet. A sofa and several leather chairs were scattered around the room.

I took all of this in before I noticed the window. It was taller than any of the Fae, almost as high as the ceiling. Four panes were separated by sashes varnished the same dark as the walls.

"Oh my gods." I dropped Tavian's hand and stepped towards the window.

We must have been several stories high at least. Below us, a city stretched out all the way to the ocean. More buildings than I could ever have imagined in one place covered a slope kilometres long. Wide streets crisscrossed between them. Square roofs, domes, and even the occasional triangular roof glistened silvery white in the morning sun. Once in a while, a building had a dark roof, but most of them were light.

The walls of the buildings themselves were a variety of colours, but mostly earthy shades of brown, green and red.

"What is this place?" I asked breathlessly.

"Lysoria." Ryze came to stand beside me and admire the view. "The Silver City herself."

"Fuck," Zared said softly.

I dragged my eyes away from the incredible sight long enough to glance at one man, then the other.

"The Silver City?" It rang a vague bell in the back of my mind, but I couldn't pin it down until Zared spoke again.

"The capital city of the Winter Court." His eyes were drinking it in too.

"The one and only," Ryze said. "Isn't she beautiful?" He sighed wistfully.

"She's incredible," I agreed. I frowned up at him. "Who are you?"

I hadn't realised Vayne was still in the room until he chuckled.

"She's onto you, Ryze."

Ryze shrugged. "It was only a matter of time."

I cocked my head at him.

It was Vayne who answered.

"He's none other than the great Ryzellius Dravenstone. High Lord of the Winter Court himself."

Vayne's words sank in a full minute after they left his lips.

"High Lord of the Winter Court," I echoed. "You're—"

"One of the four most powerful Fae in the world," Tavian said. He seemed more matter-of-fact than impressed. But then again, he already knew.

Ryze shrugged out of his jacket and tossed it over the back of a chair. "That's more or less accurate. What do you know of the courts?"

"I know there are four," I said slowly. "One for each season: winter, summer, spring and autumn. Each one has some kind of affinity with their season."

Ryze pressed a thumb to his lower lip. "It's more like an affinity with the season's magic, but close enough. I can manipulate ice and snow, but I like to be as warm as the next man." He cast a sly glance toward Zared, as though to remind him about the last time we talked about warmth. As if it wasn't only minutes ago and didn't earn Tavian Zared's animosity.

Zared glared at him, but turned back to face the window.

"That's how you were able to make a portal from ice?" I guessed.

With a start, I realised I was having a casual conversation with a man who was basically a king. A king with magic.

"Should we be calling you my lord, or something like that?"

Both Tavian and Vayne snorted laughs.

Ryze looked pained. "Please don't. At least not when it's just us, like this. In front of my court, High Lord is the correct term, or Lord Ryzellius. There's no need for formality otherwise. Although, maybe I should reconsider how Vayne and Tavian address me, since they don't display a great deal of respect for me." He peered around me toward them, but seemed more amused than chastising.

"I'd sooner worship the goddess of little, fluffy ducks than call you High Lord Ryzellius," Vayne told him. "Not unless I have to."

Ryze looked at me sadly. "See what I mean? No respect at all. None."

I smiled. "It's terrible."

"Maybe you should have them strapped," Zared suggested. "Or better yet whipped."

"I would, but I think they'd enjoy it too much." Ryze grinned.

"Then you need to do it harder," Zared told him.

Ryze raised an eyebrow at him. "I don't think I've ever been accused of not doing anything hard enough."

Zared looked disgusted, but Tavian burst out laughing.

Vayne shook his head at the rest of us and grumbled. "I need a bath." He stalked out of the room.

"We all need a bath," Ryze said. "Khala—"

"She's not joining you," Zared snapped.

Ryze looked at him like he was on the verge of tossing Zared out the window. "Not that I owe you any kind of explanation, but first of all, that's up to her, not you. Second of all, I was merely going to show her to her room, and explain how the taps work, if necessary."

To me he said, "I'll have someone organise a change of clothes for you. When we're all clean, we can sit down and eat. I'll explain everything."

"It's about time," Zared mumbled.

"You want us to stay here?" I hadn't thought that far ahead. I hadn't thought far ahead at all. Not beyond understanding why Dalyth went after me and my sisters. Or why Ryze and his companions saved us from them.

"Unless you know someone else in Lysarial?" Ryze asked. "There aren't a great many humans in the city." He rubbed his pointed chin. "There are some, but as you might imagine, they're as welcome here as Fae are in human cities. You might find the palace more comfortable for now."

I didn't get the impression we had a choice, so I simply nodded and hoped Zared would go along with it. Better the Fae you know, and all that.

"Good." Ryze offered me his arm and ignored Zared's scowl as he led us from the room.

ELEVEN

KHALA

We stepped out into a corridor bright with white stone floors and walls. Similar in size and precise cut, to those in the temple back in Ebonfalls, here, they were unstained and less marred by wear. Tapestries in rich colours, most depicting winter scenes, adorned the walls. They looked like they were completed and hung yesterday. I suspected each was older than me.

I managed to tear my gaze away to ask, "How far did we come? When we came through the portal, I mean."

"I thought that was the kind of come you meant," Ryze said with a straight face. "We travelled approximately three hundred kilometres."

"Three hundred—" I looked up at him and gaped. "But it only seemed like a handful of steps." It would have taken days to travel that far in the carriages.

"That's the beauty of magic. As long as I've been to a place, and have water or ice nearby, I can make a portal to that place. It doesn't seem to matter how far, or how many people pass through. Admittedly, I haven't tried to test the limits recently. I presume that as long as I can hold it, people can move through it."

"How long is that?" I asked.

"An hour is as long as I've ever managed," he said thoughtfully. "Ten minutes is a sufficient strain. The more the strain, the smaller the portal."

"What happens to anyone inside when it closes?" Did I want to know the answer to that?

He shrugged. "I have no idea. I can't imagine it would end well for them. They'd probably get ripped apart by magic. All the more reason to hurry up when I tell you to."

"You went through last," Zared pointed out as he trailed along behind us like a dark cloud. He sounded as though he would have been happy if Ryze was torn apart.

"Yes, I did," Ryze said over his shoulder. "I'll make sure to let you be last next time."

Zared made a rude noise, which both Ryze and I ignored.

"You can stay here." Ryze stopped in front of a door. He turned the handle and pushed it open. The door was silent, like the hinges were recently oiled. "It's not the biggest room, but it should do," Ryze said apologetically.

Zared made a choking sound I interpreted as disbelief. It mirrored my thoughts with accuracy.

The room was huge. The walls were lined with similar panelling to the sitting room, but these were painted soft grey-white. What looked like a glass candelabra hung from the centre of the tall ceiling.

Ryze pressed a button on the wall beside the door. The button clicked and the glass bulbs in the chandelier illuminated.

"What the hells?" I was starting to lose track of all things I'd stared at today. This was another one of them. "Magic?"

"Electricity." Ryze smiled but he didn't seem to be mocking me. "I suppose you could say it is magic, to some extent."

Once I stopped gaping at the light, he led me to a washroom to the side of the sleeping area.

"I trust you both know what a bath is?" he teased.

Zared grunted. "Of course we do. We're humans, not animals."

Ryze ignored the low hanging fruit and walked over to turn the tap on the side of the bath.

"Hot. Cold. Turn the tap again when there's enough water in the bath." He straightened and crossed his arms like nothing could be simpler. Like water coming out of a metal tube set in the wall was no big deal at all.

I glanced around. "Where's the fire?" Surely the water passed over it before it poured into the metallic sided tub and started to fill the room with steam?

"In another part of the palace," Ryze said simply. "Any time you want hot water, or just warm, you can get out of any of the taps. Now, here's Joviena. Can you find suitable clothes for Khala after you show Zared to his room?" He nodded to a Fae with long, dark hair, and striking green eyes.

She nodded and gestured for Zared to follow her.

When he hesitated, I said, "I'll be fine. Go and get clean."

"You'll only be next door," Ryze told him.

Reluctantly, Zared followed Joviena out, and Ryze leaned against the door frame of the washroom.

"Do you need any help getting undressed?" He gave me a suggestive, lopsided smile.

I couldn't stop myself from thinking about the way his hand felt on the inside of my calf. Part of me wanted to say yes. On the other hand, me and my clothes were revolting, and that water looked more tempting than sex.

I saw it on his face that he knew how close I was to saying yes, but when I politely declined, he smiled and backed out the door.

"I'll have Joviena come and get you when it's time to talk." He gave me a nod and disappeared out of the room.

I waited until I was sure he was gone before I stepped out of my boots and dirty clothes and into the delicious heat of the bath.

We had baths at the temple, but none as deep or as warm. I sank down until only my face was above the water. I closed my eyes and relished the feeling for a few minutes before reaching for the perfumed oils on the shelf beside the bath.

For this alone, I was glad I followed the Fae through the portal. If this was what the whole city was like, no wonder the Fae looked down on humans. I doubted even the daughters of King Mikohal of Fraxius were as pampered as this.

Did they know about electricity and taps that water came out of by themselves? Maybe their castle had all of those amenities and they simply didn't share with us regular people. Or perhaps they did share, but the Temple refused, priding itself on austerity.

I sighed at my ignorance.

I washed my body and my hair, then lay there for a while longer before I realised, if I stayed there too long, Joviena would come and find me here. Or one of the men. Nothing would keep Zared out of here for long, much less Ryze and Tavian. I couldn't rule out Vayne either. In spite of his gruff demeanour, he was as attractive as the other men.

I climbed out of the bath and wrapped myself in one of the plush towels from the shelf beside the oils.

It took me a few more minutes to realise the wooden disc on the chain at the bottom of the bath was the plug and that if I pulled the chain, it would release the water. I hesitated, wondering if I should leave the water for someone else, but then I decided if this was my room and my washroom, no one else would be bathing here.

Unless I bathed with them. The bath was big enough for two or three to fit in comfortably. How would it feel to be pressed up against the edge and fucked while the water sloshed over the side onto the tiles?

The water gurgled happily away down the plughole, taking that enticing thought with it.

I dried myself and peered out into the sleeping area. Joviena must have entered and left without a sound, because fresh clothes lay on the bed. I stepped over and picked up a pair of pants which would have fit a Fae child. Made of the softest fabric, they fell all the way to my ankles. Snug around my hips, a mirror on the wall showed they did my ass a lot of favours.

A tunic in the same shade of grey-blue fell mid way down my thighs. It was modest at the front, but plunged low at the back, exposing everything just above my rear. The temple would have found the outfit scandalous, but I felt beautiful. Sensual. I looked at myself in the mirror and did a little wriggle.

I smiled at my reflection and ran my fingers through my hair to try to tame it. In the end, I gave up and tied it back in a ponytail at the nape of my neck.

Joviena had also left a pair of butter soft shoes, which actually fit. She must be magic too if she could find clothes that fit me, after just a glance.

I was just finishing when someone tapped at the door and opened it slowly.

"The High Lord will see you now," Joviena said. Her voice was as musical as the rest of the Fae. It curled around me like a warm hug.

"Thank you— What do I call you?" Having spent the last ten years surrounded by women referred to as sister, or priestess, and men who were priest or brother, I had no idea how to address anyone else.

"Joviena is fine, my lady," she said politely.

"Oh, I'm not a lady," I said quickly. "Please just call me Khala."

She smiled briefly but stepped back out the door. "We shouldn't keep the High Lord waiting, my lady."

I sighed. Apparently I wasn't going to win that battle. I followed her out and in the opposite direction to the sitting room.

She led me through opulent corridors adorned with paintings, and the occasional window overlooking the city. I had to resist the urge to stop and stare out of each one.

We finally arrived at a door at almost the other end of the palace. It stood ajar.

As she had with mine, she tapped on the door before pushing at the rest of the way open. She nodded for me to step inside and hurried away.

Ryze sat in one of the armchairs near the window, his legs crossed at the knees. He wore black pants and a white shirt which looked clean and fresh. His dark hair was damp, brushed back off his face. He gazed towards the window, a contemplative look on his face.

Tavian sat in another chair, chewing on a piece of toast. His eyes were on Ryze until he realised I was in the room.

He turned to me and smiled warmly. "You look beautiful." The expression on his face made my heart flutter.

"Stunning." Ryze looked away from the window to drink me in with his eyes. There was hunger in those dark depths, but there was something more. He almost seemed sad.

"Please, have a seat, and something to eat." Ryze waved to the chair opposite him. "I presume you want to wait for Zared?"

"He'll want you to wait," I agreed. "Otherwise you'll have to explain everything twice."

"That sounds tedious." Ryze made a face, which bordered on his usual amused expression, but left much of that lingering pensive air he'd displayed a moment earlier.

"It sounds like a pain in the ass," Tavian said.

"That too." Ryze nodded to him. "Perhaps you could take notes."

Tavian paused with the toast halfway to his mouth, thought for a moment then said, "Let's wait instead." He bit down, his eyes smiling.

Ryze rolled his eyes ceilingward and shook his head. "No respect at all. None."

"Not even a little bit," I said with a smile. "Maybe you should try to be more scary?"

They exchanged glances.

Ryze cocked his head at Tavian. "Would that work?"

Tavian chewed on the question and the toast at the same time before he swallowed. "Doubtful. I don't find you that scary."

Ryze sighed. He opened his mouth to say something, but closed it again when Zared entered the room, Vayne right behind him.

"All right then, we're all here."

Zared flopped down into a chair so heavily it was miraculous the legs didn't snap off. "Yes we are. Start explaining."

CHAPTER
TWELVE

RYZE

I looked down into the delicate porcelain teacup. Too delicate. A direct contrast with the roughness of the last few days.

"I don't think I can do this." I glanced up from the white porcelain, to where Tavian sat slouched in another chair.

His eyes lowered. "I hear there are herbs..."

I snorted a laugh. "I can do *that*." The gods only knew I thought about it enough times since meeting Khala. "I'm talking about the rest of it."

"You want to tell her everything?" In spite of the jokester mask he wore, he was astute. He paid more attention than many gave him credit for. Myself included.

"I can't tell her everything," I said. "We don't *know* everything."

"And you can't tell her all you know or suspect, because she'll start walking back to Ebonfalls and never look back." He stretched over to snag a piece of toast from a plate on the table.

"I can tell her enough to keep her from doing that." I put the teacup aside. I needed something stronger than tea for this conversation. Not to mention the one to come.

I leaned back in my seat and looked toward the window. Usually I admired the view, but today I saw nothing. My mind was too occupied with my thoughts to appreciate it.

A brisk knock at the door broke through them, but I didn't look around until after Khala entered the room. When I did, I almost choked on my own breath.

They say no beauty can compare to a Fae woman, but this human woman was captivating. She was dainty, but strong, and her hair— I wanted to tangle my fingers in there. Drown in her eyes.

No, I didn't need any herbs. Looking at her made my cock harder.

The way she smiled while Tavian and I teased each other made me hate myself for what we were going to do to her. What *I* was going to do to her.

When Zared almost broke my chair, I was tempted to open the window and throw him out. I restrained myself both for her sake and because he was also torn out of his own life and brought here.

In spite of being told repeatedly he didn't have to come, he never really had a choice. The fact he was in love with Khala was obvious to everyone. I wouldn't let her out of my sight either if I was him, especially around dubious characters like Tavian and Vayne.

Vayne in particular. His bark was much worse than his bite. I'd seen him taking glances at her when he thought no one was watching. He was outspoken in his dislike of humans, but that was a cover for indifference at worst and curiosity at best.

I cleared my throat. "The Silent Maidens were created by the Fae. That is to say, it was the Fae who first recognised certain qualities in young women. For their protection, they were taken aside. *Chosen*, if you will."

My eyes settled on Khala, whose mouth twitched at the word.

"What qualities?" she asked carefully.

I would have welcomed an interruption from Tavian or Vayne, but for once it didn't come. Of course they'd leave this to me. Assholes.

"They were all suspected to be omegas," I said finally. I let the silence hang, ringing louder than a temple bell.

"Omegas are a myth," Zared scoffed. His eyes didn't look so sure. "They're as real as dragons."

"*Dragons* are myth," I said slowly. "I assure you, omegas are not. Neither are alphas." I said that with as little inflection as I could, but I watched as my words sunk in.

"What is an omega?" Khala asked. She looked confused, scared. I wanted to pull her into my arms and reassure her, but I couldn't do that. Not yet.

Her eyes went from me to Zared and back again.

It was Zared who responded. "They're people who...go into heat. Like a bitch. According to the legends, they were created by the gods for their amusement."

That sounded like something the gods would do. His words did nothing to settle her confusion though.

She shook her head. "I don't understand. What does that have to do with me? Or any of this?"

"Everything," I said. "The maidens took any suspected omegas aside and did what they could to suppress their heat until those girls were women."

She looked at me with a furrowed brow.

"The amethyst chokers the maidens wear," I explained. "The amethyst, specifically, has the property to keep an omega from her heat."

"Or his," Tavian said.

I nodded towards him. "Or his," I agreed. "But male omegas are even more rare than female ones."

"But the chokers stopped us from talking," Khala said.

I smiled humourlessly. "Just a strange side-effect of the amethyst. The gods only know why it does that."

"You think Khala is an omega?" Zared looked like he might open the window and throw *me* out.

I shook my head. "No. I know she is. Just like I know I'm an alpha."

Zared's face turned pink with fury. "Is that why you brought her here? For your own amusement?"

"For her own *safety*," I said calmly. "Dalyth is taking the rest of them to the Summer Court. As she has done for several years now. The rumours of what happens there... I couldn't let them take another batch of girls."

"The women who aren't maidens anymore, go to the temple for training," Khala said, her brow still just as creased.

"The women who aren't found to be omegas are sent to Havenmoor," I agreed. "Their memories are altered, so they don't remember the sisters who accompanied them. They're told those women died or, the gods knows what else."

"How can they tell if they are omegas or not?" Khala asked, but I suspected she knew the answer.

"The way they respond to an alpha's touch," I said, my eyes on hers.

"This is bullshit," Zared said. "Even if omegas are real, there's no way Khala could be one." He didn't look as certain as he sounded.

"I can prove it," I said softly. "If Khala wants proof."

She may need time to process all of this. I wouldn't push her, but the sooner she accepted who she was, and what she was, the better.

She closed her eyes for a moment. When she opened them again, she nodded.

"I need to know."

I stood and gestured for her to do the same. I closed the distance between us, although being this close to her almost set my body on fire.

"Once the amethyst is removed from an omega, the body's natural urges assert themselves strongly for the first heat. Many omegas have their first heat at around sixteen. Those extra couple of years allow it to build up. The first time will be intense. The lead up to that will be only slightly less so."

"Can I ignore it?" she asked. "I've been aroused before and not acted on it."

I smiled at her naïveté. "No, you can't ignore your heat. At this stage, you can't suppress it again, either. Afterwards, yes, but not now. And..." This was the part she might not want to hear. "An alpha can't ignore it either."

I raised my hand and brushed it lightly over her cheek. Touching her was like thrusting my hand into an open fire. Every part of me was hot, like my blood turned to lava. Not even the High Lord of Winter could ignore heat like this.

I ran my hand down the side of her face, to her neck and over her throat.

She half closed her eyes and moaned softly.

"You feel that?" I whispered. "It's more than desire. It's pure need. To touch and to be touched. To mate."

She trembled under my hand. Her lips parted. Her breath was only slightly slower than a pant. She murmured her agreement. She felt it too.

In that moment, I could have done anything to her. I could have had her. Made her mine. My body wanted that. Ached for it. Ached for her.

I lowered my hand and stepped away from her. Gods, that was difficult. Like cutting off my own limb.

She opened her eyes and looked back at me. Clearly she was thinking the same thing.

"That was what I felt when you touched my leg in the forest."

"That was when I knew you were an omega. I suspected, but I wasn't sure until then. I knew you had to come with us."

"So you can fuck her?" Zared was on his feet, hurt and outrage on his face. As much as I wanted to dislike him, that must have been difficult for him to watch.

"That isn't what this is about," I said. "By the time we found you, it was too late. She's going to go into heat, whether any of us like it or not. If I could, I'd find a room full of amethyst and put her in it until she was ready to decide for herself. The fact of the matter is, she will go into heat and I will be there. Trust me, there are worse alternatives out there."

If I said so myself.

"There are plenty of alternatives," Zared said.

"You?" I scoffed. "You're a beta. What she needs can only be satisfied by an alpha. That's not arrogance, it's a fact."

"What about them?" Zared waved a hand towards Vayne and Tavian.

"Also not alphas," I said evenly. "For what it's worth, I've considered magical alternatives, but there are none. Short of locking her in a room and letting her ride it out by herself, this is the only way." Before he could say that was a viable option, I continued, "Have you considered asking her what she wants?"

For some reason, he didn't seem to appreciate the suggestion, but he turned to her.

"Is this what you want? To be fucked by some Fae?" He waved a fist in my direction.

"He's not exactly a random street Fae," Tavian pointed out.

"Thank you," I told him.

He nodded. "Ryze is High Lord of the Winter Court. He is one of the most powerful Fae in the world. In magic as well as in influence."

"And yet he could only save one maiden from the Summer Court?" Zared said.

I had to admit he was right on that count.

"We weren't sure if the rumours that they were taking those women were true," I said slowly. "I didn't want to march an army through the countryside, in case the rumours were wrong. We were only there in the first place to ascertain the situation. Only by the luck of the gods we got there in time to save you from an arrow in your head. And to bring Khala here."

"I want this," Khala's voice broke through the tension.

All right, the tension between Zared and me. The tension in my body was a different story. That was something I'd have to deal with later.

Thundering silence fell, followed by Zared's look of disbelief.

CHAPTER
THIRTEEN

RYZE

"You want this?" Zared's voice was a hoarse whisper.

"What he felt when he touched me..." She was visibly struggling to put her thoughts into words. "I want that. If this is who I am and what has to happen, then I want to go into it willingly. This is what I choose."

Zared looked dumbfounded.

Tavian chuckled, presumably from the look on the human man's face. Sometimes it was hard to tell with him.

"How long?" Khala asked. "Until I..."

"Go into heat?" I finished for her. "I'd guess a week. Two at the most. I know your mind must be spinning. Mine was when I first realised I was an alpha."

I scratched the side of my forehead. "The first heat is...something else. That's a whole, uncomfortable story."

"Which all of us would love to hear," Tavian said. Of course he would. Asshole.

I shot him a look and sank back into my chair.

After a moment, Khala did the same. Zared remained standing, but leaned against a wall, his arms crossed over his broad chest. He looked ready to run someone through, given the opportunity.

"I was a young Fae," I started.

"About fifty," Vayne interjected.

I waved at him dismissively. "Yes, yes. Something like that. I was travelling through one of the outlying villages with my father when an omega went into heat. Thankfully, she was older and accustomed to dealing with it, because I didn't have a fucking clue. About mating yes, but not about mating heat and the role of the alpha. I was firmly in her—"

61

I cleared my throat. "Hands. The guards travelling with my father and I thought the whole thing was hilarious. My father was less than impressed."

Once I figured out what the hells was going on, I thoroughly enjoyed myself. It was an...interesting awakening.

I sat back, crossed my knees, picked up my tea and took a sip. I grimaced at how cold it was and put it back aside.

"How do male omegas find out what they are?" Khala asked softly.

She seemed to be processing everything, bit by bit. I had to give her credit for not being upset or hysterical. She was either really, really good at hiding her thoughts, or she accepted it.

"The same way females do," Tavian said softly. "An alpha's touch close to heat." He gave me a glance.

I returned it with a soft smile.

Khala's mouth formed an O. "You two..."

"That's how I know Ryze knows how to take care of an omega," Tavian said. "Believe me, you could do a lot worse."

"If anyone gives a shit, I'm a beta," Vayne growled. "Which doesn't mean my dick doesn't work." He gave us all a collective scowl.

"No one thought it didn't," I assured him.

"I suspected it might." Tavian grinned.

Vayne gave him a rude gesture with his middle finger.

"It's some consolation that they don't give each other any respect either," I said to Khala.

She smiled, but still looked troubled.

I uncrossed my legs and leaned towards her, hands on my thighs. "I know all of this is a lot to take in." I glanced up towards Zared, including him in my sympathy. "It's going to take some time to get used to, but you're stronger than you think you are. None of us are the monsters you were probably led to believe."

Zared made a sound of disbelief, which I ignored.

"What about Tyla?" she asked. "What if she's an omega too? They'll take her to the Summer Court? They'll have an alpha there? What will happen to her?"

I exchanged glances with Tavian, because this was exactly what we were discussing before she entered the room.

I looked back at her. "I don't know," I admitted. "The rumours of anything going on there might just be that. Rumours. Cavan, the High Lord of Summer, isn't known for being a reasonable, sympathetic man. All the more reason to make a move and get her out of there as soon as we can, but that has to wait until after your heat. We can't risk you being anywhere near him when that happens."

"But if she goes into—" Khala started.

I interrupted her. "If we could take the risk, I'd do it in a heartbeat. We can't."

"Don't you have people you can send?" Zared asked. "You are the High Lord of the Winter Court."

I glanced up at him and raised an eyebrow. "Am I? I had forgotten." As if I possibly could. People liked reminding me all too often.

"For your information, I prefer not to send my people to a place I wouldn't go myself. Not to mention the simple fact doing so may be seen as an act of war. Unless you'd like to provoke one of those, then we'll have to wait." I hated to do that to Khala, but war was a million times worse than what might happen to one woman, gorgeous though she was. Especially given what would happen to multiple women as a result of the conflict. The needs of the many had to outweigh the needs of the one, as they said.

Zared shrugged and paced away across to the other side of the room.

I rubbed a hand across my forehead. "I think that's enough talk for one day. After all that, I need a drink." I rose and walked to the bar in the corner, which contained several bottles of alcohol and enough glasses for half an army.

I poured myself a glass of whiskey and turned around to see Tavian grinning.

He stretched out and put a hand on Khala's arm. "Watch this."

I gave him a droll look. "So glad to be your party trick." I shook my head but half closed my eyes and drew water to me from a nearby tap. I froze it and shaped it, so when it reached my hand, it was formed into two, neat cubes. I tipped my hand so they both fell into my whiskey with a plop.

I took a sip and gave them all a sarcastic bow.

Everyone but Zared clapped. He gave me a look like he thought it was a waste of magic.

He was probably right. Whatever, I liked ice in my whiskey.

"How do you do that?" Khala asked.

I slipped back into my chair. "It's basic magic. I can't remember a time when I couldn't do it. I never think of it as a big deal until other people make it into one." I shot Tavian a meaningful look.

Of course, he was completely unapologetic. "I wish I could do it."

Khala turned to him. "Can you use magic?"

He responded with a gusty sigh. "No I can't. I've had to get by on looks and brains alone. And a bit of muscle." He raised his bicep.

"One out of three is right," Vayne said.

"Thanks for saying I have good looks." Tavian grinned at him.

"If that's how you want to interpret it," Vayne grunted.

"It is," Tavian said lightly. "But I have the other two as well. You know what *you* have, my friend?"

Vayne rolled his eyes towards the ceiling. "There's no way in hells I'm taking the bait." He looked back down and narrowed his eyes to the other Fae man.

As if Vayne went along with him, Tavian said, "You have jealousy. A great deal of jealousy. I think you should go to one of the temples and see if they can treat you for that."

Vayne stuck two fingers up at him. "Fuck off, Tave."

I looked over to Khala and sighed out my nose. "You see what I have to put up with day after day? No wonder I drink."

She smiled. "It's different from the Temple. So far I haven't had to sweep the floor, listen for a gong to tell us when to eat, and I haven't been yelled at by Sister Geralda. On the other hand, I don't have Tyla here to confide in." Her smile faded and she exhaled softly.

Zared hurried over to crouch in front of her and took one of her hands in both of his. "You have me," he told her earnestly. "I might not be an alpha, but I care about you. If anyone here understands, it's me. We are both a long way from home. We can rely on each other."

She looked back at him and for the first time since I met them both, she seemed to actually see him. Perhaps she realised they were the only humans amongst a group of Fae who were slightly insane at best, and more than slightly insane at worst. Unapologetically so. When you lived as long as we did, you got by however you could. We used humour.

"I care about you too," she told him. "I'm sorry you got dragged into all of this."

"I let myself be dragged," he reminded her. "I don't mind, as long as you are here."

"I know this is going to be difficult for you, but you have to let whatever happens, happen." Her expression was firm, yet gentle at the same time. She didn't want to hurt him, but she wasn't taking any shit either.

For a human, she was remarkably resilient. If I'd learned what she just did, I'd need at least twenty years to get used to the idea. Then again, humans didn't live long enough to have the luxury of that much time to acclimatise to sudden upheaval. They had to deal with it and move on.

Zared didn't look happy about it, but he clearly knew when he had no choice. If he wanted to be in her life, he had to deal with what and who she was. And who, I strongly suspected, he wasn't.

He looked up at me. "What happens to me? Am I supposed to sit around here for the rest of my life? Watching you make cubes out of ice?"

"You don't have to watch," I said dryly. "If you wish, you can train with the guard, or the army. I can tell them to go easy on you."

"Don't bother," he snapped. "I can hold my own against any Fae."

"Suit yourself." I swallowed down the last of my whiskey. "You can train with Tavian and Vayne. They'll figure out where you need to be."

I didn't expect a thank you, and I didn't get one. He simply inclined his head and looked away. I made a note to suggest my captains train some respect into my men and women. That was sorely lacking from my court. I supposed it was my fault for not insisting on it from the beginning. Vayne and Tavian had been with me since my father died and I inherited his role. Since before that even. One hundred and fifty years might be too long to break the habit.

"You can come with me now," Vayne said to Zared as he pressed his hands to the arms of his chair and pushed himself to his feet. "I have a few new recruits to assess anyway."

Zared glanced at Khala, but she nodded. "I'll be fine." She offered him a smile, but looked relieved. If he wasn't hovering around, ready with a snide remark or a dark look, it might be easier on her. The gods knew it would be easier on me.

Zared looked reluctant, but followed Vayne from the room.

"I also have things to do," I said with at least as much reluctance as the human had displayed. "I have yet to discern a way to have the court run itself."

"He's tried," Tavian said. "He really has. But then someone has a problem with someone else and he has to interject. And then the cycle starts all over again."

"Precisely." I put my empty glass on the table beside my cold tea and stood. "Perhaps you two could spend some time comparing notes about life as an omega? I'm sure Khala has questions."

"Only about a million," she said, looking grateful for the opportunity.

"Of course," Tavian agreed. "Let me show you my nest."

CHAPTER
FOURTEEN
KHALA

"Your nest?" I asked. My head was still spinning with everything Ryze told me. Part of me didn't want to believe any of it. It sounded far too strange. Even if it was true and omegas were real, why would I be one? I was no one special. Just Khala, former Silent Maiden. If I believed him, I was so much more than that. It was bizarre.

Yet, I did believe him. It explained the way I felt when he touched me. Every part of my body responded to him in a way it hadn't to anyone else. He could have bent me over the chair and fucked me then and there and I would have screamed for more. We both knew it.

If that was what pre-heat was like, then the idea of actual heat was slightly terrifying, but exciting at the same time. I'd never been afraid of sex, and I wasn't afraid of doing it with Ryze or any of the Fae. I was drawn to them.

Zared too, in spite of my resolve to be no more than friends.

He was right that it was just him and I here in a place so strange to both of us. That fact made me feel closer to him than I had before. I couldn't deny the connection. Not any more.

"Are all the High Lords alphas?" I asked before Tavian could even answer the first question.

He laced his fingers through mine and led me down a set of wide, marble stairs. His hand was large, comforting. The thought didn't even cross my mind that it should be awkward. I felt as if I'd known him for a lifetime. His lifetime or mine, I didn't know.

He opened a door and guided me inside before closing it behind us.

"We don't know about the other High Lords. We suspect Cavan is one because of the omegas being taken to his court. Ryze sent word to the other courts, asking their opinion, and trying to discover what they knew. If they answered, he didn't tell me." He seemed unworried.

"This is my nest." He waved towards the deepest bed I ever saw.

It stood just off the ground, on an oak frame about half a metre high. The inside of the frame was padded with cushions. Dozens more cushions lay scattered around the edges of the mattress. Three sides of the bed were surrounded by a heavy, black curtain. The fourth side was tied open with thin strips of fabric. If they were removed, the bed would be entirely enclosed.

I was immediately drawn to it. The idea of snuggling down into it was enticing. Like hiding in a cocoon. Something like a purr rose in my chest.

"You've never seen anything like this?" he asked.

I shook my head. "No. I remember building something similar out of blankets and pillows when I was a child. I'd spend hours lying in there daydreaming or reading. When I went to the Temple, I missed being able to do that. I thought it was just a thing children did."

"If it is, I never want to grow up." He lay down on his back and pulled me down with him. "This kind of space is typical for omegas. A place to feel safe and comfortable and warm. Ryze had it built for me. He's probably already organising one for you."

He wrapped his arms around me and snuggled his body into mine.

"Being an alpha is more than being there when an omega goes into heat. It also means taking care of that omega. Keeping us safe and teaching us to keep ourselves safe. Mostly I can do that myself, but if it was left up to me, I'd throw a bunch of cushions on the floor and pull a pile of blankets over my head. This is much better."

"Yes it is," I agreed. Together with the apple and cinnamon scent of him, I never felt so comfortable. So soothed. At the same time, I was very aware of him next to me. His thigh pressed against mine. "You really think Ryze will have one of these made for me?"

"Without a doubt." He rolled over on his side to face me. "He wants you to stay. He'll do everything in his power to make you feel at home here." After a moment he added, "I want you to stay too."

Slowly, he moved his face closer, until his lips brushed over mine. He watched for my reaction. When I didn't pull away, he kissed me again, deeper this time.

He explored my mouth with his lips and his tongue, caressing and tasting me.

His mouth tasted even better than he smelled. Like cinnamon and nutmeg, with a hint of vanilla. I could have devoured him then and there.

His hand slid across my midriff and up to the underside of my breast.

I pressed one of my hands against his rock hard chest, and tangled the other one in his hair. I wanted, *needed* him closer.

His mouth moved from my lips across my cheek and down to my neck.

I moaned when his touch sent a shaft of fire right through my body. It wasn't the intensity of Ryze's touch, but it was compelling all the same.

His tongue grazed my throat, before he moved down to the top of my breasts. He kissed and licked his way across, and back again.

His hands ghosted over my breast and stopped at the neckline of my blouse. He looked up at me before peeling down the fabric to reveal my breasts. My nipples were already rock hard peaks, aching for his touch.

He didn't disappoint. He kissed and licked his way down to them before taking one of my nipples between his lips and sucking gently.

I groaned softly. "That feels so good." Better than good.

"You taste so good." He moved over to the other nipple, while at the same time untying the laces at the front of my blouse and pulling fabric away from my body. "I want to..."

How adorable that he was so confident about some things but shy about others. He'd clearly had sex before, potentially a lot. I liked that he wasn't brash about it. It was refreshing.

I was tempted to tease him, but I just said, "I want to too. I want you to fuck me."

He smiled. "Whatever the lady wants."

He pulled off his shirt.

I stared. I'd suspected he was muscular, but hadn't guessed the extent. He looked like he was carved out of stone. Like an artist chiselled definition across his chest and flat stomach. He wasn't big, but every centimetre was masculine perfection.

"You're beautiful," I told him.

He grinned. "No, you are." He gripped the top of my pants and slid them down my legs. He folded them neatly and put them aside in a corner of the bed. He did the same with my panties, then sat up to run his eyes over my bare body.

"You look like the gods made you," he said breathlessly.

He moved down further and gently opened my legs with his hands. "Perfection."

He brushed over my pussy with the back of his hand, just lightly at first. He glanced at me, before lowering his face between my thighs and teasing my pussy with his tongue and lips.

I quivered with growing desire. I grabbed fistfuls of the bedcovers in both hands, and looked towards the canopy while his tongue found my clit.

He licked me slowly, tracing circles and lines like a pattern around my clit and entrance. He slid one long, elegant finger inside me, then another. He stroked me like I was some kind of musical instrument and he was playing a song on my body. He was as skilled as any bard I ever heard.

I rocked against him with increasing speed. The pressure built until it became unbearable. I arched my back and cried out as the pressure broke through my entire body. It shattered me into a million pieces, each more blissful than the last.

It lasted for at least a minute before I came back down to the mattress, panting and sighing, purring in the back of my throat.

He kissed my pussy and down my thighs to my knees before he lifted his face and smiled at me. His mouth and chin were glistening with my slick.

"You can sing. The most beautiful song of all." He shed his pants and came to lie beside me.

My eyes widened at the size of his erect cock. "My gods," I whispered.

His smile evaporated and he glanced down, looking worried. "I know I'm not big, but..."

"You are big," I told him. If he was small, then how big was average for a Fae man? If they were bigger than him, then stepping through the portal might have been the best decision I ever made.

"Really?" he asked shyly.

"Really." I kissed his mouth, tasting my slick on his lips. "I can't wait to have you inside me."

To punctuate my words, I rolled him over onto his back and straddled his hips. Trying to cover the hint of nerves, I smiled and slowly, slowly, slowly lowered myself onto his cock. I had to stop every few moments to let my muscles get used to him, but I slid my wet pussy all the way down until he was deep inside me. All the way to his balls.

"You feel incredible," he said. "So... I don't know, tight. Like you were made exactly to fit me."

"You feel incredible yourself," I said. I'd never felt so full.

His hands resting lightly on my hips, I started to rise and fall carefully, but deliberately and evenly.

He groaned. "Absolute perfection."

After a minute or two, he rolled us over and bent my knees so he could thrust in deeper still.

Every stroke hit me all the way in, caressing me in places I didn't know existed inside my own body. Places that lifted me again, driving me toward a second orgasm. One like nothing I ever felt before. Blood roared through my body, thundered through my ears. Every bit of me screamed out in pleasure that seemed to last several lifetimes.

I wrapped my legs around him and crossed my feet, drawing out my orgasm and pulling one from him at the same time.

He slowed his frantic thrusts, then went still as he shouted. His whole body shuddered. He grunted my name. Over and over. The last time, he drew it out long, and low, matching the height of his orgasm.

Finally, he released a heavy breath and sagged against me, panting and sweating.

"Gods, that was..." He shook his head. He had no words for what it was.

Neither did I. Apart from a sneaking in of reality.

I'd just fucked a Fae. Gods help me, I'd do it again, and again.

I searched his face for any sign of regret. After all, I was a human. He might have gotten caught up in the moment, and needed a body to release the tension. To spill his cum into.

He smiled. "You are perfect. The moment I saw you, I wanted to do this with you." His expression changed to worry. "You don't regret it do you?"

"No," I said quickly. "Not for a moment." I didn't regret that my feet were still pressed against his back or that his cock was still deep inside me. I could happily lie like this, in his nest with him, for a very long time.

Eventually, we untangled from each other. He drew me into his arms, slowly stroked and tangled his finger in my hair.

"How did you meet Ryze?" I asked. They obviously had a relationship that went back a long time. Could I fit into that, and if I did, where? Was this just about sex for the men, or could it lead to something more? Did I want it to? I knew them for all of a little over a day. Although, it felt like so much longer. The instinct to run, like I usually did, wasn't there with them. Was that something I should be worried about?

My mind was overwhelmed with questions I had no answers for.

"I trained with the palace guards," Tavian said. "In those days, he trained with us. He's often surrounded by guards and he has magic, but he wanted to know how to fight for himself. How to use a bow. We used to joke that he was so old he needed something to do to keep himself from getting bored."

"You became friends?" I guessed.

"Yes. Him, Vayne and me. Weird combination, but it works."

"And he spends your heats with you?" I asked carefully. "What about when you don't have a heat?"

"If you're asking if he and I are intimate outside a heat— Sometimes." He pressed his cheek against mine and closed his eyes. "We've never really talked about what we are to each other. We get caught in the moment."

"What do you want to be?" Had I accidentally stepped into territory I shouldn't have? I should back away, but he seemed unworried.

"I care about him, but whenever I think of being anything more than friends, I feel like I'm not enough for him," Tavian admitted. "He is... Ryze. Even if he wasn't High Lord, he'd still be something special, something powerful. And I'm just me."

"There's nothing *just* about you," I said firmly. "He'd be lucky to have you as more than a friend if that's what you both wanted."

"That's very sweet, but it wouldn't only be us. We both like women too much. But if you and he and I... That I could see."

"That wouldn't bother you?" I wasn't sure what to think about any of this. I didn't know either of them well enough to truly consider getting into any kind of relationship with them. On the other hand, if I did, it was good to know where I stood from the start.

"Not at all," he said. "Fae are possessive of people we love, but that often extends to more than one lover. As long as everyone agrees, then no one is bothered. What would your friend Zared think?"

I winced. "I'm not sure." He knew I fucked other men. Knew I'd be fucking Ryze. He would have seen the way the Fae man looked at me. Wouldn't be surprised that I was already laying naked in Tavian's bed. But a relationship was another matter.

"He came all the way here for you," Tavian reasoned. "I think all he wants is for you to be safe and happy."

"And with him," I said.

"And that," Tavian agreed.

"What about Vayne?" I asked. "Are you two ever..."

"Intimate? No. He's only attracted to women, as far as I know." His cheek twitched against mine.

"But not human women," I said. "He seems to really dislike humans."

"Vayne dislikes pretty much everything, including himself," Tavian said. "He hates most people when he first meets them."

"Including you?" I pulled my face back far enough to look at his.

"The first time we met, he beat the shit out of me," he said. "He claimed he was trying to teach me to stick up for myself. I wasn't very good at it then. I had to learn fast so he didn't do it again."

"Did he?"

"A couple of times," Tavian said lightly. "But then, a couple of times I beat the shit out of him, so we're even."

"It sounds like you have an interesting relationship." I wasn't sure I'd be friendly with anyone who beat me up, regardless of their motives for doing so. Honestly, it sounded like something Zared and his friends would have done to each other. Maybe it was a masculine thing.

He chuckled. "You could say that, yes."

We were silent for a few minutes after that.

I eventually broke it by asking, "Do many of the Fae have magic? You said you don't?"

"I don't. The majority of us don't these days. Those who do are like throw-backs. Or their parents mated specifically to breed children with magic. The High Lords, for example."

"They all have magic?" I asked.

"They do," he agreed. "All connected to their seasonal affinity. The High Lord of Spring, for example, can make plants grow quickly, and can channel the rain, or do interesting things with water."

"That sounds useful." I nestled into the cushions. I could get used to comfort like this. To being surrounded by soft cushions and curtains thick enough to keep the world at bay. Nest was a good word for it. I could nestle here for days.

"It is, when he bothers to share the skill with the other courts." Tavian sounded unimpressed. "If our crops are struggling, sometimes he won't do anything. Sometimes he will."

"Why?"

"Because the Fae are proud and some of them are assholes," he explained. "There's been animosity between the courts since the beginning of time. Once in a while, something will happen to bring them together. Like when we moved out to the west and left the humans to the land in the east. Some of the Fae objected, so the High Lords had to work together to get them to comply. Somehow, it didn't degenerate into full blown war. Fae tend to dislike being told what to do."

"Humans don't like it much either," I said. "It sounds like we're all as stubborn as each other."

"That's the funny thing," he said slowly. "There's been hundreds of years of mistrust and suspicion between Fae and humans, but we're not that different."

"Especially if humans and Fae can be omegas," I agreed.

He shifted beside me. "Right," he said slowly.

"Can humans be alphas?" I asked.

"Just because I've never heard of a human alpha, doesn't mean it's not possible," he said vaguely. "The gods did stranger things than that. I'll take you down to the palace garden and show you the elephant flower."

"Elephant?" I asked. That was a strange word. An unfamiliar one.

"I don't know if they're a myth, but apparently they're a huge animal that lives on a distant continent. They have a nose that looks like a giant tail. Elephant flowers look like that too. They smell amazing though. Not," he sniffed, "as good as you. You smell like honeysuckle and fresh rain. Perfect combination. Did you know only omegas and alphas can smell things like that on other people? Apparently regular people just smell peopleness."

I blinked at him a couple of times. "I've always been able to smell things like that on people. You smell like cinnamon and apples. Dalyth smelled like honey and lemon. Pleasant, but at the same time not."

"That is exactly how she smells," he agreed. "Did you ever tell anyone you can smell things like that on people?"

"I..." I considered his question. "I remember telling my mother she smelled of peaches with a sprinkling of sugar. She looked at me funny."

My blood went cold. "She knew what I was? She told the Temple so they knew to take me?"

"To keep you safe," he said quickly. "So you didn't go into heat before you were ready." In spite of his easy tone, he was frowning.

"Was she an omega?" I asked softly. "Was that how she knew what to look for in me?"

"Unless your father was Fae, then chances are she wasn't," Tavian said.

There was more he wasn't telling me, but I sensed he wouldn't, even if I asked. More because he didn't know the answers than because he was deliberately keeping things from me. At least, I hoped that was the case.

"Peaches and sugar sounds lovely," he added. "Do you remember what your father smiled like?"

I furrowed my brow. "I remember... Something metallic, like iron, but tainted. Like rust. But sometimes it was more... Like tea tree bark, or something like that. It depended on his mood."

I pressed my lips together. "If they knew what I was, why didn't they tell me? Why didn't the Temple tell me? They had ten years to do it." It explained why my parents never came to see me. They must have thought I was some kind of anomaly. Something they didn't want associated with them and their good names.

For something that happened so long ago, that stung like a fresh wound. The fact they'd turn their back on their own child for something she couldn't help. I couldn't imagine doing it to any child of mine.

"I'd imagine when the Temple was first erected, they made a rule that the girls weren't to know who was suspected of being an omega and who wasn't. Possibly for their own safety and possibly because of some other agenda. Who knows what went on back then? Either way, it's possible the priestesses weren't allowed to tell you. I know that's not much of an answer and probably not what you want to hear." He looked regretful.

"No, you're probably right," I said as I exhaled. "The temple always had their reasons for doing things. A lot of the time, things didn't make sense to us maidens."

He grinned suddenly.

I frowned. "What?"

"Maiden," he said. His expression was sly, even for a Fae.

I snorted, because I was no longer going to get in trouble for doing so. "It's a title, not a description. Although, it's a description initially, of course." Most maidens weren't maidens anymore by the time their time was up. Except those like Hycanthe, who took the title more seriously than the rest of us.

"Of course," Tavian agreed quickly. "I think it's adorable. I suppose the silence part was more the point. Were you allowed to make noise? Like clapping or stamping?"

"It was strongly discouraged," I replied. "We were expected to behave in a certain way and not cause any trouble." Seen and not heard, for sure. Geralda would have been happy if we were neither. Thinking of her gave me a small sting of homesickness, but I quickly pushed it aside. One thing was certain, I was never going back to Ebonfalls again. Not as a priestess.

"Expected," he said meaningfully.

I laughed. "What would you expect from a group of young women kept together in a relatively small place, with priests who got away with pretty much anything and everything? Sometimes I don't know who led who astray. Maybe it was mutual."

"That explains a lot," he said. "Why you didn't take much convincing to step through that portal. You have an adventurous spirit. And Ryze smells good."

"So do you," I told him. He was right, though. I hadn't taken much convincing. Even if it wasn't just for my own safety, I was curious about what was on the other side of the portal. I didn't want to live the rest of my life stifled by the Temple.

By the sound of it, I never really had much choice in the matter anyway. If I hadn't ended up in the Winter Court, I would have ended up in the Summer Court. What would it look like there? From what I saw out the window, the roofs here looked like they were made of ice or snow. Would theirs appear to be made from sunshine? What would that even look like?

"Have you been to the other courts?" I asked.

"Yes, but not recently," he replied. "Rarely the Summer Court. For some reason, they don't like us there."

"I suppose summer and winter are opposites," I said.

"Seasonally, yes," he agreed. "If you take all that stuff too seriously, which I don't. The way some people talk, you'd think it snows every day here. Or we live in a palace made of ice and spend our time giving each other cold looks. Or eating delightful sweets flavoured with rose water."

I gave him a funny look, but shrugged. "I would have thought that before I came here," I admitted. "I didn't know much about the Fae at all. Or taps." That was probably a very, very small amount of what I didn't know about the world. I'd grown up more or less sheltered. And now here I was laying naked in bed with a handsome Fae male.

Life was...unexpected.

"Does it snow here?" I asked.

"Yes, it does. Actually, it snows more here than anywhere else in the Fae realm, but not all year round. That would be tedious. Not to mention cold. Although, we could snuggle more often, so there would be advantages." He pulled me closer to him. His hands resumed wandering over my body.

I had a million more questions to ask, but they were all forgotten for now.

CHAPTER
SIXTEEN

KHALA

I spent the next few days exploring. No one told me I didn't have free reign of the palace, so I started at the top and gradually worked my way down. I caught the occasional glance of curiosity, disapproval, or even disgust from passing Fae, but for the most part they seemed disinterested. That was fine with me. I didn't want to be treated like an attraction from a travelling fair.

I spent most of my nights with Tavian, in his nest or the one that appeared in my room after that first night. To say the man was insatiable was an understatement. Some nights we barely slept. He knew his way around a woman's body already, but he quickly figured out exactly what I liked and lavished it on me.

Ryze made a point of eating at least one meal a day with me, and patiently answering my multitude of questions. Those he had the answers for. He knew no more about my parents than I did, apart from agreeing with Tavian's guesses.

I hardly saw Zared or Vayne at all. Apparently, they were busy training.

I felt their absence acutely. Zared in particular. I missed joking around with him like we used to, and sneaking out at night when we shouldn't. I was also worried he was angry with me for letting him follow me here, irrational as that might be.

Finding both men wasn't difficult once I started trying. I'd seen the training yard out of the window. From there, it was a matter of figuring out which staircase and which corridor led out there. The palace was somewhat of a labyrinth.

I finally found the way out via the kitchen, snagging a freshly baked fruit bun on the way past. I broke it open and inhaled the warm smell of cinnamon and orange zest.

The food here was also worth stepping through the portal for. I hadn't had a single bowl of lukewarm stew, or a piece of cold, lumpy bread. Everything here was fresh and tasted incredible.

In spite of what I was told growing up, the Fae were not savages. Far from it.

I slipped out the door and walked across the yard to the training area. The morning was already warm. The stiff breeze off the ocean kept Lysarial from getting too hot, while also infusing the city with the fresh smell of salt air. Everything here left me feeling like I'd lived in darkness most of my life.

I followed the sound of grunts and the clash of heavy wood on heavy wood.

Zared and Vayne sparred in a small, dirt yard, staffs taller than either of them gripped in both hands. They'd stripped to the waist, upper bodies glistening with sweat that trickled down defined muscle.

Zared wasn't as tall as Vayne, but he was broader, his shoulders wider, biceps thicker. He was holding his own against the Fae, who seemed comfortable with the weapon of choice.

I joined a group of mostly female Fae who stood leaning against the fence, watching avidly. They all appeared to be around my age, which probably made them a couple of hundred years old.

A woman with dark red hair and eyes like chips of emerald turned to look at me with interest. For a moment, I thought she might tell me to go away, but instead she smiled and moved aside to give me a place at the fence.

"I'm guessing you're Khala," she said, her voice a soft lilt. "I'm Illaria. I've never seen a human male before, but if he's any indication, I should venture east more often." She sighed in Zared's direction.

Her words made me bristle inwardly. Whatever Zared and I were, I wasn't ready to let another woman into that tapestry.

"He's one of the better examples," I said, my voice tighter than intended.

She glanced back at me. "He's taken, I see. Don't worry, I don't hunt in another woman's territory." She offered me a warm smile.

After a moment, I gave one back. "I'm sorry, I didn't mean to be prickly. It's complicated between him and I." We should work it out once and for all so he could move on with his life. He deserved better than to be left dangling on the line. Especially if women as beautiful as Illaria had their eye on him.

"Where men are involved, it's always complicated," she said with a laugh. "Sometimes I think they all get together to work out ways to make things more difficult for women. The funny thing is, they undoubtedly say the same about us." She grinned.

I laughed. "That sounds accurate." Men and women were more different from each other than humans and Fae.

Zared ducked under the staff Vayne swept towards his head. He jabbed his at the Fae man's legs, pushing them out from underneath him.

Vayne landed in the dirt with a thud.

The small audience cheered.

Zared stepped back from his opponent. He glanced over to us and caught me watching. He smiled and nodded.

The distraction was all Vayne needed. He leapt to his feet and swung his staff again, sweeping Zared's legs out from under him.

It was Zared's turn to land in the dust. Vayne pushed him onto his back, pressed his staff across Zared's chest and straddled his legs.

"Never let yourself get distracted by a pretty face," Vayne said. "If this was a real fight, you'd be dead."

"If this was a real fight, there wouldn't be a group of women watching," Zared pointed out.

"That depends on the circumstances," Vayne said with a grunt. He pressed the staff down harder, then rolled off Zared and onto his feet. "That's enough for one day. Get cleaned up. You're on guard duty."

Zared rose and glanced towards me. He looked like he might argue, but Vayne gave him a look, like they'd had this conversation before.

"Yes, sir," Zared said eventually. He smiled at me before he disappeared into a wide building, presumably the guard quarters.

"If you want to share a meal some time, you can find me in the palace library." Illaria nodded before she slipped away with the crowds.

The word library piqued my interest. I figured there must be one, but I hadn't seen it yet.

I was about to leave too when Vayne came and rested his forearms on the fence in front of me.

"It sounds like you've made some friends," he remarked.

I tried not to stare too much at his glistening torso. He was as prickly as they came, but with sweat gleaming in every groove of his chest and abs...

I swallowed.

"One or two," I agreed, my voice slightly squeakier than usual. "A few of the people here have been hospitable." I didn't even attempt to hide the double meaning. He wasn't one of them.

"Tavian in particular," he said, ignoring my dig. "He and his cock seem to enjoy spending time with you."

"I like spending time with him and his cock." I wasn't going to apologise for that, not to him or anyone else.

"I'm sure you do," he said, his tone and eyes dark. "You seem the type to enjoy being told to shut the fuck up and spread your legs like a good little human."

I didn't know if I should laugh or punch him in the face.

Instead of doing either of those things, I said, "You seem familiar with that type. Fucked a lot of humans, have you?"

He curled his lip at me. "No, are you offering?"

I snorted. "You wouldn't know what to do with me."

"Only because my standards are higher than to stick my cock into someone like you."

"And by that you mean a human?" Punching him in the face seemed more and more plausible by the minute. "What is your problem with us anyway?"

I was almost eyes to chin with him, only the fence between us. "You look at me like I'm some kind of vermin."

"Aren't you?" he threw back at me. "You want to prove yourself? Come in here and work off some of that anger with me." He scooped up both staffs from where they lay discarded on the ground. "Show me you have some spine. Zared has, can you?"

I couldn't see a gate, so I climbed up the fence and dropped down the other side, my boots kicking up dust as I landed.

I snatched the staff from him, gripped it in two hands and swung it at his head. For a second I thought it was going to connect, but he ducked at the last moment and danced back.

"That the best you've got?" he taunted.

"I thought Fae fought with bows and swords. What's up with the stick?" I swung it around in the air a few times, getting a feel for it.

"It's good practice to use different kinds of weapons," he said. "If you can't use that, I wouldn't trust you with anything pointy."

"Like your cock?" If he was going to taunt me, I'd do the same to him.

He laughed. "I've heard it described lots of different ways: thick, hard, long, skilled, but never pointy."

"Are you the one using those words to describe your dick?" I asked. "I can't imagine anyone but you wanting to talk about it."

"Except you," he pointed out. "You're the one who brought my dick into this. Been thinking about it, have you? Imagining how it would feel to have me pounding into you?"

If I hadn't been before, I was now.

"It sounds like you're the one thinking about that." I stepped towards him, staff at the ready. "Do you think about me while you get yourself off?"

I feinted, making him step back. Judging by the expression on his face, that was exactly what he did. "Do you imagine yourself telling me to shut up and fuck you?"

He lunged forward, swiping at my midsection. I barely managed to jump out of the way. Thank the gods I was wearing pants and boots and not a dress and sandals. I would have fallen on my face. No doubt he'd enjoy that.

"I imagine myself telling you to shut the fuck up," he agreed. "Why are humans so mouthy?"

"Oh, so it's my mouth you think about?" I teased. "There's nothing wrong with imagining that, you know. What does it matter that I'm human?"

"It matters," he insisted.

"Why does it matter?" I pressed.

He shook his head and swung at me again. This time, he got the back of my legs. With a grunt of pain, I fell to my knees.

Before I could stand again, he was in front of me, the tent in his pants level with my eyes. He grabbed a fistful of hair and pulled my head back.

"Yes, I fucking think about it," he growled "I think about you choking on a mouthful of cock. My cock." He scowled down at me as though it was my fault where his mind went.

I looked back at him evenly. "Why don't you make me, then?" His cock was right there, straining against his pants. All he had to do was undo them. I wanted him to. Wanted to taste him. To hear him grunt as he thrust and ground into my mouth.

He gripped my hair tighter. He seemed to be at war with himself.

Finally he reached down with his other hand, unbuttoned the front of his pants and freed his erection.

Gods, he was bigger than Tavian. Thick, tip shining with pre-cum.

He pushed me forward until my mouth was against his tip. With a grunt, he pressed himself between my lips, forcing me to open my mouth and take him in.

I swiped my tongue over his slit, revelling in the taste of his juices. Pine and something spicy, like fennel. I groaned and started to suck him down to the back of my throat.

He grunted and thrust, guiding me in and out with his hand in my hair.

I looked up at him. His eyes were closed and, for the first time since we met, he didn't look angry. He was lost in concentration and bliss.

I ran a hand up his thigh and around to cup and massage his balls.

He groaned. "Hells. I knew your mouth would be worth fucking." That was the closest he'd come to admitting maybe he didn't hate all humans. He thrust harder and harder, each stroke hitting the back of my throat.

"I'm going to come in your mouth," he said breathlessly. "You're going to swallow down every fucking drop."

Yes please.

I sucked and licked harder, while my fingers wandered up and down and around his heavy balls.

He groaned and pounded frantically into my mouth before he came, squirting a flood of pearly cum into my mouth.

Instinctively, I swallowed, then again to make sure I did get every precious drop.

He sagged and his hand loosened on my hair. He panted for a while before he slipped his cock out from between my lips.

"Fuck," he breathed. "Good girl."

His words suddenly made the day warmer still.

"Does that mean I've proved myself?" I asked teasingly.

He responded with a grunting laugh. "It's a start. I like you on your knees. It's the perfect place for you."

What could I say to that? I enjoyed it as much as he had. I'd always liked giving men pleasure just as much as I liked receiving it. I never sucked a cock that didn't taste good.

"I guess I better stay down here then," I said. "Or you could teach me how to use that stick better?"

"I don't know," he said slowly as he tucked his cock back into his pants and did them up. "You seemed to know how to use my stick pretty well. Next time, maybe I will stick it into your pussy." He released my hair and stepped away to pick up the staffs.

"These you need to learn how to use. And a bow, knife, and your hands and feet. Everyone, man or woman, Fae or human, should learn how to protect themselves. You never know when you might need to. The next time you're on your knees, might not be with your consent."

I wouldn't admit it, but he was right. He could easily have overpowered me and made me blow him off against my will. Lucky for both of us, I'd wanted to. I wanted to feel his cock in my pussy some day.

"Will you teach me?" I stood and brushed the dirt off my knees.

"I'm probably the only one with the patience for it," he said with a grunt.

I rolled my eyes. "Are you worried anyone else who trained me might like my mouth as much as you do?"

"They'd try," he agreed. "Then I'd have to beat the shit out of them."

I curled my fingers around my staff. "Does that mean you don't hate me?"

He shrugged. "I don't know, I'll think about it."

"Has anyone told you you're a pain in the ass?" I asked him.

He smiled slightly. "Frequently. Usually before I hand them their own ass. Now, spread your hands out a bit further. Keep your eyes off the staff, and on me. My movements will tell you what I'm going to do next."

He spent the next hour teaching the basics of how to use the weapon, and how not to get hurt. By the end, I was sweating and envious of men who could walk around with no shirts on. Those who disapproved of me would disapprove even more if I took mine off. I was tempted to do it anyway, but decided against it. If nothing else, Vayne was being civil to me and I didn't want that to stop.

"All right, that's enough," he said finally. "We can train again tomorrow morning." He planted one end of his staff in the dirt and leaned against it.

"See, you really don't hate me," I told him.

He gave me a slow smile. "I've found two effective ways to shut you up. We might get along after all." His gaze raked up and down my body, clearly appreciative of the way my clothes clung to me, slick with sweat.

"And I've found two ways for you to be nice to me." I playfully poked him in the thigh with the end of my staff. "That's two more ways than you are with anyone else, as far as I've seen."

He grabbed the end of the staff and pulled me to him. "Let's get one thing clear right now. I'm not nice. I'll fuck your mouth, I might even fuck you. I'll train you, but I'm not nice."

I tilted my head back to look up at him. "I'll bear that in mind."

He grabbed the back of my head and kissed me roughly before letting go and stepping away. "Get out of here, woman. I have actual soldiers and guards to work with. I've wasted enough time with you." Both staffs in his hands, he walked away toward the same building Zared disappeared into.

I shook my head to myself and found the gate so I could leave the yard without climbing back over the fence.

I stepped outside and came face-to-face with Zared.

CHAPTER
SEVENTEEN
KHALA

"What the hells, Khala?" he growled. He caught my wrists with his hands and pulled me to him. "You're fucking him now too?"

I looked up at him, my brow furrowed. "How do—"

"I saw you out the window." His tone was thick with frustration. "On your knees. His cock in your mouth."

I jerked my wrists back. "I don't need to explain—"

He gripped tighter, fingers pressing hard into my skin. "Don't you get how I feel about you?" His breath was ragged, hot on the side of my face. He smelled of warm leather and lust.

Fire burned through my veins. Liquid heat that threatened to melt my resolve into ashes.

"Of course I do." I managed to keep my tone even. "This has nothing to do with how you feel about me. This is all about me living my life the way I want to."

"It doesn't matter who gets hurt in the process," he said bitterly. "I thought we understood each other." He looked ready to shake some sense into me. "You care about me."

"You know I do." I did, but was that enough? I had no intention of being with him and no one else. Asking him to share me, much less with Fae? That seemed like too much to ask, regardless of how he felt. Ever since we met the Fae, he'd been a walking ball of anger every time I saw him. Furious about and against everything and everyone but me. *Because* of me.

I should insist he leave, but I couldn't bring myself to say the words. I couldn't bear the thought of not having him here with me. That was selfish as fuck, but I needed him.

He pushed me until my back was against the fence and leaned in so his stubble grazed my cheek.

"Why won't you let me show you? Is my cock not good enough for you? Gods, Khala, all I want is to touch you. To make you feel good. To...to be inside you. Let me fuck you before I go crazy. Please." His lips slid over the side of my face and down my neck.

He had me quivering.

"Zared," I whispered.

"Khala." He pressed my hand to the front of his pants. "I know you want me, too."

His cock was rock hard. Without thinking, I rubbed lightly over the fabric, drawing a groan from his lips.

"Are you wet for me?" he whispered.

"Drenched," I whispered back. If I was any wetter, my arousal would trickle down the inside of my leg. "But we can't do this here." Until I said the words, I didn't realise how much I wanted this. To fuck him. I needed to. Right. Now.

"I know a place." Hands still around one of my wrists, he led me around the yard, through a doorway set in the palace wall. The room was dark, lined with shelves. Each of those was filled with bottles of herbs, and boxes of onions and potatoes.

He closed and locked the door behind us, then pushed me up against the wall and yanked up the hem of my shirt.

He lifted it over my head, dropped it on the floor. His mouth was all over my neck, my chest, my breasts. He sucked my nipples like he was starving. Nipped them with his teeth to the point of pain. He wasn't gentle. I liked it.

I groaned and pushed my chest forward, driving my nipple deeper into his mouth.

He undid my pants and shoved them and my panties out of the way. He undid his own pants to free his thick erection.

He cupped my ass and lifted me up until I wrapped my legs around his waist. In one swift movement, he slammed his cock into me with all the force of his hips.

We both gasped out loud with the suddenness of his thrust. He gave my muscles half a moment to get use to him, then he was thrusting, pounding relentlessly like he was scared I'd change my mind before he came.

"Gods, gods, Khala, you feel so fucking good. So good. I needed this. We needed this." He reached down between us to rub my clit as desperately as his deep strokes.

Pressure rose like a river of fast moving lava, drawing me closer and closer so relentlessly I couldn't have stopped myself if I wanted to.

I moaned. "Zared...ahhh. I'm going to come." I was already so wet. My slick coated his cock. Every thrust made a wet sucking sound.

"Yes, yes. Come for me. Come on my cock. Let me make you mine. Mine."

He rubbed more firmly, hard but always hitting the right place. "Tell me who you belong to."

"You," I panted. "I belong to you."

"Gods, yes you do. I don't care if you fuck those Fae, or even if you fall for them, don't forget you're mine too. Always. Your body belongs to me. Your gorgeous fucking body."

His words and his touch threw me over the edge, straight into that raging volcano. I was consumed by the heat that burned in my core and radiated out through the rest of my body.

My back pressed hard against the door, I cried out his name.

"I'm going to come inside you," he said. "Inside your body."

"Yes," I panted. "Come inside me. Show me who *you* belong to."

With a series of strokes and grunts, he came hard, spilling himself deep inside my pussy.

"Gods, gods, yes." He groaned long and low, grinding himself against me to milk his cock for every drop of hot cum.

"I belong to you," he told me, even as his face twisted with the intensity of his orgasm. "Always."

He let out a harsh gasp, then sagged, his forehead pressed against the door beside my head. He panted for a while, slowly regaining his breath.

"I've waited so fucking long for that. I should have been more assertive sooner."

I laughed softly. "That wouldn't have gotten you anywhere. The time wasn't right. Until it was."

"You've changed." It wasn't an accusation, just an observation.

"I feel free here," I said. "Without the Temple, without the choker... I can finally be me. I can decide for myself. Before now, whatever we meant to each other, it would have felt temporary. I expected to be at one temple and you at another." I finally understood it was that which held me back. The idea of falling for him, only to spend our lives apart. I couldn't do that to either of us. But now...

"I wouldn't have let that happen," he said firmly. "Whatever it took, I would have made sure we were together."

I believed that he would have tried, but if the Temple wanted to separate us, they would have. They held all the power over us there. Here, in Lysarial, we could do what we wanted. In the Fae Winter Court, we could be who we were meant to be.

"I need a bath," I said as he slid his cock out of me.

He sighed. "I wish I could join you, but Vayne is putting me to work and he's a prick. If he sees I'm not at my post, he'll think up some punishment for me."

I cupped his cheek with my hands. "Poor baby. If he gives you a spanking, can I watch?"

He chuckled, but he didn't say no.

CHAPTER

EIGHTEEN

KHALA

For two more days, I searched for the library. I looked in all the obvious places, then the less obvious ones. In the end, I asked Ryze.

He smiled at me before he downed the last of his morning tea and set his teacup aside. The elegant porcelain was a stark contrast to the simple pottery cups I was used to back at the temple. Perhaps they should have looked out of place in the hands of a masculine male, but the Fae had such elegant hands, it was a perfect fit.

"I can show you, if you like," he offered. "Although, I'm surprised you haven't asked before now. You've been everywhere else in the palace from what I've heard." He arched an eyebrow at me.

I matched his expression. "Is that a problem?"

"Not at all," he said lightly. "As far as I'm concerned, this is your home too, for as long as you want. I see no reason why you shouldn't familiarise yourself with it."

If he had any idea what happened with Vayne and Zared, he gave no sign. Or he knew, but wasn't concerned. I half expected him to say something, chastise me for being on my knees in a public place. Instead, all we talked about while we ate breakfast was the weather, and how much I liked my nest. He seemed pleased that I enjoyed sleeping there as much as I did.

He nodded to Joviena who collected our plates and cups before he unfolded himself from his chair and offered me his arm.

"Let me show you the library."

I took his arm and we walked from the sitting room. His favourite room, he told me. It was where we first arrived in through the portal, with the stunning view over the city and down to the harbour. The one his portals always lead to, especially with newcomers in his company. All the better to impress them. No one could disagree that it was a striking first impression.

"How old is this place?" I asked.

"Older than me," he said with a dry smile. "I'm sure Tavian would classify it as ancient based on that alone."

I laughed. "He does like to tease."

"That he does," Ryze agreed. "However, the palace is considerably older than I am. The younger part is around a thousand years old." He waved his hand at the corridor around us.

"Younger part?" I echoed. I stopped to lightly touch one of the stones that formed the wall. How many Fae had walked past it during the last ten centuries? Thousands at least.

"Yes, younger." He seemed to be watching my hand and following my thoughts. "The lower sections, including the library, are at least two thousand years old. Probably a lot older than that. The records are unclear at best."

"How long do Fae live?" I turned my eyes from the wall, to him. He was looking at me as though trying to discern something.

"The oldest known was just over a thousand." We resumed walking. "The average is seven or eight hundred years. Less if some asshole starts a war."

"Does that happen often?" We learnt about wars at the temple, but seldom the details. Mostly, they mentioned minor altercations, usually over land.

"That depends on your definition of often," Ryze said slowly. "We haven't had a full-blown war in three or four hundred years. We have border squabbles every fifty years or so. They generally start over something ridiculous and escalate from there."

We started down the marble stairs, our footsteps echoing in the empty space.

"The library is in one of the older parts of the palace," he said. "In fact, it was built first and the rest of the palace was built around it, to protect the books and records inside. We Fae are possessive of our knowledge. We've spent a considerable time accruing it."

"Is that why it's so difficult to find?" I asked. "It's hidden so people can't find it?"

"Exactly," he said. "Something so precious shouldn't be too easy to locate and potentially destroy."

"How do people access the knowledge if they can't find it?" I asked. "Isn't that the point of knowledge? So it can be shared?"

"Of course," he agreed. "Lysarial has an extensive library accessible to everyone. The palace library, however, contains several thousand volumes of more sensitive knowledge. Perhaps *contentious* would be a better word. Arguments over the existence of the gods, for example. The last war started over that very thing. Some would insist on going to war with us if they knew we had it. People are particularly touchy when it comes to their gods."

"What do you believe?" I asked.

He smiled over at me. "Giving my opinion on the subject might start a war, so if you don't mind, I'll keep it to myself. Suffice to say, I approve of healthy curiosity and debate, and appreciate alternative points of view."

He led me down another set of stairs to the very lower level of the palace, and through a door that led out into a garden.

The air was perfumed with jasmine and roses, with a hint of autumn fruits and vegetables.

I frowned.

"It's strange, isn't it?" he remarked. "It should smell like autumn leaves slowly decaying. Instead, it smells like the height of summer."

He shrugged and led me over through a stand of trees. We stopped at a small building almost entirely obscured by vines. He swept them to one side to reveal a pair of doors made from wide slats of wood. Heavy handles in the shape of a snake swallowing its own tail, were set in the front.

"Is this the only way in?" I asked. "No wonder I couldn't find it."

"It's not the only way, but the library is warded against entry via portals, so through the front door it is."

He placed a hand on one of the handles and pushed the door open.

At first, all I saw was darkness. The air was still, the smell of yellowed paper and old binding heavy.

After a moment, lights started to pop on in the high ceiling. Row after row of chandeliers illuminated shelf after shelf covered with books and scrolls. The shelves continued until they were swallowed by a section still in darkness.

My gaze followed a shelf up to the ornately painted ceiling.

"This is the top level," Ryze said. "There are several more down below, in caverns and tunnels under the palace. We tried mapping it all once, but it's extensive and, as strange as it may sound, it never seems to be exactly the same every time."

I glanced at him quickly. "What do you mean? Someone rearranges the shelves?"

"It's more like someone rearranges the tunnels," he said. "My mother used to say an ancient magic made this place and still resides here in the library. I haven't seen evidence of anything alive in here apart from the Fae who come in and use the place, and those who maintain it."

As far as I could tell, it was only me and him here right now. On the other hand, I couldn't make out a speck of dust on any of the shelves or tables. Either dust couldn't get in, or someone was meticulous in cleaning it away. Considering how big this section alone was, I'd think by the time they got to the end, it would be time to start back at the beginning again. Unless they used magic in the process.

Hells, maybe that was the punishment Vayne gave to people like Zared when they weren't where they were supposed to be. A task that tedious would keep anyone in line, wouldn't it?

"How is it organised?" I stepped over to one shelf and ran my hand across the line of spines. At a glance, they were about a variety of topics, from gardening to philosophy. Several dozen were fiction.

I pulled out one at random and opened it. The picture printed on the page was of a woman bent over. A man stood behind her about to impale her on his cock.

The next page, she was riding him, facing away from him while his hands gripped her hips. The page after that she was with two lovers, one inside her pussy, the other inside her mouth.

"I see why you'd keep the library hidden," I said dryly. "You definitely wouldn't want anything this precious destroyed."

Ryze looked over my shoulder and chuckled. "Certainly not. We should take that with us when we're finished. It might come in useful." When I glanced back at him, he winked.

I closed the book and slipped it back onto the shelf.

"In answer to your question, it's organised by topic and age. The further down we go, the older the books and scrolls are. Some of these have only been here for fifty years or more. Some less than that. There are several sections of empty shelves for future additions."

"What happens when they're full?" I asked.

"Then we find space somewhere else," he said, as if the answer was obvious.

"And when you run out of space?"

He cocked his head. "Do we need a kitchen that badly? We could always turn that into library space."

"I think that would work right up to the point where people got hungry," I said. "Then they might resent that decision."

He sighed and picked up another book to flick through the pages. "It's always something. Either way, we'll find somewhere. Even if we have to move the palace to another location."

"Is there a section on omegas?" I asked.

He shrugged vaguely. "I'm sure there is, somewhere in here. There's not much to know beyond what I told you. Beyond what you already knew."

"I still want to read everything there is," I said. "I'm sure there's a lot I could learn about the Fae too, while I'm here."

"Probably," he agreed. "If there's a subject we like writing and reading about, it's ourselves. Evidently, we find ourselves fascinating."

"Are there books about humans in here too?" I asked.

"There's at least one whole section," he said as though that was a lot. "A couple of hundred books, unless I'm mistaken."

"Out of several thousand books, there's a couple of hundred about humans?" It was difficult not to be slightly offended by that.

He leaned against the shelf and crossed his arms. "If it makes you feel any better, there's three or four hundred about griffins. And several hundred discussing the myths around dragons."

"That doesn't make me feel any better," I said. "Are Fae so disinterested in humans?"

"Not disinterested," he replied carefully. "Just self-absorbed. Would humans want to be written about?"

"Probably not," I conceded. "Especially not by Fae. There were more books in the Temple about humans than there were about the Fae, so I suppose it goes both ways."

"Precisely," he said. "Let me show you something."

CHAPTER
NINETEEN
KHALA

I thought he was insinuating something else, but he led me over to a section full of scrolls.

"Each of these is a map of the Fae courts." He picked one up, took it over to a table and unrolled it. "This is a map of the Winter Court. There's Lysarial there." He pointed an elegant finger, before tracing it around the coastline. "I have a small house in the bay here."

"Smaller than this?" I asked.

He flashed me a smile. "Just slightly. I wouldn't want to embarrass myself by staying in a shack, would I now?"

"I've seen you sleep on a forest floor," I pointed out. "A shack would seem to be a step up from that."

"Excellent point, but it's a little bigger than a shack anyway." He turned back to the map. "This is the border with the Autumn Court, and here is the Spring Court. The Summer Court is there."

"Everyone has a bit of ocean?" I asked.

"Everyone has a harbour," he agreed. "If we didn't, we'd end up in that full-blown war we were talking about earlier. Of course, the Winter Court has the best harbour."

"They probably all think that," I said.

"Undoubtedly, but we're the only ones who are right." He pushed the map aside and reached for another. "The Spring Court has the best mountains, although we get snow caps." He pointed to a line of peaks on the map. "Right here is the best place to see griffins. They roost in the caves there."

I looked from the maps on the table, to the shelf where they were stored.

"Why are there six?"

He looked at me approvingly. "I was wondering if you'd notice. Most people might assume they're maps of all the Fae lands on one parchment. Or more detailed maps of Lysarial."

"They're not?" I guessed.

"No, although those are both around here somewhere." He gestured vaguely. "Those are maps of the other two courts. Courts a lot of Fae will suggest don't exist. In fact, some insist they don't."

"How could you have maps of places that don't exist?" I asked.

"See, that's what I keep saying." He grabbed one map and unrolled it. Across the top, the words 'Court of Dreams' were written in a neat hand. "The other is a map of the Court of Shadows."

A rough outline was sketched on the page, with minimal detail apart from a city or town here and there.

"Where is it?" I frowned at the map. If somebody went there to draw this, they weren't very thorough.

"No one knows," he said. "Hence why people are reluctant to accept their existence. For all I know, they could be right under our feet." He pointed to the floor.

"You don't think so?" I eyed the stone under my boots.

"A hidden court, deep underground. That sounds more like the Court of Nightmares than dreams, to me. Shadows— Potentially more plausible but still..."

"Where do you think they are?" He seemed very certain they were actual places.

He shook his head. "I don't know, but the way this library rearranges itself is similar to the way the legends speak of the Court of Shadows. It may be nothing more than coincidence. The Court of Dreams might exist only there, in our dreams."

"How did you get these?" I asked, running my finger down the side of the map.

"They've been in my family for several generations. The gods only know how my ancestor got their hands on them. Every couple of generations, the High Lord sends out scouts in search of the courts."

"How long has it been since the last time that happened?" I suspected I knew the answer.

"A couple of generations," he said with a smile. "It might be time to try again."

"Is this what High Lords do during their spare time?" I asked. "Hunt for omegas and courts that may not exist?"

"Life would quickly get boring if we didn't have things like that to keep ourselves amused," he said with a sniff. "Then we might have nothing better to do but start wars. I don't believe anyone wants that."

"Hunting dreams and shadows seems like a better pastime," I agreed. "What do Tavian and Vayne think about that?"

"Vayne thinks it's a waste of time," Ryze admitted. "Tavian is up for anything adventurous. He's still young enough not to be old and bitter."

I nodded. I noticed that about him.

I leaned in for a better look at the map. Along the sides were words written like a poem or song lyrics.

I read them out loud.

"IN THE COURT OF DREAMS, Fae dance,
　　Hearts flutter in a wild prance.
　　The moonlight shines so bright,
　　Lighting steps that flow all night.

THE AIR IS alive with Fae song,
　　A place where dreams hold long.
　　The scent of honey and blooming flowers,
　　Mingle with the Fae's lost powers.

THEIR VOICES BLEND, sweet and true,
　　A melody that echoes through the hue.
　　They sing of love and endless wonder,
　　Hearts aglow, spirits thunder.

THE COURT OF DREAMS is a place of wonder,
　　Where Fae reign with magic stronger.
　　Come dance beneath the moon,
　　Lose yourself to the compelling tune.

IN THE COURT OF DREAMS, time stands still,
　　All around is magic and thrill.
　　Close your eyes and take a chance,
　　Join the Fae's wildest dance."

"IT'S AN ANCIENT FAE SONG," Ryze said. "A song of scent and magic. I'll spare you my singing. Legend says it's a song from the Court of Dreams itself."

"Then it can't be underground," I said slowly. "Not if they're singing about moonlight."

He looked surprised, then down at the page, a frown on his brow.

"I've never thought about interpreting it literally, but you're right."

He placed his palm on the parchment beside the lyrics. "A place where magic is stronger, the moon shines, magic plays, and there's dew and blooming flowers."

"That sounds like a night in the late spring," I said.

He tapped the page with one finger. "It does."

"Is there a place where magic is stronger?" I asked.

He looked thoughtful, but ultimately sighed. "Probably, but I don't know of such a place. That's the kind of thing the High Lords keep to themselves. To *ourselves*, if I'm honest. I wouldn't tell anyone about it either. Some asshole would want to exploit it if they knew."

"Or start a war?" I suggested.

"That too," he agreed.

"Is there anything like that on the Court of Shadows' map?"

"Indeed there is." He hurried to grab and unroll that map. It was his turn to read.

"COURT OF SHADOWS, whispers creep,
    Fae of darkness love to sleep.
    Their magic like knives, eyes a-shine,
    They lurk and hide, await a sign.

THE TREES here bend and twist and creak,
    If they're alive, somehow speak.
    Branches reach out with spidery claws,
    Open the air, the harsh, cold doors.

FAE OF SHADOWS GATHER HERE,
    Court of secrets, place of fear,
    Dance and sway with subtle grace,
    Shadows flicker on every space.

THE MOON IS ALWAYS FULL,
    It casts a glow on the skulls,
    That line the path and watch,
    With hollow eyes, wary touch.

IF YOU DARE ENTER the court,
    To find the ones long sought.
    Fae here play a deadly game,
    They'll ensnare you, hard as stone.

. . .

HEED THE WARNING CLEAR,
    Those who wander too near,
    The shadows, where the Fae,
    Play games of darkness, night and day."

I SHIVERED when he finished speaking. "More moonlight, and a path lined with skulls. What a cheerful sounding place."

"It is," he said thoughtfully. "Nowhere you're familiar with, then?"

I wasn't sure if he was teasing or not but I gave him a playful curl of my lip anyway. "Not yet, but give me time. I'm sure I could line the corridor with skulls if you want me to. I could start with yours."

He chuckled. "So feisty. Is that why Vayne is training you?"

I should have known Ryze would know about that. "It's as good a reason as any." I tried not to smile, but failed.

"I might have to tell him not to train you, if I'm going to live to regret it. Or die regretting it." He rolled up the maps, one by one, and placed them back carefully.

"Don't give me an excuse to kill you and you'll be fine." I meant the words to be teasing, but he gave me a funny look before he turned away. Presumably Fae humour and human humour were different. Or maybe he didn't appreciate potential death threats.

When he turned back, his usual amused expression was back on his face. Had I imagined the look he gave me? He was a complicated man. Presumably most people were, after living for as long as he had. He must have seen and done untold things over all those years. You'd think he'd be used to death threats, even joking ones, by now. Unless that wasn't the Fae way. I certainly had a lot to learn where these folk were concerned.

They had a lot to learn about me too.

"What would the other Fae think if they knew those maps were here?" I asked.

"Apart from thinking I've lost my mind?" he asked. "Some would laugh. Others would want them for themselves. There may be other clues to the whereabouts of the two missing courts. Clues that can't be deciphered without our maps. Mostly, they'd think I'm foolish for holding onto them. Fortunately, I don't much care what they think. Where's the harm in imagining something that may not exist?"

"None, I suppose. Unless you're planning to create your own path of skulls in the moonlight." If that was the case, I may regret drawing his attention to those lyrics.

"That would be one interesting way to decorate the city, but I suspect the residents wouldn't agree or appreciate it. A lot of them are very conservative folk. Dew and blooming flowers in the moonlight is much more their thing. And dancing around to ancient Fae songs while drunk on their favourite wine."

"That sounds preferable to me too," I told him.

"Now I think about it, I prefer that as well." He smiled.

I wiped a hand over my brow. It came back wet. I hadn't realised how warm it was inside the library. When we first stepped inside, it felt cooler than the air outside. Now, the heat pressed down on me, like I was locked in a room full of steam.

"Khala?" Ryze looked at me in concern. "Are you all right?"

I blinked at him. He looked hazy.

"I think I need some air."

"Fuck," he said under his breath. "I thought we had more time."

Maybe he had lost his mind, or I had, because he was making no sense. More time for what?

He started to put his hands on my shoulders, but stopped. "It's not air you need. You're going into heat. We need to get you back upstairs, into your room. Somewhere comfortable for the next few hours."

Hours?

Heat?

Fuck.

CHAPTER
TWENTY

KHALA

"I'm going to make a portal for us, okay?" Ryze looked at me intently.

I stared back. "I thought you couldn't make portals in here."

I didn't care. He could have leaned me over the table and pounded into me then and there. I wanted to rip my clothes to shreds and beg him to fuck me. Blood and heat raced through me like they were competing to see which might overwhelm me first.

At the same time, I needed to be in my nest, nestled in my familiar sheets and pillows.

This was more than sex. More than arousal. It was a primal urge to seek shelter, a safe place to satisfy my alpha. To let him satisfy me. With no hesitation, no boundaries.

Ryze chuckled quickly. "No one can portal in, but I can portal out. Otherwise, I'd risk getting stuck down here if the roof caved in. That would be... unfortunate. Particularly right now." His expression was as strained as the front of his pants. If it wasn't for the imperative to take me to shelter, he'd be embedded deep inside me by now.

I suppressed a groan at the thought. The wait was already excruciating. Any longer and I may leak a river of slick on the stone floor.

He threw his hands up in front of him. A vertical white slit appeared in the air before it widened.

The door here was smaller than the one he made in the forest, barely wide enough to fit through if we went one at a time. The edges were hazy, ragged, as though he lacked the power or the concentration for anything neat and finessed.

Instead of a tunnel, I saw right into the upstairs sitting room. If I remem-

97

bered, I'd have to ask him about that later. Presumably it had something to do with the distance between the two locations.

"It will have to do," he said, his voice drum-skin tight.

I trusted he knew what he was doing right now. I hoped he did, because I certainly didn't. All I knew right now was heat and fear.

He put one arm around my shoulders, the other behind my knees and scooped me up.

"I can walk," I protested.

"Of course you can, but what kind of alpha would I be if I didn't carry you across the threshold?"

"One who doesn't get growled at later for treating me like I'm fragile." But I nestled into his arms and purred.

Anywhere his skin touched mine, he set me on fire. My whole body throbbed with need. Blood pumped through my body. I could have come then and there, but not until I was in my nest.

I tucked my legs in so my feet didn't hit the side of the portal while he carried me through.

In a rush of cooler air, we stepped into the sitting room.

Ryze called out, sending startled staff running. For what, or who, I didn't know. The sound of thunder in my ears was too loud.

He carried me down the corridor and into my room.

"Breathe," he instructed. He set me down.

I savoured the feel and smell of my bed. My nest.

I breathed because he told me to. All my instincts were to obey. Obey and mate. Give myself to Ryze. I couldn't have ignored the imperative if I wanted to. No more than I could have stopped breathing. My body gasped for his, begging to be touched, caressed, filled.

Ryze sat beside me. The bed dipped with his weight. His eyes were on mine. The last of his restraint evaporated like smoke. Like the last dying notes of his song. He reached for me and started to tear away my clothes. Every time his skin brushed against mine, the fire burnt a little hotter. His breath was harsh as he shredded fabric with his hands.

"Ryze," I pleaded. "I need—"

He paused to brush damp air off my face. "Shhh. I know what you need. I'll give it to you. All of it."

All I could say to that was, "Please."

I tore at his clothes, not caring if the fabric ripped. Not caring if I hurt my hands doing it. I needed to touch his skin. I needed to impale myself on his cock. I needed to take everything he gave me, and then some.

He ripped away my shirt and grunted his dissatisfaction when the leather wouldn't rip and he was forced to undo my pants to shove them down my legs.

I kicked them off my feet and onto the floor.

With one tug, he tore away my panties. He threw them aside. Between us, we shredded his shirt.

Like the other men, he was muscular, but slender at the same time. Smooth skin, sculpted abs, hard stomach. Right now, he was covered in a light sheen of sweat.

Hands trembling, I undid his pants. He pushed them down his thighs.

My eyes widened. "Gods. What—"

His cock was huge. Long and thick. At the base, was what looked like an extra ring of muscle, half again as wide as the rest of his cock.

"My knot," he said simply and shed his pants.

Slick was all but dripping from me when, acting on pure instinct, I rolled over and pushed myself up on to all fours. Presenting for my alpha.

"Good omega," he purred. He knelt behind me, lined up his cock, and slowly slid into me.

I groaned with pleasure and increasing need. I wanted more, deeper. All the way to his knot.

The deeper he pushed, the more my muscles were forced to relax to take him. I was so wet, so slick, so aroused, it only took a minute or so for him to be fully seated inside me. When his knot reached the entrance to my pussy, the pressure directly on my clit was so intense, I came. I bucked against him and cried out.

The single orgasm wasn't enough to even begin to satisfy the raging heat inside me.

Neither was the second one.

I came for the third time as the bed dipped again. Tavian sat down beside me. He traced the line of my face, down to my cheek before he kissed me. His tongue demanded entry to my mouth. When I opened for him, he thrust in and out, fucking my mouth like Ryze fucked my body.

I moaned with pure pleasure. I'd been with two men before, but not often. The presence of the other omega during my heat made perfect sense to me. One of my other lovers. Ryze's lover too. It was right that he was here. I suckled on his tongue and kissed him until my mouth hurt, then went on kissing him.

The bed dipped again. Vayne settled on the other side of me. He ran his hands over my breasts and pinched my aching, hard nipples.

Surrounded by three of my lovers, I was hotter than ever. I might die right here, engulfed by my inferno. Surrounded by three Fae men who seemed to have claimed me for their own. To who I wanted to belong. I wanted them to belong to me.

I closed my eyes and let the moment catch me and hold me. I wanted to make it last forever.

The pressure of Ryze's cock as he pounded into me made me come for a fourth time. I cried out Ryze's name with my lips against Tavian's. With Vayne's hands caressing and palming my nipples.

I wasn't done yet. Not even when Zared slipped into the room and tentatively sat beside Tavian. They must have been who Ryze called for after we arrived back from the library.

My pack. I hadn't thought of them like that until now, but I liked it.

I liked it when Tavian broke off our kiss, turned to Zared, and gently kissed his mouth.

Even Ryze slowed in his thrusting to watch for Zared's response.

Hesitant at first, Zared kissed Tavian back. Tavian's tongue swiped across his lips and between them into his mouth.

Evidently inspired, Vayne turned my face and pressed his erection between my lips. I opened eagerly, sucking and licking him in rhythm with Ryze's strokes into my body.

Ryze grunted as he came, his cock embedded all the way inside me. He stilled for a moment, catching his breath before finding his rhythm again.

I hadn't considered how many times an alpha might orgasm during an omega's heat. Evidently it was more than once. As for me, I was nowhere near done yet. The pace was slower now, the need less frantic. My body still ached and throbbed, but now I slowed and enjoyed the way Ryze filled me, the way his knot vibrated against my clit.

Vayne slid in and out of my mouth with deliberate, almost lazy thrusts.

All around me was a haze of groans, skin slapping on skin. the wet sound of thrusting and sucking.

I let myself get lost in it. It became my everything in those long, languid moments.

When I didn't think Ryze could be any deeper inside me, he pushed in a little further, fitting his knot inside my pussy. His muscle expanded, locking him in place as he came again.

With a storm of pressure on my clit and G-spot, I came again, and again, and again. The string of orgasms went on with barely a break between them. Barely a chance to catch my breath.

They finally subsided as Vayne came in my mouth, flooding my throat with hot cum. I managed to swallow before collapsing onto the mattress, Ryze still locked tight into my pussy.

He sagged, his weight on his hands and knees to either side of me. He rolled us so he lay behind me, his arms around me, a leg over mine.

Eventually, my vision cleared from my last orgasm. Tavian had his mouth around Zared's cock. Zared's expression was one of pure bliss. He thrust slowly between Tavian's lips, his hips rolling in rhythm.

He opened his eyes fully to see I was watching him. For a moment, I thought he might pull out, but he smiled back when I smiled at him. I liked seeing them enjoying each other. Why shouldn't they? I enjoyed both of them, and this was much better than the human-versus-Fae animosity that could have been.

"You did amazingly well," Ryze said, stroking his hand up and down my hip. "Such a good omega."

I was surprised, not just by his praise, but my response to it. I purred again.

"It's an omega thing." Vayne propped himself up on his elbow and also seemed to be watching Zared and Tavian. "Wanting to please the alpha and getting praised. Lucky us, betas don't have that instinct. We just do whatever the fuck we want."

"Yes you fucking do," Ryze agreed. He didn't sound too worried about it. Not right now anyway.

"Is that what it's always like?" I asked. "Heat, I mean. I already know Vayne does whatever he likes."

Zared's thrusts were faster now. He was close to coming.

Ryze chuckled. "It can be. Depending on the circumstances, it might have just been you and I. I thought perhaps you'd feel better with the other three present. More comfortable."

"I did, thank you," I said.

He kissed my hair. "As I said before, it's an alpha's job to anticipate his omega's needs. Yours and Tavian's."

"I didn't realise he and Zared..."

Zared closed his eyes and scrunched up his face.

"Neither did I, but Tavian has a way of endearing himself to people," Ryze said. "And you were radiating heat. They wouldn't be the only ones in the palace today responding to it."

I winced. "I hope no one has any regrets then."

"Not at all. It's like alcohol. It makes people act on things they want to act on, but they wouldn't otherwise be brave enough to. A good many relationships have started around an omega's heat. It's one of many things that makes you incredibly special."

I blushed and changed the subject. I wiggled my rear. His knot was still firmly locked in place.

"How long do we stay like this?"

"Until my knot contracts," he said. "It should only take half an hour or so. Are you in such a hurry?"

"No," I admitted. I liked the way he felt inside me.

Apparently so did Zared, because he came, groaning and thrusting into Tavian's mouth. Tavian went on sucking even after he sagged, visibly swallowing Zared's cum.

Gods, that was hot. He even smacked his lips and smiled.

Fortunately, the nest was big enough for all five of us to lie down and catch our breath. Zared lay face-to-face with me, Tavian on the other side of him.

I wanted to ask how Zared was, but Ryze slid out of me.

Immediately, the pain began.

At first, it was just a tingle, like pins and needles all through my body.

In a handful of moments, it escalated to searing pain.

Every bone in my body shattered into shards. Every nerve, every vessel, every organ was pressed tight like a thousand tiny hands squeezed them, dug in nails or talons.

I threw my head back and screamed.

And screamed.
And screamed.

CHAPTER
TWENTY-ONE

KHALA

"Her fever has finally broken." Tavian sounded exhausted. He *was* exhausted. Weary right down to the bone. And worried, but that seemed to have lessened.

"It's about time," Vayne grunted. He was tired too. "I'll get Ryze."

Tavian grunted, unintelligible, but sounded like an agreement.

Something cool and wet slid across my brow. A cloth, wiping away sweat and damp hair.

My eyelids twitched. They felt like they didn't belong to me. I wanted to open them, but they wouldn't obey.

"Hey," Tavian said softly. "You're awake? Khala?"

I managed a murmur in response, just a soft one from the back of my throat.

I forced my eyes to open a slit, and found myself in almost total darkness.

My nest.

My memory was hazy. I went into heat and then... Then the pain. Then there was nothing. Until now.

He ran the washcloth over my forehead again.

"How are you feeling? You've had a high fever for about three days. I was starting to think it wouldn't break. Here, I'll get you some water." He leaned away, and came back with a cup and a straw which he pressed against my lips.

I managed a couple of sips before he took the cup away again.

"You shouldn't have too much. Your stomach is empty. I'll send down for some soup soon."

"What happened?" I asked. "Was I sick?" I've never heard of an illness that caused so much pain. It might be peculiar to... Gods, I was with the Fae, unless all of that was a dream.

"Not sick exactly," he said carefully. "Don't worry, you'll be fine now."

He didn't quite believe his own words. How did I know that? I felt...him. His presence and his emotions. He mentioned a fever. Was I hallucinating?

I struggled to sit up and lean back against the pillows. "I remember pain. So much pain. I didn't think it would end."

"It's over now," he said gently. "You passed out and now it's over."

"What if it happens again?" My voice was a hoarse whisper.

"It won't. I promise." That, he did believe.

"Tave," I said his name slowly. "What happened to me?"

"It might be better if—"

"I'm asking you," I insisted.

He hesitated. Sighed. Twitched back the edge of the curtain.

"It might be better if you see for yourself." His tone was chilling. A shaft of fear slid all the way through me, from my head to my bare toes.

I pressed a hand to my belly. As far as I could tell, I wasn't pregnant with some human-Fae child that shattered me upon conception. Thank the gods.

How bad could it be then? Very, judging by the way Tavian behaved.

I moved my hand from my belly to push the curtain back further.

I stopped and stared.

What in the name of all the hells?

It wasn't my hand. The fingers were longer, more slender and elegant.

I made a fist.

The fingers curled into a fist.

"What is happening?" I asked in a terrified whisper.

I felt him being fearful for me.

I felt. Him. Being fearful. *For me.* I *hadn't* imagined that.

"You should look in the mirror," he said. "I can bring one to you. You'll still be weak after the fever." Before I could respond, he all but lept out of the nest and trotted away.

He returned a minute or two later, a mirror double the size of his head, in his hands.

His trembling hands.

He held it up in front of my face.

I stared at the reflection. The reflection of a stranger.

She had some of the same features as me. The same straight, blonde hair. The same eye colour. Her eyes were slanted like a cat. Her chin was pointed. Her eyebrows were perfect curves. And her ears... Her ears were elegantly pointed at the tips. Like a Fae.

Her tongue slid over her lips at the same time mine did.

"Oh gods." My breath misted the mirror.

I touched my cheek. "What did you do to me?" Ice cold fear crept through me. Along with the realisation I was looking at myself. Khala, but different.

I looked like Fae.

Ryze appeared in the doorway. He skidded to a stop at the sight of me. I felt his relief at seeing me awake, but no part of him was surprised. A whisper of anxiety was quickly brushed away. In its place, was the usual arrogant, slightly amused High Lord. His arms at his sides, he sauntered over to the bed.

"Well," he said with a smile. "You're looking much better."

"What the fuck did you do to me?" I demanded.

Ryze leaned over and placed a hand on my forehead. "You had a fever, my dear. A very high one. You've been out for a few days."

I flinched away from him. "That much I know. I remember the pain. Everything else is hazy. And when I look in the mirror, I see...someone else." I struggled to hold back anger and tears. "What did you *do?*"

Ryze's expression softened, almost to the point of looking apologetic. Almost.

"I'm sorry, Khala," he said, his voice gentle. "We suspected this might happen, but I didn't want to scare you. There was a very good chance you'd stay human. But now... Clearly that's not the case. It's important you know the truth."

"You think?" I said sarcastically.

They suspected I'd change and didn't think I needed to know about it? I thought I'd started to get to know them but now I realised how foolish that was. They were Fae. All my life I was told not to trust them. I got caught up with their charms. Where did that get me? Could I believe a single word that came out of their mouths?

I took a deep breath, trying to compose myself. Trying, but not succeeding very well.

"All right, what truth?" I asked. "No more bullshit. You've fucked around with me enough."

Ryze hesitated for a moment, then took the mirror from Tavian's hands and set it aside on the table next to the bed. He sat beside me.

"The truth about what you are," he said. "You're not entirely human. You never were."

"What the hells does that mean?" I demanded.

"You're part Fae," he said simply. "My guess is your father was human, but your mother was part Fae. Or perhaps the man you knew as your father isn't, in fact, your father. Or perhaps—" He shook his head. "Either way, when you went into heat, it triggered a transformation. That's what caused the pain you felt."

I stared at him. My mind raced.

"So, what am I now?" I asked tentatively.

Ryze hesitated again. "You're Fae," he said finally. "Like me. Like Tavian and Vayne. Like most of the residents of Lysarial. You may have magic."

This was getting better and better. Another surge of fear and confusion slid up my spine.

"What kind of magic?" I asked.

Ryze looked at me solemnly. "We'll have to figure that out."

This was all so much to take in. "What do I do now?" I asked.

"I suggest you rest. You must be tired after the last few days."

"I'll rest when I get more answers," I said sharply. "How can I feel your emotions? Yours and Tavian's? Vayne's too." I hadn't realised until now but I felt him as I was waking. I knew he was outside near the door. That was confirmed when he peered in a moment later.

Now Ryze looked surprised. "Gods, you're right. I feel yours too." He gave me a lazy smile. "You're really pissed off with me right now."

I snorted. "No shit. You didn't bother to tell me I might be part Fae and that mating with me might make me fully Fae." I frowned. "Am I fully Fae? Is any part of me human?"

"You seem to have your human temper intact," Ryze said dryly. "It's impossible to know for sure. Humans and Fae aren't biologically that much different. Except there's no such thing as a fully human omega."

That answer provoked another question. I looked over at Tavian. "Were you human before?"

He grinned. "No, I've always been Fae."

"But you knew what might happen to me?"

"We all did," Vayne said from where he stood leaning against the door frame, his arms crossed over his chest. "High Lord Ryzellius, in all his wisdom, decided you weren't to be told."

Without taking his eyes off me, Ryze said, "As I said before, I didn't want her scared. What would you have done if I told you? Running away wouldn't have changed anything except who you spent your heat with."

"They might have been someone who didn't flat out lie to me," I said coldly.

"It might have also been with someone from the Summer Court," Ryze said. He ran his fingertips over his brow. "Omegas transformed by their mating heat are almost always possessing some kind of magic. Usually strong." He chewed on his thoughts for a moment before he continued. "Always connected to the alpha they shared their heat with. What magic you have will highly likely be the ability to manipulate snow and ice and the like."

"So if this happened in the Summer Court, I'd—what? Be able to manipulate heat and fire?"

"Something like that," Ryze agreed. "High Lord Cavan has been trying to extend his influence outside his court."

"Meaning?" I prompted.

"Meaning we believe he'd like to eradicate the other courts and, with them, the other seasons," Vayne said.

Ryze nodded his agreement. "You've noticed the unseasonable warmth lately. That's due to his influence. We think he wants omegas so he can transform them and make this change permanent. And by doing so, provoke us into war. That was why we had to bring you here. We couldn't let you be used as his instrument."

"So instead, you used me as yours?" I asked bitterly.

"I can see how you might interpret it that way," he conceded. "It was never my intention to hurt you. Merely to stop you from falling into the wrong hands."

"You think yours are the right ones?" I asked.

"The fact you can feel us would suggest we are," Ryze said.

I stared at him in confusion. "Is it a Fae thing or a mating heat thing?" Did I want the answer?

"It's a bonded mate thing," he said, apparently amused at my turn of phrase.

I didn't share his amusement. "Bonded mate thing?" I echoed.

"Yes," he said patiently. "Like fated mates. Meant to be. Decreed by the gods. Joined by the—"

"Fuck." I glared at him.

"That's technically correct," he agreed. "Fucking created a bond, but I've rarely heard of someone bonding three mates."

"Four," Zared said from the doorway.

TWENTY-TWO

KHALA

"I feel her too, but I hoped I was the only one. After what you did to her, none of you deserve to be anywhere near her. In fact, you can get the fuck out. I'm going to speak to Khala alone." Zared glared at them all.

When they looked like they might all object, I nodded. "Please go. I need time to think. To understand what the hells is going on."

Before they could leave I quickly asked, "Can this be undone?"

It was Ryze who answered. "No," he said before he slipped out the door.

"Fuck." Zared flopped down on the bed beside me. "I'm sorry, I should have been here sooner. Those assholes made me leave and..."

"It's all right." I went to put a hand on his arm but saw those elegant fingers again and stopped. Lowered my hand. "This must be...difficult for you."

He shook his head at me. "Typical Khala. After all you went through, you're worried about me?"

"You don't like Fae," I said softly.

"I don't like *those* Fae." He nodded his head in the direction the other three men went. "I thought maybe... But then they went and did this to you."

He closed his eyes and shook his head. "It doesn't change how I feel about you. It's still you on the inside."

"What if it isn't?" I asked. "What if I'm not just changed on the outside? What if..." I shook my head. I didn't even know how to put my thoughts into words. Hells, I didn't know how to put them into ordered thoughts either.

I hopped up off the bed and stalked over to the longer mirror which hung on the wall.

At some point, someone put me in loose sleep pants and a shirt that barely covered my breasts. The pants would have fallen past my feet, but now, with my longer legs, they brushed the tops of my toes.

My hips were narrower too. Everything about me was more lithe and elegant. Beautiful as any of the Fae. Me, but at the same time, not me.

I ran my hands down my sides, and back up to my face.

"My mother knew. She must have known." That explained her eagerness to leave me at the temple. "Do you think—"

"I wouldn't put it past any of them." Zared came to stand behind me and slipped his arms around me. "But don't think about that. How you came about doesn't matter as much as the fact you did."

He turned me around to face him. Surprise flashed across his face when he realised we now stood eye to eye. "It's not all bad."

I slapped him lightly on the chest. "I was perfectly happy being as tall as I was."

"Me too, but..." He brushed his lips over mine without having to bend his neck. "I don't have to work as hard now."

"I'm starting to think I attract assholes," I said only half-teasing.

"I can't say I disagree," he said in the same tone. He glanced down, then back up again. "I don't want to defend any of them, but for what it's worth, they were worried about you. Tavian and I have been here pretty much since your heat. Keeping you cool and clean and watching over you. The only reason I left was because I hadn't had any sleep and they insisted.

"Ryze and Vayne were in and out all the time. Neither of them would explain anything. Tavian either." He was visibly frustrated. "I tried to get him to leave, but he refused, except for a few hours to get some sleep. I want to hate him for what he did to you."

"Did you talk about what happened between you?" I asked tentatively.

"No, we didn't talk much. When we did, it was about you. Mostly how worried about you we were. Ryze and Vayne seemed to think you'd be fine, but Tavian and I... When you started to scream...we both thought we'd lose you."

"But you didn't," I said. "Did you see me change?"

His eyes glazed as he thought back. "I thought I was seeing things. One minute you were how you were and then you weren't. I didn't understand what was going on."

"But they did," I guessed. They must have been waiting for it, to see whether or not it would happen. Hoping it would. If they needed my help to deal with the High Lord of the Summer Court, they would have been wishing for the transformation.

"Is the worst part changing, or that they didn't tell you it might happen?" Zared asked.

I shook my head. "I don't know. The whole thing is such a fucking mess. And now I have some kind of bond with all of you? I can't help thinking I deserved to know this could have happened."

The fact the bond was a surprise to all of them was no consolation. I couldn't think of anything that would make up for them keeping this from me. Ryze was right, I was pissed off. At him most of all. He was the High Lord, the alpha. If he wanted me told, I would have been. He single-handedly kept everything from me. And for what? Some supposed disagreement with another Fae court? He had no guarantee I'd agree to help him. Was he so desperate he'd take that gamble?

Did he realise he risked forming a bond with me? I had so many more questions than answers.

"You definitely should have been told," he said. "But is the bond so bad?" He stroked my cheek. "I feel your anger and confusion, but also your determination not to let this overwhelm you."

"You didn't need a bond for that," I said wryly. "How else would I feel about all of this shit?"

"Terrified?" he suggested. "Ready to kick Ryze in the cock?"

"I'm feeling both of those too," I said. The problem was, when I thought about Ryze's cock, it wasn't to kick him in it. I remembered the way he felt inside me, the way his knot locked him in place. The way his approval made me feel warm and satisfied in a way I hadn't felt before.

But his betrayal of my trust went far deeper than any of that. Bond or no bond, I wasn't sure I could ever forgive him for that, much less help him. Right now, I didn't even want to look at him.

"Lucky for you, you have me to help you get through it," he said, more than a little smug. Of course, he was the only one who hadn't screwed me over. He was also the only human left in Lysarial.

"Are you sure you don't want to go back to Ebonfalls?" I asked gently. "I can't go back now, even if I wanted to. I wouldn't be welcome."

The gods only knew what anyone there would think if they saw me now. I could just imagine the expression on Hycanthe's face. She'd probably think I deserved everything I got.

And Tyla. Was she all right, or had this happened to her too? Was it really the heat that did this, or was it from having a High Lord's cock and cum inside me? If it wasn't just the heat, and I got to her in time, maybe I could prevent the same thing from happening to her. At least warn her of what she might become. The rest of my sisters too. I wouldn't even wish this on Hycanthe.

"Because I'm human?" he asked, his tone strangely vacant. "Do you want me to leave?"

I gave him a steady look. That was easier to do now I was the same height as him. I must only be slightly shorter than the Fae men. No wonder it felt like my bones shattered. They probably had, before being put back together again differently. As long as I lived, I'd remember the agony. Was there any part of me that wasn't broken and rearranged? How could I possibly not be a different person after this?

"We both know you wouldn't leave unless you want to," I told him. "If I told you I wanted you to go, you'd feel the lie. But I don't want you to stay here just because of me. I'm not that Silent Maiden anymore. I'm—" I twisted around in his arms to look at my reflection again.

"I'm Fae." Even saying that, even *seeing* it didn't make it seem real. The face staring back at me was still a stranger, even with the familiar features.

"And I'm not," he said. "What you are doesn't make me want you any less." He rested his chin lightly on my shoulder. "Should I ask if they can change me too?"

"I don't think it works that way," I said. "Even if they could, I don't want you to change. You're gorgeous just the way you are. Besides, if you were Fae, you might be taller than me again."

He chuckled. "That's as good a reason as any not to change." He stopped and frowned at his own reflection.

"What?" I asked. The sudden change in his demeanour put me back on edge. Although, edge seemed to be the default emotion of the day. I was teetering on it, hoping not to plunge over it.

"I was just wishing I was an alpha," he admitted. "Maybe then..."

"It might not have happened?" I guessed. "If you're part Fae, it still would have."

"But then Ryze wouldn't have touched you. You know, if I knew this might happen, I would have told you. Fuck keeping quiet because Ryze said so." His expression suggested he lay the blame for that firmly on all three Fae.

"Would you?" I asked challengingly. "Knowing I might run away from you? Knowing I probably would have kept you at arm's length, as a friend, and locked myself in a room until the heat was over?"

He shrugged. "I would have broken the door down. Like Ryze said, fated mate and all that."

"They are bonded to me too," I reminded him. "If Ryze is to be believed, this was how the gods wanted it. Wanted me."

Why did they decide to invest so much interest in me? Maybe they should mind their own fucking business.

"I've always said the gods have a sense of humour," Zared sighed.

"This is definitely not how I expected the rest of the year to go," I said. "I thought I'd be at Havenmoor right now, sweeping floors and taking offerings from worshippers. With any luck, I might have been allowed to change the candles on the altars by now. Instead, I'm in Lysarial, hundreds of kilometres from Havenmoor, looking completely different. Bonded to three Fae men and a human."

"A gorgeous human," Zared said, his reflection grinning.

"A modest human," I said after I'd rolled my eyes at him. "What you're saying is I attract immodest assholes. What does that say about me?" Exactly which of the gods did I irritate? The way things were going, I might have to conclude it was several of them. Maybe all of them.

"I'd say it says you have exceptional taste in humans and that the Fae have their own agenda." His expression was serious again. "Can you make a portal?" I wasn't sure if he was scared of the idea or hopeful. A combination of the two, perhaps. Very much my response to the idea.

"I have no idea. I'm too scared to try. I might end up in the middle of the ocean or worse." If Ryze was right, a Fae could only make one to a place they'd already been. That was a fate I wasn't prepared to tempt. We already established the fact he didn't know everything, as much as he liked to pretend otherwise. The gods only know what might actually happen.

"If you could make one, you could leave here," he pointed out.

"If I walked out the door, I could leave here," I said. Where there hells would I go though? I had no idea. I wouldn't be as noticeable now as I was as a human. The Fae— the other Fae, probably wouldn't give me a second glance now. Why would they? I was one of them.

"Promise me something," he said earnestly. "Don't leave without telling me. Even if I can't go with you, I need to know."

"I don't know if I can promise that," I admitted. "I have no idea what might happen. But I promise that, if I can tell you, I will." He'd follow me anyway, so I might as well tell him.

He didn't look like it was enough, but that was all he was going to get and he knew it, so he nodded.

The door handle rattled and it swung open. Tavian pushed it with his back and elbow. When he turned around, he held a steaming bowl of soup in his hands.

"I thought you'd like to eat," he said softly.

As soon as the smell hit my nose, my stomach rumbled. Zared and I stepped apart, but he stayed close to me, protective. Possessive.

I'd eat, but then I still had many questions.

CHAPTER
TWENTY-THREE

KHALA

"I know this has been very disconcerting," Ryze started. "I also know you'd probably be happy to cut my testicles off with a rusty knife and choke me with them."

I crossed my arms, tucking my elegant fingers under my elbows. "That's both strangely specific and eerily accurate. And totally deserved."

He grinned. "There's only one thing more arousing than a pissed off woman. That's a pissed off Fae woman."

"If I didn't know better, I'd think you did this on purpose for that very reason," I told him.

He spread out his hands. "I think you're giving my magical ability too much credit. I have skills, but they don't run to transforming women to suit my particular tastes and needs."

"And yet," I gestured to myself, "you can't tell me you're disappointed that your plan worked."

"I'm as surprised as hells it worked," he admitted. "But no, I'm not disappointed. Not because your human form was any less than this. Although this," he ogled me up and down, "is very impressive."

He chuckled when I rolled my eyes. I'd been doing a lot of that lately.

"I'm not disappointed because it happened here, where we need you. The bond is, of course, an additional bonus. One I suspect would have happened either way."

"With this Cavan?" I lowered my arms. "Or are you trying to say you think I would have formed a bond with you either way?"

He grimaced. "Gods, not with Cavan. Not with anyone there."

"Is there any chance you're biased and they're not as bad as you make them out to be?" I suggested.

"I've considered that, but every time I interact with anyone from the Summer Court, they confirm their status as assholes." He shrugged. "Now, pissed off with me or not, you need to learn how to use magic. Presuming you can use it at all."

"If I can't, then all of this was a waste of time?" Wouldn't that be ironic?

"Not a waste of time," he said. "We got to meet you."

"And vice versa, so it might have been worse than a waste of time," I said, my tone icy.

He winced, but didn't stop smiling. "Ouch. Consider me eviscerated. Now, try to pull this water towards you." He waved toward a bowl on the table beside us. "Think about it coming to you like you might gesture to a person. You don't need the gesture, just the intention."

I put out my hand and thought about the water coming to me. I fully expected nothing to happen. Instead, the water immediately rose and threw itself at me, drenching my hand and dripping off my sleeve and the side of my shirt and pants.

"It doesn't surprise me at all to see how irresistible you are, even to water." He grinned.

The next gesture I gave was a rude one, aimed at him.

He refilled the bowl from a jug and gave me a smug smile. "Try again but with less..." He frowned, trying to think up the right word.

"Irresistibility?" I suggested.

"I was going to say forcefulness, but that works too. Think of the water like smoke. You want it to come to you slowly. To the palm of your hand. Then see if you can make it colder."

I shook the moisture off my arm and focused on the bowl again. More gently this time.

It lifted up out of the bowl and through the air in a trickle. The moment it touched my palm, it froze. Every drop on my hand and sleeve became ice.

"Fuck." I thought warm thoughts and shook my hand, before tucking it into my armpit to thaw it out. "Is this where you tell me there's a risk of frostbite from doing this?"

"There is a low risk," he agreed. "And all the more reason to be here and not the Summer Court. If you were there, you might have set yourself on fire."

"Because this is so much better," I said sarcastically. I pulled out my hand and inspected it. My skin was tinged blue from the cold. "What would have happened in the Spring or Autumn Courts?"

"Much the same, but less extreme," he said. "In the Spring Court, you might have set yourself on fire, but then extinguished yourself."

"Why couldn't I have ended up there?" I asked myself.

He grinned. "Because they're nowhere near as interesting as I am."

"I've never heard 'pain in the ass' pronounced that way," I told him.

"Let me have a look at your hand." He made to reach for it.

I flinched away from him.

He jerked back, hands raised. "Is this where we are now?"

"You lied to me," I reminded him.

"I didn't lie," he argued. "Not exactly."

"You didn't tell me the truth," I said. "That's the same as lying. Had it occurred to you I might not have let you near me if I knew what would happen?"

"Of course it had," he said quietly. "I couldn't allow that. For several reasons. The least of which is that omegas cannot go through their heat without an alpha. Those who have tried, or gone into heat somewhere too remote, or locked themselves away...they don't survive. Did you think I'd let that happen to you?"

"They died?" I asked.

"Died or close to it," he agreed. "Those who lived, didn't want to. They usually didn't live much past that. They withered away or took their own lives. It's not just about sex, it's about the connection between the omega and the alpha. It's like growing up without being hugged enough. The strain is too much." The sides of his mouth drew back.

"Someone you knew?" I guessed.

"My mother," he said softly. "My father was away and I was with him. Not that I would have—" He grimaced. "She stayed until we got back and then she left. Lethal dose of heartbane." He rubbed his brow with his fingertips.

"I then swore that if it was in my power, I'd never let that happen to anyone else. Regardless of the other consequences. These are desperate times. Plants are blooming out of season, and wilting. War may be inevitable. What I did, I did to prevent that."

"And to hells with who you step on along the way?" I asked bitterly. "Who you use? If you told me all of this, I might have gone along with it. I wanted you there for my heat." Even now, I wanted him, while resisting the urge to punch him. The sensation was conflicting.

"If you said no, I would have had two choices," he said slowly. "I would have had to let you go insane, or I would have had to force myself on you. Either way, you would have ended up hating me."

"Am I supposed to feel sorry for you?" I asked. "Because I don't. You should have given me the choice."

"You chose to run away from the caravan with me," he said. "You chose to step through the portal. You trusted me to agree to me being there for your heat." He placed his hands palms down on the table. "You didn't have all the information, that's true, but can you deny the attraction between us?"

"The attraction is beside the point," I snarled.

"Then what is the point?" he shot back. "That your ability to choose is more important than the lives of thousands? Tens of thousands?"

"To me it is," I said bitterly. "The fact you'd think I'd put myself before all those people..."

"Shows I didn't know you before I made this plan," he said. "If you can even call it a plan. All I wanted was to keep you, and any of the other sisters I could assist, away from the Summer Court, and ultimately prevent war. That was all."

"That doesn't mean what you did wasn't wrong," I said.

"Would you say the same thing if you hadn't changed?" he asked.

"Would you have told me any of this if I hadn't?" I countered.

"There would have been no need." He shrugged. "Until the next group of Silent Maidens was ready to leave the temple."

Without thinking, I picked up all the water in the jug and threw it in his face. I thought about throwing the jug as well, but seeing it dripping off his hair and clothes was enough.

"You would have gone on lying to me?" I could hardly believe what I was hearing.

He shook his head, droplets flying everywhere. "Thank you for not freezing that." After a moment he added, "All right, you're right. I would have told you. Certainly before we returned to Fraxius. If you'd decided to stay here after your heat, that is. I wouldn't have tried to make you stay. I won't now, if leaving is what you really want."

He swept water off his face with his hand.

"Was it the heat, or your part in it that caused the transformation?" I asked softly.

"The heat," he said firmly. "In the past, women have changed without an alpha present. That's part of the reason for the strain. Changing from human to Fae without any context or guidance. I'm sure it would be terrifying." He looked sympathetic. "It's terrible even if a woman knows it's coming."

I couldn't deny any of that. If he told me, I might not have believed him. This whole thing was going to take a long time for me to come to terms with.

Something else was more pressing than that.

"If I could have gone through my heat without you, would you have stayed away?"

"Would you have agreed to have me there if you didn't need me to be?" he asked in return.

"I hardly know you," I said.

"You hardly know Tavian or Vayne." His brows quirked upwards. So he did know about Vayne and I in the yard that day. I thought he must have, but this confirmed it.

I exhaled and considered the question. "I might have. But if I hadn't?"

"Then I would have made a portal and got the hells out of here," he said. "I know everything I did seems convoluted and self-serving. Maybe I'm the biggest asshole to have ever lived, but I genuinely care about you, as much as I care about any of my people. More so. I understand you're pissed off at me. You feel violated. Both of those are valid and justified. All I can offer are my reasons for doing what I did. It's your choice to decide what to do with that."

I stood back and regarded him. He was right, I felt all of that and more. Everything that happened between us was based on a lie.

CHAPTER
TWENTY-FOUR
KHALA

"Would you have done any of this to a Fae woman?" I asked Ryze after a few moments of uncomfortable silence. "One who looked Fae from the start?"

"You are a Fae woman," he told me. "What you looked like before and what you look like now are inconsequential. It's who you are that mattered. That matters now."

"It matters to me," I said. "Would you?"

He sighed. "Yes. Whoever it was, whatever it took, whatever it still takes. I'll sacrifice whatever I have to."

"Even if everyone ends up hating you?"

He laughed bitterly. "What's the point of being adored if everyone is dead? On the other hand, if everyone is dead, then so am I. I don't think I'll care who hates me then."

"What about Tavian and Vayne?" I asked. "They knew everything."

"Vayne would have told you the truth if I hadn't ordered him not to," Ryze said. "He wanted us to find another way. He would have killed all the Silent Maidens to keep them away from the Summer Court. He doesn't like to do things in halves."

"I've noticed that about him," I said dryly. "And Tavian?"

"I ordered him too," Ryze said. "As an omega, he had no choice but to obey a direct order like that. Believe me, he was no happier about it than you are. Especially when he got to know you. He's the kind of man who falls hard and fast. He's been beside himself the last few days, worried about you. And pissed at me for the way everything happened."

"You'll get no sympathy from me," I told him.

"I'm not expecting any." He picked up the jug and carried it over to the

118

tap to refill it. "I don't want you to blame them for what I did. I take full responsibility." He carried the jug back and placed it on the table. "If it'll make you feel better, I'll stand here while you throw a few more jugs of water at me."

"If I thought it would make me feel better, that's exactly what I'd do." I was tempted to do it anyway. Maybe I could make it snow on his head. Since all of that would be petty, I decided not to bother.

"Can the mating bond be broken?" I asked.

"No," he said simply. "It's in place until one of us dies. That won't be for a very long time, gods willing."

I blinked a couple of times. "Are you saying I'll live as long as the Fae?"

"You are Fae," he told me again. "That is likely to be the case, yes." He sighed. "I should have told you that, shouldn't I?"

"What else should you have told me?" I asked.

He looked thoughtful. "Your next heat won't make you more Fae. To the absolute best of my knowledge, as you are today is as you will always be. And I will seek out the other Silent Maidens and bring them here if need be."

"And tell them everything?" I looked at him through narrowed eyes. I narrowed them further when he hesitated.

"If you agree to stay here, I promise to discuss it with you," he said slowly. "You may agree it's safer not to tell them."

"And if I don't?" I asked.

"Then we will tell them everything," he conceded. "However..."

"However, what?"

"However, we will need to find another alpha. Now we have the mate bond, I'll only ever take part in your heat and Tavian's."

"Because the bond won't allow it?" I knew nothing about bonds like ours, but I hadn't realised it was so restrictive. It seemed to me like a hum in the back of my mind, unless I concentrated on it.

"Because *I* won't," he said firmly. "If either of you leave and choose another alpha, then I'll step aside from all heats. Who am I to go against the will of the gods?"

"I have a feeling you go against the will of the gods a lot," I said. He seemed to live life by his will and that alone.

He grinned. "And I have a feeling I can say the same about you."

What could I say to that? Geralda would agree with him.

"I don't think I would have made a very good priestess," I admitted. I wasn't entirely sure the gods existed, for one thing. That seemed like an important requisite for someone working in the temple.

"Your fate was never to be a priestess," he agreed.

"Was this my fate?" I gestured at my face.

"I think of it more as a realisation of who you really are," he said. "You never had any suspicion?"

"Should I have?" I asked. "It seems like all my life people have been lying to me. How am I supposed to believe a word anyone says?" When I thought about it, the whole thing was pretty fucked up.

I looked at him evenly. I could do that to him now, he was only a couple of centimetres taller than me.

"Can you promise never to lie to me again?"

"I never lied to you," he said. "I can't promise not to keep things from you if I believe knowing will hurt you. I don't believe anyone can make that kind of promise, even you. But I can promise not to deliberately deceive you when I know you would want to know, when the finding out will be worse than the not knowing. I misjudged and for that I am sorry." He seemed genuinely sincere. Of course, it was easy to be sincerely sorry after the fact.

I wanted to deny what he said, but I couldn't. There were nights I snuck out when Tyla was asleep and went looking for trouble with Zared. Times I never told her about. I wasn't entirely honest with Zared about my feelings for him, because I wanted to avoid hurting him.

None of that excused Ryze lying to me. I may never forgive him for that. But nothing here was black and white, nothing simple.

"If you keep anything from me, can I dump freezing cold water on your head?" I asked, only half-joking. Yes, it was petty, but it was still strangely satisfying. And much less messy than cutting off body parts. Especially body parts I might need again someday if I decided to forgive him.

"I would prefer that to having you cut my balls off, so yes," he said. "I might even let you do it in front of the entire court. I'm sure they'd enjoy the spectacle." His amused expression was back.

"I know I would," I said. "I should practice a few times, just in case I miss."

"You could do that, or we could learn some actual, useful magic." He gestured towards the jug.

"Like making cubes of ice for glasses of whiskey?" I cocked my head at him.

"That's definitely useful," he said. "I was thinking more along the lines of trying to make portals. That's the single most useful skill I can do with my magic. I can't guarantee you'll be able to do it, but we can try." He shrugged one shoulder, indicating it was up to me if I wanted to try.

I eyed him doubtfully. "Isn't that advanced magic?"

"It can be. You've already demonstrated that you can use magic, so there's no harm in trying."

"Why not move on to something dangerous?" I muttered.

"Are you ready?" he asked, his voice smooth as silk. Eyes as amused as ever.

I suspected that was a front for his real emotions. Covering the fact he very much took everything seriously when it came to protecting the Winter Court.

He clasped his hands in front of him and arched an eyebrow at me. That was a challenge if I ever saw one. Evidently he knew me well enough to know I didn't back down from a challenge.

I nodded. "I suppose so."

"Close your eyes," Ryze instructed. "Focus on your breath. Let everything else fall away."

I did as he said, taking a deep breath in and exhaling slowly. I pushed aside the doubt and uncertainty that were gnawing at me. Partly about handling magic at all and partly trusting him enough to even try. Would he have done all of that, only to put me in danger a couple of days later? That seemed like a lot of effort to me. And he didn't seem like the sort of man to waste a drop of sweat, much less a resource like he claimed I was.

"Good," he said. "Now, feel the magic within you. It's there, waiting to be used. Let it flow through you like a river. Just inside you, don't aim it at me. Leave it in the jug for now."

I snorted, but concentrated, feeling the magic coursing through my veins. It was a strange sensation, cool but buzzing like electricity humming just below the surface of my skin.

"Now, imagine a place you want to go," he said, his voice soothing with Fae melodic tones. Under other circumstances, it might put me to sleep. Or in a meditative trance. Maybe he should have been a priest.

"Picture your bedroom, with your bed in the centre. The stunning, picturesque view out the window. The tastefully decorated walls."

"I think you're overselling it a bit," I remarked.

He chuckled. "Focus, woman. It's a nice room, imagine you want to be there right now. If you like, picture me naked in your nest, waiting for you."

I cracked an eye open and looked at him. In spite of everything, that was an enticing visual image I'd have to do my best to ignore for now.

He raised a hand. "Sorry, it's too soon."

I murmured my agreement and closed my eye again.

I pictured my room, without him or anyone else in it. Neat and tidy with no clothes lying all over the floor, no half read books sitting open. Fortunately, I'd tidied up before our lesson today.

"Good," he said again. "Now, hold that image in your mind. Focus all your energy on it."

I closed my eyes tighter, trying to visualize the room with every detail. I imagined the feel of the carpet under my feet, the warmth of the sun coming through the window, the sweet fragrance of the bathroom with the oils on the shelf.

I poured all my energy into that image, trying to make it as vivid as possible.

"Open your eyes," Ryze said. "Keep that image in your mind."

I did, although it left me a little disoriented. The world seemed different somehow, as if I was seeing it through a veil. It hadn't looked like this when Ryze made the portal. Maybe it only looked like this to the person doing the magic. I made a note to ask about that later.

"Now," he said, "reach out your hand. Imagine you're touching your room, reaching through the veil that separates us from that space. Draw the water out and form the portal from it."

I tentatively reached out my hand. In the back of my mind, I drew a little bit of water, like I was raising steam from a cooking pot. Not too much, and careful not to flick any onto him or myself. Okay, mostly myself. A few more drops wouldn't hurt him.

My fingertips brushed against something firm and cool, like frozen stone, if stone was somehow yielding at the same time as it was hard.

"That's it," Ryze encouraged. "Now, pull back the veil. Open a doorway to your room."

I closed my eyes again. Power surged as I concentrated. I imagined my hand as a key, turning in an invisible lock. Slowly, the veil parted, revealing a clear view of my room and the window with the view overlooking the harbour.

"Good," Ryze said. "Now, step through."

I took a deep breath and stepped forward. Just before I walked through, the portal snapped shut and disappeared.

I let out a squeak and jumped back.

"Fuck. I'm guessing that wasn't supposed to happen."

I glanced over to see him looking perplexed.

"I've never seen that happen before. The portal should stay open until you close it. Or until you're exhausted. Are you feeling all right?"

"I'm a little tired," I admitted. "What would have happened if I stepped inside that?"

He shook his head. "I have no idea." He rubbed his pointed chin with his hand. "That might be a question for another day. Don't try that again unless I'm present."

My skin tingled. His words wrapped around me, tightened. "Is that an order from an alpha to an omega?"

He smiled slightly. "It wasn't intended to be, but yes, treat it like that. For your safety. Until we can ascertain why it went wrong and how to fix it. We don't want you getting stuck in the space between one location and another, if such a place even exists. I strongly suspect that if it does, it would suck."

"I don't doubt that for a moment," I said.

CHAPTER
TWENTY-FIVE

RYZE

"I told you you should tell her," Vayne said, over the top of his beer glass.

"If I recall correctly, you said something along the lines of her only being a human and I should explain what we were using her for," I said coolly. "You weren't giving her any consideration or credit for her intelligence."

"Same thing," he said unapologetically. "I hardly knew the woman but I figured she'd want to know what the fuck you were up to."

"That didn't stop you from enjoying her mouth." I sipped my whiskey and watched his expression. If he was surprised I knew, he gave no sign.

"That was after I got to know her," he said unapologetically. "And before she changed. No one can say I wasn't into her before she was Fae."

"She was always Fae," I said wearily.

"None of us knew that for sure," he pointed out. "Now we know, what are we going to do? With her, and with others like her."

"I've sent word to a contact in the Summer Court," I said. "I'd like to wrangle an invitation, but I suspect we may have to sneak in."

"That's one of my favourite pastimes," Tavian said. He sat on a chair in the corner, an almost untouched beer in his hand. "Sneaking, killing, and fucking. Not necessarily in that order."

"I know," I told him. "You're very good at all three of them. I suspect you'll get a chance at more of the first two soon enough."

I didn't want to talk about the third one. Every time I thought about it, I thought about Khala and the way she looked at me like I was some kind of monster. I dared to hope she might forgive me someday, but it wouldn't be anytime soon. I'd have to work hard to regain her trust and right now, I wasn't sure I could spare the time. We needed to move, and soon.

"I know we've talked about me sneaking into the Summer Court and assassinating the High Lord," Tavian started.

"No," I said simply and firmly.

Of course, he wasn't immediately done arguing the point. "It would solve a lot of problems."

"And create even more," I said. "Have you forgotten I'm attempting to avoid provoking a full-blown war?" Just because it was becoming more and more inevitable didn't mean I'd stop trying.

"Maybe it's gone past that," Vayne said. "Kidnapping omegas to fuck with the weather seems pretty provocative to me."

"To me too," Tavian said.

"An army camped on our border would be provocative," I said. "Are you two bloodthirsty or bored? Remind me to give you both extra duties."

"It might be that you're getting soft in your old age," Vayne said. "You say you'll do anything to stop whatever Cavan is up to, but what if that means striking first? What if sitting up here, enjoying the view and twiddling our thumbs is the wrong thing to do?"

"Whether it's the wrong thing to do or not, I'm not going to invade the Summer Court in the foreseeable future." The Winter Court hadn't invaded another territory in approximately three thousand years. We weren't going to start today.

"You didn't say never," Vayne said.

"I know better than to say never," I told him.

"The voice of age and experience," Vayne said to Tavian.

Tavian grinned and nodded.

I rolled my eyes at them both. "You know, that got old long ago." I held up a finger before either of them could say that I did too. A hundred year age difference wasn't that significant.

"I prefer to think of it as the voice of wisdom," I said. "Not to mention the voice responsible for thousands of Fae lives. Lives I presume you don't want to see lost either?"

Thankfully, neither disagreed with that presumption. There was a fine line between being bloodthirsty and being an asshole. A fine, often blurry line.

"You can both begin to prepare a sneaking mission to the Summer Court. Just the three of us. We have a lot less chance of being detected if it's only us." I swished my whiskey around in the glass. For some reason, it tasted slightly bitter today. An after-effect of the conversation with Khala, no doubt. With a heavy dose of guilt and confusion over why her portal snapped shut the way it did.

Magic wasn't always predictable, but it stuck to certain rules. Portals snapping shut broke that rule. Even for her first time opening one, it should have stayed open.

"Khala will want to go," Tavian said.

"So will Zared," Vayne added.

"I'm well aware of both cases," I said. "But neither of them are ready for something like this." Khala still needed to rest after her transformation, and Zared had yet to prove himself as far as I was concerned. In spite of the days spent by Khala's bedside while she recovered, he was still an unknown quantity. And a human. His presence in the Summer Court wouldn't go unnoticed any more than it did here.

Besides which, if Khala was staying behind, doubtless he'd insist on doing the same. Convincing her not to go might be another matter. I'd order her if I had to.

"I've received word that four of the former Silent Maidens were safely delivered to the Temple in Havenmoor," I said slowly. "I'll open us a portal to the border between the Spring and Summer Courts. We'll see if we can locate the remaining two, then portal the hells out of there. If they haven't transformed, no one will need to know we were there."

"And if they have?" Vayne asked. "That might be considered provocative."

"It might, but that can't be helped. It's not an outright declaration of war." I suspected Cavan might not see it that way. If he did, we'd have time to be ready.

"I hate to say it, but wouldn't it be better if they met with a mysterious, but fatal accident?" Vayne asked. "Something that can't be attributed to us? Whatever Cavan thinks, none of the other courts will agree with him. They'll want to keep their noses out of it."

"That might be necessary, yes," I agreed. "If there's no other way." In order to keep my promise to Khala, I'd have to tell her we may need to kill her former sisters. She wasn't going to like it. Hells, I didn't like it. They were innocent women, caught up in something that was only their business because they carried Fae blood.

"If we can bring them here, and keep them out of sight until all of this is dealt with, that would be my preference. But if that's impossible, then you both have my permission to do whatever you have to." The words made my mouth taste sour. I had no trouble killing, or ordering the deaths of people who deserved it. But to kill innocent women to save many more innocent people...

I had to harden my resolve. It was the right call. I wasn't going to second guess myself. I couldn't.

"And if we happen upon Cavan while we're there," Tavian said, looking cagey, "and a knife happens to slip between his ribs..."

"Try not to accidentally-on-purpose kill the High Lord of the Summer Court." I rubbed my forehead with my fingertips. "Unless you can administer some kind of poison that takes days, or even weeks to appear, and cannot possibly be traced back to us, then leave him alone. For now."

Tavian stroked his chin. "We have people in his court. They could poison his food. And anyone directly responsible for, as Vayne put it, fucking with the weather."

"That wouldn't go unnoticed," I said reluctantly. "Unless we have someone suspected of working for the Autumn Court."

I wasn't below pinning the blame on someone else and Harel was no friend of mine. If we went to war with the Summer Court, Autumn might well take their side. Harel was as ambitious as Cavan, but he thought he was a lot more subtle about it. If he could, he'd let Cavan go to war with us, then step in at the last minute to take all the credit.

Of course, he kept all of this behind a mask of civility and barely disguised sarcasm. That made him more suspicious than anything else. If you wanted my trust, you were proudly sarcastic, like me.

"I'll speak to the spymaster and see who she has in there," Tavian said. "Knowing Bravenna, she's anticipated this."

"More than likely," I agreed. The woman had been spymaster for the last two hundred years. I trusted her almost as much as I trusted Vayne and Tavian. If there was a secret we could discern, she'd find a way to discover it. If it wasn't for her, we wouldn't know what happened to the Silent Maidens at all.

"Are you sure I can't go—" Tavian started again.

"I need you here," I told him. "Sooner or later, someone there would recognise you and expose you. Besides which, we may need you to send your assassins out; you can't do that if you're working in Cavan's kitchen or scrubbing his toilets."

"You make it sound so glamorous," Tavian said sarcastically.

I snorted. "There's nothing glamorous about killing."

"Depends who you kill," Vayne said.

I looked at him for a moment, but he didn't clarify his remark.

I cleared my throat. "Anyway, I'll speak to Khala and then we can make our move."

"This is where I feel I should say the High Lord should stay here and let us deal with it," Vayne said. "We both know that's not going to happen, but I feel the words are obligatory." He hunkered down deeper in his chair, satisfied he'd done his duty.

I smiled slightly. "Your obligatory objection is noted and rejected. I'm allowed to have some fun once in a while."

As I said to Khala, I didn't like to ask my people to do things I wouldn't do myself. Besides, there was an element of enjoyment to sneaking in and out without anyone knowing we were there. I'd bet half the court's coffers Dalyth didn't know who it was that day on the road beside the carriages. No doubt she'd suspect us, but without seeing us with her own eyes, she couldn't prove anything. My only regret was not disposing of her while we were there. If we weren't outnumbered at the time...

"Sooner or later, you're going to get yourself into a pile of shit," Vayne told me.

I grinned. "That's what I have you two for. To keep that from happening, or to get me out of it if it does."

"I thought you kept us around for our good looks," Vayne quipped.

"You're half right," Tavian teased. "He keeps me around for *my* good looks."

There was a certain amount of accuracy there. I adored many things about Tavian, including his looks."It's certainly not because you're model Fae," I told them both dryly.

"Who amongst us can make that claim?" Vayne asked.

I didn't even pretend I'd suggest I could. I was sarcastic, arrogant and possibly slightly self absorbed. If I was a model anything, it was a good example of how not to behave. I had no intention of changing that.

"I'm pretty close," Tavian said lightly. "But there's something I need to tell you about. I'm not sure if it's anything serious but I thought you should know."

I knew that expression on his face. It made me worried every time. He never wore it unless the situation really called for it and things usually didn't end well when that was the case.

"Yes, Master Tavian," I said, my tone formal. "Should I have Vayne rouse the army after all?"

"I don't think that's necessary just yet," he said carefully.

"You're not filling me with much confidence," I told him. "Out with it."

"A couple of the assassins sent into the Autumn Court haven't returned yet," Tavian said reluctantly.

CHAPTER
TWENTY-SIX
RYZE

"Granted they're only a day or two later than anticipated," Tavian said quickly. "My instincts are telling me something weird might be going on."

"Who were they sent to execute?" Vayne asked. The sides of his mouth were tight. It was no secret he preferred to face the enemy head on. He enjoyed sneaking around as much as the rest of us did, but he'd prefer to incinerate the front door and storm in. The last few hundred years must have been very dull for him. Which was fine with me.

"One was sent after a minor courtier who tried to blackmail one of our minor courtiers. That was a personal matter between them," Tavian answered. "The other was something to do with a business matter between former partners. One took everything and fled to the Autumn Court. The other took exception to that."

"Understandable," Vayne said. "I'd be pissed off too."

I frowned. "Neither sound like a difficult job." If I wasn't a High Lord, I might have been an assassin. The ability to make a portal to get the hells away from somewhere was a handy skill. Not to mention assassins got to travel to all sorts of interesting places and meet new people. And kill them. What more could a Fae want?

"They shouldn't have been," Tavian agreed. "In. Slice. Out. Or whatever method they used for the kill. They should both have been back a day or two early, not late."

"Maybe they stuck around to enjoy the beach, or the Autumn Court hospitality?" Vayne suggested. "I hear their spiced coffee is tasty."

"It is," I agreed. "I've always thought it was odd you could only get it there.

It's the perfect winter beverage. Well, apart from this." I drank down the last of my whiskey.

"I can think of something tastier than that to drink," Tavian said, giving me a sly smile.

"I'm sure you can," I said. So could I. That thought made my cock harden. Not the drinking but the being drunk from.

"Let me know if they turn up. If that doesn't happen in the next couple of days, send someone after them." While I couldn't and didn't claim ownership of, or responsibility for, the assassins, they were still my people. If something happened to them, I wanted to know.

Tavian nodded. "Should we hold off sending anyone else there in the meantime?"

I considered that question while I leaned over to place my empty glass on the table in front of me.

"No," I said eventually. "Issue a warning to any of them thinking of taking a job there or in another of the courts. It might be nothing, but it might also be significant to everything else that's been going on recently. If they don't turn up shortly, we can reconsider."

Vayne leaned forward. "Can I recommend we close our borders? If this really is a matter of concern, we might be better off not letting anyone in or out."

"Then people will wonder why," I reasoned. "They might start to think we're up to something."

"We *are* up to something," Vayne said.

"Then they might start to pay attention to what we're up to," I said. "We need to keep a low profile if we can. The Winter Court is known for keeping ourselves out of other people's business, unless it's absolutely necessary. Let's keep up the appearance of doing that, for as long as we can."

I placed my elbows on my thighs and rested my head on my hands. "But quietly increase patrols along the border. If anyone thinks to incur on them, I want to know about it."

Vayne nodded. "Consider it done."

"The sooner we get in and out of the Summer Court, the better," I said with a heavy sigh.

"Who in their right mind would want eternal summer anyway?" Tavian asked.

"I suspect the right mind part might be precisely the point here," I told him. "I like being warm as much as the next Fae, but not to the detriment of all the land around us. That would be worse than eternal winter."

"Think how powerful you'd be if it was always winter," Tavian said.

"Not very powerful if I starve to death," I pointed out. "The idea is insanity. The seasons exist for a reason. It's all about balance."

"You know," Vayne drawled, "I heard that in some parts of the world there are only two. Wet and dry."

I grunted. "What a choice. High Lord of Dry or—"

Tavian laughed. "High Lord of Wet. I vote for that."

I shook my head and grinned. "I could do worse."

"Until some asshole comes along and decides to make it permanently dry," Vayne said.

"That would without doubt, very much suck," I said. "I don't think anyone is that insane."

"Hopefully not," Tavian agreed. He was still grinning, on the verge of laughter.

I rolled my eyes, but the idea was amusing. I cocked an eyebrow at Vayne.

"Who rules in the lands of wet and dry?"

He shrugged. "Far as I know, they have kings and queens, but I don't know for certain. Would you like me to launch an expedition to find out?"

I sighed. "As much as I'd like to say yes, I have to decline. For now at least. When all of this is over and we're back to being idle Fae, maybe we can think about that."

"If we ever are," he said. "If this thing results in war, it could be years."

"All the more reason to ensure it doesn't end up in war," I said. "I personally have better things to do for the next few years. I'm sure you both do too."

"Things and people," Tavian agreed. "I plan to live at least as long as Ryze is old right now."

"You're not aspiring to much then," I said dryly. "My father was twice my current age when he died." When his time came, it was brief, if not sudden. One moment he was yelling at the servants, the next minute he closed his eyes and was gone. Leaving me, his only child, to inherit the court. Fortunately, by then, I'd had a couple of hundred years' training. Stepping into the role was, perhaps not effortless, but more or less successful. Some would say more, some would say less.

"And several times as wise," Vayne said.

I drummed my fingers on my cheek. "Please remind me why I haven't replaced you yet?"

"Because no one is better equipped to be commander of your armies than I am," Vayne said immodestly. He sat back and crossed his knees, looking particularly smug, even for him.

"Ahhh. Remind me to keep an eye out for someone who is. Zared is promising. It might be worth considering—"

Vayne jerked forward, brow furrowed with annoyance. "The day a human takes over..." He finally realised I was joking and scowled at me. "You're an asshole."

I chuckled. "So I've heard. For the record, it's his inexperience, not the fact that he's human that rules him out of contention for that position. Coupled with the fact the Fae wouldn't willingly follow him."

They'd follow orders, but they wouldn't be happy about it. For people who lived a long time, we were reluctant to change. Perhaps Zared was the beginning of that. Allowing more humans into my court. Vayne's reaction was mild compared to many. That wasn't a fight I was willing to start right now.

I added that to the list of things to do when all of this was over. Or, at least, to consider.

"I'd follow him," Tavian said. "He can be abrasive and difficult, but he adores Khala. The way he helped me take care of her... He has softness down deep inside."

"Very deep," I said.

He was as pushy as any human I ever met, and more so than plenty of them. Not to mention possessive and aggressive. Traits I had myself, but I learnt to keep them in check. I had to work on that even more around Khala. She was pissed off with me enough as it was. I didn't want to drive her away completely.

Fortunately, I had time to wait and make her trust me again. And she would, even if it took me a hundred years to achieve. I've worked for things for longer than that. A hundred years was nothing.

No, I corrected myself. It wasn't nothing, it was a hundred of her heats. A hundred that she could spend with me or another alpha. In spite of assuring her I'd support her choice to find another, the idea of her fucking an alpha who wasn't me made me want to rip his spine out with my bare hands.

"What is it between you and Zared?" I asked Tavian.

He looked surprised at the question. "I... He..." His throat bobbed up and down as he swallowed.

I sat up and rest a hand, palm outward. "I'm not jealous. No more than I am of your time with Khala. I'm merely curious. I don't want to see you get hurt." I had my moments of jealousy knowing Tavian and Khala were fucking each other, and seeing Tavian with Zared, but they were brief moments. I had no right to ask any of them to keep away from each other for my sake.

That was another sacrifice I made for the people I cared about.

"It's all right if I get hurt?" Vayne asked. He didn't sound offended.

I ignored him and kept my focus on Tavian. He looked relieved.

"I don't know," he admitted. "I care about him the same way I care about you and her." He cocked a head at Vayne. "Which is different to how I feel about you, because we're friends. Although if you wanted more, I—"

"I don't," Vayne said quickly. "I'm a part of this pack, but the only one I want to touch is her."

Tavian nodded and looked back at me. "We're all bonded to her. Things could get complicated."

I rubbed the back of my head. "It certainly has the potential to get complicated. Be careful, for all our sakes. Especially Khala's. She's been through enough. This whole transition," I shook my head slowly, "has been difficult for her. I suspect it will be that way for a while. Sooner or later, she'll adjust and..."

"And?" Tavian asked.

"I don't know," I admitted. "I might not be able to begin to make it up to her."

"Which brings me back to saying you should have told her in the first place," Vayne said. "We might have avoided all of this."

"Instead of talking about this, we'd be talking about a different problem," I said. "Potentially something much worse."

I didn't know which mental image I disliked more—the one in which she was out of her mind or dead, or the one in which I raped her.

I haven't always made the right choices when it came to women, but I had to stand by the ones I made regarding her. If only because the idea of pinning her down made my cock twitch uncomfortably. That was a truth I preferred to keep to myself. One that if I ever acted upon, I would earn every drop of hate from her and from myself.

No, I had to find a way to make her mine without resorting to force or any further manipulation. I needed to weave her into the tapestry of my life and existence so fully she couldn't, wouldn't want to leave. The start of that was getting her sisters out of the Summer Court alive.

CHAPTER
TWENTY-SEVEN
KHALA

"Are you sure about this?" I signed to Zared.

He looked at me furtively, then back to the sitting room. "If you're going, then I'm going." His signing was rough, unpracticed, but he got his meaning across.

"I'm definitely going." For the first time I was grateful for the ability to speak with my hands. It meant we could watch for Ryze, Tavian and Vayne without being overheard. I hadn't realised how well Fae could hear until I was one. Our whispering wouldn't have gone unnoticed. Especially after the conversation with Ryze yesterday.

I appreciated him telling me about their intention to go to the Summer Court, even the admission that they may kill whichever of my sisters was there. I'd smiled and thanked him for being honest with me, assured him I'd busy myself in the library while he and the others were absent. I'd asked to go along and pretended to accept it graciously when he said no. He didn't try to keep me any longer once I excused myself from his presence.

I was genuinely glad for that. He was giving me time to deal with everything. The fact he wanted my forgiveness was obvious. He didn't push the matter. He'd let me turn to him when I was ready. If I ever was.

After he spoke, I went straight to Zared and made a plan.

I had no intention of busying myself in the library while they went after my sisters. I thought Ryze might have seen right through my acquiescence, but he gave no sign of it. Through the bond I sensed him holding back, giving me space. Good, because if he poked around too much, he'd know exactly what we were up to.

Zared scrounged us a couple of packs. We threw some clothes in, then found a place near the sitting room where we could watch and wait.

"Exactly how many knives did you bring?" Ryze's voice came up the corridor.

"Only eight," Tavian replied. "You don't think that's enough? I could always get some more before we—"

"Eight is plenty," Ryze said quickly. "Come on, we've wasted enough time already."

They walked past and headed toward the stairs.

Only when their footsteps faded did I gesture to Zared rise from a crouch to follow.

We slipped down the stairs silently. I kept an ear out for their banter, and the sound of their boots at the bottom of the stairs. They made their way through the palace and down to a door near the kitchen.

"There won't be anyone in the courtyard at this time of day," Ryze said.

His voice sounded louder than I expected. I froze and waved Zared back behind a corner.

"They're right in front of us," I signed.

He nodded that he understood. "This is where I should insist you stay here."

I smiled. "You can try, but I'm going. If you want to stay..." I raised an elegant, Fae eyebrow at him.

The look he gave me said he wasn't entirely used to seeing me this way. That looking at me made him a little uncomfortable.

Imagine how I felt whenever I caught a glimpse of my reflection in the mirror. Even my hair was longer. I braided it and tied it back out of the way, but it still hung all the way down my back. I considered grabbing a knife and cutting it, to spite the whole transformation bullshit. In the end, I decided I liked it as long as it was and left it.

Besides, I had enough vanity that I didn't want my hair to look hacked at.

"When you go, I go," Zared signed. He frowned and quickly corrected himself. "*Where* you go, I go."

I smiled at his minor error. He could have accidentally signed something offensive. It was easy to do. A lot of the gestures were similar, with only the flick of a finger to tell them apart. He might have called me a cockhead without meaning to. Or something close to it.

I motioned for him to be still and quiet while I listened.

The three Fae had stepped out the door into the sunshine. I wasn't sure if I felt a ripple of magic, or if that was nerves.

"Be ready," I signed.

Zared nodded, and his whole body tensed.

We had one shot at this. Miss it and...

We couldn't miss it.

"Okay, Tavian, lead the way," Ryze said.

"Yes, my Lord," Tavian said in a teasing tone.

I could almost see Ryze's eye roll.

I gestured to Zared. "Now."

We both shot to our feet and bolted to the door.

I had barely enough time to register Ryze's surprise, and the sight of Tavian stepping through the portal ahead of us, before Zared and I ran through it.

Vayne tried to grab me, but I swerved and avoided him before darting after Tavian.

"Son of a griffin-fucking whore," Vayne swore. "I told you—"

His words were cut off when we stepped out the other end of the portal.

Tavian didn't look so surprised to see Zared and I step out.

"Ryze isn't going to be happy," he remarked.

"Too bad," I replied. "They're my sisters. I couldn't stand by and do nothing."

"You could have *sat* by," Vayne growled as he stepped through the portal. "Standing was optional." He looked from me to Zared and back again, clearly trying to decide who he was the most angry at. "You're a pair of fucking idiots."

"That's approximately what I was going to say," Ryze said. He stepped through the portal and closed it behind him. "I should have ordered you to stay behind." He addressed that to both of us.

I shrugged. "You didn't, so here we are. Where is here?"

Ryze barked a short laugh. "You followed us, and we could have led you anywhere. Some would consider that foolish."

"You would have ended up 'anywhere' too," I pointed out. "We trust the plan isn't to get yourselves killed."

"She's got you there." Tavian grinned. "This is the edge of the Spring Court. The Summer Court is over that hill."

We stood in a copse of trees, most covered in flowers in a riot of colours. All of them exuded a perfume so strong it was almost overwhelming.

"I should open a portal and send you right back," Ryze growled.

"Yes, you should," Vayne told him. "Zared can start a hundred years of cleaning toilets."

"I'm human, I won't live for a hundred years," Zared pointed out.

"We'll find a way," Vayne said darkly.

"I'm not going back." I tilted my chin and looked at Ryze defiantly. "I need to be here, helping."

"You're going to get in the fucking way," Vayne snarled.

"No I won't," I argued. "I've spent my whole life learning how to blend into the background. No one will ever know I was there. Can any of you say the same thing?"

"I can," Tavian said. "I've had assassin training."

"I can be stealthy," Vayne grumbled.

"Maybe Ryze should stay behind," I suggested, not thinking for a moment anyone would agree to that.

"Hardly." Ryze snorted. "Fine, you can come with us, but both of you follow orders, or I'll open a portal and shove you through it. I may not open it to somewhere pleasant either. I know of a nasty swamp on the southern tip of the Autumn Court. It will take you weeks to get out of it, but you'll never forget the smell." He made a face that said he was remembering it right now.

"All right, let's not stand here and wait for a border patrol to find us." He pushed his pack higher up his shoulders and started towards the hill.

Vayne gave me another dark look and turned to follow him.

Tavian gestured for Zared and I to go next, then stepped in behind us.

"Are you angry at us?" I asked over my shoulder.

"Not really," he said lightly. "I would have been surprised if you didn't do something like this. You seem to act first and think about it later. I like that in my people. Although, I'm going to be pissed off if either of you get killed."

"Me too," Zared said. "I'm not planning on dying or letting Khala die."

"Then you should have stayed in Lysarial," Vayne growled. "You might wish you ended up in a swamp."

We made our way through the grass, skirting around places where it was taller.

"We don't want anyone to step on a serpent," he said. "They tend to be cranky about that kind of thing."

Vayne muttered something that sounded like, "I know how they feel." He gave us both a glance over his shoulder, but his glare was mostly for Zared.

Did I imagine a flash of worry in his eyes when he looked at me? I hoped to the gods it wasn't justified. I knew jumping in on this expedition was dangerous, reckless. But if Tyla was one of the women left in the Summer Court, I owed it to her to try to get her out. It could just as easily have been her who escaped with the three Fae men. It could have been her Ryze pounded into during her heat. It could have been her mouth...

I forced those distracting thoughts away and focused on ducking under a branch. The gods only knew what she was going through, while the worst thing I suffered was being lied to. I was pissed off, but things might have been a lot worse.

"I've never seen a real serpent," I said. "Just drawings and paintings of them. Do they really glitter like jewels?"

"Yes, they do," Tavian said. "They're beautiful. Which is the point, of course. They're meant to attract their prey before they eat them."

"Much like women," Vayne said.

"Fuck off," I told him. I hadn't heard him complaining when his cock was down my throat. Either time.

"I'm starting to understand how Ryze feels about not getting any respect," Vayne remarked.

"Does that mean you're going to start giving me some respect?" Ryze asked.

"Doubtful," Vayne said.

"I thought you might say that." Ryze stopped still. He gestured for us to be quiet and ducked down low.

We quickly followed suit just before a group of border scouts walked into view. Like us, they wore brown and green to fit into their surroundings. It wasn't surprising we didn't see them until the last moment. I was absolutely convinced they saw us until they were past us and out of sight.

Ryze jerked his head to the side and motioned for us to stand and follow him.

We kept close together, moving slowly and quietly.

After a couple of minutes, Tavian tapped my elbow to get my attention and signed, "This is the border."

I looked one way, then the other, but couldn't see how he could tell. Nothing in the landscape suggested a change between Spring and Summer. Nothing but a tingle as I took a couple of steps forward. Magic?

I signed my confusion to him.

He shrugged. "It's an invisible line. No one knows why it's there, just that it is."

"Whatever you're saying about me, it's probably true," Ryze said. He clearly knew we weren't saying anything about him, but couldn't resist the joke.

I glanced at him and then signed, "The sky is blue," in a way that suggested we were actually gossiping about the High Lord.

Tavian laughed. Out loud he said, "That's accurate."

Ryze looked completely unconcerned that we might be plotting his assassination right in front of his face. Did anything worry him for long?

"Here's where we keep our eyes out for Summer Court patrols," Ryze said. "They're inclined to shoot first and not leave anyone alive to ask questions later. Which is very unreasonable, if you ask me."

"I don't think Cavan is asking you," Tavian said.

"That's even more unreasonable," Ryze remarked. "I'm very wise."

"Cavan is a dumbass," Vayne said. "He only inherited because he was the only heir."

"I was the only heir," Ryze said dryly.

Vayne smirked. "Are we going to stand around and talk about it or get the hells out of here?"

Ryze said something about throwing Vayne into a swamp, but led the way south toward the capital.

TWENTY-EIGHT

KHALA

"How much further is it?" I signed to Tavian. I glanced over at him, keeping half an eye on the ground so I could follow the conversation without tripping.

"It's an hour walk from here," he gestured back. "As long as we don't step on any serpents or run into border patrols."

"Can Ryze open a portal to Garial?" I asked.

"Technically, yes, but without knowing who might be around, it's too much of a risk. He might open a portal right in front of a group of soldiers. Or in the middle of a cook fire."

"What would a fire do to the portal?"

"Nothing unless we stepped out into it," Tavian signed. "Which we wouldn't do, because we're not stupid. The point is, it's hard to know the ideal place when you open one to a city. Out here, it's less risky."

"Unless you step on a serpent," I signed.

"Unless that," he agreed. "But a serpent would slither away the moment they saw the portal."

"Is it possible to open a portal on top of someone?" I asked.

"I've never known it to happen." He frowned. "Although, it would account for a lot of sudden disappearances."

"What else can our magic do?" I hadn't had a chance to get into details with Ryze since my portal failed.

"Ryze can make it snow out of nowhere," Tavian replied. "That one's fun. He can make a sword or arrows out of ice. That's particularly useful if there's plenty of water around. He never needs to run out of arrows. Not to mention how many times pulling an arrow out of someone has actually killed them. Melting it out of them does the same thing."

I winced. That sounded painful but definitely useful.

I watched Ryze's back speculatively. How often did he need to use any of those? I recalled his considerable skill with the bow the day we met. Of course, he had a few hundred years to practice. Would I be as good when I was his age? Was an ice arrow more difficult to hit a target with than one made from wood? I'd have to ask him later to show me how.

"So, can the High Lord of Summer do the same sorts of things, but with heat and fire?" I asked.

"More or less," Tavian replied. "That makes ice arrows and swords slightly less useful. They tend to melt. On the other hand, an ice shield is good for neutralising heat. Ice can be deadlier, more quickly, because people can recover from burns better than they can recover from ice-holes." He grinned.

I snorted softly. I should have seen that one coming.

"So if the transformation is caused by the heat and not the alpha, why do I have winter magic?"

"I suspect that while the transformation would happen with or without the mating," Tavian signed slowly, "the magic is influenced by the alpha. It's possible that with another alpha involved, you wouldn't have magic at all. But all of this is so rare and there are so many different combinations, it's impossible to know the exact answers."

"Could he make an ice knot?" I asked. "Can I?" Did I need an alpha at all?

Tavian eyed me sideways. "Potentially, but where would the fun be in that? Unless freezing your pussy is something that appeals to you?"

"Not really," I admitted.

Zared, who was following the conversation from the other side of me signed, "I prefer warm and wet to cold and icy."

"Me too," Tavian agreed. "Although, I'll try anything once." He grinned.

That didn't surprise me at all. "Do you really have eight knives?" I asked.

He grinned. "Yes. I always like to come prepared. Part of me hopes I never need to use them, but the rest of me hopes I do."

I decided against asking. I had a feeling I might not like the answers.

He must have noticed my expression because he quickly signed, "Don't worry, I'll only use knives on you with your consent. I hope you'll let me some time, because I'm very good at knowing the exact amount of pressure to use." His eyes were on my throat.

In spite of myself, I swallowed. "Maybe when we get back to Lysarial."

"I knew you were my kind of woman," Tavian said approvingly. "Curious and adventurous. We can have a lot of fun together. Zared too, if he's game." He looked over to the other man. His expression was interested, curious, but without pressure. An open invitation rather than insistence.

"Maybe." Zared looked cagey. This was probably not the right time for this conversation.

"That's not a no," Tavian signed, a smile on his full lips.

"Give him some time," I signed back. "He's still not sure who to trust after everything." No one could blame him for that, least of all me.

"Are you?" Tavian cocked his head at me.

"Give me some time too," I replied. According to Ryze, I had plenty of that to spare, so there shouldn't be a problem with any of them giving as much as I needed. I might take a hundred years or so and decide how I felt about them then.

"Of course," Tavian signed. "Whatever you need. Both of you. Even without the bond, I'd want you to be my people, but only if you want that too."

I signed my understanding, but I couldn't give him any more than that right now. I didn't want to make any promises and have them be the wrong words, or the wrong sentiment. When everything sank in I may feel differently to how I felt in the moment.

I might take Ryze up on his offer to leave and find another alpha. What I saw of the Spring Court looked nice enough. I could find somewhere to be by myself and practice magic somewhere I wouldn't risk hurting anyone. I could even go out searching for the Court of Shadows or the Court of Dreams.

They might be led by an attractive alpha High Lord that never lies. Or possess an even bigger library than Ryze's.

For some reason, none of that sounded as appealing as maybe it should have. I needed to give myself some time too. Right now I needed to focus on why we were here and what we were doing. I didn't need to be distracted by thoughts of sex or self pity.

Wasn't it Ryze who said Fae were self absorbed? He was right. I'd never spent this much time thinking about myself when I was human. Even when all I wanted to do was talk, or live my life the way I wanted to, those were fleeting thoughts.

But now...the transformation was the first thing in my mind when I woke up. It lingered all day until I went to sleep. It haunted my dreams.

The pain, the way I looked now. A sliver of fear that I may forget how I used to look.

If I lived for a thousand years, how quickly would I forget how I looked for the first eighteen? What else would I forget? The temple? My sisters? The ones who made it to Havenmoor would be dust long before I died of old age.

I'd live to see generations of their descendants born, grow up, grow old and die.

No wonder Fae like Vayne and Ryze were cynical. I might be cynical too in a couple of hundred years. Would there be anything I hadn't seen by then? Even a beautiful sunrise might be boring after two hundred years of them.

I glanced over and saw Zared looking at me. He seemed to have similar thoughts going around in his mind. That he would be dust hundreds of years before I took my last breath. That thought was an abrupt stab in my heart, harder than any arrow.

I should work harder to convince him to return to Fraxius. He deserved to live his life with someone who was at the same place in their lives as he was. Who would keep pace with him. Not someone who would be young and frivolous when he was old and struggling, and vague.

I'd rather live without him than have him come to resent me.

Something whizzed past my head.

"Shit, take cover!" Ryze ducked behind a nearby tree and dropped to a crouch.

"Fuck." Vayne quickly followed suit, motioning for us to do the same.

I dropped down behind them, with Zared pressed against my back.

I thought Tavian was beside me, until, his body bent almost double, he ran through the bushes, keeping low and out of sight.

"Let me guess, Summer Court border patrol?" Zared asked, speaking out loud, his voice low.

His breath was hot on my ear. I wasn't sure if I imagined his heart racing. Maybe that was mine. If that arrow was another centimetre to the right, it would have hit me in the face.

"More than likely," said Ryze, his voice calm and steady. "We need to deal with them."

Vayne nodded in agreement. "Nothing we can't handle," he said. "Tavian will keep them distracted."

Over his shoulder he said, "You two, stay here. Don't fucking move."

Ryze rose, bow in hand and aimed before loosing arrow after arrow in quick succession. He ducked back down when a volley was returned in his direction.

Judging by grunts of pain and a thud or two, Ryze's arrows met their target.

While they were occupied firing at Ryze, Vayne rose and got off his own volley of shots with at least as much skill as Ryze.

I made out five, maybe six archers. Most of their attention was on Vayne and Ryze. The one on the end didn't even see Tavian until a knife was embedded in the centre of his forehead.

The remaining archers turned their attention toward the Master of Assassins, unleashing a barrage of arrows in his direction. He kept moving forward, his body twisting and turning, dodging.

He offered enough distraction for Ryze and Vayne to dispatch the remaining archers with quick shots through their heads or hearts.

The whole altercation lasted maybe two or three minutes.

Ryze and Vayne scanned the area for another two or three before lowering their bows.

"If there's anyone left alive, they've fucked off by now," Vayne said. He sounded satisfied, like he enjoyed the few moments of excitement. Perhaps he liked killing as much as Tavian did.

Ryze nodded his agreement and put his bow back over his shoulder. "Tavian?"

"I'm fine." He smiled even while he was inspecting wounds in his shoulder and thigh. "They're just grazes. I've had worse," he said with a grin.

"Well done." Ryze clapped Tavian on the back. "We should keep moving. Who knows how many more are on patrol are out here. Are you all right to walk or do you need to rest for a few minutes?"

"I can keep going," Tavian said. "It's nothing life-threatening. Not even much blood. They weren't very good shots."

"That's probably why they're border patrol and not in the main army," Vayne said with a grunt. "They wouldn't have been expecting to find trouble."

"But they did," Ryze said. "Lots of it." He wore his usual amused expression on his face, even when he inspected the dead Fae. "If only they stopped to talk to us, they would have found out we're perfectly nice."

"I don't think either of those are words that accurately describe us," Vayne said. "Perfect or nice."

"Speak for yourself," Tavian said. He frowned down at one of the dead Fae. "Now that's peculiar."

CHAPTER
TWENTY-NINE

KHALA

"What is it?" I peered over Tavian's shoulder.

The dead Fae looked younger than me. Seventeen or eighteen at most. I presumed that made him at least fifty. His face was long, ending in the same angular chin as any Fae. His eyes, still open, looked like those of a cat. His hair was as long, tied back off his face.

None of that was what caught and held my attention. Most of that was on his rounded ears and detached lobes. Judging by the way his hair lay, it usually covered them.

"He's a Fae with human blood." That didn't seem too strange to me. Why did they look so confused?

"Fae don't usually show outwardly human traits like that." Tavian's mouth twitched to one side. "They either look like one or they look like the other." He nodded at me to make his point.

"He might have more human blood in him than Fae." Ryze scratched his shoulder but seemed unconcerned. "It's bound to happen from time to time."

"The Summer Court doesn't usually take kindly to humans," Vayne said. "I'm surprised they let a half breed live this long." He cast his gaze around the rest of the dead border patrol. "That's probably why he's here. In the hope they'd meet trouble and he'd end up like this."

"If that's the case, I feel sorry for him," Ryze said. "If he spoke to us, I would have granted him asylum in the Winter Court." He squinted at the dead patrol as though somehow this was their fault.

"The Winter Court doesn't like humans either," Zared pointed out. He didn't attempt to keep the accusation from his words or tone. If the dead man was ostracised, he blamed the Fae in general. Clearly he believed if he asked for asylum, it would have been refused.

Ryze saw it too and raised his chin until Zared looked away.

"Some humans we do." Tavian glanced back over his shoulder and smiled.

"Some we don't." Vayne gave Zared a much less friendly look. "Especially when they don't obey orders."

Zared's hand twitched as if he was about to give Vayne a rude gesture, but thought twice about it. He must have some grudging respect for the commander, to resist like that. His shoulders slumped slightly, but the irritated set of his mouth remained.

"Don't blame Zared for us going through the portal." If someone didn't defuse the tension, it was going to explode and take us all with it. "It was my idea."

Vayne turned his dark eyes on me. "He could have stopped you. Or stayed behind. He's responsible for his actions. The same way you are." He wasn't relenting even half a step.

"Let's not stand here all day arguing," Ryze said. His commanding tone broke the standoff. "We still have a while to go before we reach the capital." Without glancing back, he started southward, leaving the rest of us to follow.

After a last glare, Vayne hurried to catch up.

"Come on," Tavian said to Zared and I. "Keep your eyes open for any more border patrols. These were reckless, but they still caught me by surprise." The fact he was bothered by that was obvious. Coupled with the dead part-Fae, he looked as close to rattled as I'd ever seen him.

He noticed me watching and smiled, the moment evaporating with his change of expression.

I gave the dead half-Fae a last look before walking away. It seemed to me it was either luck, or the gods' sense of humour that I didn't look the same way he did. What would have happened to me if I had?

I doubted I would have survived my first day of life, given how quick my parents were to move me along to the Temple. The best I might have hoped for was a pillow over my face, or to be left somewhere, abandoned.

I pushed the thoughts aside. None of that mattered anymore. Thinking about it was only a recipe for frustration, and questions with no answers. I needed to consider the future, not the past. The gods knew the future was full of more than enough questions of its own.

"Have you ever seen anything like that before?" I asked Tavian.

"Only once," he said. "The baby looked Fae, but had eyes like a human. No one thought much of it. Peculiarities happen from time to time. It's not as though we don't realise humans and Fae breed with each other. We've been fucking each other since the gods created us. Some of us like to pretend we don't." He looked meaningfully at Vayne's back.

"Only twice and only with Khala," Vayne said without looking back. "I have some standards."

"He likes to let on that he hates humans, but he doesn't really," Tavian said, slightly louder than necessary.

"Some of them suck," Vayne said. "Others...suck." He glanced back at me with the slightest lift of a brow.

"If the ability to suck is your requirement for someone to be worth your time, then you should know most humans can do it," I said. Some of us better than others.

"There's a difference between knowing how and having a mouth I want to put my cock into," he said. "Like I said, standards."

I didn't think Ryze was listening to our banter until he spoke. "He has a good point there. I'm also careful where I put my cock."

"Me too. Khala is special." Tavian grinned at me.

All I could give him back was a faint smile and a glance down at hands that still didn't look like mine. Part of me wondered if they were mistaken about me being part Fae. Maybe I was taken out of my body and put into a new one. One that belonged to someone else.

If I hadn't felt my whole body rearrange, I might have wondered where my original body was. But I did feel it. Every agonising minute of it. There was no doubt it was all me.

"I hate to say they're right, but they are," Zared said. "You are special."

"We're always right," Ryze said. "Well, I am. Vayne and Tavian have their moments."

"I've seen you be wrong," Vayne told him. "Recently too."

"My first mistake was leaving any witnesses," Ryze shot back immediately.

Vayne snorted. "I doubt that was your first mistake. Just the most recent."

"One I can happily rectify once we're back in Lysarial," Ryze said lightly.

"You're outnumbered," Tavian pointed out. "You'd have to work fast to take us all out." His hand hovered near one of his knives. For a moment I thought he was actually serious.

"You said omegas who go through heat alone end up crazy," Zared said slowly. "Are you sure it isn't you three who are the crazy ones?"

"Oh, without a doubt we are," Ryze agreed. "But nothing like those poor omegas. They wouldn't be able to tell you their own names or what colour the sky should be. It's as though their minds are like a young child's. More often than not, they can't even feed themselves." He sighed heavily.

"Is there no way to find them before that happens?" I asked. "Or some way to, I don't know, make sure there are alphas around?"

"Fae are educated to the presence of omegas," Ryze said. "Even then, things don't always work out the way we expect. Clearly, we have no say how humans are educated. Although Zared knew of their existence." He stepped over a fallen tree and glanced back at Zared.

"Only through reading about them," Zared said. His expression was suddenly cagey.

It should have occurred to me before to ask how and what he knew. Now I couldn't help the spike of suspicion that slivered through me. If he'd known and didn't tell me...

When he spoke again, his voice was tight.

"The Temple had books and records only available to priests and priestesses. Not to the Silent Maidens and not to people outside the temple. Things we're not supposed to talk about, under threat of severe punishment." His eyes flicked to me, full of guarded apology.

I understood. He couldn't tell me, wouldn't have even known any of it related to me. It was a secret that went above his head. It was Geralda and priestesses like her who were to blame.

"Why does that not surprise me?" Ryze asked. "Fae and humans have both been keeping important secrets from their people since the dawn of time."

"What are you keeping from us?" Vayne asked him pointedly.

"If I told you, they wouldn't be secrets," he said.

While Vayne muttered something, I said, "So, the temple deliberately didn't tell us."

"Most likely," Ryze agreed. "Especially if they have some arrangement with the Summer Court." He looked over to Zared. "What you read, was it in a place accessible to everyone easily and readily?"

Zared seemed hesitant to respond at first. "Not really," he admitted finally. "I was hunting through older ledgers that are usually kept locked away. They're only accessible to the high priest and priestess. I found a couple of other books hidden away underneath. Tucked away, like they'd been forgotten. I got curious and started reading them. They read like children's stories. I assumed they were locked away because the temple didn't think they were appropriate reading, but didn't want to burn them. I had no idea they were factual or important." He looked at me apologetically.

"There's no way you could have known," I assured him. "How could you? I never told anyone I could smell things differently. I always thought everyone could do that. I'm not the only maiden—former maiden—who enjoyed sex. Tyla was at least as..." I trailed off when I realised what I was saying.

"Enjoying sex doesn't indicate an omega," Ryze said. "It means you're a normal, healthy young woman who enjoys sex. There's nothing wrong with that, anymore than there is anything wrong with not wanting to partake. For the record, enjoying sex doesn't mean someone is an alpha either. It also doesn't mean they're not."

"Except during heat," I said.

"Except then," he agreed. "For some omegas and alphas, that's the only time they're ever with a partner. It's not always ideal, who the gods decide has which designation. Some make the choice not to take part, or to remove themselves from a heat, simply because they don't want to be intimate. It's an easier choice for an alpha to make than for any omega."

"Has anyone ever tried to make an artificial knot?" Zared asked, his gaze intent on Ryze. I could almost see him thinking if there was such a thing, Ryze wouldn't need to touch me again. Thinking and hoping.

"Tried, but not with any great success," Ryze said. "No substance locks and vibrates the way a knot does. And before you suggest it, cutting off an alpha's cock is no replacement."

"Have you tried that?" Zared asked. The hope was gone but his snark remained. "Because you seem open to trying new things."

Ryze chuckled. "No. I'm very attached to that part of my body. I'd rather offer my arm." He held one up. "It's almost as thick. My thigh might be better."

Vayne snorted the loudest of all of us.

Ryze pretended to look offended. As thick as his cock was, it wasn't *that* thick. Not nearly as big as his ego or arrogance. Those were big enough to fill an entire city.

"Usually, they find an alpha they can tolerate and do what has to be done," Ryze said finally.

THIRTY

KHALA

His words sat heavily over us while we walked in silence in the relentless warmth of the afternoon. I was lost deep in my thoughts, echoes of what Ryze said restless in my mind.

Find an alpha they can tolerate. Was that what this might come down to if I didn't forgive Ryze, or if he wasn't around for my next heat? Just find some alpha to fuck? Any alpha?

It wasn't that simple, not for me. He was right, I'd want someone I could tolerate. Someone I'd want to be locked with. Someone I'd welcome in my nest. If it wasn't Ryze, I'd have to find another alpha. Someone outside my pack. That idea didn't sit well with me either. I sighed at how something that should be easy was actually complicated.

Gradually, I became aware of a change in the air. A new smell. The sound of rapidly moving water. My Fae senses were acute enough to pick up both long before I saw the source. A river, approximately forty metres wide. It flowed steadily, like liquid glass, the scent cool and fresh.

If not for the current, I would have been tempted to jump in and swim. The swiftness would have swept me away in moments.

We stopped at the edge.

"There's a bridge downriver." Vayne looked displeased. More than usual. "It's always heavily patrolled."

"Want to try your hand at making a bridge?" Ryze asked me. He gave me an, 'it's all yours,' gesture with his hand. "Don't forget to put sides on it. Ice is, after all, slippery."

"Ryze learnt that the hard way," Tavian said with a grin.

"Yes I did, thank you." Ryze smirked at Tavian. "I slipped off and fell into the river. I should point out, I was young at the time. Somewhere around a hundred. At least I learnt my lesson. However, I regret telling you that story." He pointed accusingly at Tavian.

I tore my eyes from Tavian's grin and looked out across the river. It suddenly seemed a hundred metres wide, from bank to bank.

"Just make the water rise and freeze it how you need it," Ryze instructed.

He made it sound so basic, like turning on a tap. There was no way it would be that easy. I considered telling him to do it himself and I'd watch and learn. Stubbornness made me nod. It couldn't hurt to try. After a quick prayer to Breia.

My tongue darted over my lips. "All right." I can do this. *Please don't let me make a total fool of myself.*

I focused on the water, made it rise, but not too quickly. The last thing I wanted was to be covered in an entire river. They'd tease me about it for the next four or five hundred years. The fact they'd be drenched too was no consolation.

A small fountain of water rose, bit by bit. It hovered a handspan over the water. I tried to freeze it. Just a little, tiny exertion of pressure...

Instead of freezing over like the bridge I pictured in my mind, an elegant arch to span the river, a huge vertical section became a wall of ice. It climbed several metres up in the air. So high it blocked the flow of the river.

In a moment or two, the riverbed was exposed, a wide section which stretched all the way to the opposite side of the river. Rocks and pebbles lined the muddy bed, worn smooth from the flow of water.

"Ummm," Vayne said uneasily. "Fuck?"

The river started to spread out to either side of the wall, threatening to flood the forest around us. Creatures I couldn't see, shrieked and scuttled away in terror.

"Yes, fuck is right." Vayne nodded.

"Close enough." Ryze shouted, "Run!" He leapt down the bank, landed with a squelch, and started to bolt across the riverbed.

I had the fleeting thought he might be completely insane, but then Tavian and Vayne darted after him. I glanced at Zared for half a second and then we too were running.

The riverbed was slippery and slick with mud. My boots stuck every few steps. Once or twice, deep enough I had to stop and pull them free, the mud popping and squelching as I drew free from the suction. I don't know how I didn't lose a boot. The mud showed no mercy at all.

After a few moments, the wall of ice started to shake. Cracks appeared in the centre. The pressure of the water pushed against it, insisting it be allowed to run its course. It roared, almost deafening with its anger, a giant with fists beating against its prison, trying to break out.

I swallowed down my fear and went on running.

"Come on!" Ryze shouted. "Hurry!"

What the fuck did he think I was doing? He could make the bridge himself next time.

Halfway across, I slipped on rocks and almost fell. I windmilled my arms and managed to keep my balance before I landed face first in the mud.

"Shit."

The wall shook harder. It slanted inward, toward me, slowly losing its struggle to resist the push of the river.

Just a moment or two longer...

Tavian crouched to scoop up something, before he grabbed my hand and yanked me toward the opposite bank.

"Fish," he explained briefly before giving me a shove and climbing up behind me

"Right." Of course. I stood, palms on my thighs, trying to catch my breath. The ground was wonderfully solid under my feet.

"Zared?"

I turned to see him still running. He was tall for a human, his legs long, but he wasn't as fast as a Fae. Without realising, I left him behind about halfway across the river bed. I didn't realise I could run so fast. I suppressed the flash of guilt that wouldn't help anyone right now. I could wallow in that later.

"Khala, help me hold up the wall," Ryze said urgently. "Vayne, Tavian, grab him the moment he's close enough."

The wall cracked. Hairline at first. Water trickled through holes here and there. A heartbeat later, they were twice the size with twice the flow. At this rate, Zared would be swept away.

If there are any gods listening, please keep him safe, I pleaded silently. Right now, he needed all the help he could get. I wasn't sure me and my magic were up to it.

I gritted my teeth and pushed the water back as hard as I could. The pressure was enormous. Much more than before. The water backed up, insisting on shoving everything out of its path. I'd never felt anything like it. I could no more stop it than I could stop the sun from setting. But I could delay it. I had to.

I tried again to freeze the wall. The result was flimsy at best. The river was resisting being blocked a second time. The flood on either side of the narrow wall grew, heading towards us. Threatening to wash over us all.

If it reached us, we'd all be screwed. Nothing would stop us from being caught up in the torrent. We would die here.

"Faster!" Tavian urged Zared. He sounded desperate, scared. His tone exactly mirrored my thoughts. We had seconds to do this. If we couldn't...

I didn't bother to shake my head, I pushed my doubt away and threw everything into keeping the water from reaching Zared. Every single drop of concentration went it this. We couldn't fail.

Zared glanced at the wall that shook and quivered right beside him. He put down his head and ran as fast, palms flat to help him move faster.

"I can't hold it." The pressure pushed back at me, shoving. The water was alive and fighting back. It lapped around my ankles. I was about to belong to the river.

Ryze groaned. "Yes, you can. Another minute more." His voice was as strained as my attempt to hold the magic in place. He wasn't finding this any easier than I was. If he couldn't do it then...

"Come on." Tavian gestured frantically.

"Hurry the fuck up," Vayne growled. "My boots are getting wet."

The commander's pissed off tone was exactly what I needed. I gave the water a last shove, forcing it back for just long enough.

Zared finally reached the bank. Tavian leaned down to grab his arm. He grunted and yanked Zared up off the riverbed and onto the bank as the wall evaporated.

One moment it was there, the next it was completely gone. Not even cubes of ice floated on the current. The wall might as well never have existed. The river poured into the gap with a triumphant gush, reclaiming its territory.

I flopped down beside Zared who lay panting in the damp grass.

For the longest time, I couldn't speak. Exhaustion threatened to swamp me like the river almost had.

Finally, I managed to conjure a few words.

"I'm so sorry. None of that was supposed to happen."

"It was kind of incredible," Tavian said. His face was red, like he'd run instead of Zared. "It wouldn't have been incredible if you didn't get out in time."

"You need to run faster," Vayne remarked. He looked down at Zared and gave him a nod. The Vayne equivalent of saying he was relieved he got out alive.

"I'll bear that in mind," Zared panted. He looked up at me with something I'd never seen in his eyes before. Fear. Fear of me and what my magic almost did to him. He could have died because I fucked up.

"I tried to make a bridge, but it wouldn't do what I wanted it to." I didn't know if it was the magic or the river, but both seemed unwilling to comply with what I asked of them. Not exactly like they wouldn't behave, but like they had other ideas. Somehow they thought the wall was better than a bridge.

"At least we got some fish," Tavian said.

"Unfortunately, I don't think we have time to appreciate that fact, or cook them," Ryze said. "The minute that swell hits the bridge, they're going to know something is up. Chances are they'll come and investigate. If they do, we want to be anywhere but here."

He turned and scanned the area around us. The vegetation was thinner here, with fewer places to hide. Harder for border patrols to remain unseen, but harder for us too.

"Can you keep going?" I asked Zared.

He pushed himself to his feet. "I'm fine. I'd rather not be here when someone comes."

Tavian grinned.

"Not that kind of coming," Zared told him.

"I know, I just thought I'd lighten the moment," Tavian said.

I stood and looked back at the river. It was innocently winding its way through the landscape like nothing ever happened. Ryze was right though, the rush of water would cause a noticeable swell downstream. Big enough to look strange and out of place.

"Why couldn't we hold the wall?" I asked Ryze as I fell into step beside him. "Between both of us, shouldn't it have been easier than that?" That was logic talking, not my very basic knowledge of magic. The more I learnt about that, the more I realised I didn't have a clue.

"Magic is fickle," he said. "You felt it the minute it decided to stop playing nice. Between that and the natural pressure of the water, we were lucky to hold it together as long as we did. I couldn't have held it by myself. If it was you alone, Zared would be kilometres downstream by now. Which is exactly why magic is dangerous, and why you should practice as much as possible when we get home."

Home. Was that what Lysarial was? I supposed it was as much home as anywhere else right now. The Winter Court capital was more a home to me than the temple had ever been. The home I had before that, the memory was too faded. Tainted by the idea I wasn't wanted there, in spite of the sense of warmth and security whenever I thought back that far.

"Maybe we shouldn't have run across the river bed," Vayne suggested.

"We definitely should have done that," Ryze said with a smile. "How often do we get to do things like that?"

"Things that might get us killed? More often than we should." The army commander gave him a dark look.

"We live a long time, but we still only live once," Ryze retorted. "When did you become such an old stick in the mud?"

"When I found myself running across mud and then standing in front of a potential flood," Vayne said. "If you want to be a fucking idiot, that's up to you, but don't get me killed."

"I make no promises," Ryze told him. The lines around his eyes crinkled with amusement.

"That's what I'm afraid of. I'm starting to think your life consists of thinking up new and interesting ways I might die." Vayne gave him a dark look.

"It didn't until this moment." Ryze grinned. "I was looking for a new hobby. This one is perfect."

"We should shove you in the river and go home," Vayne told him.

"I don't think you'd enjoy the sentence for killing your High Lord." Ryze pushed his pack higher up his back. "If you're really thinking about doing that, you might want to jump in after me. It would be quicker and less painful."

"Not if we tell everyone it was an accident." Vayne glanced around at the rest of us.

"Sorry, but I'm not lying for you," I told him. "Besides, I think it's fairly obvious we need him to get back across the river. And back to the Winter Court."

"Exactly." Ryze nodded. "Without me, you're all screwed. I guess you better be nice to me then."

Vayne snorted. "Not a chance."

Ryze grimaced at him, but that seemed to be the end of their conversation for now.

We followed the river in silence for a while, before moving away as we neared the bridge. As Ryze suggested, patrols seemed to be heading back upriver to look for the source of the surge.

We managed to avoid them by keeping low and silent until we skirted around a thicket of trees and over a rise. The ground dropped away in front of us.

Ryze gestured for us to halt and let out a low breath.

I gasped.

"Behold the spires of Garial."

CHAPTER
THIRTY-ONE
KHALA

"Walk like you're not out of place," Ryze had said before we entered Garial. "Like you belong here."

The three Fae men strode through the streets, backs straight, bristling with confidence and arrogance.

I did the best I could to do the same, chin raised, eyes forward. Every so often, I glanced at Zared. He wore a cloak Ryze stashed in his pack, the hood pulled up around his face. The hem was so long it brushed the ground with every step.

If no one looked too closely, they'd see an arrogant priest in the company of four other Fae.

If they did look too closely, we'd be screwed. There was no hiding what he was with the hood pushed back of his face. We'd have to make sure that didn't happen.

Garial itself was enormous, at least as big as Lysarial. Built around a hill, a white marble palace perched on the crest. Spires jutted out of the roof like needles trying to make holes in the sky. Most of the buildings sported them, even the ones with a single story. Some were obviously decorative, others had windows, suggesting rooms inside.

The city sloped down to a harbour narrower than the one in Lysarial, but longer. One side was dotted with docks and bobbing sea craft, the other with shops and places to eat.

The breeze that blew fresh off the harbour was the only relief from the sticky warmth of the late afternoon. It brought with it the smell of salt, fish and cooking spices.

Everything was so overpowering here I thought my senses might overload.

"Charming place," Zared muttered. Like me, he was used to towns like Ebonfalls, not cities like Lysarial and Garial.

I hadn't had a chance to wander through the streets of Lysarial. For me, this was entirely new. Exciting if overwhelming.

"It's not as nice as Lysarial," Tavian agreed. "It's worse on the back of the hill. That's where all the poorer Fae live."

That was the first I'd heard of the existence of poorer Fae. It shouldn't surprise me to learn they existed. There always seemed to be people who were better off than others, whether they were human or Fae.

We followed Ryze to an inn on the waterfront and straight to rooms on the third floor.

"The owner works for me," he explained. He pulled a key out of his pocket and unlocked a plain but heavy-looking timber door. He pushed it open and waved us inside.

"We weren't expecting two extra people."

That explained why the small room had only three narrow beds.

"We'll make do." Zared pushed his hood back off his face.

"Zared can sleep on the floor," Vayne said. He swung his pack off his back and set it down on the bed that was both furthest from the window, and hard up against the wall.

Zared opened his mouth to retort but caught my warning look and shut it with a snap and click of his teeth.

"Zared and Khala can stay here," Ryze said. He swung his own pack down to the bed in the middle of the room. "The three of us are going to search for information. No, you can't come," he said before I could even think of speaking.

"We have contacts. We don't need them asking questions. The innkeeper will bring up food in an hour or so. They'll knock twice, then leave it outside. Don't open the door until you know they've gone. The innkeeper works for me, but I can't vouch for the staff. Nor can I rule out the possibility someone paid the innkeeper more than I did."

"There's always someone vying for the loyalty of people like that." Tavian put his pack down near the door, a thoughtful expression on his face.

He'd looked like that since we entered the streets of Garial. The laid-back Tavian was put aside in favour of the Master of Assassins, sneaking into enemy territory. His whole body looked loose, but I wasn't fooled. He was ready to act or react in a heartbeat to protect himself or his High Lord.

"Fae from all over the four courts come here. They bring information with them, ready to sell it or buy more," Ryze said. "The price is higher every time I step foot in Garial." He patted the full purse at his hip.

"They should be arrested for asking so much," Vayne grumbled. "Arrested and thrown in the harbour."

"I'm starting to think you have a thing for throwing people into deep water," Ryze told him.

Vayne shrugged and followed the High Lord out.

Tavian gave me a small smile and closed the door behind the three of them.

"This is bullshit," Zared growled. He dumped his pack in the middle of the floor and flopped down onto the bed closest to the window. "We came all this way just to be left behind? How are we supposed to help like this?"

I sat down beside him. "We can help by not getting in the way. When they find out where my other sisters are being held, we can help."

"How?" Zared demanded. "They could leave us behind then too. They might leave us in this room for days, to keep us out of the way."

"They can try." They probably *would* try. I didn't want to be stuck here any more than he did, but I also didn't want to risk my sisters with my own impatience. "If nothing else, they'll need us when they get my sisters out of the palace or wherever they're being kept. They're going to be confused and scared. Familiar faces will be exactly what they need."

He sighed, rose and stalked over to the window. He looked out for at least a couple of minutes before he spoke again. When he did it was with resignation.

"You're right." He turned back around to face me. "They will need that. If they haven't transformed, another human face will be welcome. And if they have, seeing you may reassure them."

"Right." And seeing them transformed would reassure me that I wasn't a one-off. Some kind of peculiarity created by the gods or circumstance. We'd all feel a bit less alone.

"So, that thing with the river..." He looked like he needed to talk about it, but at the same time didn't want to think about it. Neither did I, but we had to clear the air between us. I didn't want him to fear me. Although, if he did, that fear was justified. He came closer to dying than I could bear to think about. I never would have stopped blaming myself if he had.

"I don't know what happened," I said. I owed him the truth, as best as I could give him. "When I use magic, it doesn't work the way Ryze thinks it should. I tell it what to do and..." I stopped to think about it. "It does something else. Something I didn't expect or ask for. It's like a child who doesn't want to do what they're told. But at the same time, it's not fighting me. Not exactly." I frowned, trying to put my thoughts into words.

"It's like...it doesn't quite understand what I'm asking. Like there's a piece missing. I feel like I'm trying to communicate when I still have my Silent Maiden choker on, but the other person doesn't understand maiden hand signals. They can make out some of them, but they're mostly guessing."

I leaned back against the headboard and tucked my feet under me.

"Or it's like trying to understand someone speaking when you can't hear."

He came and sat down beside me again. "Magic speaks in a different language?"

"It doesn't really have a language," I said slowly. "But whatever it is, I'm not reaching it the way I want to. I'm sorry, I don't know how to explain it any better than that."

He put a hand on mine. His fingers trembled slightly. Through the bond, I sensed him trying to understand. Wanting to.

"It's all right. This is all very new and strange. It might just be that your body isn't used to being able to do magic. Maybe it needs time to adjust. Like...I don't know. Learning how to walk?"

"That's possible," I conceded. "Ryze likes to let on that he's an expert, but I think he's figuring things out at the same time I am. He knows more than I do, yes, but not everything about this transformation."

"Even if he did, there's no saying every transformation is the same," Zared pointed out. "He might have seen hundreds, but yours might be different in some way."

"That would be my luck," I said dryly. "I always have to be the one to stand out." I tucked my legs in tighter.

He locked his eyes on mine. "There's nothing wrong with being unique."

"Even if I nearly kill you in the process?" I asked, bitter at my own shortcomings.

"You could have been swept away downstream. Drowned, because my magic doesn't work the way it should. Or the way Ryze thinks it should." I found myself wiping a tear off my cheek.

"You said yourself, he's not an expert on everything." Zared swiped his thumb down my opposite cheek, wiping off another tear. "Maybe it's his magic that doesn't work the way it's supposed to. Maybe neither of them do. It's different, that doesn't make it wrong."

"That doesn't mean it's not," I argued weakly.

He was right though. This whole situation was difficult and strange, but that might be the way it was supposed to be. How the gods intended. I needed to give myself time to get used to being who I was now. Every part of me. His analogy of learning to walk was accurate. That was how I felt since I woke up after my fever broke. Like I was wobbling every step to get from one side of the room to the other. And falling on my ass more often than not.

"Nothing about you could ever be wrong," he said gently. "Except the dubious company you keep."

I wiped away another tear and tried to smile.

"Including mine," he added after a moment.

"Are you saying I should stay away from all four of you?" I asked.

"No, just the other three." He slipped his hand up to tangle his fingers in my hair and brushed his lips across my cheeks. "I think we should make the most of being alone, don't you? If you're ready after..."

"I'm ready." The slight touch of his lips set my blood on fire. Not the way the mating heat had. This was the slow burn of a fire under a cook pot. Taking its time to make the perfect food.

"Good, because so am I." He slammed his mouth down onto mine, his lips hungry, like he hadn't eaten in days. He pushed his tongue into my mouth, forcing my lips apart, tasting me.

His hands were on my shirt, pulling it up out of the way before he grabbed a breast in each of his hands. He palmed my nipples until they were stiff peaks.

"So perfect," he whispered.

He slid his hands down my side and grabbed my hips. With one tug, he pulled me until I lay flat on the mattress.

"I want to make you forget them," he said.

"Them who?" I said breathlessly.

He chuckled and took his hands off me.

When I looked at him in protest, he said, "Stand up. I want to watch you take your clothes off for me."

He leaned against the headboard and placed his hands behind his head. He gave me a lopsided smile and raised eyebrow.

I regarded him for a moment before I slipped off the bed and walked around to the end.

My eyes on his, I very slowly undid my pants and slid them down my hips. I stepped out of them and pulled my shirt up just enough to expose my flat stomach.

His tongue slid across his lips.

A faint smile on my own, I pulled my shirt up with agonising slowness, revealing centimetre after centimetre of skin until my breasts were exposed again.

I pulled my shirt off my head and dropped it to the floor.

I hooked my thumbs into the top of my panties and did a little wiggle before I pushed them down and let them drop to my feet.

"You're so fucking beautiful," he whispered. "Now, crawl to me."

I was beyond aroused by now. Practically dripping. He knew exactly what he wanted and wasn't afraid to insist. He took the power into his hands and I let him have it.

I placed my palms on the bed, then my knees and started the slow crawl up the mattress to him, my breasts swinging as I went.

By the time I reached him, the front of his pants looked extremely tight.

"Take my cock out," he said.

I undid his pants. Trembling with desire, I hooked my fingers in the waistband and pulled them down to free his erection. He was deliciously hard, red and throbbing with veins. His tip already glistened with pre-cum.

I ran the tip of my finger over his slit, swiping across the warm moisture.

I pulled his pants down further until he could kick them off. He grabbed the hem of his shirt with one hand and pulled it off over his head. All that training with Vayne left him even more muscular than he was before. He might not run as fast as a Fae, but he'd beat them in a wrestling match.

I was about to lower my mouth to his cock when he spoke.

"Not like that," he said. "I want to fuck you like Ryze did. On your hands and knees. Grab hold of the headboard." He stood, looking down at me, his eyes as hard as his cock.

I walked forward on my knees and gripped the timber with my fingers.

He moved around behind me and slipped his hand between my thighs. He grazed his thumb over my rear hole, while his fingers found my clit. Gentle caresses soon turned firm as he traced tiny circles with almost painful pressure.

I groaned and gripped the headboard tighter.

"You're so wet already," he said. He plunged a couple of fingers inside me and started to fuck me with them.

"That feels so good." Better than good. After the craziness of the heat, this was exactly what I needed. To touch and be touched, without the wild, out-of-control, all-encompassing heat.

"Yes, you do," he agreed. "You feel warm and wet and *mine*. Come for me."

He worked a little harder until I plunged willingly over that cliff, into the swirling eddy of pleasure that spun me around and dragged me down into bliss.

I was halfway back when he slid out his hand and knelt behind me. He positioned his cock and slammed into me. If I wasn't holding on as tight as I was, he would have pushed me all the way through the headboard, and the wall behind it.

"Harder," I panted.

"Gladly."

I braced myself as he pulled all the way out and slammed back in, pounding into me relentlessly. His fingers dug into my hips. His panting was ragged. He put all his energy and force into each stroke. Grunting and grinding into my body.

One hand found my clit again, working me as hard as he fucked me.

"Gods, yes," I panted. "So good."

I screwed my eyes shut when I came again around his cock. The muscles of my pussy clenched tight around him, sending me to oblivion and back, and forcing an orgasm out of him.

When he came, it was loud and deep, his balls slapping against my ass, cock so deep, he hit me all the way through every time.

Finally, he sagged over my back, puffing and slick with sweat.

"Gods, yes. You're special, all right." He stayed like that for a while before easing out of me and pulling me down with him. "I've always thought you were beautiful, but you're even more beautiful now, like this."

"Looking like a Fae?" I asked, not wanting to ruin the moment, but seeking reassurance.

"Yes," he replied. "It's like you were a bud, but now you're a flower. Or maybe a butterfly. Soft and elegant but strong in their own way. And beautiful." He drew me into his arms and lightly stroked my hair as he held me.

"Does that make you a bee?" I asked.

"If you're a flower it does," he agreed. "I'll eat your pollen any time." One of his hands ghosted lightly over my stomach and down over my pussy.

"I'll let you anytime."

I smiled and snuggled down deeper. I fell into a doze until a knock sounded at the door. It roused me from a dream about the temple. In it, all of my sisters went into heat at the same time. All of the priests were alphas. Every one of us changed into Fae, including the priests. Somehow Zared went from human to an alpha Fae without any pain. I didn't get to register what he looked like before I awoke.

"Sounds like food is here," Zared said sleepily.

I murmured my agreement and sat up to listen. Footsteps were heavy on the timber floor outside the room before they moved away, gradually fading into silence.

"I'll get it." I was hungry and didn't want to risk anyone seeing Zared.

I scooped up my panties and shirt and slipped them back on before I slowly opened the door and peered outside.

I couldn't see anyone. Nothing but a tray that sat outside, plates covered with a wide cloth held down by glasses in three of the corners.

I stepped out and peered up and down the corridor. It looked empty.

I crouched down to pick up the tray and carry it into the room.

I was about to close the door with my foot when it was pushed fully open again.

I let out a squeak of surprise and almost dropped the tray.

CHAPTER
THIRTY-TWO

KHALA

"I see you're making good use of your time," Ryze drawled. He stepped into the room and raised an eyebrow at the sight of Zared lying naked on the bed.

Zared shrugged, but tugged the covers up over his groin.

Ryze gave me a smile before taking the tray and carrying it over to the table in the corner of the room.

"Did you find anything?" I glanced at the door, but Tavian and Vayne didn't follow him inside.

"We got a couple of leads." Ryze pulled the cloth off the tray and tilted his head to look at the contents. "The food here is always so good."

"What leads?" Zared demanded.

"Leads the other two are following," Ryze said easily. "Unfortunately, where they're going, I'm more recognisable than they are. Fortunately, that means you get my company."

He picked up a bread roll and bit into the side of it. "Mmmm, tastes good." He picked up two more rolls and tossed them to each of us.

I caught mine and sat on the edge of the bed next to Zared. "Where are they going?" I tore off a hunk of bread and popped it in my mouth.

"A brothel." Ryze sat on the bed beside us, leaned back and crossed his ankles.

"Figures they'd recognise you there," Zared said with a snort.

Ryze grinned unapologetically. "Brothels have even better gossip than waterfront inns. It's amazing the things people will say in the middle of a good fuck. Or right after one." He toasted me with his roll before taking another bite.

I refused to blush. Instead I smiled and said, "What are they hoping to find there? Gossip about my sisters?" Not to mention women and possibly men willing to please them.

"People from Cavan's palace frequent this particular establishment," Ryze said. "If they've gone there and talked, Tavian and Vayne will find out."

"What a sacrifice they're making," Zared said sarcastically.

"The alternative was to send Khala in there," Ryze said, his expression unchanged. "I assumed no one would be happy with that arrangement. So you know, they're only going there to talk, not fuck everything in sight."

I wanted to growl, 'they better not,' but what right did I have to decide that for either of them? We fucked, that didn't mean we were committed to each other. And yet, the jealousy that coiled inside me at the thought of them touching someone else was real. As real as the bread in my hand. The roll that was getting squashed because I tightened my fingers around it.

I loosened my grip, licked crumbs off the side of my pointer finger and went on eating.

The knowing look Ryze gave me said he noticed what I did.

That was another thing I wasn't going to apologise for. Rational or not, I felt what I felt. Some kind of connection to both Fae men. Ryze too, in spite of everything. A connection that went beyond the bond.

Yes, I felt them, their emotions, in the back of my mind, but I *wanted* to. I liked having them all there. It felt...right.

"If they're only going in to talk, then why not send me?" I asked. "The men in there might open up to a woman." I was sure I could be persuasive, given the opportunity to try. Men seemed to like my company.

"No," Zared growled.

"It pains me to say it, but I agree with Zared," Ryze said. "It's not somewhere I would send a woman unless she was prepared for every eventuality. And I do mean *every*. Some of the men who go there aren't above taking what they think they paid for. In the Winter Court, there would be punishment for doing that. Here, I couldn't guarantee it. And even if there was, you couldn't do anything without exposing who you are. That would be dangerous for you and the rest of us. I know you want to help your sisters, but that's not a risk I'm willing to allow."

I wanted to argue, but he was adamant. Nothing I said would change that.

I nodded instead. "I'd suggest you could all stay close, but I doubt you'd be conspicuous enough." Three arrogant Fae and a tall human, at least two of who would spend the entire time glaring, would stick out like a griffin playing the piano. I'd never seen a griffin in person, but I assumed playing musical instruments wasn't something they could do.

"No, we'd be lurking outside with our ears to the door," Ryze agreed. "That would definitely not go unnoticed."

"Speak for yourself," Zared said. "I wouldn't even leave the room."

"That would also not go unnoticed," Ryze said. "We can all agree sending Vayne and Tavian was the best choice. They're more than capable of taking care of themselves. I just hope they don't kill anyone this time." He grimaced, but didn't look too concerned.

"Is this something you do often?" I asked. The way he was talking, it sounded like little more than an afternoon of fun for them. Something they did to entertain themselves, like drinking together and laughing over the gods knew what.

"More often than any of us would like." Ryze leaned his head back and closed his eyes. "There always seems to be something that needs our attention here."

"And you can't help yourself?" Zared asked.

Ryze cracked one eye open. "No. Nor would you if you were in my position. Keeping other Fae from provoking a war or even a minor conflict is a job in itself."

"You should learn to delegate," Zared told him.

Ryze looked at me. "He's been taking lessons from Vayne and Tavian, I see."

I grinned back at him without apology. "It would seem like it."

"Maybe we should have sent him along to the brothel." Ryze closed his eye again. "They might enjoy the novelty of a human in their midst."

"Fuck off," Zared snapped.

Ryze simply chuckled.

I leaned against Zared and finished my roll. It really was delicious, it must have been baked within the last hour or two. Whatever people might say about Fae, they couldn't complain about their food.

"Did the leads give any indication of which sisters are still in the Summer Court?" I asked, breaking the few minutes of silence.

"All we heard were whispers of women taken from Ebonfalls and brought here." Ryze said without opening his eyes. "Nothing substantial beyond that. We don't even know if they're still alive, if they've been through heat, or if they've transformed. All of this might ultimately have been pointless." He frowned. "Perhaps not pointless. Either way, we needed to know."

"Yes, we did," I agreed. "If you hadn't come, I would have been tempted to go anyway, even if I was here by myself."

He smiled. "I know."

I didn't hear anything, not even footsteps outside, until the door flew open so hard it bounced off the wall behind it.

CHAPTER

THIRTY-THREE

KHALA

Ryze was on his feet in a blur of movement, immediately putting himself between us and the Fae that stood at the door.

Zared and I tumbled off the bed. He hurried to pull on his clothes.

"Interesting." A Fae with red-gold hair regarded Ryze. "I heard a rumour the High Lord of the Winter Court was in Garial. I had to come and see for myself."

"Wornar," Ryze drawled. "I say it's good to see you but we both know that would be a lie."

Wornar laughed, but the sound was without mirth. "I wouldn't expect anything else. Perhaps Lord of Lies would be a better title for you."

"Always with the sense of humour," Ryze said. "It's good to see you haven't changed a bit."

Wornar peered around Ryze. "You always did keep some curious company. A pretty Fae." His nostrils flared. "An omega. And a human."

He looked back at Ryze, realisation on his tanned face. "You are treading on thin ice."

"Always. Are you going to stand there in the doorway all day, or are you going to come in?" Ryze moved back.

Wornar nodded to the two other Fae with him and stepped inside. He closed the door and caught Ryze up in an embrace.

"I should have known you're here to cause trouble, you old asshole," Wornar said.

Ryze snorted. "You're older than I am." He clapped Wornar on the back.

Arm still over the other man's shoulders, he turned to gesture at us. "Khala. Zared. Wornar is the cousin of the High Lord of the Spring Court. He's about as welcome in Garial as I am. He was just about to explain why he's here." He looked directly at Wornar, eyebrows raised expectantly.

164

"As it happens, no. I wasn't," Wornar said. "At least not until someone explains what a pretty Fae is doing with a reprobate like Ryze." He looked me up and down, openly predatory gleam in his eyes.

To my surprise, Ryze explained everything to Wornar in a handful of words. Wornar watched me while he listened, no hint of surprise at what he heard.

"I've heard similar stories in the Spring Court," he said finally. "Human women being brought here. Fae women," he corrected himself. "Transformed and then... No one knows what happens after that. Cavan is a secretive piece of shit at best. I assumed he has a harem of omegas locked away somewhere."

"Is that why you're here?" I asked, speaking finally. The idea of women being locked away for the pleasure of the High Lord, of any man, was sickening.

"No," Wornar said with a small measure of regret. "I'm here to speak to Cavan, to ascertain the extent of the alliance between him and the Autumn Court. They refuse to tell us anything, but Thiron is becoming concerned. Harel, the High Lord of Autumn is, how do I put it? Shady as hells? More so in recent years. Both of them together is a potential cause for concern. If they're working together for some sort of grab for power, then it's just as well we're both here. I have an audience with Cavan in the morning if you'd like to tag along?"

"If you already know I'm here, then it won't be long before everyone else knows." Ryze sighed. "I might as well make this official. Unless Vayne and Tavian can locate those women and we can get them out tonight."

"There's only one way into the palace these days, and that's through the front door," Wornar said. "Cavan has guards posted everywhere. It's almost like he has something to hide." He smiled ironically.

"And you call Harel shady as fuck," Ryze remarked. "Nothing says shady like guards on every door. Still, if anyone can get in and out it's Vayne and Tavian."

"I wish I shared your confidence." Wornar stepped over to the table and picked up a slice of cheese. "I've had several men and women try to gain access during the last week with no luck. I've had to stop trying before it looked suspicious." He bit into the cheese and nodded his appreciation.

"We wouldn't want anyone accusing you of being shady," Ryze said.

"Why not, it sounds accurate," Zared muttered.

"We're still working on teaching him some manners," Ryze said to Wornar.

"He isn't wrong though." Wornar smiled. "That description applies to both of us. Otherwise we wouldn't be in a waterfront inn, sneaking around like a pair of thieves."

Ryze pressed a fist to his chest. "You wound me."

"But I'm still right." Wornar finished the cheese and poured himself a cup of wine. "In our younger days, we would have come with an entourage of carriages and horses. And sent word weeks ahead of our arrival."

Ryze grimaced. "All of that organisation was tedious."

"You have staff to do that for you." Wornar sipped his wine.

"It was tedious for the staff," Ryze corrected himself. "Not to mention how long it takes to travel overland. Using a portal is much easier. Which reminds me." His gaze flicked over to me. "Khala has been trying to open them herself, but they snap shut before anyone can step through. Have you ever heard of that happening?"

Wornar cocked his head thoughtfully. His gaze lingered on me again. "I can't say I have. Can I see?"

I wanted to refuse. Something about him made me uncomfortable. Something more than the predatory look. He didn't seem like the kind of man who tolerated being told no.

Ryze nodded to me. "I think it's safe for you to try, as long as there's an alpha present." He nodded again, this time at Wornar. He didn't need to.

I'd smelled the scent of alpha on him the minute he walked through the door.

I moved to an empty part of the room and focused on pulling water from the nearby ocean. Creating the portal itself was almost effortless. Forming the veil and then peeling it back. In moments I'd made a tunnel that should lead straight into my room back in the Winter Court.

I raised my hand towards the portal. A couple of centimetres from it, it slammed shut and disappeared.

I let out a squeak and yanked my hand back. The gods only know what might have happened if I'd touched it. I might have lost a couple of fingers.

"You didn't let it go by yourself," Wornar observed.

"If I did, I'm not aware of it," I said. "I felt as though I was holding it and then it was just gone. It doesn't even slip away. But..." I stopped to think. "It felt like it wasn't locked open. Like when you have to put a wedge in a door to keep from slamming shut on a windy day. But without the wind." Was I making any sense?

"Like sometimes a book wants to close but you have to put your hand on it to keep it open?" Zared suggested.

"Yes, like that," I agreed. "But I couldn't hold it open because...I don't know. Something is missing."

Wornar scratched one of his pointed ears. "That's very strange. For me, I need a combination of warmth and water. The sun, a fire. A hot cup of tea is perfect. Unless you want to drink it. I don't need a great deal of either though. I've never experienced a situation where there was a total absence of one or the other."

"Are you saying she needs something other than winter magic?" Ryze asked.

Wornar spread his hands to either side, almost spilling wine out of his cup. "Or she needs more than one catalyst like spring and autumn magic do."

"What does that mean?" I asked.

"It could mean any number of things," Ryze said. "None of which I have answers for right now. When we get back home, we can experiment with various things." He told Wornar about the wall of ice at the river too.

"I won't ask you to show me that," Wornar said with a glance to the window and the ocean beyond. "That could end up messy. I suspect Vanissa wouldn't appreciate having her inn flooded just for a demonstration."

"It wouldn't go unnoticed by Cavan, either," Ryze said. "Nothing quite says, 'hello, we're in the city,' like a flood."

"That would certainly attract attention," Wornar agreed. "You might consider that in the future at some point. Preferably after I've left Garial."

"We'll bear that in mind." Ryze winked at me.

"Khala isn't going to be causing any floods," Zared said darkly. "Not on purpose. People might die." He gave both Fae men a dark look.

"People dying might be the purpose," Ryze said coolly. "If that's the case, then it may be a necessity. Right now, it's not." He wasn't giving up a centimetre to Zared. Not even a millimetre.

"I don't want to kill anyone," I said.

"Most of us don't want to kill anyone," Ryze said. "Except Tavian. He gets enjoyment out of it. The rest of us do what we have to do to stay alive and keep innocent people safe. If that means killing, then so be it. If the choice is between yourself and someone else, I assure you, you'll do what has to be done."

"Fae are bloodthirsty," Zared said accusingly.

"No, we're not. We live long enough to have a greater range of experiences than the average human. We've seen and done things you couldn't even imagine."

He didn't need to say I'd also live long enough to see or do things I couldn't have imagined as a human. We all knew it. Zared would be gone before...

I pushed the thought away. If I was to dwell on that too much, I'd tear my own heart out.

"So you keep saying," Zared said coldly. "You act as if humans are children. We're not. We have experiences and learn things. We keep doing that until we die."

"As far as we're concerned, you might as well be children," Ryze told him. "We'll keep having experiences long past your death. I've lived about fourteen of your lifetimes. Trust me when I tell you you've only just begun."

There was a weariness in his eyes I hadn't seen before. It contrasted with the comforting scent of leather and wood smoke and the reassurance he sent through the bond. How much was an act and how much was real? I'd barely begun to know the man. In a couple of hundred years, I'd probably still be learning things about him. And vice versa.

"I trust you as far as I can throw you," Zared told him. He gave him a filthy look before stalking to the other side of the small room and looking out the window.

I exhaled heavily and offered Ryze an apologetic look.

"You certainly keep some interesting company," Wornar said. "Would you like me to make a portal back to Fraxius for him?"

"He's scared," Ryze said. "Everything here is new to him. It must feel like he stepped into another world. For Khala too. She'll get used to it. Zared will if he lets himself. Right now, I don't have time to worry about it. We have bigger priorities than the ego of one human. Even one Fae."

"Bigger than your ego?" Wornar teased.

Ryze grinned. "I wouldn't have thought it was possible either, but here we are."

Wornar chuckled. "Will wonders never cease?"

"Probably not," Ryze said. "I don't want to be around for the day they do. What's life without wonder here or there?"

"No life at all," Wornar agreed. "No life at all."

THIRTY-FOUR

KHALA

While the two Fae made plans for the audience with the Lord of Summer, I stepped over to put a hand on Zared's shoulder.

"I know this is all—" I started.

"Fucked up?" he suggested. "Just when I think I understand everything and accept it, something else happens. Now he's suggesting he'd use you to kill people? As if you're a weapon like a sword or a knife?" He shook his head in a mixture of disbelief and disgust.

"I'm sure it's nothing he wouldn't do himself," I said. He made that clear a couple of times. Of course it was easy to say that. The reality might be a completely different story.

"He'd probably do it in a heartbeat." Zared's mouth pressed into a tight line, but he didn't look away from the window. "I'm not saying humans are perfect, but Fae..."

"What are we?" I tried to keep the annoyance out of my voice, but failed. At some point, he was going to have to accept the fact of what I was. He couldn't tell me he found me more beautiful, then suggest every other Fae was some kind of demon. It was hypocritical. Like it or not, I was one of them. One of *us*.

He turned to me and started to speak, but then saw the expression on my face.

"Don't tell me I'm different," I said.

"You *are* different," he said. "You didn't grow up with them."

"No, I grew up with priestesses who used the strap on us if we stepped out of line," I said bitterly. "Who kept the truth about who we were from us. Who kept us from speaking for ten years because of their suspicion about what we were. How many Silent Maidens aren't omegas? How many went through that when they didn't need to? How many went through it so the rest of us didn't come under suspicion? You think the Fae are fucked up, what about all of that?"

"According to Ryze, it was the Fae who set that up in the first place," Zared pointed out.

"With full agreement from the Temple," I said bitterly. "A temple of humans. Women who went through the exact same thing and then did it to another group of girls. And another. And another. Did they even believe in the gods, or are they only there to do whatever the Fae tell them to?" My voice got higher and higher with each word.

"I can't believe all of them knew what was going on," Zared said slowly. "Blame the high priestess and priest. I don't think the rest of them had a clue. I certainly didn't."

It didn't cross my mind until then that he might. The thought was sickening.

"You would have told me," I said, even though I wasn't sure he would. If he was sworn to secrecy, he would have had no choice but to keep quiet.

"Of course I would." He didn't look convinced either. He would have wanted to, but he knew as well as I did his hands might have been tied. It was easy to say things like that after the fact, when you couldn't be proved wrong.

One thing I knew for sure, he would have absolutely hated not being upfront with me.

"What do you think will happen?" he asked after a moment. "If Ryze can stop the Summer Court from taking omegas, maybe the Silent Maidens will be dispersed. What will happen to those girls?"

I shook my head slowly. "I have no idea. I don't think dispersing them will be easy. Especially those who are omegas. Their families might not want them back." By that I meant, as far as I knew, mine wouldn't have wanted me back. It seemed unlikely I was the only one in that situation.

"They might not want to go back," Zared said. "Lots of those girls had a better life in the Temple than they did in their homes."

"It's true," I conceded. I spent many hours communicating with my sisters about their lives before, what they remembered of it. Some were lucky to have a meal a day until they became Silent Maidens. They could hardly believe they were allowed three, even if they were hurried up by the gong. Most of them ate like the food in front of them might disappear anyway.

"I was told one of the maidens who lived in the Temple years before me was a princess." I thought back to what seemed a lifetime or two ago now. "I don't think she was better off at the Temple."

"Being married off to someone she doesn't care about because her father says so? Maybe she was." His gaze returned to the window. "Is it any better having to fuck someone just because your body says it needs it? It doesn't sound like either is a great choice."

His eyes seemed to track a small boat as it sailed past. It would be nice to catch the breeze and go wherever it took you, riding above the waves without a care. Until a storm dragged you under.

"I suppose so," I said. "I know which one I'd choose if those were my only choices."

"You'd make a great Queen," he said as though he thought that would be the choice I'd take.

I slapped him lightly on the arm. "The other one, silly. I'd rather fuck a stranger for an hour or two than spend the rest of my life with someone I hate." That would be a miserable existence for both of us.

"Wouldn't that depend on the stranger?" He glanced over to Ryze and Wornar. "If that Cavan asshole is as bad as they say... Could you do it if you hated him?" Zared asked. "Or her?"

Of course there were circumstances where people were born in the wrong body, so presumably a woman could have a knot and be an alpha. I'd have to ask Ryze about that later. I'd never been interested in another woman that way, so it was unlikely I'd find out firsthand.

As for getting down on all fours and presenting for someone I hated...

"I don't know," I said finally. "I don't know if it's possible for an omega to reject an alpha like that. Every time I find out something, there's another question waiting for more answers. Then another after that. That might be why Fae lived for so long. They're waiting for all the answers."

He snorted softly and slipped his arms around me. "I wish I could give them to you myself." He pressed his stubbly cheek to my smooth one. "I wish I could change you back, if it means taking away all the complications."

"I think I'm stuck with the complications," I said softly. "But I appreciate the thought."

"I'd do anything for you," he whispered. "Whatever you need, I'm here for you. As long as I...can be."

"Zared..." Shit, now there were tears in my eyes. "We're stuck with each other for a long time yet."

"I'm going to be one hells of an old man, with a young, beautiful Fae lover." His laugh was a warm breath of air over my ear.

"I'll be the same age as you," I pointed out. Trust a man to think of something like that.

"But you won't look it. You'll be gorgeous when I'm all old and wrinkled. Will you still crawl to me when I am?" He blew on my earlobe and made me shiver.

"Only if you ask nicely." How else could I answer that? I couldn't imagine not being attracted to him, no matter what he looked like, but the difference between us was going to cause a strain eventually.

For now, we could enjoy each other. We'd worry about what happened later when later came. That would happen soon enough.

"I don't like asking nicely," he said, his arms tightening around me. "In case you hadn't noticed, I liked telling you what to do and you doing it. You're mine, that's how it should be."

"I did notice that," I agreed. "I liked it too. As long as you don't get used to doing it outside the bedroom." I had a feeling if he could, he'd have me crawling to him anywhere and everywhere. The thought made me hot all over again.

His chest rumbled against me as he laughed. "I wouldn't dare. You're much too scary for that. You always have been."

"I am not scary," I insisted. I might not be the gentle-as-a-lamb type, but I didn't think I was particularly intimidating. Not compared to women like Geralda. She made it her life's work to scare girls like me. Until we got old enough to know how to side-step her.

"I've seen you angry," he pointed out. "Anyone with any sense ducks when that happens."

He leaned back and the smile disappeared from his face. Through the bond I felt what he was thinking, saw it on his face.

"I didn't mean to make a wall of ice and almost kill you," I said. "I know better than to try to do that again without lots of practice, and not in a safe place. Next time, Ryze can make the bridge."

"I'm not worried about what you might do on purpose," he said. "But you don't really know what magic does. There's so much potential for accidents. Or for Ryze to tell you to do something unsavory with it. Would you really use it to kill people?"

"I'd use it to protect the people I care about," I said firmly. "You can use a sword. You'd use it to protect me. It's no different to that. Not once have I practised and known what I'm doing. Then I can make sure no one gets hurt that shouldn't."

"You can't guarantee that," he said.

I wanted to argue with him, but he was right. I couldn't guarantee it. But I'd sure as hells try.

"At least you know I'm not going to try to take over the whole of Jorius," I said. After a moment I added, "Or Fraxius."

"You might not, but what about him?" Zared jerked his head toward Ryze.

"I have enough on my plate with one court," Ryze said. He'd probably heard most of our conversation.

"For now," Zared said.

The door rattled. The scent of apple and cinnamon, and pine reached my senses before it opened. I turned as Vayne and Tavian stepped into the room.

Vayne looked like his usual grumpy self, but Tavian gave me a smile.

"It took some doing, so to speak," Tavian said, "but I think we found where Cavan is keeping them."

CHAPTER
THIRTY-FIVE

RYZE

"He always did like gold everywhere." I took in the gold statues which stood on either side of the entry to the palace. Both were Fae women with bare breasts, narrow waists and ample hips. They stood with one hand out, palm raised, the other at their side. The gold plating peeled off here and there, revealing the stone underneath.

If they were mine, I'd strip off all the gold and leave the stone exposed. They'd be less gaudy that way.

"Thiron always says it's to make up for Cavan's other inadequacies," Wornar remarked.

I chuckled. "The Lord of Spring was always astute, and probably accurate." He was also the only one of my fellow lords I came even close to trusting. He and Wornar were the nearest thing to friends I had outside my court.

Whenever conflict happened in Jorius, we were invariably allied. Wornar, Thiron and I used to hunt together as younger men. Sometimes for deer, sometimes for lovers. For some reason, men and women seemed to love the red-gold hair they shared. Maybe it was their easy-going nature that endeared them.

Personally, I liked their quiet sarcasm. It was a match for my own.

Our escort, dressed in the deep green and gold uniforms of the Summer Court, glanced at us with disapproval.

I responded with a smile.

She narrowed her eyes at me, then turned away.

I glanced at Wornar and shrugged. We couldn't all be as popular as him and his cousin.

Wornar grinned and held back a laugh.

We probably shouldn't antagonise any of Cavan's people, especially those armed with swords, and likely as many knives as Tavian. Neither of us were known for taking anything too seriously, but even without a steel weapon, I wasn't unarmed. Neither of us were and everyone here knew it.

Still, nothing good ever came from antagonising a woman. I'd well and truly learned that lesson before I turned a century old.

We stepped through the wide, open front doors of the palace. Several other guards fell in around us.

"I'm starting to feel fancy," I said to Wornar. "Anyone would think we're people of importance."

"I'm sure no one is under that illusion where you're concerned."

I snorted a laugh. "Funny, I was going to say the same about you."

"I suspected as much, that's why I said it first." He grinned.

"You might have been spending too much time with bad influences," I remarked as if I wasn't talking about myself. "Before you retort anything, remember you came looking for me."

"Only because without me, you're bound to get yourself into trouble." His tone was light, but his gaze was everywhere, as was mine. We were offered an audience, but this may just as easily turn into an ambush. Or at least, something unpleasant.

Cavan was too smart to provoke an incident by murdering us outright. Too many people knew we were here. It wouldn't go unnoticed. Or in Wornar's case, unpunished. Thiron wouldn't take it well if his cousin was murdered in cold blood.

Mine wouldn't be pleased about my death either, although we weren't especially close. My oldest cousin Johah had no interest in becoming High Lord. According to his wife, my lack of an alternative heir gave him hives. He would never admit that, but it sounded more or less accurate. And if it wasn't accurate, at least it was amusing.

My family, distant though they were, shared my sense of the absurd. Maybe it was a Winter Court thing.

"I'm not sure what you consider this." I gestured around us. "Some would call it trouble."

"Morning tea," Wornar replied easily. "I hear the cake here is reasonably good."

"No offence, but 'reasonably good' doesn't sound like a very good endorsement to me. Personally, I prefer fucking amazing cake to reasonably good cake."

"It's cake." Wornar shrugged. "I'm not that picky."

I grinned. "I've noticed that about you."

"It's obvious, because I spend more time with you than a sensible person would," he retorted.

"Touché." I nodded appreciatively. I always enjoyed the banter with him, almost as much as with Tavian and Vayne. More so, because it was too easy to get under Vayne's skin, and Tavian was too sweet to go for the verbal jugular. Ironic, since he was happy to go for the literal one.

Our boots thudded on the white marble floor as we were led to Cavan's audience chamber. The walls were lined with paintings and alcoves containing small gold statues.

Some of these, I suspected, were pure gold not gold plated. They'd be worth a Lord's ransom at least. If gaudy-as-fuck was your thing.

I preferred the paintings, although by the time we reached the end of the corridor, I'd counted twenty-seven nipples. The twenty eighth was covered by a blanket. I loved nipples as much as the next man, human or Fae, but I also liked variety in my art. Cavan apparently preferred topless women. Assuming he was the one who decorated the place, that was.

Our escort stopped at another wide doorway and cleared her throat.

"High Lord Cavan, Lord Wornar of the Spring Court and High Lord Ryze of the Winter Court have arrived."

I raised my eyebrows and exchanged glances with Wornar, who looked amused. No doubt everyone here was aware that announcing a Lord before a High Lord was considered rude at best and a grave insult at worst. I assumed that was why she was told to present us in that order. To piss me off and see what I'd do.

My father might have declared his champion would fight Cavan's to the death over an insult like that. Fortunately for Vayne, I had thicker skin and a more important agenda than to dwell on petty matters like this.

"See them in." One of Cavan's courtiers hovered near the doorway, gesturing nervously.

Perhaps he thought I'd ask for his life in return for the insult. Lucky for him, I hated to get blood on perfectly good marble floors. Not to mention his death would achieve absolutely nothing.

Our escort stepped aside to let us into the audience chamber.

A massive window with a view over the harbour let in so much light I had to squint to avoid being blinded by all the white and gold. Was it there to offend the eye or to keep newcomers to the room from striking the High Lord first?

If the latter was the case, then it was brilliant. It took a couple of minutes for my eyes to adjust. If I planned to kill Cavan, I'd be dead before I could.

I made a note to lighten the walls in my audience chamber. Or maybe move it to a place the sun could slant in like it was here.

Cavan reclined on a throne made of oak, dressed in the same green as his guards. He'd left his blond hair loose to hang down his back, held from his brow only by a narrow gold circlet.

"Wornar. Ryze." He nodded to each of us in turn.

The lack of any title didn't go unnoticed.

"Cavan, how the hells are you?" I asked easily. If he wanted this audience to be casual, I'd play along. He couldn't say he hadn't started it.

"Extremely busy, Ryze." His voice was tight, blue eyes unwelcoming. Some might find him attractive. Like a serpent.

"Let's make this as quick as we can, shall we?"

He uncurled himself from his throne and stood. With the dais under his feet, he was a head taller than Wornar or me. Intentional, obviously. He was literally and figuratively looking down on us.

"What is the High Lord of Winter doing in Garial?" he asked.

"Enjoying your hospitality," I replied, as though it was obvious. "Are you going to offer us tea and something to eat?"

He glared at me, then gestured to one of his staff who stood beside a doorway at the end of the room.

"You might as well sit." He grudgingly stepped down from the dais and over to a table near the window.

"We were starting to think you'd never offer, weren't we Wornar?"

I slipped into a chair beside Wornar and opposite Cavan. I wanted him where I could see him, even knowing the feeling was entirely mutual. Antagonising him was only fun if I didn't die doing it.

"We knew it would come in time," Wornar replied. That was halfway between agreeing with me and saying Cavan was a gracious host, even though he wasn't. I admired his subtle antagonism.

We sat in silence for a couple of minutes before staff brought out a tray with tea and cake. They cut us all slices and poured tea from the same pot.

I waited until Cavan had a sip before taking one myself.

"As to why you're here," Cavan prompted.

"You were right Wornar, this cake is relatively good. Also, this was your audience, so the polite thing would be to let you go first." I glanced at Cavan to let him know his insult hadn't gone unnoticed. I wanted to tell him to stop his petty, fucking games. No wonder my cousin Johah was happy to be Lord and not High Lord. Politics was bullshit.

Wornar swallowed his mouthful. "My cousin sends his warm greetings. He's curious as to—" He must have caught the flick of Cavan's eyes at the same time I did.

I tensed and readied myself to make a sword or knife of ice if I needed to.

"Harel," Cavan drawled as the High Lord of Autumn slipped into a seat at the table.

"Well, isn't this cozy?" I sipped my tea and looked over at the red haired Fae who was glaring at Wornar and me. Mostly me.

Harel and I had a history of not getting along. We had a different sense of humour, in that he didn't have one. I thought he was boring and he thought I was frivolous. Whatever, life was too short not to enjoy it, even Fae life.

"What are you doing here?" Harel snapped at me.

"Isn't that the question of the day?" I mused. To Wornar I said, "I think we have our answer."

Wornar nodded. "So it would seem."

I pushed my teacup aside, leaned forward and pressed my forearms to the table. "Let's be blunt. We've heard reports of omegas going missing from Fraxius and turning up here. Without anyone asking their consent."

Cavan leaned back and crossed his knees. "Short on women to fuck?" He looked impressed with himself.

I grinned. "No. I was wondering that about you though. Why else would you feel the need to kidnap women and bring them here?"

I cocked my head at Harel. "Is that why you're here too? You want your share of pussy?"

Harel's face turned red with anger. "I don't need to kidnap women."

"Neither do I," Cavan said smoothly. Too smoothly. "I'm merely continuing the work my father started. To give homes to part Fae women who would be ostracised by humans. He worried they'd be treated badly in the other courts, and gave them asylum. And yet, you come here accusing me of doing something terrible."

He clicked his tongue. "Maybe you should worry about matters of your own court and stay the fuck out of mine." He gave me a sarcastic smile.

"I want to speak to them," I said. "If they're here of their own free will, I'll apologise and be out of Garial before the sun sets again." I couldn't remember a time in my life I wanted to be wrong more than I did right now. I couldn't dismiss the possibility Cavan was telling the truth. There were times when transformed omegas wouldn't have been welcome in any of the courts. If anyone knew what they were.

More than one would have gone to another court and not let on who they really were. Of course, that meant they had to leave their homes, and hope like hells no one ever recognised them. Anywhere offering asylum would have been more than welcome.

"I don't see why they'd want to talk to you," Cavan said. His gaze flicked to Harel and something passed between them. Something that was probably not good.

Since they were being cagey as fuck, I might as well address the second reason for my visit here.

"There is another rumour, just as pressing as the first. It involves the use of magic to change the weather. Specifically extending summer. Even the Summer Court shouldn't be this hot at this time of year."

I fixed my eyes on Harel. "This should be when autumn is at its strongest." I sat back. "Is that why you're here? You want your weather back?"

Harel smirked. "Now I understand. This isn't about missing omegas. You're worried there won't be any more winter in Jorius."

"I'm more concerned about kidnapped women than I am about my magic," I told him. "What has Cavan offered you that you aren't concerned about what he's up to?"

Harel twitched and I knew I was onto something. I also knew he wasn't going to tell me outright. They were both shady as fuck.

"An alliance," Wornar said softly. "Power over the other courts. Ambition corrupts even the best of us."

177

"And Harel is far from the best of us," I said without taking my eyes off the Lord of Autumn.

He sneered at me in response.

Very fucking mature.

"Did you come all this way to throw accusations around?" Cavan asked.

"No, I came to speak to those women," I said insistently. "Like I said, if they're compliant, I'll be on my way."

"There is the small matter of the alliance between these two," Wornar reminded me. "What assurance do we have that you're not planning to invade another of the courts?" His expression was uncharacteristically grave.

"I've heard enough," Cavan snapped. "I was gracious to agree to this audience. You've been nothing but rude since you stepped through the door. My guards will see you out." He gestured towards them.

"I thought we were being so polite," I remarked.

"So did I." Wornar looked troubled, but he rose at the same time I did. "I'll take your words back to Thiron." He didn't need to add that the High Lord of Spring wouldn't be happy to hear any of them. They were as good as a declaration of war, or at least intent.

"You do that," Cavan said with a smirk. "If either of you are in the city when the sun rises in the morning, I'll consider it as provocation and act accordingly."

"I think he means he'll have us executed," I said to Wornar.

"Yes, I got that," Wornar agreed.

Before I took a step away from the table I turned and waited until everyone's eyes were on me.

"Your lack of cooperation is disappointing, to say the least. Personally, I have no choice but to believe the information I was given, which is that you are holding omegas here against their will. And that for some reason, you're using them to manipulate the weather. I can only assume that's part of some bigger plan. I will be increasing patrols along my borders, and if anyone from the Summer or Autumn Courts put a toe inside, they will be dealt with."

I paused for a moment.

"If you'd like to reconsider before this matter escalates beyond this, you know where to find me. Better yet, let's put this to rest right now and we can finish that relatively good cake." The cake was underwhelming, but I'd eat it if it prevented a war. To be honest, I'd eat cock if it prevented a war. Even if that cock was Cavan's.

Cavan pressed his eyes closed tightly. "I don't know how I can express this more clearly." He opened his eyes and locked them on me. "Get the fuck out of my palace before I change my mind and have you both executed."

"So hospitable," I said sarcastically. "Fine, we're leaving." I had no concern that he might carry out his threat. I could make a portal and be gone in the blink of an eye. And Wornar with me. We all knew it. The threat was empty, if somewhat aggressive.

"Let's go," Wornar said.

"With pleasure," I said. "The sooner we're out of this city, the better." The sooner Khala was out of Garial, the happier I'd be. While I was worried for Tavian, Vayne and even Zared, I was more worried for her. That worry was increased with the almost certainty her sisters were here against their wills. She wanted to see them for herself, but if I could give her some reassurance I'd seen them and they were content, that might have to be enough.

I had a decision to make. Did I tell her the truth and risk her running off trying to find them, or did I lie to her again and risk her hating me when she found out?

That was a no win situation if there ever was one. Unless I could convince her to let the matter go. Griffins would grow three tails before that happened. Two of them was probably enough.

"Ryze," Cavan said before I stepped out the door.

I forced a smile to my face and turned around.

"There's one small matter that slipped my mind." He stepped around the table towards me, hands clasped in front of him. "I also listen to rumours. Especially ones regarding transformed omegas. According to whispers, you have one with you in the Winter Court."

I froze. I should have expected him to know something about Khala. Why wouldn't he, when we had people sniffing around his court?

"I see you know what I'm referring to." He looked smug. "Or should I say, who."

I forced myself to stay calm, although I wanted to drive a shard of ice through his heart for even talking about her.

I shrugged. "What of it? She's there of her own free will."

"Is she?" Cavan exchanged amused glances with Harel.

That look turned my blood to ice.

"Unlike you, I don't need to lock women away," I said as coolly as I could.

"I'm sure you don't." Cavan looked bored.

I wished he'd get to the point.

"But the fact of the matter is, she's not at the Winter Court," Cavan said. "She's here."

"She might have accompanied me to the Summer Court," I said carefully.

"No," he said slowly as if I was being deliberately stupid. "I mean, she's *here*. Leaving her in that inn was an oversight on your part."

"It's the first time I've ever seen you make a joke," I said with half a chuckle. I sent off a quick plea to the gods that he *was* joking.

He laughed. When he stopped laughing, he nodded to a couple of guards who stood in front of the same door the tea and cake was brought in through.

They opened the door. Someone I couldn't see shoved Khala through it. Her hands were bound and gagged tied over her luscious mouth. Tears slipped down her cheeks.

Even like that she was gorgeous, and clearly furious.

"Like I said, she's here."

CHAPTER
THIRTY-SIX
KHALA

"This is bullshit," Zared growled. He paced back and forth across the room. "There must be something we can do."

"There will be," I said. "Right now there isn't. Except to wait patiently."

He turned slightly accusing hazel eyes on me. "You have changed. The old Khala would have been climbing the walls with me."

"Maybe I realised how little wall climbing achieves." I leaned back against the headboard and closed my eyes. It shouldn't be long now. Ryze left an hour ago. Tavian and Vayne shortly after.

I barely finished that thought when I heard the sound of approaching footsteps. I kept my eyes closed until the door opened.

It didn't slam against the wall the way it did when Wornar flung it, trying to scare us. It opened slowly. Hinges creaking. Ominous.

"What the fuck?" Zared spun around, eyes wide.

I stepped off the bed, hands raised and put myself between the three Fae with drawn swords, and my human lover. His fear and anger, coming through the bond was a distraction I had to push aside.

"What do you want?" I took in their green and gold uniforms. In spite of the dark shade, they looked garish compared to the black worn by most of the residence of the Winter Court.

"Our High Lord wants to meet you." The man in the middle spoke in a deep, commanding tone, clearly accustomed to being obeyed. He had a long nose for a Fae. It made him look like a hawk.

I eyed the tip of his sword. "I guess he's not asking."

"You guess right," Hawk-nose said. "Let's go. Both of you." He glanced towards Zared and curled his lip.

I didn't need to look back to know Zared was looking at him the same way.

"Turn around." Hawk-nose put his sword back and grabbed one of two lengths of rope which hung from his belt.

"There's no need for—" I quickly turned around when the other two Fae raised their swords.

"If you think I'm going to let you take her," Zared grabbed his own sword from where it leaned against the wall near his pack.

"You can cooperate, or we can kill you," Hawk-nose said. "It's her Lord Cavan wants." He grabbed my wrists and wound the rope around them.

With my eyes and the bond, I pleaded with Zared to put down the sword and do what the Fae told him. I had no doubt they'd kill him without a second thought if he gave them an excuse to.

Hawk-nose tied a firm knot before shoving me toward the door and grabbing another length of rope.

Zared hesitated, sword gripped in both hands. For the longest moment, I was sure he would lunge at one of them. He would die, but he'd take one of them with him. Maybe two. He might give me a chance to run.

I shook my head. I considered trying to dump water on one of them and freeze it, but either Zared or I would be dead, killed by one of the other two Fae, before the first one died.

I hadn't practised enough with my magic to consider taking on all three of them at once. Not without risking Zared and myself in the process. I was almost certain Cavan wouldn't kill me. This might be the chance I needed to get to my sisters. I had to take it. And try not to get Zared killed in the process.

Finally, reluctantly, Zared placed the sword back against the wall and turned, his hands clasped behind him. His jaw was set firm, teeth gritted hard. He was hating every second of this.

Hawk-nose bound his wrists and shoved Zared towards me. He staggered a few steps, but managed to stay on his feet.

"Follow me," Hawk-nose ordered. To the other two Fae he said, "If either of them try anything, kill the human."

"Yes, sir." One of them gave a short nod and waved with his sword.

The ropes uncomfortably tight, I walked behind Hawk-nose out of the inn and down the streets of Garial.

Fae stopped to stare. Some of them stared at me, but most stared at Zared. He kept his eyes forward, chin jutted out in barely contained fury.

"If I get the chance, I'm going to kill him for touching you." He glared at Hawk-nose's back as though his eyes could sear holes through the Fae man's uniform and skin.

"I was going to say the same thing," I said softly. I hadn't realised how possessive I was of Zared until Hawk-nose was tying him up. It should have been *me* tying him up, to the headboard. Me or one of our pack.

"Quiet," Hawk-nose snapped over his shoulder. He led us over to a carriage which waited to the side of the wide road. "Get in."

If Tavian or Ryze were here, one of them would remark that Hawk-nose had no manners. The thought was almost funny, but not enough to smile at. The situation was too grim right now.

I glanced around, hoping to see one of them. I felt all of them on the other end of the bond, but none felt close except for Zared. His simmering anger hadn't let up, not even slightly. If he could, he would have wiped half the city out by now. Our captors and those who stopped to stare.

I ducked my head and climbed into the carriage. Perched on the edge of the seat because I couldn't sit back with my hands tied behind me.

Zared grudgingly climbed in and perched beside me.

Hawk-nose and the other two guards climbed in after us. The carriage started a brisk roll through the cobbled streets. It bumped and jostled us as we went, but at least now no one could stare. No one except our captors.

One looked wary, especially of Zared. The other seemed more interested in looking at my breasts. Hawk-nose seemed to have his attention on us, but also everywhere else at once. His body tensed with alertness.

Was he anticipating my pack trying to rescue us, or something else? Maybe he thought I was more proficient with my magic than I was, and was quietly preparing to freeze his brain. I'd totally do that if one of the others wouldn't kill Zared immediately after that.

I was thinking about whether or not I could freeze all three of their brains at once when we rattled through a set of gates. I caught a glimpse of them and a handful more guards, through the window. Even if I could kill all three of them, I'd still end up dead, killed by one of at least a dozen more.

The carriage rolled to a stop.

"Out," Hawk-nose ordered.

The other two, whom I assumed by now were his subordinates, scrambled out and stood to either side of the door, swords still raised. They were joined by several others. An armed escort of tall, elegant enemies.

Zared stood and stepped out first, keeping himself between me and the swords. He stood on the paved ground, his back straight, the message clear. They'd have to go through him to get to me.

I sighed and climbed out, careful not to fall on my face. The situation was shitty enough without breaking my nose in front of all these Fae.

"This way." Hawk-nose led us away from the carriage and in through a doorway that led into the palace.

I felt for my pack through the bond. Ryze was close. Tavian and Vayne were closer still.

It was Tavian who sent a sense of surprise back to me. Surprise and confusion with a layer of reassurance that things would be all right. Of course he sensed my fear on his end of the bond.

I glanced at Zared, wishing he could feel that same reassurance. If I got the chance, I'd have to ask Ryze or one of the others whether Zared and Tavian could possibly form a bond if they wanted to. Hells, I didn't even know if Ryze and Tavian had one. I was so wrapped up in myself and my sisters, I hadn't even thought to ask. There were a lot of things I never thought to ask. I sent a quick plea to the gods that I'd get a chance to.

"Lord Harel, we have the woman." Hawk-nose addressed a red haired Fae with small eyes and an expression like he hated the world.

Harel? Wasn't that the High Lord of Autumn? He stood to the side of the room talking to a woman I recognised. Dalyth, the Fae who led the attack on the caravan of Silent Maidens.

I saw from the look on Zared's face he was thinking the same thing. That confirmed what Wornar said about him working with Cavan.

"So I see." Harel's response was brisk. He stepped towards me and looked me up and down like he was appraising a cow for market.

Dalyth followed a few steps behind. She smiled at me. The same smile she gave me back in the Temple. The one that suggested she knew me better than I knew myself. She knew I'd end up here one way or another.

I turned away from her and looked back at Harel steadily. "I thought it was Cavan who wanted to see us."

He ignored me. Stepped over to Zared and gave him the same scrutiny.

"We don't need the human," he said shortly.

A hard flutter of fear passed through me. "If you kill him, I won't cooperate."

"Neither of us are going to cooperate," Zared said. "I won't let you touch her." He stepped toward Harel, eyes blazing.

Harel ignored him and looked back at me. "You'll cooperate if I assure you no harm will come to him?"

I didn't want anything to do with him, but I didn't want Zared to die. Whatever I had to do to make sure that didn't happen, I'd do. I had no choice.

I nodded. "If you can promise me—"

"Khala! No." Zared was frantic. He jerked against the ropes, trying to break free.

"Take hold of him," Harel ordered.

Four guards stepped over, converged on Zared and grabbed his shoulders and arms.

Harel pulled out a knife and stepped over behind him.

I eyed, I gaped. "You said—"

Harel cut through the ropes binding Zared's wrists, freeing his hands. He put the knife away and nodded toward Dalyth.

She smiled, moved over to Zared, stalking like a cat hunting her prey. She placed her palms on the sides of Zared's head.

Zared tried to jerk away.

"Shhh, this won't hurt a bit," she purred.

I wanted to punch her for touching him, but all I could do was stand and watch, my heart sitting in my throat.

"Fuck, you, I won't—" Zared started. His eyes half closed and he went still.

"What are you doing?" My voice was high, pulse thundering. "Get your hands off him."

"Removing his memories of the last couple of weeks," Dalyth said easily. "Taking him back to the carriage. He'll have a black spot in his memory. He won't remember your transformation. He'll think you're happy in a temple somewhere, still human. He won't come here looking for you. He'll get on with his ordinary, human life."

"No!" My voice was higher still. "This wasn't what I agreed to!"

I didn't see or hear any order given, but Hawk-nose stepped up behind me and wrapped a piece of fabric around my head. He shoved the front section into my mouth and tied the rest at the back.

Once again, I couldn't talk. Couldn't scream.

But I could sob.

I sobbed at the blank expression on Zared's face.

Watched through a haze of tears as Harel opened a portal. To Ebonfalls, I presumed.

Dalyth walked Zared over to it and pushed him through. He fell to his knees.

The portal closed.

I shook my head and groaned.

Nonononono.

If I got the chance, I would kill Dalyth. Harel too.

"Cavan will be waiting," Harel said. "Watch for the signal, then bring our guest through."

"Yes, my Lord," Dalyth said. Was that a hint of sarcasm in her tone? Evidently they didn't like each other.

I didn't care unless it was a weakness I could use at some point.

Harel disappeared through a doorway, closing it behind him.

"We did you a favour," she told me. Her voice was smooth as ever, like the honey she smelled like, laced with the acid of citrus.

"We did the human a favour. There's no place for him in Jorius, especially here. Now he gets to live his life in peace. It's a wonderful thing. You'll realise that some day."

I shook my head and growled at her. If my hands weren't tied, I'd give her a few rude gestures.

She patted my cheek. "You're welcome."

All I had were my eyes to tell her how much I hated her, but I put everything into it.

She laughed. "You'll thank me someday, Khala." She gave me that smile again and walked away.

Through the bond, I felt worry from Tavian, even some from Vayne. I had nothing to offer back but grief and anger. Where was—

I felt Ryze on the other end of the bond as the door opened and a couple of guards grabbed me and led me out.

"Like I said, she's here," a Fae man with golden hair said.

High Lord Cavan. I didn't need to be told who he was. I could tell from the way he carried himself. Arrogance, smug self assurance.

Ryze stared at me, frozen. "Yes, she is," he said carefully. "Clearly against her will."

"She's promised to cooperate," Harel said. He nodded at the guards who cut the rope from my hand and took off my gag.

Ryze frowned. "Did you make that promise?" he asked me. He took in the expression on my face, the tears on my cheeks.

"I—" I supposed I had. It was my fault for not guessing, not knowing they'd twist it around and do what they did to Zared.

"It's time for you to leave," Cavan said to Ryze. "My patience has run out. Open a portal and you and Wornar can get the fuck out."

"Not without Khala," Ryze said. He opened a portal and gestured for me to go to him.

"She's not leaving with you," Cavan said. "With or without the promise to cooperate." His gaze slid to me. "I have the answers to many of your questions. Including who your real parents are."

I gaped at him. Glanced at Ryze, then back again.

What the hells? I hadn't expected to hear that, not from him. I hated the way my curiosity was piqued. I wanted to see my sisters, but if I could learn what he knew of my family in the process...

My tongue darted over my lips.

"I'm listening."

THANK YOU FOR READING! The story continues in a Crown of Mist and Heat. If you'd love a bonus scene from Khala's point of view, of her decorating her new nest you can get it here.

CROWN OF MIST AND HEAT

COURT OF BLOOD AND BINDING
BOOK 2

CHAPTER
ONE
KHALA

" I 'm listening."

Hours had passed since I said those words to Cavan, High Lord of the Summer Court. I still didn't have any answers. Ryze and Wornar had stepped through the portal and away. Ryze eased it closed behind him after giving me a long, worried glance.

All I could do was look back and nod. I'd be all right. I made my choice. I'd stay and hear Cavan out.

Cavan, expression smug as hells, had Dalyth hustle me off to living quarters in another part of the palace.

To my credit, I managed not to kill her on the way. The temptation was incredible after she wiped Zared's memory of the last couple of weeks and sent him back to Ebonfalls thinking I was living my best life in another temple somewhere.

Picturing the look on his face when Diana touched him, the way she shoved him through the portal, was like a knife in my heart.

At the same time, in the back of my mind, was the niggling understanding it was the right thing to do. Zared would be better off without me. Without remembering I wasn't human anymore.

I hated that Dalyth did the one thing I was too much of a coward to do. Send him home. That knowledge was a twist of the knife. A searing pain I'd live with for the rest of my days. That same voice in the back of my mind suggested the person I should hate should be me, not the older Fae woman. I'd consider my subconscious' advice later.

"Your sisters will be along soon. They'll give you all the answers you need. Don't wander off." Dalyth gave me a smile like I was a child who might sneak into the kitchen and steal a cake before she left me in a wide, glass-ceilinged atrium.

The tiled floor was a pale stone I'd never seen before. Flecks of gold glittered in the sunlight that filtered through intricate lattice inset into the ceiling. The effect was that of a sparkling beach. Without the soothing lap of waves against the shore.

A variety of plants grew in pots that lined the walls: tall trees heavy with fruit, small plants dotted with dozens of flowers. Somehow they managed not to compete with each other for attention. Whoever chose their placement had a good eye. The result could have been a cluttered mess. Instead, it was a soothing garden in the top of a palace in a city. An oasis.

Low benches in stone darker than the floor, formed a ring around a circular reflecting pool placed in the centre of the atrium. Bright yellow fish darted across the water before they disappeared under lily pads covered with more flowers.

In spite of the sun coming in through both the ceiling and a picture window that overlooked the city and the harbour beyond, the atrium was comfortably cool

I could easily picture myself spending hours sitting on the benches reading a book or watching the fish. The space was serene. A moment of calm in a furious whirlwind.

That calm ended when the door opened and two women walked inside. They saw me standing beside the reflecting pool.

"Fuck," the taller one said.

She had Fae features now, like I did, but there was no mistaking the dark blonde hair and dark blue eyes.

Of course Hycanthe was one of the transformed omegas. Of *course* she fucking was.

The other was her dark-haired friend, Jezalyn.

"Khala." Jezalyn stepped toward me and took my hands. Her dark brown eyes took in the sight of me. "I had no idea."

"None of us did," Hycanthe said sourly. She gave me an accusing look. "Unless you did and didn't tell anyone." Her eyes were narrowed slits, gaze angry and unwelcoming.

I couldn't stop myself from bristling. I understood she was looking for someone to blame, but this was as fucked up to me as it was to her.

I managed to keep my tone civil when I responded. "I'm as surprised as you are. Where's Tyla?" I already knew the answer, but I had to ask anyway. Five former Silent Maidens were sent to Havenmoor. The three of us standing in the atrium were the rest of a cohort of eight.

"They sent her back to Fraxius," Jezalyn confirmed. "She's human."

"Yes, she gets to go on with her life," Hycanthe said bitterly. "While we're stuck here, trying to make sense of it all."

"Dalyth said you'd have answers." I gently removed my hands from Jezalyn's and lowered myself down to one of the benches. The stone was cold under my ass.

Jezalyn sat beside me. "All we've been told is that the Summer Court sent out Fae alphas to Ebonfalls over twenty years ago to try to make more like us."

So this was going on longer than Ryze suspected. And deliberately.

"Cavan said he knew who my real parents were." My mind hadn't stopped racing since. Speculation, which ultimately led me nowhere. For all I knew, I should be calling him Daddy.

"They kept records," Jezalyn said. "They've been keeping track of us. That was how they knew to take us into the temple in the first place. Chances are, the name of your mother and whoever fathered you are in there."

I'd already come to terms that the man I thought of as my father probably wasn't. This might be as close to a confirmation as I might ever get.

"We might be actual sisters then," I said, half-joking. This whole situation was twisted as hells. Sometimes dark humour was the only way through.

Hycanthe gave me a look like she hoped not. The feeling was mutual.

"You can ask to see if you want to," Hycanthe said. "I didn't bother. It's just a name. It's meaningless."

"It was consensual," Jezalyn said to her.

"So they claim." Hycanthe wasn't appeased at all.

"You both went through heat?" I asked.

They glanced at each other.

Jezalyn's cheeks turned pink. "We did," she said carefully.

I looked from one to the other.

"Oh."

I smelled the different scents the moment they walked into the atrium, but I didn't realise the cause and significance until now.

"One of you is an alpha and the other is an omega." That would explain the sudden unease, and the way Jezalyn put herself between me and Hycanthe.

"I'm an alpha," Jezalyn said. "But I am a woman." Her chocolate brown eyes pleaded with me to understand, to not be judgemental.

"Of course you are," I said, light but firm. "You're my sister. Both of you." Even if Hycanthe hated my guts.

"We're a pack," Hycanthe growled. "Jezalyn and me."

I looked up at her evenly. "I have no intention of getting in the way of that. I have my own pack."

The mating bond I shared with them told me three were still in the city, but not nearby. The bond with Zared was stretched so thin, I was surprised it hadn't snapped. He was alive, but that was all I knew. Either he was too far away for me to sense what he was feeling, or he was still out cold from Dalyth tampering with his memories.

"What are you doing here, then?" Jezalyn asked pointedly.

I glanced towards the door. Fae hearing being what it was, the guards outside might be listening to everything we said. Instead of speaking out loud, I used the Silent Maiden's hand language. One we were all too familiar with.

I briefly told them about Ryze's suspicion that Cavan was trying to mess with the weather, leaving Jorius in permanent summer. And then about his aspirations to take all of Jorius from the other three Fae courts.

"I came in here to look for you and try to get you out," I signed finally. "So he can't use you for whatever magic you have. You and any other former Silent Maidens who might be here. It's not just you two, is it?" From what Ryse believed, there had to be more than the three of us.

"There are six more," Jezalyn said. "Three from the year before us and three from the year before that. It seems to be a magic number." She didn't seem convinced it was anything more than coincidence.

I frowned, but couldn't see any particular significance either. It may be nothing more magical than luck. Or the gods' sense of humour. They seemed to like fucking with Fae and humans alike.

Hycanthe frowned. "You came here to get us out? Why?"

"Like I said, I don't want Cavan to use you for your magic. Do you have any?"

Whatever I pictured coming here, this wasn't it. At the least, I'd expected to find Tyla here. We'd hug each other, then find a way to get out of the city. I hadn't let myself think beyond that moment. I hadn't, I admitted, thought about what might have happened to Zared.

The plan, which he strenuously objected to, was for him to stay with the other men and for me to come here alone. We'd misjudged how long it would take Cavan's people to find us. It was a small mercy they hadn't killed him on sight. Or when we arrived here, at the palace. Sending him home was unexpected and unwelcome at the time. In retrospect, it was the least of several evils they could have inflicted on him.

Still, the blank expression on his face was seared into my soul forever.

I forced the thought aside for now. If I let it linger in my mind too much, I was going to cry. The time for that would come later.

Hycanthe ignored the question. "You came here because you didn't know it was us. You thought Tyla was here, or you wouldn't have come. Would you?"

The glance Jezalyn gave her omega was the most alpha-like expression I'd ever seen on her face. It reminded me so much of Ryze, my heart twinged.

I hadn't entirely forgiven him for lying to me, for not telling me I may transform into Fae, but he was still my alpha, a part of my pack. He'd agreed to let me come, orchestrating the situation to look like Cavan took me against my will.

"You and I haven't always gotten along," I signed. "But Ryze is convinced Cavan is planning something that will end up in an all-out war. I came here because I care about my sisters and because I don't want hundreds, thousands of people to die."

"Sounds like a no to me," Hycanthe muttered out loud.

"Hycanthe has magic," Jezalyn signed. "I don't. All the omegas here do. To varying degrees of skill."

Hycanthe huffed.

"I'm still learning to use mine too." There was no shame in my admission that I needed the practice.

"I almost set one of the guards on fire," Hycanthe said, as though throwing down a challenge.

"I almost drowned one of my lovers because I couldn't make an ice bridge properly," I said.

She pursed her lips and sighed.

I think I won that round.

I cocked my head at Hycanthe. "You have Summer Court magic. Have you tried to open a portal?"

"Yes." She shrugged. "They made Jezalyn order me not to make one without Cavan's permission."

"It stayed open?" I asked. "You could walk through it?"

Hycanthe looked confused. "Yes. Isn't that the point?"

"Supposedly." I briefly explained that mine snapped shut before I could step through, and the sensation that something was missing with my magic.

"Maybe you should stay here," Hycanthe said. "That High Lord of yours doesn't seem like a good teacher to me."

I shifted uncomfortably at her criticism of Ryze. "It's not that. I just...need to work on it. That's all."

Hycanthe smirked.

"Do you have any idea what Cavan is up to?" I signed.

Jezalyn shook her head. "We haven't seen much of him since we arrived. Mostly, we see Dalyth. She's the one who teaches the omegas how to use their magic."

"Has she taught you how to change people's memories?" I asked Hycanthe.

"No. Not beyond watching her do it to Tyla and the other sisters." Hycanthe flopped down onto the bench on the other side of Jezalyn. "Mostly I spend my time lighting candles." She curled her lip.

"Lighting candles is a useful skill," Jezalyn told her. "I can't do it." She shot her omega an affectionate look.

"You two transitioned at the same time," I realised. "That must have been horrible." Mine was bad enough and I had Zared and Tavian to cool me down, and Ryze and Vayne to watch over me. All they had was each other.

Jezalyn laced her fingers in Hycanthe's. "It wasn't easy. I kept telling the staff to look after her, but she wouldn't let any of them touch her."

"I wanted them to look after you too," Hycanthe argued. "They *were* the strangers who kidnapped us from the caravan."

After a moment, and while she was looking at Jezalyn like she was the only other person in the world, Hycanthe added, "And because they weren't you."

195

I glanced away, uncomfortable at witnessing a tender moment between them. I felt as though I was intruding.

"But we got through." Jezalyn looked back at me. "You really think we'll be safer in the Winter Court? They haven't mistreated us here. Although, we're not allowed to leave."

"We've gone from one gilded cage to another," Hycanthe said bitterly. "But I need to learn to use my magic. If I did anything to hurt Jezalyn—"

"You wouldn't," Jezalyn assured her. "I wouldn't let you." She sighed softly. "We'll have to think about it. For all we know, your information might be wrong, and if it's not, we might be able to do something from here. There's a lot to consider."

"Consider quickly," I signed. "We won't have long."

In case Hycanthe decided to be difficult, I added, "I will go into heat again at some point. It would be better for everyone if that didn't happen here."

It certainly wasn't going to happen with Jezalyn. I was quite sure Cavan had alphas at his disposal and mine, but it wouldn't hurt to push the other omega a little.

"Don't make me set you on fire," Hycanthe growled.

"Don't make me freeze your brain," I retorted. I hadn't tried doing that to anyone yet, but it was better if she didn't tempt me. Just in case.

Not to mention the fact she wasn't my enemy. The sooner she realised it, the better.

TWO

KHALA

The atrium door swung open on silent hinges. Dalyth strode inside like she was High Lady of the Summer Court.

"I see you've found each other," she said smoothly.

Her citrus and honey scent tickled my nostrils uncomfortably. If I was going to freeze anyone's brain, it would be hers. She gave me the creeps. What she did to Zared, clearly gave her pleasure. Fucking with humans as though somehow they were lesser than Fae, was ugly. And misinformed.

"I don't think we so much as found each other as were directed here." I rose and looked at her steadily. I had a ton of questions I wanted to ask, but I doubted she'd be forthcoming.

"I'm sure you're wondering why." She walked over to a tree full of apricots and pulled off one of the fruit.

She was an omega too. I smelled it on her. I hadn't realised the scent was so distinct until now. It was like a cake baking in the oven, and soft lavender. Smells which should be warm, sweet and comforting. On her, they competed with her natural scent.

Judging by the way Jezalyn raised her nose and inhaled, it was a pleasing scent to an alpha.

What would a beta make of it?

"The thought crossed my mind." I stood my ground, even when she looked at me like she could see through me. Her eyes seemed to bore into my soul.

"You would know by now the Summer Court has been working for some time to make people like us," she said smoothly. She bit into the apricot and chewed.

Us? She was a transformed omega too?

"I see I took you by surprise," she said after she swallowed. "You didn't realise I know exactly what you went through. I absolutely do. The pain of the change. Feeling like your whole body is being ripped apart. Torn to shreds before being put back together."

She took another fierce bite, shredding the fruit in the same way she was shredded.

"What difference does it make?" I asked. "You still took my sisters from the caravan and brought them here. You changed Zared's memories. Sent him to a place he didn't want to be." A place that was best for him, but that he didn't want. He made it more than clear that, wherever I was, he belonged there too. She'd taken that choice from him. From us. Stripped it away like it was nothing.

"You truly think he'd want to be here?" She swept her hand around the atrium. "Amongst Fae. Amongst alphas and omegas. Knowing he would never be any of those things. You claim to care about him. If you do, then you will realise I did him a favour. The same way I did your sisters a favour. Her heat—" she nodded toward Hycanthe "—was as inevitable as yours. As inevitable as mine. If she'd undergone that in Havenmoor, if you had, what do you think would have happened? With no alpha for you, you wouldn't have survived. If by some miracle you had, do you think the humans there would have let any of you live?"

"You don't know that there are no alphas there," I stated.

"Don't I?" She raised an eyebrow at me. She finished her apricot and tossed the stone into the base of a pot.

"Do you think that isn't something I'd look into? That Cavan wouldn't have looked into? Ryze too. I promise you, there were no alphas there apart from Jezalyn. My spies in the Winter Court say you went into heat shortly after Hycanthe. You would have gone through yours while she and Jezalyn transitioned. In the event everyone was in agreement, Jezalyn would have been unable to help you. Hycanthe's heat triggered her transition as well as her own. Jezalyn might have *tried* to help you, instinctively, but that would have killed her. Mid-transition is the most dangerous time."

Dalyth took a couple of steps towards me. "So, you see, you couldn't have stayed with the caravan or the Temple. Until we knew exactly who was an omega, or an alpha, we had to bring you to a safe place. Safe for everyone."

"Great." I raised my hands and dropped them to my sides. "We're safe. You won't mind if we leave now."

"I do mind," she said. "Hycanthe has yet to learn how to use her magic properly. I'd bet you haven't either."

I didn't have to answer, the twitch of my mouth told her everything she needed to know.

"I thought so. I can teach you how to use it."

"Why would you do that?" I asked. What the hells was in it for her?

"Like I said, I know exactly what you went through." Her voice was low now, soothing. Like an omega who wanted her alpha to buy her expensive jewelry. Like she was trying to convince me she was my friend.

"We have something else in common. A combination of hot and cold. My father was a Fae from the Summer Court. I spent my transition heat with an alpha from the Winter Court."

She looked sly, clearly trying to convince me she spent her first heat with Ryze. He'd mentioned knowing her, but never said how. Had they really—

That was a mental image I did *not* want in my brain. If anything, it made me want to freeze hers even more. I was pissed off with him, but he was still mine.

I pushed away my annoyance and shrugged. "So what?"

"So, when you try to use magic, you feel like something is missing, don't you? The power is there, but there's some key element that isn't in place. Another reason you should have been here for your heat. It's much easier to manage one type of magic than trying to combine two. If you'd had your transition heat with Cavan instead, your magic would be perfectly aligned."

"What is Hycanthe's?" I asked. Her heat took place here, but with two part Fae-part humans taking part, things might be different again.

"We're not sure," Dalyth admitted. "We only know of one other transitioned alpha. It's definitely had an impact on her magic." She shot both women a quick glance, accusing or frustrated. Either way, it didn't seem like it fit into Cavan's plans.

Excuse me if I didn't feel bad about that.

"It seems to me like you're messing with something you shouldn't be messing with," I said. "Why start all of this in the first place?"

Her expression shut down immediately. "All you need to know is I'll train you to use your magic. You'll stay here with the other omegas. And before you think it, the atrium is warded against anyone making a portal in or out. There are guards on the door all the time. For your safety, of course."

I snorted. "Of course." Hycanthe was right. From one gilded cage to another. Only this cage, I had no intention of staying in. Not a moment longer than I had to.

She smiled as though there was no hint of sarcasm in my tone. I doubted she missed it. She was too astute for that. She was the kind of woman who didn't miss much.

"Good, I'll be back first thing in the morning to start your lessons. You'll find a spare nest in the room at the end. Make yourself comfortable. You're a member of the Summer Court now. Don't worry, we'll ensure a suitable alpha is ready for your next heat. Cavan himself, if you're lucky."

Lucky wasn't the word I was thinking of. Like Ryze, Cavan had Fae arrogance to spare. He was fully aware of his power. That made him both compelling and extremely dangerous.

"Wonderful." There was more of my sarcasm. "I can't wait."

"Of course you can't," she said, all honey and light. "It's an honour to be chosen by a High Lord." She seemed to believe every word she was saying. Maybe she did. She was welcome to all of them except Ryze. Especially Harel. The High Lord of Autumn gave me the creeps even more than she did.

She swept out of the room without another word, closing the door firmly behind her.

Hycanthe made a rude sound under her breath. "I can't stand that woman. If she got the chance, she'd separate Jezalyn and me and throw me at whatever alpha she thinks I should fuck."

"I won't let her separate us," Jezalyn said, curling her fingers around Hycanthe's. "You're mine and I'm yours, and that's that."

"We should get out of here before she tries," I said. "Neither of us like the idea of being offered up to some strange alpha. Whatever it is they want with us and our magic, that's bad enough. What if they decide to go further? I don't think either of us wants to be bred to make some super-powerful Fae or whatever shit they might think."

My stomach turned at the thought.

"I'd sooner throw myself out the window," Hycanthe declared. "Or set myself on fire. Or let Khala freeze my brain." She could have gone on for hours, but we understood.

None of us wanted to be bred against our will. I hoped my mother felt something for the Fae man who impregnated her. That was something I wouldn't dwell on too much, because that was a question I may never get the answer to.

What I remembered of the people who raised me, they were warm towards each other, loving. However I came about, they had that. Did they still have it? I hoped they did. In spite of offering me up to the Temple, I wanted them to be happy. They were my parents, as far as I was concerned.

"Dalyth is right about one thing," Jezalyn said slowly. "You both should learn how to use your magic properly. For your safety, for everyone else's safety, and because we might need it if we have to run from here."

I hated to admit it, but she was right. If I had a combination of magic the way Dalyth said, the way Wornar and Ryze surmised, then I needed someone from the Summer Court to teach me. I'd have to let Dalyth do that. For a little while anyway.

I nodded. "All right, we'll stay for a while. Until we get a handle on everything. Then we make our plans. We get out of here, together."

I looked from one of my sisters to the other. Of all the Silent Maidens my age, these were the two I knew the least. By the time this was over, that will have changed. Not to mention the fact we all now had a few hundred years together.

In the back of my mind was a kernel of disappointment that I wouldn't share that with Tyla. She and I would have been laughing about all of this by now.

If we both agreed to stay for a little while longer, we would have made the most of it.

Instead, she was getting on with her human life like Zared was. Becoming a priestess and assuming I was living in some other temple, happy, and also human.

Would she write me letters and send them? She might. When she didn't get a reply, she'd eventually stop. She might assume I didn't want to be her friend anymore. Or that I met an attractive priest that consumed all my time outside of work.

She'd never know what really happened to me. That reality settled heavily on my heart. Her life would pass in the blink of my eye, then she'd be gone forever.

I wiped a tear off my cheek before the other women noticed. Not before sending sadness down the bond, apparently. I got a surge of reassurance back from Ryze and Tavian. And something from Vayne that felt like the emotional equivalent of a grunt. That was about all I could expect from the grumpy Fae commander. He wasn't chatty, but he got his point across.

I sent thanks back and assurances that I was all right. I wished I could send words and receive them. I would have liked to hear their voices right now. To explain the conversation I had with Hycanthe and Jezalyn. I'd even be happy to hear Vayne grumbling about whatever he was grumbling about in the moment.

Right now, I'd give just about anything to be curled up in my nest with them.

CHAPTER
THREE

KHALA

Hycanthe slumped on the bench beside Jezalyn while Dalyth talked me through everything she probably learned weeks ago.

The other omegas had shared a quick breakfast with us before being hustled away somewhere else. No one explained where and I didn't bother to ask. They wouldn't have told me anyway.

I recognised a couple of them from the Temple in Fraxius. I'd take them with me when I left, if I could. I didn't think for a minute any of them were here of their own free will. Truthfully, the temptation to leave immediately was great, but the need to learn how to use my magic was greater.

"Now, focus on the water and the fire," Dalyth instructed. "Think of them like two threads coming together to form a blanket. Weave them together."

I saw how to draw the magic out of the water. I could have frozen the whole reflecting pool, or formed it into tiny drops of ice. From the fire, however, all I felt was warmth with a trace of magic. Nothing more. Nothing that wanted to work for me or with me.

I placed a hand over both and tried again. A fountain of water rose up from the pool, only to splash back down.

"Try again," Dalyth ordered. She was clearly getting frustrated.

So was I.

"Maybe I'm not what you think I am," I told her. "I might only have an affinity with winter."

"Maybe you just need some help," Dalyth said stubbornly.

She waved Jezalyn over. "Order her to channel both kinds of magic." She looked pissed at having to ask an alpha for help. Maybe she wished she was one.

Jezalyn gave me an apologetic look, then cleared her throat. "Channel both

202

kinds of magic," she told me in a very alpha tone she clearly wasn't used to using. Under other circumstances, we might have giggled about it.

Today, I felt the weight of her command, and Hycanthe's glare. The omega in me was eager to obey. Not as eager as it was to obey Ryze, but eager enough. Like a puppy happy to wag her tail and sit for a treat.

I stretched my hands out and half closed my eyes.

The water rose out of the pool and danced under my fingertips. Smoke rose from the fire and became thicker.

"Combine them," Dalyth urged. "Make the magic do what you want it to do."

Considering I wanted to incinerate her, I thought I should probably ignore that advice.

I focused instead on a small plant at the edge of the garden. Carefully, carefully I nudged it with warmth and moisture. After a moment, it started to grow. Tendrils curled out from the sides and grew buds. The buds burst open, becoming vibrantly coloured flowers. The plant grew a metre, two metres.

In a blink, the whole plant wilted and slumped into a pile of wet, brown stalks and petals.

"You need to learn some restraint," Dalyth scolded. "However, we now know you have some ability, in spite of yourself. Try again."

I did, but all I managed to do was to make the reflecting pool bubble and steam. When I cooled it, it turned to slush. I thawed that quickly, but not quickly enough for the fish, whose tiny, dead, yellow bodies floated to the surface.

Dalyth sighed. "Take a break. Hycanthe, it's your turn."

I flopped down beside Jezalyn on the bench and watched Hycanthe try to light a candle in front of her.

"It's not your fault," Jezalyn said softly. When I glanced at her she added, "The fish. Or the plant. You tried. You just need to tie the tendrils of magic together more closely. You have them too loose, like a stitch that needs to be pulled firmer."

I stared at her, but forced my eyes away before Dalyth noticed.

"You can see magic?"

"I think I might be the only one who can," she whispered. "No one else has ever said anything about it."

I glanced over to Hycanthe, but I saw absolutely nothing.

"You can see hers?"

Jezalyn gave a tiny nod. "Hers isn't as strong as yours. She has the control, but she needs to work harder to do smaller things. She gets stronger every time she tries. I think that scares her. If it keeps getting stronger, how strong might it get?"

"Strong enough that she might accidentally hurt you someday?" I suggested. "But she might need to be strong to protect you."

"I think she's worried she won't be strong enough," Jezalyn whispered. "She's tough on the outside. On the inside, she's terrified."

"I know how she feels," I said. I didn't want to hurt anyone unnecessarily either.

I also wasn't convinced I could combine the two magics successfully. They felt too opposite, like night and day. They wanted to work against each other, not in unity.

I wished I'd taken the time to ask Wornar about his. Both the Spring and Autumn Courts used a combination of both magics. Only Summer and Winter used one or the other. Maybe that was the problem. In order to use both, I had to have Spring or Autumn Court blood, or to have had my first heat in one of them.

Instead, I stood on the bridge between two opposing courts. A bridge either made out of ice or fire. Since I couldn't successfully make a bridge of ice and didn't like the idea of trying to walk on one made of fire, I was stuck in the middle.

Hycanthe tentatively lit the candle over and over. Every time she succeeded, Dalyth put it out with a flick of her finger.

"Is she using magic for that?" I asked.

"Yes," Jezalyn replied. "A tiny string of heat and cold. It looks like a whisper of wind."

Her words echoed in my mind for a moment, going around and around. Something clicked into place that hadn't before. An understanding. I could actually see what I needed to do.

I half closed my eyes and drew heat from the fire to warm the ground in front of me. At the same time, I used water to cool the air. As the warm air rose, the cool air rushed in underneath it, creating an eddy of wind. It swirled around, making the leaves on the plants quiver and rustle.

It grew. The wind whistled, then howled. The flame on the candle flickered and danced. Smaller plants and branches whipped this way and that.

I barely managed to tug the wind back before it tore them out by their roots. I snuck in a bit more warmth, drops at a time, until a gentle, cool breeze blew through the atrium, soft like spring.

Only when I let the breeze drop, did I realise all three women were staring at me. Jezalyn with awe. Hycanthe with annoyance.

Dalyth looked impressed. "We may have something to work with after all. You even showed restraint."

"I saw what to do and I did it," I said, trying to sound indifferent. I didn't want her praise. Didn't want to feel good about pleasing her.

"That was incredible," Jezalyn said. "Just what this place needs, a nice breeze."

Her praise, on the other hand, warmed my omega heart.

The expression on Hycanthe's face was a bucket of ice, bringing me back down to earth.

"Thanks," I muttered. Even as I was enjoying her praise, I wanted to hear those words from Ryze. I wanted to see his usual smug amusement turn to admiration and pride. I needed him to tell me how amazing I was until all I could do was purr in response.

"Wind isn't very useful, is it, though?" Hycanthe said.

It would be if I wanted to knock her on her ass, but I just clasped my hands in my lap. "I guess not."

"Let's see if you can make something grow," Dalyth said to Hycanthe. They moved away to the edge of the atrium, to a pot in the corner.

"If she didn't hate my guts before, she does now," I said softly. I wasn't sure why it mattered. Hycanthe and I survived ten years of not getting along with each other. We could survive a lifetime.

"That's her insecurity talking," Jezalyn whispered. "I'd bet anything she wished she could do that too."

"She can do that better than I can." I nodded over to where Hycanthe was making a tomato plant grow from almost nothing, into a vine.

I stared.

In the back of my mind, a memory awakened. Slowly at first, then in a rush, like the river after the ice wall collapsed.

Not a tomato plant, but corn. My mother had nurtured seedlings in the potting shed. Dozens of them. She and my father had carried them out of the shed and planted them in neat rows in the dirt. I'd helped them, for hours, getting dirtier and dirtier, but loving every moment. After all the seedlings were safely planted in the ground, they told me to go and play.

I'd run off, but rather than playing like they said, something made me stop and hide behind the wagon. I crouched down and peered between the wheels. Watched as my mother knelt in the dirt beside the seedlings.

One by one, she made them grow. In a minute or two, several were a couple of metres tall. Cobs already grew off them, encased in their green sheath.

This was like something out of the stories my grandmother told me while I was sitting on her lap. Tales of magic and Fae. That was all I thought they were. Until that moment.

Then, I couldn't comprehend what I saw.

I snuck out from behind the wagon to get a closer look.

She must have seen my movement, because she turned to me.

I couldn't remember her face, not clearly, but I remembered the way her hair always hung over her ears. I remembered how her face paled. Turned angry.

"Khala, go inside," she snarled.

I'd never seen her so furious. She raised a hand as though she was going to hit me. I let out a squeak, and turned and ran. I scurried into our house and hid under the table.

I stayed there until it was almost dark and my mother came in to start preparing the evening meal. Neither of us ever said a word about what I saw.

I must have pushed it out of my mind until now. What did it mean? My mother was Fae? Was the man I thought of as my father, my father after all?

She used to say her ears were scarred, from an accident, that was why she covered them with her hair. She refused to elaborate. Had I ever seen them? I didn't think so. If I had, I would have remembered seeing them end in a point. I was certain now that they would.

If they didn't, then she or someone else had done something to them. Rounded the tips so she could pass as human, perhaps. Gods, how had I forgotten all of this? What did it mean that I was remembering it now?

"Khala? Are you all right?" Jezalyn asked. "You're white as snow."

I blinked a couple of times, reorienting myself. I was in the atrium, in Garial, in the Summer Court.

"I'm fine," I said quickly. "Too much Winter Court magic maybe." I gave a short, humourless laugh.

She looked at me like she didn't believe me, but wouldn't press the issue. Not in front of Dalyth. Maybe not in front of Hycanthe either.

I appreciated that. I needed time to think. My mother must have been an omega, if she had magic. If she could make corn grow like that, then chances were she wasn't from the Winter Court. Summer Court would be my guess. Dalyth had the combination right, but not the order. I didn't have a Fae father.

If I did, I'd look Fae from birth. At least, that was my understanding. The man I thought of as my father was actually my father. My mother must have given up her life in Jorius to be with him. She must have truly loved him. If anything was going to warm my omega heart, it was that.

"Where are those records of who we are?" I asked.

"There's a library across the corridor from the atrium," Jezalyn said.

"Yes there is," Dalyth said. She must have finished her lesson with Hycanthe and approached when I was lost in my memory. She was standing only a couple of metres away now. "You may use it with permission from Cavan or myself, but I don't have time right now. I have other duties to attend to. As does he," she added as though one of us was about to suggest the High Lord would bother to take the time to show us around the library.

"I'm sure you must be busy," I said. Probably doing something like sucking Cavan's cock. I kept that thought to myself. The visual image was bad enough.

"Very," she agreed. She gave us all a nod and swept out of the room with that High Lady of the Summer Court air of hers.

I suspected she wished that was exactly what she was.

CHAPTER
FOUR
KHALA

The door clicked shut behind Dalyth, leaving the three of us alone. Jezalyn turned to me, a stern expression on her face.

"All right, what was going on with you? People don't usually go white when they watch plants grow."

"Plants don't usually grow that quickly," I pointed out. "I was overwhelmed."

She gave me a look of flat disbelief. "Bullshit. Don't make me order you to tell me."

"She's not your omega," Hycanthe said darkly, her ire clearly aimed at me. "She's not part of our pack."

"No, I'm not." I stood and moved away from them both, then turned and briefly told them about my memory.

"That's all. To the surprise of no one, I'm part Fae."

"How did you remember what happened before you went to the temple?" Jezalyn asked. "I don't remember anything."

"Neither do I." A frown was etched on Hycanthe's brow. "I figured it was just me until they changed the memories of our other sisters."

Jezalyn nodded at her. "Right. We figured they must have changed ours before we went to the temple, so we couldn't remember our lives before."

I gaped. That made way more sense than it probably should. "I don't know. Maybe they left gaps. Or they changed the bits after this memory." I had no idea how old I was when I saw my mother make the corn grow, so it was possible.

"Neither of you remember anything before Ebonfalls?"

"Nothing," Jezalyn said. "Not one thing." She glanced down towards the floor uneasily.

I had a thought that made my blood run cold. "Do you think they do the same to our families? Make them forget us?" I'd waited all those years, hoping mine might drop in to visit, or send me a letter. Was the only reason they hadn't, because they didn't remember me at all?

Jezalyn's gaze shot back up. She exchanged furious glances with her omega. Neither dismissed the suggestion. I wasn't expecting them to.

"Jezalyn, did you see what Dalyth did to change their memories?" I asked.

"I did, but it looked complicated," she said slowly. "Like several strands of magic were involved."

I'd have to try to figure out a way to have multiple strands going. It would be a lot easier if I could see what Jezalyn saw, but at least she could tell me if I was close. I doubted it was a skill Dalyth would teach me, or one Ryze *could* teach me.

No, I might have to figure this one out for myself.

"Ryze said some skills are advanced magic," I said slowly. " It seems like the more kinds of magic a Fae has access to, the more complicated it becomes."

"I wonder if any Fae is one quarter of each court," Hycanthe said. "According to Dalyth, Autumn and Spring are combined but opposite to each other. Autumn needs more cold than warmth, and Spring is the other way around. She said my magic is like spring, but I can't access the cold, so it comes off weaker."

"And Khala's is a solid combination of Summer and Winter," Jezalyn said. "Like Dalyth's."

I wrinkled my nose at the idea of having anything in common with that woman.

"I bet Dalyth is pissed you didn't have your first heat here," Hycanthe said to me. "She seems to have a lot more time for the omegas who are strong in Summer Court magic. It sounds like you'd be her new favourite." For some reason, she seemed to find that idea funny. Her eyes shone with humour.

"Lucky I didn't then," I said dryly. I stepped over to the reflecting pool and looked down at the poor, dead fish. They lay with their eyes open, probably staring accusingly at me.

"Don't feel too bad about them, they've only been there a few days," Hycanthe said. "I might have boiled the water and killed the last lot. I don't know why they bothered replacing them."

"To remind you to have some self-control," Jezalyn told her. "You didn't do it again, did you?"

"No, that was all me," I said, my eyes still on the pool. I crouched and reached out my finger to one of the fish.

Without thinking, I drew a little warmth from what was left of the fire and mixed it with a sliver of cold to make some air. I pushed a drop through the fish's gills. Just lightly, I touched the fish with my fingertips.

The moment my skin touched its scales, it flicked its tail and darted away under the lily pads.

"Holy shit," Hycanthe said. "You just—" She crouched beside me, eyes huge. "Can you teach me how to do that?"

I didn't have the heart to tell her she needed a touch of Winter Court magic. I glanced over my shoulder at Jezalyn, who nodded. It would be our secret.

"Just give the fish some warmth," I said. For once, I resisted the urge to dig or tease. This was a moment between sisters. The first step in building bridges between us.

As she reached out to do as I said, I slid in some cold. A moment later, the other fish darted away to join the first one.

"You think we can do that with people?" She looked awed.

"I have no idea," I admitted. "I'm not even sure how we did that to begin with." Like with the wind, I saw how to do it and did it. I didn't have a clue it would actually work.

Whoever heard of fish being brought back to life?

I rose and wiped my brow. "When did it get so hot in here?" The sun shone through the window when we started. It wasn't now and inside the atrium was hotter than before. Nearly uncomfortably so.

"That always happens," Jezalyn said. "The more anyone practices magic in here, the hotter it gets. It'll cool down soon."

"Or sooner," I said. This I could do. Just a little water, cooled down with ice, infused into the air, and the temperature dropped almost immediately.

"I wish I could do that," Hycanthe sighed. "Or better yet, get out of here and go down to the ocean for a swim. Or sit on the waterfront and enjoy the sea air. I never thought I'd miss Ebonfalls, but I do. We had more freedom there."

"We couldn't talk to each other," Jezalyn said. "Not out loud, anyway."

"We got by." Hycanthe gave her a soft look. "There are worse things than not being able to use our voices. At least we could communicate with each other. Otherwise, I think we all would have gone completely crazy."

She was right there. When we'd arrived at the temple as eight-year-olds, trying to understand each other was hells until we learned how to speak with our hands. Now I thought about it, we learned pretty quickly, out of sheer necessity.

"Plus, it's useful when we don't want to be overheard," I signed.

"That too," Hycanthe signed back.

Since we were getting along for a moment, I ventured to ask, "Have you tried using cold magic?"

"Of course I have," she snapped. Apparently our moment of truce was over. "What do you think I've been doing all these weeks?"

"I have no fucking idea," I snapped back. "I don't think your magic is working the way it should. Either you haven't tried everything or you're not trying hard enough."

What was it about her that always made me have the need to bite back? I was never able to walk away from an argument with her, even when the last thing I wanted to do was argue. Some days it was all I could do to resist slapping her silly. Right now, that would get us absolutely nowhere. And Jezalyn would be stuck in the middle of it, which she didn't deserve. What she saw in Hycanthe, I had no idea. Love was blind, I supposed. It was yet another example of the gods' humour.

"Khala—" Jezalyn said in warning.

"No," I said back. "You said yourself she gets stronger every time she tries. She had no trouble getting the magic she needed a moment ago with that fish."

"You're one to talk," Hycanthe said. "You only seem able to do what you want to do when you feel like it. That's what you're saying about me, isn't it?"

I sucked in a breath. I supposed I was.

"If we're going to get out of here, we need to get a handle on this. Both of us. Jezalyn doesn't think your magic is weak, and neither do I. Maybe we both have a problem with authority figures, and being told what to do. We need to get past that and learn."

"I don't think so," Jezalyn said. "In fact, it might be best not to show Dalyth what you can do. I think both of you know that, but you haven't realised it. Neither of you trust her. I can't blame you for that. She killed a bunch of priests and kidnapped us. That's not something a trustworthy person does. I think both of you have a block where she's concerned. I think you should keep having it."

I chewed my lip for a moment. "You're right. I definitely don't want to do big things in front of her. That wind was probably a bad idea."

"It's a really good thing she didn't see those fish then," Hycanthe said.

I winced. "She can't see them alive." I didn't want to kill the poor things twice. That seemed so unfair. All they were doing was trying to live their best fishy lives. I mean, this was no river or lake, but it was pleasant enough.

"We don't have a choice," Jezalyn said. "We need to get rid of them, but we can put them in the toilet and hope they reach the ocean."

"They might stand a chance then." I never thought I'd be standing in the Summer Court having a conversation about putting fish down the toilet. Ryze would have found it hilarious. Tavian too. As for Zared, he would have shook his head, snatched the fish out of the water, and let them die in his hand. Whatever it took to keep us safe.

I stood back while both women grabbed bowls and started chasing the fish around the pool. Under any other circumstances, it would have been hilarious. Right now, I had too many thoughts chasing themselves around my brain.

The memory of my mother. The fact I had memories at all. Most of all, the need to practice as much as I could away from Dalyth's gaze. The sooner I had a handle on things, the sooner we could get the fuck out of here.

I winced at the realisation I'd have to tell Tavian what Dalyth and Harel did to Zared. He was going to be as devastated as I was. If I didn't kill Dalyth, he probably would. I might let him do it.

The moment I thought about the Master of Assassins, I realised I felt him strongly through the bond. He was close. What the hells was he up to?

CHAPTER
FIVE
KHALA

The nest dipped. Someone slid in beside me. A hand clamped down over my mouth, muffling my startled squeak.

"Shhh, it's me," Tavian whispered in my ear. He took his hand off my mouth.

"Fucking hells, you scared the crap out of me," I whispered. "How did you get in here?"

His teeth flashed white in the darkness. "Assassin training. No one saw me come in. If they did, they'd be dead right now. Ryze prefers I don't make a mess if I can help it. Sometimes I listen. Depends on my mood."

I noticed that about him. "Why are you here?" I asked.

He slid a hand down my cheek. "Why do you think? I was pissed Ryze let you come. Especially without telling Vayne and me. Vayne is pissed too."

"When is he not?" I asked.

Tavian chuckled. "Good point. But this time I thought he might punch Ryze in the face. He doesn't like people keeping secrets from him."

"I know the feeling," I said meaningfully.

He sighed, his breath brushing my cheek. "If I could have told you, I would have. I'll find a way to make it up to you." He sounded regretful but sincere. Clearly he was no happier with the situation than Vayne was. Than I was.

If he wanted to help, I could think of a couple of ways he could do that.

"You're good at sneaking," I said slowly. "Could you get into the library across the corridor? According to Hycanthe and Jezalyn, there are records there about us. The Silent Maidens-turned omega Fae."

"You want me to find the record on you?" he asked, like it was no big deal for him to do that. "Give me a few minutes. I'll be right back."

His teeth flashed again. The bed rose as he snuck away. It was no wonder

211

he'd crept up on me while I was sleeping. I knew he was there, and I still couldn't hear him. All I made out was a low shadow slipping out the door.

I lay in the darkness and watched the twinkling stars out the window. The same stars that shone over Ebonfalls. Was Zared looking at them too, or was he fast asleep? I couldn't feel anything down the bond apart from a faint presence. He was alive, that was all.

I missed him like an ache in my chest. As the saying went, you never know the blessings the gods give you until they take them away. I knew I cared about him, but I didn't know how deeply that ran until now. Until it was too late to tell him. If I had told him, he wouldn't remember the words anyway. I would have, though. That would have been something. Instead, all I had was regret. Regret I'd probably feel for a very, very long time.

"I'm sorry," I whispered into the darkness. The only answer was silence.

The bed dipped again a couple of minutes later. I barely managed to contain a startled gasp.

"I found it," Tavian whispered. "I didn't read it. I thought you'd want to." He pressed what felt like a few sheets of paper into my hand.

"People will notice if I turn on a light, so I'll need a candle," I said. I made no move to get up and get one. Not yet. Something else was more pressing than that.

Fuck, the words were difficult.

"What is it?" he whispered. "You don't want to know what those say?"

"I do," I said quickly. "That's not it. It's about Zared." Gods, I didn't know if I could do this. I had to. I swallowed down my emotions and tried to order my thoughts.

"I know what they did," Tavian said softly. "You told me through the bond. Not the specific details, but enough. They returned him to Fraxius."

I sniffed back tears. "They took his memories, then they sent him back. They said it was best for him if he didn't remember ever being in Jorius. He won't remember you. Ryze, or Vayne. Or that I changed to a Fae. Or that he and I ever..."

Tavian drew me into his arms and rubbed my back, letting me cry silently.

While I wept, he said soothing things in my ear, like, "They're assholes. We'll deal with them." And, "I'll sneak in and assassinate Cavan right now if you want? We probably won't get out of here alive, but I'll do it for you."

By the time my tears ran dry, I was almost able to smile. Only he could cheer me with suggestions of cold-blooded murder.

"As tempting as that is, I don't want both of us to get killed." I went to wipe away my tears, but the moment my warm skin got to within a centimetre of my face, they dried. I was barely aware of doing it.

"We'll figure something out," he said. "I don't know what, but something." He rubbed my back for a little while longer. "Do you want to see what those say?"

"I'm not sure," I admitted. I'd scrunched the papers while I cried.

I straightened them now and slipped out of bed to grab a candle from the atrium. I took it back into my room and held it in one hand while I lit it.

I had that much control over my magic at least.

I held the flame over the papers and looked at the first page. It was a list of names. My mother, my father, me and five siblings. Names that, as I read them, conjured their faces in my memories. Two sisters, three brothers. Six of us in total.

"My mother's name was Alivia Talonis. My father was Terald Fineal. He was human. She was—"

"Fae," Tavian said softly. "That explains why they kept records on you in particular. Your mother was a member of the Summer Court."

"What the fuck?" I whispered. "I don't understand."

"She fell in love with a human," Tavian said slowly. "It was quite the scandal at the time. From what I gather, Cavan didn't approve. He sent them both into exile."

"And she sent me to the Temple, putting me right into his path," I said.

"It was unlikely she had a choice," Tavian said.

I screwed my eyes shut for a moment. "Right. Jezalyn, Hycanthe and I concluded they must have wiped our families' memories before taking us to the Temple. Only— is it possible to alter the memories of someone who's full Fae?"

"No," Tavian admitted. "They may have changed your father's, but they wouldn't have changed your mother's. They couldn't."

I opened my eyes. "So she was fully aware they took me. What about my other siblings?"

"I saw no other files with your second name on them," Tavian said. "It's likely you were the only omega in the family."

"Lucky me," I said sarcastically.

"Yes, lucky you. Being an omega is the best. If you weren't one, we would never have met. You wouldn't have met any of us. You would have grown up looking human, never knowing what you really are."

"I would have grown up on the farm, growing corn and all that shit," I said. "Expected to marry some nice boy from another farm or the village. Have a bunch of babies, grow old and die."

"When you put it that way, that doesn't sound so bad," he said. He took the sheets of paper from my hand and looked over the rest of them. "Just notes on how you entered the temple and when you were expected to be moved to Havenmoor." He turned to the last page.

"Confirmation none of your siblings was an omega. Or an alpha for that matter. They tested them. Here are the dates and the results."

I glanced over. Frowned. "I think that's my mother's handwriting." The flowing script triggered a memory in the back of my mind. Nothing specific, just a general sense of having seen it before.

"Why didn't they change my father's memories before he ran away with her?" I asked. "Why not have him forget her before I was even born?"

"They might have left before anyone got the chance," Tavian reasoned. "Or they weren't doing things like that back then. They might have learned their lesson from that and started doing it afterwards."

"Maybe they didn't care," I said. "Maybe they just wanted my parents to be happy."

"That's possible," Tavian agreed. "Cavan might have seen how in love they were and decided to let them be together as long as they weren't in the Summer Court. He might not be a complete asshole after all."

I wanted to cling onto that theory. Not because I gave a shit whether Cavan was an asshole or not, but because I wanted my parents to be happy. I had to believe they were. That they gave me to the Temple for my own safety, because they loved me. Because they wanted what was best for me.

"How have you heard of my mother?" I asked.

"Like I said, it was a scandal. Fae and humans fucking isn't new, but a member of the Summer Court falling in love with one is a different story. Especially when she was supposed to be betrothed to Cavan."

I blinked a couple of times. "My mother was supposed to marry Cavan?"

"I believe their parents arranged it," Tavian said. "It might have been a relief to Cavan when she chose someone else. Although, he hasn't married yet. That was only about twenty years ago though. Practically yesterday by Fae standards."

"Either way, he let her leave with the man she loved," I said. Either Cavan really didn't want to marry her, or he loved her enough to let her go. That didn't seem like the act of a complete asshole to me.

"We could lie here all night and guess," Tavian said. He put the pages aside and blew out the candle. "Or we could make the most of the time we have. Are you ready to leave yet?"

I briefly told him about my magic and Hycanthe's. He laughed at Jezalyn's suggestion that we might have problems with authority figures.

"Me too, sweetheart, me too. I'm not gonna say I'm happy about you staying here longer, but I still want to make the most of our time." He slid a hand down my side and grabbed my ass.

"Does Ryze know you're here?" I asked.

"No. I'll tell him when I get back." He rolled me onto my back and knelt between my thighs. "I'm going to need you to be very, very quiet. Can you be a good girl and not scream when I make you come?"

CHAPTER
SIX
KHALA

His words sent white hot heat through me.

"What will you do if I can't?" I teased. I could, of course, I just wanted to know what he'd say.

He hummed softly. "Then I'll have to do this." He pulled something out of his pocket and pressed it between my lips. A strip of fabric. He lifted my head and tied it in place. "There, now you can't make a sound. Just in case."

He pulled something out of his other pocket, grabbed my wrists in one hand and started to tie a length of rope around them. He bound them firmly, but not too tight.

The other end of the rope, he tied to the headboard.

"Perfect," he whispered in my ear. "Now I can do whatever I want to you."

He started by sliding up the hem of my shirt until my breasts were exposed in the starlight.

"Also perfect." He swiped his tongue across one nipple, then the other. Feather light, but enough to make me shiver.

If he was anyone else but Tavian, I might not have agreed to give up control. I trusted him. He'd give me what I needed. What we both needed.

He brought a nipple between his lips and started to suck. He grazed his teeth over the sensitive peaks. Only the fabric in my mouth stopped me from moaning out loud. Instead, I moaned in the back of my throat, then panted out my nose.

"That sound was hot," he said with his mouth full of nipple. "I forgot you couldn't talk for all those years. You made up for it by making different noises. I like it. I might have to stop you from talking more often. Maybe another choker with amethyst hanging from it."

It was too dark for him to see my glare, so I growled softly instead. If anyone tried to put one of those on me again, I would tear them a new one.

He chuckled. "That sounds like agreement to me." He moved to the other nipple, lavishing attention on it before kissing his way down my stomach. He undid my pants and yanked them and my panties off in one, swift motion.

Then his face was between my thighs and he was lapping at my clit and entrance.

I was well aware someone could walk in and find us, but the only sounds I heard came from outside the slightly open window next to the bed. The ocean, shouts, the occasional passing wagon. The whisper of the wind.

We could have been alone in the whole palace. Even his mouth and my pussy were silent.

I closed my eyes and savoured the feel of his fingers sliding into my wet heat. He massaged me inside and out, until all I could do was roll my hips and buck against him.

He broke the silence only to say, "Come for me like a good girl."

I couldn't stop myself. Almost like he issued an alpha-order, I came.

I bit down on the gag and groaned into it, shattering into a million pieces before coming back together again.

"Good girl," he whispered. He lifted his shining face from me and kissed his way up the inside of my thighs.

He crawled up beside me, rolled me over onto my stomach. He pried my legs apart with his hands and knelt between them. He slipped his hand between us to position his erection, then slid inside me with almost painful slowness.

I wanted to feel him buried inside me, but he took his time, easing in bit by bit until he was fully seated to his balls.

He started to thrust, slowly at first.

"Sweetheart, you're more than worth almost getting caught and executed for."

I glanced at him over my shoulder, but that only made him laugh again. I was starting to think he might be a little crazy or maybe he had a death wish. Hopefully neither of those were contagious or an omega personality trait.

I closed my eyes and enjoyed the feeling of him sliding in and out of me. The sweet, wet friction, the feeling of being filled to the brim. Those were things I'd never get enough of.

He leaned forward and whispered, "Do you want me to come for you, sweetheart?"

I could only give him a muffled murmur as my response, along with a nod. I wanted to hear him groan as he lost himself the way I had only a few minutes earlier. The way I was about to again.

He kissed my temple. "Good, because I'm going to come inside you. I'm going to fill you up so much you overflow."

Those were the words that drove me over the edge a second time. I pressed my face into the mattress and bucked and groaned as my whole world exploded into sprinkles of light and waves of pleasure. All punctuated by the sound of his soft groans as he too came, spilling himself inside me.

"Gods, gods, gods." He was all but breathless as he ground into me, his stomach pressed against my ass. He let out a long, last groan and slumped over me, panting, his sweated skin sliding against mine.

"Totally worth every moment."

He lay there for a while before sliding himself out of me and flopping down next to me on the mattress.

"If we were back in Lysarial, I'd leave you like that," he whispered. "I could have fun with you later or one of the others could when they happened to find you. But it's too risky here."

The idea of Ryze, Zared or Vayne walking into my room and finding me tied up, climbing on top of me and fucking me, made me warm all over again.

The idea of anyone else walking in and doing the same, was a bucket of ice cold water on my body. I didn't want to be that kind of vulnerable in a place like this.

Tavian untied my hands, then slipped the gag off my head. He shoved them both back into his pockets.

"For later. When we're both out of here."

I swallowed to get some moisture back into my mouth. "I can't wait. It shouldn't be long. Just few days. I haven't even started to figure out what Cavan wants with my sisters. Maybe I should stay for longer, until I do."

"The longer you're here, the less I like it," Tavian said. "I still might punch Ryze for letting you come here in the first place. He should have opened a portal and sent you and Zared back to Lysarial."

"Do you think we would have gone?" Thinking about Zared made me sad all over again. I couldn't afford to get lost in that right now. I had a job to do. No matter how much I cared about him, if we didn't figure this out, thousands may die. That was what I had to concentrate on now. That and getting my sisters out. The rest, I'd deal with later.

"Probably not," Tavian agreed. He pulled up his pants and fastened them.

I hunted around for mine and slipped them back on. "You think my mother still has family in the Summer Court?" I asked.

"Considering how long Fae live, it's highly likely," he said. "Why? Do you want a family reunion with them?"

I thought about that for a few moments. "If they didn't know I existed, it was because my mother didn't want them to. If they did know about me, none of them came to stop me from going to the Temple. None of them came to tell me what I was. Not that I remember anyway. I'd like to know where I came from, but..."

"That sounds like a 'fuck them' to me," Tavian said.

I snorted. "I guess it is. For now. A day may come when I want to know them. In the meantime, I can only imagine they endorse whatever Cavan is up to. That makes them the enemy. Potentially."

"Enemy until proved friend," Tavian said. "Sometimes that's the safest way to be when it comes to Fae. Otherwise you will wake up one morning with a sword through your heart."

"That doesn't sound like you'd wake up at all to me," I said. I remembered the fish, but for some reason I couldn't bring myself to tell him. I didn't know why. I trusted him, but something like that was— I don't know. The fewer people who knew about it the better. It seemed to me like a dangerous skill to have.

Of course, I was guessing about all of this. For all I knew, Dalyth brought people back from the dead on a daily basis. Or one of the other omegas. Or another Fae who could use magic.

I wanted to ask about it, but I didn't. I'd save those questions for Ryze.

"Good point," Tavian said. "You certainly wouldn't. Unless you count waking up in one of the hells. Since people only guess what they're like, then who knows?"

"What do Fae think the hells are like?" I asked. In spite of worshiping, or pretending to worship, the gods, the priests and priestesses went into very little detail about what the hells entailed. Not much beyond 'you don't want to end up there.' Their ideal was to spend eternity on the palm of one of the gods.

I'd never given much thought as to what that actually meant. Presumably some poor deity couldn't close their hand because it was covered in souls.

"Eternity in a room full of strangers who don't like you for no apparent reason, no comfortable beds and no cake," he replied.

"Is that the Fae version of the hells, or yours?" I asked teasingly.

"Definitely mine," he said. "Although, in mine, you're not there either. Now I want to eat cake off your body. Can we do that when we get back home?"

"Sure," I said, although I wasn't sure if Lysarial was home. I didn't know where home was right now. How could I go back there and live my life without Zared? Without ever seeing him or hearing his voice? Without seeing him get angry, or watching him watch me crawl to him.

"I'm sorry I didn't try harder to get both of you back to the Winter Court," Tavian said. "I should throw you over my shoulder right now and get you out of here. Your sisters sound like they can take care of themselves."

"I'm not going yet," I said steadily. "There's more at stake than just me. But you should go. The sun will rise soon. If you're found here..."

He glanced at the window. "Fuck. You're right. I'd hide under your bed, but Ryze is going to want an update. You know what he's like."

I did know. Ryze would want every detail.

Tavian rolled over and kissed me. "I'll be back tonight, if I can. And the night after that. And every night until I can take you out of here."

"Don't put yourself at risk unless you have to," I said. "I'm fine here." More or less.

"If you've felt how your pussy feels around my cock, you'd know I have to," he said. "Besides which, it's my job as one of your packmates to keep you safe and I can't do that if I don't check up on you."

There was clearly no arguing with him, so I sighed softly. "Be careful, all right?"

"I'm always careful," he said, cocky as ever. "That's what makes me so good at what I do. I know how to avoid getting caught."

Those sounded like famous last words to me, but I hoped he was right. I didn't want to lose him too. Even though I wasn't exactly sure where home was right now, my attachment to him went beyond the bond. I was sure he felt the same way too. He hadn't *just* snuck into fuck me, he was here because he cared. Because he couldn't stay away.

And so he could fuck me.

"Will you tell Ryze about my mother?" I asked.

"Do you want me to?" He ran the pad of his thumb down my cheek.

"I think I'd rather tell him myself," I said slowly. If he was going to be angry about my connection to Cavan and the Summer Court, I wanted to see that on his face. I didn't want him to have enough time to compose himself and the perfect answer if he decided to reject me. He said he wouldn't lie to me again, but that didn't mean he wouldn't think up some half-truths to save my feelings or whatever his intention might be.

"I'll keep it to myself then," Tavian said. "It won't be long until you can tell him to his face. And Vayne."

It was too dark for him to see my grimace. I hadn't thought about telling Vayne. No doubt he'd be very forthcoming with his thoughts.

"Until later." Tavian gave me a long, lingering kiss on the mouth. Only the dipping of the bed indicated that he'd stood and slipped away, leaving me alone in the last hour of darkness before another sunrise.

CHAPTER
SEVEN
TAVIAN

"You went fucking *where?*" Ryze snarled.

"To the Summer Palace to check on Khala," I repeated. "If you're worried about it, I did the rounds with my contacts first. They didn't have much to—"

"I don't give a shit about your contacts." He stalked away a few steps, then whirled around to face me. "You shouldn't have gone anywhere near the palace. In case you forgot, none of us are supposed to be in the city. If you were caught, there would have been repercussions for all of us. Including Khala. Do you think she'd last five minutes past them finding out we orchestrated them taking her? That, in spite of telling me to leave because she wanted to know about her parents, she's still working with us."

"She's still working with us?" Vayne asked. He shook his head, visibly confused and more than slightly frustrated.

"Of course she is," I replied easily. "This is a chance for her to learn about herself and her magic, but she's still ours. She hasn't found out what Cavan wants with the omegas yet. Hopefully soon."

That was the easy part out of the way. Now for the hard part.

I took a moment, then told them about Zared.

"Shit," Ryze said softly. "That wasn't supposed to happen. We had someone in place—"

"They weren't able to act quickly enough," I said. "Thank the gods they didn't kill him."

"That was a very real, potential possibility," Ryze said. "They both knew that. Zared was willing to take the risk for her."

"Yes, and look where that got him." I flopped down into a chair. "It was a calculated risk, but that doesn't make it suck any less."

"No, it doesn't," Ryze agreed. "How is she doing? Honestly. Is she all right?" He looked as though he might open a portal then and there to go and get her. Only the fact he'd never been to the atrium stopped him. There wasn't anywhere he could portal to that wouldn't be full of Summer Court guards. He'd kill his way through if he had to, but that was a last resort.

"She was fine when I left her." I couldn't help looking smug.

"You fucking didn't," Vayne said, scowling at me. "Bad enough that you went there at all. I can almost commend you for sneaking in to check on her, but going in to fuck her?"

"Would you believe it just happened?" I asked.

"No," they both said together.

"We know you too well for that," Ryze said with a half smile. His annoyance wasn't completely gone, but it had cooled.

"Disappointed I didn't stick around to fuck you?" I teased.

His only response was to raise an eyebrow. He wasn't given to overt displays of affection or deep and meaningful conversations about personal emotions. Some days that left me not knowing where I stood with him. I knew he cared about me. It went beyond the occasional fuck, but I didn't know how far beyond. He was so busy being High Lord, it wouldn't surprise me if he didn't take the time to think about it. Whatever happened, happened and he rolled with it.

And me, I tried not to be pushy. With Khala in the picture, things were even more complicated, but in the best way. Like sugar in a cup of tea. Or the pleading look in someone's eye before I cut their throat.

"How much longer is she going to be in there?" Vayne asked.

"Not much longer." I broke eye contact with Ryze and turned to Vayne.

I told them what little I could, that I hadn't told them already.

"I don't like her being there," Ryze said. "I don't like either of you being in there. Hells, I don't like being there either. Cavan is a fucking snake."

"So is Harel," Wornar said from where he stood, leaning against the wall. His legs were crossed at his ankles, arms crossed over his chest.

He was handsome, but there was something about him I could never quite trust. I wasn't sure what, just something not right. I didn't turn my back on anyone but Ryze, Vayne, Zared and Khala, but him... I always had an extra half an eye on him.

"Now we've confirmed they're working together, I should get back to the Spring Court and let Thiron know." Wornar remained leaning against the wall.

"Knowing Thiron, he'd want more information than that," Ryze said. "What the fuck they're up to, for a start. Stick around. I have a feeling things are about to get interesting."

"Interesting in a way that might end up with us dead, or interesting in an entertaining way?" Wornar asked. "Because I know which one I'm interested in. I'd prefer not to end up dead."

"We figured that was the one you meant," Ryze told him. "As long as I've known you, you've never had a death wish. If you want to scurry back to the Spring Court, go ahead, but you know I'm right about Thiron. He'll want details."

Wornar uncrossed his legs and grimaced. "I hate to admit that you're right, but he would. What are we going to do about it then? The direct approach got us nowhere."

"Now it's time for the sneaky as fuck approach," Ryze said. "Which, incidentally, is one of my favourite approaches."

"Funny, mine too," I said. The shadows were one of my favourite places to be. Apart from snuggled in my nest, with someone I cared about around my cock. Or me around theirs. Priorities.

"You're definitely going to get me killed one of these days," Wornar said.

"I keep telling them the same thing," Vayne said. "Sometimes I think they have a bet going on about who they can get killed and how quickly. So far, we've both defied the odds. At some point, our luck is going to run out."

"That's what I'm afraid of," Wornar said, the side of his mouth pulled back.

"Isn't it better to die having a good time than live for a long time bored out of your mind?" Ryze asked.

"I'd rather have fun *and* a long life," Vayne said with a grunt.

"And yet, you became a soldier," I pointed out.

"I know." Vayne sighed. "I should have gone into my family business, making pots and vases for rich Fae."

I closed my eyes and pretended to snore loudly. When I opened them again, it was to see Vayne give me a rude gesture with his middle finger.

I grinned.

"Admit it, you'd be bored out of your mind," I told him. "You'd take up pot throwing, just for something to do."

"I might take that up anyway. Care to be my target?"

"Thank you, but I think I'll pass," I said. "Can I suggest you keep it in mind if we go to war? A pot throwing regiment could be fun."

"We do that anyway," Vayne pointed out. "Pots of hot oil."

I snapped my fingers. "That's right. I knew it was a good idea."

Vayne rolled his eyes at me.

"Are they always like this?" Wornar asked Ryze.

"Always." Ryze nodded. "I'm starting to suspect they were both born backwards. Or dropped on their heads as infants."

"That would explain why we spend so much time with you," Vayne told him.

"I thought that was because I paid you." Ryze cocked his head at Vayne.

"That too," Vayne agreed. "Otherwise, I'd be out of here."

"It's a long walk home," I remarked. "If you started now, we'd get there before you."

"As entertaining as this is," Wornar started, "it doesn't address the question of what we're going to do. Ryze, you mentioned something about being sneaky as fuck?"

"I did, didn't I? I was thinking we could sneak into the Summer Court barracks. See if they're mobilising, or training for anything in particular. Like walking on ice. Melting ice. What to do in a sudden snowstorm."

"In other words, ways to attack the Winter Court," I said.

"Precisely," Ryze agreed.

"And if they're coming after us?" Wornar asked. "I hate to admit it, but Spring Court magic isn't as dramatic. They wouldn't need to plan for any special conditions."

"That's true, but if they're training more soldiers than usual, we'll know they're up to something, even if we don't know what." Ryze tapped his finger on his lip.

"Tave, have you got people we can send in if that's the case? If Cavan and Harel's aim is a full on attack, they aren't going to turn anyone away, or ask too many questions."

"I see what I can organise," I said with a nod. "We have one or two people here in Garial who might be suitable. Assuming they're both sober, that is."

I couldn't guarantee anything when it came to the people I worked with. They wouldn't work with me if they weren't dubious characters to begin with.

Ryze nodded. "Good enough. I'd be happier if we had more ears in the palace, but it is what it is. Let's go check out the barracks."

"Now?" Vayne stared at him. "In broad daylight?"

"They won't be expecting us to turn up there, especially during the day," Ryze said. "In case we're noticed, both of you stick to Wornar or me. We'll be able to make a quick portal and get the fuck out of there."

Vayne closed his eyes and shook his head. "This isn't even the stupidest idea you've had this week." In spite of that, he picked up his sword from where it leaned against the wall and slid it into the sheath on his back.

"Thank you," Ryze told him. "I think."

Vayne responded with an eloquent roll of his eyes. Which was funny, because I knew he enjoyed all of this as much as the rest of us did. Sometimes, I thought he just enjoyed being grumpy.

Why, I had no idea.

CHAPTER
EIGHT
TAVIAN

Walking like we belonged in the city, we wound our way through the streets of Garial. Most people didn't give us a second glance. The only ones who did, made eyes at Ryze and Wornar. That was understandable. They were both attractive men, both oozing power, in magic and in authority. A heady combination for sure.

I walked a little behind the others. It was my job to be inconspicuous. Walking with them was anything but. Three men walking through the city might go unnoticed, but four? Much less likely.

In addition, the moment someone started to follow them, I noticed. She was also trying to be inconspicuous, but I could spot someone or something suspicious out of a crowd faster than most.

When she stopped at a stand on the side of the street to admire a belt, I stopped at another stand to look at a knife.

It was well made and well-balanced. If I needed another knife, I would have bought it. I made a mental note to come back later.

When the woman moved on from the belt stand, I put down the knife, smiled at the blacksmith and walked on slowly through the crowds.

She wound her way through, stopping every so often, but always keeping Ryze and the others in sight. She even bought a small cake from one of the stands and ate it as she followed. It looked so good, I bought one myself. Then one each for the others. No doubt they'd appreciate the treat later.

Unless I got hungry and ate them first.

Now, where was the woman? I glanced around surreptitiously before casually opening the bag and pulling out a cake.

I was halfway through eating it when she stepped out of an alley, right in front of me and put a knife to my throat.

"Why are you following me?" she rasped.

I looked down at the blade, then went on eating. "The question is, what are you doing in Garial, Illaria? You're a long way from the Winter Court."

"I could ask you the same thing, Master Tavian," she said.

"You could, but it's none of your business," I replied. I'd seen her plenty of times around the palace. Usually watching Fae men without shirts sparring in the practice ring. Her bright red hair and emerald green eyes were difficult to miss. Especially in the Winter Court.

I pushed the knife away from my throat with my wrist and finished the last of my cake.

"You didn't answer my question. What is a woman who looks like she's straight out of the Autumn Court, who lives in the *Winter* Court, doing here in the *Summer* Court? If you ask me, all of that is very suspicious. Added to that, you were following Ryzellius. Don't tell me you didn't notice him walking right in front of you."

She didn't flinch, but she put away her blade. Lucky for her, because if she tried to use it, she'd be dead in a heartbeat. And then Ryze would be pissed I made a mess in the street.

"I might have noticed," she said noncommittally. "I also have it on good authority Cavan ordered him out of the city. Before you say it, half the city is talking about it."

I doubted it was anything like that much, but I wouldn't call her out on it. People did like to gossip, and often didn't care what they were gossiping about. When you were a spymaster or a Master of Assassins, you tended to listen to it. On occasion, some of it was even true.

"We're starting to attract attention." I nodded for her to step back into the alley. "Now, you have approximately a minute to explain what you're doing here. Otherwise, the next set of bones drying here will be yours."

She looked huffy. "I was sent here."

"By whom?" I asked. "Not by me. Not by Ryze or Vayne either. Let me guess, direct order from Harel?"

"Fuck no," she said quickly. She actually looked disgusted at the idea. "There's a faction in the Autumn Court who are concerned about what he's doing here. They sent me to find out."

"You work for a faction that wants to rival the High Lord of the Autumn Court," I said slowly. "Why do you live in the Winter Court?"

She shrugged. "I like it."

I cocked my head at her.

She sighed. "Fine, I'm in exile from the Autumn Court. That faction, they, *we*, made a move against him a few years ago. We weren't successful, obviously. He had a lot of them executed, but some of us got out first. Now we can't go back. We'll be killed on sight."

I frowned. "Why have I not heard of any of this?" It was my job to know things like this. If I didn't know, then spymaster Bravenna didn't know either. This kind of information would have reached my ears if it reached Ryze's.

"It was all done quietly, including the executions," Illaria said. "Harel has been trying to increase his power for a long time now. His influence too. We believe he's here to do just that."

"We could have saved you the trouble of coming here," I said. "We think the same thing." I wasn't concerned about telling her that, since she clearly knew plenty already.

She almost looked sulky as she said, "I didn't know you knew. Those I work with, we're few and we're vulnerable. We have influence of our own, but Harel is aware of us. We speculated whether or not we could align ourselves with any of the other courts, but we didn't know who we could trust. We still don't."

"I think it's more or less fair to say, at this point, any enemy of Harel is a friend of ours," I said. "Any enemy of Cavan too, for that matter."

"Including Khala?" Illaria asked. "I saw her being taken to the palace. Shame, she seemed so nice. And her human friend too."

When I didn't say anything, she continued, "You're trying to get her out, aren't you? I can help."

"How?" I asked. "You can't even follow people down the street without being detected."

"You need to give yourself more credit," she told me. "No one else would have noticed me but you. You wouldn't be a very good Master of Assassins otherwise."

"That might be true," I said. "Or you might have been more obvious than you thought." I admit to getting a touch of sadistic pleasure at the look of discomfort on her face. I got it, no one liked to have their skills questioned.

On the other hand, I didn't trust anyone who tried to butter me up. She might have told the truth about a secret faction who plotted against Harel, and she might have been lying through her teeth. It seemed much more likely that she worked for Harel and was trying to keep an eye on us. If that was the case, he needed to hire some better spies.

"Are we going to stand here talking all day, or are we going to do whatever it is you're supposed to be doing right now?" she asked.

"Who says I'm not supposed to be doing exactly this?" I opened the bag of cakes and pulled out the one intended for Vayne.

"No one makes cake quite like the bakers in the Summer Court." That was a lie. It was all right, but not anywhere near as nice as what we got back home. Whatever, I was hungry.

"Basic logic says so," she retorted. "You were following them, watching out for anyone else who was also following them. And now you're not following them, so if anyone is, you're not there to see it."

I took a bite out of Vayne's cake, then dropped it back in the bag and folded down the top.

"That's true, you sidetracked me by following them," I told her. "But trust me when I say they can take care of themselves. The worst thing that'll happen right now is them missing out on cake."

The worst thing that could happen would be them being caught and killed, but missing cake was pretty high on the list of bad things to happen. Even if it was only mediocre cake.

"Are we going to catch up to them?" she asked. "We can't be that far behind."

"I'm going to keep going," I said. I stood here long enough. My skin started to twitch with impatience. That wasn't a good thing for anyone.

"I'm going with you," she insisted. "I have a vested interest in this too. The Autumn Court can't keep going on like it has. Harel is bleeding us dry. Families can't afford the taxes he's putting on them, and if they can't pay..."

I gestured for her to finish her sentence. The Autumn Court coffers were none of my business, unless innocent Fae were suffering. If that was the case, I might make it my business. Or Ryze's. I was almost sure he'd love something else to stick his nose into.

Okay, probably not, but I'd make it his business anyway. He could thank me later.

"Some of them have had to join the army," she said. "Others have disappeared."

I frowned. If that was the case, the Autumn Court wasn't the only one making people disappear. Several assassins sent to the Summer Court had gone missing. None of my contacts had any idea where they'd gone. Nothing beyond educated guesses. That likely being the case, I doubted we'd ever find their remains. Their family mausoleums, where the skulls of Fae were placed on stone shelves in neat lines, would forever miss having theirs there too.

"How many would have gone into the army?" I couldn't do anything for Fae who were already dead, but taking people into the army was extreme, even for the Autumn Court.

"More than necessary, given we're not at war." Her expression was grim, her green eyes troubled. I found it more and more difficult not to believe what she was saying.

Voices out on the street reminded me we shouldn't linger here too long. Nothing said 'suspicious' like two people standing in an alley, talking in low voices.

I thought quickly. "Fine, you can come with me. But if you get in the way, or do anything that would in any way indicate I can't trust you, I will kill you."

I thought about doing it now, just to save time, and to satisfy the urge I got all too frequently. The overwhelming desire to feel warm blood on my hand and see the light fade from their eyes. Did Ryze feel that powerful when he used magic? Surely there couldn't be anything more powerful than taking a life.

"I could say the same to you," she said. "I guess we're going to have to trust each other."

I made a slight noise of agreement in the back of my throat. "Try not to get in my way." After a moment I added, "And never put a knife to my throat again. That's the quickest way for you to end up dead."

"Don't give me a reason," she retorted.

I won't lie, my hand twitched near one of my knives. Not because I planned to kill her, but I was curious to see her response if I looked like I was going to.

I held the bag of cakes at my side and gestured towards the street. "Let's go then. We'll need to hurry a bit to catch up. Without looking like we're hurrying."

I didn't wait to see if she understood what I meant. I stepped back out onto the street and wove through the crowds. They seemed thicker now.

I walked faster than I had before, but still meandered, stopping here and there to look at stands, and to give way to wagons that crossed sidestreets.

Nothing more than a good citizen of Garial.

In the corner of my eye, I saw her catch up to me. I made a note to give her some lessons in stealth later. No wonder the uprising against Harel failed. They needed better sneaking skills.

"Where are we going?" she asked.

"North," I said. I stepped around a pair of children who sat on the side of the street, rolling marbles back and forth between them.

"No shit. Where specifically?" She glanced over at me without breaking her stride.

"Specifically north a couple of blocks from here," I said. "That's all I'm saying. If you don't want to come, then don't."

"You don't trust me," she accused.

"We don't trust each other," I agreed. "But I let you live and I'm letting you come with me. If you keep arguing, it's going to start looking suspicious."

She made a sound of annoyance, but fell quiet after that.

That left me to my thoughts, and the job of scanning the street in front of us. I saw no sign of Ryze and the others, but they couldn't be too far away. I hoped. I'd catch up with them sooner or later, but I hated the idea no one had their backs.

Yes, they could look after themselves, but it was easier this way. Easier if I could neutralise any threats before they caught up to them.

Easier if I wasn't...

I looked over to Illaria at the same time I had that thought. I saw it on her face that she knew the realisation I'd come to.

"What did you fucking do?" I hissed.

"Only what I was told to do," she said with no hint of apology. "Distract you for a while."

"Fuck." If the street wasn't so busy, I would have slid a knife between her ribs and kept going. That wouldn't go unnoticed and I had no time to waste. No time to be stealthy.

I started down the road at the fastest trot I could manage, dodging the crowds and darting in front of carriages. One almost hit me, but I managed to duck aside in time.

I was almost to the barracks when the air filled with thick, acrid smoke. Ash started to drop from the sky. When a dusting landed on my sleeve, I realised it wasn't ash.

It was snow.

CHAPTER
NINE

KHALA

I expected to see Cavan at some point. When he finally sauntered into the atrium, everyone scattered. All of the omegas suddenly found somewhere else to be.

Dalyth ended another frustrating lesson and ushered Hycanthe and Jezalyn away.

They both gave me sympathetic looks, but neither hesitated to leave. The gods only knew where Dalyth was taking them, but right now there was nothing I could do to stop her. When I started to follow, she waved at me to stay.

The place was cleared in about a minute, apart from Cavan and me. He stood near the door, appraising me with his gaze. He didn't look at me like a man would look at a woman, not exactly. This was more like the way a man might look at a newly forged sword. Or the perfect bow. Appreciative but like I was a tool he owned and planned to use.

"I trust you're settling in all right." His tone was smooth like silk. He circled around me slowly, his eyes on me at every step.

"It's fine," I said simply, not moving a hair.

"Only fine?" He stopped to tilt his head. "That sounds inadequate."

I shrugged. "A girl can only see so much of the same four walls."

I wasn't necessarily trying to antagonise him, my answers were honest. I discovered the older omegas were allowed to leave the atrium. Presumably they'd proved their loyalty somehow. I wasn't sure I wanted to know what that took. Maybe they'd kept their thoughts to themselves better than I was.

"Surely this is nicer than the temple?" He resumed walking slowly.

"I was allowed outside there," I replied. "They let the maidens enjoy the fresh air."

"That sounds like a small freedom compared to the others which were withheld. The ability to speak. The choice to worship the gods, or not."

"You don't worship the gods?" I wasn't sure why I asked. Curiosity? To make conversation? Because the way he was looking at me was unnerving?

All of those things.

He stepped back around in front of me. "When you've lived a long time, you start to question many things. Including the existence of gods. Perhaps people want someone to look up to. Perhaps they want someone to blame. Perhaps the gods created us, and perhaps we created ourselves."

"Are you saying Fae are gods?" I looked over at his hooded blue eyes. I could only begin to imagine the things he'd seen in his hundreds of years of life. So many things I had yet to see. In the scheme of things, I'd just begun.

"What do you think?" he asked.

"I don't think we are," I said. "But I think some of us like to play at being gods."

I was worried I might piss him off, but he laughed.

"Me, you mean. I'm sure Dalyth has explained why you're here. The safety of you and your omega sisters was important to me. Would you prefer I left you to whatever fate you would have had amongst the humans? I don't think you would have liked it. It's certainly not as nice as this." He gestured towards the window, and the expansive view beyond.

"I'd prefer not to have seen priests killed," I replied. "Was that necessary?"

"Unfortunately, yes," he said. "I tried to negotiate with the temple, but they were...unreasonable. The choices I had were: attack the temple in Ebonfalls, the Temple in Havenmoor, or the caravan. The caravan seemed like the option which would lead to the least amount of carnage. Wouldn't you agree?"

"I suppose so," I conceded reluctantly. Fewer people were on those carriages than would have been in either temple. Still, attacking them seemed extreme.

"Dalyth couldn't have stopped the caravan and tried to talk?"

Cavan pressed his finger to his lower lip. "Before Dalyth had the role of intercepting omegas, the job went to a lovely Fae woman by the name of Jayde. She tried this approach. Since the role now falls to Dalyth, do I need to tell you what happened to Jayde?"

Before I could respond, he continued, "They were nice enough to remove her head from her shoulders neatly enough that her skull could be placed in her family's mausoleum. They weren't as kind with several Fae in her company. The three omegas who transformed from that group of Silent Maidens were buried along with them."

"I've considered the option of bringing all of those girls, the *potential* omegas, to the Summer Court, but I suspect they wouldn't care for that arrangement. The maidens seem like a more gentle approach. Although, of course, the end isn't gentle for everyone."

I hated the fact he was making so much sense. If I was taken from my mother and brought here, I would have been even more terrified and confused than when I went to the Temple. Stepping out for fresh air in a city full of Fae might have been a death sentence. At best, I would have attracted a lot of stares.

"I see you're starting to understand," he said smoothly. "This isn't ideal, but it is for your own good. I'm sure Ryzellius has filled your head with all sorts of lies and confusion. For some reason, he seems to think we're plotting against him."

"You're not?" I asked.

"Only in as much as I intend to keep doing what's best for the omegas," he said smoothly. "I'd prefer not to let innocent young women suffer because of his oversized ego."

I managed to contain an outward response to his words, if only out of some kind of loyalty to Ryze. Loyalty I was starting to question.

"Have you told him what you're doing? Maybe he and the other High Lords would help you. They may even figure out a way to avoid any further bloodshed, or scared young women."

"I've sent messengers and envoys. Either the High Lords won't listen or the envoys don't return at all. After a few attempts, it seemed fruitless to keep trying." He sighed heavily.

I frowned. From what I'd seen of Harel, I could totally imagine him ignoring Cavan. But not Ryze. And not the Spring Court if Wornar was any indication.

"Harel is working with you," I said finally.

"The only reasonable one," Cavan said sadly. "Ironic given his...usually unreasonable behaviour."

"What does he want in return?" I asked. "Some omegas of his own?"

"Probably," Cavan agreed. "Once you're trained in the use of your magic, you're welcome to make that choice for yourself."

"Really?" I asked cautiously. "You'd let me leave the Summer Court?"

"You're not a prisoner here, Khala. You're here for your own protection. Once you're ready, your life is your own."

"If I decide to go back to the Winter Court, you won't stop me?"

"I'd be surprised if you want to go back after learning what you've learnt already, much less what you'll learn in the following months. However, if that's what you want, I won't stop you." He spread his hands.

"What do you tell the maidens when they first arrive here?" I clasped my hand in front of me and levelled my gaze at him.

His brows dipped. "We tell them the truth. It's difficult for them to accept, but those who transition deserve to know there's a possibility. Those who don't, won't remember it later." He hesitated, then drew his head back slightly, chin raised. "Ryzellius didn't tell you, did he? He left you to find out for yourself."

I couldn't help the renewed bubble of anger that boiled inside me. I didn't want to think too badly of Ryze, but he *had* kept all of that from me.

"He told me the heat would happen," I said slowly.

"But that's all," Cavan stated. "He didn't tell you you may transition?"

"Because he wasn't sure I would." I felt the need to defend him, at least a little. "He didn't want to scare me." It sounded weak, even to myself.

"Winter Court magic can't change memories," Cavan said. "Anything he told you, you would have remembered and he knew it. And so he took away your right to know what was going to happen. He lied to you."

My lips moved, but no sound came out. I couldn't deny a word. I presumed what he said about Winter Court magic was true. He'd know more about that than I would. Although, wouldn't Ryze know someone who could change my memories if he wanted it done? But he hadn't, he flat out lied instead.

"I can see from the expression on your face that was precisely what occurred," Cavan said.

I didn't feel him take my hand, but there it was with both of his clasped around it. "You don't owe him anything."

Where our skin touched, mine tingled. It wasn't attraction, I told myself. It was an alpha-omega instinctive reaction. My body wanted to curl into his, to seek his warmth and protection. To obey.

I forced myself to slip my hand away, and tucked them under my arms.

"I'm sure he didn't mean any harm."

Cavan barked a short laugh. If he was annoyed at me for drawing away, he didn't show it.

"I'm sure he didn't mean any harm to *himself*. I very much doubt he gave a shit about you. Did he tell you he did?"

"He might have," I said evasively. Those were personal conversations I wanted to keep to myself. That and the mating bond. He didn't need to know about that connection.

"I can see you're conflicted," Cavan said. "You may not wish to take up this offer, but I can ask Dalyth to put him out of your mind, so to speak."

"No," I said immediately. "Thank you. I'd rather...deal with everything and move on when I'm ready. I don't want to forget anything." No matter how fucked up it was. Or how fucked up it *might* be. Honestly, I wasn't sure who to believe right now. Who to trust.

"Ryze believes what you're doing here is messing with the weather." I might as well get an answer to that, if Cavan would give me one.

He sighed. "Unfortunately, he's right on that count. In a manner of speaking. You will have noticed it gets hotter in here after you've been practising for a while. There are dozens of omegas learning to use Summer Court magic and Fae teaching them. Here and in other parts of the court. We've noticed the more that happens, the more it impacts the temperature here and in the rest of Jorius. We've been trying to find a way to contain it, but we haven't been successful yet. As you might imagine, some of my advisers have suggested they stop practising. Some have insisted we dispose of those omegas."

He let the words hang in the air for a moment.

"I don't agree with either of those options. Thus, we're still looking for a solution. If you think of one, please let me or Dalyth know. Endless summer would be tiresome, even for the Lord of Summer."

That made too much sense too. We noticed how hot the atrium was after lessons. Every time we were done, I'd cool it down. I told him that.

He looked thoughtful. "That might be something we can try. It can't hurt."

With any luck, it wouldn't. Magic seemed a lot more complicated than anyone let on.

He regarded me for a long moment before he spoke again. "I'm not what you expected, am I?"

TEN

KHALA

"A ren't you?" I asked back. "What was I expecting?"

"Knowing Ryzellius, a power hungry asshole. Which is relatively accurate. But no more than he is. No more than any other High Lord. Most of us inherit the role, but there are always those who seek to take it from us. If the Fae are good at anything, it's biding our time. There are plots which will have been bubbling for decades. Centuries. Sometimes planning, sometimes just passing the time. Boredom can be a side effect of living so long. Some have nothing else to do but plot in the shadows. Once in a while, they'll appear and act. It makes things interesting for a while. Then they disappear again. Back into hiding, or defeated."

"Sometimes it results in war," I said. Ryze had remarked multiple times that all he wanted to do was avoid that happening again. He seemed so sure Cavan was pushing in that direction. Or maybe he just wanted me to think that.

"Sometimes war is inevitable," Cavan said.

"Nothing is inevitable," I said.

"It might seem that way when you're as young as you are. When too many times you've seen conflict escalate until all that's left is to pick up a sword and use it." He clearly spoke from experience.

"Sometimes you have to pick up a sword to defend yourself." I couldn't imagine arming myself to go on the attack. To protect me and my sisters, I would, without hesitation. And my pack? I wasn't even sure that was real anymore. If Cavan's plan was to seed doubt in my mind, he succeeded. My brain swirled with them.

"I'll always defend myself," he said. "No matter who comes after me and what's mine."

The words echoed between us for a moment.

"You know I was supposed to marry your mother." His words broke the silence.

I tried to keep the surprise off my face but failed. How did he know I knew? Or was he just guessing?

"You were?" I said carefully.

From the look on his face, he knew not only that I knew, but how.

"You look like her. Your hair is a bit lighter. Eyes a bit darker. Your nose is the same." He cocked his head. "Same forthright personality. People didn't fuck with her either. Once Alivia made up her mind about something, there was no changing it. All she wanted was Terald."

His lip curled slightly.

"If she didn't, I wouldn't exist," I pointed out.

He seemed amused at that. "You still would, but you would have been mine instead." After a beat, he added, "In a different way to the way you are now."

He brushed his knuckles over my cheek. The touch was light, but it was enough to trigger that instinctual alpha-omega connection. That tiny burst of need. Did he feel it too?

I drew my face back. I didn't want an added layer of confusion on top of everything else.

"Did you want to be with her?" I asked.

He lowered his hand to his side, then softly said, "Very much. I would have killed Terald to keep her, but she stood between us. Literally. I would have had to kill her to get to him. I exiled them instead. That's one reason I don't like humans in the Summer Court. I'm a bitter, vindictive asshole."

He smiled slightly. "I wouldn't have hesitated to kill that friend of yours if I didn't think it would put you off side. If you weren't Alivia's daughter, I wouldn't have even cared about that."

"Can you build bridges with Summer Court magic?" I asked dryly. "Because it sounds like you need to build one and get over it."

He looked surprised, then laughed. "That's probably likely. You're the first person in twenty years to say anything like that to my face. The first since Alivia. No one else would dare."

"I hear it's not healthy to surround yourself with people who won't tell you what they think," I said. "You start to believe everything you do is right."

"You might be correct," he said. "Although, everything I do *is* right. And if it isn't, I'm sure you'll tell me." The side of his mouth twitched upward.

"If I stay here," I reminded him. "I might leave and travel around the courts. Find a nice cottage in a forest or beside a beach. Live a quiet life by myself."

"You're an omega," he reminded me, as if I could possibly forget. "It's not your fate to spend your existence alone. You're meant to be taken care of, treasured. Which, in turn, is what alphas are for. To cater to your every need and whim. To bring you the stars when you ask for them. To saddle the moon."

"What would I do with the stars and the moon?" I scoffed.

"Whatever you want," he said. "But you don't need either of those. They're already in your eyes."

I snorted. "That's very...poetic. Did you say the same thing to my mother?"

He actually flinched minutely. "I might have. It didn't work on her either."

He had the grace to look sheepish. He was right, he wasn't what I expected. I couldn't decide if he was sweet or way too good to be true. Or just a good actor.

I couldn't, wouldn't, dismiss everything Ryze, Vayne and Tavian told me about him, based on one conversation. In the end, he still had Zared sent back to Ebonfalls. I had no real reason to trust him. I was basically a prisoner here.

"If it's my whim, can I go and get some air?" I gave him a challenging look.

Predictably, he responded with a sigh and a shake of his head.

Before he could speak, I said, "Let me guess. For my own protection, I have to stay here."

"I heard you froze my fish." He glanced down at the reflecting pool.

"I heard they usually get boiled," I retorted.

"I really need to stop restocking that pool," he said. "It looks so much nicer with fish swimming around in there. The alternative is to keep the omegas in the dungeon, and I suspect that wouldn't be well received."

"Nothing says 'prisoner' like putting someone in a dungeon," I agreed. "At least this cage is pretty."

He looked at me like he wanted to say something, but forced his gaze over to the window.

"Yes it is. Best view in all of Garial. Sometimes I think we're justified in changing the maiden's memories because no one would want to leave this and go to Havenmoor."

"You've been to Havenmoor?"

"A long time ago," he said vaguely. "I remember old stone buildings and new timber ones. An old well and lots of mud. Nothing to compare to Fae cities."

When he put it that way, he had a point. Not that a gilded cage was preferable to anything, including mud, but if he meant what he said about letting me go, then Garial or Lysarial were nicer places to be than anywhere I'd seen in Fraxius.

That speculation was all moot anyway, since I couldn't go back and live in Fraxius with a Fae face. Either way, I'd end up somewhere in Jorius.

"Is that why the Fae moved out of Fraxius?" I asked. "To get away from all the mud?"

"I don't know why," he admitted. "That could have been it. Plenty of us don't like getting our hands and feet dirty."

He was smiling again. I wasn't sure if he was joking or not.

"Poor babies," I said sarcastically. "My mother wasn't afraid of getting her hands dirty."

"No she wasn't," he agreed. "Or bloody. I'm guessing she didn't tell you she was a soldier."

I shook my head at him in disbelief. "My mother? Are you sure we're talking about the same woman? She didn't even tell me she was Fae. I don't remember ever seeing her ears." I lightly touched my own with my fingertips.

"You wouldn't have." He closed his eyes tightly. "She was so determined to fit in, she had them changed. The woman did such a terrible job on her, I had her executed. Thank the gods Alivia had slightly human-shaped eyes. I'd hate to think what she would have done to herself if she hadn't."

I thought back again to that memory. To the sense that I knew she said something about having an accident. But she'd done it on purpose, because she loved my father that much.

"I'm starting to think it would have been safer if she and my father stayed in Jorius," I said. I didn't bother to keep the accusation out of my tone. If he sent them away and made her so desperate she let herself be mutilated, then he should wear some of the blame for that.

"Possibly," he conceded. "Those were the choices made then. They cannot be unmade. All we can do is learn from the shit we did in the past and move on. Build the bridge, as you so eloquently said, and get over it."

"If you knew what she'd do, would you have let them stay?" I asked.

He stepped over to the window and leaned his forehead against the glass. "If I let them stay, different mistakes would have been made. By me or by... someone else." He shook his head. His breath misted the window, before evaporating again. His regret seemed genuine.

"I can't guarantee you would have been born if they'd stayed. I have no idea what would have happened. Summer Court magic doesn't allow us to see alternative presents. Or futures, for that matter."

"Do any court magics allow that?" The ability to see the future would be a useful skill to have.

"Only one and it's probably a myth." He looked over at me, gazing under long lashes. "According to legend, there are two more courts."

Without thinking I said, "The Court of Shadows and the Court of Dreams." Should have I told him I'd heard of those? The words had left my lips. It was too late to take them back.

He didn't look surprised. "According to the legends, Fae in the Court Of Dreams could see the future. They saw their own demise, and instead of letting it take them, they disappeared. Some said they planned to be gone for a thousand years."

"And the Court of Shadows?"

He turned around and leaned his back against the window. "Just like the seasonal courts, they had their opposite. The Court of Shadows and the Court of Dreams. They say those in the shadows could see the past. Lives and civilisations that are now long gone. According to legend, both courts were bitter enemies. Shadows wanted to destroy the Court of Dreams. They say if they are found again, they will destroy each other and all of Jorius."

He stopped for a moment and looked contemplative, like he wasn't sure if he should tell me more.

Finally, he continued, "I believe both courts exist. There's been conflict and strange happenings all over Jorius in the last hundred years and..."

"Let me guess, it's almost been a thousand years," I said. The expression on his face gave me chills all the way down my spine. I wondered if he and Ryze had discussed any of this, or if both of them thought they were the only ones who believed in the missing courts.

Clearly, communication between the two of them needed some work.

"That's another reason I've been helping all those omegas. I think the Court of Dreams and the Court of Shadows are about to reawaken. I believe they're about to unleash hells and we need to be ready."

He barely finished speaking when light flashed outside the window. A moment later, a plume of smoke rose into the sky.

CHAPTER
ELEVEN
KHALA

"Shit," Cavan muttered under his breath. "You'll have to excuse me."

I barely heard him. All I knew was a mass of confusion on the other end of three bonds. Chaos.

"Ryze," I whispered.

Cavan took a couple of steps towards the door, but stopped and whirled back.

"Ryze what?" he demanded. "He's not supposed to be in Garial." He drew his head back and stared at me. "How do you know?"

I blinked a couple of times.

Fuck.

"I..."

Cavan closed his eyes for a moment. Opened them again and sighed. "Don't tell me. Mating bond? I should have guessed." He shook his head. "It changes nothing. Stay here. I'll deal with you later."

"No. If he's in trouble, I'm coming with you." I followed him to the door.

"The hells you are." He put out a large hand to stop me. "I told Ryze to leave Garial. If he didn't listen, and got himself into trouble it's his own fault. I will deal with him."

"Not without me," I said firmly. If I had to freeze him to the spot, I would. I'd deal with the consequences of that later. I wasn't backing down. We both knew it.

"Just as stubborn as your mother." He exhaled out his nose in frustration. "Don't make me regret this."

"I can't make any promises," I said.

"I thought as much. Just in case." He put a hand to my cheek long enough to make me shiver. "Stay within five metres of me until I say otherwise."

I felt his order settle on me like a cloak.

"You realise that's unfair, right?" If alphas were good at anything, it was bossing me around.

He grinned briefly. "I do realise that. What's the point of power if you can't throw it about once in a while?"

"I'm starting to think Ryze was right about you," I said. "You are an asshole." Which made Ryze one too, because that's exactly the kind of thing he'd do too.

"That might be the only thing he's right about." Cavan opened the door and stepped out into the corridor.

He didn't even have to look back to see if I was following. The compulsion to obey dragged me along. I slowed to test the strength of it, but I was forced to stagger forward to keep up.

"Does this thing go both ways?" I asked. "If I ran back down the corridor, or fell down the stairs, would you have to follow me?"

"Don't fall down the stairs," was his only answer. He gestured for the guards to follow and trotted down as if he didn't have longer legs than me.

If I was still human, I would have tripped. I couldn't have kept up his pace. I suspected that was purposeful. If I was struggling, I could stay behind. All I had to do was ask.

So I kept going.

"What's over where that smoke was?" I managed to catch up and walk beside him, extending my stride to match his.

"The Summer Court barracks," he said in a clipped tone. "If Ryzellius is up to something, and you knew about it..."

"If he's up to anything, I have no idea what," I said. All I knew was that he planned to stay in Garial until it was time for me to leave. Unless the Winter Court needed him sooner, in which case Tavian would stay and keep an eye on me.

"Believe it or not, the High Lord of the Winter Court doesn't tell me everything," I said. "You saw me tell him to leave. Then he left."

"Or didn't leave," Cavan said. He looked over at me like he didn't believe a word that came out of my mouth.

Then he exhaled heavily. "An alpha doesn't leave an omega behind when there's a mating bond in place. Not if he can help it. I didn't account for that possibility. I could have ordered you to tell me everything, but I prefer the omegas to trust me. In my experience, force doesn't make people friends. You would have resented me."

"Yes, I would have." I wasn't sure whether I trusted him or not, but I certainly wouldn't have if he made me tell him everything, then acted on what I said. Pissed off with him or not, I didn't want to betray Ryze.

That alpha-omega power thing really did suck.

He led us out the back of the palace, to a wide yard, where he made a portal.

On the other side looked like pure chaos, but half of the guards headed straight through.

Cavan and I followed close on their heels, with the other half of the guards behind us.

We stepped out into the barracks. Fae were running this way and that, none stopping to give us a second glance.

A muscular Fae stepped out of a larger building made of some kind of matte black stone. He gave Cavan a nod.

"Brace, what's going on?" Cavan asked.

"We're not sure, my lord," Brace admitted. His tone was short, words concise. "A flash of light almost blinded many of us. We don't know the source of it. A moment later, a storage building went up in flames."

"None of those buildings are made of wood," Cavan said.

"No, they're not," Brace agreed. "They're not made of anything flammable. There's very little flammable inside."

"Stone doesn't usually burst into flame."

"Not usually, High Lord."

"Where's Ryzellius?" Cavan snapped at me.

"Close," I said. I couldn't tell where exactly, just a vague direction. "Winter Court magic can't—"

"No, it can't. Lead me to him."

He didn't make it an alpha order, but he could have. Doing what he requested was easier to swallow. Besides, I wanted to know where Ryze was and what the fuck he was doing too.

I felt around again, then headed towards the source of the smoke, which rose thick and steady toward the sky.

I half-heard the conversation between Cavan and Brace as we went.

"Did you say Ryzellius is in Garial?" Brace asked.

"Evidently," Cavan replied. "My omega will lead us to him. If he's behind this..."

I ignored them and wove through a group of Fae, who looked as though they were waiting for orders from someone.

"Follow behind us," Cavan snapped at them.

I stepped around the corner of the building and stopped so quickly Cavan almost walked into the back of me. He put a hand on my shoulder to steady himself, then dropped it back to his side.

"Fuck." I gaped.

The whole building—what was left of it—was still smoking. If it had burned, the fire was out. What remained looked like a pile of melted stone covered in ice.

Ryze stood beside it, weary and slightly dazed. He leaned forward, hands pressed to his thighs. Vayne was next to him, a hand on his shoulder. Wornar stood a little apart from both of them, appraising the buildings to either side of the ruin.

"I look forward to hearing an explanation for this," Cavan drawled.

Ryze glanced over. "Well if it isn't High Lord asshole himself." He gave me a glance and a faint smile, clearly trying to downplay the fact we knew each other.

"I was going to say exactly that." Cavan smirked. "What did you do to my building?"

Ryze straightened up. "I stopped it from getting so hot it set the rest of the place on fire. You're welcome."

That explained the ice.

"Why did it need your help?" Cavan asked. He stepped closer to the building, a deep frown etched on his forehead.

"I have no idea," Ryze said. "We saw a flash of light, then the whole thing was glowing. Bright red and scalding hot. If I didn't know better, I'd say it was struck by a bolt of lightning and turned into lava."

"No court has the power over lightning," Brace said. "Much less melting rock." His eyes widened and he took a step back. "If the gods—"

"I don't think it had anything to do with the gods," Cavan said quickly, darkly. "Just an accident of some kind."

He obviously didn't believe that. "We'll get to the bottom of it." He didn't bother to hide the fact he still suspected Ryze was behind this. But not just Ryze.

Brace nodded doubtfully, but moved to wave the Fae back to their duties.

"It looks like we need to talk," Cavan said to Ryze. "Not here."

Before Ryze could answer, Tavian came trotting up, his face pink with exertion. Sweat covered his brow. He must have run from somewhere.

"Looks like I'm just in time for the festivities." He pulled up to a stop and smiled. "Is everyone in one piece?"

"For now," Cavan said. "How long that lasts is up to the three of you."

Tavian was visibly resisting the urge to contradict him, but also decided to keep up the pretence we meant nothing to each other.

"Don't look at me," Vayne said. "I saw the light and followed Ryze here. Like he said, the building was glowing red. It was getting brighter and brighter. Looked like it was going to incinerate the shit out of everything. Ryze brought in a bunch of snow and ice. Building sizzled like a bitch, but it cooled down pretty fast."

"I can't believe I missed that," Tavian grumbled. "That sounds incredible."

"It was," Ryze said. "Cavan has plenty of enemies, I'm sure it will happen again soon."

Cavan rolled his eyes. "You're not above suspicion yet."

"You don't think they did it?" I asked him.

"Not for a moment," he admitted. "But we can't talk about what might have here."

"You think it was..." I closed my mouth and pressed my lips together.

"We can talk about it back at the palace." He gave me a light nod. He looked pained, but added, "You three better come with us."

"Us?" Tavian mouthed, his eyes on me.

I shrugged. Just when I thought the situation couldn't get any more complicated, it did. If Cavan was right about the other two courts, they may all have to learn to work together.

Ryze looked from me to Cavan and back again. He seemed tempted to punch Cavan in the face. The fact we were surrounded by Summer Court soldiers and a melted building served as a pretty good deterrent. For now.

"I'll make a portal," Cavan said.

Ryze gestured vaguely. "Be my guest."

Tavian stepped over closer to me and spoke softly. "Do you think we'll get to find out which one of them has the bigger cock?"

I snorted a laugh. "Stranger things have happened recently."

"My money's on Ryze," he said. "But only because I've seen it before."

"It's as good a reason as any to bet on him," I said.

"You're not honestly standing there talking about the High Lords' cock size, are you?" Vayne asked us. He spoke louder than could possibly have been necessary.

Ryze and Cavan both turned to look at us.

Tavian grinned unapologetically. "It's an omega thing, you wouldn't understand."

I could almost feel Ryze and Cavan's temptation to share a mutual rolling of their eyes. Their hatred for each other stopped them. Gods forbid they'd have anything in common. Only, I suspected they were more alike than they thought.

Wornar's face was pink with the effort to keep from laughing out loud.

Cavan shook his head and made a portal beside us. As before, half of the guards that accompanied us stepped in ahead, and half behind.

I walked between Tavian and Cavan, Ryze and Vayne on our heels. Wornar trailed a few steps behind.

"Don't forget it was you who invited us here," Ryze said. "In case you decide we turned up uninvited and think it would be a good idea to have us executed."

"I'm not sure it isn't a good idea to have you executed anyway," Cavan said. "If I didn't have more questions than answers right now, I might indulge myself."

"Always the charming host," Ryze told him. "We might be lucky enough to get some more relatively good cake."

Wornar chuckled. "We can only hope."

I glanced up at Cavan. "I feel like I should apologise for them. Well, not Wornar. I only met him a couple of days ago."

"Believe me," Cavan drawled, "I'm very familiar with them and their inter-esting sense of humour. I don't think anything exists in the world they won't make fun of. It's amusing for the first century or two. Then you spend the third and fourth centuries wanting to put an arrow in their eyes."

"The feeling is entirely mutual," Ryze said. "I can't tell you the amount of times I've almost—"

I cut him off with a sharp look. I didn't think I could put up with the needling for another day, much less a century or two. Something strange happened, and we needed to figure out what the fuck was.

They'd have to bury their animosity, not their blades in each other.

CHAPTER
TWELVE
KHALA

Cavan led us into a sitting room and nodded for the guards to stay outside. Either he wasn't worried about an attack from Ryze or one of the others, or he didn't want what was going to be said to be overheard.

I managed to plop down into one of the armchairs before anyone suggested I sit beside them. The situation was tense enough already.

"Let's start with what you're still doing in the city," Cavan said to Ryze.

Ryze sat back and crossed his legs at his knees. "I think you know."

Cavan sighed. "You're absolutely convinced I'm up to something. And you don't trust that Khala is safe here."

"I know she's not," Ryze said. "Why did you ask if you already knew the answer?"

"I was hoping for some honesty for once in your life," Cavan told him. "Without the jester act."

"Who says it's an act?" Ryze shrugged. "You know the truth. That's all there is to it. We went to the barracks to get some answers and found more questions. Including the fact you didn't look surprised at what happened. Have you been training omegas to melt stone?"

Cavan stared at him for a hard minute. Then he burst out laughing. "If that was even possible, why would I have them do it to my own building?"

"Because it wasn't aimed at the building," Tavian said softly.

All of us turned and looked at him.

He explained how Illaria met up with him in the street and delayed him.

I remembered her from outside the barracks at the Winter Court. She was making eyes at Zared at the time. Thinking about him gave me a pang of longing. I felt for him down the bond and found he was alert and confused but not alarmed. Alive, thank the gods.

"You think whatever that was, was aimed at Ryze?" Vayne asked.

"Or you or Wornar," Tavian said. "Or all three."

Ryze raised an eyebrow at Cavan. "That's not suspicious at all, is it? You could take all of us out with one hit."

"While I'm as disappointed as you are that it didn't happen," Cavan said, "I wasn't behind any of it. You can ask Khala. I was with her when that light flashed."

"Yes, he was," I said softly.

"That doesn't discount the possibility it didn't happen on his order," Ryze said. "With a convenient alibi all of us would believe."

"Why would I send anyone to distract Tavian?" Cavan asked.

"You like omegas," Ryze said dryly.

"If I wanted you dead, you'd be dead," Cavan told him. "Much more quietly. You've known me long enough to know I wouldn't have my city in an uproar to take care of a couple of problems."

"That may be true, but I'm not naïve enough to think you don't want me dead," Ryze said frankly. "However, you didn't bring us here to make death threats or go over bullshit we've gone over a million times before. You have a theory about what happened. Let's hear it." He made a, 'give it to me,' gesture with his fingers.

Cavan glanced at me.

His look didn't go unnoticed. Ryze and Vayne's bodies both stiffened. Tavian made a sound in the back of his throat. If there was anything between Cavan and me, they might rip him apart yet.

I caught Ryze's eye and held it. "He thinks the Court of Shadows and the Court of Dreams are about to reawaken."

The silence that filled was heavier than a pile of blankets. I half expected it to be broken with laughter.

Instead, Ryze tilted his head back. "Fuck."

My gaze met Cavan's. Clearly, he'd expected a different reaction.

"You believe they exist too?" Cavan asked carefully.

Ryze lowered his chin. "I've long suspected they might. During some of my wanderings, I've kept an eye out for their whereabouts. If they exist, I haven't found them."

Wornar, who'd stood until now, flopped down onto a wide sofa. "The legends say they had different magic to the seasonal courts. The ability to see the ghosts of the past and the future. To control dreams and minds. To create enough rain to make floods. Theirs was like the power of the gods themselves. The seasonal courts were terrified of them. But they hated each other and wiped each other out." He shook his head.

"Not wiped out," Cavan said. "Just hidden...somewhere."

"Don't tell me," I said. "They could harness lightning and melt stone?"

That did sound like something gods would do.

"Why would they target Ryze?" Vayne asked.

"Because I'm exceptional?" Ryze smirked sarcastically. "Maybe it wasn't directed at me. Or at Cavan. It might have been intended as a general warning. Unless there was something in that building they didn't want anyone to get their hands on." He quirked an eyebrow at Cavan.

"It was nothing but a storage building," Cavan said. "It would have been full of potatoes, grain and bed sheets."

"Maybe they're offended by cum stains," Tavian offered, his expression deadpan.

"While I'm sure everyone has the same dislike of those, that seems an extreme reaction," Ryze said. "The real question here is what do we do about all of this? Potentially, this has nothing to do with the Winter Court. Merely some random enemy of Cavan's. It might be a good time for us to leave." He placed his hands to either side of him and started to push himself to his feet.

"You're welcome to leave, but I think you know this goes beyond me," Cavan said. "The whole of Jorius has been on edge for years now. Waiting for something. Now *something* is here. I can't see another explanation for what happened today."

Ryze sat back down and put his hands in his lap. "Neither can I. Khala said you suspect the courts will awaken? What do you mean by that? Winter Court legend is similar to what Wornar said. The courts were powerful and annihilated each other. I thought if I ever found them, I'd stumble onto ruins. Fascinating, certainly, but nothing more than the remnants of long dead Fae. From what you're saying, I get the impression you think otherwise."

"Summer Court legend says they only went into hiding for a thousand years." Cavan pressed his fingertip to his lips. "The Court of Dreams that is. No one seems to know what happened to the Court of Shadows, apart from their disappearance happening shortly after. According to Harel, Autumn Court legend has them building ships and sailing to the gods know where."

"One legend says the High Lord of one court fell in love with the daughter of the High Lord of the other. They sought to bind the courts to one another. Yet another legend says the opposite. They fell in love but her father forbade them from being together and the courts went to war. The truth may lie somewhere in between blood and biding."

"Or with neither of those," Wornar said. "We're talking about thousand-year-old legends. Myths. There may be no truth in them at all."

"If I hadn't seen a bright light melt stone with my bare eyes, I may be inclined to agree with you," Ryze said slowly. "It seems clear there are forces at play here. Forces that either are or are not trying to target me or the Summer Court."

"Forces that have allies," Tavian said. "Illaria said she was working with some others. She also said she came from the Autumn Court."

"Are you sure Harel isn't up to something?" Ryze asked. "He seems eager for an alliance with you."

"I'm certain he *is* up to something," Cavan said. "Which is why I let him stay here. I trust him as much as I trust any of you."

"But you don't think he's involved in what happened today," Ryze stated.

Cavan pressed his lips together. "He's a sneaky prick, but I don't think he has that kind of power any more than you do. He's curious about the legends of the courts, but he doesn't believe they exist. He thinks they were always a myth."

"Is there any chance he's right?" I asked. "I mean, I know what happened today, but maybe there's some other explanation."

"Bored gods?" Tavian suggested.

"I'd sooner believe the gods are a myth than the two missing courts," Cavan said. "There may be another explanation, but in the last half-century, I haven't managed to find one."

Ryze stared at him. "You've been worried about this for that long?"

"Not just worrying about it, *preparing* for it," Cavan told him. "Gathering resources." He nodded towards me.

"Omegas," Ryze said flatly. "You expect us to believe you've been doing that, not because you want to go to war against us, but because you want to defend yourself and your court against the possibility the Court of Shadows and the Court of Dreams might reappear?"

"You can believe whatever you want to believe," Cavan said. "I've seen the signs and decided to be ready. If nothing else, those women deserved better than the humans would have given them."

Ryze shook his head in disbelief. "You didn't think to mention this to the rest of us?"

Cavan was still for a few moments. When he spoke, his voice was low and tight.

"I fucking *tried*. None of you would listen. Not. One. You decided long ago I was the enemy. For reasons you've probably forgotten yourself. I wasn't going to sit idly by and let your apathy destroy us all. If I had to stand between them and the rest of Jorius by myself, so be it. At least someone would be doing something, rather than all of us sitting back and waiting to die."

Ryze did sit back then, in his chair. "If all of this is true—"

"It's true," Cavan said.

"If all of this is true," Ryze started again, "I think we have some talking to do. I'm not saying I believe you, but we all saw what happened today. Maybe it was an attack, maybe it was a warning. Maybe it was a flex. I don't think it was an accident. Unless they were aiming at the palace and missed. If you're the only one, as you say, who's been preparing for this, they're going to want you out of the way first."

"That's a distinct possibility, yes," Cavan said. "Which is another reason

Harel is here. If we need to evacuate Garial, I need somewhere for my people to go."

"The Spring Court—" Wornar started.

"Is too close," Cavan said. "If Ryzellius was receptive?" He raised an eyebrow at Ryze in question.

"We'll take them, if it comes to an evacuation," Ryze said without hesitation. "Of course we will."

"It's easy to pretend to be magnanimous when you spent the last fifty years ignoring the warnings I've been trying to give you," Cavan said darkly. "But I appreciate it. I never intended to make my court a target. My only intention was to be ready."

Without thinking, I moved to sit beside him and put a hand on his arm. "I believe you," I told him. "We can do this. If we work together."

Ryze's eyes seemed fixated on my hand, but he nodded. "I think we should start at the beginning."

THIRTEEN

"Can you believe all of this?"

While the three High Lords—Harel joined the others an hour or two ago — and Wornar and Vayne talked, Tavian and I sat on the sofa and listened.

At some point, he put his arm around me. I nestled against him. Only Cavan gave us a look, which both of us ignored. I didn't know what was going on there and it didn't matter right now anyway. What did was the slight possibility they might actually agree on what to do about the potential threat.

Harel said he didn't believe a word of it, while at the same time looking cagey as fuck. After a while, I realised it was his default facial expression.

Ryze and Cavan both seemed to think the threat was real, but neither would agree to anything the other one said, even though they might have been about to suggest the same thing themselves.

Wornar seemed to find the whole thing amusing. At first, I thought he'd take Ryze's side, but then every so often he'd agree with Cavan.

"I'm starting to think that lightning strike, or whatever it was, was strategically designed to create exactly this chaos and animosity," I whispered.

"To be fair, the animosity's been there for a long time," Tavian said. "I get your point though. It was enough to make us wonder about whether or not something is coming. Not enough to prove it."

"What would it take to prove it? Thousands of heavily armed Fae attacking the city?" I shuddered at the thought.

"They'd still blame each other before they got around to responding." He made a face. "They've had a long time to piss each other off and finely hone their animosity towards each other. Even Ryze and Wornar, who get along better than the others, still have their moments. And then, sometimes when Wornar agrees with Ryze, Thiron overrules him. It's all a bunch of messy, political shit."

"We could be invaded and all they would do is sit around and argue?" That didn't sound like great leadership to me.

"Sooner or later, one of them would take a stand. Then the rest would have to, because they wouldn't want him to take all the glory. Their egos wouldn't let them sit by and do nothing."

"And how many people would be dead by then?" I asked.

"A few hundred at least. This is why every now and again someone tries to overthrow one of them. Ryze is one of the better ones. Thiron too."

"Cavan doesn't seem as bad as you said," I said carefully.

Tavian's shoulder moved against mine when he shrugged. "I can't say I know him well. If what he said about his reasons for bringing the omegas here is truthful, maybe he's not. He's certainly good to look at." He glanced over at the golden haired High Lord and sighed.

I couldn't deny that.

Cavan and Ryze looked like night and day sitting at the same table. Ryze all in black with dark hair, Cavan in light coloured clothes and blonde. Both were undeniably attractive.

Vayne too, although he scowled at everyone. He looked about ready to tell them all to shut the fuck up and take over the meeting.

"What would Ryze think if he heard you say that?" I asked.

"Are you really asking what he'd think if he knew you were thinking it?" Tavian's fingers grazed lightly over my hip. "I've noticed the way you and Cavan glance at each other. Ryze and I, we worry about you because neither of us want you to get hurt. I'm not saying we're not the possessive type, because we are, but if an omega wants someone in her pack, then who are we to deny her that?"

"Even though Ryze hates his guts?" I asked.

"Maybe it's past time they put their shit behind them. Failing that, at least things will be interesting." He laughed softly.

"And by interesting do you mean them trying to kill each other any chance they get?" I winced. The pair seemed determined to stab each other with words right now.

"That won't be boring, will it?" His smile widened.

"Is this one of those, 'when you've lived as long as we have you'll do anything for entertainment,' things?" I asked. "Because I might start to think all Fae are a little bit out of their minds."

"Only a little bit?" he teased. "Sweetheart, most of us were a little bit out of our minds two centuries ago. We're a long way past that now."

I exhaled softly. "I didn't want to be the one to say it, but now you mention it..."

He chuckled. "It's part of our charm."

"I suppose it gives me something to look forward to," I said. "Being so bored I hope someone will stab someone else. I'm surprised you're not more excited at the prospect of an invasion. That would certainly break the monotony."

"That's going to the other extreme," he said. "Too much stimulation. The occasional fight is enough."

"You can't be serious?" Harel said loudly from his side of the conference table. His face was almost as red as his hair. "There's no such thing as either of those courts. Why do you insist on perpetuating this ridiculousness?"

I wasn't sure who his words were directed at, specifically. He seemed to be looking at Ryze and Cavan, and to some extent, Wornar. Vayne, he ignored altogether.

Vayne seemed more than happy with that arrangement. His scowl toward the High Lord of Autumn was deeper than it was for the rest.

"Go down to the barracks yourself," Cavan said evenly. "If you can tell me another way that building melted, I'd like to hear it."

"Along with a list of suggestions on how to prevent it from happening again," Ryze said. "Unless you deem it to be a random event, unlikely to ever occur again."

Harel looked less than pleased that both of them seemed to be ganging up on him.

"I didn't come here to be insulted." He glared at Ryze, then at Cavan. Then at Wornar for good measure.

"Didn't you?" Ryze asked. "Personally, I've always found this a good place to come to be insulted."

"I thought you came here to dispense insults." Cavan regarded Ryze from half-lidded eyes.

"That too," Ryze agreed. "You make it so easy."

Cavan smirked. "If we can get back to the matter at hand."

Ryze sat back and spread his hands. "To summarise, Harel doesn't believe a word you said. I believe somewhere between a quarter and a third of it, because I saw the building melt. There's definitely some shit going on. I have no idea what Wornar believes."

"I believe I have to hear you out and then take all of this back to my High Lord," Wornar said. "Thiron will tell me what to believe."

"It might save time to have him come here," Vayne suggested.

"He'll want me to make sure he's not wasting his time," Wornar said, slightly apologetic. "You don't think anything will happen in the next day or two?"

"I have no idea." Cavan looked frustrated. He clearly knew this would be difficult, but the others weren't making it any easier.

Ryze looked almost as frustrated. He'd seen the building melt, but to believe everything Cavan said after so many years of mistrust, miscommunication and the gods knew what else, evidently that was a stretch.

I knew he knew how to make a bridge and get over it. Apparently that was easier said than done.

"It could happen in the next minute," Cavan said. "No one foresaw what happened today."

"Except that woman from the Autumn Court." Ryze levelled an accusing look at Harel.

"Alleged woman," Harel snapped. "Did anyone else see her?"

Tavian's body stiffened slightly. I suspected no one noticed but me.

"Are you questioning the integrity of my Master of Assassins?" Ryze's tone was dangerous.

"I question the integrity of anyone who has ever shared your bed," Harel said scathingly.

"I was right," Ryze drawled. "You are here looking for omegas to fuck. Evidently the women of the Autumn Court have better taste than to share yours."

"He's not wrong," Tavian whispered in my ear. "Anyone can do better than him."

I bit my lip to keep from laughing, but I silently agreed with Tavian. Even in the middle of heat, I couldn't imagine choosing Harel.

Whether he heard us, or sensed we were talking about him, Harel turned and gave us both a dirty look.

"What are they doing here? Neither of them belong in this room."

"Tavian was a witness," Ryze said. "And I don't trust anyone outside this room with my omegas." His gaze settled on me and he offered me a faint smile.

"Khala was also a witness," Cavan said. He looked at Ryze like he wanted to start a whole new argument about whose omega I actually was.

"So they have answers as to what caused the so-called building melting? Otherwise I see no reason for their presence." Apparently my safety was of no concern to Harel.

Ironic, because I didn't give a fuck about his either.

"They might have insight you don't," Ryze said. "Especially in light of the fact you didn't see the building at all. Perhaps we should adjourn this conversation until he's done that. You never know, he might figure it all out for us." His tone was dripping with sarcasm.

Vayne snorted loudly.

Wornar grinned.

Cavan pressed his finger to his lip so hard the skin on both turned white. He was clearly struggling not to lose his shit.

I had to give him credit for not giving in and setting everyone else at the table on fire.

"I think it would be wise for you to look for yourself," Cavan told Harel. "I can take you there, if you prefer. I'm sure you wouldn't want to jeopardise the work we've put into building our alliance." There was definitely a thinly veiled threat in there.

Harel looked as though he was ready to stand up and stalk out. Instead, he sat back and crossed his arms over his chest.

"I will look at this building of yours. It may be I have the answers you seek. All of this conjecture about—" he waved his fingers dismissively, "—missing courts, may be all for nothing. I don't know about any of you, but I have better things to occupy my time with than myths and the kind of tales ignorant humans spread."

He looked around the table like they were doing nothing more than sharing a beer and bullshit stories.

"Yes, wouldn't want to waste your precious time, Harel," Ryze said. "Shall we go then?"

"There's no need for you to accompany us," Cavan told him. "I'm sure you also have better things to do."

"Not at all." Ryze smiled. "I'm sure Wornar would like to come too. Wouldn't you, Wornar?"

Ryze clearly had no intention of letting Harel or Cavan out of his sight.

"I should be there," Wornar agreed. "In case you find something I need to know about." Evidently he had the same intention as Ryze.

"All right then." Cavan rose. I couldn't tell if he was irritated or not. I presumed he was ready to do whatever it took to get the other High Lords to listen. He looked over at me and nodded.

"Khala, you can stay here." When he spoke, I felt the order to stay close to him lift from me. I hadn't realised how heavy it was until now.

"Khala would be safer with Tavian and Vayne," Ryze agreed.

"She can return to the atrium." Cavan's tone allowed no room for argument. "I don't trust that your men won't take her when we're not here." He'd already explained that he wanted me to stay because of my magic, and the need to learn how to use it.

I suspected there was more to it than that. A lot more.

Ryze clearly thought so too. "There's no need for that. She won't be staying when I return to the Winter Court."

Cavan cut him a look. "That's her choice."

Ryze returned the look. "Really? Because I got the distinct impression you thought otherwise."

"Can we get this over with?" Harel snapped. "Argue over your whore later."

Wornar actually took a step back when every single eye in the room turned to Harel.

I slapped a hand down onto Tavian's when he twitched like he was going to reach for one of his knives.

Cavan and Ryze both looked ready to punch Harel in the face.

Vayne's face turned pink. For once, he didn't seem to have any words.

Me, on the other hand...

I stood, keeping a hand out behind me for Tavian to stay seated.

I walked towards the High Lord of Autumn, looked him in the eye and said,

"Fuck you." While he spluttered, I added, "For the record, I wouldn't. Not if you were the last man in Jorius. Or Fraxius, for that matter."

"As if I'd touch a woman with human blood tainting her," he sneered. "Filth."

His eyes widened as a knife flew so close to his head it must have shaved a couple of hairs before it embedded in the wall behind him.

FOURTEEN

KHALA

"I wasn't aiming to hit you," Tavian growled. "Next time I fucking will."

Harel quivered with rage. He barely turned his head to glare at Ryze. "Are you going to stand there and let your Master of Assassins threaten me?"

Ryze looked back at him, the soul of innocence. "I didn't see or hear anything."

"Me either," Vayne said.

"I'm staying out of it," Wornar said. "For the record, I'm almost certain I didn't see anything."

I turned to look at Cavan. If only because Ryze was playing innocent, I thought maybe he wouldn't.

He sighed and shrugged one shoulder. "That knife was already there, I'm sure."

I looked at Harel and smiled. Asshole.

He glared back. If we were alone, he'd slap me. I saw all of that and more on his face. Disgust and hatred were present too, in equal measures.

"We've wasted enough time here. Show me your melted building." His gaze slid away from me.

I had the distinct impression Cavan wanted to tell him to get the fuck out of his court. If there wasn't so much at stake, maybe he would.

Instead, he nodded graciously and stepped over to an empty section of the room to make a portal. He turned to me, but Ryze got there first.

"Stay here in the palace until I return. All three of you." The order would only settle on Tavian and I, but that was enough. We both gave him a look but nodded as if we had a choice.

Tavian muttered something that sounded like, "Fucking alphas," but he slipped his hand into mine. "We'll take care of her for you." He even went as far as to smile at Cavan as well as Ryze.

If it was his job to stir up trouble, he was doing it well. If he wasn't careful, someone might use his knife on him.

"I'm sure Vayne will take care of both of you," Ryze said. "Won't you, Vayne?"

Vayne looked us up and down. "Pretty sure they can take care of themselves. And cause me less trouble than you do."

Cavan grinned.

Ryze rolled his eyes. "Do your people give you as much trouble as mine do?"

"No. Insolence like that is usually reserved for a special kind of pain in the ass," Cavan told him.

"Ohhh." Ryze drew the word out. "Yours give you *more* trouble than mine do, then."

"Hurry up," Harel snapped. He stepped through the portal first.

"Anyone else wish the other end of that was the bottom of the ocean?" Tavian said softly.

I raised my hand.

I'd been called all sorts of things throughout my life: trouble, stubborn, difficult. Never filth. Even Hycanthe hadn't gone far enough to call me a whore.

It wasn't just the names, it was the derision on his face. Like I belonged in some isolated cave somewhere no one could look at my face. He made me feel uncomfortable in my own skin. As if I wasn't struggling with who I'd become as it was.

Tavian grinned. "That's my girl."

Both remaining High Lords gave him a look before they followed Wornar and Harel through the portal to the barracks.

Cavan gave me a longer glance, and a smile before he closed the portal behind them.

"Don't worry about Harel." Tavian led me back over to the sofa and we sat back down. "He's the worst of them. He's bitter because no one likes him, but no one likes him because he's bitter. As far as I can tell, he's always been like that."

"He certainly seems aggravated and aggravating," I said. "And determined not to believe anything Cavan or Ryze said. I get the distinct impression it doesn't matter what they say or show him. It'll only be when strange Fae from previously missing courts turn up on his door that he's going to believe any of it."

Vayne sat in the chair opposite us. "The worst thing is, he'd probably join them to spite the rest of us. Same reason he's here to begin with. An alliance with the Summer Court just to piss off Ryze and Thiron. There's probably some other agenda in there too. That's a bonus of being an irritating piece of shit."

"He makes you look like you come from the Court of Rainbows," Tavian said.

"There's a Court of Rainbows?" I asked.

"No, but there should be. What in the world could be more amazing than rainbows? Imagine the magic. We could make rainbows appear everywhere. Or make everything more colourful."

Vayne made a gagging gesture with a finger in his mouth. "The next thing you'll say is that it'll make everyone so happy they'll dance in the streets or some shit."

Tavian snorted. "That would be going overboard. I want to make things prettier, not boring."

"That sounds better," Vayne said. "You could distract people with rainbows, then cut their throat."

"I'd be living the dream then," Tavian sighed.

I shook my head. "More than a little bit out of your mind."

He grinned. "If I'm out of my mind, then I don't want to be in my mind." He stopped and frowned. "I don't think that's quite what I intended to say."

"Sounds right to me," Vayne said. "I wouldn't want to be in your mind either."

"No, you'd prefer to be in my mouth, wouldn't you?" Tavian smiled at him.

"I'd prefer to be in her mouth." Vayne nodded at me.

"How much time do you think we have?" Tavian asked. He glanced at the space where the portal was only moments ago.

"Since when did you care?" Vayne asked.

Somewhat hypocritical, since he'd fucked my mouth in the training yard where anyone could have walked up and seen. In fact, Zared had seen out the window.

He told me that right before fucking me up against the door in another building. That seemed like a lifetime ago. The ache of not having Zared here with us burned through me like a physical pain. Like part of me got ripped away, in spite of the bond which still held between us.

I hadn't told anyone about that. I don't know why. Maybe because it was my little secret to keep. Some personal, private part of myself between me and him and no one else.

"Is it possible to reverse memory changes?" I asked. "I mean, if my memory was changed before I went to the temple, but I'm remembering things from before, does that mean they're not gone? They're just...pushed down somewhere."

They exchanged glances.

"It's not a Winter Court magic thing, so I don't know how it works," Tavian admitted. "Most people don't, given it's a rare ability. Someone like Dalyth would know better than we would."

I wrinkled my nose. The last person I wanted to ask about anything was her, especially because she'd know exactly why I was asking.

"I suppose I could ask her to teach me how to do it," I conceded. "Maybe she'll let something slip."

"Fuck," Vayne said. He sat forward, hands on his thighs. "You want to change Zared's memories back?"

"Of course I do," I replied. "Don't you think he deserves the right to choose where and how he lives his life?"

"Not necessarily." Vayne held up a hand before I could protest.

"I hate to agree with anything Cavan and Dalyth did, but he might actually be happier living his life the way he is now. He's going to grow old and die along with people who will do the same at the same pace. We all know what he'll choose if he's given a choice. He'll choose you. Maybe him too." He jerked his head towards Tavian. "You might take his whole life away from him. You might not give him the choice you think you are. You both might come to regret it. How will you feel when he hates you for giving him back something he might be better off without?"

I looked over to Tavian as he shrugged.

"I don't know if you're right, or if Vayne is. I'm a big believer in choice, but I also care about Zared, and I don't want to see him hurt. I don't want to see either of you hurt. As decisions go, it's one of the more impossible ones. One thing I do know, though, it's not one that needs to be made today. Think it over. Talk to Ryze. Talk to Cavan if you have to. I'm sure if you ask, they'll take you to Havenmoor or wherever Zared is so you can see how he's doing."

He took my hands in his. "I only ask one thing. Don't rush into this. All right?"

I nodded. "I won't." They were both right. I owed it to Zared to think this through and make the right decision for him. If that meant leaving him to live his life, then that's what I'd do. Even if it broke my heart to do it. Better my heart get broken then have his life shattered all over again. He'd end up hating me and that would devastate both of us.

When the time came, I'd have to think very, very carefully. And put my faith in the gods that I'd make the right choice.

FIFTEEN

KHALA

The four men returned after around an hour, with apparently nothing changed between them. Harel looked as pissed off and disbelieving as before. The other three didn't seem to have come to any sort of agreement.

They settled in for what looked like a full night of conversation, or rather arguing.

I excused myself and returned to the atrium.

The guards were back on the door, but I got the impression they were there to keep out anyone who shouldn't be there, rather than to keep us in. A move, presumably on Cavan's part to gain our trust. Or mine, anyway.

Maybe it was easier than having Tavian throw knives at them to get to me.

In the end, I went to bed with a restless mind and more questions than I could imagine getting all the answers to. Including whether or not I was going to stay here, return to the Winter Court, or go somewhere else.

At some point, I needed to sit down with Ryze, but for now my priorities were up in the air. Getting my sisters out of here no longer seemed viable. If none of the other High Lords agreed with what Cavan was trying to do, and if those lost courts did in fact awaken, they'd be needed here. *I'd* be needed here.

I also wanted to be where my pack was. And where Zared was, all at the same time.

As far as I knew, I couldn't split myself in three.

I was still awake when the door opened slowly, almost silently. I assumed it was Tavian until I heard Ryze's voice.

"Khala? Are you still awake?" His whisper was soft enough that it wouldn't have woken me if I was asleep, but loud enough to hear.

"Yes." I sat up and rubbed my eyes. "Is everything all right?"

He took his hand away from in front of a lit candle, illuminating the room just enough for me to see him. He set the candle holder on the table to the side of the room and sat on the side of the bed.

"I feel I should apologise for... I'm not certain where to start. I never intended for you to end up in the middle of all of this. In the middle of anything."

He rubbed a hand over his face. "I don't know what to think about what Cavan said. If he's right—if he's been right all along, we all should have been doing something for the last couple of decades. How many omegas with the magic we'll need didn't make it past their heat?"

"You believe what he says, don't you?" I asked softly. "You don't want to, because you don't like him, but he makes sense."

"He does, because I've always thought the two courts still existed somewhere." Ryze lay down beside me and placed his hands under his head. "Those maps, the songs, they have to mean something. I don't know... It's possible they annihilated each other and all of this is for nothing."

"I'm new to this magic thing, but I don't think nothing melts stone." I found myself snuggling into him. He draped an arm around me.

"The only thing I know that can melt anything that hard, apart from extreme heat, is you," he said. "I'm talking about hearts of stone like mine. Like Cavan's too, unless I'm completely misreading the signs. Which I might be. I seem to be excelling at misreading things lately. Like the last hundred years or so. There's nothing more stubborn than a Fae who gets stuck in a comfortable rut."

"I'm sure there isn't," I agreed. I wasn't sure about melting anyone's heart. Mine was confused enough.

"It's possible he's wrong about the courts, but he mentioned other things happening. Tavian said assassins went missing. And then there was Illaria. Why would she keep him from the barracks if nothing was going on? Everything would seem to suggest... I don't know what it's suggesting."

"Therein lies the conundrum," he said. "No one knows. We talked for a long time and came to no conclusion. Except that Harel is a bigger prick than I thought he was. I suspect we can all agree on that. That's another thing I'm sorry for. He shouldn't be calling you names. I wanted to rip his head off. I wouldn't have shed a tear if Tavian landed that knife in his brain. Although, if it would have further complicated an already complicated situation. You can't assassinate a High Lord without consequences. Whoever inherited from him would be obligated to return the favour and assassinate me. And then my cousin Johah would have to do the same thing. If you ever assassinate one of us, make sure the finger points at someone else."

"I'll bear that in mind," I said. "You didn't tell Cavan about the maps, did you?"

"No, I didn't," Ryze admitted. "Believing he might be onto something and trusting him are two different things. I can't rule out the possibility he's working with someone else. He might have found a way to combine several kinds of magic to create that lightning bolt or whatever the fuck it was. He could have tried to use it to get rid of me. No one would know which way to point the finger then."

He toyed with my hair lightly. Every so often, his finger would brush against my skin, making me quiver.

"He might have found one of those lost courts," Ryze said thoughtfully. "He said the Shadow Court hated the Court of Dreams. The Court of Shadows was the one, according to legend, with the kind of power that could melt stone. They might be hunting for information on the whereabouts of the Court of Dreams."

"Like the maps?" I whispered. "You think he might be trying to figure out who has those maps?"

"I can't discount the possibility," Ryze said. "Those maps might give him— them, exactly what they need. The animosity between Cavan and Harel might be a pretense. An act to get us to trust Cavan."

"I suppose it could be true," I said carefully. "Cavan seemed sincere." I didn't want to believe he was using me after all.

"I'm sure he did," Ryze said. "People will do anything when there's a lot at stake. Don't forget what he did to Zared. And those priests back at the caravan. I know he explained his reasons, but those may be nothing more than pretty excuses."

If I didn't know what to think before, I was even less sure now.

"I suppose so," I said reluctantly. "This is all just so..."

"Yes, it is. That's why I came to apologise. You shouldn't be in the middle of all of this. You're not a knife or an arrow. You deserve better than to be treated like one. By the way, telling Harel to fuck off like that was the best thing I've seen in a long time. I wanted to applaud. I've been telling him that for years, but never with quite as much conviction. And the look on his face." Ryze chuckled. "I won't forget that anytime soon."

I grinned. "It felt good." My smile faded. "Unless, as you said, all of that was an act and I played right into it. The situation made Cavan look like he was on our side. Especially after Tavian threw the knife."

"That was my second favourite part of the day. Much more fun than seeing that building glowing red, and thinking at any moment now it was going to explode and take me with it. I was seriously rethinking my life choices for a while there."

This was the first time Ryze mentioned being afraid of anything. I hadn't even considered what he might have been feeling, standing on the ground, trying to cool the stone and keeping it from killing anyone.

"You really think the heat would have spread?" I asked.

"Without a doubt," he said. "Another minute or two, and the ground would have been too hot to stand on. Anything made of wood would have gone up in flames. Anyone standing there would have been incinerated."

"Including you," I said softly.

"Including me," he agreed. "And Vayne. I thought Tavian was closer than he was, but I was worried for him too. Don't tell anyone, but I was worried for the Summer Court Fae too."

"If you're not careful, people might start to think you're not an asshole after all," I warned.

He turned his face to look at me. "Shit, really? We can't have that happening. People might start to like me, or something ridiculous."

I hadn't realised how much I missed his amused expression until it was right in front of me. He didn't take anything too seriously for long. On the surface anyway.

Inside, he took everything a lot more seriously. His humour was a way to conceal that. In the end, Ryze would do anything for his people, the same way Cavan would do anything for his.

Or would he? Shit, I didn't know what to think about Cavan right now.

"Trust is a precious commodity," Ryze said softly, as though reading my thoughts. He must have sensed them through the bond. Or he was that astute. Maybe both.

"Once it's lost, it's difficult to get it back again. But it's the one thing we should try never to lose, or take for granted. If I could go back again and do everything over—"

"I know why you did what you did," I said. "I was pissed off at you for not telling me everything, but I understand. And you're right, I would have freaked out. I would have been terrified of my heat. That might have all been for nothing. You did it to spare me. Honestly, if you had told me and I didn't transform, I would spend the rest of my life thinking what if it happened at the next heat, or the one after that."

"I've never heard of that happening, but I can understand why you'd think that way. No one ever said brains were logical. Sometimes they tell us things that aren't true."

"Like trusting Cavan?" I asked.

"Or mistrusting him," Ryze said. "I stand by every decision I've ever made as High Lord, but this one... This one might come back to bite me on the ass. No matter what I do, I might end up screwing us all."

"Is there any way to know what the right choice is without jumping straight in?" I asked.

"There might be," he mused. "Does this mean you're not angry with me anymore?"

"I'm not as angry as I was," I said. I couldn't go too easy on him. He wouldn't want me to anyway.

"It's a start." He lowered his mouth to mine and kissed me. Tentative at first, as if he thought I might slap him for it. Deeper when he went unslapped.

"What are you going to do to make it up to me?" I asked between kisses. Every time our lips met, my body burned a little more. It wasn't just the alpha-omega connection. It went far deeper than that.

I wanted him because I cared about him. Through the bond, I felt his emotions. In a matter of moments, I could barely tell my need from his.

"I can think of a couple of things. Do you trust me not to hurt you?" He pulled back and looked at me intently.

"Yes." I wasn't sure what I was getting myself into, but I knew he wouldn't. Not deliberately.

"Good." He grabbed the hem of my shirt and pulled it up over my head. He tossed it aside. "Roll over onto your stomach." He climbed off the bed and walked over to pick up the candle.

A spike of nervous excitement buzzed through me but I rolled over.

He sat back down beside me, legs tucked under him.

"One advantage to Winter Court magic is the ability to prevent people from burning badly."

In the centre of my back, a patch of cold grew. He held the candle over it and waited.

The wax dripped from the candle onto my skin. One careful drop at a time. Where it landed warmed my skin again, almost to the point of pain.

"Do you like that?" he whispered.

"Yes, I do," I whispered back. It felt fucking amazing. "You can make it hurt a little more if you want to."

"That's my omega," he said approvingly.

Once again, he made a patch of my skin cold, but not as cold as the first time. The hot wax made a pleasant sting against my bare skin. Each drop sent a surge of heat to my centre.

I hummed with pleasure. "Hotter than that. Please."

"Good girl," he said. "Needy and polite. I can give you everything you need. Even if you don't ask nicely." He chuckled.

He held the candle over my shoulders and let the wax drip without cooling my skin first. Each drip was an exquisite point of pain that lasted only a moment. I knew he must have been cooling the wax so it didn't burn me, but left it hot long enough to feel incredible.

I moaned. "I had no idea that could feel so good."

He moved down and grabbed the top of my pants with one hand. He pulled them down just enough to expose my ass.

"Let's see how you like it here."

The first couple of drops were almost enough to make me come on the spot. The wax wasn't the only thing dripping at this point. My pussy was too.

"Oh my gods," I breathed. I'd never felt a sensation like this before.

Exquisite pain while at the same time, the absolute knowledge he wouldn't let me come to harm. My trust in him wasn't misplaced.

He let a few more drops land on my ass, then rose and put the candle back on the table.

Before he sat back down, he pulled my pants off the rest of the way. He dropped them aside, then parted my thighs with his hands. He kissed his way around my ass, and down the inside of one thigh and up the inside of the other. He teased around my rear hole with his tongue, before finding my clit and licking with firm strokes.

I shivered under his touch. Wanted more and more.

I felt his need match mine. Knew his cock was hard and aching. He'd make sure my needs were met before he even thought about his. Through the bond, I knew all of that and more.

"You taste delicious," he told me. He pulled his face back, rolled me over and bent my knees to open me out to him. "All the better to feast."

He lowered his head back down to me and put all his attention onto my clit.

I bucked lightly, slowly against his mouth before I came, pleasure was washing over me in a warm wave that included his response to my orgasm. He was more turned on than before.

I floated back down to earth, but he didn't stop licking and teasing my clit, his hands on my thighs to keep my legs open.

His eyes on mine, he watched as my desire rose again. My second orgasm was deeper and more intense than the first.

I flopped down against the mattress.

He lifted his face long enough to say, "I'm not finished yet." He went back to licking and sucking, his teeth grazing my clit, tongue sliding inside my pussy.

I thought I was done until he worked me up to a third orgasm. This one made me arch my back and shout his name to the ceiling.

He still didn't stop.

"Ryze, I can't—" I pleaded.

"Yes you can," he insisted, his voice muffled. "One more, like a good girl."

I almost pushed him away, but I knew he'd persist until I came for him a fourth time.

His tongue must have been aching more than his cock, but he didn't stop, didn't slow. He worked me until my body felt like it didn't belong to me anymore. All I knew was his mouth on me and another rising flood of pleasure.

This time when I came, there wasn't a part of me that didn't feel it. Blood raced through me like a raging inferno, like dripping wax through my veins. Every bit of me was on fire, engulfed in pure sensation. The whole world could have ended right then.

Maybe it did. Maybe it shattered along with me in a burst of tiny lights, pants and moans.

Only when I flopped to the mattress, boneless, did Ryze move to kneel between my legs. I hadn't seen him shed his pants, or the rest of his clothes, but he was naked, lying over me. sliding his thick cock into my pussy.

This was the first time we'd been together outside my heat. This wasn't the frantic coming together that was; the primal urge to fuck.

This was slow, deliberate and careful. This was an alpha taking care of his omega, while satisfying his own needs. And me taking care of him.

I hooked my legs around him, rolled us over and straddled his hips. While I slowly moved up and down the length of his cock, he ran his hands from my stomach and up to massage my breasts.

"Has anyone told you you're perfect?" he asked.

"Not recently," I said. He was pretty fucking good himself. I rose all the way up to his tip, then lowered myself all the way down to his knot and his balls. His knot wouldn't lock outside my heat, it was still thick, and amazing.

"Khala, you're incredible," he said breathlessly. "Absolutely perfect."

"If you're not careful, saying things like that will go to my head," I teased.

"You're certainly going to mine." He closed his eyes and thrust up into me. "I don't mean the one on my shoulders."

I laughed softly. "I didn't think you meant that one." I started to ride faster, enjoying the way his breath became ragged pants. The way his fingers rolled and pinched my nipples.

"Such a good girl," he said. "My omega. My beautiful omega."

"My alpha," I said back. My feelings for Cavan were confused, but I knew what I felt for Ryze. He was my alpha. We were a pack. A pack who was missing one member, but I intended to fix that. One way or another.

He grunted, thrusting harder and harder, all the way inside me. He gritted his teeth and groaned.

"Gods, you feel incredible. So warm, wet and perfect."

He let out a low cry and came. Through the bond, I felt the way his balls tensed before exploding inside me in a rush of hot, pearly cum.

He flopped back down and tilted his head back, puffing lightly until he caught his breath.

"When is your birthday?" he said when he was able to speak again.

"My birthday?" I still straddled him, his cock still inside me. I could happily have stayed that way for hours.

"Yes, your birthday. I think I want to give you a crown." He looked up at me. "We don't have queens like humans do. We only have High Ladies if they rule. But I think you still deserve a crown."

"I don't need a crown," I told him.

"You might not need one, I still want you to have one. And if you won't wear it, I'll have to imagine." He half closed his eyes and smiled. "Even if it's only a crown of mist. Or smoke. Or starlight. Or a light dusting of snow."

"You're such a romantic," I told him.

He opened his eyes fully. "Not usually. You bring it out in me. Or maybe I am, but I've spent too long with Tavian and Vayne." He grimaced playfully, but it quickly turned back into a smile.

"You don't want to give Tavian a crown?" I asked.

"Now that's someone who'd actually wear one." Ryze grinned. "He'd want one made of knives he could pull out and throw. And stab people with."

"That would be practical," I said. "Something like that would suit him, except it wouldn't be very subtle." He'd looked fabulous in it, but it probably wasn't the perfect headwear for an assassin.

Ryze chuckled. "No, it wouldn't. I might hold off on ordering one of those to be made then." He gripped my hips and helped me off so I could lie beside him.

"Can I ask you something?" I snuggled close to him.

"Anything," he said.

"Are you sure? There might be things you don't want to answer." I pulled the blankets over us.

"If that happens, I'll let you know," he said. "Otherwise, ask away."

I straightened the blankets around our feet and lay back to get comfortable. I wondered if he was as surprised to end the day in my bed as I was to have him here. I had to admit, he looked good lying there, dark hair against the pale coloured pillows. Like midnight on snow.

"How does a pack add more members?" I asked. "You said it's unusual for one person to bond with four others. How unusual are packs?"

Apparently I had more questions than even I was aware of. For every answer, I'd probably have a dozen more. Or a dozen-dozen.

Fae and human might not be that different, but throw in the whole omega thing and I had a lot more to learn. And a sneaking suspicion I'd still be learning in a decade or two.

"To answer your questions in reverse, packs are slightly less common than omegas. Some omegas prefer to be monogamous with one alpha. Some prefer one beta, except during heat. Some are lucky enough to surround themselves with several others who may be alphas, betas or omegas, like you."

"So having more than one alpha in a pack is normal?"

"It's normal in that it happens," Ryze said. "There's no right or wrong way to be a pack. They come together in whatever way works for the pack members."

"And if one member of the pack objects to another?"

"Then there's friction, but if they want to make it work, they will. Sometimes a pack member will tolerate another because they can't bear to be away from the others. Of course, it helps if everyone gets along. It's all a matter of communicating and being respectful. If either of my omegas wanted someone else that badly, it's my job to help them get what they want. For your sake or Tavian's, I'd tolerate almost anyone. Please don't tell me you've fallen for Harel?" He made a rude noise in the back of his throat.

I matched it with my snort. "Gods no. Almost anyone but."

I wouldn't go there with Hycanthe, Jezalyn or Geralda, the priestess from

Ebonfalls, either. But I felt the way my body responded when Cavan touched me. I had a hard time putting it out of my head. In spite of everything, I found him intriguing.

Whether it would ever go beyond that, I didn't know. It certainly wouldn't if we found out he was playing us.

"What do we do now?" I asked. "Do we go back to the Winter Court and wait?"

"Actually, I have an idea," Ryze said.

I closed my eyes and listened to his deep, musical voice while he spoke.

SIXTEEN

I woke up warm, wedged between two bodies in my narrow nest. I inhaled the scent of leather and wood smoke on one side and cinnamon and apple on the other.

Ryze and Tavian.

I didn't know when Tavian slipped into the room. I had a vague memory of waking with his fingers on my clit, cock already inside me and a quick, almost frantic fuck before we both went back to sleep.

Movement caught my eye and I lifted my head as the door opened. Hycanthe peeked inside, gave me a disapproving glare and disappeared again.

Evidently, she hadn't gotten over her past prejudice against me liking sex. Or maybe it was the company I was curled up with. I dropped my head back down.

"Friend of yours?" Ryze asked sleepily.

"Sort of," I said. "I should talk to her." I reluctantly managed to untangle myself from them and quickly pulled on my clothes.

They both looked like they wanted to tug me back to bed, but they also got up and dressed.

We stepped out into the atrium just as the palace staff were serving breakfast. Neither man hesitated to grab some tea and toast, in spite of the looks the staff gave them.

The expression on Jezalyn's face was remarkably similar. The moment she caught sight of them, she put herself between them and Hycanthe. She and Ryze eyed each other, alpha to alpha. They reminded me of two angry cats, circling each other, sizing each other up for weaknesses.

Tavian looked appraisingly at Jezalyn, which earned him a scowl from Hycanthe.

Ryze seemed to find the whole thing hilarious. Of course he fucking would.

"Everyone relax," I said. "Jezalyn and Hycanthe are together. Ryze and Tavian are together. No one needs to be threatened by anyone else."

Jezalyn looked from Ryze to me and nodded. "As long as we understand each other." She took Hycanthe's hand and led her to sit down at the table.

I thought that was the end of it, but Hycanthe couldn't let it go.

"They don't belong here," she said. "Who are you?"

Someone like Harel would have been offended. Maybe Cavan too.

Ryze grinned.

It was Tavian who answered. "Allow me to present High Lord Ryzellius of the Winter Court. I'm Tavian, Master of Assassins."

"You shouldn't be here," Hycanthe told them. "Does Cavan know?"

I told her briefly about what happened yesterday and why the men were staying in the palace. Nothing I said wasn't information everyone here would know by now, so it wouldn't matter if the other omegas or the staff overheard. Evidently no one told Hycanthe or Jezalyn.

I didn't mention anything about the lost courts. I'd have to save that for when we were alone.

"I thought I saw a flash of light, but then I assumed I was seeing things," Hycanthe said. "Jezalyn didn't see it at all." There was something else she wasn't telling me. I saw it in her eyes. I couldn't tell if she also didn't want to share too much information in front of other people, or just me.

She surprised me by saying, "Can I speak to you for a moment? Alone."

I glanced at Ryze, who nodded.

"We'll be right out here enjoying breakfast." He bit into his toast while watching Tavian, who'd sat himself beside another omega and was having a friendly conversation.

I followed Hycanthe to the room she shared with Jezalyn, and stood near the window while she closed the door.

"I wanted to talk to you, but you were...not alone," she said awkwardly.

I didn't want to get into that with her right now, so I jumped straight in. "What did you want to talk about?"

If she took me aside to judge me, I was going to be pissed off.

She glanced nervously towards the door, before stepping deeper into the room. It was the same size as mine, but reflected the fact they'd been here longer. The nest was full of pillows. Discarded clothing lay on the floor. It looked comfortably lived in.

"Something happened when the light flashed," she said. "Apart from some weird building melting. Just for a second or two, it felt like... Like a rush of magic through me."

She frowned, trying to put thoughts into words.

"I was stronger. It was as if the bit of me that's missing during classes was right there. I could have set the city on fire. And then it was gone."

She looked down at the white tiled floor. Kicked a sandal aside in frustration.

"Jezalyn believes me, but she didn't feel anything. Did you?"

I chewed my lip for a moment. Shook my head. "Nothing like that, no. Not that I recall. I saw a light, and then a bunch of smoke. Then I made Cavan take me down there with him. I didn't feel any burst of magic, just worry."

I told her about feeling Ryze and Vayne on the other end of the bond.

"I believe you," I added. I gave the closed door a quick glance too, before telling her everything else I knew. Everything except Ryze's plan.

"You don't think I had anything to do with that?" she demanded.

"No," I said firmly. "It sounds like whatever happened had some kind of impact on your magic. Have you tried using it since?"

"Yes, but it's as weak as ever." She sighed heavily. "It's as though none of that happened. I'm starting to think I imagined it."

"You didn't imagine it, but you should talk to someone who knows more about magic than I do."

"I'm not talking to Dalyth," she said quickly.

"I wasn't suggesting Dalyth," I said. "Ryze, or even Cavan. Either of them might have more answers than I do."

"Not Cavan either," she said. "I don't know if I can trust Ryzellius. He's one of them."

"A man?" I asked.

"A Fae High Lord," she replied. "I've seen Cavan and Harel. They all seem to have their own agenda and don't care who they use to get their way."

I couldn't argue the accuracy of her words. They did have their agenda, but who didn't right now?

"You can trust Ryze," I promised. "If you prefer, I can talk to him for you. I can try to keep your name out of it, but he knows we're in here talking."

She hesitated. "Make him promise not to tell anyone else," she said. Her mouth moved a couple of times before she continued. "Does this mean we're not leaving the Summer Court?"

"It might mean we're leaving sooner than I thought," I said. "But I'll let you know when I know." That was all I could give her right now.

She nodded and opened the door before following me out.

Ryze gave me a questioning look, but I shook my head. I'd tell him later.

"As much fun as this has been to spend so much time with so many beautiful women, Tavian, Khala and I are needed downstairs." Ryze gave the gathered omegas a bow and ushered us out the door.

Several of the women sighed as he left.

"You've still got it," Tavian told him.

"Do I?" Ryze asked. "I hadn't noticed." He slipped an arm around me. "I noticed you two."

We exchanged glances, rolled eyes and walked with him down the stairs and into another room where the staff were serving breakfast. As if they hadn't eaten already, both of them slipped into a chair and helped themselves to toast and eggs.

"How nice of you to join us," Cavan drawled from the head of the table. An empty plate set in front of him, but he was sipping from a delicate, porcelain cup. The smell of coffee mixed in with his eucalyptus and musk.

Wornar must have returned to the Spring Court. He was nowhere to be seen now.

"Isn't it though?" Ryze asked. "We thought about waiting until you left the room, but decided that would be impolite."

Both High Lords exchanged sarcastic smiles.

I slipped into a chair beside Ryze and reached for toast and black tea. I took my first bite when Harel finally shuffled into the room.

"Have any of you given up on the fantasy of the other courts?" He flopped heavily into a chair before reaching for three pieces of toast and a large pile of eggs. A member of staff poured him coffee, which he poked his finger into before half closing his eyes. Judging by the steam that rose a moment later, he'd heated it.

"No we haven't, Harel," Ryze drawled. "Have you finally figured out what actually happened? I'm sure everyone around this table would love to hear it."

Harel shrugged. "I have no further explanation. Unless you believe in dragons."

"Dragons are a myth," Ryze said wearily.

"So are the Court of Dreams and the Court of Shadows," Harel retorted. "At least a dragon would explain the excess heat. Maybe it wasn't a light in the sky. Maybe it was a flash of fiery breath." He smirked. "It's as likely to be true as any other bullshit you've mentioned so far."

Tavian was staring at Harel. When I managed to catch his eye, he responded with a quick hand signal. "Later."

I couldn't tell if Ryze noticed, he seemed occupied looking lazily at Harel with a raised eyebrow. He stayed that way for a minute or two, then turned to Cavan.

"Quite some time ago in my library back in Lysarial," he said slowly, reluctantly, "I saw a map. It made mention of the Court of Shadows."

Cavan stopped with his cup halfway to his lips and jerked upright. "A map?" He echoed.

"For fuck's sake," Harel muttered. "More of this nonsense."

We all ignored him.

"I hadn't thought about it until now," Ryze lied. "It's vague at best. The general consensus was that it wasn't a map to a real place. In light of yesterday's happenings, perhaps I was mistaken in that assumption." Had he decided that they'd spend the rest of their days talking around in circles if he wasn't forthcoming about the maps?

"Perhaps you were," Cavan agreed. "This might be exactly what we need to find them. Can you bring the map here? Does it mention the Court of

Dreams?" He was sitting forward eagerly, elbows on the smooth, mahogany table.

Ryze looked thoughtful. "There may be mention of the other court on another map. As I mentioned about the other one, it was vague. They may be no use at all, but I'd be more than happy to go and get them. On the condition Khala and any omega who wants to accompany her comes with me."

That spoke more volumes than the library contained about how he felt about me and helping my sisters. He was willing to share those maps in return for our safekeeping. I knew exactly how important those maps were to him. He'd kept their existence to himself for this long. I couldn't overstate how big a deal this was. To him, it would be like conceding a part of his court.

Cavan was visibly conflicted. He wanted to keep us here, but he needed to see that map.

"As long as they choose of their own free will," he said finally, as reluctantly as Ryze was to mention the maps. Another huge concession.

"If you're so concerned for their welfare, you're welcome to come with us," Ryze offered. "You're welcome to bring a few of your guards with you, in case you think this is an ambush."

Cavan clearly considered it might be. He thought quickly, then nodded. "I will accompany you. I'd like to see this map for myself."

"Excellent," Ryze said before turning to Harel. "Will you be joining us?"

"Hells no," Harel snapped. "It's long past time for me to return to my court. Send word when you're finished with this nonsense." He hastily finished his breakfast and stalked out of the room.

"If you'll excuse me, I have to take care of a couple of things before we leave." Cavan rose, nodded graciously and hurried out.

It wasn't until we were safely alone that Ryze turned to Tavian.

CHAPTER
SEVENTEEN
KHALA

"All right, what was that? The moment Harel mentioned dragons, you twitched." Ryze lifted his chin and regarded Tavian.

"I did not," Tavian protested.

"Something certainly happened," I said. "Are you about to tell me dragons are real after all?"

"Dragons—" Ryze started.

"Are a myth," we both finished for him.

"What was up with you?" I levelled my gaze at Tavian.

"I don't know," he said slowly. "When the light flashed, I had the impression of something. I thought it was ash, but then it was snow. When I put my hand out, I could feel it. But it wasn't in Garial anymore. I was on a field. Somewhere I didn't recognise. In the middle of a battle. Something flew over my head. I saw wings. White and grey with feathers."

"A griffin?" Ryze asked.

"That was what it looks like, but only saw a flash." His eyes glazed over as he thought back. "When Harel was talking about dragons, it came back to me. I realised something. Griffins can fly."

"That's not exactly news," Ryze said dryly.

"I know, but that light was in the sky. What if it wasn't a light? What if it was a portal? Opened by someone on the back of a griffin for just long enough to throw heat through before they closed it again?"

Ryze sat back. He pressed two fingers to his upper lip, and his thumb to his chin.

"Fuck. It may not have been aimed at me. It might have been an example of what they can do." He stood. "We need to get a look at that map."

"Yes we do," Cavan arrived back in time to see Ryze stand. Had he heard anything else? His expression gave away nothing.

"Perfect timing," Ryze said smoothly. "We were about to leave without you."

"I'm sure you were," Cavan told him, clearly not believing that for a moment.

Tavian pulled me to my feet and nudged me with his elbow. When I turned to him, he was grinning.

"What?" I asked.

"This is the bit where we get to watch two alphas argue over who's making the portal. It always gets interesting."

"I'm sure it does," I said. A smile tugged on the side of my lips. "Your portal or mine?"

He laughed. "That sounds perfectly inappropriate. Who wouldn't want watch them fuck each other?"

Before I could answer, I caught Ryze and Cavan staring at us both.

Tavian grinned broader. "It's an omega thing."

"If you keep saying that, I'm going to open a portal to that swamp we talked about," Ryze started. "Push you through it. And close it behind you."

"He wouldn't really do that," Tavian told me.

"I've heard he's done it before," Cavan said. He arched an eyebrow at Ryze. "Who was it? Someone spilled a drop of milk on your shoe?"

"If anyone spilled milk on my shoe, they'd deserve to end up in the swamp," Ryze said. "If you must know, they tried to kill me. Did you send them?"

"Not on that occasion, no," Cavan said.

"So you don't deny sending people to kill me?" Ryze pretended to be offended, but the humour in his eyes said he wasn't really.

"I'm sure you deserved it," was all Cavan said. "You can make the portal. You know where we're going better than I do."

Ryze looked surprised but nodded. "Khala, are your friends coming?"

"They're already waiting outside," Cavan said. "Hycanthe, Jezalyn and a couple of others who are scared to stay in Garial after what happened yesterday. As soon as I stepped out of the room, I sent word to the atrium."

"How magnanimous and efficient of you," Ryze told him. "I'm almost impressed."

"I almost give a shit," Cavan said in return. "Actually, no, I don't. Not even a small one."

"Liar." Ryze nodded his thanks to Vayne, who stepped into the room carrying all of their packs. "You care about my opinion much more than you'll admit."

"Keep telling yourself that," Cavan said dryly. "That will never make it true."

Ryze smirked and slipped his pack onto his back before taking my hand. "Ready to go home?"

I wasn't sure how to answer that. I knew he wanted me to tell him I was, and that the Winter Court was home, but I wasn't sure I could say that yet.

"I'm ready to get back to my nest," I said finally. I knew he saw through my hesitation, and understood the reason for it. I also knew he'd do whatever it took to make Lysarial home for me. He squeezed my hand as we walked through the door together out into the open hallway.

As Cavan said, Hycanthe and Jezalyn were waiting there with two other omegas, a few guards and, to my annoyance, Dalyth.

"These three haven't finished their training," Cavan said. "I'm sure you'll agree it's important they keep up with that." He didn't look like he cared too much whether Ryze agreed or not. Like me leaving wasn't negotiable, neither was this.

"On the condition she returns here the moment they're ready," Ryze said. He turned away before anyone could argue, and opened a portal.

The same as the first one I ever saw him make, this one wound around a bend, the end disappearing out of sight. Garial and Lysarial were obviously a great distance apart.

Ryze pushed me gently towards Tavian and Vayne. "Stay near them. You three go through first. Cavan and I will go through last, so we can keep an eye on each other."

Cavan nodded, apparently satisfied with that arrangement. What would it take for those two to trust each other? Would they ever? They might need to, sooner or later.

Evidently, today was not that day.

To my surprise, Vayne took my other hand. The three of us stepped through together.

In spite of having done this before, I still expected it to be cold inside the portal. Like always, it was warm all the way through until we stepped out the other side. Not into the sitting room at the palace in Lysarial, as I expected, but rather in a yard near the kitchen.

We hurried to move out of the way of everyone else coming through.

I glanced around, half expecting to see Zared come running out to greet us. Possibly to stab Dalyth and Cavan for sending him away. Of course, he wasn't here. He was a long way from Lysarial. Closer now, according to the bond, but still too far from me.

"It's nice to be back here," Tavian said. He and Vayne seemed to be scanning the area, looking for trouble or anything out of place.

As far as I could tell, none of the buildings were melted, exploded, imploded, or otherwise impacted in any way. Everything looked just how we left it.

By twos and threes, everyone stepped through the portal. Ryze and Cavan still looked at each other dubiously until Ryze closed the portal.

"Would you like to get settled first, or shall we get straight to the library?" Ryze was asking Cavan.

"I see no reason to wait," Cavan said.

Ryze nodded. "I didn't think you would." He waved one of his staff over and told them to take care of Jezalyn and the omegas. And to find separate accommodation for Dalyth. Clearly he had no intention of taking her into the library.

She scowled, but went quietly when Cavan gave her a nod.

Another member of staff took everyone's packs. The rest of us headed to the library.

"This is impressive," Cavan admitted once we stepped inside. He tilted his chin and looked around, taking everything in.

"Everything is bigger and more impressive in the Winter Court," Ryze remarked.

Cavan snorted softly and continued his appreciation of the shelves and shelves of books.

Ryze shrugged to us and placed his hands on his hips. "Now, the maps are in this section."

Cavan had pulled a book off the shelf and was looking at it with raised eyebrows. "I didn't realise Winter Court Fae were as adventurous as those of us from the Summer Court."

"We're not," Ryze said absently, as he scanned the racks. "We're much more adventurous. Aren't we, Tave?"

"I don't know," Tavian admitted. "I don't have any experience with anyone from the Summer Court." To Cavan he said, "Are you offering?"

Cavan's eyes slid to me. He gave me a smile which clearly said he'd extend me the offer any time.

My pulse actually fluttered.

I managed to look away, but not before I saw what page Cavan was looking at. I'd like to try that, whether it was him or someone else.

"Anyway, the maps." Ryze drawled. "If you don't mind." He stepped in front of us. "They're precious and brittle. You're welcome to watch over my shoulder."

That was exactly what Cavan did. I stood on the other side, Tavian and Vayne behind me.

Ryze carefully turned page after page, saying what each one was as he went. "Map of Lysarial. Map of the land surrounding Lysarial. Map of the Winter Court. Map of our border with the Autumn Court. Map of our border with the Spring Court. Map of..."

He tilted his head, and lowered his face for a better look. "Something so faded I can't make it out." He handed it over his shoulder to Cavan.

"That might be the swamp you were talking about." Cavan shrugged and handed it back.

Ryze looked again. "Ahhh, you might be right." He placed it with the others.

He kept turning over pages. They crackled under his touch and some of the corners started to split. He winced a couple of times.

After about ten maps, Cavan put a hand on his arm. "Wait. There. Right where you put it whenever you put it there. One day you might appreciate the fact I wasn't born yesterday either."

"I don't trust you," Ryze said simply. "Of course I'm not going to tell you everything straight away."

"One of these days, people will die because of that," Cavan says scathingly. He shook his head and turned his attention to the map.

"You were right about one thing, it is vague." He ran his finger down the centre of the piece of parchment. "Those mountains look familiar."

"They do?" For once, Ryze was sincere. "They don't appear on any map I've ever found. I've spent decades comparing them."

Cavan responded with a grunt of annoyance. "If you listened to me sooner, we might have found what we were looking for by now." He turned back to the map, tapped on it absently with a fingertip. "If I could just remember where I've seen a mountain formation like that."

"Somewhere there's griffins?" Tavian asked casually.

Cavan's finger stopped tapping. "What did you say?"

Tavian glanced at Ryze, who shrugged.

"I said somewhere there might be griffins," Tavian repeated.

Cavan mouthed the words. *Somewhere there might be griffins.*

"What is it?" I asked.

"I think I know where this is," Cavan said.

EIGHTEEN

TAVIAN

"Are you going to force us to guess?" Ryze asked. "Like I said, I've spent decades looking for where this is. I'm somewhat out of guesses."

He looked pissed Cavan might have the answers to questions he'd had for such a long time. We'd spent a good many nights drinking, talking and speculating about this.

Like with most things, Vayne thought it was a waste of time. I wasn't sure I disagreed with him, but it was important to Ryze. That meant it was important to me.

On those occasions he got it into his head to go searching for lost courts, I went with him. All we ever found were local legends from all over Jorius. When we weren't ducking Autumn Court border patrols and the like.

No one ever said life with Ryze wasn't fun.

"I'm only guessing myself," Cavan told him. "Obviously it's not in Jorius."

"I concluded as much," Ryze said. "I've never seen a formation of mountains like that in Fraxius either. I haven't spent much time in the lands beyond that."

"There are lands beyond that?" Khala tilted her head and looked up at him.

Like it did every time I looked at her, my heart skipped a beat. I'd never seen a woman as fucking gorgeous as her in my life. She smelled of lavender, fresh rain and omega sweetness. Between her and Ryze, my cock ached more often than not.

I loved every minute of it.

"Gerian and Freid," I told her. "Human land. Very unwelcoming to Fae. Even less than the Autumn Court is welcome to outsiders."

She turned her pretty eyes towards me. "Sounds like a good place to hide if you don't want to be found by other Fae."

"Not so much if you are Fae and object to being shot on sight," Ryze said. He looked toward Cavan. "That wasn't what you meant."

Cavan shook his head slowly. "Natanya."

Ryze, Vayne and I all stiffened.

Khala looked from one to the other clearly confused. "What is Natanya?"

"Some call it the forbidden lands," Ryze said. He spoke softly as though not wanting to be overheard by the gods. "The land beyond the mists."

"Superstitious?" Cavan asked mockingly.

"When it comes to that place, yes, I fucking am." Ryze glanced back at the map. "I tried to go there once, when I was young and stupid." He shuddered.

"What makes you think the map is leading there?" Khala asked Cavan. "Apart from the fact hiding somewhere even Ryze is scared to go is potentially a good place to hide."

"I didn't say I was scared to go there," Ryze snapped. "I just said I've been and it freaked me the fuck out."

"There are records in the Temple in Havenmoor," Cavan said. "Specifically, a map carved into the wall. It dates back to when Fae occupied Fraxius. Before the seasonal courts were formed. Before the mists. On that map is a mountain range that looks like this." He tapped the map again.

"That could be nothing more than a coincidence," Ryze said.

"Or it might not be." Cavan straightened and crossed his arms.

"Are you suggesting the Court of Shadows put mist around itself to keep everyone out?" Khala asked. "That it was there all along?"

"Doubtful," Cavan said. "The mists appeared at least a hundred years after the courts disappeared. But the clues to their whereabouts might be there."

"Or they might be here." Khala leaned over the map and read out loud.

"Court of Shadows, whispers creep,
Fae of darkness love to sleep.
Their magic like knives, eyes a-shine,
They lurk and hide, await a sign.

The trees here bend and twist and creak,
    If they're alive, somehow speak.
    Branches reach out with spidery claws,
    Open the air, the harsh, cold doors.

Fae of shadows gather here,
    Court of secrets, place of fear,
    Dance and sway with subtle grace,
    Shadows flicker on every space.

. . .

281

THE MOON IS ALWAYS FULL,
 It casts a glow on the skulls,
 That line the path and watch,
 With hollow eyes, wary touch.

IF YOU DARE ENTER the court,
 To find the ones long sought.
 Fae here play a deadly game,
 They'll ensnare you, hard as stone.

HEED THE WARNING CLEAR,
 Those who wander too near,
 The shadows, where the Fae,
 Play games of darkness, night and day."

"So POETIC," I said.

RYZE LEANED OVER THE MAP, beside Khala.
 "If I didn't know better, I'd think they were suggesting we ask a tree for the answers. I've gone over that bit in my head a thousand times."
 "To seek the Court of Shadows," Cavan read. "As if they're alive, they somehow speak."
 "Trees don't talk," Vayne said. "How are they going to have any answers?"
 "There's more than one way to speak," Khala pointed out.
 "Yes there is," Ryze agreed.
 "What does the other map say?" Cavan asked.
 Ryze pulled out the other map. He unrolled it and placed it beside the first.
 Cavan shook his head slightly and read:

"IN THE COURT OF DREAMS, Fae dance,
 Hearts flutter in a wild prance.
 The moonlight shines so bright,
 Lighting steps that flow all night.

THE AIR IS alive with Fae song,
 A place where dreams hold long.
 The scent of honey and blooming flowers,
 Mingle with the Fae's lost powers.

. . .

THEIR VOICES BLEND, sweet and true,
  A melody that echoes through the hue.
  They sing of love and endless wonder,
  Hearts aglow, spirits thunder.

THE COURT OF DREAMS is a place of wonder,
  Where Fae reign with magic stronger.
  Come dance beneath the moon,
  Lose yourself to the compelling tune.

IN THE COURT OF DREAMS, time stands still,
  All around is magic and thrill.
  Close your eyes and take a chance,
  Join the Fae's wildest dance."

"That sounds like my kind of place," I said. "Music and dancing. Much more fun than trees trying to claw your eyes out."

"It shows the same place as the other map," Khala said. "If the two courts hated each other, then they weren't going to live on top of each other, right?"

"Right," Cavan agreed. He seemed to be lost in thought.

I couldn't deny how attractive he was. If Khala and I were able to coordinate our heats, we might have a lot of fun with both alphas. And Vayne. And Zared too.

Thinking about him made me as conflicted as Khala must have been. I missed him like an ache in my heart, but if he was content living his human life, then what right did I have to yearn for him at all? I should be happy for him. I wasn't, and that made me feel like a selfish prick, but it was what it was. No one ever said love was logical or even selfless.

We chose who we wanted to walk with on this road, and I chose him along with Ryze and Khala. Even if it wasn't meant to be.

"This might be nothing more to a clue as to the last spot they were before they wiped each other out," Vayne said.

"Or a warning to stay away," Khala added.

"Or a map leading to a huge vault where the treasure of those courts is buried," I said.

"I hate to say it," Ryze said, "but that seems unlikely. Although, it would explain why I have both the maps here. What other court could be trusted with a secret like that?"

"The other courts might be smart enough to solve the riddle." Cavan smirked.

Ryze raised an eyebrow at him. "Interesting theory, but with absolutely nothing to back it up." He smirked in return.

"We can all agree the Winter Court is a better place for them than the Autumn Court," I said.

"Under its current High Lord, yes," Cavan said. "Harel would have these burnt."

"If it means going into the mist, I'm not sure he'd be wrong to do that," Ryze said. "I like an intrepid adventure as much as the next man, or woman, but that place isn't right."

"You don't have to go if you don't want to," Cavan told him. "I'll go with a contingent of my people. If you're lucky, I might tell you what we find."

Of course that was exactly the thing to make Ryze respond to the way he wanted him to.

"I'm going," Ryze said firmly. He never could back down from a challenge or a dare. "But there's somewhere we need to go first. I'd like to see that map in Havenmoor. If we can match that with this, we might have a better idea where we're going."

"I'd like another look myself," Cavan agreed. "And for the songs on the maps to be transcribed. Unless you prefer we carry these around with us?" He waved his hand over the maps.

"I'll do it," I said. "I presume we don't want anyone outside this room to know about it?"

"I think that would be wise." Ryze nodded. "These maps are too fragile to remove from here. Make a sketch of the maps too, so we can take them with us to Havenmoor."

I nodded. "Khala, want to help me?"

"Of course," she replied. "On the condition I get to go to Havenmoor too."

No one needed to ask why.

The High Lords exchanged a glance. Ryze looked as though he was waiting for Cavan to say no. Cavan simply pressed his lips together, leaving Ryze to answer.

He looked at the way Khala's chin jutted out in determination and reluctantly nodded.

"Fine, but if we bump into Zared—"

"I just want to see if he's all right," she said quickly, firmly. "I want to see that map for myself anyway."

Ryze held up his hands in surrender. "All right. Get to work. We'll leave first thing in the morning."

I nodded and went in search of paper and something to write with.

By the time I returned, everyone left except Khala. She stood pouring over both maps, a frown on her pretty forehead.

I wanted to tear off her pants and fuck her over the table, just like that. But I had a job to do first.

"Do you think it is a riddle?" I placed the paper down beside the first map and started a careful sketch.

"It could be a silly children's song for all I know," she said. "The Court of Shadows sounds like a nightmare. The Court of Dreams sounds like, well, a dream. Do you think they really existed?"

I paused in my sketching for a moment. "Until yesterday, I would have said I don't know. Going with Ryze... It was something to do. You know? Indulging his fantasy of the glory of finding missing Fae or some shit like that." I shrugged one shoulder.

"And then yesterday?" she prompted.

"Then I saw griffins right above my head that weren't there. I have a good imagination, but this was something completely different. It was happening in front of me."

I'd smelled smoke in the air. Felt the rush of wings above me. I heard the screams of people dying, and the clash of steel on steel. I was right there. In the middle of a field of battle. Hells, I could even smell blood and fear. It coated the insides of my nostrils, heavy and thick. Several metres away, a man sobbed in agony before he twitched and felt completely still. His eyes stared up at the sky, accusing and scared.

The moment passed, I found myself standing in the streets of Garial, surrounded by people going about their lives. Nothing about it seemed real. It took me a solid couple of minutes to reorient myself again. To convince myself I wasn't really on a battlefield. I was nowhere more extraordinary than a street in the Summer Court.

"It's too strange to disregard anything at this point," I concluded.

"Can you keep a secret?" she asked.

"Sweetheart, I wouldn't be a good Master of Assassins if I couldn't," I told her.

She smiled and lightly kissed my mouth. Then told me about Hycanthe and her magic.

"Whatever happened yesterday, something happened to both of you." She looked worried, for her sister and for me. Not for herself. That was typical Khala. She was beyond sweet. Especially when she told High Lords to fuck off. That was literally the best thing I've seen in years. That and the look on Harel's face.

I nodded, and said, "I think we should keep both of these things to ourselves. For now at least. We can trust Ryze and Vayne, but Cavan would feel obligated to tell Dalyth and fuck knows what that bitch would do."

"I trust her as far as I could throw a mountain with one hand," Khala said eloquently.

"What about Cavan?" I went back to sketching. "You wouldn't kick him out of your nest, would you?"

She smiled and laughed softly. "No, but that doesn't necessarily mean I trust him either. Physical attraction doesn't always make sense."

"Is that all it is?" I carefully drew the outline of the mountains, and shaded where the map was shaded. "He's also intelligent, powerful, and doesn't take crap from anyone. Not even Ryze."

"It sounds like you have a crush on him," she teased.

I looked over and flashed her a smile. "Is it that obvious?" I pushed my hair back over my shoulder and went back to sketching. "Like you said, physical attraction doesn't always make—"

Khala was gone.

The whole library was gone.

NINETEEN

TAVIAN

The mountainside overlooked a wide valley. A sheer drop ended in a river, which meandered through the middle, glittering in the afternoon sun.

I traced its progress with my gaze until it reached the delta and flowed out to sea.

A stiff breeze ruffled my clothes and hair. Strands blew across my eyes. I pushed them back, tucking them behind my ears. I straightened my long tunic.

"Are you listening, Patric?" a voice snapped behind me.

I turned.

The man beside me turned too. "I hear you Yala, but it's not time yet. The chicks are too young."

"Old enough to be ridden," Yala snapped. "What are we waiting for? The next clutch of chicks? The clutch after that? You always say it's not time yet." Her eyes flicked to me and she curled her lip before looking away.

"When the time is ready, we'll know," Patric said patiently.

"Tavian?"

Whose voice was that? There was no one here but me, Patric and Yala.

"Tavian?" It came again, more frantic this time.

"How will we know?" Yala demanded.

"The five will come—"

Patric's voice faded and he was gone, replaced by the library and Khala's worried face.

"Tave? Are you all right?"

I shook my head. "Yes. I'm fine. I was just...not here for a moment."

"I saw that," she said. "You looked deep in thought, but your face was pale." She brushed hair off my forehead with warm fingers. "You're so cold."

"It was—"

The sound of screaming outside the library interrupted me.

"Stay here." When she started to argue, I grabbed her wrists and pulled her closer to me.

"Whatever's going on, someone needs to finish transcribing those songs and sketching the maps. Can you do that?" I looked firmly into her eyes. I needed her to do this. Ryze needed her to.

She nodded. "I can do it, if you promise me you'll be safe."

I kissed her mouth quickly. "I always do." I let her wrists go and started out of the library at a trot. I was used to dealing with all sorts of shit, but this had me on edge. Whatever I saw, whoever those people were, had something to do with this. I was certain of it.

I slowed to a walk before I stepped out into the sunshine.

Into chaos.

Like in the Summer Court barracks, Fae ran back and forth. There, it was from fear. Here, it was with purpose.

They ran to refill buckets, to throw water on fires that blazed in the trees and various buildings. Debris lay everywhere. Branches, brooms, random pieces of cloth, what looked like a smashed wagon.

I grabbed the arm of a young man as he ran past.

"What the hells is going on?" I asked.

"A huge whirlwind," he panted. "Came through from the sea. Grabbed up everything in its path and threw it around like it was nothing. Then it was gone."

"Any flashes of light?"

He gave me a funny look. "Not that I saw. I saw the wind and ran like hells until it was gone. Now it's got things on fire." He nodded towards another wagon, this one fully ablaze.

I nodded. "Go." I dropped my hand and he went on running.

I supposed it could have been a coincidence, an act of nature or the gods. My instincts told me otherwise.

I was about to head inside when a portal opened beside me. Ryze, Cavan and Vayne stepped out so fast Ryze almost barrelled into me.

He grabbed me at the last moment. "What the fuck happened?"

I told him what the young man told me.

"No winter magic can do that," he said.

"Not summer either," Cavan said. "A combination of it can."

"Khala was with me. She didn't do it," I said quickly.

Ryze eyed Cavan. "Where was Dalyth?"

"Training the other omegas," Cavan said coolly. "Hycanthe isn't strong enough to do something like this."

I wanted to contradict him, but not in front of Ryze and not after telling Khala I wouldn't say anything to anyone about Hycanthe's magic getting stronger during yesterday's attack.

"We don't get whirlwinds at random here in Lysarial," Ryze said.

"I think we can all agree it wasn't anything random," Cavan said wearily.

"Nothing happened here yesterday," Vayne said. "I've spoken to my second-in-command, she said it was as boring as shit. If this was the same asshole as in Garial, then I suggest they're following one of you around."

"They might be following *you* around," I pointed out. "You are pretty cute." I couldn't resist the flirt, if only to see the expression on his face. He was too easy to rile.

Vayne snorted. "Yes I am, but they can fuck off. I'm not interested."

Ryze patted him on the shoulder. "You'd have to be slightly flattered if they've gone to all this trouble to get your attention. Wouldn't you?"

Vayne jerked away. "It's not about me," he growled. "Tavian was the one Illaria tried to keep away from the barracks. Maybe it's about him. Or you," he said to Ryze. He glared at Cavan but didn't say anything further. He didn't need to. It was obvious to everyone where he thought the blame really lay.

"Extreme heat and high wind," Cavan said thoughtfully. "Both destructive forces."

"So?" Ryze asked. "They haven't done much damage so far."

"Exactly," Cavan agreed. "It's like a hen pecking at a hunk of bread."

"A hen can't swallow a loaf of bread whole," I said. "All she can do is peck at it."

"Until what?" Cavan asked.

I frowned. "Until she manages to tear it apart. You think that's what's happening here? That if they nibble at us here and there, we'll tear ourselves apart?"

"Considering our struggle to remain civil to one another, I'd say they're assuming that will be the result," Cavan said. "Whether or not it is, is up to us."

"I think he's trying to tell you to play nice," Vayne said to Ryze.

"I always play nice," Ryze said. "But why do something different here than in Garial?"

He thought for a moment before he answered his own question. "They misjudged. They didn't think there'd be anyone in Lysarial who could deal with extreme heat. And they didn't think there'd be anyone here who could stop that wind."

"Khala didn't stop it," I said. "Either someone else did, or it stopped by itself."

"Dalyth might have," Cavan said. "But no one would have anticipated her being here in Lysarial. Whatever they're basing their information on, it's out of date."

"Or a bunch of coincidences," Vayne said.

"Or that," Ryze agreed. "If we can ascertain what they think they know, maybe we can get ahead of them."

"If they think we're looking for them, chances are they'll know we'll go to

Havenmoor," Cavan said slowly. "If they can only act once a day, we should go there now."

"They might be anticipating that we assume they can only act once a day," Ryze said.

"Whatever we decide we can assume, they assume," I pointed out. "Maybe we should be as prepared as we can."

"That goes without saying," Vayne said with a grunt.

"Why did you ask about the griffins?" Cavan asked me suddenly.

I glanced at Ryze.

He closed his eyes for a moment, then reluctantly nodded. "If they want us to tear ourselves apart, the best we can do is to not let them. Let's go back into the library."

Cavan regarded Ryze for a moment, but followed us back inside.

"Just in time," Khala said as we approached. "I've finished writing out the songs." She handed the paper with her neat handwriting on it to Ryze.

"I can't remember the last time I saw handwriting I could read so easily," Ryze said. He folded the paper and placed it into his pocket. "I'm so used to writing that looks like a spider was crawling along the page and got squashed."

"In other words, your own writing?" Cavan asked.

Ryze smirked. "No, not mine." He turned to me. "You might as well tell Cavan everything you told us. If nothing else, it will save him from complaining later about things he didn't know."

He leaned against one of the shelves, cocked his head and waved a hand to give me the floor. A faint smile graced his full lips.

Cavan smirked back. "You'll thank me when your court isn't in ashes." He turned from Ryze and raised an eyebrow at me. He was too attractive for his own good. Probably mine and Khala's too.

In as few words as possible, I told them what I saw both times. Standing on the battlefield and standing on the mountainside. They all listened intently while I spoke.

"Have you ever seen anything like that before?" Ryze asked with a frown.

I shook my head. "Never. I'm not sure I want to again. I felt like I was standing in someone else's body." I couldn't contain the shudder that passed through me. If something like that were to happen when I was supposed to be killing someone, I may end up being the dead Fae. I didn't much care for that idea.

"Did you get any sense of whose body it was?" Cavan asked. "Thoughts that weren't your own?"

I considered his question, but eventually shook my head again. "No, it was me. Just...not me. I didn't think to look down at myself or anything like that. I'm not sure I was able to. I think I could only look where they were looking. Whoever's body I was in."

"The people you saw didn't see anything out of place?" Cavan asked.

"They were too busy being angry with each other." I shrugged. "But the griffins and the mountains would seem to track with all of this." I gestured towards the maps still lying on the table.

After a moment I added, "There's something else. I didn't get the impression they were the same timeframe. The battlefield on the mountain didn't happen at the same time. I think one was the past and the other the future. Or the present maybe?"

"Let's hope the battlefield was the past," Ryze said. "If that's the future, I'm going to be really, really pissed off."

"That might be the first thing you've said that I agree with," Cavan said. "I suggest we get to Havenmoor now. Take a look at that map before it's too late."

"I think we should take Hycanthe with us," Khala said softly. She sighed and started to explain.

"I can't believe you *fucking told them*," Hycanthe snarled. Only Jezalyn's hand on her arm kept her from lunging at me. She looked ready to scratch my eyes out.

Perhaps it was the proximity of two High Lords, the Commander of the Winter Court army, the master of assassins, and Dalyth that stopped her. All of them were watching us with varying degrees of interest or amusement. Or annoyance, in Vayne's case.

"I didn't have a choice," I said regretfully. "You put out that wind, didn't you?"

Hycanthe leaned back and glared at me. "I don't know what you—"

"You might as well tell her," Jezalyn said softly, her voice only loud enough for the three of us to hear. "Dalyth was there too."

Hycanthe gave her a glance that bordered on resentful before she exhaled loudly.

"Fine, yes I did. I got a burst of magic and somehow managed to put a bunch of warm air under the wind and force it up. I don't know how I did it, I just did. And then my magic went back to normal after that."

"You're tied to all of this," I told her. "You and Tavian. Ryze and Cavan. Maybe the rest of us too. Do you want to understand what's happening to you?"

"Do I have a choice?" she snapped.

"Of course you do," Ryze said. He stepped over and placed a hand on my shoulder. "You can stay here and let us figure it out, if we can. Or you can come with us and help us. I have a feeling what we find may be enlightening. You might be much more powerful than anyone realises."

She was clearly unsure whether she liked that idea or not.

I had to remind myself she'd been through the same thing I had, at around the same time. People deal with traumatic events in different ways. The only person she was sure she could trust was Jezalyn.

She'd trusted me enough to tell me about her magic and I'd betrayed that. I regretted hurting her, but not being forthcoming.

Cavan was right, keeping secrets was getting us nowhere. We had to be open with each other and work together to figure this out. The alternative was waiting for Hycanthe to speak out for herself, or asking Jezalyn to order her. I'd rather Hycanthe hated me than herself or her alpha.

"Aren't you at least a little bit curious about what we'll find?" Ryze asked. "Lost courts, forgotten magic." He grinned like a little boy.

"What if they don't want to be found?" Hycanthe asked. "What if the wind and that lightning bolt, or whatever it was, was a warning to stay the hells away?"

"Taking aim at my court isn't the best way to warn me off," Ryze said. "On the other hand, it's a really good way to *piss* me off. Either way, we're going. You can come with us, or you can stay here with Dalyth. Or you can go back to the Summer Court. Perhaps Cavan will lock you in the atrium again."

Cavan grimaced, but didn't rise to the bait. Evidently a hundred was enough times to say he only did it for our own good.

Hycanthe and Jezalyn stepped back and spoke in whispers for a minute or two. Finally, Jezalyn stepped forward.

"We're coming with you. But no matter what happens, Hycanthe and I stay together."

"I wouldn't have it any other way," Ryze said. He nodded and turned to Cavan. "You know Havenmoor better than I do. Will you make the portal?"

Cavan nodded. "I thought you'd never ask."

"I didn't want to," Ryze admitted, eyes twinkling. "But here we are." He spread his hands out to either side.

Cavan shook his head but half closed his eyes and placed his palms outward in the air. Where Ryze's portals looked like ice, his looked like fire.

I expected heat to radiate from it, but it was the same temperature as the air in the courtyard. Still, stepping through it was tentative at best. I half-expected to be roasted alive.

Ryze took my hand and walked through with me.

"Disconcerting, isn't it?" He looked up at the—was it a ceiling?—above us. "Walking through ice and snow makes more sense than walking through fire."

"I find them both disconcerting," I admitted. "Is that why mine won't stay open? Because walking through portals freaks me the fuck out?"

He laughed and pulled me closer, to tuck me to his side. "Possibly but probably not. The first time I went through one I made, I felt the same way, and it stayed open."

"It's just me then," I said with a sigh.

"I don't think it's just you," he said. "No more than it's Hycanthe's fault her magic isn't strong except at certain times. And Tavian seeing visions? Probably not a coincidence either. I don't know what any of it means yet. Hopefully we can get some answers."

"Hopefully," I agreed.

We stepped out into a stand of trees. Was it the same forest we'd spent the night when we ran from Dalyth and Cavan's Fae? That seemed like years ago now. Being here in their company was more than a little strange. Not until my feet were on the leafy ground did I realise I'd expected armed Fae to still be here waiting to attack.

In spite of everything Cavan said, trust was thinner than the layer of leaves under my boots.

Cavan closed the portal behind us and glanced around. "I see no sign anyone knows we're here, but us."

"Keep your eyes open for portals in the sky," Ryze instructed. "Or stray griffins."

"Or dragons," Tavian said teasingly.

"At this point, if a dragon appeared, I'm not sure how surprised I'd be," Ryze said wryly.

"Things certainly couldn't get stranger," Cavan said. "Who could have guessed you and I might be civil to each other for more than a minute or two?" Before Ryze could respond, he added, "Don't get too used to it."

"I wouldn't dream of it," Ryze told him. "Are we going to stand here talking, or are we going to Havenmoor?"

Cavan responded with a curt nod and started away to the north.

Tavian slipped over next to me. "Can you feel Zared?"

I'd been putting off feeling down the bond until now, scared of what I might find. While Tavian held my hand, I reached out.

"He's close," I whispered. "He can't be more than a kilometre or two away."

He seemed tired and angry. What was it that had him so upset? He felt like he was ready to punch someone. Could he feel me too? Should I send nice thoughts, or stay out of the bond?

I didn't know how he'd react to feeling anything from me. He might have felt me all along, and he might not. Better to wait until I saw him face to face.

Tavian squeezed my hand. "I still haven't ruled out stabbing Dalyth for messing with his memories." He looked ahead to where she walked a few steps behind Cavan.

"Me either," I said. She looked like she enjoyed it at the time. She seemed to take pleasure in the suffering of others. Pleasure that went way beyond doing what she was ordered to do.

I still hadn't resolved the fact Cavan was the one who told her to do it. Regardless of his reasons, it was difficult to forgive and impossible to forget.

Unless Dalyth made me forget.

"We may need her someday," Ryze said. He walked on the other side of me.

"Her magic anyway. She seems to be the only one who understands how yours works."

"Did you just admit you don't know something?" Cavan asked over his shoulder.

"Yes, but you don't know it either," Ryze retorted. "Mixing magic has always been complicated."

"Winter Court usually only breeds with Winter Court?" I asked.

"Not so much that," Ryze said slowly. "Usually if Fae from different courts breed, the offspring have one kind of magic or the other. Cases like yours are rare and special."

"How do spring and autumn magic work then?" I asked. "Isn't it a combination of hot and cold too?"

"Not really," Ryze said. "Spring magic is the magic of birth, rebirth and growth. Autumn magic is the magic of—not death exactly. Change, endings. Clearing out of old things to make way for the new. If summer magic can raze a field to the ground, autumn magic can turn the dirt, air it out to plant new seeds. It's good for cleansing things too."

"Nothing gets blood out of clothes like autumn magic does," Tavian said.

"That's good to know." I gave him the side eye.

"You never know when something like that will come in handy," he told me unapologetically.

"I suppose not," I agreed.

We moved quietly through the trees. I kept half an eye on the ground in front of me and half of my attention on the bond. The other three around me were comforting, but I couldn't help but focus on Zared. Every step drew me closer to Havenmoor. Closer to him.

"Are we going to walk into Havenmoor looking like this?" Hycanthe asked.

"You have another suggestion?" Dalyth asked, her tone scathing. "At some point, you're going to have to accept you're Fae now. The sooner you do that, the better."

Hycanthe stewed on that for a minute or two. "You don't think a bunch of Fae walking into Havenmoor won't go unnoticed?"

"They'll notice," Cavan said. "They've seen Dalyth and I there before, along with some of my guards. Not usually in these numbers, but I wouldn't be concerned. It's nothing we can't deal with if they give us any trouble."

"You're going to march into Havenmoor and start killing people?" Hycanthe asked in disbelief.

"There's no need for anyone to die," Cavan told her.

"Even your magic is strong enough to deal with anyone throwing stones or insults." Dalyth smiled at her sarcastically.

One minute Dalyth was standing there looking smug as fuck, the next minute she was flying through the air. She slammed into the trunk of a tree and dangled there, halfway off the ground, face red with annoyance.

"My magic is strong enough for that," Hycanthe said. Now who was looking smug?

"Put her down," Cavan said wearily.

"Where's the hurry?" Ryze asked. "I don't know about the rest of you, but I like her like that. It's nothing she doesn't deserve."

"Fuck off," Dalyth snarled. "Let me down."

She barely finished talking when she was struck in the centre of her chest. Her eyes widened. She opened her mouth to scream. No sound came out before she burst into flame.

"Fuck!" Ryze raised his hands and half a blizzard of snow roared out from the air. Where it met fire, it sizzled. The flames died out in moments.

Even before the smoke and steam cleared, the smell of roasting meat told me it was too late. Dalyth was nothing more than a blackened corpse, now lying at the base of the tree.

"Oh my gods." Hycanthe took several steps back before Jezalyn managed to grab her. "I didn't mean to... Oh gods."

"It wasn't you," Vayne said. He was looking at the sky over her shoulder. He shook his head. "It opened and closed so quick, I almost missed it."

"Another portal," Ryze said. He was staring at Dalyth's remains.

I turned to stare at Tavian. He seemed to be frozen on the spot, like he was in the library. There, but at the same time not there.

CHAPTER
TWENTY-ONE
KHALA

"Ryze," I said, to get his attention.

"What is it?" He too turned and saw Tavian. "Shit." He stepped over closer to the assassin master. Put a hand on his cheek. "He's colder than ice. Tavian? Tave?"

Tavian blinked a couple of times and shook his head. "Sorry, I was..."

"Let's sit you down." Ryze led him over to a tree and helped him to the ground. "What did you see?"

Tavian's eyes were glazed. "The same Fae as last time. They were talking to someone. I couldn't see who. It was dark. I wasn't supposed to be watching."

I crouched beside him. "What were they talking about?"

He shook his head slowly. "I have no idea. I could only hear a word or two. It sounded like they were arguing. Then the woman, Yala, she saw me."

"The person whose body you were in?" I asked.

He frowned. "No. She saw *me*. I don't know how. She looked shocked. She started to point to me, and then... I was back here." He looked around. Caught sight of the burnt mess on the ground. "What... Who?"

"Dalyth." Ryze sat down next to him. "Vayne saw another portal open and close. Something came out of it and hit her."

His gaze flicked towards Hycanthe and back again. "Where was she each time?"

I thought back for a moment. "The first time, I don't know. She was with Jezalyn. The second time, she was training with Dalyth."

I suspected Hycanthe had something to do with this, but not to this extent. Whatever 'this extent' was. To me, it seemed like she was stuck right in the middle of it. A place she clearly didn't want to be any more than I did.

297

"And the third time, Dalyth ended up dead," Ryze said thoughtfully. "And Tave keeps eavesdropping on strange Fae."

"Not on purpose," Tavian protested. "If it's all the same to you, I'd rather not do that again." His wide mouth twisted to the side like he tasted something unpleasant.

"Do you think Hycanthe did this somehow?" I whispered. Hycanthe wasn't my favourite person ever, but I couldn't really imagine her attacking people with anything but her words.

"Not purposefully," Ryze said. "At least, I don't think so." He looked over to Cavan and jerked his head to indicate that he should join us.

Both he and Vayne crouched down beside us.

"You're the closest thing to an expert in Summer Court magic," Ryze started.

Cavan raised his eyebrows, but didn't say anything. He gestured for Ryze to continue.

"Can you pin someone to a tree, open a portal, aim a blast of fire and actually hit the target, all at the same time?"

"At any other time, I'd make the claim I could," Cavan replied easily.

"So, no," Vayne said.

"No," Cavan agreed. "I could pin someone to a tree and make a portal at the same time, or do the other two, but not all of it at once. If you're volunteering, I could demonstrate." He smiled sarcastically.

"Only if I get to pin you to a tree afterward," Ryze said dryly.

Tavian made a choking sound in the back of his throat.

I had to bite my lip to keep myself from smiling.

Ryze sighed exaggeratedly. "Do your omegas have filthy minds too?" he asked Cavan.

Cavan grinned and glanced at me. "I hope so."

"There's no one to find you if I kill you and bury you out here," Ryze growled.

"You'd have to get past my guards first," Cavan pointed out.

"Our guard contingents are evenly matched," Ryze said. "But I have Vayne, which tips the odds in my favour."

"As fascinating as this conversation is," Vayne said, "I'd like to be somewhere not so open if whoever, or whatever, killed Dalyth decides to try again."

"It's good to see someone from the Winter Court has some sense," Cavan said. "I was starting to wonder." He gave me a look that suggested he didn't consider me part of the Winter Court. Presumably because of my mother, he thought of me as a Summer Court Fae. That was a conversation for another day.

He stood and offered me his hand.

I took it and stood, but released it the moment I was upright. Partly because I didn't want to create more conflict, and partly because the heat his touch sent through me made me want to pin him to a tree myself. That wouldn't go unnoticed.

"I have sense," Tavian protested. He pushed himself to his feet. "Right now my sense of smell is almost overwhelmed by the intoxicating scent of alphas. Maybe you can relax a little." He nodded toward Jezalyn to include her too.

Now he mentioned it, the scent was strong. Two alphas competing with each other and one protecting her omega. My own scent flared in response.

Ryze groaned. "Let's get out of here before we end up with an impromptu orgy in the middle of the forest." He adjusted the front of his pants.

"You say *impromptu orgy* like it's a bad thing," Tavian said.

"It's the middle of the forest thing that would be a bad thing," Ryze told him. "And as Vayne reminded us, we are somewhat out in the open."

"Yes we are," Cavan said in a way that made us all look at him. "Unless something has taken place that we're not aware of, then this always happens outside."

"And from the sky," Vayne added. "All the more reason to get inside."

Cavan nodded and turned to Dalyth's remains. He instructed a couple of his guards to remove her head and pack it carefully, then incinerate the rest of her. His expression was tight. Not exactly grief. More like annoyance with a dose of caution. What happened to her could have happened to any of us.

I made a note not to get in Hycanthe's way. Right now, she was standing with Jezalyn's arms around her, staring at what was left of Dalyth. Her eyes were wide and glossy. If somehow she did this, she definitely didn't do it on purpose.

I stepped over to them. "Are you all right?" I asked as gently as I could.

"What do you think?" Hycanthe asked. She exhaled a ragged breath. "I'm sorry. I just..."

"Khala understands," Jezalyn said. "We all know it wasn't you." She looked over at me meaningfully.

I wasn't sure we did know that, but I nodded anyway. "Of course we do," I said. "Whoever is on the other side of the portal took advantage of the moment. That's all. Dalyth was being obnoxious."

She deserved to get thrown against a tree, but did she deserve to die like that? I didn't have the answer. Or maybe I did and didn't want to admit to being bloodthirsty. After what she did to Zared, I couldn't bring myself to regret her death.

"Did your magic get stronger again?" I asked.

"I felt like I could have ripped the tree out by its roots," Hycanthe said. "I almost did, and then... What hit her? It looked like lightning."

"Lightning does seem to be their method," I said. "Lightning and wind." And strange visions of unknown Fae.

"You think the Court of Shadows is responsible, don't you?" Jezalyn asked.

I closed my eyes for a moment and tried to shut out the chopping sound as Dalyth's head was removed from her shoulders by a sword.

"Cavan thinks it is," I said finally. "I don't think the rest of us know what to believe. They'd have to exist, for one thing. For another, they'd have to have a grudge against one of us. For all we know, they were after Dalyth and now it will stop."

"I wish I could believe that," Jezalyn said.

Hycanthe hummed her agreement.

I didn't blame them. I wished I believed it too.

"Let's go," Cavan said when Dalyth's head was suitably wrapped and placed inside one of the guard's packs. The idea of carrying that around made me want to vomit.

The Fae method of preserving skulls was something else I'd have to get used to.

I remembered the line in the song about rows of skulls and wondered if somehow that had something to do with any of this. A pathway of the dead sounded nasty as fuck. Then again, opening portals and firing at people was also nasty as fuck.

"What are you thinking?" Ryze was in front of me, looking at me intently.

"I was thinking life as a Silent Maiden was a lot simpler than this," I said. "The worst thing we had to worry about was getting caught putting salt in the sugar containers. Or whether the cute priest would notice me."

He smiled and kissed my nose. "I know they would have noticed you. Although, if we see any of them at Havenmoor, let me know. I'll have Tave poke their eyes out."

I jabbed him in the side with my elbow. He grabbed my arm and pulled me in for a deeper kiss. We broke off when Vayne cleared his throat behind us.

"I don't think Cavan will leave without Khala, but he would totally leave without the great Lord Ryzellius."

Ryze waved Vayne away. "We'll catch up."

I laughed, grabbed Ryze's hand and pulled him behind me. "We all agreed we don't want to be out in the open. Let's get to Havenmoor."

He pouted, but let me drag him along.

As much as I liked the idea of being sidetracked and pinned to a tree, I needed to see Zared. I needed to know he was all right and could live his life without us. If I never saw him again, I'd have this. I could settle my mind, if not my heart.

We wound our way through the forest, moving carefully. We all glanced at the sky every few moments, always on alert for anything weird. Any strange sound, smell or sensation or sight.

Of course, that had me jumping at rustling from the bushes, or a bird soaring overhead.

One of the guards stepped on a twig, which cracked loudly, making us all jump.

If Jezalyn hadn't stopped Hycanthe, he might have ended up pinned to a tree, she was so startled.

By the time we reached the edge of the trees, we were all as twitchy as fuck.

"I think it would be a good idea if we stay close together," Cavan said.

"All the better to keep an eye on you," Ryze told him.

Cavan gave him a rude gesture with his middle finger, which for some reason made Tavian giggle.

"Maybe we can not argue amongst ourselves for a while," I suggested. "If we stay close together, we can help keep each other safe."

"Exactly," Cavan said, giving Ryze a long look.

Ryze nodded. "No one get complacent." He pulled me closer to him. "Keep your magic ready, in case you need it. You too, Hycanthe. If they come at us again with wind, we'll need all the heat we can get. I'll be ready with a shield of ice if they throw lightning at us."

"That sounds like a solid plan to me," Vayne said. He stepped in closer to the rest of us. Not having any magic, he must have felt slightly vulnerable. Not that he'd ever admit to it.

"Of course it is," Ryze said. He gave Vayne a cocky smile, but it wasn't as cocky as usual. He couldn't know what might come at us, if anything.

We walked for a few minutes until we found the road.

"Havenmoor is half a kilometre away, approximately," Cavan said. "I would have opened a portal closer, but the humans tend to... How do I put it? Shoot arrows first and ask questions later. Walking in won't scare them so much."

"Have you had to dodge arrows often?" Ryze asked him.

"More than I'd like to admit," Cavan said. "Humans are a twitchy bunch at best."

"And at worst?" I asked. I was half-human after all.

"At worst, they'll happily kill any Fae they see, just for sport. They won't stop to see if they recognise you. Were they to do that, they may suspect we did something to you to make you one of us."

Tavian grinned. "We did do something to her. I think she liked it."

I felt a tug on the bond and froze. "It's Zared."

CHAPTER
TWENTY-TWO
KHALA

"Where?" Ryze asked.

"Not far," I replied. "Up ahead. But he's upset, excited, angry. He's coming this way. I think they know we're here."

"Are you ready to dodge more arrows?" Ryze asked Cavan.

"If I have to," Cavan said. "It would be better to slip around them. Stay out of their way. We can get into Havenmoor, look at the temple and get back out again."

Ryze considered for a moment, then nodded. "Everyone off the road. We'll go through the bushes." He waved us ahead of him.

I gave him a pleading look, but he waved me off too.

"You heard what Cavan said. They won't look twice at any of us, including you. That bond might be confusing the hells out of him."

Reluctantly, I followed the others into the thick bushes, and kept low, close to Tavian.

"It'll be all right," he whispered.

I didn't know what he was basing that on, because right now it didn't feel all right.

"The smoke was coming from around here," a voice said.

Zared.

"It might be nothing," another voice said.

"I'm telling you, Ianic, there's something fucked as hells going on," Zared insisted. "It wasn't a random event. I can't explain how I know, but I know."

He stopped in front of the bushes. He was close enough to touch. Close enough to smell his cedar scent. He turned his face.

I'd swear he looked right at me.

"I don't see anything," Ianic said. "It was probably nothing more nefarious than a hunter cooking a rabbit."

"You're right," Zared said a bit too quickly. "I'm sure it was nothing. Let's get back to the temple. Tyla is probably waiting for you to fuck her mouth again."

Ianic chuckled. "She does like being on her knees."

I stiffened at the way they were talking about my friend. Not because I was ashamed of anything she did with Ianic, or anyone else, but he didn't seem to have much respect for her.

"You go on ahead," Zared said. "I'm going to take a piss."

"All right. I don't want to keep her and her mouth waiting." Ianic's footsteps crunched away down the road.

I held my breath while Zared stepped in front of the bush again.

"All right, you can come out and explain what the fuck is going on," he snarled.

"We're right here with you," Tavian whispered.

At the same time, Ryze gestured for everyone else to stay out of sight. He sent reassuring thoughts through the bond and pulled his bow off his back. He readied an arrow, then nodded to me.

Hopefully he wouldn't feel the need to use it. If he hurt Zared...

I put my hands in the air to either side of me and slowly stood.

"Hello." The smile I gave him was forced at best. Tentative in the face of his expression.

Zared stared at me with utter confusion. He squinted. Recognition, then shock crossed his features.

He shook his head and took a few steps back.

"What the fuck? I thought I could feel Khala. You look like her, but..." He reached a hand back and gripped the hilt of his sword.

"I am Khala," I said evenly. "I look a little bit different, that's all. It's still me. Your...your friend."

Dalyth said she removed his memories from after the attack on the caravan. We were only friends back then, although he'd wanted more. So had I, but I hadn't wanted to ruin things between us.

"The hells you are," he snapped. "What did you do to her? Why can I feel you? What did you do to me?" He looked at me with such fear and loathing, like I was some kind of monster.

I was starting to think I should have tried harder to stay away from him.

"I am Khala," I insisted. I took a step toward him. Then another.

He drew his sword and held it out in front of him, a hand away from my throat.

"Don't come any closer. I don't know who you are or what you've done, but you're not her. She's not *Fae*." He spat the word like he was disgusted.

I stopped still. "What do you remember of her? When did you see her last?"

He frowned. "I can't—"

"When did you see her last?" I insisted. If I knew that, I'd have some idea how much Dalyth took from him. Right now, she was lucky she was dead, because if she wasn't I'd kill her for this.

"Right after she had her choker taken off by that Fae. Did she do this? Khala was supposed to go to Havenmoor. Then... She was supposed to go somewhere else. Where is she?" His hands trembled slightly. The blade dipped and weaved in front of me.

"She's safe." I put up a hand to push the blade away, but he managed to hold it steady again.

"I don't believe you," he said. "What did you do to her?" He sounded so devastated a piece of my heart broke.

"You're right, that Fae woman did something. She wanted you to forget Khala. She changed your memories, but she's dead now. She won't be able to do the same thing to anyone else."

"Why would she do that?" he demanded.

"Because she was a sadistic bitch." That was accurate, if not entirely truthful. "She got pleasure out of messing with humans. I came here to see what damage she'd done. I'm sorry she did this to you. You didn't deserve this."

His mouth twisted. "She's dead?"

"Yes. That smoke you saw? That was her. She's been dealt with." I felt like a real Fae now, skirting around the truth while not lying.

I tentatively raised my hand and pushed the blade to the side.

"I know it's hard to believe anything I say, but Khala is fine. She... She wishes she could see you again. She hates what Dalyth did to you." I blinked back tears. If he couldn't accept I was me, then maybe this would give him what he needed. A final close of the door between us. A twist of the key in the lock.

"Why can I feel you?" he asked in a rough whisper. He dropped the sword down until the point almost touched the road. "Why do you feel like her?" His voice was choked with emotion.

All I could think to say was, "So I could find you. To make sure you're all right after what was done to you. It's a thing Fae can do. Are you all right?" I hated lying to him, but if the truth was too hard for him to take, I had no other choice.

He looked down at his sword for a minute or two, then put it back in its sheath.

"Of course I'm all right. It takes more than one Fae bitch to fuck with me."

That was the Zared I knew.

I forced a smile. "Of course it does. I'm glad you're doing well. I should let you go on your way. I have to make another stop before I return home. A visit to the Temple in Havenmoor. I have business there. An offering to make." He wouldn't refuse to let me go if I had a gift for the gods. The Fae visited rarely, but were always generous when they did. I overheard Geralda mention the fact once. Something about fine wine and a bag of money. Recompense for taking care of the maidens for the Summer Court, perhaps?

"That's where I'm going," he said reluctantly. "I can show you if you want."

"I'd appreciate that," I said graciously.

Without thinking, I reached out and touched his hand.

He jerked away as if my touch stung his skin.

Froze.

He clapped his hands to either side of his head and felt to his knees in the dirt. A jolt of pure agony surged through the bond.

"Shit, Zared!" I dropped down beside him and grabbed him before he could topple.

Ryze and Tavian darted out from behind the bushes and helped me lower him until he lay on the ground. His legs kicking, body writhing.

"Gods, what did I do?" His pain was so intense I swear I felt it too.

"Stop panicking," Cavan ordered as he too stepped out of the bushes. "You have the magic to ease his pain."

"I'm not going to—" I started.

"I'm not suggesting you kill him," Cavan snapped. "Focus."

Without knowing what I was doing, I placed my hands on either side of Zared's face, beside his. I pushed a combination of numbing cold and soothing warmth into him. That was when I found it.

"She didn't change his memories," I said absently. "There's a block. If I move it, will it kill him?"

"If you don't, this may kill him," Ryze said. I felt a sliver of his cold magic curl around mine. A moment later, Cavan added a dash of warmth.

"We've got him," Ryze said. "We'll try to keep the pain at bay while you deal with the block."

Zared still writhed, but the agony wasn't quite so bad.

I sucked in a breath. Cavan's order not to panic kept me from losing it completely.

I focused my attention and my magic on the block in Zared's mind. It felt like a wall made of pure thought. Like Dalyth created an idea and pushed it into place there.

Ideas, once settled into the mind, were always difficult to shift. This one was no different. It clung to him stubbornly even while he rejected it.

I closed my eyes and sent my own thoughts down the bond.

I am Khala. I was transformed into a Fae. I was always part Fae. You know all of this, you were there. I'm an omega. I went through heat and changed. You were there for that too. You're part of my pack. You were always meant to be part of my pack.

The block started to disintegrate, bit by bit. It clung on stubbornly, tendrils trying to dig invisible claws into Zared's mind. I teased away each one, until only one large piece remained. One particularly stubborn section. I poked at it with my magic.

Zared arched his back, threw his head back and howled in pain.

"Quickly," someone urged. I didn't know whose voice it was. It might have been Ryze's, or even Tavian.

I had no choice but to reach in and shatter the last piece of the block. For the longest while, it resisted. I growled in the back of my throat and pushed harder. Eventually the shard disintegrated along with the remaining fragments. A heartbeat later, nothing was left.

Zared writhed a couple more times before he finally fell still. His brow was covered with sweat, but his skin was frigid.

"Is he dead?" Hycanthe asked.

I didn't know when she and Jezalyn stepped back onto the road, but they were here now, leaning over us all. Hycanthe looked as worried as I'd ever seen her. Jezalyn clutched her arm.

"No," Ryze said. "But we won't know if he's all right until he's able to speak." He and Cavan both sat back.

I smoothed hair back off Zared's brow. "I shouldn't have come here. I shouldn't have touched him. That must have triggered something. Did Dalyth set booby-traps in people's minds in case things like this happened?"

"If she did, it's a good thing she's dead," Cavan growled. "I certainly didn't ask anything like that of her."

Ryze glanced at him, but turned away. "It's more likely to be the bond. You two being that close together, the bond fought against what Dalyth did. Zared's memories wanted to resurface. Chances are, this would have happened sooner or later anyway. If it happened when we weren't here, he'd be dead."

"He fought to remember me," Tavian said to lighten the mood.

I managed to give him a smile. "Of course he did. You're unforgettable."

"I am, aren't I?" He grinned.

Zared groaned and shifted slightly.

The next thing I knew, I was lying on my back in the dirt, Zared straddling my thighs. I was ready to fight back, but then his mouth slammed down onto mine.

"I think he remembers her," Tavian remarked with a laugh.

Zared's tongue thrust into my mouth. I managed to get my arms around him and opened my mouth so our tongues could tangle.

He tasted so good. The pain was gone from the bond, replaced by hunger. For me. For my body.

He slid his hands up my shirt and over my breasts. My nipples went hard under his palms.

"We can't just—" We were lying on the road in full view of everyone.

"Yes we can," he growled.

"We don't mind," Tavian said.

"I do," Hycanthe said. Because of course she would. I was tempted to fuck him then and there just for that.

"We've been out in the open long enough," Ryze said. "Your cock will have to wait a while longer."

Zared exhaled loudly and pressed his cheek to mine, his stubble scratching my skin. "Fine, but you all have a fuck ton of explaining to do." He rolled off me and helped me to my feet.

"You can start by telling me what the fuck he's doing here." Zared's hand was back on the hilt of his sword, his eyes on Cavan.

"We'll catch you up while we walk to Havenmoor," Ryze said. "Wait until you've heard all of that before you run Cavan through."

"Fine." Zared dropped his hand and took hold of mine. We walked side by side and I told him what he missed during the last few days. Including all the reasons why he probably shouldn't stab Cavan.

CHAPTER
TWENTY-THREE

KHALA

"So this is the shit you get up to when I'm not around," he said. "Lost Fae courts, melting stone and excessive wind. I can't believe I missed watching Dalyth become toast."

"One of the guards has her head in their bag if you want to look." I wrinkled my nose. "I don't recommend it. It's not pretty. Is Tyla all right?"

"She's fit right in at Havenmoor. She thinks you were sent to a temple in Freid or Gerian and that you're content."

"She's happy?" Since we didn't have a bond, there was no reason to expect her mind would fight the block. And if she was happy, there's no reason to remove it, even if she wasn't at risk. She was probably better off not remembering her time in the Summer Court.

"Happier than I was," he said. "I kept feeling like something was missing. The bond tugged at me. I thought I was imagining it. How could I be feeling someone else's emotions? I knew they weren't mine, but they had to be. Only they weren't." A heavy frown sat on his brow.

"No, because they were mine." I squeezed his hand. "What happens now?"

"What do you mean?" His brow uncreased. "This doesn't change anything. We're a pack. It sounds like we have a world to save or some shit. I don't belong in the Temple. But I can show you where that map is. No one will ask any questions about why you're there if I'm there too."

"Maybe the gods planned for this to happen," Tavian said. "It's the kind of fucked up thing they'd do. Mess with Zared so he could help us later."

"That's most fucked up thing I think I've ever heard," I said.

"That's because you're young," Ryze said. "When you get to our age, you will have heard a plethora of stuff way more fucked up than that. Although, that is pretty fucked up."

"As if the gods don't have better things to do," Hycanthe said scathingly.

Zared looked over his shoulder at her. "It's nice to see you haven't changed. Still as sweet as vinegar."

She stuck her middle finger up at him. "You're still annoying."

He turned to me. "You must have been really happy to see she was one of the maidens who transformed too."

I shrugged. "We have to learn to get along at some point."

"At least Hycanthe and I transformed together," Jezalyn said. "It would have been really awkward otherwise."

"Not necessarily," Tavian said. "You still would have been alpha and omega. Call me a romantic, but I think you would have ended up together anyway."

Jezalyn gave Hycanthe each other a loving look. "That's true. If I wasn't an alpha, it might have been difficult, but all I want is what's best for her." She leaned over to kiss Hycanthe's cheek.

Zared grimaced. "There's no accounting for taste."

I socked him lightly on the arm. "Be nice. Hycanthe is trying to save the world too."

"Exactly," Hycanthe said, looking smug. "All you're doing is being a distraction."

"He's an attractive distraction," Tavian said. "I, for one, am glad he's back with us." He didn't break his stride to put an arm around Zared and give him a hug.

"We're all glad," Ryze said. He gave Zared a warm smile. "Even though the last time I saw you, you would have happily cut my throat."

"The last time I saw you, you were happy to let Khala go into his palace." Zared jerked a thumb towards Cavan. "You were engineering a plan to have her get taken."

"As I recall, I suggested you leave Garial," Ryze said. "You insisted on staying. You were supposed to hide, remember?"

"You misjudged," Zared said.

"At least I didn't have him executed," Cavan pointed out.

"We're very grateful for that," I told him.

"You did all of that to help Hycanthe and me?" Jezalyn asked.

"They did all of that not knowing it was you and me," Hycanthe said. She glanced over to me. "Would you have bothered if you knew?"

"It didn't matter who it was," I said firmly. "I thought my sisters were at risk and I wanted to get you out, whoever you were."

Hycanthe looked disbelieving, but Jezalyn patted her arm and whispered in her ear. Soothing words, presumably, because Hycanthe backed down and fell quiet.

"Imagine all the hassle that could have been avoided if more communication took place," Cavan said.

"You're never going to get past that, are you?" Ryze asked.

"Twenty years of trying to tell you there's a risk that might destroy our courts? No, probably not."

"In that case, if you're wrong, I get to remind you every chance I get," Ryze told him.

"Since you're also walking on the road to Havenmoor, to look at a map, I'd suggest you're as wrong about this as I am," Cavan said. "At this point, we're equally invested."

"Maybe I'm just humouring you," Ryze said.

"I'd literally pay money to see them kiss each other," Tavian said with a groan.

Ryze and Cavan both turned to give him a look.

Tavian shrugged. "What? The sexual tension around here is hotter than that melted building."

Cavan and Ryze shared a look.

Ryze grimaced. "It is not sexual tension between me and him. It's a genuine, carefully cultivated dislike. Honed by years of him being an asshole."

"I was about to say exactly the same thing," Cavan said. "Although, I was going to say stubborn, ignorant asshole."

"I might be stubborn, but I'm not ignorant," Ryze protested. "We have years of mistrust between us. It's a centuries' old pattern. I had no reason to think anything changed."

"Except me sending envoys to try to get you to listen," Cavan snapped.

"See, sexual tension." Tavian sighed.

Ryze stopped in the middle of the road. "What envoys? None ever came from you talking about any of this."

"Because you didn't listen—" Cavan stopped too.

The only sound was the wind in the trees and the crunch of the guards' footsteps until they caught up with us.

"Not one word," Ryze said. "The Winter Court never got a word about any part of this from you or from anyone else. The first I heard of any of it were rumours about Silent Maidens being taken to the Summer Court, and the weather being screwed with. That was all relatively recent."

"They never returned." Cavan closed his eyes tight. He exhaled loudly out his nose, like an angry bull. "They never *arrived*."

His words fell in silence that lingered for a couple of minutes while we all absorbed the meaning and the implications.

"Who thinks they didn't make it past the Autumn Court?" Tavian raised his hand.

I raised mine as well. Ryze raised his, but Zared shrugged.

"Whether it's Harel or some other faction, someone has been working against us for a long time. Sowing the seeds of division between us. And we let them grow." Cavan opened his eyes. "Khala, what was it you said? Something about building bridges and getting over things."

"I was talking about you and my mother, but this is a good example too," I said. "We're all on the same side here. We don't have to like each other, but we need to stop being divided. That might even include Harel." I added that grudgingly because I really wanted to punch him in the face.

Cavan sighed and ducked his head for a moment before looking back up again. His generous mouth was pressed in a tight line.

"Let's get a look at this map first," he said. "Then we can make a plan."

"I can agree with that," Ryze said. "Although I have the horrible feeling that means going into the mist." He seemed more resigned when he talked about it now.

"It means whatever it means," Cavan said. "I think you all realise I'll do whatever it takes to stop our courts from being destroyed. Even if that means going into the mist and never coming back."

Ryze opened his mouth, probably to say something sarcastic, but he closed it again and nodded.

"You're right. I'll do whatever it takes to keep the Winter Court safe too. Even if I have to be nice to Harel."

"I'll tolerate him," Tavian said. "I don't promise to be nice."

"Me either," I agreed. I wouldn't rule out the possibility of telling him to fuck off again, if I had to. Especially if he called me names.

"I didn't see much of him and I also don't promise to be nice," Zared said. "He seemed like a prick to me."

"He definitely is," Ryze agreed. He resumed walking, but his expression was troubled.

I had a feeling realising Cavan tried so hard to warn him was a hit to his ego. He was so certain Cavan couldn't be trusted. That he was the one causing all the trouble in the first place. And now, it seemed he was very much wrong. Or at least misguided. He couldn't have known those envoys were sent and went missing, or were killed.

I stepped close enough to Tavian that I could speak low and not be overheard.

"Those assassins who went missing in the Summer Court, who were they sent to assassinate?"

Tavian glanced over at me. His apple and cinnamon scent was a comfort I needed amidst the turmoil and chaos. He was like a warm hug even when he didn't have his arms around me. Sometimes it was hard to remember he had anything to do with assassins at all. He seemed more likely to be in a bakery making cakes and tasty pies.

Instead, he could cut a person's throat without them knowing he was even there. Should that be as hot as it was? Possibly not, but it was anyway.

"Mostly business people who cheated on their business partners. Why?"

"Are you sure they disappeared and weren't working for someone else?" I asked. "Is there any chance they were keeping an eye out for any envoys, taking care of them and then slipping away?"

"It's not impossible," he agreed after a minute or two of thought. "Assassins tend to be loyal, but that doesn't necessarily mean they were loyal to me. If that's the case, they were in our midst for a long time. Creating discord and division and watching us."

"How long was Illaria in the Winter Court?"

"Years," it was Vayne who replied. He'd veered close enough to us to hear the last question. "I saw her there watching training at least once a week for years. I never considered her a threat."

"Whatever's going on, they're playing a long game," I said. A game that started before I was even born.

When would it end?

CHAPTER
TWENTY-FOUR
KHALA

The temple at Havenmoor was twice as large as the one in Ebonfalls. Weathered pale stone stood tall. Carvings around the doors had long since lost their definition. They might have once been flowers and vines, or random patterns. I couldn't tell.

In spite of that, everything was in a good state of repair. None of the stones were cracked. The mortar in the gaps seemed relatively new.

The biggest difference was the sound. Not just because my Fae hearing was better, but because priests, priestesses and those in training moved around, talking and laughing amongst themselves. It was a far cry from the Silent Maidens.

Until they noticed us.

Then they stopped to stare or hurried on their way.

"No arrows yet," Ryze remarked.

"Yet," Vayne said ominously.

"Give them time," Cavan added.

"They won't do anything," Zared assured them. "You're here with me."

"That doesn't fill any of us with as much confidence as you want it to," Hycanthe told him.

"If you prefer, I can tell them you forced me to bring you here." He pretended to genuinely consider the idea.

"How about you don't?" Vayne growled. "If you're sticking with us, you're still serving under me." He pointed a finger at Tavian before the Master of Assassins could comment on the potential innuendo.

Tavian raised his hands and grinned with mock innocence. "I wasn't going to say a word."

"Bullshit." Vayne lowered his hand. "We know you better than that."

"Where is this map?" Ryze was unusually tense. He didn't stop to banter with the others. His attention seemed to be everywhere at once.

I felt his high alert through the bond. Not alert against anything in particular, just on guard.

"This way." Zared looked relieved to change the subject.

I reminded myself he still hadn't gotten used to the whole idea of the Fae in the first place, much less his attraction to Tavian or any other man. That was something none of us would push, although Tavian would flirt. That was him. Unapologetically so. It was one of the things I adored about him.

We followed Zared through a side door, and into the cool interior. The dimly lit passageway was a stark contrast to the bright sunshine outside. Some people might have found it enclosing, but I found it comforting. Not just because of the attacks, but because it felt cozy.

As Tavian would say, it's an omega thing. We liked to feel safe and snug.

The layout of the temple was familiar. The passageway led to a wide hall for receiving gifts intended for the gods. That in turn led to a bigger hall, this one for prayers.

Several people knelt on the floor, heads down. None looked up as we walked past as silently as we could.

"Back here," Zared said softly. He opened the door to another room at the rear of the temple.

Another room for prayer, this one looked older than the rest of the temple. The stone was more worn, a faded rug on the floor. Cobwebs hung from the ceiling here or there.

Cavan stepped past Zared, and raised his hand. What looked like flame flickered over his palm and fingers, illuminating the wall.

I stared for a moment before realising I could do the same thing. I raised my hand and called on the magic. Instead of the warm, yellow-orange flame, mine was a silvery-white, like a cross between ice and fire. It lit up the wall where Cavan's didn't reach.

"Nice," he told me. "You're learning."

"Of course she is," Ryze said. "Khala is smart and competent. And gorgeous." He stepped into the light of my magic, kissed my mouth, then moved aside to look at the map.

"I noticed all of those things," Cavan told him, although most of his attention seemed to be on the wall in front of him. "Have you got that transcript and sketch?"

"I do." Tavian pulled the paper out of his pocket and unfolded it. He held it up in front of the wall, below the mountain range so we could all see.

"Havenmoor is down here." Zared pointed. "That's Ebonfalls. They look really close together here." They were less than a fingertip apart.

"Freid and Gerian are there," Cavan gestured. "Seasonal courts here, here, here, and there. Natanya is there."

"The mists are around here." Ryze traced a circle around the base of the mountains. An area that must have been at least fifty kilometres long.

"What is this?" I leaned in to peer at the area that was indicated on the paper map. Symbols were carved into the wall.

At first I didn't recognise them. It took me a moment to realise. "Those look like Silent Maiden hand signals."

"What does it say?" Ryze asked.

Tavian leaned in and squinted. "It says something about death. Death awaits... Death..." He looked over his shoulder at me.

"The closest I can interpret is death seeks," I said. "Death is looking. Looking for... An end? Or a beginning. Those two are similar, but neither are quite right."

I made the signs with my hands, but shook my head. "Either they wanted it to mean both, or the meaning has changed over time."

I looked at the next line. "Bone in rows. The song talks about skulls in rows."

"Anything about trees?" Ryze asked.

"The... Plant... Bush? That could be tree. The tree has answers or accepts the sacrifice. To open a... Window is the closest interpretation. To open a window, one must remain behind. Two who are one. Or one who will give everything." I shook my head. "That's about as much sense as it makes."

"So feed someone to the tree and get answers?" Tavian asked, possibly facetiously.

"The hells kind of tree is that?" Vayne asked.

"I'm going to go out on a limb here and suggest it's a hungry tree," Tavian said. "Pun not intended."

"That pun was totally fucking intended," Vayne told him.

Tavian grinned.

"Like I said before, I'm new to this Fae stuff, but I've never heard of a hungry tree," I said. "Hungry people, hungry animals—"

"Hungry pussies," Ryze said.

I snorted softly. "But never a hungry tree. I'm guessing they don't mean fertiliser." I looked around at them all.

"Why are they using hand symbols as a language?" Hycanthe frowned.

"It might be the language that came first and was turned into hand symbols," Ryze suggested.

"Or they did it so only a... select few could read it," Cavan said.

"You were going to say handful, weren't you?" Tavian asked him. "We don't mind puns around here."

Cavan gave him a funny look, then turned his attention back to the map. "There's more symbols down here. That's the pass leading into the mountains. Before Ryze's beloved mist."

"I'd say I can't wait to see the expression on your face if you go there," Ryze said. "But that shit is so thick, I wouldn't see it anyway."

Cavan ignored him. "Khala, what do these say?"

I had to crouch down to make them out. "Fire, ice, birth, death. A... Junction? Crossroads?" I shook my head. "Where all four meet comes a path." I stood. "I don't know what that means. Do we need someone from each of the seasonal courts?"

"Yes, but it's worse than that," Ryze said. "There's one place where all four courts meet. Neutral ground during times of conflict. Each High Lord, or a representative, has a key."

"It's called Nallis," Cavan said. "It can only be entered with all four keys."

"So we need Harel?" Vayne scowled.

"We don't need Harel, just his key," Ryze said. "Which he's not going to give up, no matter how nicely we ask."

Cavan pressed a finger to his lip. "So we're going to have to figure out how to get it without asking."

"High Lord Cavan, are you suggesting we steal it?" Ryze cocked his head, a faint smile gracing his lips. "I'm absolutely shocked."

"Try to contain it," Cavan told him, his expression deadpan. "Yes, we may have to steal it."

"So you really don't have an alliance with him?" Vayne asked. "Because it seems to me now would be a good time to have one of those. Or at least fake it."

Cavan's expression didn't change. "I never fake," he said. "I could probably get in the front door of his palace, but beyond that..."

"This would be easier if Harel wasn't an asshole," Ryze said. "But if there is a pathway through Nallis that means not going through the mists, I'll do just about anything to get there."

"Have you been there before?" I asked. "To Nallis, I mean."

"Once," Ryze replied. "There hasn't been a need ever since. I don't remember seeing a tunnel there, but I wasn't looking for one. Unless..."

"Yes, unless," Cavan agreed.

"Don't keep us hanging, unless what?" Tavian asked.

"Nallis has a guardian of sorts. No one really knows what it is, but it lives under the building itself. Every so often, you can feel it moving around. The earth rumbles. If I was going to have a hidden tunnel, that's where it would be."

"I think we should include Harel in this," Tavian said. "He can supply his key and then this guardian can have him for lunch while the rest of us run like hells."

"I can get behind that suggestion," I said.

"Me too," Zared agreed. "So, how do we steal his key?"

"We make a plan," Ryze said.

"Khala and I will go," Cavan said softly. "I can get us in, and keep him distracted. Any of the rest of you would be too suspicious."

"I did tell him to fuck off," I pointed out. I wasn't sure how I felt about any of this.

"But then I punished you and you've learnt your lesson," he said. "He'll believe that I wanted to show you off. To prove that you're beaten."

Ryze snorted.

I was inclined to agree. Pretending to be broken seemed like a stretch, regardless of what was at stake.

"If I have to, I'll order her to behave like she's scared of me, and won't dare to disobey." Cavan gave me a heated look like he wouldn't mind acting out this fantasy.

A sliver of heat went through me and pooled between my legs. I liked when Zared ordered me around. I suspected I'd like it very much if Cavan did it too.

"I hate to say it, but that makes sense," Tavian said. "If you can get both of you in, I sneak in and help where I can. No one would believe Ryze is paying Harel a social call. That puts Vayne out too. And if somehow those attacks have something to do with Hycanthe, she's better off staying out of sight somewhere."

"You go in, do what you have to do and get out immediately," Ryze told Cavan. "And if you get her killed..."

"I won't get her killed," Cavan said evenly. He closed his hand and the magic light went out. "We should leave first thing in the morning. Zared, is there somewhere we can spend the night?"

"Yes, there are visitors' quarters beside the temple," Zared said. "I'll show you where, but then I'd like some time alone with Khala. There are some things we need to sort out."

After getting his memories back, he probably had at least a million questions. I'd answer them as best I could, although I wasn't sure how much I knew. I didn't know why my touch made the bond push back so hard. I didn't know if it would work on anyone else, bond or no bond. I didn't know if everyone had a block like he did, and I didn't much want to find out. I didn't want to be like Dalyth, violating other people's minds.

Did he feel like I'd violated his? He said he wanted to stay with us, with me, but what if he changed his mind? I hoped like hells he wasn't about to ask me to put the block back. Even if I wanted to, I wasn't sure I knew how.

If he asked me to, I'd try. That was all I could do.

CHAPTER
TWENTY-FIVE
KHALA

"If I haven't said it before, I'm sorry you got dragged into all of this in the first place."

I turned to Zared as he closed the door behind us. "We should have been better prepared back in the Summer Court. Or stayed in the Winter Court. Or—"

There was a lot I felt I needed to apologise for. He'd been dragged over the proverbial coals because of me. He could have died. I never would have forgiven myself if he had.

He shrugged. "None of that matters now." He grabbed my wrists and pulled me to him. "Be honest. How much of you coming here was about seeing that map and how much was it about me?" He looked me dead in the eyes.

I met his gaze unwaveringly. "The map was an excuse to see you. I had no idea touching you could bring back your memories."

His grip on my wrists tightened. "If you knew, would you have touched me?" His pretty hazel eyes searched mine, unashamed desperation burning there.

I knew what he needed to hear. I had to take a few moments to consider the question. I wanted to give him total honesty. He deserved that.

"If it wasn't for the bond, you would have accepted what I told you when I said the human version of me was content," I said slowly. "You would have returned to the temple and that would have been that."

He shook his head, dark hair falling over one eye. "I would have known something was missing. I would have tried to find out where you were. And when I couldn't find you... I couldn't just move on. The gods meant for us to be together. I fully believe that."

"You believe in the gods?" I couldn't help the light tease. "I remember now.

Your favourite is the god of jokesters. If he intended for us to be together, then what does that mean?"

Zared grimaced. "It means we make each other laugh?" he ventured.

He closed his eyes and exhaled out his nose before he opened them again. "You didn't answer the question. Would you have touched me?"

I glanced down towards his muscular chest, then back up again. Gods, he was so handsome it was ridiculous.

"I know people seem to think I'm selfless and caring. I'm not. I'm selfish. So many times I knew I should push you away but I couldn't. I didn't, because I wanted you to be with me. So, yes, I would have touched you if I knew it would make you remember me. I need you. I'm sorry, that probably makes me a total bitch." If he had any sense, he should have run away from me.

Instead, he immediately said, "Not at all. If the situation was reversed, I'd touch you too, in a heartbeat. I always had trouble keeping my hands off you anyway." He raised my wrists, tugging me until our chests met.

"Really?" I teased. "I hadn't noticed."

He grinned, then slammed his mouth down onto mine. His tongue shoved its way between my lips and rammed almost down my throat.

I sucked like it was his cock.

I didn't hear the door open and close, but then Tavian spoke. "Do you mind if I join? I brought a little something."

Zared and I broke apart and turned to the Master of Assassins.

Tavian raised his hand. In his palm he held a bottle of lubricating oil.

I glanced back at Zared. Anything that happened between him and Tavian had to be his choice. Truthfully, the idea of them together sent wet warmth right between my legs. If they both wanted it, I was one hundred percent here for it.

After what felt like a lifetime of held breaths, Zared finally nodded. "Are you as obedient as Khala?"

Tavian grinned with relief and excitement. "Definitely. Tell us what you want your dutiful omegas to do."

The heat between my legs grew to inferno level. My whole body trembled with anticipation.

Zared rubbed his chin in thought. "Take each other's clothes off." He grabbed a chair from the side of the room, turned it to face the bed and sat down. He leaned back and crossed his knees, one eyebrow raised.

He reminded me a little of Ryze, but now was not the time to vocalise such a comparison.

"You heard the man," Tavian said. He started oh-so slowly unbuttoning my shirt and slid it off my shoulders. When it pooled on the floor, I did the same to him.

He undid my pants and I shimmied out of them, and my panties. I kicked them aside and helped him out of his.

319

I glanced over to see Zared with his own pants undone, stroking his hand over his own erect cock.

"Lie down on your stomach," Zared said to Tavian. "Your feet are still on the floor."

"Yes sir." Tavian did as he asked. He lay face first, his legs hanging off the end of the bed, legs apart, ass in the air.

Zared grabbed up the lubricating oil and handed it to me. "Prepare his ass for me."

Holy gods, yes please. Just when I thought I couldn't get any hotter and wetter with anticipation, I did.

Surprised by his confidence and eagerness, I took the jar, unscrewed the top and dipped my fingers inside. I warmed it with a bit of magic and eased a finger carefully inside Tavian's rear hole. He was warm and tight. The idea of Zared's cock sliding in there...

"Is this all right?" I asked.

Tavian groaned. "More than all right. Use more fingers to stretch me. Don't be afraid to hurt me. If Ryze can fit in there, your fingers can."

Now there was a mental image to keep a girl warm on a cold winter's night.

I slid in another finger, and another. My body throbbed and ached while I finger fucked the Fae man. I slid my fingers in and out, harder and faster while he writhed and moaned with pleasure.

"My turn," Zared said. He waited until I slid my fingers out before tentatively replacing them with his own, larger fingers. His throat bobbed as he swallowed, but in a matter of moments he thrusted as firm as I had.

"Gods yes," Tavian groaned.

He rolled onto his side until I was able to slip my lips over his cock. With both of us working him from either side, he was powerless to do anything but cum with a series of breathy groans and grunts, spilling his cum into my mouth.

"Swallow it," Zared said insistently.

I lifted my head up high enough for both of them to see, then deliberately swallowed down every delicious drop.

"Good girl. Come here," Zared ordered. He pushed Tavian gently back onto his stomach and grabbed my hand until I was sitting on Tavian's back, my legs to either side of me to take most of my weight.

Zared ran his hand up and down his cock a couple of times, then positioned it just outside Tavian's ass. His eyes half closed in concentration, he pressed himself inside. At the same time, he slid his hand down to rub over my clit and kissed my mouth.

I leaned back a little and wrapped my legs around Zared's waist.

Feeling him sliding in and out of Tavian while working me was one of the hottest things I'd ever experienced.

Judging by the moans and groans from Tavian, he felt the same way.

"Fuck, this is..." Zared ground out between kisses. "So fucking good." He thrust into Tavian with smooth, even strokes, matching those with circles around my clit. "Come for me."

I didn't want to come so quickly, but I couldn't contain it. Everything about this was so erotic. I tipped over the edge, groaning and dripping all over Zared's fingers and Tavian's back.

Zared came a moment or two later, his body still with heavy tension until his balls released his hot cum into Tavian's ass. He bit down on my lip at the same time, forcing a second orgasm out of me from sheer delight at the pain. Not even the coppery taste of my blood could deter me from the burst of pleasure.

Zared panted against my mouth for a long while before sliding his cock free.

"Any time you want to do this again, I'm all for it," Tavian said. "Although, my cock is already hard again." He made a face of mild discomfort.

"Good," Zared said. "Fuck her." He placed his hands on my hips and raised me up so Tavian could roll over onto his back. Carefully, he lowered me onto Tavian's erect cock.

"Yes, sir," Tavian said breathlessly. He placed his hands on my waist, just above Zared's and thrust up into me as I looked Zared in the eyes.

Zared worked his hand back between us and over my clit again. "I want you both to come at the same time."

I didn't think I had another orgasm in me until I heard those words. The moment they were out of his mouth, another burst of desire rose inside me. The need to please him as well as the need to feel good. It wasn't the same as the need to please an alpha. This was the desire to please my lover, to let him dominate Tavian and me. In this moment, he could have asked almost anything and we would have done it. An orgasm seemed like a small thing to give him.

When it came, it was a big thing, intense, travelling all the way through my body, clenching Tavian's cock and drawing a second orgasm out of him at the same time.

My breasts bounced as I ground onto Zared's hand and Tavian's cock. All thought went out of my head except the extreme pleasure as I shattered completely, coming apart around them in a flood of my cum and Tavian's.

I cried out long and loud until I came back down to earth with a sag and breathless pants. Tavian sounded much the same way, puffing and sagging back against the mattress.

"Gods, you two are amazing," Tavian whispered.

"I was going to say the same about you two," I said.

"I'm glad you came for me," Zared said. "In both meanings of the word."

"We'll always come for you," Tavian told him. "Always."

An exhausted murmur of agreement was all I could manage. I was definitely eager to do this again.

CHAPTER
TWENTY-SIX

KHALA

"Do you come here often?" I asked. We stepped through the portal and onto the paved street that led to the Autumn Court's palace. Cavan raised his elegant eyebrows at me but didn't answer.

Marial was undeniably magnificent. Tall towers swept toward the sky, each looking as though they were made from red-brown leaves.

Elegant bridges stretched across a river that glimmered like polished copper in the early morning light. The iron railing on either side was formed into the shapes of leaves, the top rail worn smooth from countless years of hands swiping past.

The streets were lined with shops, all in neat rows. Their storefronts were each adorned with autumnal colours of orange, red, and gold.

Even this early, the conversations of merchants and patrons filled the streets. Each one seeming tense, forced.

The buildings closer to the palace were all constructed of dark stone and iron, also giving the appearance they were made of leaves.

I stopped to appreciate the way they were cut and placed with such careful precision. Masons must have taken years to perfect the art. Constructing each one would have taken the better part of a year. The effect was striking.

I felt as if I was encased in autumn.

"Through here." Cavan led me toward a set of tall gates with the same pattern as the bridge railing. "Remember you're obedient, broken and very sorry you were rude to him."

"I'm not sure I can fake the last one," I muttered.

"Try, or I'll order you," he said simply.

"Have I mentioned how unfair that is?" I glanced sideways at him.

"You might have mentioned it. In this instance, it might work in our favour.

Perhaps I should order you now and save any potential hassle later." He gave me a speculative look in return.

"I think you just want me on my knees." I kept my eyes down, as though I really was beaten.

"I definitely want you on your knees," he replied. "But not if I have to order you. Where's the fun in that?"

"You're not shy about asking for what you want," I observed.

He chuckled. "I've always found it easier to be forthcoming. So to speak."

"Even if Ryze wants to stab you every time you look at me?"

"Especially then," he agreed. "I've never let someone like him get in my way. I don't intend to start now."

I was attracted to him, in spite of the complications. Maybe in part because of it. Nothing worth having was never easy.

For now though, I needed to concentrate on why we were here.

I deliberately flinched away from the guards as we walked through the gate, and wrapped my arms around myself. I felt the weight of their gazes on me, but none made a move to stop us. As far as they knew, we were what we appeared to be. The High Lord of the Summer Court and his broken omega.

The palace itself was a sprawling building made of a lighter stone than the rest of the city. If Marial was the red of autumn, the palace was the yellow and gold. Towers, spires, and domes topped the vast complex, each one covered in what looked like shining gold leaf, adorned with intricate carvings of autumn leaves and vines.

"Walk a little behind me," Cavan muttered before we stepped through the enormous doors that led into a wide courtyard. "But stay close. Act like I own you now and you know it."

"You're having way too much fun with this," I whispered back.

"Yes, and I intend to keep having fun with it. Quiet now. Let me do the talking."

I swallowed hard. Gods, that was hotter than it should be.

I followed him through the courtyard, my eyes on his way too perfect ass.

I was enveloped in the rich, spicy scent of autumn.

The air was cool and crisp. The leaves on the trees rustled gently in the breeze. Here, it felt like the unseasonable warmth everywhere else didn't exist.

I sensed it was exactly like this regardless of the time of year, or the season. Undoubtedly the result of some kind of magic.

We were greeted by more guards in front of a door that led into the palace. They looked like they might stop us from entering until they realised who Cavan was.

"High Lord Cavan." One snapped to attention. His eyes slid to me for a moment, then away like I was nothing more than a dog at Cavan's heels.

I forced my eyes down lower before my annoyance was too obvious. We'd never find the key if we didn't even make it through the door.

"You can announce my arrival to High Lord Harel," Cavan instructed.

"Yes, my Lord." The guards jumped to do as he was told. He hurried inside and spoke to someone.

After what felt like ages, he re-emerged. "My Lord will see you." He stepped aside to let us in.

"Of course he will." Cavan swept past like he owned the place. He was the absolute epitome of arrogance. If I had to decide who was cockier, him or Ryze, I'd be hard pressed to do it.

I hurried along behind him, keeping as much distance from the guards as I could.

I even managed to ignore when one of them muttered something about me being, "The Lord of Summer's slut." Apparently the Autumn Court Fae were all judgemental assholes.

The inside of the palace was as stunning as the outside. The walls were covered with tapestries of golden leaves, and richly coloured murals depicting the different seasons.

The floors were made of polished red-brown stone which reflected the sunlight that slanted through wide windows set high in the wall. Chandeliers dangled from the ceiling, dripping with gold and glass. Like everywhere else, they were shaped like leaves.

We were greeted by a courtier dressed in autumnal colours, and a couple of other guards.

"Lord Cavan," the courtier said smoothly. "To what do we owe the pleasure of your presence today?"

"Daniek." Cavan sounded bored. "I've come to meet with Harel. I'm sure you wouldn't want to keep him waiting."

Daniek smiled ingratiatingly. "Of course not. Come along then." He barely managed to contain his irritation at Cavan's obvious disinterest in telling him anything.

Hopefully I was better at containing my smirk. People like Daniek liked to gather up gossip, and didn't mind spreading it around. I'd bet the moment he was away from us, he'd be telling someone about us, and speculating about the reason for our visit.

Once again, I hurried along behind Cavan as if I was scared to let him out of my sight. I kept my gaze at the floor, trying to cover my annoyance.

I'd never been shy, or timid. Pretending to be so now was difficult and uncomfortable.

Better than being ordered to behave this way. If nothing else, the situation reminded me how vulnerable omegas were to alphas.

The throne room was perhaps the most magnificent thing I'd seen since stepping foot in Marial.

The walls were lined with mirrors that reflected light from two ornate chandeliers, making the room glow with warm, golden light.

The throne itself was carved from dark mahogany, and inlaid with rubies

CROWN OF MIST AND HEAT

and topaz, and yet more gold leaf in the shape of leaves. No one would ever mistake which court we were in.

I glanced up briefly to see Harel on the throne, legs crossed at his knees. He looked at Cavan like he was a supplicant come to beg for his favour.

He looked at me like I was less than nothing.

I forced my eyes back down before I told him to fuck off again.

"Isn't this an interesting surprise," Harel drawled. "Cavan, and Ryze's whore. Or is she yours now? Perhaps she spreads her legs for both of you?"

I ducked my head down lower, as though ashamed of his words instead of being pissed off as fuck.

"Ryze got tired of her attitude," Cavan said. "He gave her to me to teach her how to behave. She didn't learn quickly, but she learnt thoroughly. I thought you'd appreciate seeing her, since she put our alliance in jeopardy. She's been a lot of trouble, but she's very sorry for every, every moment of it."

He gave the impression he beat me until my skin was raw and I was begging him to stop. Which led me to wonder what it would feel like if he spanked me.

Focus, I told myself.

"Is she now?" Harel slid off his throne and stepped towards us. He grabbed my chin in a tight grip and forced my face up.

I averted my eyes and swallowed like I was scared instead of in pain from the way his fingers dug into me.

"This is a delightful change from the mouthy slut. If I'm convinced she really is as broken as you say she is."

"Why would I bother to lie about something like that?" Cavan asked, sounding bored again.

"Perhaps your new allies proved unreliable," Harel said. "You wanted a way back into my good graces."

Only by sheer will, I managed to contain a snort. He wasn't just an asshole, he was delusional.

"I was never going to align with Ryzellius or Thiron," Cavan said. "They believed my reasoning for bringing all those omegas to my court. As a gesture of good faith, Ryze left this one with me. She's used goods, but when she's on her knees, she can do incredible things with her mouth."

"They actually think those other courts are real?" Harel asked derisively.

"I don't care what they think," Cavan said. "They'll stay out of my way the next time the Temple moves any potential omegas. Out of *our* way."

"So you're keeping your promise to send some to me." Harel leaned in until his breath brushed my cheek.

I didn't need to fake my trembling. Being this close to him made me want to jerk my face away and drive my knee into his groin. I smelled alpha on him, thick and unyielding.

Cavan better fucking know what he was doing.

"Of course," Cavan said lightly. "We have an agreement. We build our magic and our courts become more powerful. When the time comes, we move against The Spring and Winter Courts."

That was exactly what Ryze assumed Cavan and Harel were up to in the first place. It sounded chilling coming from his mouth. Hopefully it wasn't the truth after all. If it was, he'd get a whole lot more than a knee in his groin.

Harel shoved me away so hard I almost fell on my ass.

I managed to keep my footing and moved closer to Cavan, as though scared of Harel. Honestly, I was ready to see if I could freeze or boil his brain. Maybe one, then the other.

Harel chuckled. "I like her much better like this. I'd insist on borrowing her, but I don't like 'used goods,' as you put it. Especially if Ryze had his cock in her. Broken or not, she's still a tainted whore. What will you do when you tire of her?"

"I'll give her to my men to play with," Cavan replied. "They aren't so fussy about where their pussy comes from."

As disgusting as this conversation was, I was relieved Harel had no interest in touching me. For a moment there, I thought he might insist on being shown I was broken.

The last thing I wanted was any of his body parts inside any of mine.

I shuddered.

Let them think it was because I was fearful of a future in which I was passed around Cavan's guards. That wasn't a lie, I didn't want that to happen either.

TWENTY-SEVEN
KHALA

"It seems we have a lot to discuss." Harel flopped back onto his throne so heavily I was surprised it didn't break. Judging by the wear on the seat and the arms, it was as old as either of the Fae men. It must be well made to withstand that kind of treatment.

"Indeed we do," Cavan agreed. "I appreciate the opportunity to enjoy your hospitality."

"I'm sure you do." Harel hadn't offered, but Cavan worded it in a way that he'd be rude to decline.

I didn't think Harel gave a fuck about being rude, but presumably there was some protocol between High Lords, especially when there were courtiers hovering nearby.

Harel waved one of them over and told them to tell the kitchen to prepare for a lunch guest. Evidently I didn't exist. That was fine with me. The sooner he forgot about me, the better.

"Make a room too," Harel added. "I'm sure Cavan will want to stay for a night or two." He looked like he wanted Cavan to refuse, but Cavan smiled.

"It would be my pleasure. Only for a night or two. I wouldn't want to impose any longer than that."

"Of course." That was obviously too much by Harel's standards, but if nothing else, he needed the alliance. Wanted the omegas and their magic.

What did Ryze say about Autumn Court magic? That it was related to death. That didn't sound like a power Jorius needed more of.

"If you'll follow me, I'll show you to your room," Daniek said. "I'm sure you'd like to rest before lunch."

"Certainly," Cavan agreed.

Considering the day's exercise consisted of making a portal from Havenmoor, stepping through it, and walking through the streets of Marial for ten or twenty minutes, I didn't think a rest was warranted.

On the other hand, I was happy to be away from Harel and his courtiers. I hadn't looked, but I knew they were watching, listening and judging. I didn't care what they thought, but I didn't want to be on display either.

I stayed close to Cavan as we followed Daniek out of the throne room and down the ornate corridor.

Like everywhere else in the Autumn Court, the bedroom the courtier led us to was opulent.

The air was thick with the scent of sandalwood. The walls were adorned with tapestries depicting scenes of what I assumed were Fae mythology. Rich autumn colors adorned every surface, from the yellow-gold curtains to the russet velvet cushions piled high on the enormous four-poster bed.

The bed was made of carved oak, with intricately detailed posts which reached almost to the high ceiling. Silk sheets embroidered with gold thread were tucked in neatly across the top of the mattress and pillows.

Matching nightstands sat on either side of the bed, their carved wooden legs gleaming. A plush armchair stood in each corner, their front feet sinking into thick woven rugs on the polished wooden floor.

Sunlight poured through a set of double doors that led out to a balcony overlooking lush gardens below.

At the far end of the room, a fireplace dominated the wall, its stone mantel intricately, and somewhat excessively, covered with carvings of flowers and animals. It looked as though a fire hadn't been lit in there for a long time.

"Thank you." Cavan dismissed Daniek with a nod.

The courtier looked less than pleased, but he backed out the door and closed it behind him with a bow.

Cavan sighed and his posture relaxed visibly.

"He doesn't spare any expense, does he?" I looked around at everything. It must have cost a High Lord's ransom just to decorate this room.

"Not when he's trying to impress his guest," Cavan agreed.

"Guest, singular." I raised an eyebrow at him. "He doesn't like to make a girl feel welcome, does he?"

"Harel isn't a fan of women," he said.

"You don't say," I said sarcastically. "He doesn't seem to be a fan of anyone but himself. You didn't mean any of that, did you?"

I placed my hands on my hips and gave him a level look. The ability to look him almost eye to eye might be one of my favourite things about being Fae. If I was human, I'd have to crane my neck.

"Which bit?" he asked, feigning innocence.

"Most of it," I told him. "You're not really gathering omegas for our power, right? You're not planning to invade the other courts? You're certainly not handing me over to your men."

"No. No. And definitely *not*," he said. "I bet I wasn't lying about your mouth."

He stepped towards me, gripped my shoulders and pushed me until my back was against one of the bed posts.

Heart racing, I looked back at him. "Did you and my mother ever..." I wasn't sure why I needed the answer to that, but I did.

His responding smile was brief, but he clearly understood why I asked the question.

"No, never. Her heart and body were always with your father."

Relief rushed through me. I wasn't sure what I'd do if his answer was yes, but I was fucking glad it wasn't.

"And mine are with you," he added before he slammed his lips down onto mine.

I'd thought about doing this a lot, in spite of my connection with the other four men. He didn't disappoint.

I slipped my arms around his neck and kissed him back.

"How's that?" I asked when I finally broke off the kiss.

"Good for a start." He scooped me up like I weighed nothing and placed me on the bed.

While my heart raced, he started to slowly undress me, bit by bit, kissing my skin as he bared it.

"I've been thinking," he said as he traced lines across my stomach with his tongue. "If you're supposed to be broken, shouldn't you know how it feels to be spanked?"

"How do you know I don't already know?" I replied.

He picked up his head and cocked it at me. "Do you?"

"Yes," I admitted. "I wasn't always perfectly behaved when I was a Silent Maiden."

He chuckled. "Why does that not surprise me in the least?"

"I have no idea, I'm sure," I said innocently. "Maybe they strapped me for their own enjoyment."

His mouth drew back. "That wouldn't surprise me either. What about you, though? Did you enjoy it?"

"Is it wrong if I say I did?" I winced.

"Not even a little bit," he assured me. "Would you like to feel it again?" He kissed around my belly button.

Fuck yes, please.

"Do I have a choice?" I asked teasingly. "If you own me, shouldn't you do whatever you want with me?"

He turned his face to the side so his cheek was resting on my belly. "Good point. I think I will. But tell me if I go too far for you."

"If you go too far, you'll know about it," I assured him.

"Just make sure to be loud," he said. "No doubt someone will be listening. You might as well make it sound convincing."

"It sounds like we need a safe word then," I said. "If I'm supposed to be screaming at you to stop, then I might send you the wrong message."

"Good point," he said. "Let's go with something in context, but that you might not shout out in pleasure. Something like, *I hate you*."

I grinned. "It's good to see you're as crazy as all the other Fae. If you're supposed to be sadistic, that isn't going to stop you."

He blew a warm breath across my stomach. "You're right. Maybe something like 'yellow.' If anyone was listening at the door, it would sound like, hells no."

"Suitably sadistic, but just about right." I nodded.

"Good. Now be a good slut and roll over onto your stomach."

I gave him a look but did what he said.

"I've been waiting for this for too long." He nibbled at my ass cheek until I wriggled. Chuckling, he propped himself up on his elbow and brought his hand down hard on my bare skin.

A shock of pain and pleasure surged through me, sending heat to my core. I groaned in pleasure.

"You like that?" He brought his hand down again, harder this time.

I gasped out my nose. My whole body was trembling with need. I wanted him to keep spanking me. At the same time, I wanted him to drive himself deep inside me. To pound into me until I screamed.

"Harder," I said breathlessly.

"Is that how an omega talks when she addresses the alpha who owns her?" he asked.

I whimpered. "Harder, please, alpha."

"That's better." He slapped me harder and harder, until my eyes started to water.

My pussy was dripping by now. My senses were in overdrive. I sucked in a breath. The dominant alpha scent of him filled my nostrils and flooded through me, right down to the heat between my thighs.

I cried out louder with each strike, part pleasure, part pain. Right before I shouted out yellow and begged him to stop, he stopped.

I wasn't aware of him removing his pants, but then he was parting my legs with his hands and sliding his cock inside me.

He leaned over and spoke into my ear. "Your ass is a perfect shade of red."

"Perfect for the Autumn Court, alpha?" I asked jokingly.

"Perfect for anywhere, omega," he replied. He began a series of slow, lazy thrusts into me. "You're perfect for anywhere."

His cock felt so incredible, driving into me, pure pleasure after all the pain.

He slipped out of me, rolled me over into my back and knelt between my legs. He slid his hands under my thighs and cupped my ass. He pulled me forward until only my shoulders and head rested on the mattress, my back suspended in the air between us.

I wrapped my legs around his hips as he pressed his cock back into me.

I placed my arms to either side of me, bracing me and using my hands to rock my hips in rhythm with his thrusts.

I locked my eyes on his and watched his expression of bliss as he pounded over and over again into my body.

"Gods, you feel incredible," he whispered.

"So do you," I said back. With every thrust, his knot rubbed and nudged my clit, driving me ever closer to an orgasm.

"You don't hate me?" he teased.

"I definitely do," I joked. "Such an asshole, alpha." I rocked harder, drawing closer and closer.

"It seems I didn't spank you hard enough." He grinned.

"Oh you did," I assured him. I scrunched my eyes closed.

"Keep them open," he said. "I want your eyes on me when you come. Look right at my face."

I opened them and focused on his intense blue eyes. The colour of the sky in the middle of summer. He was the epitome of his court. Bright and hot and compelling. The more I got of him, the more I wanted. The more I needed.

I arched my back as I came around his cock. The smile that graced his lips brought me higher and higher, before breaking me apart in the most perfect, explosive way possible.

My pussy milked his cock, pulling an orgasm out of him. His whole body went rigid and still. He grunted hard, grinding himself against me, spilling himself inside me.

"Fucking gods, yes," he breathed. "Khala you are...everything." He sagged forward, panting heavily before lowering us both down to the mattress and pulling me close to him.

For a long time we lay there in silence, enjoying each other's company and letting the sweat on our bodies dry.

CHAPTER
TWENTY-EIGHT

KHALA

My breath held, I moved through the shadows of the palace halls.

Cavan was dining with Harel and his favourite courtiers, keeping them distracted for as long as he could.

Apparently I was confined to his room as punishment for something. Presumably they bought that story, because when I slipped out an hour later, there were no guards at the door. If anything bad happened to me, it would be my fault.

So hospitable.

On bare feet, I stepped silently. The only sound was the occasional swish of fabric on fabric, and laughter from somewhere else in the palace.

Harel's booming voice echoed, followed by more laughter. The polite kind, as though the listeners were humouring him, not enjoying his humour.

I hurried on as quickly as I could, the map Cavan drew etched in my mind.

"I'm not certain the key is here, but it is a possibility," he'd said, his fingertip pressed to the shape of one room. "I don't know this place as well as I probably should."

"I'm guessing you know it better than Ryze, or even Tavian," I said. "I'll look there, but what if I don't find it?"

"Then keep looking. Otherwise, I'm going to have to do something drastic." He ran a hand over my slightly sore ass.

"Spanking me again won't make the key magically appear," I pointed out.

"No, but we'd both enjoy it." He pinched my ass and grinned when I jumped.

I batted his hand away. "I'm also not going to try to seduce Harel to find out where the key is. Even if he was interested in used goods." I grimaced.

"Then you better find the key," he said.

"You better be right about it being where you think it is," I retorted.

The dimly lit walls were covered in intricate tapestries showing scenes of hunting and feasting. Their appearance seemed distorted somehow, like they were stretched too thin or at too much of an angle. Perhaps the loom wasn't set straight.

Hells, for all I knew, it was a preferred style here in this court.

I froze as voices came up a corridor that crossed the one I was in. I ducked back and tucked myself into an alcove as a group of courtiers passed by.

They laughed and chatted, their voices echoing down the hall. I only half-listened to what they were saying. Something about the weather and an upcoming wedding. None seemed particularly interested. If anything, I got the impression they were mocking the couple preparing to exchange vows.

As soon as they were out of sight, I pressed on, keeping to the shadows. The palace seemed endless, with hallways branching off in every direction. Every so often, I stopped to picture the map in my mind. I would have carried it with me, but as Cavan pointed out, I had no reason to be sneaking around the palace with a map in my hand.

Or without a map in my hand, but I could make up an excuse if anyone saw me.

Finally, I reached a small room tucked away at the end of a long hallway.

It wasn't opulent like the rest of the palace. That in itself was peculiar. On the other hand, where better to keep a hidden key than in a room that seemed ordinary and uninteresting?

Although, now I thought about it, that was as suspicious as fuck. Since pretty much everything I'd seen since we stepped foot in Marial fit into that category, I slipped into the room and closed the door behind me.

I illuminated the room with magic and started to hunt around.

"What the hells?"

I moved closer, my breath catching in my throat as I stared. In the center of the room was a throne made of twisted branches and thorns. It reminded me of the song on the maps. Twisted branches that had the answers, or something like that.

Did Cavan know this was here?

I stepped around it, eyes on it as though it might jump out at me or something.

"It's just a chair," I told myself.

My whisper almost made me jump. It sounded too loud in the silence. This whole sneaking around thing had me on edge, it was totally not the weird throne.

All right, it was equal parts of both. I'd seen some odd things in the last couple of months, this was just the most recent.

I tentatively put my hand out to touch it, careful not to prick myself on a thorn.

I remembered a tale I was told as a young Silent Maiden, of a goddess who did exactly that. She bled so much from that tiny pinprick, she passed out.

When she woke up, a thousand years had passed. Her children had all grown up. Her husband gave up on her ever returning from wherever she supposedly went, and married some other goddess.

Heartbroken, she killed her husband and his new wife before disappearing into the sky to become a shooting star.

Since all of that would suck, I was careful to avoid anything pointy and sharp.

The branches were still ragged, the wood rough under my fingertip. It felt like someone picked a bunch of sticks up off the ground and formed them into a throne. And yet, where my skin touched, I felt a faint tingle, like there was magic embedded in the chair.

"It doesn't usually let anyone touch it," a voice said from behind me.

I jumped back from the throne and whirled around. I hadn't even heard the door open, but now Illaria stood in the doorway, a candle in her hand.

"You scared the shit out of me," I told her. "What are you doing here?"

I couldn't immediately tell if she was armed or not, but after she distracted Tavian back in Garial, I could only assume her agenda was suspicious as fuck.

Fitting for the Autumn Court.

"I could ask you the same thing, but I already know," she said. "You're looking for the key."

"I don't know what you're talking about," I said, shrugging one shoulder.

"Why else would you be in my father's court, unless you are searching for some way to find the missing courts?"

"Your father's court?" I echoed. "Harel is your father?"

She sighed and stepped further into the room before closing the door behind her.

"Unfortunately, yes. I've been in exile in the Winter Court for a long while. I thought it was time to come back and beg for my father's forgiveness." She grimaced.

"You're looking for the key?" I guessed.

"I know where the key is," she said. "I'm here to help you find it. I went back to the Winter Court, only to hear you'd gone to Havenmoor. I could have saved you that time. Would have if it wasn't for the first attack. I was supposed to distract Tavian, so my contacts could speak to High Lord Ryzellius. They suspected the attack might come. They wanted Tavian away from it, so he wouldn't be harmed."

I shook my head. "I don't understand. Who are your contacts?"

"Other people in the Autumn Court who believe in the other courts," she replied. "We believe the Court of Dreams will be the salvation of the seasonal courts."

She sounded dogmatic, and slightly unhinged.

"Salvation from what?" I asked.

"From division, apathy and antagonism," she said. "You know of how High Lord Cavan has tried to unite the seasonal courts. He's been ignored and ridiculed. Vilified. We believe Fae from the Court of Shadows have been working for a long time to create exactly that environment. When they awaken the rest of the court, that will be to their advantage. If the seasonal courts are pitted against each other, they can use that weakness. Even if it means stepping over bones and ashes."

Her words reminded me of what Tavian said of his vision.

"They want us to go to war against each other, so they can step in at the end and defeat all of us?" I said slowly.

"Exactly." She nodded. The movement made her candle flicker.

"And you think the Court of Dreams can help stop that from happening?"

"They already are. Every time the Court of Shadows opens a portal, they piggyback their magic on to whatever is being sent through. There are Fae in the seasonal courts with the blood of the Court of Dreams. And the Court of Shadows," she added.

"When the portal opens, they can use that magic," I said.

"I think you know people who can," she said. "Who are."

I certainly did. Tavian's visions, for one. If he had the blood of the lost courts inside him, he might be a seer. Hycanthe, whose magic increased in strength whenever a portal opened, for another.

"Shouldn't that blood be diluted by now?"

Illaria laughed softly. "Fae can bear children at hundreds of years old. Those with the blood of those courts may be children of the lost Fae. Grandchildren at most."

"Is it possible those attacks are aimed at someone in particular?" I asked carefully.

"Not only possible, it's likely," she said. "The lost courts can only be returned by a coming together of a Fae with the blood of the Court of Shadows, one with the blood of the Court of Dreams, and one whose blood transcends courts. There are some who believe it's possible to return one court and not the other. Both of those courts are trying to stop the other from being awakened. As far as we can determine, the Court of Dreams has only been defending itself."

"You sound like you know a lot about all of this," I said.

"The people I work with have been looking into this since before Cavan," she said. "We've been working in the shadows, trying to help him be heard. That's why I got exiled. My father doesn't believe any of it. A lot of people don't. Some of us wanted to approach Cavan directly, but we didn't dare reveal ourselves. If my father knew I was talking to you right now, I'd be executed in the morning. In public, as a warning to the others."

"Sounds like a loving parent," I said sarcastically.

"There's nothing my father won't do to get his way," she said. "To save face. Having a daughter who openly disagreed with him caused him humiliation. It would have been bad enough if I stood outside and told him the sky was pink. When it comes to the other courts, he has no room for leniency. Or forgiveness, which is why I'm leaving before the sun rises. I needed you to find what you came here to find. I would have taken it, but he would have known. He has eyes on me; he thinks I haven't noticed. I don't know how long it'll be before they realise I'm out of their sight."

"You should talk to Cavan," I said. "It sounds like you have the answers to a lot of his questions."

"I only know what I've told you," she said. "And that my people suspect Tavian has Court of Dreams blood on his father's side. The High Lord had a brief relationship with a priestess. Thirteen months later, he was born. That's the gestation period for Fae."

I winced. Nine months sounded like long enough to me.

"And you have suspicions about Hycanthe too," I said.

"I wasn't sure if it was her, you or Jezalyn," Illaria said. "We figured it was one of you, because things escalated after the removal of your chokers. They were dampening more than the mating urge, or your ability to speak."

"One of us has lost court blood?" I presumed it wasn't me, unless my mother carried the blood and Cavan didn't know.

"Wait, Tavian's father might be a High Lord? Does that make him the heir?"

"We can only guess at that," she replied. "We don't know who amongst those Fae still live. For all we know, one of you former maidens might be the heir to the Court of Shadows."

"My money is on Hycanthe," I said dryly. If they were as nasty as they sounded, that fit. Her money would probably be on me, so I supposed that made us even.

"You might be right, you might not. Either way, you need to find the key and, from what I gather from the map in Havenmoor, that will lead you to the place that has the answers. What might happen there, I have no idea."

"How do you know about the keys?" I asked.

She smiled humourlessly. "I'm my father's heir. He'd dearly like a better one. Preferably a male who does what he says. In the meantime, I had to know where it is, in case something happened to him."

"Where is it?" I asked.

She explained where, and how to get it.

"The trick will be getting in and out without being seen."

"Right." Of course it couldn't be easy. Nothing about this had been yet, why would it start now?

"This is the real throne of the Autumn Court." She brushed the tips of her fingers over the back of it, apparently not worried about being pricked. "My father replaced it when he became High Lord. He said it was too uncomfortable."

"It doesn't look very comfortable," I said.

"It's not supposed to be. It's a symbol of our court."

"Is that your way of saying it's a chair, but no one is supposed to sit on it?" I asked.

She laughed softly. "Something like that. You have to want to be High Lord very much to sit in a chair like that."

"Or you have to have to be willing to change out the chair," I said.

"That too," she agreed.

"Are you sure you can't get the key for me?" I asked. Presumably she could go places in the palace without being asked questions, unlike me.

"I've lingered for too long already," she said. "I need to return to my father's banquet. I'll stay to say my good nights. As soon as I slip away, he'll check to see if the key is still there. Once he's left, you can make your move."

"How can I be sure this isn't a trap?" I asked. "You might be working for this faction you talk about, or you might be working for your father. He may be waiting for me if I sneak in there."

"He might be," she agreed. "But if he is, it's nothing to do with me. I can promise you that."

I wasn't sure if I could believe her promises, but she was forthcoming with a lot of answers to a lot of questions. Assuming it wasn't all a bunch of lies.

"You can keep searching for the key, or you can look for it when I said it was. When you find it there, then you might believe me. Since you won't find it anywhere else, it's worth a try. Right?"

"Those sound like famous last words if I ever heard them," I remarked.

"I need to go. I'm sure we'll be seeing each other again. Especially if that handsome human is with you." She flashed a smile.

A totally irrational surge of annoyance passed through me. I knew she didn't mean anything by it, but Zared was mine. A part of my pack.

She gave me a knowing look, then slipped out the door.

I waited a minute or two, then followed her. I didn't know which direction she'd gone, but there was no sign of her now. Or anyone else in the corridor outside. Judging by the talking and laughter, the banquet was still in full swing.

I slipped back into the room I shared with Cavan without seeing anyone else.

CHAPTER
TWENTY-NINE

KHALA

"That complicates things," Cavan said.

"Just a little," I agreed. "I'm sure you have a plan."

"While I appreciate your faith in me," he said slowly, "you'll have to give me a moment."

I couldn't resist teasing him. "I knew I should have brought Ryze. He seems to know all about sneaking around. He'd be in and out of there by now."

"Do you want me to spank you again?" he growled.

"Maybe I do," I replied tartly. "Or maybe we can figure out a way to get this fucking key and get out of here."

"First that, then the other." He placed his hands to either side of him on the bed and pushed himself to his feet. "Come on then."

"You have a plan?" I rose to follow him.

"No, I figured we'd work it out as we went along. Harel and everyone else turned in hours ago. Judging by the amount of wine they drank, they won't be up early, so we have some time. We need to keep an eye out for guards. Whatever I say, play along."

"Why do I think that sounds like the start of a very bad idea?" I asked.

He smiled before he opened the door and stepped out, leaving me to scurry along behind him.

Like he did everywhere else, he strode along like he owned the place. Between him and Ryze, they had at least three quarters of the confidence that existed in the seasonal courts.

We approached a couple of guards who were patrolling the corridor. Against what, I didn't know. People like us, I supposed.

"Hurry up," Cavan snapped over his shoulder. "Unless you enjoyed your punishment for being too slow the last time. I can give you double."

338

I didn't hate the sound of that, but I kept my eyes down and trotted until I caught up. "Sorry," I muttered.

He stopped so quickly I almost ran into the back of him.

"Sorry what?" he growled.

"Sorry, alpha," I said quickly. Asshole was enjoying this way too much. If he wasn't careful, I'd bite his cock. Not in a good way.

He glared at me, then turned and stomped on.

The guards looked at me and one of them actually chuckled. He was an asshole too.

I followed Cavan around the corner, before punching him in the arm.

"Ouch what was that for?" He rubbed the spot which probably didn't hurt, because I didn't punch him *that* hard.

"I felt like it," I said. "Are you suggesting you didn't deserve it?"

He grinned. "Stay in your role. You never know when someone else might appear."

"Yes, sir," I said sarcastically. I sighed and slumped back down beside him.

"I like the way that sounds," he said.

"Of course you do," I whispered.

He gestured for me to be quiet as we walked down another corridor and into the one leading to the throne room.

"You'd think he'd keep it somewhere safer, like a treasury," I remarked. "Or under his pillow. No one would want to go there to find it."

"Lucky for you it's not under there," Cavan said. "Otherwise I'd have to send you for it. Whatever happened there, you'd have to play along."

"I'm starting to think the sadistic thing isn't an act," I told him. I was almost certain he didn't mean he'd let Harel do whatever he wanted to me. I sure as hells wouldn't.

"Quiet." He tried the door to the throne room. It was locked. A quick flick of his finger and flare of magic, and it clicked open.

"Locks are only there to keep out honest people and people who can't do magic," he said.

"I know which of those you fit into," I said sweetly.

He snorted.

We stepped inside and he closed the door behind us.

The darkness inside was almost suffocating. The only light came from the moon. It cast an eerie glow through the window, illuminating the room in patches. It was quiet, too quiet. the stillness broken only by the sound of our footsteps on the cold, hard floor.

"I don't know about this," I said. "It feels..."

"Like we shouldn't be here?" he asked.

"Exactly," I agreed. "Entering places like this was something Zared and I used to do when I was a maiden."

"Why is that a problem now?" He cocked his head as he illuminated the room with magic on his hand.

"I don't know. I suppose I think Fae should behave differently. More mature or something. Aren't we supposed to be regal and elegant?"

"Of course, but that doesn't mean we have to be boring." He waved his hand across the arm of the chair and looked down and around. "Nothing on this side."

I looked around the other. "I can't see— Wait." I slid my hand across a groove in the wood. It was round and smooth. "If I stick my finger in this, am I going to end up dead?"

"Potentially," he said. "Do you want me to do it? I can if you're scared." He gave me a challenging look I was almost certain he knew I'd have to refuse.

Asshole.

"I'm not scared," I said. "All right, I am, but if I end up dead, I'm going to be really, really pissed off at you."

"Save your pissed off for Harel," he said. "If there's a booby trap in there, it's because he put it there."

"That would be no consolation if I was dead." I placed my finger into the groove and pressed down into it. I heard a soft click and a drawer slid out from under the arm of the throne.

Inside was what looked like a rusty, old key.

"Please tell me that's what we're looking for," I said.

"You were expecting something shiny?" he asked.

"Well...yes." My fingers hovered over the key. "I think this is the first rusty thing I've seen since I left Ebonfalls."

"Ryze and I are about as rusty as that," he said with a smile. "Pick it up."

I tentatively touched the key, then gripped it between my thumb and forefinger. When I lifted it up out of the drawer, it glinted in the moonlight.

"What the fuck?" It didn't look rusty anymore. It was as shiny as one of Tavian's knives.

"A little autumn magic. Making it look like nothing when it's really something. Here." He reached into his pocket. "You didn't think I'd come unprepared did you?"

He held a similar-looking key on the palm of his hand.

"If Harel has a quick look, he'll assume the key is still there." He handed it to me and pocketed the other one.

I placed the replacement in the drawer and shook my head as it turned rusty.

"Can I learn to do that?"

"You could if you had your first heat with Harel or an alpha here. I'll let you decide if it's worth it or not."

"That would be a big no," I said. "We should get out of here."

"We could," he said slowly. "Or we could stay here a little longer." He reached over and closed the drawer, then grabbed my wrist and pulled me until I was sitting on Harel's throne.

"You like living dangerously," I observed.

340

"If those guards talk about seeing us in the corridor, we can say I brought you here for this. It's the kind of depraved thing Harel would expect of any of the other High Lords."

He hooked his fingers into the top of my pants and tugged them down my hips. He pulled them until he was able to slide one leg off my foot.

"Would you want any of them to do this on your throne?" I asked as he pressed my thighs apart with his hands and knelt in front of me.

"If anyone other than me fucks on my throne, I'll have them executed." He lowered his mouth and ran his tongue all the way from the bottom of my pussy to the top.

I shivered. There was something both enticing and arousing about him fucking me in a place like this. I should have told him to stop, but I didn't want to. Instead, I leaned back against the mahogany and enjoyed the way he devoured me.

"You taste like divine sin," he said. "Absolutely delicious."

I groaned and rocked against his mouth, slowly, building the friction. He certainly knew what to do with his tongue. And his fingers, three of which he slid deep inside me.

In the moonlight, in the throne room, the High Lord of the Summer Court fucked me with his hand and tongue. He drove me to the edge and drew back to let me come down before driving me harder still. Several times, he pushed me right to the brink, only to pull back before I tipped over.

After the fourth time, I growled at him.

He chuckled and worked me mercilessly, licking and nipping my clit. This time he let me drop over the edge of the cliff. I came so hard I had to bite my lip to keep from screaming.

He finally lifted his shining face from me and grabbed a fistful of hair. He drew my face to his and kissed me. His mouth tasted of the tang of my arousal.

"See how delicious you are?" He kissed me again, tracing around my lips with his tongue.

I reached forward to undo his pants and slide them down his hips. His erection happily sprang free, thick, red and hard. His tip shone with precum.

I raised my legs and pressed my heels into his back, pushing him insistently until his cock slid inside me.

"Pushy omega," he teased.

"Shut up and fuck me, alpha," I growled. "Please," I added sweetly.

"Only because you said please." He grabbed my hips with his large hands and pulled me forward until I was only perched on the edge of the throne. He grunted and thrust into me, slowly at first.

"What is it about you that the more I get, the more I want?" He asked, his voice already breathless with exertion and concentration.

"I'm amazing," I said jokingly. I gripped the hand rests of the throne and used them to roll my hips in time with his.

"Yes, you are," he agreed. "And I'm going to come inside your beautiful, amazing body. If anyone sees us walking back down the corridor, they won't know you have my cum dripping down your thighs."

Gods, yes, please.

I was tempted to make a comment about anyone here in the palace expecting me to have his cum on my face, but instead I concentrated on squeezing my muscles around his cock and driving him to oblivion.

His fingers tightened on my hips. He thrust once, twice more before he came.

He groaned, the sound so deep and compelling it forced another orgasm out of me. This one was quick and shallow, but no less pleasurable than the other.

We held each other and panted for a while before we somehow managed to remember where we were.

We quickly pulled our clothes back together and slipped out of the throne room before anyone knew we were there.

CHAPTER

THIRTY

KHALA

"I trust you slept well." Harel gave Cavan a meaningful look.

It seemed the guards did their job and told him where we were in the middle of the night. If his expression was any indication, he'd checked and found the replacement key in place.

I'd wanted to leave right after we left the throne room, but Cavan reasoned that nothing said suspicious as fuck like sneaking away in the middle of the night.

"We might need him yet," he'd said.

"If you say so." I thought I was going to get another lecture about, 'When you're as old as I am, you don't burn bridges.'

Instead he smiled and said, "I do say so."

"Do you have to take smug lessons to become High Lord?" I asked. "Or is it something you're born with?"

"It's a skill we hone over time," he said. "We can't be seen to lack confidence or no one will follow us."

"Confidence or arrogance?" I teased.

"Is there a difference?" He grabbed my wrist, pulled me to him and smacked my ass. "That's what you get for questioning your alpha."

"One of them." I twisted around until I was facing him.

He sighed. "Yes, one of them. If it wasn't for that bond, I'd talk you out of any desire to be with Ryze. I'm sure he's as happy to share you with me as I am sharing with him."

"According to Tavian, it's an alpha's job to make sure his omega is happy, regardless of what he has to do to achieve that. Even if that means sharing with someone you don't like. Maybe if you get to know each other..."

"Tavian is right," Cavan conceded. "Liking each other might be a stretch,

343

but we may come to respect each other. In the end, we both want the same thing. A happy, content, satisfied omega. Especially satisfied." He kissed me lightly. "Come on. Let's have breakfast and say our goodbyes."

"Gladly." The sooner we were gone from here, the better.

"I slept very well," Cavan said, his words bringing me back to the present. "It must have been all the fine wine and company."

"Autumn Court wine is undeniably the best in Jorius or any of the human lands," Harel said.

He said nothing about the company.

"It's very drinkable," Cavan agreed. "I'm glad we were able to come to an understanding as well."

I forced myself not to glance at him. I kept my eyes down on my cereal and sweet tea and tried to contain my curiosity.

Understanding about what? What concessions had he given to Harel to buy me time to look for the key?

"It will be mutually beneficial," Harel said.

Either he didn't want to talk about it in front of me, or he enjoyed being cagey as hells. Maybe both. I'd ask Cavan about it when we left.

"It definitely will," Cavan agreed. "I can return to the Summer Court knowing our alliance is stronger than ever."

"And I can look forward to expanding my lands. For too long, we've been confined to this one corner, while the humans let their lands fall into ruin. It's past time for the Fae to return and rule as we should have been doing."

I almost choked on my mouthful. I coughed a couple of times while Cavan patted my back.

"Does the part-human whore object?" Harel seemed amused.

"Of course not," Cavan said smoothly. "She's Fae now, and knows better than to question her High Lord. Her food just went down the wrong hole for a moment."

Harel grunted and I could almost hear him thinking that I didn't have any wrong holes. All of mine were there for the taking. If not by him, then at least by whomever Cavan gave me to.

"Good," Harel said. "I'd hate to miss seeing the look on her face when the humans kneel to us."

Lucky for everyone, I had one hand in my lap. He couldn't see me curl it into a fist that I wanted to pound into his face. I struggled to keep my body from stiffening. Everything in me wanted to respond, but I couldn't.

I felt a surge of concern from Tavian through the bond. That was what kept me from losing my composure entirely. I sent back thoughts that I was fine.

I managed to take a calming breath and continue eating.

"You may get to see that yet." I felt Cavan's eyes on me, but I ignored them. He was definitely having way, way too much fun with this. I wouldn't rule out using that fist again.

"She's broken, but there are others like her who aren't," Cavan added. "Not to mention the humans themselves. I'm sure you'll enjoy toying with them."

"In the same way a child likes to play with a puppy," Harel said. "Humans are, after all, nothing more than animals."

"Of course." Cavan set his teacup down on the table. "Now, if you'll excuse me, I need to return to my court."

Evidently, it didn't matter that I wasn't finished. Of course it didn't. It was only a courtesy that I got any food in the first place.

Whatever, as long as we got out of here, I didn't care. I'd have a proper meal later, somewhere a long way from here.

When Cavan stood, I hurried to follow. I managed to avoid looking at Harel. There was no way he'd miss seeing the disgust on my face.

I bit my lip while we walked down the corridor towards the courtyard that led out into the city.

"Don't say anything, we're still being watched," Cavan said, his hand around my upper arm. "Something is wrong."

It certainly was, but I managed to contain myself for a while longer.

I thought we'd portal out from the courtyard, but we kept walking out into the city.

"He put wards in place to stop me from opening a portal," Cavan said in my ear. Anyone overhearing, would have assumed he was growling at me.

"You, or anyone?" I asked.

Hopefully I managed to look like I was scared of him. Truthfully I was scared, because his tone put me on edge. We'd come this far. Being stopped now would be frustrating as hells. Not to mention potentially deadly.

"I don't know, the wards feel strange. I can't put my finger on it. It's not like anything I've felt before."

"Should we get inside somewhere?" I asked.

He glanced at me, then nodded. He all but pulled me over to a tall inn, and through the front door. He pushed me over towards a table, then turned to look out the window, firmly putting himself between me and anything out there.

"Do you see anything?" I stood behind him and ignored the stares of the patrons eating breakfast.

He shook his head slightly. "Nothing, but it still feels wrong. I don't think it's autumn magic doing that. Don't use any of your own. In case they're looking for it."

I didn't need to ask who 'they' were. If this was something new to him, then chances were it was related to one of the lost courts.

"They don't want us leaving with the key," I whispered.

"That would be my guess," he said. "Either Illaria told them, or someone else did. The map in Havenmoor wouldn't tell you anything unless you already knew."

"Who else knows?" I asked. "You, Ryze, Harel, Illaria. Tavian, Vayne and Zared."

"Ryze's designated heir, Johah," Cavan said softly. "I don't have one. And then only Thiron and—"

"His heir, Wornar," I said as Wornar stepped through the crowds out on the street, and moved towards the inn.

"And him," Cavan agreed.

"Fuck," I said softly.

"Potentially," Cavan agreed.

"If he betrayed us, can I rip his head off?" I asked.

"Certainly, but wait for my go-ahead. This might not be what we think it is."

"Excuse me if I don't take that bet," I said dryly.

Wornar stepped through the door to the inn and nodded at us.

"I apologise for sidetracking you both, but I believe you have something I need."

"Oh really?" Cavan asked. "What might that be?" He crossed his arms and kept himself between me and the Spring Court Fae.

"You can try to pretend you don't know, but we both know you do," Wornar said.

"Humour me," Cavan said. He looked completely unmoved.

"The key to Nallis." Wornar's tone was as friendly as ever, although his eyes spoke of his impatience.

"What about it?" I asked.

"I know you have it," he said.

"So what if we do?" Cavan asked. "What would you need it for? Are you planning to open the place yourself?"

"It doesn't matter what I need it for," he said. "Only that I need it and you have it." He held out his hand. "No one needs to get hurt here today."

"I don't know about that," I said. "You're here demanding a key we may or may not have, and you're not telling us why. If you're so sure we have it, then you'd know the reason for that. If you do, then you wouldn't want to stop us."

Wornar stepped around Cavan, who moved to keep himself between us. He grunted softly.

"That might be exactly why I'm here. To keep anyone from opening that place."

"Why?" I asked. "It seems to me the sooner we deal with those courts, the better."

"Or we can keep them contained where they are," Wornar said. "Thiron agrees it's better to leave them alone. He wants me to get the keys so we can hide them. We'll find a way to stop them from waking."

"Unless you haven't been paying attention, it's already started," Cavan said. "Our best allies against the shadows might be the Court of Dreams."

Wornar shook his head. "Thiron doesn't want to take the risk. Give me the key."

"No," Cavan said.

"Then you leave me no choice," Wornar said. He looked around at me and said, "Take his knife and slide it between his ribs."

I shook my head and tried to back away, but the alpha-order settled on me. I didn't even have time to fight it before I was slipping Cavan's knife out from the sheath at his hip and driving it into him.

Warm blood spurted over my hand, coating my fingers. I let out a sob.

Gods, no, no, no.

My eyes were wide, staring. This couldn't be happening. None of it. I felt like I was watching myself through the eyes of someone else.

But I wasn't. I had done this. Me, because being an omega meant I had to obey.

Somehow...somehow this was all my fault.

Cavan's eyes widened in surprise and pain. His knees started to buckle.

Wornar grabbed him and held him up long enough to slip his hands into his pockets. He searched for a few moments until he turned up the key.

"Let the hilt of the knife go and come with me," he ordered.

Hot tears ran down my face. Every part of me was screaming not to do what he wanted me to do. My movements stiff and tight, I moved towards Wornar.

"Asshole," I ground out.

"Quiet," he ordered. His words were like a choker around my throat.

I tried to growl and found I couldn't even do that.

I was a Silent Maiden again.

Cavan dropped to his knees, his hand around the blade of the knife. His fingers were covered in blood. Eyes wide with pain and fury.

I could only mouth his name before the order forced me to follow Wornar out the door.

THANK YOU FOR READING! The story continues in Sword of Balm and Shadow. If you'd like a bonus scene of Khala visiting Tyla, you can get that here.

SWORD OF BALM AND SHADOW

COURT OF BLOOD AND BINDING
BOOK 3

TRIGGER WARNING

Chapter 7 contains a scene of sexual assault. It's contained to that chapter, with another warning as a reminder. This chapter can be skipped without losing any elements of the story.

CHAPTER
ONE

KHALA

I stepped out of the portal to the sight of the Spring Court palace.

Stark, white marble was formed into the shape of a giant lotus. Massive petals sat half-open, ready to greet the sun. At dawn, it would be tinged pink. At sunset, red and gold.

I might have been impressed if I was here voluntarily.

I shook my head, trying in vain to dislodge Wornar's alpha-order from my mind. It was lodged harder than Dalyth's block in Zared's mind. Heavy and unyielding.

I hated it, hated *him*.

Wornar.

Cousin and heir of the High Lord of the Spring Court.

Cavan's blood was still wet on my hand. Red stained my sleeve. The image of him falling to the ground played over and over in my mind. The knife embedded in his side. The knife slid in there by me, under Wornar's fucking order. Words that gave me no choice but to stab one of my lovers.

I wanted to stab Wornar. Wanted his blood to coat my hand. I wanted him to look me in the eyes as he died, knowing who held the knife.

My grudge was the heaviest thing I held right now, but I clung to it. Whatever happened, he'd regret what he made me do.

Tears ran down my cheeks. I let them. Maybe Wornar would feel bad if he saw them. Some hint of guilt at forcing me to shed Cavan's blood. A shred of remorse.

That seemed less than unlikely. He strode in front of me, chin raised, anything but repentant.

Fucking asshole.

On the other end of the bond, all four men were frantic. I sent back the plea

I'd sent since the moment Wornar made me slide the knife between Cavan's ribs.

Help him. Go to the Autumn Court and stop him from dying. I needed them to do that for me. If Cavan died...

Ryze sent back that they were on their way, then they were coming for me. Coming for Wornar. He sent reassurance, but also fear tinged with confusion as to what happened to Cavan.

The bond was good for sending emotions, but not solid information, not words. That they knew I was all right would have to be enough for now.

"I know you must be confused," Wornar said. "You'll understand soon enough." He smiled at me as if we were friends. "You can talk now if you like. We're safe here."

That part of the alpha-order lifted, a slight shift in weight, like loosening his grip around my throat.

I wanted to tell him to fuck off, but held my tongue. He was worth my rage, but not my words. After decades as a Silent Maiden, unable to speak, I'd learnt the value of not speaking. Often silence says more than the most eloquent speech.

He continued as though oblivious to my anger. "I'm sure you'll agree, all the conjecture about the other courts has done nothing but cause friction and conflict. We should be searching for a way to seal them off forever, not release them back into the world."

I was unable to contain my response. "That's a conversation for all of the High Lords," I said bitterly. "Not for just one to decide."

"Tell that to Ryze and Cavan," Wornar said easily, undeterred. "They didn't seem concerned about not consulting Harel or Thiron. Cavan even went so far as to take you into the Autumn Court to steal the key from Harel."

I shrugged. "The consensus seems to be the Court of Shadows and the Court of Dreams will find their way back, with or without our help. Ryze and Cavan wanted to do it while we were united enough to stand against them if they posed a threat."

Wornar stopped, turned around and faced me. "*If* they pose a threat? How many Fae have to die before they recognise that they *already* pose a threat?"

I stood my ground and stared him down. "They know there's a threat. Right now it's a small one. They want to stop it from becoming worse later." So far, we'd seen nothing more than random attacks and only one, arguably deserved, death. Dalyth.

Wornar stepped closer. We were almost chest to chest. "They won't be a threat if we seal them away forever. *When* we seal them away." He smelled of oak, alpha and determination, tainted with something else. Ambition and the burning desire to be right. To win against anyone who might think to stand in his way. The combination left a bitter sensation on my tongue.

Did the High Lord of the Spring Court know who he had in his midst?

Wornar had fooled Ryze. The High Lord of the Winter Court considered him something close to a friend. The gods only knew what Thiron thought.

"Is that what you need me for?" I managed not to flinch.

He was so close I was sure I could hear his heartbeat. His harsh breath all but scraped the side of my face, rough like a desert breeze.

"Potentially." He brushed hair off my cheek and tucked it behind my ear. "We also need you to keep Ryze and Cavan from doing anything stupid. If they do, it won't end well for you."

"So I'm a hostage," I stated. Fuck. I shouldn't be too surprised. Why else would he bring me here?

"Of sorts," he agreed. "The Spring and Autumn Courts have one thing in common. Lack of omegas. That's something Thiron has been trying to rectify for quite some time. He's not going to want to let you go too easily. Fortunately, you'll like it here. The Spring Court is so much nicer than any of the others. You won't find all the dreary red and gold here. Or the ice, or the relentless summer."

"I'd rather be anywhere but here with you," I told him. If he thought anything different, he was delusional.

I didn't see the slap until my cheek was stinging from the impact. I was forced back a step. My hand flew to my face. I raised the other to hit back, but he grabbed my wrist and yanked me closer.

"You will never try to strike or hurt me in any way," he ordered. "Ever. You will obey me and Thiron, and any other alpha from the Spring Court. You'll watch what you say, or you can look forward to being a silent omega."

I closed my eyes and tried to ignore the order. Tried to stop it from wrapping itself around me and tying itself tight like a noose. So tight I could hardly breathe.

"Do you understand?" His nose almost touched mine. "You will respond with *yes, alpha*."

No matter how much I wanted to, I couldn't stop the words from leaving my lips. My whole body felt like it wasn't mine anymore. Like I was a shell for something darker.

"Good girl." He skated the back of his knuckle down my cheek. "One more thing. From now on, unless I say otherwise, pleasing me will be the only thing that will give you any satisfaction. Me and any other Spring Court alpha. That seems to have been missed in your training, somehow. My role is to take care of you, your role is to please me. Understand?"

"Yes, alpha," I said automatically. Inside, I felt like I was being torn in two. Part of me wanted to grab his sword and run him through with it. The rest of me wanted to get down on my knees and let him fuck my mouth.

Gods, this was worse than having the choker around my neck and not being able to talk. Then, I could communicate my honest thoughts and feelings. Now, I was in a battle with myself.

"Come with me." He let my wrist go and stepped back.

We made our way past a contingent of guards dressed in long tunics and fitted leather pants. Their tunics were either a soft green, or the blue of the spring sky. Each wore their pale red-gold hair long. They watched me with either blue eyes or green, tracking every step. Everyone was armed to the teeth.

They watched us as we walked past, gazes following, bodies tense and ready. They were a far cry from the indolent, disinterested guards from the Autumn Court, or those from the Summer Court who seemed innately mistrustful of anyone from outside the court. The guards from the Winter Court were as arrogant and laid back as Ryze.

I thought Wornar would lead me to the throne room, but instead he led me to a wide chamber with a stone balcony that overlooked a stunning garden.

A Fae with a striking resemblance to Wornar stood near the railing, a heavy clay cup held in both hands. He didn't turn until we stepped out onto the balcony, and waited for at least a handful of minutes. He must have known we were there, but decided to deal with us when he was ready.

Finally, he turned to face his cousin. His blue eyes were striking. His glance bore into my soul.

He wore alphaness like a cloak. And smelled of it. As with Wornar, the scent of oak lingered on his skin, along with something else. Something between lavender and a spice I couldn't identify. It wasn't unpleasant, but it wasn't compelling either. Not exactly.

He didn't seem concerned about the blood on my skin and clothes.

When he finished drinking me with his eyes, his attention turned to Wornar.

"You got the key?"

"Not without a slight altercation, but I got it, yes. Once we destroy it, no one will be able to open Nallis." Wornar pulled the key out of his pocket and held it out on his palm.

Thiron looked at it for another long, slow moment, then nodded. That seemed to be the way he did things, slow and deliberate. Like the flower-dotted vine that wound its way up the side of the palace, and around the stone railing. It looked like it had been working to get there for a hundred years. The white flowers gave off a soft fragrance, in contrast with the two men.

I glanced off the balcony, to the stunning garden below. It was beautiful, a riot of colours and fragrances. Completely enclosed by a wall too high for me to climb. I wouldn't get out that way then.

"Good. We can work on a way to seal the courts." Thiron nodded. Slowly, of course. He looked like he was trapped in a vat of honey. Unable rather than unwilling to move quickly.

"I have good reason to believe she knows exactly where to find them." Wornar turned his blue eyes to me.

I really, really wanted to tell him to fuck off, but that was overridden with the need to tell him everything I knew. The words spilled out of my mouth.

"According to Ryze and Cavan, the best way to go is through Nallis," I said.

"Otherwise, the only other way is through the mist. Ryze hated the mist. It scared him. He said he'd rather go through Nallis and some dark tunnel than go through the mist."

I hated myself for babbling all of that.

"Did he say why he didn't like it?" Thiron asked. He blinked at me, his long lashes brushing the tops of his cheeks. He'd be ridiculously handsome under other circumstances.

Had he told Wornar to bring me here? I assumed he had. Asshole until proven otherwise.

"He said he couldn't see where he was going," I said. "I always got the impression there was more to it, but he didn't say." It was the kind of thing he wouldn't elaborate on unless he was ready to. He was relieved when another way through the mountains presented itself.

Thiron's full lips drew back to the side in what looked like contemplation. "According to legend, people have tried to enter the mist and haven't returned."

"The mists engulf the side of a mountain," Wornar pointed out. "They probably couldn't see where they were going and fell to their deaths."

Thiron's gaze slowly swung towards him. For a moment I thought he might suggest Wornar go find out. Instead, he nodded.

Shame, I supported sending Wornar to die.

"It's possible that was what occurred. It's also possible there's more there than an unlucky misstep."

"So the only way through is through Nallis," I concluded.

"This will require further thought and research," Thiron said. "In the meantime, no one will be able to enter Nallis. That may keep them from exacerbating the situation further."

I wanted to scream at them that wasn't how this was going to go. I'd seen the results of those portals opening and magic being thrown through. The Court of Shadows and the Court of Dreams weren't going to sit back and give up because Ryze, Cavan and the others couldn't take a shortcut to find them.

Wornar nodded and closed his fingers over the key. "I'll put this somewhere safe, until you're ready to have it destroyed." He didn't look sure that was what Thiron intended at all.

The order he put on me would keep me from stealing it a second time. Otherwise, that's what I'd do. Then I'd try again to make a portal and get the hells out of here. For Fae Ryze considered friends and allies, these two were anything but friendly and trustworthy.

"I'll get our guest settled," Wornar added.

Thiron nodded and turned his attention back to the garden.

"Follow me," Wornar snapped.

TWO

KHALA

I had no choice but to do what he said, but I didn't have to like it.

The order gave me enough freedom to turn back and look at Thiron. He looked like a man who had the weight of a thousand stars on his shoulders.

Strangely enough, he reminded me of Cavan. Maybe even Ryze. Both were trying to do what they thought was right for their court. For Jorius as a whole.

I hated to admit it, but I had no idea who was actually right in any of this. Maybe it was Thiron. Maybe we *should* find a way to stop the other courts from returning. Maybe in trying to free them, we'd bring about our own destruction.

One thing I knew for certain, Harel, High Lord of the Autumn Court, was wrong to sit back and do nothing. He wanted to believe the other courts didn't exist, that if he ignored them long enough, they might go away.

Wornar stepped back inside and I was forced to hurry to catch up to him.

"Ryze gave you absolutely no indication what he thought might be in the mist?" he asked. "Nothing at all?"

"Just that there was something." I shifted my shoulders, trying to see how far away from him I could get. No further than I was. Close enough that he could reach out his hand and touch me. "You must know I can't lie to you."

"I know if anyone could, it would be you," he said. "You're smart enough to find a way around the order, if there is one. Of course, I could order you not to lie to me."

"You're enjoying this, aren't you?" I asked. What was it with Fae men and the need to be controlling? Cavan enjoyed it too much when we were pretending I was broken. Now this.

I ignored the bond for the last while, but I felt for it now. The response was a jumble of confusion. Something about working to get to Cavan and at the same time, needing to reach me. They seemed to be having trouble doing both of those things.

Zared was angry at everyone, but that was nothing new. Vayne was equally angry. It felt like Ryze was struggling to keep them and everything else together.

I sent thoughts that I was all right, then turned my attention from the bond.

"Why wouldn't I be enjoying it? I've been heir to the Spring Court for two hundred years. Do you know what that means?"

"It means you'll be High Lord some day?" That was technically correct, but I suspected he meant more than that.

"Some day," he said bitterly. "Some day that may be another two or three hundred years coming. And will only come if Thiron doesn't father a child."

"You're worried you'll never get to take over from him?" Honestly, being High Lord looked like a big pain in the ass to me. Far too much responsibility and hassle.

"I'm sure I will eventually," he said. "In the meantime, it means doing whatever he tells me to do. I speak on his behalf, but only with his permission."

He stopped at a door before pulling down the gilded handle and pushing it open. "Sometimes he doesn't override the things I've said or the decisions I've tried to make."

"Sometimes? Most of the time he does?" Did he think I gave a fuck?

I followed him into a sumptuous room decorated in dusky shades of pink, blue and yellow.

Gold thread was woven into plump cushions which sat neatly on the wide bed.

Mahogany and glass doors lead out to a balcony covered with potted plants, each full of scented flowers. The whole place smelled like lavender, roses and magnolia.

"Not directly." He closed the door behind us. "Usually he finds some sort of fault with whatever I do. He might as well tie my hands behind my back."

I started to say I didn't care, but the words wouldn't come.

Instead what came out was, "That seems tedious."

What was the point of making a decision when someone else would override it anyway? Hopefully he didn't mistake my words for sympathy. Whatever situation he was in, I didn't give a shit.

"I agree. He should trust me to advise him, and listen to what I say. I'm the one who travels around Jorius speaking to people on his behalf. I know what the fuck is going on."

Wornar stalked out to the balcony and snapped a magnolia off at the stem. He started to tug petals off, shredding them as he went. He reminded me of a petulant child, frustrated that he never got his way, and willing to take it out on anything, or anyone who didn't have the power to fight back.

"Ryze respected your opinion," I said. "You two seemed to agree on things."

He shredded harder at the mention of Ryze's name. "Ryze is a fool. I would never have let you go to the Autumn Court with Cavan. I would never have you out of my sight. Or my bed."

He tossed the decimated flower aside and turned to me.

"Fortunately, I won't be making that mistake. In case you think they're coming for you, we have wards all over the Spring Court to keep anyone from portalling in from anywhere else, unless they have spring magic. We've also increased patrols along the border, so they won't be getting in that way either. No one will be coming here until Thiron is ready for them."

I shook my head.

"I don't— I won't—" My voice was high with the strain of trying to speak the words that the order kept suppressing. I couldn't tell him I had no intention of sharing his bed. The words wouldn't come.

On the inside, I was screaming them. Shouting so loud they should have heard me all across Jorius. I couldn't even growl out loud.

My fingers twitched to scratch his eyes out, but when I tried to curl my hands and step forward, I failed.

He smiled. "Yes, you can, and yes, you will. You were born to give pleasure to alphas. That's what you're for. You are going to give me a lot of it." He gripped my hair and pulled me towards him.

He leaned in and slid his tongue over my lip, tasting my mouth.

I wanted to bite it off, but between the order, and my omega instinct to please him, I couldn't move. Couldn't break away when he kissed me. I couldn't stop myself from kissing him back, even though my stomach turned.

"See?" He pulled back enough to smile smugly. "You want to satisfy me. Don't you?"

I fought with the words, but they slipped out anyway. "Yes, alpha."

I wanted to pick up a chair and smash it into his smug, asshole face. Or better yet, grab a knife and cut off his cock. I'd probably live for about thirty seconds after that, but it would absolutely be worth it.

"You asked me if I'm enjoying this. The answer is yes. I've spent the last two hundred years being powerless. But you—"

He gripped my hair so tight it hurt. "With you I have nothing but power. You'll do exactly what I say when I say. At first because you have to, but then because you *want* to. You'll come to learn that obedience to me will be rewarded. When I lift the order, you'll stay. You'll beg to stay because that will be what you want."

He pressed his forehead to mind. "You'll beg to be on your knees, sucking my cock dry. Beg for me to fill that pussy of yours. And I will. I'll fill you with my cock and my children. Our child will be the heir when I'm High Lord."

He made a pleased sound in the back of his throat, like he had it all thought out and everything was going to work out so perfectly. That he'd break me and make my belly swell with the gods only knew how many baby Fae.

I'd often thought the Fae were slightly out of their minds, but he was worse than the others. Did he really believe I'd turn to him? That I'd willingly have his babies? If he did, he was more delusional than the rest.

"You're looking forward to that day, aren't you?" he asked. He actually kissed my forehead.

No, I'm fucking not.

"Yes, alpha." I was going to throw up on his boots. If there was ever a time to believe in the gods, I had to believe in them now. That they'd find a way for Ryze and the other men to get to me.

If I didn't believe in the gods, I believed in those men. None of them would let anything stop them from reaching me. Whatever they had to do, they'd do it. I had to believe in that. Cling to it with everything I had.

"Good," he said, his tone soothing, laced with triumph. "Because you belong to me now. Every part of you." He ran his spare hand over my hip and up to my breast. He squeezed my flesh, then pinched my nipple hard.

I let out a tiny squeak of pain. At the same time, my body betrayed me by registering pleasure. I struggled to contain my response. If he knew I enjoyed pain, he wouldn't hold back in inflicting it on me.

He chuckled, seemingly oblivious to anything but his own enjoyment in hurting me.

I'd accused Cavan of having a sadistic streak, but with him, it was playful. A tease because he enjoyed pretending I was beaten, and broken.

Wornar, I knew, would get a great deal of pleasure in breaking me for real. He must have hidden that side of him well for Ryze to have any respect for him at all.

I'd almost liked him myself. Zared, I remembered now, was the only one who didn't. Although, the sentiment was more him disliking Fae in general, than disliking Wornar in particular.

Still, it was more than the rest of us saw.

"You're going to be so much fun to play with, omega," he said. "I can't wait to pound my cock into your pussy. Unfortunately, that will have to wait. I have things to attend to first. And you could use a bath. Get yourself cleaned up. Change into some fresh clothes."

He nodded towards a wardrobe placed at one side of the room. "I'll have someone bring food. Don't leave this room. Get some rest if you feel the need. Otherwise, wait for me to return. Spend your time thinking about the ways you're going to please me. How your pussy is going to be dripping wet for me. How much I'm going to punish your mouth, and your pussy. Your whole body. Every sweet centimetre of it."

He pinched my nipple, harder this time. Hard enough to bring tears to my eyes.

"Make sure to wash his blood off you," he added. "Don't leave any sign of him on any part of your body. Inside or out. Tonight will be a new start for both of us."

"Actually, definitely get some rest. You'll be needing it." He chuckled as though he said something hilarious and not repulsive.

He let me go then and pushed me towards the bathing room.

I would wash all right, but I felt dirtier from his touch than I did from Cavan's blood all over my hand and wrist. How the hells were we all so wrong about him?

I had to try to find a way out of here somehow. Like he said, if anyone could find a way around the order, it was me. The problem was, I was finding it difficult to figure out a way how, and that was making me start to panic.

Whatever happened, I wouldn't let him break me. I'd find my way through this. He might make me do things I didn't want to do, but I could still be strong. I'd survived this long, I'd keep surviving.

I held myself together until the door closed behind him, then I allowed myself a couple of minutes to cry before pouring myself a bath and slipping under the warm, refreshing water.

CHAPTER
THREE
ZARED

I stood near the doorway, hand hovering over my knife, and stewed.

When Khala's frantic rush of emotion came down the bond, I wanted to go straight to her. I'd insisted, but in typical Fae fucking form, the other two ignored me.

"We need to get to Cavan first," Ryze said. "We can't afford to lose a High Lord. Even with a clear heir, it can take years to settle succession. We don't have years." Those were the words that came out of his mouth. The expression on his face said he wanted to go right to Khala.

I wanted to slap his priorities straight.

"Isn't that exactly what Wornar wants? To distract you while he does the gods knows what to her?" Everyone seemed surprised by Wornar's betrayal. Everyone but me. I hadn't trusted him for half a heartbeat. Not just because he was Fae. No, the fucker always seemed way too nice. In my experience people that smooth were usually faking it.

When I felt Khala's confusion and then fear through the bond I wasn't even slightly surprised, but I was furious. Blindly, murderously furious.

The next time I saw Wornar, he'd better hope he was already dead, because if he wasn't I would kill him. I didn't give a fuck if that messed with the succession of the Spring Court.

I'd more or less come to terms with Tavian, Ryze, Cavan and Vayne touching my woman, but no other fucker got away with it.

"We will get her back," Ryze said definitely. "He only has a couple of minutes' head start on us, and Khala is capable of taking care of herself." He was trying to look like he wasn't as worried about her as I was, but he wasn't fooling anyone.

Vayne and I gave him the same flat as shit, disbelieving look.

Vayne shook his head. "You better be right." In spite of having to work with Cavan, the commander of the Winter Court army, clearly still didn't trust him either. Trust was as thin on the ground right now as snow.

"I'm always right," Ryze said, his expression his usual smug arrogance. Prick.

"Except when you're not," I told him.

"He better be right about this, or we won't let him forget it," Tavian said.

He stood near the other side of the door, his eyes on the street. He hadn't questioned Ryze, but he was clearly as antsy as I was. I didn't want to admit it to myself, but it was only his presence which kept me from completely losing my mind.

In spite of his obvious anxiety, he was keeping more or less calm. He probably wanted to slice a bunch of throats open to let off steam.

Ryze had muttered something about not getting any respect, and opened a portal to the Autumn Court.

That was an hour ago. He, Vayne and a healer were still crouched beside Cavan, who finally had some colour back in his face. He was pale, and covered in so much blood when we arrived, I'd thought he was dead already.

As Fae went, he was tolerable, but if it was too late for him then we could go straight after Khala.

When Ryze detected a heartbeat, he ordered me to stay near the door and stop anyone from entering. I was going to tell him I didn't take orders from him, but Vayne nodded.

Since I'd apparently been recruited into the Winter Court army, I *did* take orders from Vayne.

So I stood, guarded the door with Tavian, and waited.

Waited while Wornar and Khala were so far away. The bond was stretched thin, like my patience. She seemed unhurt, but also unhappy. Angry. Scared. Alone.

For the first time in my life, I wished I was Fae and had magic to make a portal of my own. I would have left these assholes behind and gone after her myself.

The reminder I was a powerless human didn't do much for my state of mind. Especially when the staff from the inn kept giving me looks like I was tomorrow's breakfast. Literally.

I bared my teeth at one who got too close, but ignored them after that. Let them think I was a feral animal, as long as they stayed the hells away.

"Can you stand?" Ryze was asking Cavan.

"Only if you give me some room," Cavan replied.

Apparently being stabbed hadn't improved his personality. Nor had the fact Ryze seemed to have saved his life by freezing the area around the knife and pulling it free. His magic had cauterised the wound and stopped it from bleeding. That in turn gave the healer enough time to arrive and do whatever she did to close it completely.

Apart from the blood all over his clothes, no one would know he had a knife embedded between his ribs only minutes ago. Put there by Khala on Wornar's orders.

Gods, I knew how badly she must be feeling about that. She would have felt worse if he'd died. For that reason alone, this side quest to save Cavan might be worthwhile.

If we didn't, it would gnaw at her for the rest of her life, her choice or not.

I hated the fact any alpha could manipulate her. Loathed it every bit as much as she did. No one should have that kind of control over my woman. No one.

Fucking alphas.

I hated that I wasn't one. If I was, we could have run away and lived our lives away from all of the Fae.

I wouldn't dwell on the fact she might not have run away with me at all. For some reason, she seemed to genuinely care about these men. They cared about her too, but not as much as I did. None of them knew her as well as me. She and I were friends when she was still a Silent Maiden. When I used to tease her by pretending I didn't understand every single one of her hand symbols, including all the nuances she probably wasn't even aware of throwing in. The little flicks of her fingers or her wrists that showed more irritation, or humour than the symbols themselves allowed for.

Ryze and Vayne stood and gave Cavan room to stand on wobbly legs. He held his hands out to the sides until he regained his balance and nodded.

"We need to go after Khala." He teased the edges of his shirt apart and frowned at the fading stab wound. The skin was still puckered and red, but even as we watched, it became paler and smooth.

"That's the most sensible thing anyone said all day," I grumbled.

So sensible I could *almost* forgive feeling him fuck Khala through the bond last night. And yesterday. He hadn't taken long to make his move once they were alone.

Like Wornar's betrayal, that wasn't a surprise either. He was as hot for her as the rest of us. Of course he'd take advantage of the time they had together. It's something we all would have done, given the chance. It was something I'd done whenever I could. The woman was irresistible.

Tavian murmured his agreement. He pulled out his knife and was using it to clean under his nails. His body language suggested he'd throw it in half a heartbeat, just because he could. That and the other eight or nine he had on him.

Cavan stared at me for a moment, then at Ryze. "Why are you here? Wornar has the key and her. You should have gone after them first."

"That's what I told them," I said. "They seemed to think you were more important."

Tavian grunted under his breath.

"We never said he was more important," Ryze argued. "Just that—" He shook his head. "We can stand here and argue or we can go after them."

I gestured toward the door and almost struck my hand on High Lord Harel's chest as he stomped into the inn.

I dropped my hand and moved away. Not because I was intimidated, not a chance. No, I moved because he was an even bigger asshole than most Fae. The best place to be when he was in a room was on the other side of it. Or better yet, in a different room.

He looked at me like I was the worst kind of vermin he'd ever seen, and walked past me, chin high like he was king of the gods. Since the gods didn't have a king, he was shit out of luck with that assumption.

"I shouldn't be surprised to find you all here, and in each other's company," he drawled. "Did you think I wouldn't hear of it?"

Tavian watched him through narrowed eyes. His fingernail cleaning paused. I could almost see him calculating the distance and how hard he'd have to throw to embed the knife in Harel's brain. He even gripped the hilt of the knife and checked the balance, right before he slipped it up his sleeve instead.

"I figured you would, sooner or later, Harel," Ryze said. "We were just leaving." He started to step towards the door, but the way was barred by several guards in deep red and gold uniforms.

"Or we could stay a bit longer. I didn't realise you enjoyed our company that much." Ryze smiled sarcastically, but there was worry in his eyes. Not for the guards or Harel, but for Khala.

When this was over and she was safe, I was going to enjoy telling him I told you so, in as many different ways as I could. Just because I was human didn't mean I was wrong. And I was right about that. Even if Cavan died. All right, I might have regretted his loss almost as much as Khala would. He was part of our pack. His magic might be needed to get her back.

Harel smirked at Ryze, then looked Cavan up and down. "It looks like someone tried to save me the trouble of having you executed for stealing my key. Did you think I wouldn't know? That I'd see the replacement you put in its place and not know it for what it was?"

Cavan shrugged unapologetically. "We only needed to fool you long enough to get out of the Autumn Court. I didn't anticipate taking quite this long."

"From the report I heard, it was your pretty, broken omega who did this." For some reason, Harel seemed to find that amusing.

"If you know that, then you also know I don't have the key anymore," Cavan said wearily. "It went with her."

"It would have gone with Wornar," Harel corrected. "As it happens, it didn't go anywhere. I haven't kept the real key to Nallis in the side of my throne for years. Not since I exiled Illaria. I expected, at some point, she'd give that information to someone."

Ryze's laughter broke the momentary silence. "I don't mind being outsmarted by you, if it means outsmarting someone who betrayed me. Who betrayed all of us."

"It won't matter if he plans on destroying, or hiding the key. He'll be destroying a fake." Cavan pressed a finger to his lower lip. The side of his mouth twitched upward.

"It matters because we still have access to it," Ryze said. "Admittedly, I'd like to be there to see him try to use it and fail." He sighed. "You can't have everything, I suppose."

"You can't have the key either," Harel said. "I'm sure I didn't give you the impression I intended to give it to you."

"After the effort we went to, to try to get it from you, do you really think we'd do that for nothing?" Ryze asked rhetorically. "I know you don't believe in the other courts, but what if we're right and not following through means dooming us all? Are you really willing to take the chance?"

"Does any of this matter right now?" I asked. "We need to go after Khala."

"If you can just give us the key—" Cavan started.

"The key stays in the Autumn Court," Harel said firmly. "I've wasted enough of my time here. You have two minutes to make a portal and get the fuck out of my court. If you don't, I will have you apprehended and executed. With any luck, this nonsense will end there."

"We'll go," Ryze said after a couple of moments' pause. "But we can assure you, this will not end here. You can bury your head in a pile of leaves as much as you like, but Jorius is under threat. Pretending it's not won't make it go away."

"One and a half minutes," Harel said impatiently.

Ryze rolled his eyes and ushered all of us towards the door. "Your hospitality is worse than Cavan's. No offence, Cavan."

"Offence taken," Cavan said dryly. "Don't compare me to Harel."

I decided they were all as bad as each other, but kept my mouth shut and hurried into the morning sunshine.

Judging by the expression on Tavian's face, he was thinking much the same as me. He was unimpressed by the High Lords bickering with each other. More was at stake than their fragile fucking egos

Ryze waved a few people aside until a space in the middle of the wide plaza was empty.

Apparently opening a portal too close to people was dangerous or something. Right now, I didn't give a shit. I wanted to be gone from here. I wanted to hold Khala and punch the crap out of Wornar. Not necessarily in that order. I'd play that by ear.

Ryze frowned, but eventually had a portal open and waved us through.

I didn't much care for the expression on his face as he did it. Enough was wrong right now. What the crap *else* was happening? We needed to focus our attention on getting Khala back.

I followed Vayne and Cavan through the portal, with Ryze and Tavian right behind me. Ryze closed the portal the moment he stepped out.

The very same moment Vayne turned around to stare at him. "What the hells?"

"This isn't the Spring Court," Cavan added.

"No, it definitely isn't." Tavian's knife was in his hand again. As long as he didn't plan to use it on me, and he acted quickly, I didn't give a shit who he used it on. We'd wasted more than enough time already.

We were standing in a field, a few metres from a stand of trees. Somewhere in the distance I heard what sounded like a waterfall. Or rushing water of some kind. Nothing gave me any indication what court we were in. We could have been back in Fraxius, for all I knew.

"Where the fuck are we?" I demanded.

"In the Winter Court," Ryze said. "On the border. I tried opening a portal to the Spring Court, but it wouldn't let me. They've put wards around the entire court."

"Fuck," Vayne said under his breath.

I looked from one to the other. "What does that mean?"

"It means," Ryze said slowly, "Thiron was planning for a while to keep us out. It also means we can't get to the capital through a portal."

"So we walk." I raised my hands and dropped them back to my sides. Whatever it took to get to her.

"Even without dodging border patrols, it will take us a few days to walk to Lanrial from any point along the border." Ryze kicked a rock in frustration.

I gaped at him. "There has to be another way."

"Can you fly? Because unless you can, there is no other way." Ryze looked ready to tear off heads. He could get in line behind me.

"Now would be a really good time for dragons to exist." Vayne looked as stabby as the rest of us.

"Griffins exist," Tavian said.

"Would you happen to have one in your pocket?" Ryze asked him. "Because if you don't, then they're as useful to us as dragons."

"If one fit in my pocket, it would be as useless as shit," Tavian said. "Unless you have magic to make it big enough for us to sit on its back."

"None of this talking is getting us to the Spring Court any faster," I said, irritated with their banter.

"What would?" Tavian asked. He directed the question to Cavan and Ryze.

It was Vayne who responded. "If we are where I think we are, there's a river not far from here. We could borrow a boat. That would save at least half a day's walking."

"More than that, if Ryze and I can work together and make a breeze to move us along faster," Cavan said.

"By borrow, do you mean steal?" I asked.

"Do you have a problem with us stealing?" Ryze asked. He seemed genuinely curious.

"Fuck no," I replied. "Whatever gets us to her faster." There was nothing I wouldn't do right now to achieve that. *Nothing.*

"Good. Let's go then." Ryze led the way through the trees.

CHAPTER
FOUR
ZARED

"She'll be all right," Tavian said as we walked as quickly as we could through the late morning. "She's tough and brave and smarter than all of us put together. Which is saying something, because we're all pretty smart."

"Says you," Vayne said over his shoulder.

"We're all smart except Vayne," Tavian teased.

Vayne stuck up his middle finger behind his back without glancing back at us.

Tavian managed half a smile which was half more than I did.

"If he touches a hair on her head..." I wasn't even sure which he I meant. It didn't matter. Wornar, Thiron, whoever. I'd cut off their balls and jam them down their throat.

"We can either take turns making him suffer, or we can do it at the same time," Tavian said. "I don't care which it is."

"You can get in line," Ryze said. "In the meantime, we need to be quiet." He waved us down.

I dropped to a crouch and moved over beside him.

There, nestled between the trees and tall grass, a handful of huts sat beside a river that wound silently through the countryside. It must be fed by the waterfall I'd heard earlier, For now it was a tranquil, but rapid flow.

"Can't you just commandeer a boat?" I asked.

"Firstly, I don't want word of my presence here to get out. Approaching people would potentially do that," he said slowly.

"And secondly, we crossed the border into the Spring Court about ten minutes ago. Even if they aren't looking out for us, we won't be welcome here."

"I thought you and Thiron were friendly?" Cavan asked.

"It's as much a surprise to me as it is to anyone else," Ryze admitted. "I'll be having stern words with Thiron the next time I see him. All of this division is exactly how we *shouldn't* be right now. We spent too many years getting complacent and snarky with each other. This is the result of that."

"Maybe having four separate courts is a bad idea," I pointed out. "Why do you have four when you can have one?"

"Because we'd argue over who was going to be king," Cavan said.

"And then there'd be war," Tavian added.

"Unless everyone agrees I should be king," Ryze said. "I'd be a good Fae king."

"Because you're good at faking it?" Cavan suggested.

Ryze snorted a laugh. "I never fake, but that is a faking good joke."

Vayne groaned. "Now you've started them off on puns. I hope you realise, Ryze won't stop until they're out of his system. That could take hours."

"That's the faking truth," Tavian agreed. He grinned, but it wasn't with as much humour and joy as usual. Dampening his spirits was a challenge at the best of times. Just now, he looked like someone dumped a bucket of snow on his.

"Can you point me in the direction of the capital," I said. "It might be less painful to go there by myself."

"I'll go with you," Vayne agreed. "Anything to get away from the puns."

Ryze patted him on the shoulder. "Some day you might lighten the fake up."

"If you don't stop it, I'm going to get my knife and ram it through your faking eyeball," Vayne growled.

"None of us would stop you," I told him.

"Quiet," Cavan said suddenly.

To the surprise of all of us, we immediately fell silent.

I froze on the spot, listening, while wishing I had Fae hearing. I made out the faint sound of voices, and movement through the trees. A crack of a twig here, rustle of leaves there. Nothing anyone would hear if they weren't paying close attention.

Vayne gestured to the south of us and Ryze nodded.

"We need to get to the village and find a boat," Ryze whispered.

"We need a distraction," Cavan added.

He sighed, but rose and headed in the direction Vayne pointed. He staggered with exaggerated steps until he caught the attention of the border patrol. Apparently being covered in blood was useful once in a while.

Ryze gestured us towards the village, if you could call it that. It was little more than a handful of small wooden buildings and a dock that jutted out into the river. A couple of small boats were tied to the worn pilings. A larger dock occupied a chunk of the opposite bank, a wide ferry bobbing against it.

Shouting came from behind us, accompanied by a couple of flashes of light. It wasn't until I smelled the smoke that I realised the light was flame.

The acrid smell was followed by heavy footsteps as Cavan ran to catch up.

"I think I got them all," he panted. "Hurry." He looked tired. After losing all that blood, he probably needed to eat and rest.

Like the rest of us, he wasn't going to rest easily until our mate was back with us.

Even then, I might stay awake until the end of time to make sure no one tried to take her from me again.

I tried to ignore the smell of burning meat as I ran to the closest boat and started to untie the rope that held it in place.

"Never mind that," Cavan said. "Get in."

I glanced at him, but nodded and did what he said. I realised why when all of us were in and another flash of flame burned the rope away.

"Don't set the boat on fire," Ryze warned. If I didn't know better, I'd almost think he was enjoying himself.

"That's what you're here for," Cavan told him. "To make sure I don't." He gave Ryze a smirk.

Ryze gave him one in return.

I moved to sit closer to Tavian while the two High Lords quickly figured out how to combine their magic to make wind.

"Khala could have done it by herself," Tavian whispered. His hand found its way to mine. He gave it a squeeze.

"You really think she'll be all right?" I asked, my voice low so no one could hear the tremble in my tone. "You know these Fae better than I do. Would they hurt her?"

He took a while to respond. "I thought I knew them," he said slowly. "But now I realise I didn't know them at all. Before I met you, I would have said Cavan is an enemy and Wornar is a friend."

"Now?" I absently stroked my thumb across the inside of his wrist.

"Now I trust Cavan almost as much as I trust Ryze, but Wornar... He's an alpha. He got his hands on an omega, possibly for the first time. I can only guess what that might do to him. We seem to have a way of getting under people's skin without meaning to."

He gave me a glance, but didn't smile. He didn't mean Wornar might fall for her. He honestly didn't know whether he'd hurt her or not.

"That thing where alphas order you," I started.

"We can't fight it," he said, his tone and expression hollow. "I can't explain it. If he orders her to do something, she'll do it. No matter what it is. Even if she hates the idea. Even if it hurts her. You only have to see what he made her do to Cavan. You can't think for a moment she wanted to stab him. She'd only do that if she was angry with him, and she wasn't."

"No, she wasn't." I felt that much through the bond. She was horrified at what Wornar made her do. I didn't want to imagine how much worse it might get for her.

However fast Ryze and Cavan made the boat go, it wasn't fast enough.

The sunset painted the sky with streaks of pink and gold. A woman of middle years brought me a tray of soup and fresh bread.

For a Fae to look as she did, she must have been old. Of course I didn't ask.

I waited until she left and sat down to eat. I didn't waste time worrying that it might be laced with something. If they wanted me dead, they'd kill me. And if they wanted me incapacitated in some way, they'd order me.

So I ate and enjoyed the flavours of the vegetables in the soup and the freshness of the bread.

I could say this about the Spring Court; they knew how to cook.

I was just mopping up the last of my soup when Wornar slipped in the door. Almost immediately, the food threatened to sour in my belly.

"It looks like I have perfect timing," he said smoothly. "You can speak freely. I'd prefer you to be willing."

I hadn't realised how heavily his orders lay until he lifted them. When they were gone, I felt like I could breathe again.

"If you were here a couple of minutes earlier, I could have dumped my soup on your head," I said with mock sweetness. I probably shouldn't provoke him, but he gave me permission to speak my mind, so I took it.

He laughed. "So feisty." He propped his elbows on the table and leaned towards me. "I would have liked to see you try."

I managed to resist the urge to sit back away from him. "It would have been worth it." Maybe I could singe his face with magic instead.

Before I could even try, he held up a finger and pointed at my face. "No using magic on me. That's an order I won't be lifting. Omega magic is too dangerous to be on the loose."

"I still have a spoon." I held it up as though to stab him with it.

"Terrifying." He snatched the spoon and tossed it into the bowl with a clatter. "I thought we could have a little fun. A chance for you to get your freedom. If you dare to try." He arched an eyebrow at me.

"I dare if it means getting away from you," I told him. I still felt dirty from his touch. If there was a chance I could escape the Spring Court, I'd take it.

"I was hoping you'd say that." The smile he gave me was dark, brutal. Shivers slid up and down my spine.

What had I gotten myself into? Whatever it was, he wasn't going to make this easy.

"Come with me." He stood and made a portal in front of us.

Wherever we were going, it wasn't far. I saw right through into a forest, where the last rays of the sun gilded the trees. It was beautiful in a chilling kind of way.

Night would fall soon. I had a feeling we'd be out there alone.

"I see you're starting to appreciate what I have in mind," he said. "Step through."

Not because he told me to, but because this might be my chance to flee, I stepped through.

He followed me and closed the portal behind us.

The forest was almost silent, the air cool and still. A lingering scent of lemon and eucalyptus hung in the air, along with the faint smell of roses and lavender.

I wrapped my arms around myself and moved across the forest floor, away from him.

"Where are we?" I asked.

"We're a few kilometres from the border." He leaned back against the trunk of a tree and regarded me through half-lidded eyes.

I wished I had a knife I could use on him right now.

"Why are we here?" I felt for the other men through the bond, but they were even further away now.

"Have you ever been hunting?" He cocked his head at me. He spoke in such a pleasant tone, he could have been asking if I'd ever had chocolate. Or if I'd been in love.

"No, never. It's not really the kind of activity Silent Maidens get up to."

"Seems a shame to miss out on all the fun." He clicked his tongue. "Never mind, we can make up for it tonight."

I swallowed and started to wish I hadn't eaten anything. The soup and bread turned to lead in my stomach.

"What are we hunting?" I asked carefully. I was almost certain I knew the answer to that question.

"We're not hunting," he said easily. He straightened up and lowered his hands to his sides. "*I'm* hunting. I'll give you a couple of minutes head start. If you can make it across the border before I catch you, you can go free."

My shivers turned to cold fear.

"And if you catch me?"

He stepped over to me and leaned in. He smiled as he spoke. "Then I get to keep you. One word of advice. Run."

I didn't stop to think, I turned and fled into the trees.

His laughter followed, mocking, unhurried. Like he was so certain I'd panic and he'd catch me easily.

Don't panic, I told myself. *He wins if you do.* I couldn't run blindly and hope to outrun him. I had to reason clearly. Where exactly was the border?

I wouldn't let myself think about what might happen if he decided to break his word, if I crossed before he caught me and he decided to keep me anyway.

I had to focus on getting across.

The sun was setting, so I knew which way was west.

I pictured the map in my mind. The placement of the four courts. The Spring Court was north of the Winter Court, and west of the Summer Court. If I ran west, I'd run deeper into Spring Court territory.

I veered off towards the east. Running into the deepening shadows.

No doubt that was his plan. He assumed in my fear I'd head for the part of the forest where I could still see where I was going. Logical, given how quickly it became difficult to see much of anything in front of me.

I considered using magic to illuminate the way. If I did that, I might as well stand amongst the trees and shout. Any light would give my location away. The only chance I had was to find my way in the dark.

I slowed, moving quieter. Snapping twigs under my feet would resound like thunder out here. The crack of several behind me said he'd started to follow.

Don't panic, I told myself again. What would Tavian do? He was a trained assassin. He'd slip away and be across the border before Wornar could blink.

I tried to put myself in his mindset. How exactly did an assassin move so quietly? Become one with the trees or something?

I tripped over a root and almost fell to my knees. I managed to save myself at the last moment and staggered on a few steps.

"You smell delicious, sweet omega," Wornar called out behind me. "Like a spring rain on a field abundant with lavender. Good enough to eat and drink."

I shivered and went on moving. Now he mentioned it, I could smell him too. The scent of an alpha mixed with that of fresh grass and that first warm breeze of spring.

I needed to cover my scent. He said I couldn't use magic against him, he didn't say I couldn't use it at all.

I paused for maybe half a minute, winced at the flash before the tree behind me caught fire. For once, the unseasonable warmth worked in my favour. The bark was drier than it might otherwise have been. Flames roared up into the canopy in moments, down to ignite the leaf matter on the ground.

The smoke would help to cover my scent, but the fire spread quickly. I turned from it and fled.

"You'll be punished for that," Wornar called out.

All the more reason to get away.

I glanced over my shoulder to see he'd stopped, and was using magic to douse the flames. I couldn't see what he was doing, but it seemed effective.

I sent a quick request to the gods that it would be enough to delay him until I reached the border. I didn't try to be quiet now. I ran.

A couple of times I tripped and fell, wincing as my knees scraped, digging into twigs. I immediately pulled myself back to my feet and kept on running.

By now, the sun was little more than a slight blush behind me. Everything in front of me was so dark I was forced to run with my hands up in front of me to keep from slamming face first into a tree.

I glanced back again. The fire was out. The sun was completely gone. The forest was entirely dark and stank heavily of smoke. He might have more difficulty finding me, but I also had no idea where he was. And no way of knowing when I reached safety.

What had he said? A couple of kilometres to the border? How far had I run? Not that far, not yet. Even if I had, I'd run twice that, just to be sure. And then go on running until the sun rose.

I dashed tears off my cheeks. I told myself they were from the smoke, not because I was scared. Not because I thought at any moment now, he'd catch up to me. If I was a human, he would have caught me by now. But I was Fae. I was taller, faster. I could evade him.

"Are you getting tired?" he asked.

Fuck.

There was no way he was as close behind me as he sounded. He couldn't be. I didn't dare to look back and check.

"I'm not," he called out. "I could go all night. And I will, the moment I catch you."

If he was trying to make me run faster, he succeeded. The threat of what he'd do to me gave me renewed energy.

In spite of that, I slowed down. If he couldn't smell me as easily, then I needed to rely on stealth to evade him. Stealth and cunning.

I ducked past a tree and formed a sheet of ice across the forest floor behind me. The moon was starting to rise, but not enough to illuminate it.

Let's see how you deal with that, I thought.

I rose and kept on moving.

After what felt like an eternity, but was probably a minute or two, he gave a short cry of surprise. That was followed by a heavy thump.

When I was at the temple in Ebonfalls, they taught us about the rules of the gods. Things that just were. Rocks can't fall up. If something doesn't have wings, it can't fly. I'd added a couple of others myself, like it's extremely difficult to fit more than two cocks into my pussy at the same time.

I added a new one now. Ice is slippery. Don't try running across it. The thud of his body hitting the forest floor was satisfying as fuck.

"Fucking bitch," Wornar snarled.

Not sorry, I thought. Was it too much to hope he'd broken a leg and couldn't keep after me? Judging by the sound of stomping and the angry smashing of branches, he hadn't broken any bones. Shame.

"I'm going to make you regret doing that," he called out. He was gaining on me again. "When I'm finished with you, you'll beg for my forgiveness."

In your dreams, I thought. What I could use right now was one of those portals in the air, a gift from the other courts, and some magic aimed at him. It was effective in getting rid of Dalyth. Why not Wornar as well?

No portal appeared. I hadn't expected it to. It seemed to follow Hycathe around, not me. That was something I didn't have time to dwell on right now.

I darted through the trees and ducked low as I crossed a section of open grassland. I half waited for him to pounce, exposed as I was for a minute or two. By the time I dove back into the trees, he seemed further behind somehow. I didn't stop to wonder why until the ground tilted down.

I lost my balance and rolled and slithered all the way down, painfully bumping over rocks and sticks. Finally, I landed with a splash in frigid water.

The shock of the sudden cold made me gasp out loud. I was covered in scrapes and bruises, but as far as I could tell, nothing was broken.

Suppressing a grunt of pain, I forced myself back to my feet. I was standing on the edge of a river. In the starlight, I made out its progress as it flowed past.

"Fuck," I whispered. It was flowing west, straight back into the Spring Court. Of course it was. He must have hoped I'd get caught in the flow and dragged back. Asshole.

I'd never managed to make a bridge like Ryze could, but I grabbed enough magic to make an ice wall. The last time I did it, I almost killed Zared. This time, if anyone behind me got caught in it, I wouldn't spare any sympathy or tears.

The flow of the river was blocked for a couple of metres in either direction, but it wouldn't hold for long. It would overflow right to where I was currently standing in a minute or two.

I sucked in a breath for bravery, then bolted across the river bed, my feet slipping on mud as I went. Every few steps, I had to pause and yank my foot free. I lost one shoe, then the other, but kept on going.

I managed to reach the other bank and scrambled up, breaking fingernails and skin as I pulled myself free of the mud.

I turned to look back over the river.

Wornar stood looking at the wall. The moon had risen high enough to illuminate him. The admiration on his face. He didn't seem to be breathing as heavily as I was. Perhaps he made a habit of chasing women through the forest.

"Nice trick." He clapped his hands together a couple of times.

"I thought so," I called back. I used a bit of summer magic to help melt the wall and let the river flow back to its bed. I must be close to the border now, and he was on the other side.

His teeth flashed right before he opened a portal and stepped through.

The other end appeared right beside me. I wasn't good at keeping portals open, but I was good at closing them. I grabbed all the magic I could and focused on trying to do just that.

If I could snap it shut at this end, he might get stuck in there. Or better yet, squashed to death. I was absolutely all right with that.

He growled and staggered back out, before closing it himself and opening another one.

I did the same with this one, teeth gritted, fighting to not only shut it, but push it. Push it where, I didn't know. Just...away.

Something made me glance over to the opposite bank. He'd moved away from the portal and was getting ready to make another one.

I stopped pushing on the portal in front of me, turned away and ran. I considered trying to make my own portal and getting the hells out of here, but if it behaved like they always had in the past, he'd catch me while I was trying to keep it open. I couldn't afford to waste that time.

"Are you having as much fun as I am?" He was on the same side of the river now, but he was dry and still had his boots on.

I had bare feet and wet clothes holding me back. I also had the determination not to let him catch me.

"It's adorable that you think you can make it," he added. "You're close, so close. But not close enough. You might as well give up right now. I know there's a part of you that wants to. A place in your omega heart that wants to surrender to me. Embrace it. Save your energy for other things. Better things."

Yes, there was a very small part of me that instinctively felt the need to please the alpha in him, but it was small enough to ignore. And overridden with thoughts of Cavan, Ryze, Tavian, Vayne and Zared. Pleasing two alphas, two betas and another omega was much more important to me. My pack. They overrode everything. Everything I was, belonged to them.

I was tiring, but I clung to what Wornar said about being close to the border. Had he expected me to get this far? Maybe he hoped I would, just for the thrill of the chase. From some deluded idea that he could teach me who was in charge here. He wouldn't win. He couldn't. Nothing in me could accept that.

I realised the air smelled different. It was clear of smoke. Instead, it smelled like the honeysuckle and wildflowers of summer. I might have imagined the increase in temperature, and it might just be from exertion. Either way, he was right, I was close.

This wasn't like going from one season to another, it was a sensation... A trickle of magic between each court that formed the border. Something only Fae could feel.

There. I wasn't imagining it. There was something ahead, drawing me closer. Something warm like a nest, but more soothing. More compelling.

Safety.

Just another minute or two. A few dozen handfuls of steps.

I didn't know he was right behind me until he grabbed me. We crashed hard to the ground. The impact drove a sob out of my lungs.

He held me down, his weight on mine. He chuckled in my ear.

"Caught you."

CHAPTER
SIX

KHALA

I writhed and fought, trying to push him off and get away. He was too heavy. His weight pinned me to the ground.

I struggled to scream or shout, but landing heavily winded me. It took me a few moments to regain my breath.

Before I could utter a sound, he spoke.

"Don't make any loud noises. I don't want anyone to disturb our fun."

"Get off me," I hissed.

"I want you to feel something." He grabbed my hand.

I pushed back against him. The last thing I wanted to do was touch his cock.

He pulled my hand forward until the tips of my fingers tingled. "You feel that? Do you know what that is?"

I wanted to both bask in the magic and draw away from it at the same time.

"The border." I managed to speak in a small, bitter whisper.

"That's exactly what it is," he said triumphantly. "See how close you were. You put up a good fight. I'm genuinely surprised. I thought I'd catch you at the first line of trees. But here you are. Just centimetres away from escape. Another couple of steps and you would have done it. But you didn't. You failed. I won, and now I get to keep you."

I curled my fingers away from the border. "I'll never be yours. Ryze, Cavan and—"

"Didn't reach you in time," Wornar finished for me. "It doesn't matter what they do now. It doesn't matter what *you* do. I don't want to force you to comply. I don't want to break you, but if that's what it takes, so be it. Remember this. It's your choice to make. You can force me to force you, or you can be agreeable."

What sort of choice was that?

"If I have a choice, then I choose neither," I said. "Get off me and let me go."

He clicked his tongue. "I can't do that. We had a deal. If you reached the border first I would have let you go. Besides, I don't want to. I own you now."

He rolled off me, grabbed my hands and pulled me to my feet. "No running away now."

I couldn't run, couldn't use magic against him and I couldn't shout. I was becoming more and more powerless. Stripped down, layer by layer until I was raw.

I refused to give in to despair. I would find a way out, no matter what it took. I would not let him get the better of me.

"You're a stubborn one, are you?" He cocked his head at me. "I can see you thinking about your next move. This doesn't have to be bad. As Fae go, I'm not the worst of us. I'm not going to beat you, or lock you away."

He slid the tip of his finger down my cheek. "All I'm going to do is fuck you. Is that really so terrible?"

I jerked my face away. "Without my consent it is, yes."

"Then give your consent," he said as though it was the easiest thing in the world. "I don't need it. With a few words, I can make you want me. I can make you do whatever I say. I'd rather you didn't force me to do that. Whether I have to or not, is up to you."

He made it sound like he was the victim. That if he took me with force, it would be entirely my fault for making him do it.

"I will never voluntarily fuck you." My voice wavered, betraying the depths of my emotions. The cold fear that started to settle on me.

He shrugged. "So be it." He made a portal beside us and grabbed my wrist to push me through. "Go and have a bath. You smell like smoke and dirt."

I wished I'd incinerated him. So much more than that, I wished I'd made it those handful of steps. To be so fucking close...

"Wait," he said before I started towards the bathing room. "Take your clothes off here. I want to see what I'm getting when you're clean."

The order settled on me, like an executioner's sword. Sharp, heavy and final.

I'd never hated anyone more than I hated him right now. I was a puppet, made to dance on his strings. A puppet who wanted to stab him in the eyeball with a fork.

Tears slid down my cheeks. I gritted my teeth. My body moved beyond my control. I slipped out of my pants and pulled off my shirt.

I dropped them on the floor and looked back at him with resentment, his face blurry through the haze of tears.

His eyes travelled up and down my bare body. The front of his pants tented. For a while, I thought he might not bother to wait until I was clean.

My whole body trembled. Without touching me he made me feel violated. Dirty. Beyond dirty, filthy.

381

He nodded. "Go and get clean. I'll be back in a few minutes."

"Take a year if you have to." At least I still had my sassy mouth. Maybe I shouldn't provoke him, but I couldn't see how any of this could get much worse than it already was. If I was lucky, he might get furious enough to kill me.

A flash of anger crossed his face, but it was gone before I could blink. His customary smile was back.

"I could take a year," he said slowly. "It might be interesting to see the effect of the anticipation on you, dear omega. Wondering exactly when I'd return and what I might do when I get back. At some point, you'd become complacent. That would be the exact moment I reappeared. Fortunately, I have no interest in clinging to the anticipation any longer than necessary. Blue balls are much less fun as they sound."

He cupped a hand around his erection, then smiled and left the room.

I swallowed hard and headed into the bathing room to start the bath. Like in the Winter Court, the Spring Court had running hot water, which still fascinated me in spite of my present situation. It was a luxury humans didn't have.

I filled the bath to the top and stepped into the slightly too hot water. It enveloped my skin like a wet embrace, wrapping around me and washing away everything, at least for now.

While I was under there, I could pretend this was all there was in the world. That I wasn't being held against my will by a Fae man who intended to force himself on me. Who seemed to be looking forward to doing that.

It was all I could do to hold myself together and not duck under the water and stay there. That would solve one problem, but it would create too many more. Not the least of which was the potential Ryze and Cavan might go to war with the Spring Court over me.

They still might, but without doubt they would if I was dead. They needed to focus their attention on the other courts and dealing with them. Not worrying about me.

They were, though. I sensed that through the bond with the four of them. I doubted Cavan was any less worried and determined to reach me.

Right now, they felt so far away. Too far. What were they doing? They didn't seem to be fighting with each other. That was a bonus. They all seemed tense. If I had to decide who was the most strung out, I couldn't. Vayne and Zared were the usual simmering pots of anger waiting to boil over. Ryze was cold, determined fury.

I wouldn't like to be on the receiving end of any of their ire.

I sent them thoughts that I was all right, but I wasn't sure how convincing I was. I certainly didn't convince myself. I was terrified of what might happen tonight. And tomorrow night. And the gods only knew how many nights after that.

I tried not to think about it, but it dominated my thoughts. Of course it did. What else did I have to think about? The idea of being violated enveloped me tighter than the water.

This was exactly what Wornar wanted. It wasn't enough that I knew what he was going to do to me. He wanted me to think about it, to be scared, terrified of the moment he'd step back into the room.

I washed quickly and dried myself off before dressing in clean clothes I found in the wardrobe. Soft pants in pale blue, and a short-sleeved blouse that barely covered my breasts. The fabric moulded around them, leaving little to the imagination.

I stepped into a section of the room out of sight of the balcony and rubbed my temples for a moment.

If I didn't at least try, I'd never know if I could make a portal here. I knew I could make one, I'd done it before. Then, they hadn't stayed open. But I hadn't been desperate before.

When Ryze tried to teach me, I was angry with him. Not receptive to everything he was trying to tell me. I was angry he'd lied to me. That he hadn't told me there was a chance I'd transform into a Fae. All he told me was that I would go into heat and I'd need him and want him.

It seemed to me as if every part of being an omega meant surrendering my choices. I'd liked him before my heat, but he hadn't presented me with a ton of other alphas to choose from. Or any, in fact. I'd fucked him because my body needed me to. Not because I'd been able to make any conscious decision.

I wasn't only angry because he lied. I was angry because of that too; my lack of choice.

I wasn't angry with him anymore. Now I could calmly, rationally think about what he told me about forming a portal and keeping it open.

I had no choice. I *had* to get it to work. Wornar thought we had some kind of deal where he got to do whatever he wanted to me because I didn't run fast enough.

As far as I was concerned, we had no such deal. Even if we did, keeping me didn't necessarily mean he got to touch me. He could lock me away in this room forever. As long as he gave me books, it might be a tolerable life. Certainly better than being violated.

I drew together winter and summer magic. If I had no luck with one, maybe I would have luck with the other, or with both. If I did it right, I might convince the magic it was spring magic. Magic wasn't alive, so how hard would it be to trick it?

Gods, please let it be easy.

The air quivered in front of me, like I was looking through a cloud of smoke. A chair in the corner danced and writhed on the other side of the wall of magic.

I ignored it and focused on opening a portal to the first place I could think of. My bedroom in the Winter Court. It was a place of confused and conflicting memories, but also safety.

It was the place where I learned I was part Fae. Where I first discovered that my mother used to be involved with Cavan, before she ran off and married my father. It was a place where Tavian and I spent hours curled up together, talking and touching.

Best of all, it was anywhere but here.

I couldn't see all the way into my room, the portal was too long. The walls were made of what looked like a combination of ice and fire. Crystalline, but at the same time glowing faintly red. I didn't care what it looked like, as long as it got me out of here.

I took a step towards the portal, my heart racing. So far, it was staying open. At any moment now, it might snap shut.

I held my breath and took another step.

A hand clamped around my throat from behind.

"What did I say about not running away?"

A blink later, the portal was gone. And my hope with it.

CHAPTER
SEVEN
KHALA

Warning This chapter contains sexual assault. It's contained within this chapter and only vaguely referenced beyond this point. If you're uncomfortable, you can skip this chapter and not miss out on elements of the story.

"You needn't have bothered to get dressed again," he said. He slid his other hand to the front of my shirt and grabbed my breast. He pinched my nipple between his fingers. "I've been giving this a lot of thought."

"You've decided to let me go." I knew that wasn't what he was saying at all.

He chuckled near my ear. "No, dear omega. I've been deciding whether or not to let you fight me. You will fight me if I let you, won't you?"

"Yes." I tried to jerk myself out of his grip.

He pinched harder. "I thought you might." He slid his hand out of my blouse, grabbed the front and tore it down the middle.

"Listen carefully, little omega. You won't fight me. You'll do exactly what I tell you to do. You want to please me. You want me to fuck you more than you've ever wanted anyone in your entire life. You're going to enjoy every moment of it. When I tell you to, you're going to come for me, and it will be the best orgasm you ever had. Not just tonight, but whenever I want you. You'll be willing and compliant. Eager. Dripping."

Every word he said was another layer on top of an order that was as twisted as fuck. My body immediately throbbed for him. I wanted, needed, him to touch me everywhere. I wanted to spread my legs wide and take him inside me.

And I hated myself for it. The need to scream and cry was pushed into the back of my mind, overpowered by lust.

"Undress yourself, then undress me."

I couldn't stop myself from turning around to face him while stripping quickly. I all but tore the clothes off him, revealing a toned, muscular physique and thick, erect cock. I was trembling again, but this time with the need to feel him fill me.

"Isn't this much more fun?" He looked so smug.

I wanted to punch him in the face.

I managed to whisper, "Please, don't," before he led me over to the bed and laid me down on my back.

He ignored me and parted my thighs with his hands. He slid his hand up one leg and slipped two fingers straight inside my pussy.

"You say don't, but your pussy is dripping wet for me. I think, secretly, you want this as much as I do." He slid in another finger and started to pound me with his hand.

Tears trickled down my cheeks while my body betrayed me by bucking and moving my hips until my clit found the heel of his hand.

"See? In the end, all omegas are whores. All you want is to be fucked. It's what you live for." He ground his hand into my clit, rubbing firmly until I was on the verge of coming. "You're enjoying this, aren't you?"

I wanted to tell him to fuck off, but the only thing that came out of my mouth with the words, "Yes, alpha."

I didn't know what I hated more right now: his ability to control me, him, or myself. My body wasn't my own anymore. As long as I was stuck here with him, I'd never be able to do anything except what he told me to do.

I should have sunk under that bathwater while I could. Any of the seven hells would be better than this.

"Come for me, omega whore," he ordered.

I came hard and fast, rocking and crying out as the world shattered and my body betrayed me even more completely than it already had.

I was barely down when he pulled his fingers out of me, rolled me over and pulled me onto my hands and knees.

"Tell me you want me inside you," he ordered.

No no no. Gods no.

My lips moved and the words came out anyway. "I want you inside me."

Not as much as I want to die right now.

He slipped a hand between us to position himself, then pushed himself deep inside my body.

I couldn't contain a sob, even when it turned into a moan of pleasure. I hated how good he felt inside me. How full I was. I hated that I could have stayed like that for hours. I hated how good it felt when he started to pound into me over and over with even, firm strokes.

I wanted it to stop and I wanted it to go on forever.

He grabbed my breasts and kneaded them while thrusting.

"You feel good, omega whore. Worth all the waiting. Worth all the preparation. If Ryze and Cavan ever reach Lanrial alive, you'll tell them you want to stay with me. And you'll mean every word of it. If they come. I'm sure by now they have realised all the effort isn't worth it for one omega slut. They'll go back to the usual petty squabbles and we'll get on with our lives. We'll raise the child I'm about to put into your belly. You'll spend the rest of your life adoring me, even if I have to tell you to do it. I'd prefer it if you turned to me, but it doesn't much matter. I don't want you for your companionship, just your body and your womb. Both of those are mine now."

He thrust harder several more times, then stilled as he came inside me.

I screwed my eyes shut and tried to block out the noise of him and his orgasm. He could make me say I wanted and do things I didn't. He might make me feel things I didn't want to say. But he couldn't change the fact that, at my core, I hated him.

He slumped and panted over my back for a couple of minutes before pulling out of me and flopping down on his back on the mattress.

He looked over at me and smiled at the expression on my face. "Conflicted? That's perfect. I don't care what you want as long as you do what I say. You know why? Because it's an alpha's job to have power over his omega. And your job to obey. I'm sure Ryze has told you something ridiculous like he's supposed to cater to your every need. On the contrary, you're here to take care of mine. Now, get comfortable. I have things to do, but I'll be back later."

He patted me on the ass, then rolled off the bed and pulled his clothes back on.

It wasn't until the door clicked shut behind him that I scrambled off the bed and refilled the bath. I needed to scrub every centimetre of myself clean. To rid myself of his touch. By the time I got into the bath, it was hot as in the first one. Hotter.

My skin turned red the moment I was immersed. I grabbed a brush and started to scrub myself everywhere. When I was done cleaning the outside, I still needed to clean the inside too.

He said I couldn't use magic on him, but he didn't say I couldn't use it on myself.

I focused my thoughts on everywhere between my pussy and my womb. I scoured myself inside with magic so hot I thought I might incinerate myself. I didn't care.

Everywhere his seed might be, I scrubbed. There was no way it could take hold inside me. No way a child that belonged to him could grow inside my body.

In the back of my mind, I understood this might stop me from ever having children, but I didn't care. *Couldn't* care.

I wanted, needed every drop of him gone from me. If this was what I had to do every time he touched me, I would.

387

I lay back, sank under the water until only my mouth and nose weren't submerged.

I tried to sink a little deeper, but I couldn't bring myself to do it. If I did that, then he won. He got the satisfaction of forcing me to the point where I didn't want to live. I wasn't there yet.

I would *not* let him push me there. No matter what he did, or made me do, I couldn't let him reach every part of me. I could not, would not let him break me.

If I had to endure him using my body every day for the rest of my life, he would *not break me.*

I promised myself that. If he ordered me to rip my own soul in two, I wouldn't let him. Even if all that was left to fight was a small part of me in the back of my mind, I would stand against him.

He would never completely win.

I dragged myself out of the bath for a second time, dried and dressed, and slipped under the covers to curl up into the smallest possible ball.

I forced a wall between me and my three bonds and let the tears come.

I didn't know how long I sobbed. Maybe minutes. Maybe hours. I hated myself again for showing this much weakness, even though I was the only one here to see it.

I had to be stronger than this. I had to be harder than stone. Harder than diamonds. I couldn't afford to be fragile or brittle. I couldn't let anyone put a toe past my walls. Not ever again. Even half a toe would make me vulnerable, and I was done being vulnerable. I was Khala. I was tough.

I told myself that over and over while I sobbed.

I ignored Ryze's attempt to push through my walls and reach me. I shoved him back out.

If I could break the bonds right now, I would. What was the use of them when they couldn't help me when I needed them? Surely there was a way for the men to reach me, even with the wards in place? Had they tried hard enough to get to me?

On the other end, all I'd felt was concern and determination, not battling and struggling to break through into the Spring Court. What use was their worry while I was in here having Wornar force himself on me?

The bonds were useless. All they did was make me vulnerable, because the men on the other end knew what happened to me. They knew what I went through, and they couldn't do a thing. Not one thing. They couldn't stop it, or make it go away. They couldn't give me a place to hide while it happened.

No, all they could do was fucking sympathise. Their fucking sympathy was no fucking use to me. None at all.

Those thoughts made me hate myself even more. They were worried because of me. They shouldn't be.

Wornar and Harel were right, I was nothing more than an insignificant omega whore. My pack should be finding a way to stop the other courts from destroying the seasonal courts. Not wasting time on me. On someone who couldn't even control her own body. Someone who, even now, ached to have Wornar's cock deep inside me again. Who wanted his hands and mouth on my pussy. If he walked into the room right now, I'd spread my legs for him and let him sink deep into me. I'd let him do it again and again and again. Until my body was raw.

I was made for fucking. Why else would the alpha-order exist? Whether the gods had a sense of humour and created omegas for shits and giggles, or not, this was how we were. We were made to be compliant, obedient, willing.

Even when we wanted to be none of those things.

If the gods had a sense of humour, it was the most fucked up thing in the world.

I added the gods to the ever growing list of things I hated right now.

None of those things I hated as much as I hated myself.

CHAPTER
EIGHT
ZARED

"We need to hurry the fuck up."

How the hells could any of the others stay so calm? I wanted to burn the whole fucking world down right now. Before Khala shut us out, I felt exactly what that asshole did to her.

If he was in front of me right now, I'd tear him into a million pieces. Bad enough that he touched her at all. The whole omega-alpha thing was screwy without being abused.

Without *her* being abused.

Fuck, I wanted to choke that asshole with my bare hands.

"Don't you think we'd go faster if we could?" Cavan whispered.

He gestured at me to keep my head down so I wouldn't be seen by the passing patrol. They were far enough away they wouldn't hear us whisper, but they'd see us if we moved excessively.

They were the third border patrol we'd seen this morning and the sun was barely a hand span high in the sky.

I glared at him, but looked away.

This was his fault. If he hadn't insisted she go to the Autumn Court in the first place, she wouldn't have been there for Wornar to take. All of that was for nothing, since we didn't have the fucking key anyway. Everything she was going through, was for *nothing*.

If it wouldn't waste time, I might rip him apart too. I still might, later.

A hand touched my shoulder. I didn't have to look to know it was Tavian.

"Fighting amongst ourselves isn't going to help her," he said softly.

The two of us and Ryze felt the same thing from her, but it seemed to hit Tavian almost as hard as it hit me.

In spite of his apparent love of killing people, the Master of Assassins had a

390

sensitive side. And, given he was also an omega, the same thing might have happened to him. Had it happened in the past?

That was a question I couldn't bring myself to ask. Not in front of the other men. It was something best kept for a quiet conversation, when and if he was ready to share. If the expression on his face was any indication, he'd at best been in a similar situation.

"Hiding in the bushes doesn't seem to be helping much either," I said. "Can't we just... I don't know."

"Go home and come back with an army?" Ryze suggested. When I turned to look at him, he gave me a wry look. "Don't worry, I've considered it. The five of us have a better chance of getting in and out quickly, and with minimal loss of life. On both sides."

He must have seen what I was about to say. I didn't give a shit about loss of life from anyone belonging to the Spring Court. If they supported Wornar, then they were the enemy. They deserved to be smashed to pieces by the combined armies of the Winter and Summer Courts.

"I hate to say that Ryze is right," Vayne said, "but in this case, he is. It would take too long to mobilise our army and transport everyone here. Besides, the five of us make up a pretty fucking good army."

"I disagree," Tavian said. "I have a better idea."

"I'm coming with you," I said once he told us. "I know how to keep quiet." He'd have to tie me down or kill me to keep me from following. He might as well let me accompany him.

He wanted to tell me no, that was obvious from the expression on his face, but finally he nodded. "Fine, but if I tell you to do something, don't argue. This is what I do and I'm good at it. Listen to me and we should be all right. If I tell you to stay behind somewhere, you do it. Agreed?"

I considered for a moment, then nodded. "Whatever it takes."

Ryze rubbed his chin. "I don't like it, but I think it's the only way. We'll be ready for your signal." He nodded to Cavan and Vayne and rose. They headed off east.

After several minutes, Tavian gestured to me and started off to the north.

"You're about to get a crash course in assassin skills. Personally, I think everyone should have them. You never know when the ability to sneak in and out of places will come in handy."

"I get the impression you do that often," I told him.

He gave me a broad smile over his shoulder. "Quite often," he agreed. "Wouldn't want my skills to get rusty."

"Who taught you?" I asked as we slipped through the tall grass and into the shelter of a thicket of trees.

"I was apprenticed to the last Master of Assassins," he said. "I wanted to join the regular army, but he saw something in me and took me under his wing. He taught me how to be silent when it mattered, and told me I could get paid to kill people. He was right, it was the perfect job for me. I would have hated peacetime as a soldier anyway. The constant training is all very well, but it's pretend."

"You prefer real killing?" I asked.

"Only people who deserve it," he said, his tone dark. He didn't try to suppress the undercurrent of violence. It gave me the shivers while at the same time making my cock twitch. He was charming and dangerous, and it would be easy for me to fall for him as hard as I had for Khala.

"I can think of a few of those right now."

"Me too. We can argue later over who is going to kill Wornar. And whether we do it quickly or slowly."

"I don't care how fast it is," I said. "As long as he can't touch her ever again."

Tavian stopped and turned to put a hand on my bicep. "We will get to her. He will pay for what he did."

"I know, but how many more times will he do it before we get there?" She shut us out so firmly, I didn't know if it was happening right now. All I knew was she was alive.

Literally nothing else. All this not knowing was ripping my heart straight out of my chest.

Tavian shook his head. "I don't know. Once is too many. But we need to keep our heads for her sake. If we get caught and killed, it won't help her. The most important part of assassin training is learning how to turn your anger into something productive. Focus on what we'll do when we find her, and what it takes to do that. Don't let your hatred and anger make you do something to jeopardise her. All right?"

I closed my eyes for a moment, then nodded. "I'll try."

"It's okay to think vengeful thoughts, just not rash, angry ones," he said. "She's locked us out right now, that doesn't mean she's going to continue to do that. She needs calm thoughts on the end of the bond. If she reaches out, *when* she reaches out, she'll need reassurance. Can you do that?"

"I can," I said firmly. He was right. Khala didn't need my emotions in turmoil. For all I knew, she felt everything flowing from us to her.

I immediately regretted my fury. What if I made things worse for her? I might be as bad as Wornar if I did that.

"I know you can." Tavian gave me a quick kiss on the mouth. "You're one of the most amazing people I know. Now— we should keep going. We're about half a day from Lanrial. If we hurry, we can be there by nightfall. By the time the sun rises again, we'll be back home. All of us safe and sound."

My lips tingled where his touched mine, but I didn't have time to think about that right now. Khala was what mattered, not whatever was growing between me and Tave. That was something we could deal with later.

"I like the sound of that."

His whole body went stiff. He pulled me into a crouch beside him.

I didn't question him, I dropped and listened.

He leaned over to whisper in my ear. "Stay here. I'll be two minutes." He crept off silently.

It couldn't have been more than half a minute later when a short cry was followed by a soft thud. Another came half a minute after that. Someone shouted, but it was cut off as quickly as the first two.

A few seconds later, Tavian reappeared. He was wiping blood off a knife with a piece of what looked like someone's shirt. He grinned at my questioning look.

"Border patrol. By the time anyone finds them, we'll be long gone." He slipped his knife away and waved for me to follow him through the trees.

We stepped silently past three Fae men, each with their throats sliced open.

I should probably find it disturbing how pleased Tavian looked with himself. I didn't. I actually found it hotter than a sane man probably should. He'd killed them all so quickly and efficiently, before any got the chance to raise any kind of alarm.

"Can you teach me how to do that?" I asked.

"Of course," he agreed. "There's a fourth man maybe twenty metres from where we are. As far as I can tell, he's alone. He's all yours." He gestured ahead of us.

I hadn't known anyone was there until he mentioned it. Now he had, I listened and looked. At first, I thought he was wrong, but then I heard the snap of a twig. They had no reason to try to keep silent. That worked to my advantage.

I slipped out a knife and crept through the trees, moving carefully around a fallen log or anything else that might make noise if I stepped on it.

I peered around a wide trunk. A Fae man with red-gold hair that hung down his back faced away from me.

He was slightly taller, but I had the advantage of him not knowing I was there. I'd have to be quick and careful. I didn't have the hearing or reflexes of a Fae. I had to rely on my human senses and skills, and the training I got at the Temple and in the Winter Court.

I bent down to pick up a rock that lay at the base of a tree. I pulled my arm back and threw it as hard as I could.

When the man turned towards the sound, I rushed out of the trees and drove my knife into the side of his neck.

His eyes widened. He stared at me before he started to fall. I grabbed him, supported his weight, before lowering him silently to the forest floor.

I slid my knife out of his neck and watched the blood flow and pump out onto the ground. He let out a last, ragged breath, then fell still.

It wasn't a quick, clean kill like Tave's, but he was just as dead.

"Nice work." Tavian was leaning against the trunk of a tree, his arms crossed over his chest. He nodded his approval, then pushed himself off the trunk and stepped over.

"I'm sure he won't mind if you take his knife and his sword. He doesn't have any use for either of them anymore. His sword is better than the one you're carrying. The steel one anyway." He grinned.

I snorted softly and drew the sword out of its sheath. The blade was long, slender and sharp. The hilt was a perfect fit for my hand, although the design was nothing fancy.

I didn't need fancy, I needed deadly. Made by a master.

In comparison, mine was made for the Temple, with lower quality steel, and a less than honed skill by a human swordsmith.

"It will do," I said casually, as though the weapon in my hand wasn't considerably superior to the one on my back. I swapped them over, leaving mine in the Fae man's sheath.

"Now you have two good quality swords." Tave grinned.

I snorted softly. "And I know how to use both of them."

That only made his grin widen. "Yes, you do."

I also swapped my knife for the one the Fae man carried and followed Tavian deeper into Spring Court territory.

CHAPTER
NINE
ZARED

"This place stinks of flowers," I muttered. Everywhere we went, the city smelled of them. They cascaded off balconies and spilled out of pots in front of every building. Every block seemed to contain a park where they crept across the ground, over the neat grass.

I quickly lost track of how many shades of pink bloomed all over the place. Added to that, multiple shades of yellow, purple, red, blue and the gods knew what else. There were even colours I'd never seen before.

"You don't like flowers?" Tavian plucked one as we crept past and tucked it behind his ear.

"Not this much," I said. "What would anyone do if they were allergic to flowers?"

"Live somewhere else." He shrugged. "I like it, but it is more difficult to smell alphas. On the other hand, it's also harder to smell feet."

I snorted softly. "I suppose so." That probably depended on the feet.

"We're almost to the palace. We should use Silent Maiden hand-talk for a while."

I nodded and signed that I understood. He told me once that his mother was a priestess and she taught him how to speak with his hands. I'd learned from living in the Temple and communicating with Khala and the other maidens.

I felt like crap now for pretending not to understand everything she said. When we got her back, I'd apologise for being an ass. I knew how much she hated not being able to talk and I'd teased her. It would serve me right if she hated me for that.

We'd both grown up a lot in the last few months. Especially since finding out she was part Fae. I hadn't completely come to terms with that. Or the fact I was only ever going to be human. I'd grow old and die while she stayed young.

I didn't want to think about any of that, but it was inevitable. It was almost as strange as Khala fucking her mother's former lover. As far as I knew, Cavan was in love with Alivia, but she hadn't returned the feeling.

If they were all human, the whole situation would be weird. Since Fae aged differently, Cavan didn't appear much older than Khala and me. In reality, he was a few hundred years older than both of us. All of the Fae were. I didn't know exactly how old Tave was, but he didn't act like he was older than me.

Tavian signed. "The palace is at the end of this street. If everything we've seen so far is any indication, it's going to be heavily guarded. We have to wait for the right moment."

I followed him down a side street, which led to the back of the palace.

"This would be a good place for the Court of Shadows to open a portal and attack someone," I signed. "We could use the distraction to sneak in."

Tavian looked skyward, eyes moving back and forth before he shrugged. "No such luck, evidently."

That was probably just as well, because with my luck, they'd attack us instead. I had no intention or desire to die here. Not unless it helped Khala to get free. If that was the case, I'd stand straight in front of any lightning bolts. I'd readily give my life for her to escape. There wasn't a fucking thing in this world I wouldn't give to get her away from here.

"If Ryze can't open a portal here, then neither can they," I reasoned.

"That depends on the kind of magic they have," Tavian replied. "Or to be more accurate, the kind of magic the wards are designed to keep out."

"I feel much less safe now," I signed, hoping he'd pick up on the sarcasm.

He smiled. "You're safe with me."

I followed him for a couple of minutes before the smell of flowers gave way to something much less pleasant.

"Where are we going?" I signed.

"Where else?" he replied. "The back door."

It took a moment for me to realise what he meant. I grimaced. "The sewer?"

"You can handle a little bit of shit, can't you?"

"A little bit, yes. A lot of it..." I reminded myself why we were here. Khala was more than worth swimming through shit for. I didn't have to relish the idea.

Tavian patted my shoulder. "No one ever said the life of an assassin was glamorous."

I assumed that was what he signed. As far as I knew, the Silent Maidens didn't have a gesture for assassin. Slicing his hand across his throat seemed clear enough.

The way into the sewers was via a creek that stank worse than anything I'd ever smelled before. I copied Tavian's example and pulled out a handkerchief to tie over my mouth and nose.

"This is the poorer part of the city for a reason," he signed.

"They need more flowers here," I signed back. Lots and lots and lots of them.

Tavian chuckled and led the way along the side of the creek to a wide opening that disappeared down into the darkness.

"We can talk a bit," he said out loud. "The only people here are also people who shouldn't be here." His voice echoed slightly off the sides of the tunnel, but it was mostly absorbed by thick walls and thicker water.

Although the smell was vile, the tunnel had a kind of shelf along either side, just wide enough to walk. Every so often, ladders led up to grates which let in some air, but did nothing to diminish the stench.

"I have to give Thiron credit for how well maintained the sewer is," Tavian said.

"His cousin is an irredeemable asshole, but at least he has some of his shit under control," I said sarcastically.

Tavian chuckled. "Just picture Wornar walking here instead of us."

"I don't want to picture him at all." If I did, I'd have an image of him touching Khala in my mind. Of his cock...

I shook my head. I didn't want to think about that. Feeling it through the bond was difficult enough. Not as difficult as living it of course, but fucked up anyway.

"Me either."

Tavian led the way in deeper and deeper, before he stopped to pull out a torch from his pack. He lit it by striking a flint on the wall. It wasn't much light, but it illuminated the way and cast eerie shadows that danced around us.

"Have you been here before?" I asked, trying not to let the shadows get the better of me. *That is all they are*, I told myself. Shadows of our movement and the flickering flame.

"Here specifically, no. We need to keep a lookout for— Oh. That." He raised the torch to illuminate a side tunnel. "By my estimation, that will lead straight under the palace. Fortunately I have a very good sense of direction. Most of the time."

"Most of the time," I echoed under my breath. It was the rest of the time that worried me.

"Don't worry, I'm not going to get us lost in the sewer." He started up the side tunnel.

I had no choice but to follow his flickering light.

"Is this the kind of place most assassins go?" I asked. If a person wanted to sneak into the palace, it seemed like a logical way to do it.

"Hells no," Tavian replied. "Most assassins prefer the rooftop. Or waiting until their target goes out into the city. This is a different circumstance though. They'll be looking for me on the rooftop. And if Wornar has any sense, he won't show his face in the street until he knows we're dealt with."

"So they won't be expecting—" I stopped talking when the tunnel started to rumble. "Us."

"Maybe they do and maybe they don't. We need to hurry." Tavian started to trot carefully, torch high in his hand.

"What was that?" I asked.

The tunnel rumbled again. The ground shook under our feet. "Please don't tell me there's a giant worm, or a serpent down here."

"No, it's much worse than that," he said over his shoulder. "Every so often they have to flush the sewer."

I mouthed his words as they sank in. "And by flush you mean..."

"We need to find a ladder. Now."

The water that ran past us started to rise quickly. In a matter of moments, it was almost up to the shelf we walked on.

I glanced up the side of the wall and saw the line where the water reached in the past. It was well above both our heads. If we didn't find a ladder, we'd be swept away. That would be shitty, to say the least.

A couple of moments later, water sloshed over my feet. It was frigid. I tried hard not to think about why it was lumpy. My stomach rebelled enough as it was.

"Here!" Tavian waved me forward. "It'll be a squeeze, but I think we can manage."

Torch held in one hand, he scrambled up the ladder, all the way to the top. He moved over so he was dangling off one side.

I threw myself at the ladder and hurried up just before a sudden gush of sewage poured past.

The water rose higher and higher, washing over my feet, my legs, my torso. I half closed my eyes and gripped with all my strength to keep from being swept away. I tried not to think about things that bumped past me as they went, before they swirled away.

What looked very much like an arm struck my leg before it twisted and disappeared. I had a feeling it was attached to an entire person.

I swallowed down my last meal before it joined the rest of the sewerage.

After what felt like a lifetime or two, the water level started to drop again. The tunnel stopped rumbling.

Everywhere from my chest down was wet and sticky. Oozing.

"This is disgusting." I grimaced.

"Yes, but I didn't get you lost," Tavian said as though that made it all right.

"I don't know, but I think lost may be better than this. Did I imagine seeing a dead body float past?"

"No, I saw it too," Tavian said. "That might have been the reason they were flushing the sewer. Destroying the evidence."

I quickly felt for the bond. It was still walled off, but Khala was alive. Thank the gods it wasn't her they disposed of. I hoped it was Wornar, but that seemed unlikely. How unfortunate. The cousin of the High Lord would probably get a more dignified disposal than to be thrown into the sewer.

"We should get out of here, in case they did that because they suspected we're here," Tavian added. He started to climb back down the ladder.

"Any chance it was a coincidence?" I followed him down.

"Possibly, but I don't believe in coincidences. They know we're coming for Khala. Chances are, they're flushing more often until they can be sure where we are."

"I thought Ryze and Wornar were friends," I said. "It seems like they hate Ryze as much as Cavan does."

"Fae are complicated," Tavian said. "For all I know, they may have held some grudge for the last two hundred years, and they've been covering for it, waiting for a chance to strike out."

He exhaled out his nose. "Or it might be the new grudge Wornar made it out to be. They may simply want to keep the lost courts from waking up. I can only guess."

I sighed and adjusted the handkerchief. I wasn't sure if Fae were complicated or just pains in the ass. With the exceptions of Khala and Tave, of course.

I occupied myself by looking at the wall and the way the shadows danced again in the torchlight. The stone was wet now. When the light glinted off carvings, I initially thought I was seeing things.

I blinked a couple of times and shook my head.

"What the hells?"

CHAPTER
TEN
KHALA

I jerked from a doze to completely awake. Every muscle in my body was on full alert, tense. Eyes wide open, listening.

"Psst, Khala," Tavian's voice whispered from the darkness.

Was I dreaming?

I sat up, eyes scanning the shadows.

"Tave?" I whispered.

"Yes, it's me. And Zared. We've come to get you out of here."

Zared too?

I lowered the walls around the bond enough to feel for them both.

It wasn't a dream. And yet, I could hardly bring myself to believe it. What if this was some kind of trick? I tempered my hopes, just in case. Hardened my heart against a potential break.

"How did you get in here?" I felt for the others. They were close, but not as close as Zared and Tave.

"Through the sewers. We managed to...acquire some clean clothes along the way. After a quick bath in one of Thiron's fountains."

"How did you find me?" I asked.

"Through the bond. It led us to the balcony," Tavian replied. "I prefer not to go back that way. They were looking for us. We were almost caught three times."

"We had to hide in the flower bushes," Zared said. "Fucking thorns." He sat down beside me. "I'm sorry. A few thorns are nothing compared to..."

The moonlight that came in through the window illuminated his hand as he raised toward me. He let it hover near my shoulder for a moment before he lowered it again.

I understood. I wouldn't want to touch me either. I was tainted. Dirty. Even after that second bath, I felt *him* all over my skin.

"You shouldn't be here," I told them. "There are more important things—"

"There's nothing more important than you," Tavian interrupted. "You're the centre of our pack. I'm sorry we couldn't get here sooner. We will help you through this. And we will deal with Wornar and anyone else who stands in our way." He sat on the other side of me and lightly touched my cheek with the back of his hand.

I wanted to jerk away from his touch and lean into it at the same time. My emotions were conflicted, but overpowered by one pressing need. We had to get the hells out here.

"Can we go? Please?" I whispered.

They'd come for me.

"Of course we can." Tavian dropped his hand to mine and helped me up off the bed.

"Are you...injured?" Judging by the sound of his voice he'd base how quickly or slowly Wornar died on my response.

"No." Not physically. "I can keep up."

"Of course you can," Tavian said proudly. "But if you need a rest at any time, you only have to say so. All right?"

"I'll rest when we're not here," I said. If I could ever truly rest again. I still wasn't completely sure my mind wasn't playing tricks on me. I might be asleep and dreaming about both men. If that was the case, I didn't want to wake up.

I followed them over to the door on silent feet.

Tavian gestured for us to stop. He cocked his head and listened, then eased the door open.

"Wait there," he signed. He slipped out and disappeared into the darkness.

"Khala..." Zared whispered. "I wish I could..."

I shook my head and signed it, "I'm not going to tell you I'm all right, because I'm not." There was no point in lying about that, he'd know. He knew me better than almost anyone. Even without the bond, he'd understand what I left unsaid.

"What happened wasn't your fault. It was *his* fault." And mine for being an omega. But it wasn't Zared's fault.

"I should have insisted you not go to the Autumn Court with Cavan," he signed. "I shouldn't have allowed him to take you there."

"It wasn't your decision to make," I pointed out. "I went knowing the risks."

"I didn't even try to stop you." His gestures were short and sharp, showing his aggravation.

"When have you ever been able to stop me from doing something I wanted to do?" I asked. Exactly never. I was too strong-headed and stubborn for my own good. Sometimes it was an asset, it helped me get through hard times. And sometimes it got me into those hard times.

He could argue all he wanted, it wouldn't have changed anything. The only way he could have kept me from going with Cavan was if he was an alpha.

I couldn't contain the shudder at the idea that he could have ordered me not to go. What would have happened then? Cavan could have ordered me to accompany him anyway. I may have torn myself in two, obeying them both. Would one order override the other? Did a High Lord's order hold more weight? Or maybe an order given first was the stronger of the two. I had no idea, except that it made me vulnerable in a way I'd never experienced before. One that made living in my own skin harder.

"I should have tried," he insisted.

"The corridor is clear," Tavian whispered. His sudden reappearance made me jump. "Sorry," he said quickly. "Occupational hazard."

I shrugged and tried to ignore the way my heart raced. It was just this place. I'd feel less jumpy later. All right, I was lying to myself, but whatever it took to get through this next while.

"Follow me," Tavian gestured. "Stay close."

We stepped behind him. I didn't look too closely at the guards who lay on the ground, or the shining puddles of blood on the marble floor. They probably hadn't even seen Tavian coming. I couldn't bring myself to conjure any sympathy for them. They worked for *him*. That made them complicit as far as I was concerned. Not one of them tried to help me. Not one.

It felt like three days passed before we reached the end of the corridor, we were moving so slowly and carefully. Any minute now, someone would hear my heart racing, or smell my fear. Or they'd come looking for the dead guards. Or—

I stopped at the end of the corridor, completely unable to move.

"Khala? I know it's scary, but we have to get out of here," Tavian whispered.

"I... That's not it." I moved my upper body, but my legs wouldn't follow. Panic started to settle in.

"He ordered me not to run away." My voice broke as I spoke. "I can't leave." I was as frozen to the spot as if Ryze turned me into an icicle.

"Fuck," Tavian said under his breath. He took my hand and tried to pull me forward.

I took a step, but then stopped again. "I can't." Tears slid down my cheeks. "You have to go. If he finds you here..."

"We're not leaving without you," Zared said. Before I could protest, he put an arm around me, another under my knees and scooped me up. "Maybe you can't run, but I can." He nodded to Tavian to lead on.

I tangled my hand in the front of Zared's acquired tunic and hung on while he took several tentative steps.

At first the pressure in my mind was light, but it increased with every step. By the time we reached the corner and headed into another corridor, my head was screaming.

A whimper slipped out from between my lips.

"It's all right, I've got you," Zared whispered in my ear.

"It hurts," I replied, my voice high and strained.

Tavian stopped mid-step. "Can you manage to go a bit further?"

"I... I don't know," I stammered. "You should go. Leave me here. I..."

I didn't want to spend the rest of my life here, being raped by Wornar, but I'd never forgive myself if anything happened to either of them because of me.

Oh gods, he was going to appear at any moment and kill them both. Their blood would be all over my hands.

He might make me do to them what he made me do to Cavan. He might make me kill them, just because he could. Panic became barely coherent thought.

"Not going to happen," Zared said.

Tavian looked to be thinking. "We need to make it to the front of the palace. If we can do that, we can get you out of here."

They weren't giving up, that much was obvious.

"I can... I can hold on." I had to. It was increasingly clear I had no choice. The only way to get us all to safety would be for me to endure the incredible discomfort.

I closed my eyes, gritted my teeth and did my best to ignore the pressure. Any more and my brain might explode. If it became worse, I might welcome it.

"Good girl," Tavian said. "Stay here for a moment, I'm going to clear the corridor in front of us." He slipped away into the shadows again.

A minute or two passed before we heard a shout, followed by Tavian calling out. "Run!"

With a grunt for the extra weight he was carrying, Zared turned and ran back the way we came.

Tavian was right behind us in moments. The pressure in my head eased as we approached the room Wornar put me in, but worsened again as we ran past into another corridor.

"I guess they know we're here?" Zared said between pants.

"No, I just felt like the exercise," Tavian said sarcastically. "Yes, they know we're here and they're not happy about it. Apparently they didn't appreciate me killing a bunch of them." He didn't sound even slightly guilty. If anything, he sounded like he enjoyed it immensely.

I looked back over Zared's shoulder to see a handful of guards, swords in hand, flying around the corner. Five, no, six of them. All of them looked like they knew exactly how to use those swords.

"There they are," one of them shouted. As if they couldn't all see us bolting through the shadows. Moonlight spilled in through the windows that lined the corridor. There was nowhere to hide.

"Put me down," I insisted.

"We're not leaving you behind—" Zared started.

"No, you're not," I agreed. "Put me down."

When he finally did, I turned and gripped a bunch of magic. I focused for a moment before coating the floor between us and our pursuers with ice.

I could have incinerated them without a second thought, but I wanted to slow them down. I wasn't ready to kill that many people in cold blood. Not yet. Not unless they gave me a reason to. They worked for Wornar, but they weren't him.

There was a chance, however slight, they didn't know what he was really like, I'd give them the benefit of the doubt. For now.

One by one, they slid and slipped. One slammed straight into the wall and let out a grunt. Several fell on their asses and growled in pain and frustration.

Tavian laughed. "That's fucking awesome. It's only going to slow them down for a minute or two."

They were already climbing to their feet. A couple of them managed, only to slip and fall again.

I froze their shoes to the floor.

They struggled to pull their shoes free, or pull their feet out of them.

Under other circumstances, it would have been hilarious. Considering what would happen to me if they caught me again, I couldn't bring myself to raise a smile.

One pulled out a knife and aimed it.

I squinted at the blade. It turned bright red and melted it in his hand before he could throw it.

The scream of agony as the hot steel poured down over his fingers was one I'd hear for the rest of my life.

Blame Wornar, I thought. *He didn't tell me I couldn't use magic against anyone else.*

"Remind me not to piss you off," Tavian said admirably. "That looks like it fucking hurts."

"Good," Zared snarled. "They all deserve it."

The sound of footsteps approaching from the other direction told me we had more company. Another handful of guards appeared around that corner. They took one look at their companions still scrambling on the ice, and drew their swords.

"Unless you want to end up like them, I suggest you get out of the way," Tavian said to them. He sounded very calm. Almost enough to silence my own panic.

"Lord Wornar is coming," one of them said. "You're not going anywhere."

I shuddered. Not just at the thought of seeing him again, but at the way my body responded to the mention of him. It was somewhere between recoiling and pure need of him.

"Lord Wornar can kiss my ass," Zared muttered.

I acted without thinking. I didn't know my hands had moved until they were in front of me. I didn't know I'd tapped into any magic until it was full of it. I could have frozen them all, or boiled them on the spot.

Instead, I opened a portal right in the middle of where the guards stood. One minute they were there and the next they were replaced by an opening.

I couldn't tell where it led and I didn't care. All I knew was that it would stay open until I closed it again. This might be the only time in my life it worked, but it worked now and that was all I gave a fuck about.

"You're going to have to push me," I said, my voice tight with concentration.

"Gladly." Tavian and Zared both grabbed hold of me and pulled me through the portal.

I slammed it closed behind us.

CHAPTER
ELEVEN
KHALA

The pain was excruciating. I felt as though my skull was going to cave in on itself. My body was going to rip itself apart. Nothing existed except agony and the burning need for it to end.

If it wasn't for Tavian and Zared holding onto me, I would have opened a portal and gone back. I would have thrown myself at Wornar's feet, because that was what my instincts were begging me to do. He'd take away my pain.

But I let them hold me, because I'd rather die than give myself back to him.

"You're going to be all right," Tavian said. "You're safe here. Ryze and Cavan will be here soon."

"What the fuck are they going to do?" Zared snarled.

"A lot more than us arguing with each other will," Tavian snapped. He shook his head at Zared before turning his attention back to me. "How far away are they?"

"I don't know," I sobbed. "I can't... I can't...." All my walls around the bond were shattered, but I couldn't feel past the pain. The four of them were on the other end, that was all I knew. That and some vague sense that they were trying to reassure me.

Except for Vayne, who seemed irritated, as usual.

"Khala." Tavian put both his hands on my cheeks.

I jerked away from his touch. That had nothing to do with the strain of the alpha-order. It was pure reaction to what Wornar did to me. I barely tolerated being held down, but the intimate contact was too much.

"Fuck." Tavian dropped his hands back to my arms. "I'm sorry. Hold on a little longer."

"Where are we?" Zared asked. I'd never seen him look so helpless. I knew if he could take my pain, he would.

There was nothing he could do and we both knew it.

"Just inside the border to the Summer Court," Tavian said. "I could throw a stick and it would land in the Spring Court. For some reason, the portal came here."

If I could speak, I'd tell them exactly why. This was the place I would have been safe from Wornar if I'd only run a few more steps before he caught me. What he did to me wouldn't have happened. Unless he went back on his word.

I didn't bother to think how likely that was. I was here now, and safer. This might also be as far as I could go without being literally ripped apart by the order.

"So it's not—" Zared started to say.

I startled violently and squealed at a flash of light in the corner of my eye. The sight of a portal opening made me want to get up off the ground and flee.

Until Ryze stepped through, followed by Vayne and Cavan. They were all by my side before the portal even shut.

All shared the same expression. If Wornar was in front of them, he'd last another half a heartbeat before they ripped him to pieces.

"Gods, Khala," Ryze said softly. "He's going to regret the day he took his first breath."

"We need to undo this," Cavan said briskly. "Khala, listen to me. Look at me."

I turned to look at him through a haze of pain. His blue eyes were intent on mine. Whatever he planned to do, he looked confident, self assured. That reassured me in a way no words could have.

"As one of your alphas," he started, his tone firm and commanding, "you will forget everything Wornar ordered you to do, think and feel. You will put what he did to you in the back of your mind. If you think about it, remember it's in the past. He can't hurt you ever again. Furthermore, you will *never* accept an order from another alpha, including myself, for as long as you live. Our words will be nothing but words."

His order settled on me. The pain gradually evaporated, leaving only a dull ache behind my eyes.

"I should have thought of that," Ryze muttered. "Making sure she's never susceptible to any other alpha ever again."

"I wasn't sure if it would work," Cavan admitted. "I've never needed to try anything like this before. You should try giving her an order, but later. She's been through enough for now." He stroked the inside of my wrist with his thumb, but made no move to do any more than that.

"I'll give Tavian the same order too," Ryze said. "I don't want either of them to be vulnerable to some asshole like Wornar."

The mention of his name made me flinch, but the order went further than keeping me safe. When Cavan ordered me to forget what Wornar made me do, that was more or less what happened. Some of it I remembered. Some of it I didn't. The pain of that ordeal was reduced. It wasn't gone, it would never be fully gone, but it wasn't as raw.

In a way, I was glad he didn't make me completely forget. What happened was something I had to deal with and move past. Erasing it from my mind meant I didn't get to do that. My mind wouldn't remember, but my body would. I needed to heal both of them. Only time could do that.

"Thank you," I said softly. "Thank you for coming for me."

"I'm always ready to come for you," Tavian said with a small smile. "Which you may not be ready for for a while, and we all understand that. We're here to give you everything you need, including space."

"Exactly," Ryze agreed. "Anything you need, no matter what it might be, you only have to ask."

I wiped tears off my cheeks and nodded. Tavian was right, it was going to take some time before I could bring myself to be intimate with them again, but someday I would. Because I wanted to, and because if I didn't, Wornar won. I wasn't going to let him win.

"We should get the keys together and open Nallis," I said. "Figure this out once and for all."

They exchanged glances.

"We didn't get the key," Cavan said. He briefly explained how Harel switched them before we went into the throne room.

"Harel is a smug fucker," Vayne growled.

"Like most Fae," Zared muttered.

"Most, but not all," Tavian told him.

Zared looked back at him for a moment before nodding. "Yes, not all."

"I, for one, am epic," Ryze declared.

"If you say so," Vayne said to him.

"I do say so," Ryze agreed.

"Anyway," Tavian said. "We may not need the keys. There may be another way through the mountains that doesn't involve going through Nallis or the mists. At least, we could sidestep most of the mist."

When we all turned to look at him, he nodded at Zared.

"We found carvings on the walls inside the sewer," Zared said. "In the same symbols as the temple in Havenmoor. The Silent Maidens' hand language. It spoke of a tunnel in Nallis and where to find it. The symbols looked old. Worn down by the flushing of the sewer. But we could read them clearly enough."

Tavian hummed his agreement.

I stared at them. "Who would leave carvings in there? Was it always a sewer?"

"For the last thousand years it has been," Ryze said. "Whoever put it there either didn't want it seen or knew it would be some day."

"Wait a moment." Zared stared at him. "Are you saying that some Fae thousand years ago had a vision of Tavian and me going into that sewer and left carvings for us to see?"

"Is that honestly the strangest thing you've ever heard?" Ryze asked. "I don't think it's even the strangest thing I've heard *today*. Someone from the Court of Dreams knew you were coming and wanted you to find that. And you did. I suggest keeping your eyes open for anything similar that might have been left for you. For any of us."

"The Fae of the past is a fucker too," Vayne growled. "If they saw what happened to Khala and all they did was leave symbols behind..."

"They may not have known that part," Cavan pointed out. "If they did, what could they have done?"

"They could have stopped us from going on a wild griffin chase after the keys," Ryze said.

"Exactly," Vayne said with a grunt.

"They wouldn't have known we'd jump to the conclusion that we need the keys," Cavan said.

"It doesn't matter now," I said softly. "What happened, happened. We need to focus on what happens next. Do we need to take Hycathe and Jezalyn to Nallis with us?"

"The first thing we need to do is return to the Winter Court so you can get some rest," Ryze said. "The other courts have waited this long, they can wait a little longer."

He smiled, but it was strained. He'd spent a lot of time since we met worrying about me. I'd do my best not to give him any more reason to do that.

"You're all welcome at my palace," Cavan offered. "Since we're already here, it's not far to go. And when the Spring Court notices our little distraction, we'll have a good vantage point to see it."

He smiled lopsidedly. It made him look much younger than he was. He and Ryze both had a mischievous side, although Cavan hid his better than Ryze. Ryze never tried. Never held back from being exactly who he was. It was one of the things I liked most about him.

"Distraction?" I asked. Did I really want to hear the answer to that? I'd come to realise I didn't always need to have my curiosity satisfied. Some things were better not known.

"I might have sent in a few of my most trusted men who can also use Winter Court magic," Ryze said. "Let's just say the Spring Court harbour is going to look a little icy for a while. They may have trouble getting ships in and out."

"And some of their flora may spontaneously burst into flames," Cavan added. "It's a shame to attack innocent plants, but no one takes our omega without consequences."

I smiled at the idea of both of those things happening. As distractions went, they were creative.

"That's where you were when Tavian and Zared came to get me?"

"If they got into any trouble, we would have initiated all of those things sooner," Ryze said. "As it was, we were only a few minutes away from giving the nod for them to happen." He didn't seem too disappointed it hadn't come to that.

"If you hadn't opened the portal, I would have given them a signal," Tavian told me. "It would have distracted them enough for us to run. Although, you were doing very well with your magic. You should have seen her melt a knife." He grinned at Ryze.

"That's my omega," Ryze said approvingly.

I twitched at his use of the word. I didn't want to be known for being an omega. Wasn't it enough just to be Khala?

I'd spent enough of my life being defined by what I was, not *who* I was. Silent maiden, Fae, omega. All I wanted to do was be me. That didn't seem like too much to ask.

"Can we go?" Zared asked. "Didn't you say it was dangerous out in the open?" That was a concern, but I doubted it was uppermost in his mind. His eyes were intent on me. I knew he saw my discomfort. I wasn't in pain anymore, but I was still overwhelmed with...everything.

I wanted another long soak in a bath and to take some time to think and clear my head. Not too long, because if the Court of Shadows attacked again, people may die just so I could come to terms with what happened. That didn't sit well with me. I wasn't going to mope around and let people be killed.

"Yes, let's go," Ryze stood and offered me his hand.

I forced myself not to shrink away from him. I slipped my hand into his and let him pull me to my feet. I could tell he wanted to embrace me, but didn't know how far to push.

I gave him a quick hug and then stepped back but kept hold of his hand. The warmth of his touch was comforting.

I'd need that and more in the coming days.

TWELVE

KHALA

Almost as soon as we arrived in Garial, Ryze and Cavan took Zared and Tavian aside to talk about what they found in the sewer.

I wanted to listen, but they closed ranks and Vayne escorted me to the atrium instead. He wasn't much of a talker at the best of times, but he didn't say anything until we reached the sun drenched space.

The room I stayed in when I was learning magic from Dalyth was still empty, so I slipped inside and sat on the edge of the nest, my legs hanging over the side.

Vayne followed me in and sat beside me, his movements and expression heavy.

"The others are going to say the same thing, but I blame myself too." His tone was just as heavy. "It's my job to anticipate threats. I saw the way Wornar looked at you when he first saw you. I should have seen it for what it was. I thought he was just looking at you because you're beautiful, not because he..." He shook his head.

"No one else saw it," I pointed out. I'd noticed Wornar's appreciative glances, but hadn't thought much about it either. I had my hands full enough as it was and that was before Cavan was part of my pack.

At some point, we'd have to sit down and talk about that, because that was how I thought of him, but the others may not. Except Tavian. He seemed open to anything, as long as I was happy.

"All the more reason for me to be on guard against him," Vayne groused. "We should have tried a direct approach to getting that fucking key."

"Like marching an army up to Harel's door and demanding it?" I asked, only half teasing.

"Exactly," Vayne agreed. "What's the point of having an army if you can't flex your muscles once in a while? Ryze would do anything to avoid a war, but as far as I'm concerned, Wornar declared one when he touched you." He gave me an unexpectedly tender glance.

"You're not going to invade the Spring Court over what happened to me," I told him. "How many innocent people would die as a result?"

Vayne sighed. "That's the problem with war, you can't just kill the guilty. And of course the guilty hide behind the innocent."

He crossed his booted ankles. "I promise you this— if any of us gets the chance, Wornar is a dead Fae. I'm tempted to fight the others for the privilege, but in the end it doesn't matter how the fucker dies, as long as he dies. Painfully."

I leaned back against the headboard and sat cross-legged. "Good, because you'd have to fight me too." Although, I admitted to myself I didn't know if I could deliver the killing blow, no matter how much I hated Wornar.

Vayne grunted. "I'm not going to fight you, but we know I'd win anyway. Unless you used magic, in which case I'd be fucked." He gave me a glance which bordered a smile. It was the closest I'd ever seen him come to doing that.

"I'll bear that in mind. I'll use every advantage I can get, fair or unfair." I picked at a thread on the knee of my pants.

"That must be a thing amongst people who can use magic. Ryze would cheat if given half a chance too." He grimaced.

"I don't see it as cheating," I said. "Just using what the gods gave us."

Vayne nodded slowly. "So if we have a fight, I get to use my good looks?" His eyebrows twitched.

"That really would be cheating," I told him. "Totally unfair to us ordinary looking folk."

He grunt-laughed. "There's nothing ordinary about you. You're even more beautiful than I am. I realise that's saying a lot, but it's true." One side of his mouth rose slightly.

"I don't feel very beautiful right now," I admitted. "I feel messy and... Like maybe I'll never be clean again."

He looked down at his feet, then back up again. "Can I tell you something?"

"Anything," I said. I wondered if maybe these feelings were too big for him, at least for this early in our relationship. He wasn't as open about things as Tavian, Ryze and even Zared. Or Cavan for that matter.

Vayne cleared his throat. "When I was a young Fae, maybe around fifty or sixty years old, there was a woman. She was a friend of my mother. I knew her ever since I was born."

He shook his head slowly, and his eyes glazed as he thought back.

"One time when we were alone, she decided to touch me. She was like an aunt to me and I didn't want to...but she pushed and told me it must be what I wanted because my cock...you know."

"I know," I said quickly. It wasn't difficult to understand what he was trying to say. "She made you be with her."

"Yes. I never told anybody because I think they'd just, you know, agree with her. That I must have wanted it."

"You didn't?" I asked gently. My heart ached at the expression of pain in his eyes. The memory was a difficult one, especially to deal with alone. Telling me now must have taken a lot from him. I was touched that he trusted me with something this traumatic and important.

"No." He looked back down at his feet. "Afterwards, I felt angry with myself. With her. With the whole fucking world. I've been angry ever since."

"You had every right to feel that way," I assured him. I reached over and lightly placed a hand on his leg. "What she did to you was the same as what *he* did to me. There's a difference between your cock wanting something and you wanting it. She was wrong to do what she did." Very wrong. "Is she still—"

"Alive? No. She died about a hundred years ago now. And good riddance. But I still remember how...messy I felt. Ever since then, I haven't let anyone get close to me. Not until you." He placed his hand over mine.

I offered him a smile. "Thank you for telling me. I'm sorry for what she did to you." I couldn't help asking. "Did you kill her?"

Both sides of his mouth twitched. "No. I kinda wish I had, but I didn't. She got old and sick and died in her sleep. As far as I know, poison wasn't involved. Don't quote me on that though. She had a few enemies. By the time she was gone, not too many people regretted the loss. Granted, that happens a lot to us Fae. If you live long enough, you accumulate enemies and pissed off people. Still, she was an evil bitch, even compared to some others I've known."

"It sounds like she would have gotten along well with...*him*." I couldn't bring myself to say Wornar's name.

"They would have killed each other. That sounds just about perfect to me," Vayne said. "Which is odd, because Thiron is a genuinely decent Fae. Wornar is his sister's son, but not the only one. I never gave much thought as to why Wornar was his heir. But now—" He frowned. "Doesn't make much sense. Unless Thiron has no idea what the asshole is really like."

He stroked his thumb over the side of my hand. "Don't waste too much thought on it though. We get no say in who is High Lord of any other court. Not unless we go to war with them and win. Then we can install anyone we want, but it's a high price to pay just to do that."

"That brings us right back to innocent people dying to protect the guilty." I hated the idea of Wornar ever being High Lord of anything. "What sort of power does the High Lord have?"

"Absolute," Vayne replied reluctantly. "They have advisors, but at the end of the day their word is law. If we have a decent High Lord like Ryze, we don't have too much to worry about. He tends to listen to Tavian and me. A lot of the time, he pretends he doesn't, but he does. If we tell him something he's doing is shit, he'll rethink it. He'll take all the credit, but we don't give a crap. As long as he doesn't continue. Others, like Harel, do whatever the fuck they want and they don't care what anyone thinks."

He was silent for a few moments. "I'm pissed off at Cavan for taking you to the Autumn Court, but I admit he's not as bad as I thought he was. I thought he was like Harel. Turns out he's a lot more like Ryze. Arrogant, self-centred, but basically decent. It's gotta be eating his insides what happened to you. At least you got to stab him for it." He quirked an eyebrow.

I snorted. "I should apologise for stabbing him. Even though I had no control over it. Maybe if I'd tried harder..."

Vayne scowled. "As far as I can tell, no amount of trying harder would have countermanded what that asshole told you to do. It wouldn't matter if you were the strongest Fae in the world, that alpha bullshit would have done what it did anyway. It's like if you fell off the roof of the palace. Nothing is going to stop you from falling and landing."

"It would if I put wind under myself," I pointed out.

"You'd still land on the wind," he said. "You'd land on something. Point is, once you start to fall, there's nowhere to go but down. Once you're dead, you're dead. Can't undo that either."

I gave him a measured look.

He frowned back at me. "What?"

"The last time I was here, when I was trying to help my sisters run away from the Summer Court, I...might have brought a fish back to life. Possibly two of them."

His head jutted forward and he blinked. "Come again? I thought you just said you brought a fish back to life?"

"That is what I said," I agreed. "With magic. I accidentally killed them." I nodded towards the reflecting pool in the centre of the atrium. "Then I touched them and they were alive."

"So...they weren't really dead?"

"Oh, they were definitely dead. Somehow I combined winter and summer magic to undo that." I raised my hand in an, 'I don't know either,' gesture, then lowered it to my thigh.

"Do Ryze or Cavan know about this?" Vayne asked.

"No. I didn't trust Cavan at the time, and it didn't seem like the right time to tell Ryze. Hycathe and Jezalyn are the only ones who know. Unless it's something lots of Fae can do?"

Vayne shook his head slowly. "As far as I know, it's not something anyone can do. Not even the gods."

He chewed on his thoughts for a moment. "This might be best kept between us for now. When we get a chance, we can tell Ryze and he can decide who else should know."

He scratched his forehead. "This is knowledge that would be very dangerous in the wrong hands. Fae have gone to war for less than a skill like that. If word gets out, everyone will want you to bring back their lost relatives."

"I don't think I can bring back long lost loved ones," I said.

"They'd want you to try anyway," he said. "Knowing Ryze, he'll want us to kill him, and have you bring him back just to know how it feels."

That did sound like something Ryze would do. How many times had they mentioned how bored Fae got being alive for so long? He might think it was worth doing, even if there was a risk he'd never be brought back.

Shits and giggles knew no boundaries.

"I'll keep it between us," I assured him. For now. Sooner or later, Ryze would have to know, if only because I hated keeping secrets. We'd done enough of that already and it cost us dearly in time and frustration.

"I should let you get some rest," he told me. "I'll be right outside the door if you need me. Me or one of the others. Fair to say, you're not going to be alone for the foreseeable future."

CHAPTER
THIRTEEN
KHALA

I woke to voices outside my door. They were low. but I recognised Vayne, Ryze and Tavian. After a minute or two, Cavan said something, then Zared.

Were they all standing guard outside?

I crawled out of my nest and padded over to the door on bare feet. I pushed it open further and peered out. They all stood near the reflecting pool, illuminated by a sun that was a finger width above the horizon. Their voices were still hushed, but there was urgency in their tones. An urgency that was immediately contagious.

"What's going on?" I asked.

They turned to me, each looking guilty for having woken me.

It was Ryze who moved first, stepping to my side. "I'm sorry, we should have taken this out into the corridor."

"Like I suggested," Vayne said darkly.

"We couldn't all listen and be near Khala at the same time," Zared pointed out.

"We could have——" Tavian started.

"Does it matter now?" Cavan asked.

"It doesn't matter to me," I said. "Is someone going to tell me what's happening? Was there another attack?"

"In a manner of speaking," Ryze agreed. "Thiron is dead."

It took me a moment for his words to sink in. "The High Lord of the Spring Court? How? Did he..."

"If you want to know if he was assassinated, that's my guess," Ryze said. "Wornar has declared himself as his replacement. He's also declared that anyone that crosses his border without permission will be dealt with."

"Executed," Vayne said.

"Yes, that." Ryze gave him a short, quick nod. He glanced at the others.

"What else?" I demanded. "If it's about me, I deserve to know."

"It's not precisely about you," Cavan said. He closed his eyes and looked pained. "He's ordered that every omega in Spring Court territory be brought to the palace in Lanrial, irrespective of age and status."

My blood froze in my veins. "So he can do to them what he did to me?" I wanted to curl up and disappear under my own skin.

"We've already put out the order that any omega is welcome in the other courts," Ryze said. "And suggested that any alpha should give his omega the same order Cavan gave you, to protect them from Wornar. Or anyone else."

"We still don't know if that's going to work," Tavian pointed out.

"It's too soon," Zared argued. "She's been through enough."

"That's up to her," Tavian said.

"Are you ready to try to find out?" Cavan asked gently.

"If it helps any other omega, yes," I said straight away and without reservation. If I could save one from going through what I went through, then I'd do it.

"Khala..." Now it was Zared's turn to look pained. "You don't have to do this."

"Yes I do," I told him. "It's all right. Ryze won't ask anything I don't want to do." I turned to him. "Will you?"

"Definitely not," he said firmly. He looked me right in the eyes and said, "Put a hand on the top of your head."

My hands remained by my sides. I felt the slightest push in my mind, like Cavan's order was shoving Ryze's aside. There was absolutely no temptation to obey.

Ryze tried again. "Touch your nose."

I smiled, my hands nowhere near my nose. "I guess it worked."

"Perfect." Ryze rubbed his hands together. "Tave, I order you to ignore and disregard any order from any other alpha, as long as you live."

"*Other* alpha?" Zared looked unimpressed.

Ryze sighed. "Fine. Tave, disregard any order from me as well. As long as it's an alpha-order and not one given as a High Lord to his Master of Assassins. Those you should absolutely regard."

Tavian grinned. "I'll disregard your alpha-orders and consider the others on an order by order basis."

"I really need to find some better subordinates," Ryze said.

"Good luck with that," Vayne told him. "There are no better than me or Tavian. Right Tave?"

"Right, Vayne." Tavian patted his shoulder.

"Do you have the same problem with your subordinates?" Ryze asked Cavan.

Cavan smiled and shook his head. "I think it's a problem unique to you. You could do a lot worse though. You don't have an heir who assassinated you."

"That body," Zared said suddenly. When we all turned to look at him he gestured towards Tavian. "We saw someone dead in the sewer. They floated past when the system was flushed. Is there any chance..."

"That it was Thiron? If I was going to assassinate my High Lord, I'd dispose of him quickly too," Ryze said. "That would give me time to make up some kind of story."

"What does this mean for us trying to find the Court Of Shadows and the Court of Dreams?" I asked.

"It means he'll try to stop us," Cavan said. "Worst case, he'll ally with Harel and they'll both try to stop us."

"Is there any chance they're right?" I asked. "That maybe we should be trying to bury them deeper or...something?"

"It's too late for that," Cavan said. "If we try that, we'll make enemies of them both. Right now, we might assume we have an ally in the Court of Dreams. At the moment that's the best we can hope for. To help them and stop the Court of Shadows from annihilating us all."

"Who would have thought we'd end up working together?" Ryze asked Cavan.

Cavan looked back at him, his mouth slightly twisted to the side. "No one is more surprised than I am."

"It's going to be harder to get to Wornar now?" Zared asked.

"For now," Cavan said. "I promise you all, as long as there's breath in my body, I will search for a way to separate his head from the rest of him. Even if I die doing it."

"You and your personal sacrifices," Ryze said. "Is that a Summer Court thing, or just you?"

"It's not just Summer Court," Vayne said. "I feel the same way."

"It's not even just a Fae thing," Zared added. "I want to rip off his balls and choke him with them."

"Me too," Tavian said. "I'd be more than happy to sneak in and do the job tonight."

"They'll be looking for you," Ryze said. "No doubt Wornar expects you to do exactly that. We have to wait until he's not on his guard anymore. If it takes a hundred years, he will be dealt with."

"We need to get to Nallis as quickly as possible," Cavan said. "While Wornar is occupied with becoming High Lord." This was the culmination of years of work for him, but he looked less than enthusiastic. He, more than the rest of us, knew what was at stake. It might not be much consolation that at least he wasn't working alone anymore.

I doubted he appreciated the years of trying to shout and being unheard. We could try to make up for it now.

"Right," Ryze agreed. "I'll return to the Winter Court and get Hycathe and Jezalyn. I have a feeling we may be needing them." He rubbed a hand over his weary face.

When was the last time any of them got any rest? I had a feeling it was a while. I'd suggest we wait another day or two, if I thought they'd agreed to it. They all had a ridiculous amount of stubbornness in common.

"We can be ready to leave in an hour." Cavan turned to me.

"If you're about to suggest I stay here, don't," I told him. "I'm coming too. I'm just as involved in this as the rest of us."

"I was going to suggest you might need some new boots," Cavan said. "I know better than to suggest you wouldn't involve yourself. If we tried to leave without you, you'd follow."

"Yes, I would," I said. "And now I know how to make a portal that stays open, following you will be a lot easier." It wasn't that simple but none of them corrected me. They didn't need to. Whatever I had to do, I wouldn't let them leave me behind.

"Also, I'd love some new boots," I said. I didn't take the time to dwell on where mine were. It didn't matter, they were only shoes. If we were heading up into the mountains, I'd need better footwear. "Some new pants and a jacket wouldn't hurt either."

"I'll have the staff organise everything we need," Cavan said. He regarded me thoughtfully, but before I could ask what he was thinking, he nodded and left the atrium.

"Vayne, you can come with me and help me organise Hycathe and Jezalyn, and our provisions," Ryze said. "Tavian and Zared, I don't think either of you need me to tell you to stay here and keep an eye on Khala."

"No, you don't," Zared agreed. "We'll keep her safe." He looked at Ryze as though accusing him of not being able to do the same.

If Ryze noticed, he gave no sign. He slipped out of the room, followed by Vayne. Of course, he couldn't portal out from here.

"Are you sure you won't stay here?" Zared asked once the three of us were alone. "We all could. What do they need us for anyway?"

"We were the ones who saw the symbols in the sewer," Tavian reminded him. "They were meant for us to see. We might both be needed to interpret them when we get to Nallis. But you might be right about Khala staying here."

He shrugged apologetically. "You'd be safer here. Vayne could stay and—"

I interrupted him. "No. I'm coming with you. And if either of you try to insist, remember what I did to that knife." I would never do that to either of them, but it didn't hurt for them to remember I could take care of myself.

"Please don't do that to my cock." Tavian crossed his hands in front of his groin. "All three of us are very attached to him."

"Don't give me a reason to," I mock growled. I gave him a meaningful look, but smiled.

"So, about you two. You seem to be getting along well." Was it too early for a conversation about that? I couldn't take the words back now anyway, but it effectively turned their attention away from me for a while. Who knew how long that might last?

I appreciated how much they cared about me, but I wasn't a fragile flower petal, broken under the heel of Wornar's boot. I was tougher than that. I had to be.

They exchanged a glance.

"I think I speak for us both, when I say there's an attraction there," Tavian said. "But neither of us is going to choose each other over you. But..." His face turned slightly pink. "If I can have both of you, and Ryze, I'd be ecstatic."

"We're a pack," I said. "All six of us have each other, including Cavan and Vayne. Within that, as long as everyone is happy, and consenting then I don't see why we can't have whoever we want."

Zared swallowed audibly. "I only want Khala and Tavian. At least...for now." He looked like he wanted to say more, but then fell silent.

His eyes on me to make sure it was all right, Tavian leaned in to kiss me lightly on the mouth. He did the same to Zared.

"That sounds like the perfect arrangement to me."

"Me too," I said softly. All we had to do was survive potentially bringing two lost courts back to Jorius and deal with the growing animosity from the Spring and Autumn Courts.

I was starting to miss the simple life of a Silent Maiden.

CHAPTER
FOURTEEN
KHALA

ycathe looked at me like I was the last person in the world she wanted to see. Since that was basically her default expression, I shrugged it off. The smile I gave Jezalyn was genuine though. She was sweet. In time, the alpha woman and I might even be friends.

If Hycathe lightened up, we might be friends someday too.

"Jezalyn has ordered Hycathe not to listen to any other alphas as well," Ryze said. "All three omegas will now be able to ignore us and do whatever the hells they want."

Vayne grunted and Tavian grinned.

"Isn't it adorable that he thinks we didn't already do whatever the hells we want?" Tavian asked me.

I smiled. "Definitely. It's like he hasn't met any of us."

Ryze shook his head indulgently. "Your impertinence is so cute. I can't decide whose ass I want to smack more."

"He's such a flirt today. Is it because you now have some competition?" Tavian's gaze slipped over to Cavan.

"I'm always a flirt," Ryze said. He turned to Cavan. "Your portal or mine?"

Cavan hefted his pack higher up his shoulders. "Does it matter?"

"It might," Ryze said. "My portal might be better than your portal."

"I don't think it's possible for a portal to be better than another one." Cavan gave him a funny look.

Tavian sighed loudly. "I hate it when daddy and daddy fight."

I put a hand over my mouth to stifle a laugh.

"See, you've upset the omegas," Ryze said.

"Are we going to stand here wasting time, or are we going?" Hycathe asked. "Because we all have better things to do than listen to you argue."

"I think what she's trying to say is that someone needs to open a fucking portal," Vayne said.

"Yes, I got that," Ryze told him. "All right, I'll do it." With a snap of his wrist, he split the air in front of him.

The tunnel on the other end of the portal was dark. Not completely dark. It was light enough to see where to put one foot in front of the other, but it wasn't the bright, icy illumination I was more used to.

"It's further to Nallis than anywhere I've taken you before," Ryze explained. He must have seen the expression on my face. "It might feel disconcerting walking through, but it should be perfectly safe."

"Should be?" Hycathe repeated. She looked disbelieving.

"It's a magic portal, there are no absolutes," Ryze told her. "Especially with missing courts opening portals in the sky. While the chance of anyone making another that dissects with mine is slim, it's not impossible."

"What happens then?" Jezalyn asked. She moved closer to Hycathe and looked as though she was about to refuse to let her come with us.

"I have no idea," Ryze said lightly. He glanced at Cavan.

"I don't know either," Cavan said. "I'm assuming it won't be good, so we should hurry." He punctuated his words by turning and stepping into the portal.

"That kind of bravery is kinda hot," Tavian said. He grabbed my hand and Zared's in his and we all stepped inside together.

Ryze was right, it was disconcerting inside. The further we got, the darker it was. The only sounds were echoing footsteps and my heart racing in my ears. Both were unbelievably loud. For the longest time, I thought we might have been the only creatures in the world. Eight Fae and one human.

Ryze closed the portal behind us. We were plunged into darkness which lasted for a minute or two before he and Cavan illuminated the tunnel with magic.

I almost wished they hadn't. The way the light bounced off the walls, never quite penetrating the shadows, made my skin crawl.

"Sometimes I wonder what it would be like to be stuck in a place like this forever," Tavian whispered. "How long would it take for me to completely lose my mind?"

"Less time than it would for the rest of us," Vayne told him. He followed a handful of steps behind. "You already have a headstart on being crazy."

"Thank you," Tavian said over his shoulder. "I love you too."

"That perfectly illustrates my point," Vayne said. "Only Tave would take that as a compliment."

"You didn't mean it as a compliment?" Tavian asked. "I wonder what it would be like to kill someone in here." He seemed to be seriously considering the suggestion, but a smile tugged at the corners of his mouth.

"If you don't shut up, you're going to know how it feels to *die* in here," Hycathe told him.

Tavian laughed. "Have you ever thought about becoming an assassin, Hycathe? You could slice open people's veins with that tongue of yours."

Whatever she thought of that, I didn't know because we were suddenly faced with daylight so bright, I had to blink for a while to let my eyes get used to the glare.

My hand still in Tavian's, I stepped out into a late morning that was considerably cooler than the Summer Court. The air was crisp and refreshing.

Cavan was already standing a few metres away, his eyes on what I assumed was Nallis.

I expected something that looked like one of the temples in Fraxius, but this was nothing like that. It was nothing like anything I'd ever seen before. My breath caught in my throat with awe.

Made entirely of dark stone that seemed to absorb the sunlight, the base of the building was rounded. Every few metres a groove was set into the surface for rainwater run-off.

Three towers jutted out of the centre of the building. Each was shaped like the wing of a butterfly made from iron latticework, which gave the appearance of fine lace.

"It's so old, no one knows who built it," Cavan said thoughtfully. "There's nothing like it anywhere else in the world. Not on this continent, anyway."

"Some believe it was built by the gods." Ryze stepped out of the portal and closed it behind him.

"What do you believe?" I asked, addressing the question to all of them.

"I believe whoever built it was a master," Cavan said. "If they were still alive today, they'd be extremely busy creating wonders like this." He was clearly in awe of the creation.

That was understandable. I couldn't even begin to imagine how they did the ironwork, much less made towers that looked like wings. And the stone— I'd never seen stone so dark and imposing, but beautiful at the same time.

"There are ruins in a remote part of the Winter Court that use a similar stone," Ryze said. "They were built close to the coast and smashed apart by centuries of storms and massive tides. This has lasted by being isolated. Unless you count that." He pointed behind me.

I turned slowly to look.

"Oh." The side of the mountain dropped off into a thick wall of mist.

"It's closer than it was the last time I was here." Ryze looked more concerned than I'd seen him before.

"You're right," Cavan said. "It is." He gripped the handles of his pack and stepped toward the edge of the mountain.

For once, Ryze didn't claim he was always right. He frowned and watched the other High Lord like he was worried he'd disappear, never to be seen again. If he wasn't careful, I might start to think he liked Cavan after all.

They seemed to have come to some unspoken agreement between them to get along with each other. Although, they still needled each other as well. I suspected that was a habit they wouldn't break, possibly ever.

"Maybe you shouldn't go too close to the edge," I suggested.

After all the years of trying to be heard, we didn't want to lose Cavan to what was surely just a thick curtain of air and water droplets. I couldn't blame Ryze for the way he felt about the mist. It really did look like it might swallow all of us whole. What it would do with us after that, was anyone's guess.

Cavan turned his face to look back at me and smile. "It's harm—"

He gaped at something behind us. His eyes widened.

"Run!" He dropped his hands and headed toward the building.

"What—" I started after him a second before a flash of lightning lit up the sky behind me. That was followed by a sizzling sound and the smell of burning dirt and grass.

It missed me by a hair.

Fuck.

We bolted towards the building, zigzagging to avoid more bolts of lightning. A pair of them landed on either side of me, so close the fabric on the sleeve of my jacket singed.

Fucking gods.

I followed the others around the base of the building, to a wide doorway that was deep enough to hold all of us. Just barely.

I turned as Ryze threw a wall of ice between us and the lightning. I caught a glimpse of a portal hovering maybe twenty metres above us.

Inside that, was a helmeted figure on the back of a winged creature. I'd never seen one before, but I recognised a griffin from pictures in books.

Before Ryze put up the wall completely, I flicked off a shot of fire in the direction of the griffin's rider. They ducked and the portal slammed shut.

We all slumped against each other, breathing heavily.

"Fucking hells," Vayne growled. "Fucking griffin riding asshole." Part of the sleeve of his jacket was burnt away. "That was my favourite leather jacket too."

"I'm starting to take things like that personally," Ryze said.

"There is something very fucking personal about people throwing lightning at you," Vayne growled. He glared in the direction of the sky where the portal had been. If he could have bored a hole through the sky and incinerated our attacker, he would have. Although, an arrow would have done just as well.

I had to agree with the sentiment. "Tave? Hycathe? Are you both all right?"

"No visions this time," Tavian said. "I'm fine."

I nodded at him, then turned to Hycathe. Her face was pale, eyes wide. She grasped Jezalyn's hand which rested on her shoulder. She was trembling.

"I... I felt so powerful. Like I could have blasted them both right out of existence. But I couldn't." She shook her head.

"You don't want to hurt anyone," Jezalyn said gently.

"It wasn't that." Hycathe focused all of her gaze on her lover. "I couldn't hurt...*them*. Something was stopping me."

"Like a shield around them?" Vayne asked. He gestured towards the ice wall, which was already starting to melt.

"I don't know. I just couldn't." She didn't seem to have any more explanation than that. None of us pushed her any further.

"Whatever it was, Khala didn't feel the same way," Cavan said.

"No, she almost got him," Zared said proudly. "Or her. Whatever." He put his arm around me and gave me a squeeze before realising what he was doing. "I'm sorry, I..."

"It's all right," I said quickly. "I can handle hugs. Especially when you're telling me how amazing I am." I gave him a watery smile.

"Very amazing," he said. "The most amazing woman I ever met." He kissed my cheek lightly.

"I agree, but we should get inside before they come back," Cavan said. He placed his hands on two massive handles and pushed the pair of heavy, wooden doors inwards. They groaned in protest, but slowly opened.

"We didn't need a key," Zared said.

"Not to this part," Ryze agreed. "The outer part of Nallis is accessible to almost anyone. It's the interior we need keys for. It's... Go on inside. You'll see."

Zared and Tavian's hands still gripped around mine, we stepped through the doorway and I lost my breath.

CHAPTER
FIFTEEN
ZARED

I squeezed Khala's hand and stared up. And up.

What looked like towers from the outside, were hollow. At least in part. Walkways crisscrossed far above my head. I could only guess at how anyone would get up there. They'd have to be more out of their mind than Tavian.

"This is where the keys would go." Ryze led us over to another door. At least, I assumed it was a door. It had no handle, no knob. In the wall beside it, was a set of four key holes.

"If we had the keys, it would lead up to there." Ryze pointed straight up. "There's a staircase on the other side."

"Is there another door?" Khala asked. "The carvings in the sewer, what did they say?"

I glanced around. Met Tavian's eyes. "It wasn't clear. It said..." I signed the symbols.

"Shadows and dreams," Khala interpreted. "On the underneath."

"Underside," Hycathe corrected. "Like...the belly."

"Right." Khala nodded to her. "Underneath the inside. On the underside of the outside. Beneath the wings. Four palms to open. Two to guard the gate. One to open the sky."

"I like a good puzzle as much as the next man, but what the hells does that mean?" Ryze asked.

"Are you sure we don't need the keys?" I asked. If I didn't know better, I'd think they were guessing their way through all of this. And hoping none of us got killed along the way.

When that fucking lightning was thrown at us, I ran as hard as anyone, but

426

as close to Khala as I could. I was prepared to throw myself over her to keep her safe.

If anything else bad ever happened to her again, I wouldn't be able to live with myself. I felt like all I'd done since the Summer Court's attack on the caravan was let her down.

Letting her go with Ryze, for a start. We would have managed through her heat somehow.

Everything after that... I felt like I was hanging on by a thread. I half expected her to send me away. To tell me to go back to Fraxius and live my life without her. If that was what she truly wanted, I'd go.

I knew she didn't though. She wouldn't have gone to all the trouble to find me in Havenmoor and give me back my memories if she didn't want me.

But the doubt remained. Although I cared almost as much for Tave as I did for Khala, I couldn't keep from comparing myself to him and the other Fae men.

If I could decipher this puzzle, maybe I could start to redeem myself.

I sifted through the clues in my mind. "The underside of the inside..." I moved away from them, my gaze scanning the floor.

"Shit, he's right," Ryze said. "Underneath the inside would be something under the floor. Spread out and keep looking."

I moved slowly, keeping half of my attention on the floor in front of me and the other above.

"Here." I stopped in the middle of the building, where the floor was decorated with a chequerboard of tiles. "It's directly underneath the wings."

They all hurried over to stare.

"There are sixteen squares," Vayne pointed out. "Are we supposed to press four of them?"

"There are four of them," Cavan said softly.

"No offence, but there are sixteen." Vayne gestured toward the floor. He started to count them.

"Cavan is right," Khala said. "I mean, you're both right. There are four sets of four."

"Four palms could mean hands," Jezalyn said.

"I don't see any trees, so hands makes sense," Ryze said. He gave Jezalyn a smile.

She returned it and nodded. "So, four of us are supposed to press one of the sets of four?"

"But where within the sets of four?" Khala frowned.

"My guess would be the middle," I said. "Right where four intersect."

"That's possible, but I have a feeling if we're wrong, we're screwed," Ryze said. "Not to mention we don't know which four of us the symbols are referring to."

"Two have to be Hycathe and Tave," Khala said. "They're the most affected by the portals opening to the other courts. And the symbols were left there in the sewers for Tave to find."

"Or for Zared to find." Tavian cocked his head at me. "You could be just as important to this as anyone."

"Possibly." That was all I could say.

"We've come this far based on clues," Cavan said. "It seems unlikely they'd keep us guessing completely."

"They haven't exactly left us a big arrow pointing in the direction we need to go, complete with implicit instructions," Ryze pointed out.

"That would be too easy," Cavan said. He crouched beside the chequerboard tiles and peered at them. He tentatively reached out and touched one.

"I don't think they're dangerous. If there were, they would have dropped out from under the feet of people who have spent the last who knows how many centuries walking over the top of them."

I thought for a moment, then stepped onto the tiles. Like he said, they didn't drop out from under me. I knelt and tapped on the floor with my knuckles. Frowned. Tapped on the floor *beside* the chequerboard.

"It's hollow."

"It would be hollow if there is a secret door under there," Ryze said.

I shook my head. "No, it's not hollow under those tiles. It's hollow over here." I tapped around in a circle. "Khala, Tavian, Hycathe, come over here."

Hycathe gave me a doubtful look, but stepped over to crouch down beside the others.

"There's room here for four hands." I traced a circle on the floor. "I think it's a good idea to get off the chequerboard." I shrugged. If it dropped out from under Cavan, that was his fault.

He gave me a look, but rose and moved away from it.

"Let's all press at the same time," I instructed.

I placed my hand, palm down against the cold stone. The other three arrayed their hands beside mine. "One. Two. Three."

We all pressed downwards.

Nothing happened.

"Maybe we should try *on* the chequerboard," Ryze suggested.

"I think I should try," Vayne said. "The riddle said that two are supposed to stay behind and guard. Stands to reason one of those would be an alpha." He nodded to Jezalyn. "Hycathe isn't leaving without her. If whoever put this in place had visions of us, they'll know that."

"Why not me or Cavan?" Ryze asked.

"If anyone was going to stop us from doing this, they'd come after either of you," Vayne reasoned. "That might be the point of the attacks. I'm in the background of this. There was a much greater chance of me ending up here than either of you two. And if it doesn't work, you can try."

"All of that makes sense to me," Khala said.

"Me too," I agreed. I shuffled aside to give him more room.

Hycathe stood and moved over beside Jezalyn. She looked relieved. Sometimes it was easy to forget she got dragged along on all of this as much as the rest of us. Maybe more. I should cut her some slack.

"Let's try this again," I said. "One. Two. Three."

The floor started to rumble and shake. The section under our hands crumbled around the circumference and dropped down a centimetre or two.

Then it stopped.

I waited, my hand still in place.

"Please tell me we didn't come all this way just for that," Hycathe grumbled.

"That can't be all that happens." Cavan frowned.

Ryze matched his expression.

"On the underside of the outside," Khala said softly.

I stared at her. "Right."

"What the fuck are you talking about?" Hycathe growled.

"The riddle," Khala told her. "The underside of the outside might mean outside of the building. Whatever we did here—"

"Did something outside," I finished for her. "We should go and find out."

She stood and grabbed my hand to pull me towards the door, leaving the others to follow.

We tentatively stepped out through the double doors, keeping our eyes open for portals in the sky. So far, the sky seemed empty. The gods only knew how long that would last.

We moved slowly around the outside of the building, looking for holes, tunnels, anything that wasn't there before. There definitely wasn't an arrow pointing in the right direction. Nothing looked disturbed. The ground didn't look broken anywhere. There was no sign of the rumbling. No sign anything happened at all.

"I'm starting to think whoever did this has the same sick sense of humour as the gods," Khala said. "Do you think they're up to something somewhere else, while we're here trying to solve a riddle that has no meaning?"

"There's a special place in the hells for them if they are," I said. I rubbed a hand over my chin. We had to be missing something. It could be staring us right in the face, or it could be hidden by centuries of dirt, dust and grass. Were we supposed to dig? I didn't think so, but I could be wrong. Only, I didn't want to be wrong. I figured out where to put our hands. I wanted to figure out the rest too.

She snorted softly. "I hope the gods make it hurt."

I gave her a half smile and leaned back to get a good look at the top of the building. "Do you think there's a way up there?"

"Not without the keys," she replied. "Unless you can fly?"

"Unless you can fly," I echoed. "One to open the sky. Can you freeze those wings? Or set them on fire?"

"I can, but so can Ryze and Cavan," she said. "If I'm supposed to do something, it has to be something they can't do. Right?" She cocked her head at me.

I wasn't sure if she wanted me to agree with her, or tell her I had a different answer. I didn't have one. What she said made perfect sense to me. She was special, I'd known that for a very long time. Only now she was coming to realise how special. She'd always be my Khala, as far as I was concerned. No matter what the world did to us.

"Dalyth could do the things you can," I said slowly. "That might be why they killed her. It had nothing to do with Hycathe being angry with her. They wanted to stop her from doing whatever it is you need to do."

"Wind," she said softly. "I can create wind."

"Do it," Ryze said, appearing from around the other side of the building. "Cavan and I will keep an eye out for another portal. If it's going to come, it's going to come soon."

Khala nodded and half closed her eyes. She had that expression on her face that meant she was doing magic. Pure concentration. She was even more fucking gorgeous like that.

I watched the sky with half an eye, the other on the wings on the roof of Nallis. Watched as they started to shake. Dust rose into the air, followed by chunks of stone. Small at first, then increasingly larger.

I put a hand above my eyes to protect them from falling debris.

"Hurry," Ryze said urgently.

I thought he saw a portal, until I realised the mist was rising up the side of the mountain. It seemed to have ghostly fingers, reaching for us.

Reaching for Khala.

A strange, mechanical grinding filled the air, followed by a clunk. The wings moved. slowly spreading out like a flower opening its petals. The grinding sounded again, then the wings started to move. Slowly at first, but then with increasing speed.

The ground under my feet shook so hard I barely managed to stay standing.

The wings moved faster and faster until they became a blur.

Then the ground opened up right in front of me.

CHAPTER
SIXTEEN
ZARED

"**S**hit!" I slithered downward as the ground slanted hard, one arm windmilling, reaching for Khala with the other.

After two tries, I grabbed the corner of her jacket. A fistful of fabric in my hand, I yanked her towards me. She staggered a couple of steps until she was close enough for me to grip her arm.

She clung to me, eyes wide as the ground became steeper and steeper.

I managed to get my arms around her before the ground virtually dropped out from under our feet.

She let out a squeal and held on tighter.

We slid and rolled, dirt and rocks tumbling with us.

"Hold on!" Khala shouted.

Wind whipped around us in a frenzy, slapping my hair across my face.

Magic. Khala slowed our descent, but there was nowhere to go but down.

I tried to shield her, but we both slid painfully over jagged rocks that threatened to shred us to pieces. My jacket was the only thing keeping me from losing most of my skin.

Finally, we hit the ground with bruising force so hard it knocked the wind from my lungs. I lay there holding her while I struggled to suck back a breath.

"Khala?"

She groaned. "I'm all right."

Another groan sounded from the other side of her. "I'm all right too," Vayne said.

"Me too," Ryze agreed. "Tave? Cavan?"

"Over here," Tavian said.

Cavan grunted something right before the sliver of sky above us disappeared.

"We seem to be under Nallis," Ryze said. The darkness was broken when he illuminated the space with his magic. A lot of the time, magic freaked me out, but this once I was glad to see it. If only to break up what seemed like complete darkness.

The air smelled stale, like it was trapped for a thousand years.

"Hycathe and Jezalyn," Cavan said. "The mist took them. I tried to seize them, but... It was though hands reached out and drew them in." He shook his head, his expression haunted. There was more to that story, that was obvious, but he wasn't going to share right now.

"I told you the mist was dangerous," Ryze said. He didn't sound triumphant. Instead, he peered around, and looked deeply troubled. "I'm not sure this is any less fucked."

I helped Khala to her feet. She and Cavan used their own magic to add a further light to the space.

We stood in a vast room, clearly not natural. The walls were constructed of blocks of the same stone as the structure above our heads. It seemed to suck in light the moment it touched.

"This isn't the sky," Ryze mused.

I wasn't the only one who gave him a questioning look.

"One to open the sky," he quoted from the riddle. "Khala opened this space, but it's not the sky."

"It might be if you live underground," I reasoned.

Now they were all staring at me.

I shrugged. "The lost courts went somewhere, didn't they? Who's to say that wasn't down?"

"It's certainly possible," Cavan conceded. "It wouldn't be the strangest thing I ever saw."

"It wouldn't be the strangest thing any of us ever saw," Ryze said. "But it doesn't explain the griffins."

I glanced over to see a thoughtful look on Khala's face. "What is it?"

"I'm not sure," she admitted. "Just a thought, but I might be wrong." She walked a few steps away, raising and lowering her hand as she went. "There has to be a way out of here."

"We certainly can't go back the way we came," Vayne said. He brushed dirt off his clothes and inspected his sleeve.

"Not unless there's a way to open it back up and climb," Ryze agreed.

"I don't think we're supposed to," Khala said. "Look." She held her hand down lower, illuminating the ground.

"Are those—" I started.

"Bones," she agreed. "And that's a knife. If I had to guess, I'd say those were Fae bones."

"Does that mean we don't get out of here?" Vayne asked. "That would fucking suck. I knew I shouldn't have followed Ryze. You were always going to get me killed horribly someday."

"While I can't deny that, I didn't predict *this*," Ryze said. "Should we decide now who is going to eat who?"

"I call dibs on eating Khala and Zared," Tavian said.

"No one is going to be eating anyone just yet," Khala said. She turned to Ryze. "Remember the song on the map that led to the Court of Shadows? It talked about darkness and a row of skulls." She followed the bones into the shadows until she reached what looked like a pathway.

On either side, placed neatly, was a line of skulls. They stared at us, each positioned precisely the same distance from the one before, as if someone took the time to measure them.

"That's creepy as fuck," I remarked.

"That same song also said to stay away," Ryze pointed out. "Something about deadly games and knives?"

"I'd rather take the risk of a deadly game, than sit here and wait to die," Cavan said. He walked with deliberate steps down the centre of the macabre row, chin raised like he wasn't bothered at all.

Tavian said something under his breath about bravery being hot, and followed along behind, Khala on his heels.

Not wanting to be left behind, I hurried to catch up. Ryze and Vayne walked behind me.

The trail led farther and farther away from where we landed. As we went, the ceiling became lower, the walls closer. The cavernous room became a considerably narrower tunnel.

"It smells better than the sewer," Tavian observed.

"Anything would smell better than that," I said.

"He's right though," Ryze said. "Not only does this smell better than a sewer, it doesn't smell like a tunnel."

"What do you—" I started. I sniffed. I smelled dirt and slightly stale air, but something else as well.

"Trees," Khala said. "Maybe Zared was right and the courts are underground." She didn't seem convinced.

I didn't blame her. Underground trees didn't seem very plausible to me.

"Any more of that riddle?" Cavan had stopped and was now staring at another wall. It was covered with symbols. The same as the Silent Maidens' hand talk.

Khala stepped forward to look at it more closely.

She frowned adorably. "It's all... Not quite gibberish. It looks like they carved every symbol they could think of into the stone."

Ryze rubbed his chin.

"The moon, it seems, is always full,
And casts a pall upon the skulls."

"That was written on the map. Is there a moon symbol on there?"

"There's three of them," Khala said. "Full moon, crescent moon and half-moon. Should I press the half-moon?"

433

I glanced down at the floor. It didn't look like it was going to fall out from under us, but neither had the mountainside. At this point, I wouldn't rule out anything.

"Maybe we should hold hands or something," Tavian suggested. "If anything happens to one of us, it will happen to all of us."

"We might end up added to the row of skulls," Vayne said.

"That's going to happen anyway if we don't get out of here," I pointed out.

"I think it might be a better idea if the rest of you stand back," Ryze said. "The song mentioned treachery. Pressing that moon might do the gods knows what."

"Shouldn't you stand back too?" I ask him.

"Someone needs to stay near Khala, and I've already volunteered myself," he said. "I'm still your High Lord. When I say stay back, you'll stay back." He turned to Cavan. "I'm trusting you to keep them safe."

Cavan nodded. I thought he was going to argue that he should stay near Khala, but he moved back, putting himself between us and the wall full of symbols.

I didn't like any of this, but I stood beside Tavian and watched with my breath held. He slipped his hand into mine and moved closer until our shoulders touched.

"She'll be all right," he said softly.

I didn't know what he was basing that on, but I nodded. If this didn't do anything, we'd be fucked anyway. We'd die down here. We'd never know what happened to Hycathe and Jezalyn. Were they still alive?

The mist had looked like a living thing, reaching out with fingers and claws. Did it also have a mouth? This whole thing was so, unbelievably fucked up. Moving buildings, rows of skulls, mists that may have eaten people. More than ever, I was regretting not running away with Khala.

"Wait," I said when she raised her hand to touch the moon.

She stopped and turned around.

I pushed past Ryze, put my arms around her and kissed her. After a moment of surprise, she kissed me back, albeit more tentative than usual.

Fucking Wornar.

I forced myself to pull back before I pushed her too far, but I looked her in the eyes and smiled.

"I needed you to know I love you," I told her. "In case anything bad is about to happen."

Her expression softened. "I love you too."

I kissed her once more, quickly, then stood back again.

"That was sweet," Tavian told me.

I shrugged and tried to ignore the way my face heated. I wasn't usually given to displays of sentiment, especially not in front of other people, but this was important. Too important not to step up and say what I needed to say. I needed her to know exactly how I felt about her. It went so far beyond caring, it had for a long, long time.

Ryze cleared his throat. "All right. Let's try this then."

"Wait," Vayne said. "How do we know Khala is the one who is supposed to touch that moon? Or anything else, for that matter?"

"That's a good point," Ryze said thoughtfully. "It could be meant for any of us. Or none of us."

"It was me who moved the wings," Khala said. "It makes sense I'm supposed to do this too." She was more resigned than convinced. "From what we've seen so far, if it's not meant to be me, then nothing will happen."

"Assuming they haven't changed the rules on us," Cavan said.

"That is a big assumption." Ryze rubbed his chin. "I could press it and if I die..."

Before he finished talking, Khala turned and firmly pressed her fingers down on the full moon symbol.

Nothing happened.

"That was anticlimactic," Vayne said. "I guess we all get to try."

One by one, we stepped forward and pressed the symbol. Nothing discernible happened at all.

"At this point, I'd be happy for anything to happen, rather than nothing," Ryze said.

"You'd prefer this tunnel to flood and drown us all?" Vayne asked.

"It would break up the monotony," Ryze said like it was no big deal.

"It would completely end all monotony," Vayne agreed. "Personally, I'd prefer monotony for a while longer to a watery grave."

"You're starting to sound like an old man," Ryze told him.

"That's what I get for spending time with you." Vayne gave him a faint smile. "After a while, I started to become like you."

Ryze raised his middle finger at Vayne.

Khala rolled her eyes at them.

"The end of that song," she said, "it mentioned night and day." She turned back towards the wall and placed a hand on the moon and one on the symbol for the sun. She pressed down hard on them both.

"What do you know?" Vayne said dryly. "That did nothing either."

"Do you have a better idea?" Khala asked. She looked like she was just about out of patience with us.

I totally understood that. I was just about out of patience with us too. Not to mention this whole ridiculous fucking quest. Maybe we should have left the courts to get themselves out of the shit.

All right, I understood the reasons for helping them, but I couldn't shake the feeling it might come back to bite us in the ass.

"Maybe two people have to press it?" I suggested. "Tavian and I found the symbols that led us here, maybe we're supposed to do it."

Tavian grinned suggestively.

I smiled back at him. He was too fucking adorable. Being around him made my cock twitch just as much as it did around Khala.

"Let's start with this first." I moved past Khala and placed my hand on the sun.

Tavian placed his on the moon.

In unison, we pushed down on the symbols.

The response was immediate. The whole wall trembled, then started to move to one side. Something shot out of the gap and struck me in the chest.

Tavian ducked and another struck Vayne.

I glanced down. I barely had time to register anything at all before my whole body began to turn to stone.

CHAPTER
SEVENTEEN
KHALA

"Oh my gods!" I stared in horror as Zared and Vayne both became encased in the same black stone. It happened so quickly they both barely registered their shock and horror before they were consumed entirely.

The whole thing took only several, silent seconds. Neither men let out so much as a sound. Their jaws dropped and then they were gone, obscured and still. Even the scent of fear was a flash, immediately suppressed.

"What the hells?" I threw myself at Zared, battering at the stone and trying to break it away from him.

"They're still in there. I can feel them!" Both were confused and terrified. Their fear tangled with my own, until I wasn't sure whose emotions were whose.

Tavian did the same with Vayne. "We have to get them out of there." His tone was full of anxiety laced with guilt. If he hadn't ducked when he did...

"You cannot," a new voice said.

In my haste to try to free my men, I'd forgotten about the wall opening.

A Fae woman with hair as dark as midnight stood in the doorway, her hands clasped together in front of her. Her expression betrayed nothing but calm, the epitome of serenity.

"What did you do to them?" Ryze demanded. He and Cavan put themselves between me and Tavian, and the woman.

"I did nothing," she said. She barely even blinked in the face of accusation. "They were chosen to be guardians. They will remain as surety for your behaviour. When you have proven you will pose no threat to the Court of Shadows, they will be released. They will not be harmed."

Court of Shadows? Fuck. We were screwed.

"How can we be sure you'll do what you say you'll do?" Ryze asked.

"Because I have told you I would," she said easily.

"Because no one has ever lied before," Tavian muttered.

I put a hand on his wrist to stop him from doing anything rash. Or maybe to contain myself. Encasing two men, my men, in stone wasn't an act of welcome.

"Court of Shadows," Cavan breathed. He looked awed. "And the Court of Dreams?"

The only change in her expression was a slight dipping of her eyebrows. "We have much to discuss. Follow me." She turned in a flow of skirt and long tunic, both black with slashes of gold through the fabric.

"We can't leave them here," Tavian argued. He looked ready to pull out a knife and chip the stone away from Zared and Vayne, bit by bit if he had to.

"They will remain here and be unharmed," the woman said. She kept walking without looking back, clearly expecting to be obeyed.

"She smells like an alpha," Tavian muttered.

I hummed my agreement. She also smelled like a combination of chocolate and roses right after their peak. Not unpleasant, but not compelling either.

"What's your name?" Cavan asked. Of all of us, he was the least intimidated. If anything, he seemed validated after so many years. Only a glance back over his shoulder at Vayne and Zared showed his true concern. That was the first sign of anything other than animosity between them and him. The gesture would have been heartening under other circumstances.

"You may address me as Lyra," she said simply. "The High Lady is waiting."

The tunnel opened to another cavernous chamber. This one with other tunnels and doorways leading off in different directions.

In the centre of the chamber, a massive lake was surrounded by trees. Light shone from somewhere in the ceiling of the cavern. What looked like a huge full moon, hung in the centre.

"The magic of night and shadows," Ryze said softly.

Lyra stopped and turned to look at him. "Some call us the Court of Night. Or the Court of Darkness. We prefer shadows, because the other two suggest the absence of light. Shadows cannot exist without illumination."

"Night cannot exist without day," Cavan said.

"Indeed," she agreed. "But there is no Court of Day."

"There's no Court of the Sun either," Ryze said.

"Some would say there are four courts which live in the sun," she said indifferently. "But this is a conversation for another time. Best not keep the High Lady waiting." She clicked her tongue and turned to hurry on.

She led us around the edge of the lake, to a wide doorway that led into a grand chamber.

I stepped inside and gaped.

The walls were entirely covered with a mural that looked like a garden from the Spring Court. Amongst the flowers, trees with autumn foliage nestled. Leaning over to smell bright yellow roses, was a Fae girl with pale blonde hair the same shade as Cavan's. A man stood near her, his eyes closed as though asleep, dreaming. Shadows reached across the ground behind him.

Behind them, buildings that looked like the Winter Court palace sat amongst wispy trees, each covered in a dusting of snow.

"All six of the courts in one," a woman said. She rose from where she sat on a plush chair with high arms. Her hair was as dark as Lyra's. She was dressed in a flowing skirt and tunic in the same style. Where Lyra's eyes were blue, hers were brown.

She turned to Lyra and smiled fondly. "Thank you, my love."

Lyra returned the smile, then sank into a chair to the side of the room.

"Let me introduce myself. I'm High Lady Vernissa. We've been expecting you for quite some time." She addressed the statement to Tavian and me.

Tavian stared at her. "You're an omega."

"Of course I am," she said with a tinkly laugh. "So are you. Both of you. And your alphas are your protectors."

Ryze looked amused. "That's more or less accurate. I'm High Lord Ryzellius of the Winter Court. You can call me Ryze." He introduced the rest of us.

Vernissa looked surprised.

"I assumed things had changed in the last thousand years, but I didn't expect you'd have alphas in a superior role to omegas." Vernissa exchanged glances with Lyra.

Lyra looked downright offended.

"This is what I've been trying to tell Ryze for the last two hundred years," Tavian said.

"I'd laugh, but he really has," Ryze said dryly.

"Likely it was something akin to suggesting he'd make a better High Lord than you, not that omegas should be in command," Cavan said. He looked like he couldn't decide what to make of all of this.

"So, you mostly have women leading?" I asked Vernissa, trying to make the question sound innocuous. That was an idea I could appreciate. I didn't see a reason for any particular preference toward men leading.

"I've been High Lady for five hundred years," Vernissa said. "Before me, it was my aunt. She was the one who found this place, to keep us safe from the Court of Dreams."

"Court of Nightmares," Lyra said sourly.

"Legend has it that *you* were trying to destroy *them*," Ryze said, the slightest hint of accusation in his tone.

"Legend *they* started," Lyra said, just this side of snippy. She sniffed, then pushed her mask of serenity back into place.

"The Court of Dreams captured and trained griffins for the sole purpose of invading and destroying us," Vernissa said. She seemed more accepting of the past. She'd certainly had time to get used to the idea. "They forced us into hiding, before the seasonal courts did the same to them. They've been trying to find us ever since."

"Why did they try to destroy you?" I asked.

If they were to be believed, everything we were told was backwards. Unless they were full of shit. They seemed sincere. Although, that's how I'd act if I was trying to get sympathy. I'd keep my judgment to myself for now.

"That's a long tale," Vernissa said. "I've been remiss as a host. Let us share a meal and I'll go into further detail."

"Actually, what we would like is for you to remove Zared and Vayne from the stone," I said. "They are our pack. We need them with us." I glanced at Tavian, who nodded.

"Right. They're along to protect us." He forced a smile, but looked like he might start stabbing if they didn't agree to our request.

"I apologise," Vernissa said smoothly. "I cannot undo that magic until we come to an understanding. I can assure you, they are well and alive. But you know that, because your bond with them is intact." She addressed that to me.

"They're alive," I agreed. "But they're terrified." I did my best to assure them, but it did little to calm their minds. If they could smash their way out, they would. Hells, if anyone could glare their way out, it would be them. Doubtless they'd tried.

"Then we better talk quickly." Vernissa gestured for us to follow her through a side door that led into a narrow room with a long table in the middle.

Fae, all with dark hair and clothes, bustled about setting down plates and pottery cups. A large teapot sat in the centre of the table, beside a tiered tray full of cakes.

For the first time since we stepped out of the tunnel, I saw Fae men. Their hair was as dark as the women, and just as long. The same dark skirts brushed the tops of their feet.

They moved around with their eyes down, each step silent as though trying to be as unobtrusive as possible. This was a stark contrast from any man I met in the seasonal courts. Or in Fraxius for that matter. None of the priests in the Temple at Ebonfalls were subservient like this.

We sat, they served us cake and tea before they hurried out.

"People who work for you and don't talk back," Ryze remarked with a side glance at Tavian.

Vernissa laughed her tinkly laugh. "They don't work for me. I own them."

We all stared at her then.

"You...own them?" Cavan asked. He glanced at me, but then away again before I could dig my elbows into his ribs for whatever he seemed to be thinking.

Fae men.

"Of course," she said lightly. "Some of them used to belong to my aunt. Some of them are sons of those men."

"Are all the men in this court owned?" I asked carefully.

"Oh no, not at all," she said with a wave of her hand. "Merely those born to it, or who choose to surrender themselves. It's not easy to live underground the way we do. Many have long struggled with my aunt's decision to confine the court to these caverns. They want to see the sunshine and feel the wind on their faces. And they will soon enough. But there is much to be considered first."

"If you didn't send the griffins, were you the ones who put the symbols in the sewer of the Spring Court?" Tavian asked.

She gave him a blank look. "We've had minimal interaction with the seasonal courts for the last thousand years. The first warning we had of your arrival was when the cavern above us moved."

"The Court of Dreams did all that?" Tavian surmised. "Because they wanted us to find you."

"They wanted someone to find us," Lyra said. "Be it you or them. Undoubtedly, they're tracking your progress."

"They tried to attack us aside Nallis," I said. "They didn't seem to want us to find you at all."

"The fact they didn't kill you suggests they were merely trying to scare you," Vernissa said. "That is the manner in which they behave. With aggression and force."

"You don't seem worried they followed us here," Cavan pointed out.

"No one can enter here without our knowledge," Vernissa replied. "If they tried, they could only enter several at a time. We'd deal with them before they became a problem."

"By turning them to stone?" I asked bitterly.

"That's certainly a possibility," she agreed. "The presence of your betas will provide additional warning. Hence they are the two guardians. The magic that holds them in place will respond to any further incursion."

"You said you want to come to some kind of understanding," Ryze said. "Let's cut straight to that. I don't want my people in stone any longer than necessary."

I murmured my agreement. As far as I was concerned, them being in stone in the first place was longer than necessary.

"Yes," Cavan said. "What is it you want?"

"We want to return above," Vernissa said. "We've spent enough time underground. It's time for us to regain our place in the sun."

CHAPTER
EIGHTEEN
KHALA

"What do you make of all of this?" Ryze asked us. We'd finished our tea and cake with small talk before Vernissa insisted we rest. Further discussion and negotiation would take place after that. Both High Lords tried to steer her back to her declaration, but she wouldn't be drawn.

Cavan was pacing back and forth across the room, arms crossed, frown on his face.

"I spent a lot of time thinking about all of this but nothing is the way I visualised it. Everything I ever knew painted the Court of Shadows as the antagonist. Including those songs on Ryze's maps. Now they're suggesting all of that was incorrect?"

Ryze reclined on the wide nest in the middle of the room, hands behind his head, legs crossed at his knees. Even piled high with cushions, it was big enough to sleep ten people comfortably.

"In my experience when dealing with two opposing points of view, the truth is usually somewhere approximately in the middle." He glanced meaningfully in Cavan's direction.

"Is that your way of admitting you were wrong about Cavan?" Tavian asked. He'd guided me over to a couch that sat against the wall and pulled my feet onto his lap. He took off my boots and started to massage my feet.

"To some extent," Ryze said. "As wrong as he was about me."

Cavan stopped pacing to quirk an eyebrow at Ryze. "I'm not entirely certain I was wrong. But you are more tolerable than I expected."

"That's not surprising, I'm extremely tolerable." Ryze uncrossed his legs and crossed them the other way.

"Yes, you are," Tavian told him.

Cavan snorted softly.

"It looks like we have a way to go." Ryze shrugged.

"At least they're trying," Tavian said to me.

"We should be trying to get Vayne and Zared out of the stone," I said. Neither was as frantic as they were before. In fact, they seemed to be asleep, or perhaps unconscious.

"Unless you want to try melting it, there's no way out of there until Vernissa frees them." Cavan sighed. "I hate it also, but we have no choice but to do what she says."

"Do you hate it?" I asked. "You seemed only too happy to get rid of Zared once before. Have you forgotten how you had Dalyth took his memories?"

He stopped pacing. His body stiffened. "I haven't forgotten. You know I only did that for his own good."

"So you said." I tried but failed to keep the bitterness out of my voice. Zared knew going to the Summer Court might end in his death, or worse, and he'd gone with me anyway. In spite of Cavan's reasoning, the whole thing still stung.

"Khala—" Cavan started.

"We've all been through a lot," Tavian said quickly. "I think we all need to relax and unwind." He massaged my toes one by one.

I exhaled softly. He was right. This was not the time to tear each other apart.

I lost myself in thought for a while.

Finally, I said, "I admire Vernissa. She seems like the kind of woman who would never let anyone take power away from her." I pressed my lips together, but they all knew what I was referring to.

"You didn't *let* anyone take power from you," Tavian said softly. "He took it. He took complete advantage of the fact you're an omega. The only person who did anything wrong was that prick. I look forward to stabbing him in the eyeball."

I managed a faint smile. I was looking forward to the same thing.

"My point is that I don't have to let him take anything from me," I said. "Including being...intimate. I don't know what I'm ready for, but if you can be patient with me, I'd like to try."

Maybe it was too soon, but I wanted to take the power back for myself. I needed the closeness with the pack I had here with me. If it wasn't for Cavan's order that dimmed the memories of what Wornar did to me, I wouldn't have been ready for anything.

Because of that, I was done being a victim. I wanted to touch and be touched. To show these men how I felt about them.

Ryze sat up. "We can be as patient as you need. Why don't we start with a snuggle?" He held out his hand.

"A snuggle sounds good," I agreed. I swung my legs off Tavian's lap and stood.

I grabbed his hand, and Cavan's, and tugged them both towards the nest. We all climbed in and lay down, Ryze and Tavian on one side of me, Cavan on the other.

For the longest time, no one moved.

I lay still, Cavan's hand on my hip, Ryze's just above.

Tavian was the one who made the first move, sliding down and undoing the front of Ryze's pants.

Ryze twisted to lie on his back while Tavian freed his erection and started to slide his hand up and down his length. He groaned softly.

"I don't expect you to call me sir," Cavan started.

"Maybe I want to." I offered him a smile. Being dominated by someone I felt deeply for was entirely different to what Wornar did to me. Consent was everything.

Cavan lifted his eyebrows. "You want me to spank you?"

His words elicited a rush of heat through my entire body. Heat that was tinged with trepidation, but made my pussy wet as fuck.

"Same safe word?" I asked.

He nodded. "Yellow it is." Eyes on mine at every moment, he unbuttoned the front of my pants and slid them with almost painful slowness down my hips. He paused every time I even looked like I was uncomfortable. A couple of times I had to smile and nod for him to keep going. Every moment, I was in control. If I said to stop, he'd stop immediately.

A couple of times I thought about it. My mind flashed me back to the Spring Court, back to another man's hands on my body. His cock...

I pushed them away. What mattered was here and now, and proving to myself I wasn't broken. Later, I may regret pushing myself too hard, but I'd worry about that when later arrived, if it did.

By now, Tavian was licking and teasing the tip of Ryze's cock. Ryze's eyes were half closed in enjoyment. It was the first time I saw them together and it was hotter than hells. Knowing they fucked and seeing it were two different things.

I kept my eyes on them while Cavan flipped me over onto my belly.

They watched me as he kissed my ass, nibbled on it then brought his hand down on my skin.

The first spank was tentative, almost gentle.

"If that's your idea of spanking..." Ryze teased.

"I'm more than happy to show you how hard I spank," Cavan told him.

"That's some wish fulfillment right there," Tavian muttered.

I hummed my agreement, but looked at Cavan over my shoulder. "How about you show me instead."

"With pleasure." Cavan brought his hand down harder the second time. And harder again the third.

I groaned from sheer bliss brought about by a combination of the stinging slaps and the sight of Tavian with Ryze's cock deep down his throat. Every slap and suck drove the bad memories further and further to the back of my mind. Nothing else existed but this.

Cavan's order was stronger than I thought; it went deeper. It kept the worst of the darkness from reaching me. More than that, it knitted that part of me back together, like magic closing a wound.

With every spank, I healed a little more.

Between spanks, Cavan slid his hand between my legs, grazed his fingers over my pussy.

The moment he touched me, I froze.

"I'm so sorry—" He pulled his hand back immediately.

"No," I said quickly. "It's all right. Please don't stop." I needed to know I could be touched by someone who respected me and my boundaries. The fact he was paying close attention spoke more volumes than the library in the Winter Court. The last thing he wanted to do was hurt me.

"When you touch me...I feel more myself again. Please..."

He hesitated for a moment longer, then slipped his hand back to trace slow, deliberate circles around, and over my clit.

I shivered under his touch. The more he gave me, the more I wanted. The more I needed.

He parted my legs a little wider and swirled his fingers several times more around my aching clit, before sliding one inside me.

"Mmmm. More of that please, sir."

"Whatever my omega wants," he rumbled. He slid in another finger, then another.

Ryze slowly bucked his hips, driving himself deeper into Tavian's mouth.

Cavan slid his fingers out of me and turned me over onto my back. He bent my knees and lowered his face between my legs. He slipped his fingers back inside me but traced swirls around my clit with his tongue.

It only took me a matter of moments to almost came apart.

"That's it," Cavan said between licks and nibbles. "Come for me." He sucked my clit into his mouth and bit down lightly.

My whole body quivered. When I came it wasn't with a rush of intensity. Rather, it was a gentle, perfectly blissful wave of pleasure washing over my body and sweeping my soul clean.

In that moment, I knew Wornar could never hurt me again.

It wasn't until Cavan lifted his face from me that I realised Tavian moved away from Ryze and was busy undoing Cavan's pants and drawing out his cock.

My eyebrows rose. I watched, curious to see Cavan's reaction to Tavian's touch.

He looked bemused at first, but he didn't pull away. If anything, he was completely still until Tavian lowered his mouth onto his tip and started to suck.

Holy gods, that was as hot as seeing Tavian suck Zared or Ryze's cocks.

Ryze took the opportunity to roll over to me and smile before he straddled me. "I apologise for the lack of hot wax. I can get a candle if you like."

He started to stand.

I quickly grabbed his arm and pulled him back.

"Next time. Right now I just want your cock." I manoeuvred him so he was straddling me and wrapped my legs around his hips. If spanking and finger fucking could heal me, I wanted to see what being fucked would do. I ached for it.

"Whatever the lady wants." He slowly, slowly pressed himself inside me, filling me bit by bit until he was fully seated inside. He closed his eyes and savoured the sensation before he started to slowly thrust into my body.

Like Cavan had, Ryze watched me carefully for my reaction.

All he would have seen was my enjoyment. My overwhelming need to live in this moment.

Gradually, he thrust harder, his knot sliding against my clit and driving me towards the edge again.

With a rush, I came again, this time the intense inferno that had me bucking my hips and grinding myself against him for every precious drop.

My breathy cries pushed Ryze and Cavan both over the edge, thrusting and coming inside me and Tavian.

I glanced over to see Cavan looked surprised at himself for spilling his pearly cum into Tavian's mouth.

Ryze panted, then slid out of me and rolled away, leaving space for Tavian to replace him.

Tavian lay beside me and pulled me over so I straddled him. I slowly lowered myself onto his cock. He groaned in pleasure as I rode the other omega to his orgasm, and a third for me.

I sagged down, sweating and panting, but satisfied and feeling whole for the first time in a long while.

I was right, this was exactly what I needed.

CHAPTER
NINETEEN
KHALA

When I woke, the cavern was dark and silent. Presumably they turned off the illumination to simulate night-time. According to my body clock, it was close to morning.

I felt through the bond for Vayne and Zared. They were both still alive and surprisingly calm. Even Vayne didn't seem as aggravated as usual. Maybe he was getting some much-needed rest in there.

I managed to slip out of bed without waking any of the men, and padded over to the door.

Without knowing why, I slipped out into the corridor. I headed towards the lake just as the fake moon started to glow, faintly at first. Its reflection glinted off the still water, making the whole place strangely beautiful.

I stood watching the light gradually grow brighter. After several minutes, I sensed that I was also being watched. Nothing malevolent. At least, I didn't think so.

I turned to see a Fae man, his curious gaze on me. He was one of those who served us tea and cake yesterday.

"Morning," I greeted. I spoke low to keep my voice from echoing around the space.

He nodded in response.

"It's pretty here," I said for something to say.

He nodded again.

"Are you not allowed to talk?" I asked. None of them said a word the day before. "Can you talk?"

When he didn't respond, I asked the same question with my hands.

That pleasantly surprised him, judging by the widening of his eyes.

He signed back. "I am not permitted to speak out loud to an omega. I am... beneath them. In my role here."

His gestures were different to the ones I knew, but I understood the general meaning. He was subservient to Vernissa. And perceived himself to be subservient to me and Tavian too.

"Are you allowed to speak to alphas?" I asked out loud. He could clearly hear.

"That depends on their rank. Some, yes. Some, no."

I took that to mean he couldn't speak to Lyra.

"You're a beta? What's your name?"

"Yes," he signed. "Rijal. And you are Khala." He glanced around nervously like he shouldn't be standing here too long communicating with me.

"Yes I am. Am I allowed to give you permission to talk out loud to me?" I didn't see myself as superior to him in any way, regardless of my designation.

He shook his head vigourously. He even backed up a step or two, like he was scared I'd insist.

I put my hands up to placate him. "All right, I won't ask. Why are you not allowed to talk to people of rank? Is it considered offensive?" The way some people talked certainly was.

I pushed any thoughts of Wornar out of my mind.

"It's considered rude," Rijal signed. "We're expected to know our place. To be silent. Those who rule want to forget we're here except to receive the food we bring and to see that we cleaned for them." Again his gestures were different but understandable.

"It sounds like they don't see you as people," I told him.

He looked down at the ground. "We are less. Those who cannot own ourselves. We are less."

"You're only less because they want you to think you are," I said firmly. "Why does she own you?"

"Because her family owned my father, and my father's father. And his father." He shrugged.

"Is there any way to stop that?" I asked. Of course, that was assuming he wanted to. He didn't seem too concerned with his circumstances. Or maybe he was resigned to them.

"If we ask," he signed.

I blinked. "All you have to do is ask?" He nodded again. "So you don't mind?"

He cocked his head slightly. "Sometimes I mind. We get punished if we're too loud. But here—" He gestured around the cavern. "There are a few ways to...live. To get food. Some hunt through the tunnels. Some go above to hunt there, or try to catch fish. Some train in the army. Some serve."

"So there aren't too many jobs down here," I concluded. "Vernissa makes sure you eat?"

No wonder they were ready to return to the surface of Jorius. If being owned was better than starving, then what choice would they have?

"If you go back up to the surface, the whole court, what would you do?"

"I would grow food," he signed. "I would look at the sun and watch food grow."

"You'd be a farmer," I said. "That sounds fabulous." Assuming there was farmland available for him. Where would the Court of Shadows go? I wasn't even sure where it was before. I'd have to ask Cavan.

Rijal grinned. "What is the sign for this word?"

"Farmer?" I asked. I showed him the sign I knew and he copied it back to me.

"How do you know these signs?" he asked.

I could have asked him the same thing. "I guess your ancestors taught mine. Then they made sure we couldn't forget them."

The Silent Maidens seemed to be a bridge between this court and the world above. Was that intentional? Cavan once said the Silent Maidens were established as a means to eventually return the two courts to Jorius.

Someone was definitely playing the long game. Vernissa's aunt, perhaps.

"How many people are there like you?" I asked. "Are they all men?"

"There are a few thousand throughout the caverns," he replied. "All men, yes. Women are for leading, or having children. Not for serving. Is it the same?" He pointed upward.

I snorted softly. "No, it's usually the men who lead. Women serve and have children. Although some join the army or become guards. Some are even farmers."

He gaped at me in disbelief. "In the Court of Shadows, women do not grow food. Or hunt. They would get... Ground and blood on their hands."

"Dirt?" I suggested. I pointed to the base of a nearby tree, then showed him my hand symbol for dirt. "Women aren't allowed to get dirty?"

He shook his head vigorously. "No, no dirt. No mess. Only men have a mess on them."

"Only men get messy?" I said. "Some people would say men get messy more often up there. But women get messy too."

He looked horrified. "Why? Why would a woman get mess on her?"

"Because she wants to." That was the only explanation I could give. It sounded like we had more freedom than they did down here, but maybe I shouldn't judge too harshly. They did what they had to do to survive. If the lake was their main source of water, then it would be easier to stay clean than it would to wash off a mess. After a thousand years, that might have become a rule, as well as a necessity.

"Those men with you," Rijal signed tentatively. "Do you—" He made the symbol for fucking.

My face heated slightly at the direct question. "With them? Yes."

"Because you choose to?" he asked. "Because they choose to?"

449

I smiled. "Because we very much choose to, yes. Do you not get to choose?"

He glanced down at the ground again. "Vernissa decides who is best for breeding with whom. For the strongest. If we are weak, we don't get to fuck."

It was my turn to look horrified. "She decides who you sleep with?"

I supposed that made a twisted kind of sense too. With limited space in the cavern, those here needed to be strong enough to survive. And to fight whatever may come on their way back to the surface.

He looked confused. "Not sleep, no."

I laughed. "I'm sorry, it's another way of saying fucking. It doesn't make much sense I guess. Although, often sleep happens after fucking. And some snuggling."

He gave me a funny look like maybe intimacy was something he wasn't familiar with.

Each court had their peculiarities, but this, this one was different again. The seasonal courts had more in common with the way humans lived than they had with the Court of Shadows. A thousand years apart had made a great deal of change between them.

I wasn't sure what they'd all make of each other. I didn't want to think about Wornar, but I couldn't shake the feeling he'd love telling his people who they could and could not screw. He'd probably find that hilarious. Asshole.

The light was brighter now and Fae were starting to emerge from various tunnels and doors.

"How many live here?" I asked.

"I think, maybe twenty thousand," he said. "So many no one is allowed to breed right now. If we do, there will be too many. Too many to feed and not enough food."

He paused for a moment before he continued. "Vernissa has announced the culling will happen in two days."

"The...culling?" That didn't sound good.

"Yes, when Fae get old and aren't strong anymore, they're culled. There hasn't been a culling in a hundred years. But for going above, she wants us at our strongest."

I closed my eyes for a moment, trying to get my head around what he was telling me.

"They kill Fae because they got too old?"

"Old and not strong," he agreed.

"What about their wisdom?" I asked. "I hope to be wise when I've been around for a few hundred years."

"I don't get to decide," he said evasively. This culling seemed to be something he approved of. Or at least was accustomed to, so he didn't question it anymore.

"How old are you?" I asked.

"Only one hundred and twenty-three," he signed.

"Young then," I said. A hundred years older than me, but not old enough to worry about the culling for a very, very long time. It was easy not to worry about something that wouldn't affect you for centuries.

"Barely more than a child," he agreed. "I was one of the last bred here. Only Leopol and Geris are younger."

My eyebrows rose involuntarily. "Does that mean no one has fucked anyone they might get pregnant for over a hundred years?" No wonder he wasn't familiar with intimacy.

"Yes. Hands, mouth and ass only."

"What happens if someone puts their cock into a pussy?" I asked.

"They are culled," he said simply.

"How would anyone know?" Did they have any idea what we got up to last night? For all I knew, they'd watched our every move through a hole in the wall.

"The court is small, with many Fae," Rijal explained. "It's difficult to be alone anywhere. The risk... Most won't take it."

"Fucking isn't worth dying for," I reasoned. Most of my men would agree to disagree on that point. So would I, when I thought about it.

"I should go and serve," Rijal said. "If I'm late, I'll be punished." He gave me a bow and hurried away.

I watched him disappear down a side tunnel then made my way back to my room.

CHAPTER
TWENTY
KHALA

"You want what?" Ryze stared at Vernissa. "You realise it's not in my power to give. Humans live in Fraxius, Freid and Gerian. Even if I wanted to forcibly remove them, which I don't—"

"There is no choice to be made here," Vernissa said evenly. "We cannot remain under the ground indefinitely. Unless you have sufficient land in the Winter Court, and are ready to concede power to me..."

"Not a chance," Ryze said immediately. "Land we have. Me stepping aside as High Lord is not an option. Nor is it an option for Cavan to step aside." He glanced at Cavan.

"Not a matter for consideration," Cavan agreed. "Nor can we offer the Spring or Autumn Courts." In spite of the animosity toward both High Lords, that would likely result in bloodshed.

"The Autumn Court has an heir," I pointed out. "Illaria doesn't agree with Harel. If something happened to him, a reasonable replacement exists." I couldn't say the same about the Spring Court.

"Then the human lands remain," Vernissa said reasonably. "Are you trying to suggest Fae aren't a higher priority than humans? That we should remain down here in the darkness and continue to stagnate? We cannot continue to live like this. We are safer here, certainly, but this is a miserable existence in comparison to our former glory."

She leaned forward and tapped the tip of her finger on the table in front of her. "We held those lands. They're rightfully ours. We ruled over the humans and lived in a harmonious relationship with them."

"I thought the Fae moved out of Fraxius," I said.

"We did." She turned her eyes to me. "We moved here. None of the seasonal courts ever held land there. Only the Court of Shadows and the Court of

Dreams. And now your High Lords—" she used the title like it was an insult "—are suggesting we can't return."

Ryze sat back and laced his fingers behind his head. "I'm not suggesting anything. I'm saying it outright. That land is not mine to give. It's not Cavan's. If it belongs to anyone here, it's Khala and Zared. Perhaps you could remove him from the stone so he could give his say. He might even agree with you." No one in the room believed that for a moment.

"He's a beta," Vernissa said coolly. "He will remain where he is, for now."

She turned her gaze to me. "You're an omega. And a Fae. Why is Ryzellius suggesting you have any say over our former lands?"

"I was born there," I said simply. "I—" I glanced at my three men before turning my attention back to her. "I'm part human. I transformed during my first heat."

She looked slightly disgusted, but thoughtful. "Then you know the way humans live compared to the way Fae live. Do you truthfully believe humans live better? Or do you think they would benefit from things the Fae have, like running water? We would provide them with those things."

"That's not my decision to make," I said. "Every human I know would love running hot water, but what would they be giving up in return? You said the Court of Dreams wants to destroy you. Would you put innocent humans in the middle of that?"

"I believe we can adequately protect them if they choose to accept our protection," she said smoothly.

"Yet, you had to come here because you can't protect yourselves," Ryze said.

"With the assistance of the seasonal courts, we can adequately protect ourselves and them," she said. "It's in the best interest of all of us to work towards eradicating the Court of Dreams entirely."

"How would it help us?" Ryze asked.

"They keep trying to attack us from the back of a griffin," Tavian pointed out. "Or multiple griffins. Didn't you say that was starting to feel personal?"

"Not enough to go to war for," Cavan said. He pressed his thumb against his lips. "There's a lot to consider here. And a few pieces of the puzzle that need to be placed. The whereabouts of the Court of Dreams, for one thing."

"That's a good question," Tavian said.

"I was wondering the same thing myself." Ryze cocked his head at Vernissa. "Perhaps you can enlighten us."

"We're not entirely sure," She admitted. "We believe they may be higher up the mountain, but the summit is out of reach on foot. And protected by wards, so no one can try to portal in or out. We've sent people to climb there and look, but they've never returned. Whether that is from the court, or natural hazards, is unknown. I'm unwilling to send anyone who is bonded, because of the potential impact on their mate who remains behind."

She didn't seem too worried about the impact on me of having two of my mates encased in stone.

Lyra, who was silent until now, spoke. "I have suggested placing a bond on a pair and sending one of them. If it isn't a natural, gods given bond, it may not have the same impact."

"I haven't dismissed the suggestion, merely the idea of sending someone else after so many failed attempts," Vernissa said heavily. "It's possible the court is hiding in the mists, or somewhere across the ocean. I don't want to send anyone else on a fool's errand."

"What you mean *placing a bond?*" I asked, crinkling my brow. "You can do it without having to wait for one to form?"

Cavan was sitting forward, listening with interest.

"One of the idiosyncrasies of our magic," Lyra said. "It's not a common ability, but it's one I can perform."

"Can you do it for us?" Cavan asked, nodding towards me. "If Khala wanted to?"

"I do want to," I agreed. All this time, it was strange to be bonded to the others and not him. But there was more than just me to consider here.

"If the others agree." They had to be all right with it or I wouldn't go ahead. I wouldn't risk what I had with any of them for anything, not even a bond with Cavan.

"Definitely," Tavian said without hesitation or reservation.

Ryze eyed Cavan speculatively. "I suppose it wouldn't hurt for you to keep a connection with her when she spends most of her time in the Winter Court with me."

"That's one hells of an assumption," Cavan said. One he seemed to find amusing rather than offensive.

"I can also dissolve bonds," Lyra said helpfully. Her serene expression didn't change except a twinkling of her eyes.

"Hmmm," I hummed as though actually considering it.

Ryze frowned at me.

Tavian looked amused, clearly knowing I wouldn't break the bond with him.

"I don't want to break any bonds," I said finally.

I had a good idea what Zared would think, but I took a moment more to consider Vayne's reaction. In the end, all they wanted was for me to be happy.

"I would like to have one with Cavan."

He looked pleased. "Can you do it now?" he asked.

"You're very impetuous for a Fae," Vernissa told him.

"I wasted enough time trying to convince them you exist," he said evenly. "I think it best not to delay things anymore. If that makes me impetuous, then so be it. I don't want to wait two hundred years to have a bond with her."

"I feel the same way," I agreed. Besides, the gods only knew when we'd get another opportunity to do this, if ever.

Vernissa seemed annoyed that the conversation was sidetracked from taking land from humans, but she nodded anyway.

"It's time for a break. Do what you feel you need to do and then we'll finish this conversation. With your cooperation, we can have your other two bonded out from their incarceration before another night falls."

She rose and swept from the room.

Ryze sighed and closed his eyes. "She's under the impression all of this will be easy, isn't she?"

"It is easy," Lyra told him. "I need only to touch both of them and—"

His eyes popped open. "I didn't mean the bond. I meant the whole thing about human land."

"I know," she said lightly. "That is easy too. We must put Fae before humans. That seems straightforward to me. Are we not superior in every way? We live longer, we have magic. We don't have round ears." She wrinkled her nose.

"I like round ears," I said quietly. "Can we do the bonding? Please." I didn't want to have any more conversations like this. The whole dislike of one race for the other was frustrating. More often than not, I felt like I was caught in the middle. I looked Fae, but I felt human. More and more I started to feel like a Fae, but I couldn't forget where I came from and who my father was.

Ironic, given I could barely remember my father at all. I knew enough not to turn my back on my roots.

"Very well." Lyra rose and moved to stand between Cavan and I. She placed a hand on each of ours and closed her eyes.

"Do we have to do anything?" I asked. We were putting a lot of trust in her. Considering she was also not bothered about having two of my lovers encased in stone, perhaps we shouldn't trust her to do anything magical to us.

On the other hand, if she tried to screw us over, she'd lose any trust Ryze might have put in her or Vernissa. Any chance of being allies would be shattered.

This might be their way of trying to get us to trust them. Perhaps we'd view them more favourably if they did this. Perhaps we would.

My hand felt warm and tingly where Lyra touched it. Gradually, my skin grew warmer and warmer until it was almost hot, but not uncomfortably so.

One minute I couldn't feel Cavan's presence, the next I could. He was just... there in the back of my mind. This new bond felt no weaker or stronger than the others, but his presence was a comfort. I didn't know how much I needed it until now.

I smiled.

"This is different," he said thoughtfully. "I like it." He sent me adoring thoughts down the bond, which I returned.

"Now you know exactly when she's angry with you." Ryze looked amused.

"Lucky I never do anything to piss her off," Cavan said.

Tavian laughed.

"Are you sure about this?" Lyra asked me. "I can break it again if you like."

I grinned. "I'm sure. It's easier to keep track of them this way anyway."

"Assuming you want to keep track of them," she said dryly. "Rather you than me."

"You don't know what you're missing," Tavian told her. "Khala is someone very special."

"I'm sure she is," Lyra said. "She'd have to be to want to bond with so many men. Vernissa only has three of them, and me. Between we two women, we keep them in line."

"We're pretty good at keeping ourselves in line," Ryze said.

Cavan laughed at him. "I see you're exceptionally good at deluding yourself."

"Everything I do, I do exceptionally well," Ryze told him, unflinchingly. "Good or bad."

Cavan shook his head and rolled his eyes.

"He's telling the truth," Tavian said. "Whatever Ryze does, he throws all of himself into it. We have that in common."

"All five of you do," I said. I could hardly believe I was bonded to five men. Five strong, intelligent, very different men.

"Did you just say I'm like Cavan, Vayne and Zared?" Ryze asked. He looked like he wasn't sure if he was offended or not, but his amusement didn't falter for a moment.

"In that you are all incredible, yes," I said.

"Yes we are," Tavian agreed. "We're all very special."

Lyra gave us a look and said, "I'll show you to the lunch room. You'll want something to eat before the conversation recommences. That will also give you some time to confer with each other and perhaps you will agree to Vernissa's suggestions."

I would have called them demands, but it seemed like a good idea to keep that thought to myself for now. Somehow, we had to find a way to compromise and get Vayne and Zared out of the stone.

CHAPTER
TWENTY-ONE

KHALA

"We're ready to negotiate a compromise," Ryze said as soon as we walked back into the meeting room. "We'll mediate a meeting between you and the King of Fraxius, so you can discuss your needs and see if he can accommodate them. I can't offer anything else. In that regard anyway."

I glanced over to Vernissa who seemed unimpressed with this compromise.

"What do you mean by that regard?" she asked cautiously.

"I mean that there's no point in returning to the outside world if there's still potential for conflict with the Court of Dreams," Ryze said. "We're prepared to help you find them and negotiate some kind of peace so, wherever you end up, you can be assured it will be better than this." He gestured around the room.

"Even if it means going into the mist?" Cavan asked Ryze.

Ryze's mouth twisted in a barely contained grimace. "Even if we have to do that. Conflict between the two courts will affect all of us. Better to deal with this before it becomes a major problem."

Vernissa glanced at Lyra. The other woman's expression gave away nothing. Either they were communicating through a bond, or they knew each other well enough to know what the other was thinking.

"Very well," Vernissa finally said. "We'll accept your assistance with both matters. However, your people will remain here, in stone."

"No," I said. "You said you'd free them when we came to an understanding. We've done that. If you want us to keep our side of this deal, then you need to keep your word."

I was well aware that might piss her off, but it could take weeks to find the Court of Dreams, and longer to get them to listen. Assuming we found them at all.

Then there was the matter of speaking to the King of Fraxius. He might not be receptive to speaking to Fae. Zared and Vayne could be stuck in the stone for a thousand years. That was unacceptable.

Vernissa and Lyra exchanged another look.

"How do we know you'll help us after we free them?" Lyra asked.

"Because we said we would," Tavian said. "Ryzellius is a man of his word. If he says he'll do something, he will."

"So will I," Cavan said.

"Me too," I said. "I'll do anything to avoid innocent people dying."

I understood their reservations. They were locked away from the world for so long, it must be difficult to know who to trust. As far as they were concerned, we were strangers who turned up on their doorstep.

Technically, we didn't even knock.

Although, technically there wasn't a door to knock on. Still, we could have been anyone who stumbled upon the cavern. How could they be sure we were who we said we were?

Ryze and Cavan both displayed the arrogance of a High Lord, but so did many other Fae. Dalyth had had arrogance to spare.

"You can send people with us, or come yourself," Ryze said. "I'm sure you must be curious about the world out there."

"You should take a look before you decide to rejoin it," Tavian said. "You might not like what you see. Believe it or not, there are some real assholes out there."

That was all too accurate.

"What will you do if you don't like it out there?" I asked.

"My people have made their feelings clear," Vernissa said. "They don't want to remain here. What we find out there, we'll deal with. We'll adapt. Or the world will have to adapt to us. Remaining here is not a viable option. We're stifling here."

"Will you cull your people on the outside?" I asked.

"If doing so is necessary," she replied.

I didn't expect her to be apologetic, or regretful, and she wasn't. Killing older Fae just for being older was something she endorsed. A decision she made because she thought it was the best thing for all her people.

And yet, I had the impression she was holding onto her leadership by a very fine thread. Her people wanted out of the shadows, and the gods knew what they might do when they got there. Not to mention what they might do if she denied them.

"Do you have an heir?" I asked, without thinking.

"I do but he'd prefer to be a farmer." Her lip curled slightly.

I blinked a couple of times. "Rijal? Rijal is your son?"

She was surrounded by strong men she owned. Why not let one impregnate her, so she could have an heir? It was no different to a man marrying a woman for the same reason. Except men didn't usually own their wives. Or any other woman, for that matter.

"He is," she agreed. "I hope he wasn't too bothersome. He was born with far too much curiosity for his own good."

"He wasn't bothersome in the least," I said. "He seemed to want to live his best life, that's all."

"That's all any of us want," Vernissa said. "Which is why we need your help. Living here was a safer option, but it is far from our best lives. This is merely...existing."

I felt that acutely. When I was a Silent Maiden, I felt like I was moving from one day to the next, always waiting for something to happen. Hoping for something to break the monotony, to change the daily routine.

If I knew what came after, I might have better appreciated the peace in those days.

I would have tried to spend more time with Tyla if I knew our time was limited.

Guilt twinged inside me for not having thought about her for days. So many other things occupied my thoughts, pushing her to the side.

What would she think about all of this? She probably wouldn't believe any of it, and if she did, she'd find it hilarious. Especially the part about me being bonded to five men.

Would things be different between Zared and me if I'd known we'd be here right now? I suspected it wouldn't. The way we came about was right for us, although he'd spent a lot of time frustrated as fuck, and hoping I'd see what was right in front of me.

"No one should go through life just existing," Tavian said. "Life is meant to be grabbed by the balls and lived."

"That's a very interesting analogy," Lyra told him.

He grinned. "I'm all about interesting, especially analogies. Although, that one is literal some of the time."

"I don't doubt that. You say you're an assassin?"

"Former assassin," he said. "Now I just organise other assassins. Although, I have been known to dabble here and there when the need arises."

He gave me a glance and I knew he was thinking about Wornar. I wouldn't regret for a moment if he used those skills on *him*.

"We haven't had need of an assassin for a long time," Vernissa said. "We may have to make use of your services in the future. Or those of your subordinates. Do you own them?"

Tavian laughed. "No, they just work for me. If I tried to suggest I owned them, I might end up dead myself. That would be...unfortunate."

"Very unfortunate," Ryze agreed. "I've become attached to you."

"Thank you," Cavan said as though Ryze was talking about him.

Ryze rolled his eyes, but smiled. "You're all right, I suppose."

"Can we get Vayne and Zared out of the stone now, please?" I asked.

Lyra glanced at Vernissa, who nodded reluctantly.

"If we must. However, if we detect any signs you plan to betray us—"

"We won't," Ryze said firmly.

"Very well. I see no reason for further delay. If you'll excuse me, I have pressing matters to attend to." Vernissa rose and swept from the room, leaving us to follow Lyra.

I STOOD BESIDE ZARED, gripped by a mix of anticipation and anxiety.

Lyra insisted she could free them. I'd believe it when I saw it with my own two eyes.

She stepped forward, her presence almost radiating with raw magic. Her eyes were focused, her expression her usual serenity.

Her hands moved gracefully through the air, tracing invisible patterns. Not the Silent Maidens' hand language, but similar.

I hadn't seen anyone do magic with any kind of gestures before. I didn't know what it meant that she did just now. Maybe it was more complex magic and maybe it was a habit.

Some people spoke with their hands, she removed stone from my lovers with hers.

Whatever got the task done.

The air around us seemed to hum. A tingling energy enveloping the space.

I held my breath. My eyes never left the frozen figures of Zared and Vayne, hoping like fuck that Lyra's magic was enough to shatter the stone.

A surge of energy pulsed through the room, thick enough to feel. My heart leaped in response.

I saw subtle changes in the stone encasing Zared and Vayne, faint cracks forming, bit by bit.

Lyra's focus intensified, her magic swirling around the statues, coaxing them back to life.

A moment of intense silence hung in the air, broken only by the sound of my own heartbeat pounding in my ears. And then, from one moment to the next, the stone began to crumble, revealing the two men trapped inside.

As the fragments fell away, Zared and Vayne took their first gasps of air, their features shifting from rigid to alive and animated.

My breath caught in my throat as Vayne's eyes found mine. A combination of awe, gratitude and pissed off as fuck flashed across his face.

He took a tentative step forward, finding his balance, and then he was standing in front of me, his warmth palpable.

I reached out, trembling, as he pulled me into an embrace, the weight of his arms reassurance for us both.

"Khala," he whispered, his voice filled with relief. "Thank fuck."

Unable to speak, I nodded against his chest, tears streaming down my face.

The joy of seeing him free, the overwhelming flood of emotions, threatened to consume me.

As I held onto Vayne, I stole a glance at Lyra. Her face was beaded with sweat, and a mixture of exhaustion and satisfaction.

A silent acknowledgment passed between us. Gratitude for her returning my men to me. And from her, the understanding that I would do what I could to help her and her court.

I mouthed, "Thank you."

Zared joined our embrace, then Tavian, Ryze and finally Cavan, completing our circle of relief.

The echoes of magic faded and the world righted itself.

Silence fell for at least a few minutes until Tavian broke it.

"Thank fuck you two are all right."

I laughed softly, but I couldn't agree more. If somehow Lyra couldn't get them out of the stone alive, a piece of me would have broken. I suspected that might be the point. Either they held my men to ransom, or they relied on our gratitude for releasing them from the magic they, themselves, put into place.

I suspected none of us missed the way we were manipulated, but for now we'd just enjoy the moment.

TWENTY-TWO

ZARED

My muscles were still stiff as fuck from being stuck in the fucking stone for more than an entire day.

For the first while, I'd tried to kick my way out, or pound my hands against my prison. I quickly realised that achieved nothing. Trying to shout got me nowhere too. I could move my mouth, but no sound came out.

Once I got past my initial fury, I focused on the bond, and Khala's presence on the other end of it.

Eventually, the minimal air made me drowsy and my brain became fogged.

I was barely aware of anything after that, apart from the other men gently making Khala feel good. I was worried they were pushing her to a place she wasn't ready to go, but she seemed to enjoy what they were doing. Just as well, or I'd strangle them myself when I got out of the fucking stone.

"Are you all right?" Khala asked gently.

Of course she'd be thinking of me right now instead of herself. She looked at me like what I went through was a million times worse than what that asshole did to her. Honestly, it wasn't a competition as to who went through the most trauma. They both sucked. We'd get past it.

Working with the people that did what they did to Vayne and me, that was another matter.

I shrugged and winced with how stiff my shoulders were.

"I'm fine, but if I don't ever get stuck in stone like that again, I'll be all right." I managed a slight smile. "That was bullshit."

"Bullshit is a good word for it," Vayne growled. "I had a fucking itch over my eyebrow and I couldn't scratch it. If I was there another minute, I would have gone out of my mind."

"That sounds like a cruel and unusual torture," Tavian remarked thoughtfully. "On the other hand, it might be a fun way to get information out of someone who doesn't want to talk."

"Itch torture, that sounds terrible." Khala grimaced.

I murmured my agreement. Of course right then my head was itchy. Not just mine. I caught Ryze scratching his cheek in the corner of my eye.

"Only a fucked up person would think of using something like that for torture," Vayne said.

"I see you've met me," Tavian said, grinning.

Vayne grunted and went on eating, even though the bread was dense, and the fruit small. He looked like he hadn't eaten for days.

I didn't have much of an appetite, but I chewed on a corner of bread. "We're not really working with them, are we?"

"We have to," Ryze said. He'd explained the agreement they'd come to in return for releasing Vayne and me. "I don't see any reason to stay here past this meal."

"Where are we going first?" Khala asked. "To look for the Court of Dreams, or to Fraxius, to speak to the king?"

I wasn't sure if they weren't both a waste of time. There was no way the humans in Fraxius were going to allow the Fae to move onto their lands.

As for the other court, it could stay hidden as far as I was concerned. They seemed determined to kill us, so excuse me if I didn't want to help them. Same for the Court of Shadows. They could both get fucked.

"We'll look for the Court of Dreams first," Cavan said. "Let's not alarm the humans for no reason. Until both courts can come to some accord, it seems likely they'll remain where they currently are."

"And reaching an accord could take a century," Ryze said. "The present King of Fraxius will be dead by then. Potentially his successor too. Any agreement we make now would be null."

"Vernissa really would have left Zared and Vayne in the stone for a century?" Khala asked.

"It felt like a fucking century anyway," Vayne grunted. "Even with Hycathe and Jezalyn coming to check up on us. Where are they anyway?"

We all turned to him and stared.

"What do you mean they checked up on us?" I asked. "I didn't hear them."

Vayne frowned and stopped eating for a moment. "I don't know. I had a sense they were there. It only lasted for a few minutes. Why? What the fuck is going on?"

"That's a good question," Ryze said. "As far as I know, they're still in the mists. We haven't seen them since they were taken."

Vayne blinked a couple of times. "I guess it's possible I hallucinated, but I could have sworn they were just on the other side of the stone."

"You don't have a bond with them, do you?" Cavan asked.

"Definitely not." Vayne shook his head. "I felt Khala, but this was different. I can't explain it except to say I thought they were there."

463

"Maybe you had a vision," Tavian suggested. "When you're in the middle of one, they feel real, but they're not."

"Unless..." Khala said softly.

"Unless?" I prompted.

"Unless they found the Court Of Dreams, and somehow their magic projected a dream of Hycathe and Jezalyn into your head," she said. "I don't know if that's possible."

"They're not called the Court of Dreams for nothing," Cavan remarked. "Did they say or do anything? Were they scared?"

"First of all, the Court of Fucking Dreams can stay the fuck out of my head," Vayne growled. "Second, I had the feeling they were trying to tell me something, but I have no idea what. There weren't any words, as such. They were just...reaching out."

He gestured with one hand to indicate he didn't know how better to explain what he experienced.

"Fuck," Ryze swore. When we all turned to look at him he said, "This more or less confirms that we have to go into the mist."

"Did you have much doubt of that eventuality?" Cavan asked.

"No, but I had hope," Ryze said. "Don't tell me you are any more excited about venturing there than I am. Because if you try, I'm going to call you a liar."

Cavan pressed the back of his knuckles against his lips. "Excited wouldn't be an accurate word, no. Resigned. Wishing we brought an army with us."

"What if we tell Harel and Wornar there are multiple chests of gold and virgin omegas in the mist?" Tavian asked, a mischievous smile on his face. "If they don't come back, we'll know it's not safe for us to go."

"It's highly unlikely to be safe for us to go," Ryze said. "It seems we don't have a choice."

"We don't?" I asked. "It seems to me if we leave, what are they going to do?"

"We made a promise," Ryze said, like that was the end of that. "You saw no sign of Hycathe or Jezalyn? None at all?"

"Nothing," I said. "The only one I was aware of was Khala." I frowned. "And I knew Vayne was still there too. I don't know how I knew."

"Wishful thinking?" Vayne suggested. "I had the same thought about you. Hoping they hadn't gotten you out and left me the fuck behind."

I regarded him for a moment. "I'd ask if that's something they'd do, but I am, after all, me. If they could have only gotten one of us out, then the choice is obvious."

He grunted. "If I wasn't hungry, I'd throw the rest of my bread at you. Give me a few minutes to eat and I'll happily toss you in the fucking lake." In spite of his gruff tone, the faintest smile tugged at the corners of his mouth.

"We wouldn't have left either of you behind," Khala said unfalteringly.

"Not if we had a choice," Ryze agreed. "For what it's worth, I'm glad we didn't have to choose between you. That would be an impossible choice."

"No it wouldn't, you'd choose me," Vayne told him.

"I agree with Ryze, it's an impossible choice," Khala said before I could respond. "I hope I never have to choose between you, because I want to choose all of you. We're a pack. Whatever happens, we belong together."

"And if anyone goes missing, we'll find you," Tavian said. "We'll leave no stone unturned."

Vayne tossed his bread at Tavian. "The joke is worthy of Ryze."

"My jokes are much better than that," Ryze said, pretending to be offended.

"No they aren't," Vayne said.

"You tell daddy jokes," Tavian said. "But it's one of the things we love about you."

"Thank you," Ryze told him. "I think." He held his hands out to either side.

"You're welcome." Tavian gave him a sideways hug from his chair.

"You know," Ryze said slowly after a minute or two of quiet, "Vayne and Zared should be grateful they were encased in stone underground. If that happened out in the open, for example outside the Winter Court palace, you would have had the birds landing on your head and crapping on you."

Tavian laughed.

"That isn't fucking funny," Vayne told him.

"It kinda is," Tavian said. "But, to be honest, I would have been more worried about griffin attacks out in the open. One well-placed bolt of lightning magic and you'd both be encased in melted stone."

His words brought us crashing back down.

"I'll take bird crap any day," I said. "Or better yet, never getting stuck in stone again. What sort of fucked up booby trap was that anyway?"

I hated to admit to any vulnerabilities, but I was going to have nightmares about being stuck in there for a while after this. I'd never enjoyed enclosed spaces, except my cock in Khala's mouth or pussy. That unease would be worse now.

None of them would blame me if I freaked out, but I'd be pissed off at myself. I was supposed to be the big, tough human priest. Former priest. I'd do the best I could to live up to that, if only in my own head.

"One that would have been worse if we were all encased," Cavan said. "I get the impression if that happened, we'd all be stuck in there forever, or until we died. Whichever happened first. Since the magic seems capable of sustaining life for a prolonged amount of time, we'd soon end up wishing we were in one of the hells instead."

"And you're still working with these people," I pointed out.

"We might be the best chance of brokering peace between the two courts," Cavan said. "And between them and the humans. What they did to you is unfortunate—"

Without thinking, I slammed my fist down onto the table.

"Unfortunate? It was completely and totally fucked the fuck up. How do you know that's not what they're planning to do to everyone up there?" I pointed to the ceiling.

"We don't," Cavan said evenly. "But that sounds to me like a good reason to keep our eye on them. If we walk away, we won't know what they're doing. This is the decision we've made. If you don't like it, Khala may be able to remove your memories again and send you back to Fraxius."

That sounded suspiciously like a threat to me.

"I'm not going anywhere," I told him. "If I have to go along with this, I will. But when all of this goes completely sideways, don't think I won't say I told you so."

"Noted," Cavan said simply. "We'll trust you to keep the closest eye on them of all of us."

"Don't worry, I will," I replied. I was going to watch anyone from the Court of Shadows like a hawk. They wouldn't get away with anything without us knowing about it.

Not one thing.

CHAPTER
TWENTY-THREE
ZARED

"It's not too late to walk away from all of this," I said to Khala as I adjusted the straps of my pack. "I've heard there's a nice, secluded beach at the very top of Freid where the fish practically leap out of the water into your hands. We could grow some potatoes and corn and live a simple life."

"Would you really walk away without knowing what happened to Hycathe and Jezalyn?" She brushed hair off her forehead.

She looked weary. Not just tired, but feeling the pressure of everything that happened since Dalyth took the choker off her neck.

I felt the strain myself. A quiet beach sounded like just what we both needed right now.

I decided the straps were as even as they were going to be, and placed my pack beside the door.

"This might make me the asshole, but if it meant keeping you from going through anything else, then I would." I tentatively reached out and took her hand. I stepped towards her slowly like I'd approach a wild animal. Not wanting to scare her, but hoping she wouldn't run.

"As tempting as it is, I can't spend the rest of my life scared." She let me pull her into my arms and rested her head against my shoulder.

"You're the bravest person I know," I told her. "But sometimes the bravest thing you can do is walk away. Let other people deal with the shit. I know we couldn't drag you away, because you want to finish what's been started. Because even though you and Hycathe never got along, you want to make sure nothing happens to her. I've never met anyone with such a big heart. Except maybe Tave, which is strange considering he's an assassin."

"I suppose it's possible to kill people for a living and still be sweet," she said with a laugh. "That is very discordant though, isn't it?"

"Just a little bit," I agreed. It wasdifficult not to adore him. As difficult as it would be not to adore her. I wasn't ready to proclaim my undying love to him, there were strong emotions there. Ones which got stronger every day.

She raised her head and looked at me.

I didn't move a muscle. When our lips met, it was because she initiated it. I had to keep myself from devouring her then and there.

"Zared," she whispered.

"I'm sorry." I pulled back. I wasn't sure what I was sorry for, but it seemed like the thing to say. Maybe somehow I encouraged her to do something she wasn't ready for.

Although, this was Khala. When had she ever let me push her into anything she wasn't ready for?

"Don't be," she said. "Seeing you like that, in the stone... For a while I thought we'd lost you. How could anyone be alive in there? Even when I knew you were still alive, I was scared we'd never get you out. I would have done anything to free you, even if I had to take your place."

I wiped a tear from her cheek with my thumb. "I never would have forgiven myself if you did that," I told her. "I wouldn't wish that on you. On anyone."

All right, I'd wish it on a few people, but I wasn't going to bring them into the conversation. We both knew what I didn't say.

"I know you wouldn't," she said. "But I would have done it anyway. For you. For any of you. It made me realise how important you are to me. How important it is for me to tell you, and show you."

"I don't want you to do anything you're not ready for," I told her. Even as I said that, my cock twitched. I wanted—needed to touch her. I wanted to bury myself deep inside her and never come out.

"Neither do I," she said. "But I'm not going to let someone stop me from living and making the most of life." She leaned back in and kissed me again. Then her hands were under the front of my shirt and she was pulling it off me.

I let her take the lead. When she pushed me over to the nest, I didn't object. I lay back just where she wanted me and watched her undo my pants and work them down my hips.

She glanced at me and smiled, clearly enjoying being in full control. She knew she could stop at any moment and that would be completely all right. My balls would hurt, but I'd understand. This had to be on her terms.

She freed my erection and wrapped her fingers around my cock. I didn't even try to contain the quiver her touch sent through me. That quiver increased when she licked the tip of my cock, then wrapped her lips around me.

"Am I interrupting?" Tavian said, slipping in the room. "I came in to say the others are waiting, but let them wait."

Khala went on sucking, but her eyes were on Tavian. She was clearly taunting him and enjoying every minute of it. Hells, so was I.

He groaned and adjusted his pants. After a while, he couldn't take watching any more. He stepped over to the bed and lay down beside us. Watching carefully for her reaction, he undid Khala's pants and buried his face between her legs.

Her breathless, little moans nearly made me come undone already. I didn't want this to end yet. Not this quickly.

"Did you bring any of that oil of yours?" I asked, my voice hoarse with lust for them both.

Tavian looked up. His mouth shone with Khala's arousal. "Of course." He slipped off the bed and stopped to kissed my lips, letting me taste her. He flicked his tongue around my lips and inside my mouth.

I groaned. The combined taste of both of them was like nothing else.

"Delicious." I watched his cute little ass as he stepped away, shedding his clothes all the way to his pack which lay in the corner.

I tangled my fingers in her hair, savouring the way her mouth felt sucking me slowly.

I waited until Tavian was back between her legs and reluctantly eased her mouth off my cock. I took the oil and moved around behind him.

I opened the oil and dipped my fingers in. With one hand, I drew Tavian up until he was kneeling, ass in the air, face between Khala's thighs.

I slipped a lubricated finger slowly into his rear hole, stretching him and feeling the warmth of his muscles around me. Another finger joined the first, then a third. I worked my fingers in and out of him slowly, deliberately.

I glanced up to see Khala watching me, eyes half closed in bliss. She was slowly rolling her hips in rhythm to Tavian's lips and tongue.

I slid my fingers out of his ass and replaced them with my cock. I used my hand to position my tip, then slowly pressed myself inside.

"Gods, you're so fucking tight," I breathed. I'd done this before, with other partners but none ever felt as good as him. If I never had anyone else around my cock but these two, for the rest of my life, I'd be fucking content.

Tavian made a sound that suggested he was enjoying himself as much as I was. As much as Khala was.

Her eyes were locked on me, watching me thrusting in and out of Tavian with slow, firm strokes, while I watched her buck and writhe.

If I wasn't close already, I was after she arched her back and cried out. That and the wet sound of Tavian's mouth on her pussy, drove me right to the edge.

Tentatively, I reached around to wrap my fingers around Tavian's cock. He was as iron hard as me. Bigger than me, but whatever. It wasn't what a man had, but how he used it. And right now, I was using it to drive Tavian and I closer and closer to the precipice.

I slid my fingers up and down his cock in rhythm to my thrusts.

Tavian groaned and went on licking and sucking Khala, pushing her back to the edge.

When she tipped over, I went with her, coming hard into Tavian's ass. At the same time, he came, spilling hot cum over my hand.

Our moans mingled and echoed around the room, sweeter than the temple chorus. The music of bliss and orgasms. Nothing in this world could compare. Not even close.

I sagged over Tavian's back, breathing heavily, heart racing.

For the longest time all I could do was catch my breath and say, "So fucking good."

CHAPTER
TWENTY-FOUR

KHALA

No one said a word when we finally met up with the others beside the lake.

Ryze took in our flushed faces with amusement.

Cavan looked slightly uncomfortable, with the front of his pants tented. Clearly he felt every bit of it through the bond.

Vayne was off to the side, talking to Rijal. Evidently the younger Fae was allowed to talk aloud to a beta. I couldn't hear what they were talking about, but Rijal stopped the moment he saw me.

"Vernissa is sending him with us," Ryze said. "And them." He waved towards a couple of other Fae. "Willum is one of her bonded mates. Jistun is his brother."

All three had night black hair which hung down their backs. Where Rijal had brown eyes, Willum and Jistun had blue. Their bodies were slender, contrasting with Rijal's muscular frame. He was one of the biggest, broadest Fae I'd ever seen. Presumably his role serving his mother saw him do more physical tasks than most others.

Willum nodded at me, then gestured for all of us to follow him to the tunnel through which we'd entered. We walked in silence until we passed the spot where Vayne and Zared were imprisoned.

"How do we get back up?" I asked. "We fell down an incline to get here."

"Please don't say there's a staircase back up," Vayne said with a grunt.

"Scared of a little walking?" Ryze asked him.

"Scared, no. Fully aware how far down we came, yes."

Willum gave them both a funny look. "We're going down. A tunnel leads directly to the mists. We don't go there."

"Today you are," Ryze said.

"Today we are," Willum agreed. His expression was so guarded I couldn't guess what he thought about any of this. Had Vernissa told him to go or had he volunteered?

I wasn't going to ask. What went on between them was their business.

It wasn't until Willum illuminated the tunnel before we headed into it, that I realised he was also an alpha. From the scent of them, Jistun and Rijal were both betas.

I fell in beside Rijal as we stepped into the tunnel. "Are you related to either of them?" I asked out of curiosity.

He glanced over to me and signed. "Jistun is my father. So, Willum is my uncle."

"And your mother is bonded to Willum?" I asked. That sounded awkward.

Although, I was in no position to make any judgement. I was bonded to my mother's former lover. Cavan could just as easily have ended up bonded to her. Perhaps it should feel strange, but it didn't. I felt what I felt and I'd never seen my mother and him together. If Cavan found it uncomfortable, he didn't mention it, or show any indication.

Sometimes I wondered if he saw me as a replacement for her, but I put that thought out of my mind whenever it popped into my brain. He cared about me for who I was, not who my mother was.

"Yes," Rijal signed. "My mother and my father..." He searched for the words.

"Don't like each other very much," Jistun finished for him. "We butt heads more often than not."

"Jistun believes we should stay in our cavern," Willum said over his shoulder. "It's not a popular opinion, especially with Vernissa."

"We're safe where we are," Jistun said, a light growl in his tone.

"We're slowly dying out," Willum contradicted. "You and I will be old enough for the culling after the next one. If we returned to the world above, there will be no need for the next culling. Nor the one after that. We can return to breeding young, like we used to."

"Young who will come under attack." Jistun shot his brother a resentful look.

Clearly this was a conversation they'd had many times before.

"Might those who want to remain stay behind in the cavern?" I asked. "While the rest leave for up there?"

They both gave me a look which suggested I'd hit on a contentious, if unifying topic.

"We are one court," Rijal signed. "Where one goes, we all go."

"Where Vernissa orders us to go, we all go," Jistun said. "Whether we agree with her choices or not."

"If she orders you to do something, you just do it?" Ryze asked. His voice echoed as we moved deeper into the tunnel.

"She is our High Lady," Willum said proudly.

Ryze huffed a breath. "It sounds like my people need to listen to you. They could learn a thing or two."

"Or we could teach them the meaning of anarchy," Tavian said with a grin.

"The last thing they need to learn is that," Ryze told him. "There's more than enough anarchy in the world as it is."

"How to say you have no control over your court without saying you have no control over your court," Cavan remarked.

Ryze stuck his middle finger at him. "I have control over most of them. Just not Tavian and Vayne."

"If they don't obey, you should have them culled," Jistun told him. "If you tolerate disobedience, it grows."

"Vernissa has tolerated yours," Willum said.

Jistun immediately looked defensive. "I obey. I only give my opinion when she permits me to do so."

"She permits you too often then," Willum said. He waved his hand ahead of us. "We continue down this way."

We fell into silence for a while until Tavian broke it.

"The row of skulls that led the way in. Whose were they? Your enemies or your friends?"

"Those who were culled from age," Willum said. "It's their honour to present the way to those who were chosen to come and free us from the caverns."

"So they were killed for us," Tavian concluded. "We're honoured you went to so much trouble, aren't we Ryze?"

Ryze murmured something that may have been an agreement. "I would have settled for a glass of whiskey."

"Me too," Vayne agreed. "At least your ancestors told us which way to go."

"I can tell you where to go any time you like," Tavian teased.

Vayne grunted and rolled his eyes at him. "How about you don't."

Willum gave them a glance like he thought they might be out of their minds.

"In case you're wondering, yes they're always like this," I told him. "Ryze, Vayne and Tave have been together for a long time. They give each other hells, but they would do anything for each other."

"And to each other," Tavian said.

"Speak for yourself," Vayne said. "I don't want to do anything to you or Ryze. Except maybe stab you when you annoy me too much. With a knife, not my cock."

"Cavan and Ryze give each other hells too," I said.

"Do they fuck each other?" Willum asked.

We all gave both High Lords a speculative look.

In the end, it was Tavian who answered. "Not yet, but if they do, I want to either watch or participate."

"Noted," Cavan said simply.

473

"No doubt you'll be the first to know," Ryze said. "And by first I mean third."

"Fourth is more likely," Tavian said. "Khala would know before I do." He seemed unworried.

"Either way, you won't be unaware," Ryze said. He glanced over at me. "What would you think of that?" He seemed undecided with a measure of hopefulness that I'd agree.

My gaze dropped to the bulge in his pants, before I looked back up again."As long as you both want it, then I'm all for it," I said.

Of course, now my mind was running away with thoughts of seeing them together the way Zared and Tave were only an hour or so ago. The idea of Ryze on his knees with Cavan's cock in his mouth, or vice versa, made me wet as hells.

"I think she likes the idea," Ryze said. He must have felt my arousal through the bond.

I smirked at him, then noticed the expression on Rijal's face.

"I suppose you don't talk like this if you're not allowed to do what you want, with who you want." I kept my voice low so Willum and Jistun couldn't hear.

Right now, they were engaged in a conversation about something I couldn't make out. Whatever it was, their exchange seemed intense. Their voices were low, but their expressions suggested agitation.

"We talk like that too," Rijal signed. "We talk about when we're above and we can do what we please. There is much speculation as to who might fuck who. Much...teasing?" He looked unsure as to whether his last gesture was one I understood.

"No different to us then," I concluded. "Do you ever... Do alphas ever order omegas to do things? Maybe things they don't want to do?"

He looked horrified. "An alpha knows their place as inferior to all omegas. To order one would be to face culling. There would be no mercy. No sympathy. This would be a terrible crime."

I couldn't argue with that. It certainly deserved to be considered a criminal act. They could get into the growing line to cull Wornar if they wanted to.

"Does that happen above?" He looked concerned, like he hated the idea an alpha could abuse their power in such a way.

I sighed. "Not often, but sometimes. But there are ways to keep it from happening." I quickly explained what Cavan did to me, and that Ryze ordered the same thing of Tavian.

Rijal nodded thoughtfully. "When we return, I'll recommend this to my mother. She will not want to be vulnerable to any alpha from above."

"She definitely wouldn't want to," I agreed. The idea of Wornar doing to her what he did to me made me shudder. Or Harel, for that matter. Either of them may order her to step aside as leader of the Court Of Shadows, and take her place, or the gods knew what else.

"Are we nearly there?" Vayne asked. "By my estimation, we must be close."

"Very close," Willum said over his shoulder.

Indeed, the walls had become rougher, like they were carved by nature and not hand. The air became colder. Something about it felt ominous and uncomfortable.

"We're getting closer to the mist," Ryze whispered.

He didn't need to tell us that, we all felt it. Like we were being watched by something malevolent. Something big. Something that lived in the mist because it could be all but invisible until it struck.

I found my hand wrapped around Zared's. His palm was somehow cold and sweating at the same time. So was mine.

"I feel I should apologise," Cavan said softly. "I hadn't realised they would feel quite like this."

"Apology accepted." Ryze's tone wasn't as light and full of humour as usual. He sounded like he wanted to be anywhere but here.

"Do you have any idea what caused the mists in the first place?" I asked Rijal. Hadn't Ryze said they appeared one day out of nowhere?

"According to Lyra, it's old magic," Rijal signed.

"Yes," Willum agreed. "Something from before the days of Fae. Somehow released back into the world or brought here from somewhere."

"That sounds ominous as fuck," Vayne remarked. "If I haven't mentioned it before, do we really need to go looking for the Court of Dreams?"

"You might have, and yes, we do," Ryze told him. "Don't let the way the mist feels scare you."

"You've let it scare you for quite some time," Cavan pointed out.

"It's not so much the way it feels, as the way..." Ryze shook his head. "You'll understand when you step out into it."

"Which won't be happening," Jistun declared. He stopped dead and pulled out a knife.

Rijal did the same, with an apologetic look to me.

"You're outnumbered—" Willum started to say.

Several figures stepped out of the shadows, all armed. All looking ready to use them.

"Fuck," Zared whispered.

CHAPTER
TWENTY-FIVE
KHALA

"What the hells?" Willum demanded. He pulled out a knife of his own. "This insurrection nonsense has gone on long enough. Stand aside and you may walk away without being culled." His tone didn't convince me they weren't completely fucked. It didn't seem to convince Jistun and his co-conspirators either.

"There are more of us than you realise," Jistun said. "You feel how the air is in here. It's evil. It's telling us to stay here. They feel it." He nodded toward Ryze specifically.

Ryze raised his hands. "We have nothing to do with this. All we want to do is get out of here. Even if it means going through evil."

I glanced at him. I didn't think he truly believed the mist was evil. The Fae behind it maybe. The mist itself was no more malevolent than smoke. Bad for you, but without bad intentions.

"Step aside," Willum said. "I will not ask again—"

He was interrupted by Jistun, who lunged forward and drove his knife into Willum's throat. The Fae man's eyes widened with surprise. He let out a gurgle before falling to his knees and then heavily to the ground.

"Let that be a warning that you will not proceed past us." Jistun pulled his knife free and stood with it held out in front of him.

In the corner of my eye, I saw Tavian slip out a blade of his own. With barely any movement or effort, he flicked it. It embedded in the left side of Jistun's chest, killing him immediately.

Tavian had two more knives out before he even hit the ground. "You don't have to be next if you don't want to."

Rijal and the other four insurrectionists all took a step back.

"We don't have to kill any of you." I looked straight at Rijal. "I know you're scared, but we are leaving here. With or without you." Fear sometimes led to people making bad choices. That included dying for no good reason.

"You wanted to leave here," I reminded him. "What happened to your dreams of being a farmer? Your people need you. You're going to be their leader someday. What happens if you die? Your people won't have a leader and you won't get to live your dreams of growing food in the sun. You know what your mother is doing is for the best for the whole court, right?"

I wasn't sure if it was right for everyone, but staying down here didn't seem right either. If nothing else, they deserved the chance to make an individual choice.

"Put the knife down," Ryze told him. "Put it away and let's get on with what has to be done."

Rijal sighed and slipped the knife back into the sheath at his hip.

"Coward." One of the insurrectionists lunged towards him, but stopped when a knife was embedded in the centre of his forehead.

Rijal stepped aside as he toppled and landed with a sickening thud.

"Anyone else?" Tavian asked pleasantly. He seemed to be having way too much fun with this. I should probably not find it as hot as I did, but he really, really enjoyed killing and was obviously good at it. His pleasure was compelling and attractive.

The other three insurrectionists raised their hands and slipped their knives away.

"If you want to go out there, it's your death." One gave us a dirty look, then moved past us and headed back to the main cavern. The other two were close on her heels.

"Are you coming with us?" I asked Rijal. I glanced down at the three dead Fae. Their blood pooled on the ground, but had already started to mingle and dry.

I'd hate to be whoever explained this to Vernissa. Had she felt Willum die? She must have. That kind of loss would burn. I felt for her. She probably felt as though he was ripped away. And for what?

"I will accompany you," Rijal signed.

I wasn't sure if that was his choice because he didn't want to face his mother or because she'd instructed him to accompany us, but I nodded.

"No," Zared snapped. "He would have killed us or let us be killed. How can we be expected to trust him?"

"I say we leave him behind," Vayne said.

Rijal ducked his head. "I have shamed my court. I let my father lead me the wrong way. I should have followed Willum's lead. I submit myself for punishment."

"We don't have time for punishment," Zared said. "I vote he just fucks off."

Ryze and Cavan exchanged looks while Rijal looked at me.

Apparently everyone had different expectations as to who was making the decisions here. I liked Rijal's assumption in general, but not in this case. I couldn't argue against what Zared said about trusting him. I truly believed Rijal when he said he wanted to leave the cavern, but he was quick enough to pull a knife on us.

"He's accompanying us as a representative of the Court of Shadows," Cavan said finally.

"And he's still young enough to do stupid things," Ryze added. "We will keep an eye on him. If he looks like he's going to betray us, he'll end up like them." He gestured toward the bodies on the ground.

"I will not betray you," Rijal signed.

"You say that now," Zared said, taking away any need for me to interpret for Ryze, Vayne and Cavan. "I'd prefer not to end up with a blade in my back while I'm asleep."

Rijal's hand went to the hilt of his knife.

Everyone stiffened.

The tunnel was silent except for the echo of steel sliding free. Rijal turned his knife around and offered it hilt-first to Zared.

Rijal gestured awkwardly with one hand that it was his only knife.

Zared took it.

"Better?" Ryze asked.

Zared shrugged and put the knife away. "I still don't trust him."

"You don't have to," Ryze said. "We just have to tolerate each other until all of this is over."

"For the record, I agree with Zared," Vayne said. "But it seems the decision is made."

Tavian hesitated for a few moments before putting his own knives away. "Let's get on with it then. Before the rush of killing them fades and I need another hit."

"Things get ugly when that happens," Vayne said. "One time he almost stabbed me in the ass, just to stab someone."

Tavian grinned but didn't deny it.

"If we give you permission to talk out loud in front of Khala, will you?" Ryze asked. "Can you?"

Rijal glanced at me, then shook his head. "I've shamed myself and my court enough. Talking in front of her would be further shame. I'd deserve to be culled."

"He said no," I interpreted. The specifics of what he said didn't matter. The others would have gotten the gist of it anyway.

Ryze nodded. "I had to ask. Now, how do we get out of here? Please tell me there's not another puzzle. That didn't go too well last time."

Rijal shook his head and gestured down the tunnel before he started off that way.

"This is madness," Zared said softly to me. "He pulled a knife on us. The gods only know what else he might have planned."

"I don't think he has anything else planned," I said. "I think he was led

478

astray. He regrets what he did. We've all made mistakes, haven't we? Where would we be if we hadn't given each other second chances? Ryze and Cavan wouldn't be working together. You and Vayne haven't always gotten along. Hells, Ryze basically kidnapped us from the side of the road and made us go to the Winter Court with him. Where would we be if he hadn't? I think Rijal deserves the same second chance." I hoped like hells I wasn't wrong. This could just as easily go very badly.

"I hope you're right, and your soft heart doesn't get one of us killed," he said. "Especially if that someone is you."

He stopped, grabbed my arm and pulled me in for a quick kiss. "I don't want to lose you."

"You won't lose me." I quickly kissed him back, then followed the others. I didn't want to get left behind in here.

Although, even after a session with Zared and Tavian, I wouldn't have minded an hour or two alone in the dark. It was difficult not to be aroused by so many attractive men. I was lucky to have all of them.

"I better not," he growled. "Because if you go, I'm coming with you. And I'm not ready for that for a long time."

"Neither am I," I agreed. We had a lot more living left to do yet.

I shivered. "Is it colder in here suddenly?"

He glanced around. "It feels the same to me. Cold, dark and not my idea of fun."

"It's definitely colder," Tavian said. His eyes seemed to be everywhere, searching the tunnel for I didn't know what.

Ryze raised his hand to stop us all. "It doesn't feel colder to me either."

"Doesn't feel any different," Vayne said.

Cavan shook his head. "To me either."

"Really?" Tavian asked. "It feels like an icy breeze coming from somewhere."

"Yes," I said immediately. "That's exactly what it feels like. Like a cold breath blowing or—"

"Cold fingers," Tavian finished for me. "Reaching. Stretching out towards us." He shuddered. I'd never seen him look so disconcerted before. If he was uncomfortable, then I had good reason to be.

"The mist," Cavan said. "Is it reaching for all of us or just you and Khala?"

Tavian paused and shook his head. "I don't know. It's just reaching." He pointed in the direction we were headed. "It's coming from there." He moved forward, every step slow and careful.

Zared kept hold of my arm as we followed. Evidently he was taking his promise seriously. If I was dragged away by icy fingers of mist, he was coming with me.

The feeling grew stronger and stronger until we reached the end of the tunnel.

Ryze and Cavan raised their hands to illuminate what looked like nothing more than a dead end wall.

There, in the centre was an indentation the size of a hand.

Rijal pointed towards it. "We press that and the door opens. Then we will be in the mist."

"It's not too late to make a portal and go home," Vayne said.

"We can't portal out from here," Cavan said. "I tried. The cavern and tunnels are warded against making one."

Rijal looked at me questioningly. "What is this..." He was clearly trying to think of how to sign the word portal.

I didn't know that one myself. "It's a magical doorway," I explained. "You don't have those?"

He shook his head. "We have the doors that open and close by magic, but not ones that are made from magic." He seemed intrigued, if slightly scared at the prospect.

I didn't blame him. The first time I ever saw a portal it freaked me the fuck out. Considering I'd just seen a bunch of priests die and Fae trying to take my sisters, pretty much everything freaked me the fuck out at the time.

"How do you get out of here unless you go via the mist?" Vayne asked.

"There are other ways that lead off the mountain," Rijal signed. "Long tunnels."

I interpreted for him. "Looks like the quickest way to get the hells out of here is through that door."

I didn't relish the idea any more than they did. Especially with the way the icy fingers still tugged at me. They were becoming harder and harder to ignore.

Harder still when I felt like they wrapped around my waist and pulled me towards the door.

"Khala." Zared was dragged along behind me.

My hand didn't feel like it was my own. It rose involuntarily to the centre of the door. I slapped my palm against it, then pushed.

The stone door slid slowly aside, and I was ripped out of Zared's grip.

CHAPTER
TWENTY-SIX

KHALA

I heard him shout my name before the sound was ripped away, along with my breath.

I tried to reach back for him, but there was nothing there. Nothing but damp air so cold and thick, I felt like I was encased in ice.

I tried to grab on to some magic. To do what, I didn't know, but I couldn't get a grasp on anything. I couldn't tell which way was up or down. I wasn't even sure if I was still alive, or if this was the portal to one of the seven hells.

Was I dead? Would I be able to tell if I was?

I sucked in a breath. I couldn't do that if I was dead, could I?

I reached out through the bond. Four of my men were frantic, the other, Vayne, was close.

"Vayne!" I called out. My voice was thrown straight back to me, as though bouncing off a wall.

"Khala?" I wasn't sure I'd imagined that, but it sounded like him.

"Where are you?" I still had the sensation of moving rapidly, right up until I hit something that felt solid, but not hard enough to hurt. It was like colliding with a mattress or pillow.

I grunted and flopped to the ground. I placed my hands to either side of me and tried to catch my breath.

"Fuck," I managed to gasp out.

Everything around me was white and thick. I held my arm out as far as it would stretch. My fingers disappeared from view.

I quickly pulled them back.

"Khala?" Vayne called out from somewhere nearby.

"Vayne?" I shouted back.

"Keep talking. I'll find you."

"What do you want me to talk about?" I asked. It was a rhetorical question. It didn't matter what I said, as long as I kept saying it.

"This kind of sucks," I said. "When I woke up this morning, I didn't think I'd end up in the middle of a cloud. That's what this is isn't it?"

"It looks like a fucking cloud," he grumbled.

"It doesn't smell like one." I sniffed the air. "It's like nothing I've ever smelled before. I don't know how to describe it." It was like old ashes, fresh flowers and some kind of spice. "It's strange."

"I don't suppose you know where the others are?" He sounded closer now.

"I think they're right where we left them," I said. "Near the entrance to the cavern. They're all right." As all right as they could be, under the circumstances.

He appeared right in front of my face, making me startle violently.

"Sorry." He grabbed my wrists when I held them up in front of me reflexively, and pulled me to him.

I wrapped my arms around his neck and leaned against him. "There's no point in asking where we are, is there?"

"You can ask, but I don't have any fucking answers." He leaned back and looked up and all round. "This is why Ryze hated the mist so much. It's creepy as fuck. As far as I can tell, it's more or less harmless. Except the part about bringing us here. Wherever the hells here is."

I kept one arm firmly tangled around him and felt around for whatever it was that stopped my momentum. As I expected, it wasn't a mattress or pillow. It seemed like nothing more than a wall of mist, only...somehow more solid than the rest of it.

None of that made any sense, but that was the best impression or explanation I had.

"Whatever or whoever brought us here, this was as far as they wanted us to go."

"For now," he added.

I sighed. "Yes, for now." The gods only knew how long that might last. "Any idea why they want us?"

"Apart from the fact we're both incredibly attractive? Tave or Ryze would probably say it has to do with the blood that runs in your veins. The visions he keeps having suggest he has Court Of Dreams blood. Either Hycathe does as well or they wanted to keep her away from the Court of Shadows. Unless it's Jezalyn who has the blood of one of them." He shrugged.

"And you think my mother has the same blood and so do I," I concluded. "Couldn't they have sent an invitation? I can read."

He snorted bitterly. "That would have been the polite thing to do. Maybe the fuckers can't."

"And maybe they don't want to," I said. "They might have brought us here to kill us."

"If that's the case, they're screwing with the wrong Fae." He smiled. "Killing us won't be that easy."

"I hope you're right," I told him.

"Of course I'm right," he grunted.

"You sound like Ryze," I said.

"In two or three hundred years, you'll sound like him too." He grimaced. "Now, can you portal us out of here?"

"Right." It hadn't occurred to me to try until he said that. Sooner or later it would have. Neither of us were inclined to stand here and wait for something to happen.

I tried to grab on to even a small amount of magic. I half expected it to be as elusive as it was when I was moving.

Instead, I got a rush of power stronger than anything I'd felt before. Winter magic, summer magic and something else. It was like... Nothing I could wrap my head around. Whatever it was, it was new and it was powerful.

I opened a portal in the middle of the mist, trying to reach the door to the tunnel, where the others were. The portal seemed to fight me somehow. As though it would go...somewhere, but it wasn't going to go *there*.

Perhaps it was too close to the wards, or couldn't guarantee it wouldn't open onto one of my men. Realising the latter might be the case, I stopped trying and directed it a different way.

I had no idea where we might end up. I frantically thought about my bedroom at the Winter Court, or the sitting room there. Or the atrium at the Summer Court.

A thought popped into my head just as the portal settled into one spot.

Vayne grabbed my hand and we ran through to the other side.

"All right," he said slowly. "Where the fuck are we?"

I put a hand over my eyes to shield them from the glare of the sun. I looked across grasslands to a forest beyond. Further away still, a castle perched on top of a hill which rose above the canopy.

"I have no idea," I admitted. According to the bond we were a long way from the others.

A very, very long way.

THANK YOU FOR READING! The story concludes in Whisper of Frost and Flame. If you'd love a bonus scene of Vayne encased in stone, you can grab yours here

WHISPER OF FROST AND FLAME

COURT OF BLOOD AND BINDING
BOOK 4

CHAPTER
ONE
KHALA

"We're not in the Winter Court anymore," Vayne remarked.

"No. No we're not," I agreed. The question was, where the hells were we?

We'd been in the mist, pulled there on ghostly fingers. I'd made the portal to get us out of there. To get back to the rest of the pack.

Now, we stood on the edge of a vast expanse of grassland. A breeze rippled the green-gold grass for unbroken kilometres. Behind us, a copse of trees gradually thickened into a forest that meandered up the shallow slope of a hill. A castle sat perched at the apex, squared towers made of large blocks visible above the canopy.

"Does anything look familiar?" I asked.

"You're the one who brought us here," he pointed out. "It must look familiar to you, or that wouldn't be possible. You can only make a portal to a place you've been."

I turned around in a slow circle. "If I've ever been here, I don't remember it. But..."

The commander of the Winter Court army fixed me with a look that said he knew he wasn't going like what he was about to hear. "But?"

I winced at his expression.

"In my room back at the Temple, back when I was a Silent Maiden, a triptych of paintings hung on the wall. They made this." I raised my hands and framed part of the landscape with my fingers.

"Fuck," Vayne said softly. "Once upon a time, I would have said it's a coincidence or a bunch of bullshit. But now, I've seen enough to know some past asshole put it there to bring us both here. I knew being this good-looking would go badly for me at some point."

487

He gave me the faintest upward jerk of the side of his mouth. More a twitch than a smile. Mostly, he glared at the landscape as though somehow it was to blame for us being here. "Did it give any indication of where 'here' is?"

I lowered my hands to my sides and thought back to the paintings. "No. There was no writing on any of them. Not on the back of them either." I got curious one day and took them off to look. I'd asked one of the priestesses about them once, but they had no more answers than I did.

"Wild guess, the castle belongs to the Court of Dreams." He nodded toward it.

I pinched him.

"Ouch, what the fuck was that for?" He squinted at me.

He wasn't wrong about how attractive he was. Dark hair, dark eyes and a muscular body, the usually grumpy Fae was part of my pack. One of the mates I was bonded to. One of five. The other four were on the end of the bond, wondering what the hells happened to us.

"Just making sure we're not dreaming. I figured it would be more effective than pinching myself."

I jumped as he pinched my ass hard. "No, not dreaming."

"I guess that means we found the Court of Dreams." His hand lingered on my ass. "The question is, can you make us a portal back to somewhere that isn't here? Maybe after we take advantage of being alone." His dark eyes were suddenly darker.

What was it with men that we could be in the middle of wide grassland, in the gods only knew where, and he could still think about sex? And get me going with the suggestion.

"We could—" Movement in the sky interrupted my train of thought.

A shadow soared over us, followed by an enormous, winged beast. And another. And another.

"Shit. The portal might be a good idea right now." Vayne grabbed my arm and pulled me to him, putting himself between the three griffins and me.

Before I could begin to open one, the first of the griffins landed a few metres from us. Wind from its wings ruffled my hair and clothes. I threw my hand up to protect my eyes from dust thrown up by massive taloned feet hitting the ground.

I turned as the other two landed behind, circling us in.

"When I woke up this morning, I didn't think I'd end the day as lunch for griffins," Vayne said with a grunt.

"Me either," I agreed. All thoughts of opening a portal went right out of my head, shoved out by awe for the magnificent creatures surrounding us. Along with a healthy dose of fear.

Each had a long, wicked looking beak, and round, orange eyes. The one in front of us blinked slowly, upper and lower lids closing and opening again. Golden feathers on a birdlike head led down to golden fur and haunches made for pouncing. Huge front paws were tipped with claws that looked ready to tear us to shreds.

A spicy scent, like cinnamon, accompanied each of them, a strangely pleasant balance to their fierce appearance.

Seated on the back of each griffin was a helmeted figure dressed in dark leather moulded to their bodies like a second skin. One slipped off her helmet and tucked it under her arm. Her hair was as golden as her griffin, ears delicately pointed. She regarded us with eyes the colour of Ryze's whiskey.

"You have come from the seasonal courts," she declared.

I exchanged half a glance with Vayne, trying to come to some agreement as to how we should respond.

"We have," Vayne said slowly, carefully. "Who the hells are you?"

She regarded him, barely blinking.

I couldn't tell what she was thinking. As far as we knew, these were the Fae who attacked the seasonal courts. Who killed Dalyth. Who were about to kill us.

My hands twitched. I should have asked Tavian to teach me how to use a knife the way he did.

"You'll come with us," she stated. "You may ride on the back of Patric and Gavil's griffins." She spoke like she was used to being in charge. She expected to be obeyed.

"What if we don't want to go with you?" Vayne asked. "As it happens, we were just about to get the fuck out of here. You might want to move your griffins out of the way before we open a portal in the middle of one."

She looked unimpressed, bordering on angry at his response. The griffin shifted underneath her, as though sensing her annoyance. He made no move to attack. Yet.

Another of the riders chuckled.

"They're feisty, Yala." He pulled off his helmet and grinned. "Don't worry, the griffins don't bite unless we tell them to. I'm Patric, that's Gavil."

Gavil gave us a nod, but left his helmet on. His whole body was tense. So taut it might snap at a sneeze.

I looked back to Patric. He seemed friendly at least. "Are you planning to tell them to bite?"

"That depends on you," Yala said darkly. Her annoyance seemed to be directed at Patric. That was confirmed when she glared at him.

"I'd apologise for Yala, but she hates it when I do that," Patric said. "She'll loosen up when she gets to know you. So, who's riding with me?" He looked from me to Vayne and back again.

"We're not riding separately," Vayne growled. "If we agree to go with you, and we haven't done that yet, Khala stays with me." He tightened his grip on my arm.

"You'll hurt Gavil's feelings, right, Gavil?" Patric grinned at his companion.

Gavil responded with a very Vayne-like, eloquent grunt.

"Sounds like he doesn't give a shit to me," Vayne said. "What do you want with us anyway? Why did you try to kill us?"

While he and Yala had a glaring competition, I sniffed. I expected to find at least one alpha, or omega, but none of the riders were either of those things. All three smelled like betas. What did that mean, if anything? I sensed somehow it was significant, but right now, I couldn't see how.

"The griffins are perfectly capable of carrying you in their claws," Yala said darkly. "You might find it slightly less comfortable than riding on their backs."

"Has it occurred to you we might go willingly if you told us why?" Vayne said. "A simple explanation doesn't seem like too much to ask. Does it, Khala?" He turned his head towards me, but didn't take his eyes off Yala.

"There is a reason you've been brought here," Yala said. "It's not my duty to disclose that. I assure you, we meant you no harm. None of the incursions into the seasonal courts was intended to kill either of you. If they had, you'd be dead." She sniffed.

"What was the reason behind the incursions?" I could probably set all three griffins and their riders on fire, then get the hells out of here. Whatever their intent was, they *had* fired lightning bolts at us. They'd almost hit Vayne and me. That wasn't a friendly act, as far as I was concerned.

"As I said, I may not disclose that," she said, visibly becoming further irritated.

"You don't know, do you?" Vayne stated. His tone was derisive now, almost taunting.

"We were sent to collect you," Patric said. "Believe it or not, it's an honour to be permitted to ride on the back of a griffin."

"Says you," Vayne growled.

Patric was undeterred. "I didn't expect you to believe me. How about we show you?" He leaned over and stretched his hand out to me. "Come on, ride with me."

His grin and the slight upward movement of his eyebrows confirmed what I already guessed. He was flirting with me. He seemed like the sort who would flirt with everyone, like Ryze or Tavian. They flirted every chance they got.

"It can't hurt to give them a chance," I said. We *had* come in search of the Court of Dreams, after all. I didn't trust these three, but this might be the opportunity we needed. The chance to learn what this court's intentions were towards the Court of Shadows. Perhaps to broker peace between them. Some kind of understanding that wouldn't end in all-out war.

"It *could* hurt, but if you're going, then I'm going." Vayne looked less than pleased at the prospect. He kept his eyes on Patric while the golden-haired Fae man helped me to slide up behind him on the griffin. He glared at him, a silent warning to keep his hands to himself.

Before anyone could stop him, Vayne vaulted up behind me and gripped my waist with his wide hands.

"See, there's plenty of room on the back of this thing," Vayne grunted.

"There is, but I suggest you refrain from referring to Nami as a thing," Patric said over his shoulder. "She tends to take exception to stuff like that. It would be unfortunate if she decided to buck you off mid-fight."

"Don't threaten me," Vayne rumbled.

"I'm not threatening you, I'm telling you what might happen if Nami gets upset. Now, I suggest you wrap your arms around my waist and get as close to me as you can."

While Vayne grumbled, I shimmied forward a couple of centimetres and slipped my arms around Patric. His leather was butter soft and smelled like a combination of griffin and woodsmoke. Obscurely, it reminded me of Ryze.

I felt down the bond for him and the rest of my pack. They seemed to have left the mist and the Court of Shadows. They weren't close, so they hadn't figured out how to follow me here. If I had to guess, I'd say they were in the Winter Court, probably trying to figure out how to find us.

I sent thoughts that we were fine, and that I'd keep the bond open in case anything happened.

Vayne tightened his grip as the griffin crouched and jumped skyward. Her massive wings snapped out as she rose, sweeping the air to push us higher.

"Fucking hells," Vayne whispered. "Don't look down, *don't look down*."

I wasn't sure if he was talking to me, himself or both of us. He put on the façade of being a big bad army commander, but in the end he was a person with fears like the rest of us. This particular one, I hadn't known about.

"Scared of heights?" I said over my shoulder, no judgement in my tone. As far as I was concerned, it was a perfectly rational fear. Especially while sitting on the back of a griffin.

"It's not the heights I'm scared of," Vayne replied. "It's the landing. Falling off this thing would suck."

"Don't fall off," Patric told us. "But don't worry. If you do, Nami will catch you."

"That's fucking great," Vayne said sarcastically. "I can't wait to dangle from those claws." He held on so tight, I could hardly breathe. In turn, I did the same to Patric.

It really *was* a long way down already, and if the griffin didn't catch us, the landing would kill us. Wind roared past, threatening to sweep us off the griffin's back.

"Isn't the view from here incredible?" Patric asked.

The other griffins flew on either side of us, a magnificent sight for sure, but a glance at the ground below took my breath away.

"This is insanity," Vayne said. "If Fae were supposed to fly, we'd have fucking wings."

Patric chuckled and leaned back against me as we soared toward the castle perched on top of the hill.

CHAPTER
TWO

KHALA

The griffins landed neatly inside the castle walls. Their feet kicked up dust in a yard big enough to fit several of the beasts. The large stone structure off to one side, with huge wooden doors standing wide open, suggested they were housed here.

"Imagine having to clean out their shit," Vayne said as we landed in the centre of the yard.

"That might be why they brought us here," I said, half-joking.

"Fuck that," he growled. "If they wanted people to help them clean up after their animals, they could have brought Zared here instead."

Patric chuckled. "Don't worry, we have plenty of help to clean up after the griffins."

Indeed, the moment we stepped off her back, a group of Fae children came running to lead Nami inside the building. They must have seen her a thousand times before, but they all looked at her and the other two griffins with awe.

Patric and Yala slipped their helmets off again, but it was Gavil who caught my eye.

When he pulled his off, I saw his face was heavily scarred. Almost every centimetre of his skin was covered in what looked like burn scars.

I tried not to stare, but it was difficult. Fae tended to heal injuries with magic, if they were lucky enough to get to a healer in time. I'd never seen any with injuries like this.

He noticed me staring and turned to glare. He shot daggers at me with his eyes, before he turned and stalked away.

"What happened to him?" I asked softly.

"Fire," Patric replied with an indifferent shrug. "He was a kid at the time. He probably doesn't even remember, but he's still touchy."

"You don't have any healers?" Vayne asked.

"That's a matter for our leaders," Yala snapped. She gestured for us to step through an archway that led towards the castle.

I glanced back over my shoulder before I followed. The children who took the griffins into their stable building came running back out and started to kick a ball around the yard. They laughed and shouted while they played, carefree and joyful.

I smiled before I turned away. "I didn't realise how few Fae children I've seen." There were none in the Court of Shadows; their High Lady forbade her people from breeding.

Here, they seemed to have space in abundance. If I had to choose between the two courts, I might be inclined to choose this one. If I trusted anyone here that wasn't me or Vayne.

"Most of them are occupied with studies or chores," Vayne said. He frowned at the playing youngsters as though they were wasting their time somehow.

"Here, we like children to be children," Patric said with a shrug.

Vayne muttered something I couldn't catch, then laced his fingers through mine and tucked me against his side. He gave Patric a look as though if he thought about touching me, Vayne might stab him through the eyeball.

Patric merely grinned in response. He seemed like the kind of man who wasn't bothered by much. Nor was he easily intimidated, judging by his interactions with Yala.

We followed them through the arch and a set of worn, stone steps to a wide terrace. Yala led the way across to a set of doors which were thrown open to the afternoon sunshine.

We stepped into a room tastefully decorated with mahogany furniture and pale, timber floors. Everything in the room was simple, and placed with care. Couches and armchairs sat within reach of several tables, and footstools upholstered in dark fabric. If the room was occupied with people, no one would sit with their back to anyone else. Nor would anyone sit with their back to the doors.

The space was comfortable, cosy. The perfect room to sit and read a book, or share too much wine with friends.

Yala took us all the way through that room and out the door on the other side.

We stepped into a darker, more utilitarian corridor. No art occupied any part of the walls. The windows we walked past were narrow slits, as though for defence against invaders.

"This is an older part of the castle," Patric explained. "It dates back over a thousand years. The terrace and sitting room are only about five hundred years old."

"Only," I echoed. Sometimes I forgot how old Fae got. Five hundred years was young for a lot of them.

Patric chuckled. "I was a child when it was built. Before that, the front of the castle was a crumbling ruin."

"This way," Yala snapped, as if we weren't keeping up with her steps. Perhaps she was irritated with our small talk. As far as I could tell, she was easily irritated.

She led us down the corridor, into a large reception room. This one looked like a combination of the old castle and the new. The windows were slits, but the room was full of the same style of furniture as the sitting room. Simple, hand carved and comfortable. Each of the chairs was padded and upholstered in similar dark fabric.

Several Fae looked up as we entered the room, all of them with hair in varying shades of gold. None was more than a shade or two darker, or lighter than the griffins's fur.

Back when I was still a Silent Maiden, I saw pictures of lions in the Temple library. Creatures that looked like the back half of a griffin, but with heads like cats, with heavy manes around their faces. I was reminded of those now. These Fae looked like a pack of lions and lionesses.

"High Lord Dennin, High Lady Ramela," Yala greeted two of them. "I have brought the outsiders. They come with many questions."

She said that as though having questions was a bad thing. Like we were children who needed to know the answers to anything and everything.

"Thank you, Yala." Ramela rose from her chair, took Yala's hands in hers and pressed her forehead lightly to the other woman's. She released Yala's hands and did the same with Patric.

Vayne's hand tightened on mine, not with possessiveness this time, but hoping she wasn't expecting him to do the same thing with her.

I remembered what he told me about an older Fae woman taking advantage of him when he was a much younger man. He was grumpy with everyone, but particularly women who weren't me. When we met, I thought he hated me. Now I knew it was only his past talking. Nothing I could blame him for, especially given what Wornar did to me. Thanks to Cavan, that was now a slight pinch in the back of my mind, not the heart-shattering event it was at the time.

Ramela cast a glance at us, but didn't offer either of us her hands. Presumably the greeting was reserved for members of her court, or her friends. Instead, she waved us over to chairs.

"Please, sit. Patric, darling, go and organise us some refreshment." She waved him away like he was still a child.

Far from looking offended, he grinned and nodded before he backed out the door.

"I'd imagine you have a great many questions," Dennin started. "So do we."

Ramela gave him a glance. "Let's start with their names."

Vayne introduced us and then said, "You have a High Lord and a High Lady? Which one of you is really in charge?"

Dennin offered Ramela a sly smile. "In theory, we're equals, but anyone who knows us, knows I often defer to my very wise wife."

The look she gave him back was openly adoring. "And he calls me the wise one. A wise man knows when to listen to a woman, wouldn't you agree, Khala?"

I couldn't help but smile. "That sounds accurate to me. More men should listen to what women say."

"I always listen to what you say," Vayne argued. "So do the rest of the pack."

"Pack?" Ramela asked. "Are you not husband and wife?"

Vayne grunted. "Not yet."

That was the first time any of my men mentioned marriage. I hadn't even thought about it before. Could I marry all of them? I liked the idea, but would they? That was a thought for another time and definitely another place.

"I have five mates," I said finally. I realised, to my surprise, no one else in the room was an omega or an alpha. I hadn't smelled the scent of either since arriving here. What did that mean, if anything?

"All male," I added.

"Five men," Ramela mused. She looked at Dennin sideways.

He snorted. "Don't even think about it. I'm not sharing you with four other men."

She sniffed, but smiled. "We might have to talk about that later."

"Only if you want me to start having to kill anyone you take an interest in," Dennin said. "I could start with Patric."

Ramela laughed. "Breia forbid. He's too young and frivolous for me."

"You worship Breia?" I asked without thinking. The temple that housed the Silent Maidens was dedicated to the goddess Breia. I hadn't known any of the Fae believed in her, much less worshipped her. Granted, I hadn't had much in the way of theological conversations with any of the Fae, beyond Cavan's apparent disbelief the gods existed at all.

Ramela cocked her head at me. "Of course. She is our goddess. The goddess. Mother of all existence."

The Temple didn't mention her as more than one of the minor gods, in spite of having her own temple. She certainly wasn't considered the mother of anything other than a couple of younger gods.

Beliefs certainly had changed in the last thousand years.

"You were a Silent Maiden, were you not?" Ramela straightened her head and raised eyebrows in question. Her expression remained pleasant, but with an air of urgency. Of the need to know. Whatever was going on here, a lot was at stake for them.

Me too, I thought. I hoped I was whatever she needed me to be, because I didn't know what would happen if I wasn't.

I wasn't sure how much I should tell them, but I nodded. "I used to be, yes," I signed. If the Court Shadows still understood maidens' hand language, then logically the Court of Dreams would as well.

495

Both Ramela and Dennin followed my symbols and nodded. Clearly they both knew what I was saying. Or at least, enough to get the idea.

"I see you're wondering what that has to do with you and the Silent Maidens," Ramela said. "It was us, the Court of Dreams, who founded the order. Based on a vision from one of our own that one day the Silent Maidens would be our undoing and our salvation."

For the first time, she looked uncomfortable. I wanted to ask what her perception of the Court Of Shadows was. That the two courts were very different was obvious. Apart from Yala, everyone here seemed friendly, almost warm. They were a stark contrast from Lyra and Vernissa, and the division inside the Court of Shadows.

I sensed we would get to that subject when they were ready to steer it that way. So far, I saw no sign of animosity. No hint that these Fae drove the other court literally underground.

What was it Ryze said? When there were two opposing views, the truth was often somewhere in the middle. I suspected that might be the case here. Either way, they seemed more receptive to peace than I'd anticipated. That immediately put me on guard.

It was Zared who said if anyone seemed that nice, those were the ones you shouldn't trust. No one was ever *that* nice.

I could have used him and the rest of my pack with me right now. What would they have made of this place?

Dennin sat forward in his chair and placed his hands on his knees. "Undoing and salvation. The question is, which of them are you?"

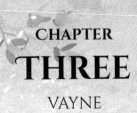

CHAPTER
THREE
VAYNE

"What the hells sort of question was that?" I growled.

I looked over to Khala who was standing near the window face turned towards the late afternoon light. She was so fucking beautiful she almost made my heart stop. Even when she looked human and I was pretending to hate her, and all other humans, she was still the most beautiful woman I ever set eyes on. Gorgeous on the outside and feisty and sassy on the inside.

She saw right through my gruff façade, past my inner asshole and into the deepest parts of me. If I had to admit it, I'd say I fell in love with her the moment I saw her step out of the carriage into the rain. The way her clothes clung to her body, displaying her peaked nipples, full breasts and the curves of her hips. She transitioned to the way she looks now, but she didn't lose her curves, or a drop of her attitude. We gave each other hells and I loved every minute of it.

"One I don't have the answer to." She turned around to face me, and crossed her arms under her breasts. "I'm just me, Khala. Why should I be anyone's downfall or their salvation?"

I finished kicking off my boots and stood to take her hands. "This is going to sound corny as fuck, and if you tell any of the others I said this, I'm going to deny the hells out of it."

I took a moment before I spoke again. "You're *my* salvation. Before you, I thought I was stuck with Ryze and Tavian, spending most of my time training soldiers for a war that may never come. Following Ryze on his insane missions and quests in my spare time. Trust me when I say you haven't seen anything yet, when it comes to Ryze and his harebrained shit. Tavian too.

"But now, things make sense." I hesitated again. "All right, a lot of things still don't make sense, like how the hells you brought us here when you've never been here. But you... *You* make sense."

I put a finger to her lips when she started to speak.

"Let me finish, or I won't." When she nodded her understanding, I lowered my hand.

"I guess what I'm trying to say is, I love you. Even when I thought you were nothing but a human pain in my ass, I loved you. I thought my heart was cold and dead, but some of it is still alive. What's left is all yours."

I swiped a tear off her cheek and cursed myself. Great, now she was fucking crying because of me. I assumed I'd misjudged her feelings, but at least I told her what I was feeling. I got that off my chest and now we could get on with figuring out more important things.

I dropped her hands and started to step away.

She grabbed my arm, pulled me back and placed her hand on the back of my head. She drew me closer and pressed her lips to mine.

Gods, the taste of her mouth. She was better than wine, more intoxicating. Immediately more addictive. When she pulled her mouth away, I felt bereft. Like she took away my air.

And then she spoke.

"I love you too," she said softly.

I let out a breath I was *totally* aware I was holding. "Thank fuck for that. This could have gotten really awkward." I managed a faint smile. I didn't smile often, but for her I would try to do it more. I *wanted* to do it more. She gave me things to smile about.

She laughed, a sexy little sound from the back of her throat—one of my favourite parts of her—and kissed me again.

"Once, you said someday you might put your cock in my pussy," she said. "Why not today?"

After our meeting with the High Lord and Lady, we were shown to one of their fancy ass rooms to rest and contemplate Dennin's question. I couldn't remember the last time I was alone with her, but it seemed like a smart move to take full advantage of it. I wasn't going to make it too easy on her though.

"I don't know if your pussy is ready for my cock," I teased. "I wouldn't want to wreck her." That was a flat-out lie and we both knew it. I wanted to wreck her and then some. I wanted to fuck her so hard she couldn't walk for days. As far away from everyone else as we were, I would take full advantage of it. Every second. Every drop.

"You really think you can?" she asked, the lift of her chin matching the challenge in her eyes.

I returned her look with a mild one, then snaked my hand around the back of her head and grabbed a fistful of hair.

"You like to live dangerously, don't you, woman?" I growled. "You know what provoking me gets you? Do you?"

She let out a tiny gasp of surprise, but leaned into my hand.

"Are you going to punish me, Commander Vayne?"

I grabbed hold of my belt buckle and worked it loose. I slid the belt free of my pants and pulled her over to the bed. It wasn't one of those nests omegas prefer. It was a regular, four poster bed with curtains of the same dark fabric they seemed obsessed with around here.

I pulled her wrists up and looped the belt around them. I pushed her until she knelt on the bed and tied the other end of the belt to the bed frame. She had to kneel all the way up, arms stretched above her head.

Her cheeks were pink with excitement.

One of the best things about the bond was knowing how much she was enjoying this already. She was so aroused, her pussy would be dripping.

I leaned in until my face was almost touching hers. "You're right, I'm going to punish you. I'm going to punish you until you learn to do what I say. Do you understand?"

When she didn't respond, I raised my eyebrows at her. "I said, do you understand?"

"Yes, sir," she replied. Practically purred the words.

"That's better." I undid the front of her pants and yanked them down her hips. I worked them off her legs and threw them over my shoulder. I hooked my fingers in the waistband of her panties and tore them off.

"Remind me to get you some leather panties, with a lock only I have the key for," I said.

They wouldn't keep any of the other men from getting to her pussy, but it would slow them down. Plus, imagining her like that made me harder than stone.

I turned her until her cute little ass was facing me. I ran my hand over the smooth, rounded surface of her skin. She was taut, but soft at the same time.

I crouched down and nipped her before giving her a gentle slap.

"Wait there for a moment." She could work her hands loose if she wanted to, but I wanted her to stay dangling where she was.

"Yes, sir," she replied.

Gods, hearing her say that made my balls heavy as fuck.

I pushed myself off the side of the bed, hurried over to her pack and pulled out her hairbrush.

I sat down beside her and ran the bristled side lightly over her ass.

"Do you want to use the same safe word you use with Cavan, or do we want one just for us?" I watched in fascination as her skin quivered in response to the brush.

"We need our own, sir," she replied. "One just for us."

I nodded slowly. "What about turnip?"

She laughed softly. "Turnip?"

"Why not turnip? It's not something most people shout out during sex. Not in my experience anyway." The gods only knew what other people did. That was their business.

"Turnip it is then," she said.

"Turnip it is then what?" I pressed the bristles against her skin.

"Turnip it is then, sir," she replied. "Are you going to punish me for that?"

"Definitely." I turned the brush and brought the hard side down on her ass. She jumped slightly, but didn't flinch away.

Through the bond, I felt the sting of pain, but the rush of pleasure. Yes, she enjoyed that very much.

I smacked her cheek again, then gave the same treatment to the other side. Her ass was soon a lovely shade of red.

"Harder," she groaned.

"You want it harder? You don't get to decide, remember? I'm in charge here. If you want it harder, you have to beg me for it." By now, my cock was harder than my sword. And desperate to slide into her sheath.

"Please, sir." Her voice was breathless. "Please, spank me harder."

I spanked her hard enough to make myself grunt with the exertion. The impact made her cry out, but that tapered off into a moan.

"You like that?" I spanked her other cheek just as hard.

"Yes, sir." Her voice was almost a whimper. "Please, sir, I need your cock. I need you to fill me. Turnip. Turnip, please."

I tossed the hairbrush aside and reached up to release her hands. While she flopped down onto the mattress, I shed my clothes, and stroked my hand up and down my throbbing erection.

"You want this?" I raised one eyebrow at her. "You have to touch yourself first. Touch your beautiful pussy."

She locked her eyes on me and dipped her hand down between her legs. She started to trace circles around her clit with the tips of her fingers.

"Put your fingers inside yourself," I ordered. I was turned on so hard right now. The sight of her with her fingers sliding up and down, then inside her pussy almost made me lose my load in my hand.

"Let me taste."

She slipped her fingers between my lips.

I sucked them, tasting her sweet flavour.

"Good girl, make yourself come." I sat beside her and watched her finger fuck herself, while I traced circles around her nipples with the pad of my thumb.

Her breath came in short pants. She closed her eyes.

"Open them. I want your eyes on me when you come."

Her eyelids fluttered open again. She locked her gaze on mine and moaned softly. She rocked her hips against her hand until she cried out. I watched her shatter at the same time as I felt it through the bond.

"Good girl," I said. "I think you deserve a reward now. You deserve my cock." I gripped her legs and pulled them, and her, toward me until I could drape them over my shoulders.

I positioned my cock at her entrance and finally, finally sank inside her beautiful body.

There was nothing better in this world than being inside the woman I loved. Feeling her around my cock, enjoying the way she felt so full that it radiated through the bond.

I forced myself not to come undone too quickly. To thrust slowly and evenly into her, drawing out every moment as long as I could. I wanted to do this all day, and all night. I might have, but she came again, stealing an orgasm from me like a little thief.

I thrust inside harder and harder, faster and faster until my balls exploded my heated cum inside her delicious pussy.

I panted for a while before I lowered her legs down to the mattress. I drew her to me and kissed the top of her head.

"I trust you've learnt your lesson," I teased.

"What I've learned is that being bad is good," she replied. "I might need to keep being bad so you can punish me more later."

"Remind me to spank you harder later." I would, and I knew she'd enjoy every fucking moment of it.

CHAPTER
FOUR
CAVAN

I paused my pacing to regard Ryze.

The High Lord of the Winter Court looked calmer than I felt. He couldn't possibly have been. Ever since we left the Court Of Shadows, we'd gone back and forth about what to do.

All we knew was that Khala made a portal in the mist and she and Vayne stepped through it. Wherever they were, they were so far the bond was stretched almost to breaking point.

So were we.

Zared and Tavian barely said a word. Instead, Tavian played with a knife while Zared favoured Ryze and I with glares, as though somehow all of this was our fault.

"What do you mean Harel is right?" I asked Ryze.

Ryze swirled his whiskey around in his glass. "I didn't say he was right. I said he *might* be right. Or at least, Autumn Court legend might be right. They believed the now not-so-lost courts jumped on ships and sailed away."

"I hope he's wrong, because that's a lot of ocean you need to freeze to get to Khala," Tavian remarked.

I watched his mouth move as he spoke. I shouldn't be thinking about his mouth right now, I certainly shouldn't be thinking about how his lips felt wrapped around my cock. The memory made my balls heavy.

I pushed the thoughts away and shook my head. "If Khala can open a portal to wherever she is, then we should be able to do the same."

"In theory, yes," Ryze agreed. "I'm sure you've tried. I know I have."

I resumed pacing. I *had* tried. Multiple times. I even tried piggybacking on the bond, to force a portal to open where she was.

That was a tentative effort at best. I was scared of breaking the bond if I

502

pushed my magic at it too hard. I resolved to try again later though, because her safety was more important to me than my ego. More important than the ability to feel her emotions in the back of my mind. Right now, it seemed she and Vayne were having fun. Presumably, their lives weren't in immediate danger.

I wished I'd gone through the portal with her. Not just because I'd be the one spanking her right now, but she wasn't as experienced in the creation of portals as Ryze and I were. As far as I could tell, she hadn't tried to make one back here yet.

Of course, she managed to achieve what we had been trying to do anyway. She found the Court of Dreams. When she and Vayne weren't fucking, no doubt she was talking to their High Lord and trying to broker a peace between the two formally lost courts.

I was sure I wasn't the only one hoping she wasn't adding another High Lord to her pack. We would support everything she did, but two massive egos was enough for one pack. The gods knew Tavian, Zared and Vayne had enough arrogance to spare as well.

"Did we try hard enough?" I asked rhetorically. "It might be we don't have the right kind of magic to make a portal to her current location."

"We are not asking Wornar," Zared growled.

"Or Harel." Tavian's tone matched the human's.

I had to give Zared credit for so fully shaking off the block Dalyth put in his head. I'd hated asking her to do it. Blocking people's memories, messing with their minds...

It wasn't something I relished. It was simply something I'd had to do, a decision I made sometimes in the last twenty years, because I had no choice. I knew the lost courts would return and I had to do whatever was necessary to be ready.

Humans running around Fraxius with the memories of the Summer Court, and being taken from the Temple, weren't in the best interests of that goal. From what Khala told me about her friend Tyla, the women with altered memories got on with their lives, exactly as I hoped.

When I ordered Dalyth to block Zared's memories, I firmly believed it was in his best interests. And to some extent, mine.

The moment I saw her in my reception room, I had to have her. It didn't hurt to have Zared out of the way.

When he regained his memories, I was convinced she would turn from the rest of us, back to him. But she hadn't. She chose all of us, and for that I was eternally grateful.

"No, we're not asking either of them," Ryze agreed. "There must be someone. Some way."

I rubbed the back of my neck. "I know of no one who has the same ability Khala does. I would suggest we try Hycanthe, but no one knows where her or Jezalyn are. Or if they're still alive."

I got no impression that Khala found them in the Court of Dreams. They might still be lost in the mist.

Try as I might, I couldn't get the image of the mist curling around them out of my mind. It wound round their eyes and mouths and drew them inwards. The expressions of terror on their faces, the way they opened their mouths to scream, but no sound came out...

Those were images which would stay with me for the rest of my life.

I fought in wars. I've seen death and fear. But I've never seen misty claws gripping bodies, clenching them close, claiming them, pulling them until all signs of them were gone.

All that was left was a wall of mist, taunting me. Telling me I couldn't have them. It hadn't wanted me. It wanted the two women.

In that moment, I understood Ryze's fear of the mist. Not to mention the legend of something living under Nallis. Whatever kind of monster it was, I didn't want to see it again.

"I don't understand why she hasn't tried to come back yet," Zared said.

We all knew what he meant. He did understand, but he didn't like it. He was talking out of frustration and a growing sense of powerlessness.

We had agreed to approach the Court of Dreams on behalf of the Court of Shadows, but we hadn't agreed to this.

"We will get her back," Tavian told him. He slipped his arm around Zared and pulled him close. They were adorable together. The human man and the male Fae omega.

While I had no interest in Zared, my feelings for Tavian were complicated at best. I'd had male lovers in the past, but never as part of a pack. Certainly never one who wanted me to kiss another High Lord. The idea was...intriguing.

I wasn't sure Ryze and I didn't share too much animosity to contemplate any kind of romantic relationship between us.

I stopped pacing, leaned against the wall and crossed my arms over my chest and my legs at my ankles.

"If Ryze is right about Harel and the Autumn Court's legend, they may have some idea where the Court of Dreams went." They may have left people, or documentation, behind. As Ryze would say, an arrow to point the way would have been very helpful.

"Potentially," Ryze agreed. "Why go so far though? If they were the antagonists, the Court of Shadows were chased underground. Why leave Jorius altogether?"

"Maybe they weren't leaving Jorius," Tavian said. "Maybe they were going somewhere."

"So they weren't running," Zared said slowly. "They were deliberately going...wherever they are, for some particular reason. Griffins?"

"Potentially," Ryze agreed. "Vernissa said they tamed the griffins for the purpose of attacking the Court of Shadows."

"I saw a vision of them doing just that." Tavian shivered.

504

"Right," Ryze agreed. "It's possible they moved away to put a plan in motion to finish what they started."

"That is some foresight," I remarked. Most of the Fae I knew were planners, but not usually to this extent. Abandoning their lands and cities just so they could later annihilate their enemies was something very different. Whatever went on between the two courts, that was a lot of time and work to invest in a grudge.

"We've always thought they were in this for the long game," Ryze said. "Everything seems to indicate the Fae of a thousand years ago had plans that are only now coming to fruition."

"What about Illaria?" Tavian asked. "She's the heir to the Autumn Court. If anyone knows where the Court of Dreams might be, she would."

I remembered her from the dinner with Harel. She'd claimed to want to reconcile with her father, before helping Khala steal what turned out to be a fake key. Harel had switched out the real one and not told his daughter.

Wherever her loyalty lay, it wasn't with him.

"I saw her in the training yard earlier," Zared said. "She's always very friendly to me."

Tavian grinned. "I bet she is. Whenever you're around, she needs a handkerchief to wipe the drool off her chin."

He seemed unconcerned. He was the kind of man who didn't mind sharing his lovers, as long as he got his time with them too. He was easily the sweetest assassin I ever met. Most of them were quiet and kept to themselves. Occupational hazard, I presumed. But Tavian, he was nothing like that. He was deadly as hells, but he'd smile and say nice things while he cut your throat.

Zared shrugged one shoulder, unabashed. "I can't help being irresistible."

Ryze snorted. "That's my line." He favoured us all with a rakish smile.

I couldn't deny that he was attractive too, but that was something I wasn't going to dwell on right now. We'd only just learned to trust each other. Whatever else might come, would take time.

"You're both irresistible," Tavian said. He gave me a sly look. "You too."

I returned his glance with a nod. There would be time for flirting later.

"We should find Illaria and talk to her," I concluded. "It seems like Zared should be present for that conversation. She might be more receptive to opening up to him."

"I'm not going to—" he started.

"I don't mean that kind of opening up," I said quickly. I was starting to think a large percentage of our minds were occupied thinking about sex. "I simply meant she might tell you more than she would tell the rest of us. If she has a crush on you, we might as well use that to our advantage, if it means reaching Khala sooner."

"If we find out they're on some continent, on the other side of the world, what then?" Zared asked.

"We've stolen a boat before," Ryze said. "If we have to steal a ship to get to her, then that's what we'll do. Between us, Cavan and I can create enough wind to push it along faster. And if we can't, you and Tavian can row."

He spoke the word lightly, but we all knew he wasn't precisely joking. If we had to do exactly that, then we would.

"It's times like these I wish dragons were real," Ryze mused.

"Griffins are," Tavian said.

Ryze stared at him, then snapped his fingers. "Yes, they are. On this continent too."

"Please tell me you're not suggesting we ask them to fly us to wherever Khala is." Zared grimaced.

Ryze smiled.

Zared groaned. "Vayne is right, you are trying to get us all killed."

None of us doubted he would be right there with us, even if it meant soaring over vast oceans on griffin wings.

"I don't know about any of you, but this is the most interesting time I've experienced in the last three hundred years," Ryze said.

I didn't bother to argue with him. Interesting certainly was one word for it.

"Zared, let's go find Illaria," I said.

Just as I expected, Tavian and Ryze rose too. Whatever happened, we were all in this together as a pack.

Khala's pack.

CHAPTER
FIVE
CAVAN

Tracking down Illaria took longer than I anticipated. Longer, I suspected, than any of us anticipated.

"She's usually hanging around near the training yard," Zared said. "I have no idea where she goes when she's not."

"Where would you go if you were the heir to the Autumn Court?" Tavian asked. "If you were working with people who also believed in the lost courts, even when the people around you didn't believe the same?" He gave me a meaningful look.

Ryze gave me the side eye, clearly expecting me to say something. To remind them I tried for years to warn them about the present situation.

"If I was her, I'd keep a low profile," I said finally. "High enough for people to find me if they wanted to follow me, but low enough to keep from becoming a target for my father's assassins." The fact she was the only heir was undoubtedly the sole reason she was still alive. Regardless of Harel's feelings towards her, he needed her until he had a replacement.

A court without an heir could be an ugly place. The preference was for an alpha who could do magic, but they were becoming fewer. Very few in the Autumn Court, by Harel's admission.

That left the succession up to anyone and everyone if Illaria was dead. Evidently the situation wasn't dire enough yet for any prospective successors to have her assassinated themselves. Or perhaps they were biding their time. Making sure the blame could be pinned on someone else.

Ryze rubbed his chin. "Where would I go if I was going to keep a low profile?"

"Do you know how to?" I asked. For once I wasn't ribbing him, not exactly. I was genuinely curious as to the answer. He'd tried to be stealthy in the Summer Court, but wasn't successful. Someone like him always stood out, regardless.

"In theory," he agreed. "Keeping a low profile is more Tavian's skill than mine."

We all turned to Tavian.

He shrugged. "I tend to keep to the shadows. And if I can't, I go somewhere everyone sticks out. Places where there are lots of people." He looked thoughtful. "There's a tavern on the corner that's always busy. Fae from all over Jorius converge there. People might not look twice at a woman with hair as bright red as hers."

"Let's try there then," Ryze said. "If we can't find her, we'll be able to find a drink."

Zared muttered something about priorities and trudged along behind us.

I couldn't argue with his sentiment. If there was anything most Fae were good at, it was being patient. Since meeting Khala, that became more difficult.

Unlike Ryze, who seemed to enjoy a life of adventure, I was impatient to put the matter of the lost courts to rest. I was ready to settle down and live my days with Khala and the rest of the pack. Admittedly, I wasn't sure what that would look like. The rest of them were settled here, in the Winter Court. At some point, I'd have to return to the Summer Court.

Thankfully, we were only a portal away. If we were all willing, and I believed we were, we'd find a way.

As Tavian said, the tavern was busy. With the curious name of the 'Dragon and Griffin', a sign hung out the front with both creatures chasing each other around in a circle.

"Are you sure dragons aren't real?" Tavian asked Ryze teasingly.

Ryze rolled his eyes. "They're as real as men with two cocks."

"I once knew a man who had two cocks," Tavian remarked. "And since I know you're all wondering, yes, they both worked. I never could decide if he was blessed or cursed. He could fuck two people at once, but two erections is a lot to handle."

"Only if you have one hand," Ryze said. "Still doesn't make dragons real."

"What do you think, Cavan?" Tavian asked. "Do you think dragons are a myth?"

"As far as I know, they are," I said slowly. "But until recently, you all thought the lost courts were a myth."

Ryze groaned playfully. "Don't encourage him. Otherwise when all of this is over, Tave will want to go searching for them."

I raised an eyebrow at Ryze. "You mean, *you'd* want to go searching for them. You'd lay the blame on Tavian, especially when you don't find any."

Zared snorted a laugh. "That sounds accurate."

Ryze turned to him. "Meaning?"

Zared stopped in the middle of the street. "Meaning Cavan is right. You're only honest when it's in your interest to be. You don't give a shit who you step on, as long as the great Ryzellius gets his way."

Ryze regarded him for a few long moments. "You've spent too much time with Vayne." He didn't deny the accusation. He turned and hurried into the tavern.

Tavian put a hand on Zared's arm. "We shouldn't be arguing with each other. We need each other right now."

Zared didn't shake off Tavian's hand. "I know, but tell me it's not true. You know what he's like."

"Ryze likes to get his way, but his heart is in the right place," Tavian said. "He cares about all of us. Whatever you think, he'd put all of us before himself. He'd also go off and hunt dragons, given half a chance. He'd be the first to admit he likes to live life to the fullest. Now, let's go in and see if we can find Illaria."

Zared nodded and the pair hurried inside. I followed a step or two behind.

The tavern was packed with Fae sitting around tables eating their lunch, or reclining against a wide, timber bar. Here, Autumn Court Fae sat with Summer Court Fae, and Winter with Spring. Most looked like they'd come here on business. They had that air about them, like they were engaged in intense negotiation. Haggling for the best deals, angling for the best goods.

Men and women moved between the tables, collecting empty plates and cups and taking them away to be washed.

There was no sign of Illaria, but Ryze nodded toward the table of Autumn Court Fae and moved to lean against the bar.

That was clearly a cue to Tavian, who slipped over to sit in a chair at the table beside them.

Deciding inconspicuousness would be the best approach, I slipped into a table in the corner. Zared sat beside me, his back to the room.

"I know this can't be easy," I started.

He crossed his arms and gave me a level gaze. "What can't be easy?" He frowned slightly.

"Any of it," I said, albeit unapologetically. "Everything that has happened since you and Khala left the Temple. Finding out what she is. Being a human amongst Fae."

"Having to share my woman with four other men..." He lowered his arms. "Your— what was she to you? Dalyth would have let your people kill me back at that caravan."

Before I could respond to that, he continued, "All because the other High Lords had their heads stuck up their asses so far you didn't think you had any choice but to kidnap innocent women. No offence, but the way you four Fae lead Jorius is shit. You even have a meeting place to resolve differences and you don't use it. What way is that to govern? A fucking ineffective one, that's what. I bet none of you gives a shit that innocent humans get caught up in your schemes."

I sat through his accusations until he ran out of steam and words. Then all I could do was nod.

"You're right. We're disorganised and contentious. We let ambition and suspicion get in the way of matters which should be a higher priority than they become. Two more courts into the equation and the coming centuries will be a challenge."

He flinched. A reminder that he wouldn't be here to see any of it. I was truly sorry for that. If I knew of a way to extend his life like the rest of the Fae, I would do everything in my power to see it fulfilled. For Khala, for Tavian and for him. Perhaps somewhat for myself as well.

In spite of his often abrasive attitude, I was fond of the man. His dedication to Khala was apparent and as strong and solid as my own. I couldn't fail to admire that. Both of us would do anything for her. And *to* her.

For me, the next eighty years would pass in a blink, and then he'd be gone. However, he was here now and I would do what I could to make the most of these years.

"When this is over, we could use your assistance to mediate between us, to find a better way to govern. That should include the human kings. We've all been divided for long enough. It's past time to end the suspicion between not only the courts, but the Fae and humans as well."

In the corner of my eye, I saw Ryze sipping a glass of whiskey. He was watching Tavian, who seemed to be engaged in conversation with the Autumn Court Fae beside him.

I thought Zared might tell me to get fucked. Instead, he nodded. "I'll help in any way I can. If only to stop people like Ryze and Dalyth from using humans." He gave me a look that clearly included me in that.

I nodded to acknowledge the silent accusation. I wouldn't deny it if he ranted and raved at me, but I was relieved he didn't. That wouldn't equate to a low profile.

"Dalyth can no longer harm anyone," I pointed out. "As to your question, what did she mean to me? She was an omega who helped me to gather other omegas. She was ambitious. Probably too much so. She had little regard for humans. She was nothing to me personally. We weren't lovers."

"She wanted you to be," Zared stated.

"I believe so," I agreed. "That was never even likely. If she wasn't an omega, I would have sent her away. She was a tool. A means to an end. One of the few who could block memories. Unfortunately, I needed her."

"Past tense," he said.

"Yes, past tense," I agreed. "Although, as long as the Silent Maidens continue as they are, someone will be needed to block their memories. Other- wise we need to find a way to safely separate the omegas from the others."

He sat forward, his elbows on the table. "Since I'm helping any way I can, let me give you some advice."

I waved for him to go ahead.

"Go to the Silent Maidens and tell them the truth," he said. "When we get Khala back, we can all go. Let the choice be theirs. You owe them that much."

"How do you think Khala would have reacted to the truth?" I asked slowly.

He glanced down at the table, and sighed out his nose. "Not very well, but she still deserved to know. She might have gone with you willingly."

"Would you?" I asked.

He looked back up. "Anywhere she goes, I'd go. If I haven't proved that by now—"

I held up a couple of fingers. "You have. I admire that very much."

He looked surprised. "You admire me?"

I chuckled. "Is that so difficult to believe?"

He shrugged one shoulder. "Maybe. I'm not a king or a High Lord. I'm not even a priest anymore."

"No," I agreed. "You're more than that. You're a member of Khala's pack. That makes you extraordinary. She has impeccable taste."

It was his turn to laugh softly. "You Fae have no modesty at all."

"That is unfortunately true," I conceded. "We are the absolute worst. Fortunately, at the same time, we're the absolute best."

Before he could respond, Tavian appeared at the table beside us.

"I know where Illaria is."

CHAPTER
SIX

KHALA

Not long after dawn, a man came to escort Vayne and I down to breakfast. Neither Dennin nor Ramela were present. One of the serving staff, a woman with bright blue eyes, told us they would speak with us later. She seemed disconcerted, but unwilling to offer any further answers. The sense of urgency about the place lingered, along with one of anticipation. It put me further on edge.

We were left alone after that and no one directed us anywhere in particular, so we decided to make our way back to our room. We were barely out the door of the small dining hall when I realised we were being followed. Not by guards, but by someone or something else.

"We should step apart a little bit, and see if they'll approach," Vayne whispered. His hand hovered near his hip, ready to pull a knife if necessary.

I nodded and stopped to gaze out of one of the narrower slits that passed as windows. Vayne moved away to look out another. He meandered around a corner and out of sight.

A figure shot out a doorway. I found myself pinned to the wall beside the slit. A hand went over my mouth before I could make a sound.

"Shhh, come with me." I recognised Gavil, the scarred griffin rider. He jerked his head towards the room he recently exited.

My whole body was frozen with fear, and the memory of Wornar. The way his hand felt on me. The things he'd done. I thought Cavan's alpha-order suppressed the worst of the trauma, but now it came back in force. My heart raced so hard it hurt. If not for Gavil's cold fingers tight over my lips, I would have screamed. I managed a squeak of fright.

"I'm not going to hurt you, I need to talk," Gavil urged. "Before someone comes." He sounded earnest. His brown eyes were full of sincerity.

512

I glanced up the corridor. Vayne would come barrelling back the moment I asked him through the bond. I asked him to wait, sensing Gavil meant me no real harm. I hoped to the gods I was right.

I nodded once.

"I'm going to take my hand off your mouth, if you promise not to scream."

I nodded again.

He lowered his hand.

"What the—"

"Not here," he said quickly. Again, he jerked his head towards the room. "You don't have to be scared of me. I know I look like a monster, but I promise I'm not one." His voice was hoarse, like he was burnt on the inside too. Something in his tone made me look at him again. Through my fear, I saw a man who was rejected by the people around him. Discarded because of his scars.

"I'll listen to you, but you need to let me move," I said.

"Oh, shit, I'm sorry." He stepped back away from me and waited for me to enter the room before he followed. His body language suggested he was sure I would flee the first chance I got. For that alone, I wouldn't.

Instead, I sent reassurance down the bond and attempted to calm my pounding heart.

"What is this about?" I asked.

He looked up and down the corridor, then closed the door behind us.

"You're an omega," he stated.

"And you're..." I stopped to inhale the scent of him. Frowned. He smelled like nothing I'd smelled before. Beta, but not. Familiar, but at the same time, unfamiliar. The closest I could come to an explanation was that he smelled like a Silent Maiden with her choker on.

"I don't understand." I shook my head. "Are you a beta? So far everyone here I got close enough to smell, is."

"That's precisely what they want you to believe," Gavil said. "Dennin and Ramela will tell you they came here to seek safety from the Court of Shadows, from the seasonal courts. The truth is, they believe alphas and omegas to be lesser than betas. They wanted to eradicate everyone who wasn't a beta. They came here because this was a place they could set up wards."

"Wards against what?" I asked.

"Wards against magic," he whispered. "Wards against those who are not beta. They killed many omegas before they found a way to suppress us."

"You're an omega?" That explained his scent. He smelled like nutmeg and magnolias, but the way they'd smell if you were at a great distance.

He waved at his face with undisguised bitterness. "You can see what they did to omegas. I was a child. Only because my foster mother intervened that they didn't terminate me. Instead, they disfigured me and suppressed my heat."

I tried not to gape. I didn't want to stare, but the idea of anyone doing that to a child was chilling. It didn't matter who or what they were, no one deserved what he must have endured.

"I'm so sorry, that's terrible," I said, my voice rough with sympathy.

He closed his eyes for a moment. "It's the past. Now we are simply suppressed."

I had to push my emotions aside and focus on what he was saying. That was the message he was trying to get to me here. This was about more than what was done to him.

"With wards," I mused. "Like Amethyst." I'd assumed it was the stone, but maybe something was done to them. Some kind of magic. What, or how, I could only guess at. "But you can talk."

He smiled wryly. "The initial wards prevented everyone from talking, so they had to find another way. Now, they can suppress heat without suppressing their voices."

"If they could do that here, they could do that to the Silent Maidens too," I reasoned.

"If they cared to," he agreed. "I fear they prefer a more permanent approach."

"They don't want to destroy the Court of Shadows," I said slowly, horror crept up my spine. "Just the alphas and the omegas?"

"Exactly," he agreed.

"But they don't only exist in the Court of Shadows," I said.

"A thousand years ago, they mostly did. Then the Court of Shadows started to breed with humans. Then the other courts bred with their offspring. Humans reproduce so quickly and live for such a short time, there began to be more and more of them. The Court of Dreams tried to stop it from happening. In the end, they licked their wounds and came here."

"And tamed the griffins so they could ride them," I said. "But betas can't do magic, can they?"

"No, only suppressed omegas and alphas, and only above the wards." He sighed and stalked over to the other side of the room before turning and walking back.

That explained the portals in the sky and the attacks, but not why.

"I—"

I was interrupted by the door opening. Vayne looked inside. He glanced at Gavil like he better not think about touching me, then turned back to me.

"We've been *summoned* by the High Lord and Lady," he said. He looked unimpressed at his wording.

"I must go," Gavil said quickly. "I've taken too long as it is. Thank you for listening to me." He gave me a long look before he hurried out of the room.

"What—" Vayne started.

I shook my head. "I'll explain later." I had to get my head around it first. Why would anyone want to eradicate all omegas and alphas? The gods knew we had our moments, but we weren't all bad. Were we?

"You said we were summoned?"

He grumbled something under his breath. "That's right. Wouldn't want to keep them waiting."

"For someone in authority, you seem to have a problem with people in authority," I teased.

"Because I have enough authority to know most people in authority don't know what the fuck they're doing," he growled. "No offence to Ryze, or Cavan, but it's stupid to choose a High Lord because of who his father was. Or his cousin. I'm Commander of the Winter Court army because I know what the fuck I'm doing. Tavian is Master of Assassins for the same reason. No one gives a shit who our fathers were."

I nodded. "Right." Except Illaria speculated that Tavian was the son of the High Lord of the Court of Dreams. Either she was wrong or Dennin was one hells of a hypocrite. Assuming Dennin was the High Lord in question. Or it may have been his father, making Tavian his brother. Did either of them have a clue about that?

I suspected not. I hadn't had a chance to mention it to Tavian, and he hadn't said anything to me. If he didn't know, then how did Illaria? She hadn't elaborated before she'd slipped away that night. As with so many other things, she left more questions than answers.

"Did they tell us where to go?" I asked.

"Same place as yesterday." Vayne laced his fingers in mine and we walked in what I hoped was the right direction. The Fae did like palaces and castles that were like labyrinths.

"For the record, if they decide to be assholes, I'll tell them where to go. I might only be a beta, but I'm still a badass." He nodded his satisfaction with himself.

"Of course you are," I assured him. The fact he was a beta might hold him in good stead with Dennin and Ramela. If what Gavil said was true, it was better that I was here with him than any of the rest of my pack. Although, that begged the question, did the High Lord and Lady realise I was an omega?

I pulled Vayne to a stop. "Can you tell I'm an omega?"

"Beautiful, I have vivid memories of that heat," he said, looking sly.

"That's not what I meant." I frowned at him. "Can betas smell omegas and alphas?"

He gave me a funny look. "Not...distinctively. I mean, I can smell you. You always smell nice. But you don't smell omega-ish, if that's even a thing. I guess it's a thing, Ryze talks about it. Why?"

"Do I smell different at all?" I pressed.

He hesitated for a moment, then leaned in and sniffed.

"Now you mention it, you do smell slightly different. It's probably all my cum on you." He leaned back and grinned. He looked very pleased with himself.

I suspected his favourite part of the previous night was coming all over my hair. Remembering it now made me feel hot all over again. There was something about warm, sticky cum hanging in strings from my hair, and past my face.

I batted him on the arm. "I had a bath after all that."

"I know, I was in there with you." He gripped my hand again and we resumed walking. "What's with all the questions?"

"I don't know," I admitted. "I'll explain everything when we're alone."

I wasn't sure what to make of it anyway. If he couldn't smell omega on me, then all they knew about me was that I was a Silent Maiden. Any other knowledge about me might be nothing but a guess.

I had a feeling it wasn't that simple. Nothing had been yet.

"I have a feeling about this place," he said. "It looks the opposite of the Court of Shadows. No mist. No rows of skulls smiling at us. No puzzles to get in. No underground tunnels. But I feel like it's a cover for something. Like Tavian smiling before he stabs you in the throat. I wouldn't trust any of the Fae here as far as I could throw them. I know that's saying a lot, since they haven't once encased me in stone. Yet."

"I believe in your instincts," I told him. "There's definitely something off about this place." I'd thought that before I spoke to Gavil. My instincts were also telling me to be very, very careful around here.

I felt for the rest of the pack through the bond and got a sense of them being cagey, but not towards me. Whatever they were up to, I hoped they didn't get themselves into trouble. Especially since Vayne and I weren't there to bail them out. The sooner we were done here and back home, the better.

"Who was your father?" I realised I hadn't asked after he brought up the subject. "And your mother?" Hadn't he mentioned a family business making pottery vases or something?

"That's a story for another day and after a lot more alcohol," he said. "Suffice to say I'm a distant relative of Ryze. Too distant to mention, really. And nothing I'd admit to anyone else. In fact, if you tell anyone I said that, I'll strenuously deny it." His mouth turned down, but his eyes were smiling.

"I won't say a word," I said.

We stepped into the reception room together, my pulse racing.

SEVEN

KHALA

"You must have a great many questions," Ramela started.

"We presume you have a great many answers," Vayne replied. He sat against the back of the couch and crossed his legs at the knees.

Her smile held a menacing edge. Nothing I could put my finger on, or accuse her of, but it made me tense, alert.

"That depends on the questions," Dennin said. "We may not have all the answers you seek."

"Let's start with why the griffins were attacking us." Vayne's tone was blunt, bordering on rude, even for him.

Ramela raised a dainty cup to her lips and sipped before she put it aside on the table between us.

"They weren't precisely attacks," she started.

Vayne snorted. "I beg to fucking differ. I saw that first bolt, what it did to the building in the Summer Court barracks. What the wind did in the Winter Court. The burnt meat Dalyth ended up as, although good riddance to the bitch. And this." He held up his seared sleeve. He seemed the most annoyed about that.

"Any harm caused is regrettable," Ramela said lightly. "Except to the Summer Court woman. However, let me begin at the beginning."

"What a novel idea," Vayne said sarcastically.

I put a hand on his knee. Not to stop him from expressing how he felt, but to remind him he wasn't alone. And to remind myself.

Ramela gave Vayne a look of reproach, but it was Dennin who replied.

"Some of us have the ability to foresee future events."

I nodded. I knew that about them already. His words backed up the suggestion Tavian was related to them in some way.

"Not only that," Dennin continued. "At times we can see those points... Those...crossroads, if you will. Moments which can be altered to set events along a different path." He let the words hang in the air.

"Those attacks," Vayne stuck stubbornly to his term, "were intended to distract us and make us make different decisions?"

"Precisely," Ramela agreed. "In the first instance, we foretold a continuation of the division between the seasonal courts. Indeed, a plan was in place to assassinate a member of the Winter Court and place the blame on the Summer Court."

Vayne leaned forward. "Who?"

"It is of no consequence now," Dennin said. "That path didn't occur."

"No consequence, my ass," Vayne growled. "If someone was trying to assassinate me, Ryze or Tavian, I want to know about it."

"The details aren't always clear," Dennin said apologetically.

"What about the second instance?" I asked. At the time, Tavian and I were making copies of the maps to the lost courts. The rest of the pack was inside the Winter Court Palace, making preparations to go to Havenmoor.

"The assassin followed you to the Winter Court," Ramela explained. "We foresaw her carrying out a variation on her original plan."

"Her..." My lips dropped apart. "Dalyth? You think Dalyth was working against us?"

"It would seem so," Dennin agreed.

"Makes sense to me," Vayne said. "If Ryze and Cavan got along with each other, what influence she had with Cavan would be diminished. If we all weren't working together, we wouldn't have found our way here. Plus, if anyone was up to shit like that, it would be her. She always was a sneaky, ambitious bitch. And she had people who followed her. Assholes who liked to kill humans for sport."

I pressed my lips together. Yes, I'd seen those very Fae, saw them kill the priests.

"So you killed her," I said.

"When the opportunity arose, we took it," Dennin said. "We hoped to remove you and your sister from the situation, but we were unable to do so."

"My sister?" I echoed. "Hycanthe or Jezalyn?" What did either of them have to do with this? When the portal opened, Hycanthe's magic became stronger. She was clearly connected to this court in some way. For the first time, I couldn't bring myself to think of her in a negative light. She was just a woman trying to find her way in this world. A world that ripped both of us out of what we knew and threw us into whirlpool in the centre of a cauldron.

"We're not certain which one," Dennin said. "The visions are unclear. Merely that one is pertinent to us. Thus the last incursion. We needed you all to move away from the mist before it consumed you. Our tactics may have been slightly heavy-handed—"

Vayne snorted. "Slightly? You could have shouted out a warning."

518

"That wouldn't have been enough," Ramela insisted.

"It might have," I said. "But the mist took Hycanthe and Jezalyn anyway. What is it?"

Their reaction to the mention of mist was immediate and telling. Stiffened bodies, wider eyes, faster breaths; as fearful of it as Ryze always was. As the rest of us came to be when we were face-to-face with it. Especially after it took Vayne and me. What would have happened if I hadn't opened a portal to this place?

Ramela and Dennin exchanged a glance. Dannin's throat bobbed as he swallowed. He nodded for Ramela to continue.

"We believe it's a shadow of magic, if you will. Like smoke or steam. A kind of residue. More than that, we don't know.."

"What happens to the people it takes?" Vayne asked.

"We have no answer to that," Ramela admitted. "There have been no visions of either woman since our last incursion. We cannot know if they still live."

I glanced at Vayne. He sensed their presence while he was encased in stone, but he might have imagined it. There was also the possibility he was in contact with their souls on the way to the gods, or the seven hells.

I surprised myself with a flood of emotion at the idea that Hycanthe might be dead. I was genuinely sad over the possibility of Jezalyn's loss. I liked the sweet alpha woman. But Hycanthe...evidently I cared about her more than I realised. When it came down to it, she was still one of my sisters.

I could almost see Vayne wondering if Hycanthe also made a portal away from the mist. It was better he didn't ask, although it seemed unlikely anyone had the answers.

"Have you had any more visions about me?" I directed the question to Dennin. I got the impression he was the one who had the foretellings. Another potential confirmation of his relation to Tavian.

"Or me," Vayne said. He seemed mollified knowing that if anyone was trying to assassinate him, they were already dead.

The idea Dalyth wanted to kill him made me dislike her even more than I already had. Which was saying something, because the woman had got my back up even more than Hycanthe. I'd always hold a grudge for her enjoyment at putting the block on Zared's memories.

"I have not," Dennin replied. "It would seem events have caught up to themselves, in a manner of speaking. We have changed much of the past, but now we can only alter the present by the things we say and do now."

"Which is what, exactly?" Vayne asked. "You wanted us here for a reason. What is the reason?"

"It was foretold that the return of the two courts to Jorius relied upon a Fae with the blood of our court, one with blood of the Court of Shadows and one whose blood transcends courts." Ramela picked up her tea and took another sip. "A good many have the blood of our court, of course."

I nodded. Judging by the shared hair colour, they had that in abundance.

"We believe your blood transcends the courts," Ramela said.

I knew that already. I at least had a combination of magics. I suspected this was less about blood than it was about the type of magic wielded by the omega or alpha. The specifics weren't relevant right now.

"We hoped to draw out someone from the Court of Shadows," Dennin said. "Someone who could play their part." His mouth turned downward.

"Why do you need them?" Vayne demanded. "What are they supposed to do? You don't look stuck here to me. And the other court... They can leave any time they want to."

"In ones and twos, they can leave," Dennin agreed. "Or they could, before the mist encroached. They may not realise it yet, but it keeps them from leaving entirely. Just as the wards around our court keep us from leaving. They were never intended to be removed. It will only take a great act of magic to remove them."

Ramela shuddered at the word magic. She looked like she'd be content to use any method necessary, as long as it didn't involve magic. Why was she so scared of it?

Even as I had that thought, I had the answer. Because, at times, magic was scary as fuck. It could be used for many things, including killing.

I tried not to think too hard about the magic that was the alpha-order. That was evil in the hands of the wrong alpha.

I wouldn't dwell on him now. The discomfort of having Gavil's body pressed against mine had faded significantly. I still felt slightly uncomfortable at the thought of it, but nowhere near as panicked.

"So you got yourself stuck here and now you want help to get out," Vayne stated.

"That is a simplified version of the situation, yes," Dennin said. "Just like the decision to live in caverns underground was made by the previous High Lady, and regretted by the present, the decision to come here has proven to be unfortunate."

"You seem to know a lot about them," Vayne remarked.

"We have our spies in the seasonal courts, just as you have them in each other's," Dennin said unapologetically. "They have had occasion to speak to those from the Court of Shadows. Their dissatisfaction with their current situation was made clear."

"Why not ask them for help?" I asked. The situation was all too similar to the hostility between Ryze and Cavan when I first met them. Fae were good at a lot of things, but their communication could definitely use some improvement. All right, that was an understatement; their communication sucked.

"Past animosity suggests they would decline," Ramela said. "In truth, we believe they are unaware of our vulnerability. They would assume if we asked for help, we were setting a trap for them."

If Gavil was to be believed, that assumption would be right.

"All they want is to live out in the sun," I said. "They wanted us to speak to you on their behalf, to work out a peaceful resolution that everyone could be happy with. I think, if you ask for help, they'll be happy to give it."

Happy might be a bit of a stretch. Unless I was mistaken, it would be someone like Lyra, whose magic would help bring down the wards. Happy was definitely not a word I would associate with the alpha woman.

Dennin glanced at Ramela. "If it's within your power to bring someone from that court here, they'd be welcome." His expression suggested they be as welcome as a pimple on his ass, but they had little choice in the matter.

"And then what?" Vayne asked. "You all live happily ever after?"

"That is our intention," Ramela said. "This land, Brentius, looks like paradise. In some ways, it is." She placed her now empty cup back on the table and sat back in her seat.

"It's better than a fucking cave," Vayne said.

"Indeed, but it's not without its limitations," Ramela said. "Including the difficulty interacting with other Fae. We haven't been part of our own people for a thousand years. It's past time to end the isolation."

Her words were punctuated by the ripple of the ground under our feet. The whole building started to shake.

CHAPTER
EIGHT
CAVAN

"I thought you said you knew where she was." Ryze directed the question to Tavian.

"This is where they told me she was," Tavian argued. "They had no reason to lie to me."

"Unless they didn't want you to know where she was, or they really didn't know at all," Zared said. "They wouldn't be the first Fae to lie." His gaze slid across me and Ryze, before returning to Tavian.

I wanted to tell him the lingering animosity wouldn't help anyone, but making a comment would only perpetuate it.

"I'm usually good at telling when people lie," Tavian said. He stepped into the abandoned tannery. "It's possible this was her last known location." He glanced into a couple of empty barrels. "She's not in there at least."

"That's good to know." Ryze followed Tavian and glanced into the barrels himself. "It's possible she returned to the Autumn Court."

"Highly unlikely." I also glanced into the barrels. They contained only patches of damp right at the bottom. Nothing which might be blood or dead Fae. Rather, they smelled like nothing more innocuous than the substances used to tan leather.

Nothing in the entire tannery smelled like anything freshly dead. Although the smell was so strong, the gods only knew what it might cover.

"The last time we saw Harel, he was unhappy with her. I have no reason to believe she'd be welcome back there anytime soon." He was well aware his daughter had told us where she thought the key to Nallis was. Where he kept it before he became suspicious that she might betray him.

"That might be what they both want you to believe," Zared suggested.

I shrugged. "Potentially, but doubtful. Harel very much believed the lost

522

courts didn't exist, and she believed they did. According to Khala, Illaria was convinced he'd have her executed if she spoke out against his beliefs again."

"I'd love to see the expression on his face when he discovers how wrong he was," Ryze said gleefully. He rubbed his hands together.

"Me too," Tavian agreed. "Almost as much as I'd like to see Wornar's face when he learns nothing he did stopped us. That would come right before I stick a knife between his ribs."

The further we moved into the tannery, the more and more apparent it was that the place was empty. That is, currently empty. Here and there were signs of recent habitation. A fire that was still slightly warm. A plate and cup drying on a table beside a barrel of water.

"If she was here, she's not here now," Ryze concluded.

Not long ago, I would have responded to that with something sarcastic, or pointed out how obvious his statement was. Now, I didn't bother to antagonise him, especially with such low-lying fruit as that.

"I don't think she's coming back," I said instead. "We haven't seen any sign of personal items. Wherever she went, she went there recently, but with no intention of returning." I expected a sarcastic comment from Ryze, but it didn't come either. Perhaps he was as weary of fighting as I was. Petty squabbles weren't worth the time. Not when Khala was the gods knew where. I'd tried several more times to make a portal to her, but with no success whatsoever. I wouldn't give up trying until she was in my arms.

"Why now?" Zared asked. When we turned to him he put out his hands. "She's been here this long, why leave just when we're looking for her? "

"Because she knew we'd come looking?" Tavian suggested.

"How?" Zared shook his head. "We didn't even know until just before we did."

"Unless she has visions," I said. "Or unless one of us is in contact with her." My gaze scanned all three of them.

They regarded me back.

"None of us is in contact with her," Ryze said. "I don't think she has visions, but she definitely has contacts. She always seems to know where we'll be, and when we'll be there."

"She said she worked with other people," Tavian said. "I put out feelers with my own contacts, but haven't been able to find out any more than that. Whoever they are, they're almost as good as me at keeping secrets."

"That's saying something," Ryze said admiringly.

"It definitely is," Tavian agreed. "In this case, it doesn't help us much. We could use one of Ryze's arrows, with implicit instructions written beside them, right now."

"The lack of giant arrow is very inconvenient," Ryze remarked.

I snorted softly, before moving away from them and taking another look around. I fervently hoped this wasn't another puzzle we had to solve. I'd had more than enough of those for one lifetime. I suspected this was simply a case of Illaria moving on, the timing coincidental.

I pressed my finger against my bottom lip. If I was the disinherited heir of a court, where would I go? An heir who knew about Havenmoor. Who knew about the lost courts. Who said she was working with others and had tried to support me when no one else would listen. I suspected she knew we went to Nallis, and she must have known we returned. People often had little better to do than gossip about the comings and goings of High Lords, especially when two were consorting with one another.

Had she concluded we'd found one of the courts? Assuming she had, what would her next move be? Would she go and speak to whomever she worked with? Would she go to Nallis herself to see if she could find what we found?

I sighed. No, she wouldn't have done either of those things.

I turned to the others. "I think I know where she went. Where would you go if you wanted to say I told you so?" Ryze and Tavian mentioned it only minutes earlier.

"I don't usually have to go very far to do that," Ryze said lightly. He smiled at Tavian.

"Funny, I was about to say the same thing," Tavian said. He returned Ryze's smile.

"You think she went to the Autumn Court?" Zared said, completely unsmiling. "Just to tell her father he was wrong?"

"I have a feeling she's there to do more than that," I admitted.

"Anarchy is contagious." Tavian seemed pleased at that.

"You think she's gone there to overthrow Harel?" Ryze asked. He rubbed his chin. "If she was going to do it, now is as good a time as any. If nothing else, it will distract him from getting in our way."

"Yes, but if she has gone there to stage a coup, we can't go there to ask where she thinks the Court of Dreams is," I pointed out. "We're no closer to reaching Khala."

I was silent for a moment, then turned to Zared. "In theory, we can't open a portal to a place we've never been. Have you got any idea where she might have been that we don't know about?"

"I've thought a lot about it," he admitted. "I've gone over every conversation we had. I can't think of a single place except where she lived before she was a Silent Maiden. You'd probably have a better idea of that than I would."

He was right, I knew exactly where Alivia was. I kept tabs on her after I exiled her from the Summer Court.

"Not the Court of Dreams," I said. "She didn't have visions, so she didn't find her way there through those."

"This is probably a stupid question," Zared said slowly. "Is it possible to open a portal to a place I saw a picture of?" In a rush he added, "I remember feeling through the bond that the place she ended up seemed familiar somehow."

"You're right," Ryze said thoughtfully. "I got that from her too. It was familiar, but at the same time, not. Like she'd never been there, but she'd seen it. She was thinking back about... Something."

"There was a triptych of paintings on the wall in her bedroom back at the temple," Zared said. "Grassland, forest—"

"And a castle," Tavian finished for him. "She portalled to wherever that painting portrayed. That's where she is." He looked excited.

"Have you got any idea where?" I asked Zared. "Where was the place in the paintings?"

"I have no idea," he said, looking downcast. "She told me she asked the priestesses a couple of times, but none of them knew. There's no way that was there coincidentally, was there?"

"When was the last time anything coincidental happened?" Ryze asked rhetorically. "I'm starting to think there's a reason for every little thing we do, right down to what type of whiskey I prefer." He frowned as though trying to discern whether whiskey tied into everything else or not. After a couple of moments, he gave up.

"What else has happened that can't be coincidental?" Tavian asked. "Maybe we're missing something here."

I ran through everything that happened in the last few weeks specifically.

"Of every group of Silent Maidens, three transition," I said slowly. "None of them seem to have anything to do with this. They're ready to defend themselves and those around them, but I don't think they're the key. Nor are the five who don't. Perhaps that is coincidental."

"Is it a coincidence that Khala is the daughter of your former betrothed?" Ryze asked.

"I don't think it's pertinent, but it is lucky," I said. "She could have been my daughter instead." Thank the gods she wasn't. That would have been a thousand kinds of awkward. Especially having to fend off men like Ryze when they sniffed around her.

"You could have been my father instead of my daddy," Tavian joked. He wiggled his eyebrows.

I snorted softly. His words made my balls slightly heavier.

"Is it a coincidence that Zared didn't die in that caravan?" Ryze asked.

Zared looked confused. "I don't think I have anything to do with any of it. No more than anyone else. Is it a coincidence Vayne went to the Court of Dreams with her?"

I cocked my head slightly. "It can't be." I'd seen the mist curl itself around her and Vayne. We all tried to reach out to them both, but they were yanked away between one heartbeat and the next. "Why him?"

"Why not him?" Tavian asked.

"He's not an alpha, or an omega," I said. "He has no magic."

"Apart from his personality," Ryze remarked.

"Apart from that," I agreed with a slight smile. He was certainly an interesting man. Grumpy as fuck, but loyal and intelligent. If he wasn't dedicated to Ryze, I'd steal him away to command my army.

"If he has no magic, he's no threat to them," Zared pointed out. "But the mist pulled Khala out of my arms. Why not take me? I have no magic either."

"No offence, but you're a human," I said. "Believe it or not, some Fae don't much care for humans." I knew he was well aware of that fact. That was yet another thing I wanted to fix. It seemed like that list grew ever longer, even when I took points off it. For every problem we solved, two more popped up in their place.

"No shit," he muttered. "But why take anyone with her at all?"

I shook my head slowly. "I have no idea. It could be nothing more than the mist thinking they were both a tasty snack. We're assuming someone is in control of it, but I don't think that's the case. The mist is a mindless entity that likes to eat, or at least steal, Fae."

"That might mean I'm safe to go there," Zared said. "Now, who's going to open a portal to Havenmoor? It seems to me, we have a triptych to take a good, hard look at."

Before any of us could respond, a portal opened right beside us.

CHAPTER
NINE

KHALA

Vayne threw himself over me as the ground beneath us dipped and rose.

Ramela's cup slid off the table and shattered on the floor. The glass in the windows rattled and cracked, sending shards flying.

I threw a hand over my face to protect my eyes. I tried to grab some magic to make a wall of ice, or...something. Anything to protect us. I couldn't reach a drop of it. It wasn't even out of reach. It just... Wasn't there.

Gavil said the court had suppressed magic. He was right. I couldn't access it at all.

I forced myself not to freak out, even when the shaking became worse. I was sure my bones were going to be rattled apart.

"Fucking hells," Vayne growled. He gripped my shoulders so tight it hurt, but I didn't make a sound.

Smoke filled the air, making my eyes sting and water.

"We need to get out of here," Dennin shouted.

"No shit." Vayne pulled me off the couch with him, and tucked my head down. We staggered out the door after Dennin and Ramela.

The smoke was thicker here. Thicker still further we ran.

"It's like the fucking mist," Vayne said.

I glanced up. "Are you sure it's only smoke?" I dashed tears off my face with the back of my hand.

"I wouldn't assume anything." He pulled me forward, holding me tighter as the building shook more violently. "If we die here, I love you."

"I love you too," I said back. "But we're not going to die here." I hoped.

Dennin and Ramela stopped so suddenly we almost ran into the back of them.

"We can't go this way," Dennin shouted.

The ground had cracked open in the middle of the corridor, leaving a huge gap. Too far to jump. Too far, I presumed to drop to whatever was below this level. I couldn't make out whatever that was, between the smoke and the darkness below.

We turned and hurried back the other way.

"Where's the nearest exit?" Vayne called over his shoulder.

The ground shook again and I clung to his arm. Chunks of stone from the ceiling started to break away and fall around us.

Before either of them could respond, the ceiling cracked and fell on Dennin and Ramela. At the same time, the floor beneath them gave way, taking them down with it.

I caught a glimpse of shock and fear on their faces and then they were gone.

Another gaping hole slanted across the building.

"Fuck," I muttered. I stood staring at where they were just standing. I blinked, unable to believe what I saw. They were right there and then...

"I wish," Vayne replied. "Fucking would be better than this bullshit. Come on, we'll need to find our own way out."

The gap behind us was widening, the floor falling away as though chasing us.

Now would be a really good time to be able to use magic, but there was still nothing there. I was going to be pissed off if I died here because of that.

"I think we came in this way." I pointed down a side corridor.

"They all look the same to me, but it's as good a direction as any."

We staggered down past the narrow window slits, all but feeling our way by the time we got to a wide entrance hall.

The smoke was so thick, I felt like it was coating my lungs, making it hard to breathe. We both started coughing.

"I think I found a door— Fuck." Vayne grunted.

"What?" I asked.

"It's locked. We're going to have to kick the fucking thing down. Stand back a bit."

I took a step or two away.

He raised his booted foot and slammed it hard against the lock. The door didn't budge. He kicked again and again, until it finally began to give way.

"Just one more—" He kicked and the door flew open. He flew through it and disappeared.

The entryway was flooded with light, but the smoke was thicker than ever.

"Vayne?" I called out. My hands in front of me, I felt for the doorway. I found the door frame and moved slowly past it and outside.

"Vayne?" I called out again. The only response was shouting coming from other parts of the castle. All muffled by the smoke.

I shouted his name out several more times, but the smoke kept throwing my voice back at me.

I walked carefully, looking for holes in the ground he might have fallen into. I felt for him through the bond. He was there on the other end, but I couldn't tell where. I wasn't even sure if he was hurt or lost. He was just...alive somewhere, somehow.

I kept moving, hoping the smoke would thin as I made my way away from the building. And hoping like hells I didn't fall down the hill. Was that what happened to Vayne? I didn't think so. He had to be here somewhere.

Every so often, I called out his name. If it wasn't for the bond, I'd assume he met the same fate as Dennin and Ramela. I presumed they were both dead. If the ceiling falling didn't kill them, the drop would have. What would that mean for the Court of Dreams? I could only guess at how many people agreed with Gavil. Was it possible they were behind whatever was going on?

As if to punctuate my thoughts, the ground shook again. I put my arms out to either side to keep from falling, fingers splayed. Someone not far from me screamed. Female, by the sound of it.

I turned towards the sound and stepped carefully.

"Hello? Is anyone there?" I called out tentatively. As soon as I did, I wished I hadn't. If this was some kind of attack, it might be better if the attackers didn't know where I was. They might mistake me for an enemy. Hells, depending on who they were, I might *be* the enemy.

I tripped over something and almost fell to my knees. I caught myself at the last moment and glanced down.

A woman lay on the ground, eyes open and staring, golden hair fanned around her head. I couldn't see what killed her, but she was definitely dead.

Was she the one who screamed?

I crouched down and brushed hair off her cheek. She was still warm. She must have died only minutes earlier. I gently closed her eyes.

"I'm sorry I couldn't do anything for you," I whispered. What could I have done? I had no idea, it seemed like the thing to say.

In case whatever killed her was still nearby, I rose and hurried off through the smoke.

I tried to orient myself. I recalled seeing a road leading up the hill to the castle. If I could find that, I could get down to the forest and grassland. The smoke might not be so thick down there. Better yet, it might not be there at all.

I walked slowly, gradually heading downhill, but across at the same time. Sooner or later, I'd find the road. Unless the gods decided to fuck with me. Since they seemed to enjoy doing that, I walked more carefully, while at the same time, moving as quickly as I could.

I kept my senses open for sounds and smells, anything that would give me a clue to where I was and where to go. And where Vayne was.

The smoke didn't let up, but the smell faded. It became less acrid, but thicker. This wasn't smoke anymore. It was mist. How was it here, in this place? Was it also hungry for Fae? Had it taken Vayne?

Had it somehow followed me here? When I opened the portal, it might have found a way to slip in with Vayne and me. If that was the case, I was responsible for at least three deaths. Judging by the eerie silence, more than that.

I started to get the feeling I was alone here, in the middle of a white wall of nothing. A heavy cloud of mist.

"Well this sucks," I said out loud to myself.

"Yes, it fucking does." Vayne's voice came out of the mist right before I ran into him. "I've been looking everywhere for you." He folded his arms around me and pulled me to his chest.

I checked through the bond to make sure it really was him before pressing myself against him and inhaling his scent.

"You disappeared," I said. "I was starting to think—"

"You can't get rid of me that easily." He drew his head back and kissed me.

I kissed him back, my tongue skating across his lips. "Lucky I don't want to get rid of you." My words were muffled by his mouth. "What happened to you?"

He shrugged against me. "I kicked the fucking door in and then I couldn't find you. But I found them."

"Them?" I asked. Who...

I tilted my head to the side and looked past him. My eyes widened.

Standing behind him were Hycanthe and Jezalyn, their arms around each other.

"You're alive," I said. I untangled myself from him just enough to give each a one-armed hug. "How are you here?"

"We don't even know where here is," Jezalyn said. "One minute we were outside Nallis, the next we were bumping into Vayne. He said we're in the Court of Dreams. How is that even possible?"

"What did you do?" Hycanthe demanded. "Wherever we go, you somehow turn up and tip everything on its head."

"I'm glad to see you too," I said drolly. "Can you use magic here?"

"Of course I..." She stopped suddenly.

"It's all right if—" Jezalyn started.

Hycanthe interrupted. "No. I *can't*. Not because I'm not able to. It feels like there is none. What the hell is going on?" She sounded as frustrated and powerless as I felt. Maybe we should be used to that by now, but I, for one, wasn't. I doubted I ever would be. I knew her well enough to know she wouldn't either.

"I don't know," I said. I quickly told them what Gavil said and what I felt.

"Whenever the portal opened, your magic got stronger, so we know you have Court of Dreams blood," I added slowly.

"We need someone with Court of Shadows blood to undo the wards," Jezalyn said.

"Khala," Hycanthe said simply.

I shook my head. "My mother was from the Summer Court, my magic was from the Winter Court, because of my heat."

"And somewhere in there, you have Court of Shadows blood," Hycanthe insisted. "According to Cavan, people thought their magic was from the gods. How else would you explain your ability to bring those fish back to life?"

My lips dropped apart. "You knew?"

"Of course I knew," she scoffed. "You didn't think I believed *I* brought them back, did you?"

I had thought that. I should have realised she wasn't fooled. She might be a burr in my ass at times, but she wasn't stupid. I wasn't convinced she was right about my heritage, but at this point, it was the only lead we had.

"So, if we have all the blood we need to, all we need to do is find the wards and we can shut them the fuck down," Vayne reasoned. "How hard can that be?"

"Without being able to see more than a metre or two in front of us, maybe very hard," Hycanthe said.

"We can do it," Jezalyn said with complete conviction.

"We might have to do it," I said. "If we don't, we can't open a portal. And if we can't do that, we're stuck here unless a griffin happens by."

We all looked skyward, but there was no sign of anything but more mist. The sun was nothing more than a ball of light in the haze.

"We better start looking," Vayne said. He took my hand and I grabbed Jezalyn's. She laced her fingers tightly in Hycanthe's hand.

In a chain, we carefully made our way through the mist.

CHAPTER
TEN

VAYNE

I've done some bullshit things in my life, but this was close to the top of the list. The rest usually involved Ryze dragging Tavian and I into some stupid adventure that somehow didn't result in us getting killed. That included trying to save the Silent Maidens from Cavan and Dalyth. I still couldn't get my head around that whole fucked up situation. Especially the part where Cavan ended up part of Khala's pack. I'd do anything for her, to make her happy, but I wouldn't rule out giving her the side eye a few more times before I accepted his role in our lives.

To my surprise, I actually missed Ryze and Tavian. Knowing Ryze, he would have found the wards by now, and Tavian would have kept us laughing the entire time. Or the other way around. I would have shared my honest opinion as we went, like I always did.

Instead, I kept a tight grip on Khala's hand, eyes scanning the ground in front of me. Every so often, I glanced back to make sure the other two women were still with us. I wasn't the biggest fan of Hycanthe, she reminded me too much of myself, but if we lost them, we'd have to back-track and look for them. That might be an impossible task given the thick fucking mist.

It was impossible to see very far in front of us, but it would have been good for just that—fucking. If it wasn't for Hycanthe and Jezalyn, I might stop for a break and make Khala suck my cock. I can say many things about the woman, including how willing she always was and how amazing her mouth was. Thinking about her made me hard.

Maybe we could lose the other two women for a little while. Surely they wouldn't mind.

Unfortunately, I'm a realist. I didn't want to have to find them if we lost them, and I didn't want to be in this gods forsaken mist a second longer than I had to.

"What are we looking for?" Khala asked. "I'm guessing there won't be an arrow here either?"

"I'm guessing not," I agreed. "I don't know what we are looking for, but I think we'll know when we find it."

"How?" Hycanthe asked.

"I don't know that either," I said with a grunt. "You and Khala are the ones who can use magic. Why don't you tell me?"

That shut her up for a while. Me too, to be honest. Right now, the best thing we could do would be to listen and keep our eyes open. I'd spent most of my life as a soldier, but my tracking skills were as good as anyone's.

Those skills were what made me stop so quickly I didn't know I was going to until I did.

I pulled Khala around back behind me and gestured with my spare hand for everyone to be quiet. We all fell still as statues, unfortunately reminding me of being stuck in that stone in the Court Of Shadows.

I managed to contain a shiver at that crappy memory. That sucked harder than most things I'd done in the last two hundred or so years. Especially that fucking itch.

Something crunched in front of us. Crunched again. Slow, deliberate footsteps. Moving carefully but not concerned if anyone heard. Nothing says suspicious like someone who doesn't care if we knew they're there.

I swapped Khala's hand over to my other, and slowly slid my knife out of its sheath. I scanned the mist for any sign of movement. Anything that might give away whoever was there.

I caught a glimpse, a flash of something. There was definitely someone there.

I moved forward slowly, silently. Watching for further movement.

There it was again. A hint of dark fabric, maybe a hand.

My knife in front of me, I stepped forward again. Tentatively I called out. "Who's there?"

A second later, a face appeared, followed by a body.

"What the—" I lowered my knife.

"Rijal." Khala spoke his name as she exhaled. "What are you doing here?"

That was a good question. If he was here, did that mean the rest of the pack was too? No, if they were, Khala would have told me.

He was about to speak out loud, until he saw her. For whatever reason, he wasn't allowed to talk out loud in front of an omega. I presumed that meant he couldn't talk in front of two of them. Not that any of us would tell on him, but whatever. If that was the Court of Shadows custom, then who was I to question it, even if I thought it was strange.

He started signing in Silent Maiden hand language instead.

Khala interpreted.

"After we were taken by the mist, the others went back to the Winter Court. Ryze made a portal."

Rijal didn't look happy as he explained that bit.

I understood that. Portals were disconcerting, to say the least. Useful, but not my favourite mode of transport. I preferred my own two feet, or a horse. Still, if I had to choose between a portal and the back of a griffin, I'd choose a portal all day, every day.

"Vernissa sent Rijal back to the mist to look for us. He told them what happened with Willum and Jistun. He brought great shame on himself. The High Lady was disappointed at his actions."

"So she sent her own son away because he made a mistake," I concluded. All right, he and his co-conspirators pulled knives on us, but they only did it because they were scared to leave the caverns. Sending him out into the shitty mist was a fucked up thing to do, if you asked me.

It was probably better I wasn't High Lord, because I never wanted to make decisions like that. I preferred to punish my men and women by making them clean toilets and other, similar nasty things. Not potentially sending them to a pointless death. Ironic, given that's what war usually resulted in. Of course, it was my job to make sure those deaths weren't pointless or numerous.

"He says he earned his punishment," Khala translated. "Shame seems to be a big part of their court. Anyway, then he ended up here. He was trying to draw the mist's attention so it could end his shame."

"He was stomping around so he could get killed?" Hycanthe asked, disbelieving.

Khala glanced at her. "He considers it appropriate punishment for his rebellion. Fortunately, he found us instead. He can redeem himself by helping us find the wards."

Rijal perked up at her words. He signed something quickly.

"He says he doesn't know if that will be his redemption, but he's willing to help us and start working towards it." She hesitated for a moment. "He also says I own him now."

I snorted a laugh. "He can come with us, but we don't do owning people around here. Not like that anyway." I gave Khala a grin.

"That's great," Jezalyn said. "I'm glad we found each other. We could have been wondering about for days."

"We still might be," Hycanthe said, but in a gentler tone than she used for the rest of us.

"We won't be," I said firmly. "If we keep heading in a straight line, sooner or later we'll find the wards, or the edge of the bubble."

Rijal signed something else, his hand gestures moving quickly, excitedly.

"If she owns you, can she command you to talk out loud?" I grumbled.

He looked horrified and hastily shook his head. Instead, he went on signing.

"He said he walked until he couldn't walk anymore," Khala said. To Rijal she asked, "What do you mean by that?"

He frowned and signed again.

"He doesn't know. He tried to keep walking but the mist wouldn't let him. I don't think it was the mist. Rijal, which way was it?"

Rijal signed again. His hands moved so quickly, at times they were a blur. Strange how different the symbols were to those used by Fae who couldn't hear, such as my sister. If they used a universal language, I could have followed better. Since they didn't, all I could do was listen.

"He doesn't know, but it was close," she said. "He came from this direction, so with any luck, that's where it is."

"Because no one has ever been led astray by luck before," Hycanthe said.

Khala looked ready to snap at Hycanthe.

I could just imagine what she was going to say. Something along the lines of, "Do you have a better idea?"

Since Hycanthe clearly didn't, there was no point having that argument. I had to commend Khala for her restraint.

And since I was the commander here, I took command. "We're going this way." I indicated the way Khala had.

Jezalyn took Rijal's hand in her spare one and we went on walking through the relentless fucking mist.

Not being able to see very far was starting to get on my last nerve. I'm the first to admit I'm not the soul of patience, but this was getting ridiculous. Although, I admit to being relieved the rest of the pack made their way home safely. I never would have heard the end of it if Ryze didn't. Not that he ever listened to my advice if I tried to keep him safe. He was a stubborn asshole. A bit like me at times.

While we walked, Khala spoke to Rijal. "What do you know of the mist?"

He signed back awkwardly while clinging to Jezalyn's hand. Again, Khala interpreted.

"He says it's punishment from the gods."

"What for?" I asked over my shoulder.

"He doesn't know. He said the mist swallows his people if too many go out at once. The gods must want the court to stay in the caverns."

"That was what Dennin and Ramela said," I remarked. "That the mist wouldn't let them leave. It seems to me like a harmless annoyance right now. Maybe people left the caverns and decided not to go back." I wouldn't have, if I got away from that shithole.

"They would bring great shame on themselves if they abandoned their court," Khala said.

"I'm sure that's what Vernissa wanted them to think," I said. Call me cynical, but she seemed to like being in control over her people. Not in the same way Ryze or Cavan were. Not even the same as Harel was or Thiron had been.

Instilling superstitious ideas into people's heads was worse than just being an asshole. Making people scared of gods and monsters was reprehensible.

On the other hand, if they were to be believed, people leaving the Court of Shadows would have fallen victim to the Court of Dreams. In the end, maybe all she was doing was what she had to do to keep her people safe. Or maybe she believed her own bullshit.

If I hadn't been dragged through the mist myself, I would have thought she was completely full of it. As it was, I figured there had to be a better explanation for it than simply punishment for leaving. It was more likely to be some fucked up kind of magic. Magic had a way of messing with things when it shouldn't.

We kept walking carefully for what felt like an hour, maybe more. I gradually became aware of a strange shift in the air. Something I couldn't put my finger on at first. Everything looked the same. It smelled the same. I took a moment to listen and couldn't detect any new sounds. And yet, something was different.

"You feel that too," Khala stated.

"I'm no expert, but it feels like a fuck ton of magic," I said. Only magic had that way of making my skin crawl. It made me want to climb inside myself and never come out.

"I'm guessing we found the edge of the bubble," she said.

Half a second later, the world exploded in a blast of pure agony.

ELEVEN

Vayne's hand was ripped out of mine. He was picked up off his feet and thrown through the air. He disappeared into the mist, before landing heavily with a crunch.

"Vayne!"

All but dragging the others, I raced through the thickened air and dropped to my knees beside him. His arm and leg were twisted, bone gaping out of his thigh. His head lay at an odd angle, as though his neck was snapped. His skin was paler than usual. Breathing more shallow.

He was alive, but barely.

"We need to get that ward down, now," I snapped. The only thing that was going to stop me from losing him was magic. If we didn't get the ward down in time...

"Jezalyn, Rijal, stay with him." I glanced up at them both, silently beseeching them to take care of him.

Jezalyn knelt down beside me. She looked me straight in the eyes with a steady gaze.

"We'll look after him," she promised. "You two go and do what you need to do. We'll all be right here."

Her alpha scent was suppressed, but it was enough to soothe me. That and her words.

For once, Hycanthe didn't bristle as Jezalyn gave me attention. Not even when Jezalyn leaned over and gave me a quick hug. She even let me take her hand and lead her back to the edge of the bubble.

"Who's to say it won't throw us too?" She sounded scared.

"It might," I agreed. "I have to take the risk. I can't let him die." I wiped a tear off my cheek. "If we don't do this, I don't think any of us will get out of here alive."

I thought she might argue, but she nodded. "If it was Jezalyn, I'd risk everything too."

I managed a faint, forced smile. "I know you would. Love has a way of making us do things we otherwise wouldn't do."

Like bonding five, incredible men. I'd only told two of them I loved them. When we got out of here, I was going to tell the other three. I wasn't sure when I'd fallen in love with Ryze, Tavian or Cavan, but I had. A long time ago, if I was honest with myself. That was yet another reason to succeed now.

"Just in case we don't make it through this, I'm sorry for being a bitch," she said. "I was envious of your confidence, and the way people are drawn to you. I always wanted to be more like you."

I didn't think anything could surprise me at this point, but her words did.

"I'm nothing special," I said with a shrug. "I could have tried harder to be nice to you too."

She smiled wryly. "I'm sure you could, but I didn't make it easy. Now, are we going to bring down these wards or not?"

"Let's do it." I gripped her hand.

We stepped forward, our palms outstretched, both trembling with anticipation and fear. The magic could embrace us, or it could kill us.

"I feel like it's right in front of me," she said. "I don't know, but I feel like we need to touch it at the same time."

"And just like that, we're back to the puzzles," I said with a sigh. "It has been a theme up until now, so we might as well try." I could feel it too, on the edge of my skin.

"On three?" she asked.

I nodded. "On three."

We spoke together, in unison.

"One."

"Two."

"Three."

When our palms pressed the magic, sparks lit up around our hands.

"We're not dead," she remarked.

"That's a fucking bonus," I replied. Magic rushed into me like a flood.

"Do you feel that?" I said, in awe.

"It feels like it knows me," she said in the same tone. "Like it's recognising me."

"Exactly," I agreed. "The question is, will it obey?"

"Let's not give it a choice," she said.

I glanced over as she closed her eyes. An expression of pure concentration came over her face. I'd never seen her like this. If this didn't bond two people, nothing would.

I turned my attention back to the magic and closed my eyes.

Images tumbled through my mind. Memories, visions, pasts and possible futures. Most of it was a blur, but now and then I saw faces. No one I recognised, although one or two looked familiar. A woman with my hair and Ryze's eyes. A young man who looked strikingly like both Hycanthe and Jezalyn. Another who looked like Gavil, but without the scars. A woman who looked to be about thousand years old. Another young, a baby in her arms.

I realised this was the magic of the Court of Dreams. All the foresight, tangled in a web of thought. Past, present and future blended into one.

At the edge of my mind was a tug of a different kind of magic. Lightning bolts and whirlwinds. Beginning lives and ending them.

Court of Shadows magic.

Here and there were hints of heat and cold, frost and flame. Buds and leaves that turned when the weather changed.

And something else. Something I couldn't quite put my finger on. Something I'd have to think about later.

The magic called to me and I bent it to my will. Bit by bit, I tore down the bubble, dismantled the wards, shattered the gilded cage around the Court of Dreams until nothing was left but a tiny spark of magic.

Then it was gone too.

The mist around us didn't disappear immediately, but rather slowly, gradually floated away. Patches lingered here or there, but mostly the air cleared in a matter of minutes.

I lowered my hand and exhaled.

"That was incredible," Hycanthe said. She actually pulled me in for a hug. "All that magic. I can feel it all now. I'm not blocked off from it anymore. And I can heal Vayne."

"Do it," I said, choked with emotion. "Please."

I followed her back to him at a trot, clinging to the bond like it was a lifeline.

"You did it," Jezalyn said. "Good girls. I'm so proud of you both."

Her words warmed my omega heart. I smiled, then dropped to my knees beside her.

Carefully, I took Vayne's hand in mine. "He's so faint," I said softly. His presence through the bond was little more than a whisper. A faint hint of the vibrant, grumpy Fae. If I lost him now...

"I've got him," Hycanthe assured me. "You've got him too. Whatever you did to those fish, you can do that if you need to."

She was right, but I didn't want to bring Vayne back from the dead. I wanted him to stay alive.

I reached for magic. Finding it was more difficult now, but not impossible. Some Court of Shadows magic lingered. Everything else felt distant, like magic from the other courts was more closely connected to Jorius than it was to heat or cold. That was something else to think about later too.

I squeezed Vayne's hand and pushed the magic into him, keeping him alive and calm while Hycanthe healed his bones, one by one. She started with his snapped neck, her face scrunched up in concentration.

He groaned, his face twitching with the pain.

Jezalyn and Rijal knelt on either side of him, holding him carefully to keep him from throwing Hycanthe or me off.

I felt his agony through the bond. He was even weaker now. The thread that connected him to life was thin. Painfully so. It was stretched so thin I was certain it was about to snap.

"Stay with me," I urged. "If you die, I'm going to be really, really pissed off. So is the rest of the pack. I'm sure Tavian could find a way to stab you in the ass, even if you're dead. If anyone can, he can. And Ryze... Imagine all the things he'll get up to if you're not around to keep him from doing anything too stupid."

I wiped tears off my cheek with my sleeve.

"And Zared. You know he's fit in really well with the army." I didn't know that at all, but it seemed like the right thing to say. "If you're not careful, Ryze will make him command of his army. A human, imagine that."

I was getting through to Vayne. I could tell by the sudden burst of outrage through the bond. Zared would take his job over his dead body, literally.

I pushed on. "That whole spanking me with a hairbrush thing, I really enjoyed that. I was thinking that could be just for us, but now I think about it a bit more, that would be something Cavan would enjoy too."

Vayne groaned. Or was it a growl?

He felt stronger now. He was fighting back with every drop of cranky, stubborn, Fae male arrogance he had. Considering this was Vayne, that was a decent amount.

"Hold him still, so I can fix his arm and leg," Hycanthe ordered.

We all held him while I continued.

"If you want that to be our thing, maybe we can experiment with other things. Some of the priests in the temple liked to play a game with a small ball and a paddle. They hit the ball over a table, but the paddles look like fun. Maybe we could—"

Vayne's eyes popped open and his back arched. He let out a long, low cry of pure agony. His eyes were wide, skin covered with a sheen of sweat.

We held him harder until his body flopped down onto the ground. He lay there panting.

"Fucking mother of a fucking griffin fucking fuck," he said, his voice hoarse. "That hurt like a bitch. And no one paddles your ass but me," he added.

I snorted in relief and flopped down over him.

"Thank the gods." The bond felt stronger now, clear and solid. He wasn't going anywhere. After all this, he'd be lucky if I let him out of my sight. No doubt that would make him even grumpier than usual. I was all right with that, as long as he was alive.

"Thank the *omegas*," Jezalyn said. She sat back and pulled Hycanthe into her arms. They both looked exhausted. Hycanthe in particular.

I saw something on her face I'd never seen before. Contentment. Satisfaction. The realisation of who and what she was. She finally fit into her own skin.

I was happy for her. Everyone should feel like that.

Rijal looked at both of us with awe. I had a feeling what he just witnessed made him think omegas were even more special than he believed.

I pressed my cheek against Vayne's chest and rested for a while.

I didn't want to be idolised, or treated like I was special. I was just me. Just Khala.

Through the bond, I felt the rest of my pack asking if Vayne and I were all right. I sent reassurance back that we were fine.

"Dennin and Ramela are dead, we should go and see who is in charge now," I said.

I just finished saying that when a shadow rose above the hill where the castle used to stand. Wave after wave of griffins. Each with two or three people on their backs.

Portal after portal opened in front of them. They started flying through.

"Fuck," I said softly. They must have been waiting for the wards to be lowered so they could leave. I didn't have to think too hard to guess where they were going.

"We need to get out of here," I said.

I had a sinking feeling it was already too late.

CHAPTER
TWELVE
KHALA

I opened a portal the moment Vayne was able to stand. I tried to visualise my bedroom at the Winter Court. So much time had passed since I was there, the memory was hazy around the edges. I forced myself to focus on what I could visualise, and the bonds waiting for us on the other side.

I supported Vayne's weight on one side, while Rijal supported him on the other.

"You two go first," I said to Hycanthe and Jezalyn. "We're right behind you."

"Hurry up," Vayne growled when they hesitated. "Let's get the fuck out of here."

Hycanthe frowned at him, but let Jezalyn take her hand and pull her through.

"Let's go home." The portal was already a drain on me. I didn't want to risk it snapping shut if we took too long going through.

"Home sounds perfect." Vayne staggered a couple of steps, but we managed to keep him upright and walking into the portal.

When we stepped out the other end of the long passage, home wasn't where we ended up.

"Khala," Ryze drawled, as though he fully expected me to appear. "There you are. Vayne, good to see you looking so well."

Vayne responded with his customary grunt, but gave Ryze an awkward hug before being pulled into a bigger one from Tavian.

"We were worried." Tavian drew me into the hug too. "Not too worried. We knew you could take care of yourselves. It seems like you found the Court Of Dreams faster than we did. Nice work."

Zared stood back until Tavian loosened his grip, then pulled me in for a firm embrace and a kiss. "Thank the gods."

Cavan waited patiently until we were done to give me his hug and kiss, his tongue sliding across my lips and into my mouth.

"What is this place?" Hycanthe asked.

"It's a tannery," Tavian told her. He briefly outlined their search for Illaria.

When he was finished, Vayne and I explained what happened to us.

"We think the griffins are on the way to attack the Court Of Shadows," I said. "We have to help them." We'd wasted enough time already.

"You need to rest," Ryze contradicted.

"We can't just—" I started.

He interrupted me. "How many griffins did you say it was? It's going to take more than nine of us against that many. We need to rouse all the alphas and omegas we can. Not to mention as many archers as we can muster. If we go after them now, we are as good as dead."

"I've almost died enough for one day," Vayne said. "Ryze is right. We can't go in half cocked."

I wanted to argue, I really did, but there was too much logic in what they said. On top of that, I was tired. I needed a couple of hours' sleep. During that time, they could gather together what and who they needed.

"A couple of hours," I agreed reluctantly. I hoped to the gods there would be something left of the Court of Shadows when we got there.

Ryze pulled me in again and kissed my forehead. "This is one of the most difficult parts of being a High Lord. Making the tough calls."

I nodded, but that didn't settle my unease. Especially knowing how frantic Rijal must be. I glanced over to him. He looked calmer than I would have been under the circumstances.

In fact, he looked at me like he was confident I would fix this. Me and my pack.

Gods, I hoped his faith wasn't misplaced, because I wasn't so certain.

Without any argument or conversation, Ryze opened a portal to the sitting room in the Winter Court Palace. We all filed through.

"I'll make sure Khala rests," Tavian said.

"Me too," Zared agreed.

"How many orgasms is that rest going to include?" Ryze asked facetiously.

Tavian grinned. "As many as we can manage." He grabbed my hand.

"Wait," I said quickly. "There's something I need to say."

As if he knew what I was going to say, Ryze shook his head. "There will be time for that later. In the meantime, we need to rally the troops. Cavan?"

Cavan nodded. "I'll return to the Summer Court to organise my people." There was more to what he was saying, but he opened a portal and was gone before I could ask.

I sighed and gave Ryze and Vayne a quick kiss each before I let Tavian and Zared pull me away down the corridor to my bedroom.

"I never really wished I could do magic," Tavian said as he closed the door behind us. "Until today. If I could have, I would have found a way to get to you."

543

"How?" Zared asked. He pulled me toward the bathroom and started to help me out of my clothes while Tavian turned on the water. "Ryze and Cavan couldn't help. None of us could." His frustration was very much evident.

I understood it. None of us liked to feel powerless. This was something he couldn't kill or charm his way through. That must have chafed.

"We would have found a way," Tavian told him. "But since we didn't, we can make up for it." He grinned broadly.

Zared glanced at us both for a moment, then said, "Yes, we can." He turned off the tap and tested the water before helping me to climb in.

I sank underneath the warmth and exhaled softly. I didn't know how much I needed this until right then.

The water level rose as first Tavian and then Zared slipped in with me. The bath was so big, the rest of the pack could have fit, but this was just right for now.

Tavian grabbed the soap and started to wash my body as Zared started on my hair.

"You know I can do all of this myself." I was fully aware that wouldn't deter them one bit. They were determined to spoil me and that's what they'd do. All I could do was lie back and enjoy it. Especially when Tavian ran soapy hands over my breasts, making my nipples harden.

In spite of my tiredness, I was immediately aroused by the touch of both men.

"Tavian." I opened one eye crack. "I love you."

"Khala, I love you too," he replied. "And I love Zared."

Both of my eyes popped open. I twisted around to watch for Zared's reaction.

He scratched his forehead, covering his face with his hand for a moment. He lowered it.

"I... I love you both too."

"That's good, since we're all naked together in the bath," Tavian said, grinning broadly. Water dripped off his chin, back into the bath.

Zared laughed softly, but didn't object or pull away when Tavian slid up to him, sloshing water over the side.

Tavian kissed him, then kissed me. "Both of you are so perfect," he said dreamily.

"No, you," I replied, equally dreamy.

Tavian chuckled. "All right, we're all perfect." He went back to washing me, taking his time with my thighs and pussy. Even when I was clean, he went on washing every centimetre like I was a statue that had to sparkle, just for them.

Every so often, he brushed against my clit, making me shiver. I wanted more, but at the same time, I wanted to draw it out and enjoy it. These men never failed to make my body throb and ache for them. The water of the bath masked the fact I was dripping everywhere with my arousal.

Zared rinsed my hair, then started to lavish attention on my breasts. He rolled my nipples between his thumbs and forefingers, pinching lightly every so often. This wasn't about spanking and dominance. This was slow and loving. A reunion of hearts, souls and bodies.

"We missed you," Tavian whispered.

"Yes we did. I missed your breasts." Zared kneaded my breasts and palmed my nipples until they were hard as rocks and begging for more.

"I missed this beautiful pussy." Tavian slipped a couple of fingers inside me. His heel rubbed over my clit as he fucked me with his hand. Every movement was deliberate, perfectly hitting me inside and out.

Slowly, languidly, my hips rose to meet him. Delicious pressure built gradually, unhurried.

When I finally came, it was hard. I gasped out loud. Arched my back and cried as my muscles clenched around him. Water sloshed over the side of the bath and onto the floor with a splash. That, coupled with the wet sound of Tavian's hand, drove me harder still, over the edge and into the abyss.

I floated back down to earth and lay with my back against the side of the bath, catching my breath before Tavian slid his hand free.

"I bet she missed our cocks." They exchanged a glance. Something passed between them.

Without another word, they made sure I was fully rinsed, then turned to face each other. Tavian put one of his legs over Zared's, locking them together like they were scissors. Their hard cocks pressed against each other.

Holy gods.

Zared gripped my hips and moved me so I straddled both of them.

Carefully, slowly I worked myself down until both of them were inside me. Every few moments, I needed to stop and stretch to fit them both inside. I didn't doubt they would, but I didn't, couldn't rush. I wanted to make this last for all of us, for as long as possible.

Finally, I lowered myself all the way down until they were both seated deep inside me.

"Oh my gods," Zared breathed. "You both feel incredible."

I felt so fucking full. I closed my eyes and savoured the feeling for a minute or two. Oh-so-slowly, I started to move. Rising and falling, rolling my hips, keeping both of them inside my pussy at the same time.

I glanced over my shoulder at Tavian, who looked blissed out. His eyes flickered open. He gave me a smile.

I smiled back and went on pumping them both while they thrust up into me. Knowing their cocks touched drove me wild. I loved that they cared about each other, and were as into each other as much as they were into me. My heart was as full as my pussy. More so.

I rode them both slowly and deliberately until I couldn't stop myself from coming again.

My whole body was on fire with the delicious, beautiful orgasm that flooded my vision and made my heart thunder through my body. Every drop of blood boiled hot in the most incredible way.

They both came a moment after, spilling their cum into me and around each other. The sounds of both men panting and groaning in unison was the most beautiful music.

"Gods, you two are both so..." Tavian groaned. "I love you so... Gods, yes, yes, fuck."

Zared moaned his agreement, milking his orgasm for every drop before he sagged, panting against the side of the bath.

Tavian flopped back a moment later, his handsome face turned toward the ceiling. "So fucking perfect."

I panted for a while, still straddling them until I caught my breath. By now, the water was getting cold and weariness was settling in deep.

Reluctantly, I climbed off them and out of the bath. I grabbed my towel and dried myself quickly. They dried themselves and followed me over to my nest.

Lying down naked amongst the cushions gave me a last burst of energy. I might as well put it to good use.

I smiled at them both, then kissed my way down Zared's body. I gripped his cock and ran my fingers up and down slowly, deliberately, until he was hard again.

"Khala..." he breathed.

"Shhh." I fastened my lips around him and started to suck.

He dropped his head back and exhaled out his nose, apparently done arguing before he really began.

Tavian ran his fingers down my back and over my ass. He squeezed the flesh gently before kissing and nibbling his way down my ass, to the top of my legs. He spread my thighs and lowered his face between them to bite, lick and tease my clit.

I cupped Zared's balls and massaged them gently while I sucked. His hips rose and fell to meet me, pressing him deeper down my throat with each thrust.

"That feels so good," he said breathlessly.

I murmured my agreement. He tasted good, and Tavian's tongue on my clit was perfection. He worked me firmly, relentless until I came against his mouth.

I took mine from Zared's cock so I could breathe through my orgasm. Tavian didn't stop licking for a moment, not until I was well and truly back down and the stars in my vision faded.

I drew Tavian up until I was lying between both of them. I shifted my upper body and fastened my lips over Tavian's cock while running my hand up and down Zared's length. I sucked, licked and worked until they were both gasping, hard and lingering on the very edge.

I slowed in pumping Zared until Tavian came, groaning and squirting his salty cum deep into my mouth.

Instead of swallowing, I slipped my mouth off him, held his cum in my mouth and shimmied up to kiss Zared. I let Tavian's cum trickle from my mouth into his.

Zared looked surprised, but even more aroused.

I wriggled back down and wrapped my lips around his cock once more. He thrust once, twice before he came undone fully, bucking hard against my mouth.

"Mmm," he grunted, his lips pressed tightly together. He squirted his own cum into my throat.

I held it again and shimmied up to a smiling Tavian. When he opened his mouth, I trickled Zared's cum inside.

"Mmm, tasty," Tavian said around his mouthful. He exchanged glances with Zared. I realised neither had swallowed. Not yet.

They rolled me over into my back. Zared, then Tavian trickled all of the cum back into my mouth. The combined taste of them both was divine.

I smiled and swallowed the delicious mouthful.

"Gods that was hot," Tavian said. "We should include Ryze, Vayne, and Cavan next time. It's probably the only way you get to taste Vayne's cum."

"Doesn't it all taste the same?" Zared asked.

I couldn't tell if he was curious or disbelieving.

"Not at all." Tavian propped himself upon his elbow. "It depends what a person eats or drinks, or whatever. Some are tastier than others, right Khala?"

"Right," I agreed. "You all taste delicious." How did I get so fucking lucky? Sometimes, I thought maybe the gods didn't hate me after all. How could they when I was surrounded by five incredible men?

"You should get some sleep," Tavian said. "I'm going to go and see what Ryze needs. Zared, stay with her and make sure she actually does rest." He slipped out of the nest and pulled on his clothes before he disappeared out the door.

Zared pulled me to him and kissed the top of my head.

"Are you really all right? It sounds like what you went through was...traumatic. Vayne is a pain in the ass, but it would suck if he died. Especially if you were right there to see it. I know you, you'd never forget it."

"No, I wouldn't," I agreed. "I really am all right. It's just a little weird knowing I owe most of that to Hycanthe, of all people. I'm starting to realise she's not as bad as I thought she was. Although, both of us have grown up a lot since we left the temple. A lot has happened. So much has changed. My whole life is different."

There wasn't an aspect of it that wasn't touched in some way. Some bigger than others. "I never would have thought I'd end up here."

"With me?" he asked.

"I think that was inevitable," I replied. "The rest of it is slightly crazy." I stifled a yawn with my hand.

"Just slightly," he agreed. "Get some rest. I'll watch over you. You're safe now."

I snuggled into him and closed my eyes. It didn't take long before sleep claimed me the way my five men had.

Deep and satisfying.

CHAPTER
THIRTEEN
CAVAN

I huffed a breath as I strode out of the portal.

The last time I was in the Autumn Court things didn't precisely go according to plan, to understate the case.

I didn't blame Khala for a moment for stabbing me, although it hurt like a bitch. No, that act was all Wornar's fault. Recalling what he did to her afterward, I fumed. I dearly wanted to rip off his head and shove it up his own ass. He would be dealt with, I'd make sure of that, but first I had something else to attend to.

I strode towards the palace, senses on alert. At first glance, it appeared nothing was different. Nothing amiss.

I knew full well by now looks could be very deceiving. My instincts told me to be careful. I was inclined to give heed to them.

It quickly became evident someone was following me. Likely more than one someone.

I didn't look back. They weren't making any effort to hide their presence. They may have intent, but they weren't ready to act upon it yet.

The guards at the gates knew me by sight. None made the slightest move to stop me from passing. That in itself was curious. Harel made it clear I wasn't welcome here. Either that changed or no one informed the guards.

No, something else was going on here. I had the unshakeable sensation I walked in on something.

Even more cautious, I stepped towards the doors that led into the palace. As before, the guards let me pass.

"This is fun, isn't it?" Tavian spoke behind me as he followed me in.

I kept my eyes forward. I should have guessed it was him. Ryze must have sent him after me.

"Have you come to assassinate Harel?" I asked.

"Officially? No." He hurried to catch up with me. "Unofficially, if a knife happens to find its way into his forehead, I don't think too many people will mind." He grinned over his shoulder at the guards.

None of them made a move to stop either of us.

Evidently I wasn't the only one they recognised on sight.

"You know a High Lord doesn't pay well when people aren't willing to die for him," Tavian remarked.

I snorted softly. "Perhaps they realise he's not worth losing their lives for. Aah, Daniek."

I presumed the courtier would be slithering around somewhere. He seemed to have a sense for gossip and trouble. I glanced at Tavian and wondered if he'd seen anything with his sixth sense, since the Court of Dreams was released. I'd ask him when I got a chance.

"High Lord Cavan," Daniek said in his nasally, ingratiating tone. "What a surprise. Are you still busy chasing fables?"

His question clarified two things. Harel was still in charge, and Daniek was still a dickhead. The latter would never change. The former...

"Why don't you be a good boy and tell your High Lord I'm here to see him?" I said.

Beside me, Tavian twitched. That small movement spoke volumes.

I put that information in the back of my mind and raised an eyebrow at Daniek. I owed him no explanation and we both knew it. The best he could hope for would be for Harel to let him sit in on our meeting, or tell him details afterwards. No doubt he'd be salivating for every one of them.

Daniek gave me a slimy smile and waved his hand toward the throne room. "Of course."

He started there ahead of us so he could open the door and announce us.

I'd let him have his moment of pretending he was important.

Harel sat on a plush armchair near the window. He seemed less than pleased to see us. The polite thing for him to do would be to rise and greet us.

He remained sitting.

"Dropping in unexpectedly is becoming an unfortunate habit," he told me. "Have you brought me another broken omega?"

I didn't have to look to know Tavian's hand was hovering over a knife. One word against Khala and he'd use it.

"The Winter Court's *Master of Assassins* has accompanied me to speak on behalf of High Lord Ryzellius," I said. In case Harel forgot who and what Tavian actually was.

He was unique, and in some ways sweet, but Tavian was very, very dangerous. I wasn't entirely comfortable with how much he seemed to enjoy killing, but that was merely one facet of him. One of a great many.

"Is Ryze too much of a coward to come himself?" Harel sneered. "Or is it too much effort to come and say he was wrong?"

"On the contrary," I said smoothly. "He's busy gathering together as many Fae as possible who can use magic. I myself have just been in the Summer Court, organising the omegas I've been helping for the last twenty years."

I needed to get back to them as quickly as possible, and get them all to the Winter Court. All of this nonsense was wasting precious time.

"The Court of Dreams has awakened and been released," Tavian said. "As we speak, they're on their way to attack the Court of Shadows."

Harel regarded him for a moment, then threw his head back and laughed. "I see you've been hit in the head too many times with Ryze's cock. Even if this was true, what concern would it be of mine? If they destroy each other, perhaps you'll stop coming to my court and talking about them." He clearly didn't believe a word we said.

"They have griffins and magic," I said steadily. "Do you think they'll stop at the Court of Shadows?"

"They absolutely won't," Tavian said. "The Summer and Winter Courts will be ready. What about the Autumn Court?"

"We'll be ready," another voice said behind me.

Harel's face turned a delightful shade of pink. He looked like he might explode.

"Illaria, you are exiled from this court, under punishment of death." His voice was high, barely controlled.

In spite of the pressure we were under, I wouldn't have missed this for the world.

Illaria strode past us, chin high. "I challenge your authority. I declare you no longer fit to hold the title of High Lord. I have come to assert my claim and take my place as High Lady."

Harel spluttered. "You've lost your mind. Guards, seize her and take her to a cell. She'll be executed within the hour." He glared at her like she was something he scraped off the bottom of his favourite, and most expensive, pair of shoes.

Believing they were related to each other was difficult. Sometimes, family was a group of people who came together, not necessarily those who were related.

"I bet she has daddy issues," Tavian muttered.

The guards didn't move. Not one stepped forward to take her arm. They remained by the door, watching. After a minute or two, they were joined by others. Those from the front doors and the gate. And others still, moments later. None made a move to do as Harel ordered.

Now Harel stood and spluttered. "How dare you?"

"I dare," she replied. She glanced at Tavian and me. "Will you witness the change of leadership?" Her gaze was unwavering and unapologetic. She was entirely prepared for this. Completely ready to step up and take her place as leader.

I had no authority over who led another court, no say in it. Perhaps it was past time that changed.

I nodded. "I bear witness to your claim as High Lady of the Autumn Court."

"On behalf of High Lord Ryzellius, I bear witness to your claim," Tavian said formally.

Harel looked outraged and scared. "You can't do this. I am High Lord here."

"Not anymore," Illaria said. She nodded to the guards. Four of them stepped forward immediately and surrounded him. Two gripped his arms and looked pleased to do it.

Harel struggled for a moment before he was forced away.

"To his credit, he didn't piss himself," Tavian remarked. "Yet."

I shook my head at his comment and turned to Illaria. "I have a feeling you've been planning this for quite some time." That would explain the lack of reaction from the guards. They were expecting something to happen and knew I'd be on their side if it did.

Illaria wouldn't have to pay them too much more to die for her. She'd be a much better High Lady than her father was High Lord. Although, he lowered the standard quite a bit.

She gave me an innocent smile. "Perhaps I have and perhaps I haven't. Now, you were saying something about the Court of Dreams? What can the Autumn Court do to assist?"

"You can start by arranging any alpha who can do magic to come to the Winter Court immediately," I said. This was the conversation I'd come here to have. Granted, it would have been easier without the time we'd already wasted. "And any omegas you can, if there are any Harel doesn't know about."

The expression on her face confirmed what I suspected. There were indeed such omegas present. They'd done well to stay away from Harel's gaze.

"Consider it done," she nodded. "Fortunately, my father's unpopularity was far-reaching. Much more than he realised. The whole court has been waiting for this move. They might not have backed me, but the return of the two courts... Let's say they're happy to have someone more competent leading. As far as I'm concerned, the Summer and Winter Courts are welcome here anytime."

"And you're welcome at the Winter Court." Tavian grinned. He seemed to enjoy playing the part of the High Lord's emissary. He didn't even seem too disappointed the coup was, so far, bloodless. No doubt he would have jumped in with two feet if Illaria took the court by force.

"And the Summer Court," I agreed. "But I need to get back there." I glanced at Tavian.

"I'm coming with you," he said. "I've decided I like your portals just as much as I like Ryze's."

I raised my eyebrows at him, but nodded.

"I've already had the wards removed," Illaria said. "You should be able to portal out from here."

I admired her ability to organise quickly. She must have put years into this coup. Her timing was nothing less than impeccable.

"I already like you much more than Harel," Tavian told her. "If you need help executing him, let me know when we've dealt with the Court of Dreams. I'm only too happy to assist."

She laughed softly. "I suspect I will have many offers of help. If you'll excuse me, I have alphas and omegas to assemble. We won't be far behind you."

Before I could take a step, she put a hand on my arm.

"Do you have a plan to deal with Wornar?" She couldn't possibly have known what happened to Khala, but from the look in her eyes, she understood what the man was like.

I suspected it was first-hand experience, but I wasn't going to ask, especially not now. If that was the case, she'd be as eager to see Wornar with a knife in his chest as the rest of us.

"Thiron might have assisted us, but Wornar won't," I said.

"He wouldn't live long enough to say no," Tavian growled.

I glanced at him to acknowledge what he said, then looked back at her.

"We can't worry about him right now. When we've dealt with the Court of Dreams, then we'll deal with him." I was sorely tempted to take Tavian there to dispense with him right now, but we didn't have the time.

Not to mention that I suspected Khala would want to be there. She should have a say in what happened to him. If she wanted to wield the knife, I'd let her. None of her pack would stop her. If anything, we'd hold him down for her.

Illaria nodded and lowered her hand. "We'll see you in a few minutes."

I nodded in return.

Without another word, I opened a portal back home to the Summer Court and hurried through, Tavian on my heels.

CHAPTER
FOURTEEN
KHALA

The scent of alpha and omega was almost overwhelming.

Until now, I had no idea how many of us there really were. Several hundred from the Winter and Autumn Courts, along with sixty former Silent Maidens and more alphas from the Summer Court.

We gathered in the yard outside the Winter Court Palace. Us and several contingents of archers. A few thousand more had swords on their backs and steely looks in their eyes.

Wherever their High Lord led, they would follow and fight.

"Are you ready?" Ryze laced his fingers through mine and kissed my temple.

"Is anyone truly ready for something like this?" I asked.

"They are." Tavian had a faraway look on his face. "I've been getting bits and pieces of visions all morning. Things keep changing. One keeps reoccurring, though. Patric telling Yala and me the time has come. Whoever's visions these are, they're not happy about any of this."

"Gavil," I said softly. "I don't know how, but I think somehow you're getting his visions." I quickly told them about him.

"He foresaw all of this," Ryze mused. "In his visions and in his lived experience. I wonder if he knows how it will all end."

"Badly for them," Cavan said confidently. "I wonder if he told them that and they ignored him." He looked sly.

"You're never going to let us forget that, are you?" Ryze asked.

Cavan smiled.

Ryze shook his head. "Get a portal open, man. We have a court to help."

Cavan smirked and opened a portal to the side of Nallis. He stood beside it, keeping it open while Vayne ordered his people to march through with him.

For someone who almost died a couple of hours ago, the army commander was looking surprisingly well. He was clearly tired, but he was too fucking stubborn to admit it. Not to mention the fact he wasn't going to sit out of a perfectly good, potential battle.

He gave me a quick kiss before he strode past and disappeared into the long tunnel to Nallis.

The alphas and omegas went next, followed by the former Silent Maidens. I walked with them, side-by-side with Hycanthe and Jezalyn. Rijal trailed along behind.

"Does anyone else think this is a bad idea?" Hycanthe asked.

"It's your court too," I pointed out. "Unless you can convince them to stop?"

"She would if she could," Jezalyn said. She gripped Hycanthe's hand tightly.

"Yes, I would," Hycanthe agreed. "Also, I take no responsibility for what they do. I had no idea I had anything to do with them."

"I know you didn't," I said gently. No more than Tavian did. Blood didn't always equate to influence.

"Be ready," someone shouted from up the front.

A rumble came from behind and I turned back to see Zared push his way through to me.

"I wish I could throw you over my shoulder and take you away from here," he said. He slipped his hand into mine.

"Funny, I could say the same to you," I said lightly. "I'm sure I could carry you if I had to."

He smiled. "I'd like to see you try. In fact, let's go back to the Winter Court and do that right now."

Before I could say no, he squeezed my hand. "I know you won't go back. You're as stubborn as I am. Maybe more so. Make me a promise though. Don't take any risks unless you have to. We've come too far for me to lose you now." His voice was choked with emotion.

"I won't do anything stupid if you don't," I told him. "I love you."

"I love you too." He kissed me quickly before we stepped out of the portal and onto the side of the mountain.

"The mist is gone." Jezalyn sounded astonished.

"I don't see any griffins," Hycanthe was equally surprised.

"They could be trying to find a way into the caverns," Zared suggested.

"I know where they are," Tavian said. He hurried over to me and took my hands. "I can see the vision. Can you see it too, through the bond?"

I felt for it and got a hazy image, but that was all.

"I don't know if it's enough to open a portal there," I admitted.

"Can you try?" Ryze asked.

I hadn't seen him approach, but the portal was already closed behind him. We all stood on the side of the mountain, a stiff breeze blowing on all of us.

"I— I suppose so," I agreed. What was the worst that could happen? I'd open it to another place instead. A place we didn't have to walk through to. I'd close the portal and we'd try something else.

"Good girl," Cavan said, coming up behind me.

"Isn't she?" Vayne was close on his heels.

All of that praise was going to go to my head if they weren't careful. I turned my face so they couldn't see me blush too hard.

I nodded and stepped away from them into a clear space. I formed the portal in the air in front of me and peeled away the veil.

On the other side was pure chaos.

A wide plateau was set into the side of the mountain. At one end, a doorway led inside.

At the other, at least two dozen griffins hovered. They'd discharged a number of their riders. The ones who remained on the back were raining lightning down on the doorway, trying to blast their way in.

Bodies lay here and there. Mostly with golden hair, but a couple with black. Vernissa must have sent some of her people out here when the griffins arrived. By the look of them, they'd received no mercy at all.

"This is the place the mist took us," Vayne said, peering over my shoulder.

"It's the place I saw in my first vision." Tavian sounded haunted. "The place I saw all the death and destruction."

"Death and destruction aside, that's where we're going," Ryze said. He waved everyone over before stepping through himself.

Cavan was half a heartbeat behind.

Tavian, Zared and I were right on their heels, followed by everyone else in neat, disciplined order. Each archer, each swordsperson, knew exactly their position. They kept a precise distance between themselves and their comrades. Half a metre. Down the centimetre by the look of it.

"Aim for the riders, not the griffins," Vayne shouted out.

Almost as one, the archers pulled out their bows, took aim and fired.

The Silent Maidens separated amongst the ranks, before loosing shots of fire at the griffin riders.

Cavan did the same, while Ryze used blasts of ice.

What looked like an icicle speared one of the riders straight through the heart. She didn't even have time to cry before she fell off her mount and landed on the ground below with a sickening thud.

"Fall back to the doorway," Vayne ordered. The message was clear. The Court of Dreams would get to the Court of Shadows past us. We weren't going down without one hells of a fight.

We all fired off shots of ice and fire, frost and flame, while ducking lightning and sudden, violent eddies of wind. Several of our people were struck, or swept off the plateau.

The smell of burning hair and flesh soon pervaded the air and turned my stomach.

One of the griffin riders landed a shot of lightning right in the centre of the archers.

"Cover them!" Vayne shouted.

The Silent Maidens used hand language to communicate across the plateau, before working together to form a shield of heat in front of the archers. That gave them time to regroup and reorganise their ranks.

The griffin riders battered at the shield until it finally collapsed. One of them narrowed his eyes and aimed at a group of Silent Maidens, who stood near the back.

Before he could gather enough magic to attack, I speared him through the eye with a shard of ice. He flew backwards off his griffin and was thrown heavily to the ground. The griffin, apparently freed of her obligation along with her burden, banked and flew off towards the top of the mountain.

Another griffin wasn't so lucky. He got caught in the middle of a blast of flame. His scream of agony while his feathers and fur burnt was one I'd hear for the rest of my life.

He veered away before he crashed down in a heap on the edge of the plateau. The gods only knew if he was alive or not.

The griffin riders retaliated with an attack on the centre of our lines.

"We only need to concentrate on those five," Zared said.

Without taking my eyes off the riders, I asked, "Which five?"

"The middle one, the two on either side and there's two more mixed in. They're moving in and out of the others. The rest aren't doing magic, they're just covering for those five. There were seven, but we've got two of them."

Seven was a peculiar number. And it wasn't right. It was eight. Gavil was the last one, but he wasn't using magic against us.

He and his griffin were in front of another, shielding them from attack. They'd barely managed to dodge flames several times. Gods, he must be terrified. After what he went through as a child, he was having to face what had to be his worst nightmare.

There was that number again, eight. Eight Silent Maidens per year. Three transitioned. If I had to guess, I'd say Gavil was born looking like a Fae.

"Three of them are alphas," I guessed. "We need to focus everything on them." I twisted and sighed frantically to the closest of my sisters. She turned and signed to the sister who stood near Vayne. She, in turn, spoke to him quickly.

He nodded and stepped amongst the archers. He barked another order.

As one, the archers turned their bows and loosed their arrows. Everyone standing on the plateau who could use magic aimed at those three alphas.

All three of them realised quickly what was going on. Two of them were too slow to react. They were incinerated.

The third turned his griffin and tried to flee. He got maybe ten metres before he froze. Literally. He was encased in ice from head to toe. The griffin shuddered and bucked, eyes wide in terror. Her rider was thrown clear. He landed on the ground and shattered into a hundred frigid shards.

"What a way to go," Zared muttered.

Without the three alphas, the rest of the griffin riders fell into disarray.

Some returned fire with their own bows, but most turned their griffins and scattered. In moments they'd disappeared, some to the top of the mountain, and some below.

Three remained behind. None with a bow or any other, visible weapon, apart from their beasts and those huge talons, and sharp beaks. Those could do inestimable damage in moments.

The lead rider raised a hand. A gesture of surrender, a plea for mercy. It was more than Vernissa's people got.

A rumble went through our ranks. I wasn't the only one who glanced at Vayne for orders.

"Hold!" Ryze shouted before the archers took aim again. "Fire if they move to attack further."

Vayne nodded for everyone gathered to do as ordered.

No one relaxed a muscle, but we watched and waited.

Eyes on us, the riders directed their griffins to land and slid down off their backs.

Gavil and two other omegas.

Gavil sank to the ground and covered his face with his hands. His whole body shook. He was clearly terrified. Scared both of the flames and of what might happen to him now.

Somehow, I'd make sure everyone understood what he was subjected to, and what he risked speaking to me back at the castle. The blame for today shouldn't fall on his shoulders.

The plateau fell into silence, broken only by the groans of injured archers and Silent Maidens. The air was thick with smoke. It stung my eyes, making them water.

The two female griffin riders stepped away from their beasts, hands raised to either side. Both looked stricken.

I knew that look. That was the same look I saw in the mirror after Wornar made me run Cavan's knife through his side. The look of someone who only did harm because they were ordered by an alpha.

"How did you know?" Zared asked softly.

"I didn't," I admitted. "I guessed based on the way Dennin and Ramela talked about omegas. They saw them as something disgusting. That seems to lead to people assuming it's all right to use them. Like they're nothing more than tools. They couldn't help the things they were made to do."

"Neither could you," he reminded me. "You still blame yourself though, don't you?"

I leaned against him and shrugged one shoulder. "I probably always will. Whether it's rational or not."

"It certainly isn't," he agreed. "I guess this is where we leave the leaders to sort shit out."

"If you don't mind, I want to be part of that," I said. "Those omegas are going to need all the help they can get."

CHAPTER
FIFTEEN
KHALA

I stayed close to Ryze and Cavan as they addressed Vernissa and Lyra.

The High Lady regarded the new omegas with undisguised scepticism.

Calm radiated from Lyra, as always, although her brows creased every so often. That was as rattled as I ever saw her.

The three omegas knelt on the stone floor, Gavil in between the two women. He hadn't said a word since he slipped off his griffin.

Instead, a golden haired Fae with her hair in several braids spoke for the other two.

"You say you were given no choice," Ryze asked. He paced back and forth in front of them, keeping himself between them and Vernissa. Not so the High Lady couldn't see, but to protect. An alpha protecting omegas. No one in the room missed what he was doing.

The omegas seemed grateful as well as forthcoming.

The woman, who said her name was Saminta, nodded eagerly. "High Lord Dennin ordered Patric to give us an alpha-order. As soon as the bubble was gone we were to take our griffins and come here to attack the Court Of Shadows. The moment Patric was shattered, the order stopped. We were free to choose. We choose not to fight against our fellow Fae. Especially omegas."

Both she and Betha, the other female omega, didn't seem surprised to learn the Court of Shadows was led by one.

"You knew that would happen," Cavan said softly to me.

"I hoped it would," I said. "It was Zared who realised we needed to focus our offence."

Before that, we were concentrating on defending the doorway into the caverns. No doubt I wasn't the only one who was intimidated by the presence

559

of the griffins in the first place. If all of the riders could do magic, we'd be dead right now.

"If it didn't, we would have dealt with them," I added. "There was no way to know the rest would leave once Patric was gone."

"Without anyone to do magic, they had only their griffins and regular weapons," Cavan said. "Against all of those former Silent Maidens, they wouldn't have stood a chance."

I reached for his hand and laced my fingers in his. "All of that work over all of those years—"

"Was worthwhile," he finished. "The eradication of Patric and the other alphas. And Yala too, from what I gather. Without them, we might not have got the upper hand in time. Although, we do have you."

"And you. And Ryze." I glanced over at Cavan and smiled. "But you're right, we needed them too." Out of sixty, we lost five. And as many archers.

"Can we expect the Court of Dreams to come after us again?" Ryze asked.

"The Court of Dreams is no more," Saminta said. "Outside the griffin riders, our numbers were few. Those who existed, the majority resided in the castle and the surrounding outbuildings. When the mist caused the earth to shake, most were lost. The attack on the Court of Shadows was a last effort to annex the court and save ours."

Vernissa sat forward. "Only a couple of hundred of you remain?"

Saminta nodded, her expression sombre. "That is correct, High Lady. We are at your mercy."

I caught a glimpse at the expression on Rijal's face. He stood near the wall, watching the proceedings intently.

He was clearly surprised to see omegas on their knees, much less suppli-cants to his mother. In some ways, he was like a child. Innocent of the world around him. He reminded me a lot of myself.

Vernissa sat back and glanced at Lyra. "I've long wanted to see the Court of Dreams at its end, but I find myself conflicted. Now Ramela and Dennin have gone, perhaps there is no need for animosity. Did they have an heir?"

"Yala was their heir." It was Betha who responded. "They have no other."

I glanced over to Tavian, who stood near Illaria. She'd arrived right after the battle was over and insisted on watching the proceedings.

"They may have another," I said. I nodded to Illaria to explain.

She told everyone what she told me about the High Lord visiting Tavian's mother and her becoming pregnant.

Tavian looked amused but not surprised. I should have known he already knew.

Saminta looked over to him. "I apologise, but the succession may only pass through the female line."

He grinned. "That's all right, I didn't want to be High Lord anyway. Being in a pack with two of them is plenty. May I make a suggestion?" Before anyone could tell him he couldn't, he continued. "What we need is someone with the blood of the Court of Dreams, right? Someone who understands how it feels to be an outsider. Someone with intelligence and compassion. Someone who isn't going to start any further antagonism towards omegas or alphas. Someone who doesn't take shit from anyone."

Slowly, dramatically, he raised his hand and pointed right at Hycanthe.

"What the fuck?" She stared at him like he was out of his mind. "Me?"

"Why not you?" Jezalyn asked proudly. "You're all of those things and more. I can't think of anyone better."

Neither could I. Tavian was right about her. The court was going to need someone strong to guide them and settle everyone back into their new lives. If anyone could do that, it was her.

"We approve of this arrangement," Saminta said after a quick, quiet few words with Betha and Gavil. She lowered her head. "High Lady Hycanthe."

"That's not going to go to her head at all," I said out of the side of my mouth.

Cavan chuckled. "Were you hoping it would be you?"

I snorted. "Fuck no. I have enough to deal with without leading a scattered court."

"A wise Fae once said the best person to lead is the one who is reluctant to do so," he said. "Someone who isn't merely concerned with their own ambition."

"So not someone like Harel or someone like Wornar," I said dryly.

"Definitely not," he agreed. "Although, now I think about it, I'm not sure Ryze or I fit that description either." He shrugged, seemingly unconcerned.

"Maybe that Fae wasn't that wise after all," I remarked. "Personally I'd suggest the best leader is someone who isn't an asshole."

Cavan hummed his agreement. "That is wise indeed. I'm thinking of suggesting we form a council of High Lords and Ladies, so we can make decisions together, instead of acting against each other when there's no need to do so. The first topic of conversation should be making that rule. No assholes."

"That's the smartest thing I've heard all day," Vayne commented. He'd walked up to us in time to hear. "Can we eradicate all assholes, not just the ones who lead?"

"You'd have to decide on the definition of asshole first," I said. "I suspect that might cause more trouble than it solves."

"Not if you appoint me judge of who is an asshole and who isn't," Vayne said. "I'm an excellent judge of character."

"Until recently, you thought I was an asshole," Cavan pointed out.

Vayne grunted. "Yes, well... We all make mistakes. I'm a big enough man to admit to mine."

We turned back to the proceedings as Vernissa stood. "I'm satisfied we've settled the matter of the Court of Dreams. We have two further matters to discuss. The presence and subsequent absence of the mist, and the matter of the returning of land to the Court of Shadows."

"The mist lifted from here the same time it lifted from the Court of Dreams?" I asked.

"As far as anyone can tell it did," Cavan agreed. "No one thinks that's a coincidence."

"Right, but the mist was around here for years, and only around the Court of Dreams for a matter of hours," Vayne said.

"Also probably not a coincidence," Cavan mused.

"How many years?" I asked.

"Around twenty," he said. He leaned back and looked at me. "About as long as you've been alive."

"And Hycanthe, and Jezalyn," I said. "And the gods know how many others. They were there along with me."

"The mist took them there," Vayne said. "It made sure you and Hycanthe were in the same place. It protected this place all those years. It kept out people like Ryze. And Ramela and Dennin."

"That doesn't mean it has anything to do with me," I said. Until I spoke, I didn't realise the room had fallen silent and everyone was listening.

"I figured you had Court of Shadows blood," Hycanthe pointed out. "I was right about that."

"How is that possible?" I directed the question to Cavan. "My mother was from the Summer Court. My father was—"

"Part human," Cavan finished for me. "He looked human, but he was half Fae. He must have been. He wasn't an alpha or an omega, so he didn't transition. I'd always thought he looked younger than he was. I should have realised it sooner."

"So one of my grandparents was from the Court of Shadows," I said slowly. "I never met my grandfather. My grandmother said he died before I was born."

The memory was vague, like most of my memories of those days. Just a few words I'd long since accepted as truth. Only now I realised they weren't.

My gaze drifted around the room before settling on Rijal.

"He didn't die, did he? The reason you always want to stay close to me is because you're my grandfather."

He started to sign, but Vernissa cut him off.

"You may speak," she said sharply.

He sighed. "I wanted to see the sun." His voice was gravelly and choked with emotion. "We fell for each other. Her parents and my mother did not approve. When she became pregnant, they forbade me from seeing her ever again. Whenever one of our people would go above, I'd ask them to check on our son. When he was born and looked human, they stopped going. It seemed better for him to get on with his life without knowing what he was."

His eyes were glazed. "But then when I saw you, I knew. You look like her."

Vernissa was visibly unimpressed, but this was clearly an old transgression. One she'd more or less come to terms with. Was this part of the reason her people weren't allowed to fuck each other? Because it created more problems than it solved?

To think a man who looked no older than me was my grandfather was strange. That would take some time to get my head around. Hopefully we'd get a chance to sit down and get to know each other.

"So you're the High Lady's great-granddaughter," Vayne remarked. For some reason, he seemed to find that funny.

Zared gave me a long glance. "Is there any way to find out if someone is part Fae?"

"You're talking about yourself?" Tavian asked him gently.

Zared shrugged. "It seems like something a man should know about himself. If Khala's father was half Fae and never knew, he's not going to be the only one, is he?"

Tavian smiled. "Unlikely. A lot of us struggle to keep our cocks in our pants."

Zared snort-laughed. "I noticed," he said without a hint of accusation or condemnation. "Anyway, is there?"

It was Lyra who answered. "There is, but we have a more important issue to resolve first. The matter of our land."

Vernissa nodded. "Yes. That must be resolved."

"We will speak to the King of Fraxius on your behalf," Ryze said. "However, I must remind you I have no say." He cocked his head. "Although, you know there's land available where the Court of Dreams were hiding."

"That land belongs to them and their griffins," Vernissa said. "I'm sure High Lady Hycanthe agrees."

Before Hycanthe could say anything, Vernissa continued. "We want our own lands. That way, both courts can thrive and return to their former glory."

Ryze gave her a bow. "We'll see what we can do." He didn't look confident, but somehow, one way or another, we'd find a solution to suit everyone.

CHAPTER
SIXTEEN
KHALA

"This isn't Fraxius," I remarked as I stepped through the portal into the sitting room in the Winter Court Palace.

"No it's not," Ryze drawled. "I made the arbitrary decision that we all needed a rest first. For one thing, we all smell like smoke. Except Vayne, he smells like feet."

"I fucking do not," Vayne protested. "I smell like good, honest sweat and blood. I smell like a warrior."

"Yes, you do," Tavian told him. "You smell like a warrior who is outnumbered by a pack that largely consists of High Lords and High Ladies." He grinned.

Vayne stuck his middle finger up at him. "You're not a High Lord. You and Ryze are trying to make me add you to my list of assholes."

I stepped up behind him and wound my arms around his neck. I kissed his cheek.

"None of you are assholes." They would never stop needling each other. I liked that they were close enough to tease each other and not get offended about what the others said. They pretended at offence, but that was all it was. A game between brothers.

"By rest, you mean..." Vayne grabbed my hands and pulled me around to face him.

"A bath and a nap," Ryze said. "Maybe with a few orgasms in the middle."

"That was what I thought." Vayne grabbed my ass and lifted me until I wound my legs around his hips. He brought his lips to mine and kissed me, deep and demanding.

He carried me like that all the way to my room and into the bathroom. He lowered me to the floor and I found myself surrounded by my entire pack.

All of the bonds felt close and warm. Like a blanket.

They helped me and each other out of their clothes and we all washed each other. Soap and water and wash cloths were everywhere, making the floor and each other slippery.

"Isn't that interesting?" Tavian remarked as he washed my back and Zared's at the same time, a cloth in each hand.

I looked in the direction he nodded, to see Ryze swiping a cloth down Cavan's back. Both of their cocks were half erect.

"That's going to feature in my fantasies for a while," Tavian remarked.

I smiled. "Mine too." The air temperature rose suddenly.

Ryze and Cavan both turned to us and raised their eyebrows. They turned to each other.

I couldn't have been the only one holding my breath, waiting to see what they'd do. I didn't let it out until their lips met, lightly at first, then more deeply.

"Gods, yes," Tavian sighed.

I murmured my agreement. My whole body throbbed watching them kiss.

Ryze's hand slipped down to circle Cavan's cock. He slowly drew it up to his balls and back down to his tip.

Cavan groaned.

Vayne grabbed a towel and started to dry the front of me, then dropped to his knees with a faint splash. He parted my legs with his hands and flicked his tongue over my clit.

It was my turn to groan.

Tavian helped Zared to dry off and dropped to his knees. He curled the fingers of one hand around Zared's cock and cupped his balls with the other.

Zared groaned and pulled me over close enough so he could kiss me while Tavian and Vayne licked and sucked both of us. Between that and the sound of Ryze and Cavan's mouths on each other's, my whole body was on fire.

I rocked my hips, bucking against Vayne's mouth. He reached around to squeeze my ass, pinching every now and again. He gave me an especially tight pinch.

I gasped in a breath before I came. My orgasm pounded through me like thunder, hot blood racing through my ears. I arched my back and cried out.

Vayne lifted his face and, on a signal from Tavian, lay back on the wet tiles. Tavian and Zared lowered me, carefully sliding me down onto Vayne's thick cock.

"Lean forward," Tavian told me. He grabbed some lubricating oil and dipped his fingers inside before pressing them into my ass. His fingers stretched me, making me ready before he slid his cock inside my ass.

My eyes widened at the feeling of two cocks inside me at the same time. It soon became a third, when Zared stood beside me and tapped on my lips with his.

"Open your mouth," he said.

I opened eagerly and let him slide his cock between my lips. After a few thrusts, all three men and I got a rhythm of sucks, licks and smooth strokes.

"Gods, you feel so fucking good," Tavian groaned. "You too, Vayne. I can feel your cock inside her."

Vayne grunted in response, but kept his eyes closed and pushed up into me.

"Oh my gods," Zared breathed.

I looked up and saw him with his gaze behind me. My hand on his cock, I lifted my mouth off him and looked over my shoulder.

Ryze was behind Tavian, the bottle of lubricating oil in his hand. He gave me a smile and prepared Tavian the way Tavian had prepared me.

Cavan stepped over to the other side of me. I curled my fingers around his cock and licked and sucked his tip before drawing him all the way down to the back of my throat.

Tavian stiffened for a moment and groaned. "Fuck yes." When Ryze thrust into him, he pushed Tavian deeper into my ass. His momentum knocked me forward onto Vayne.

Ryze set the pace for all of us, thrusting slowly while I alternated between Cavan and Zared's cocks, my hands around their lengths the whole time.

The pressure built inside me again until I thought I might burst. I came for a second time, and a third.

That stole an orgasm from Vayne, who thrust up into me harder and faster before he shouted my name to the ceiling. He gritted his teeth and groaned long and low, the intensity of his orgasm flooding through the bond.

Tavian came next, deep strokes stilling as he spilled himself into my ass. Through the bond I felt a perfect, tight heat, and the delicious sensation of pure bliss that lasted before he finally floated back down to earth.

Ryze followed a moment later. I couldn't see him but I felt him too, the bond was full of emotion as well as bliss.

This wasn't just sex to him, this was about him giving everything to his pack. To our pack. Something he'd never had before. Something that made him feel complete. Content. Even more than being a High Lord, his place was here. He could have been a farmer or an executioner and still he would have belonged to us.

Our connection told me all of that and more.

Zared quickly followed Ryze, coming while his thick cock was almost down my throat.

"That's it. Suck me harder," he panted. "Gods, yes, yes, yes."

A squirt of hot cum blasted out of him and into the back of my mouth. It flooded my mouth with the smooth, salty taste. I held it there. Forced myself not to swallow. Instead I turned to Cavan and sucked him harder, my fingers massaging his balls.

I looked up at him to see him watching me.

"Good girl," he crooned. "Hold his cum. Wait for mine."

I sucked and licked him harder, grazed my teeth up and down his length and forced myself not to swallow. It took all of my focus. Everything else in the world disappeared except my mouth and his thick, throbbing cock.

His hips moved, driving him almost all the way to his knot. The tip of his cock was swimming in Zared's cum and the warmth of my mouth.

He grunted and thrust harder, fucking my mouth with even strokes.

I reminded myself to breathe as he came, spilling another half a mouthful of hot cum down my throat. It quickly mingled with the first, making a ball of hot liquid in the back of my mouth.

"Good girl," he said breathlessly. "Take every drop but don't swallow." He went on thrusting until his cock lost some of its hardness. Only then, he slid out of my mouth and took half a step back.

"Such a good girl." He kissed my brow, then turned my face to Tavian as he slid his cock out of my ass. He manoeuvred me until our mouths met. I kissed Tavian, but kept my mouthful where it was for now.

I broke off the kiss and slipped off Vayne's cock.

Looking around deliberately, I stood and wound my hands around the back of Ryze's neck. I pressed my mouth to his and squirted my mouthful between his lips.

He swished his lips from side to side as though tasting a fine wine. "Mmm." He eyed all of the other men speculatively.

Vayne shook his head, but Zared, Tavian and Cavan simply gazed back. Each with an expression of curious interest on his face.

I had to give it to them, they were adventurous. Lucky for me, because so was I.

Finally Ryze stepped over to Cavan and pressed his mouth to his, passing on the tasty mouthful to the other High Lord.

I wasn't sure how Cavan would react, but he did the same as Ryze, tasting and appraising before he grabbed Tavian by the back of his head and slammed his mouth down onto his.

"Delicious," Tavian said, licking his lips. He turned from Cavan to Zared, tipping Zared's head back and dribbling the cum inside.

I thought Zared would swallow it, but he didn't. He took his turn in tasting before he grabbed me and gave it back where it started. Pressing the warm, wet ball into my mouth.

I accepted it, even licking his lips to make sure I got all of it.

By now, it tasted different, but no less delicious than it started. I smiled at all of them and swallowed it down. Every last drop.

"Well, that was hot," Tavian remarked. "Ryze, I thoroughly enjoy your idea of a rest. We should definitely all *rest* more often."

"We absolutely should," Ryze agreed. He stepped over to me and cupped the back of my head in his hands.

"You are amazing. After everything you've been through since we met, most would be ruined. But not you. You're stronger, tougher and even more beautiful." His throat bobbed with emotion. "I need you to know I love you."

"I love you too," I told him. I kissed him, putting all of my emotion and warmth into it.

I broke off and turned to Cavan. "I love you too."

He smiled. "And I love you."

It felt good to say that to them. I wasn't sure if I'd get the chance to do it.

"I hate to interrupt," Tavian said. "But I just want to say I love Ryze. I told Khala and Zared, but I never told you. I thought it might make things awkward, but I want you to know."

Ryze grabbed his arm and pulled him over. "I love you too." They kissed each other lightly, tentatively at first.

Seeing them like that warmed my heart and my body.

Vayne and Zared both slipped an arm around me and leaned into me.

"It's like one big happy pack," Vayne remarked. "We managed to avoid full-blown war and everyone loves everyone else."

"Does that mean you love Zared?" I asked.

Zared leaned and looked around me to him, his eyebrows raised.

"I love him like a brother," Vayne said with a grunt. "Just like the rest of them. I don't want to touch you, but I don't mind your company once in a while."

"Thanks," Zared said sarcastically. "You too. I guess we're back to training when we return from Fraxius?"

"Definitely," Vayne agreed. "We don't want you getting soft."

Zared scoffed. "I could never get soft. I could get hard again though." He grinned.

While Ryze and Tavian kissed, Zared, Vayne and Cavan slipped off with me to my nest.

SEVENTEEN

"This is going to be strange." I gripped Zared's hand and found it as sweaty as mine.

"Going to Havenmoor was weird enough. Then, I was thinking about seeing you. I wasn't thinking so much about being surrounded by humans again. Going to Phikus, knowing they'll only see me as Fae..."

"And they'll only see me as a human in the company of Fae," Zared said.

His tone made me turn to him. The expression on his face was sad, reflective.

"You're hoping to discover you're part Fae, aren't you?" I asked gently.

"Wouldn't you?" he asked back. "Think about what it might mean for both of us. I'd age slower. I might even live almost as long as you. We could grow old together. Before any of this happened, that was all I wanted for us. Now..."

He sighed. "I know it never would have happened. You were always going to become who you are."

"Why do I get the feeling you're saying goodbye to me." I cocked my head at him. "If you want to stay in Phikus, I won't stop you." Tavian might try, possibly the rest of the pack as well, but it had to be his choice.

"Not a chance," he said easily, immediately. "Whatever happens, you're stuck with me. I feel like..." He frowned.

"What do you feel like?" I prompted gently.

"When I first came here to the Winter Court, I felt angry. I wanted to force you to go back with. Even after you changed. I wanted to be anywhere but here amongst the Fae. But now, I know they aren't that different to any of the humans in Ebonfalls. It's taken me a while, but I know it now. In most cases, they're better than anyone there."

"Here, they ask for permission to strap my ass," I said with a smile. "That seems like a dozen lifetimes ago. I watched Hycanthe have her choker removed before me. Now she's literally High Lady of the Court of Dreams. Tyla is living her best life, enjoying what Havenmoor has to offer. And I'm the great-grand-daughter of the High Lady of the Court of Shadows."

"And I'm a part of your pack," he said. "And somehow I have two Fae lovers." He didn't elaborate on any potential for him to form a relationship with Ryze or Cavan. There was plenty of time for that.

"But you wish you were Fae too," I said.

I hesitated for a moment. Frowned. "I wonder if I could do what Lyra says she can. In theory, I have some of the same kind of magic as she does. I should be able to remove stone from people if you get stuck again."

It hadn't occurred to me at the time that might have been possible. If it was, what else might I be able to do?

"I trust you," he said without reservation. "It can't hurt to try."

Those sounded like famous last words to me, but I took him farther aside from where the others were getting ready to go to Fraxius. Ryze, Tavian and Vayne were arguing some point about how armed they should be. Cavan was watching on and adding a word here or there. They didn't notice us move away.

Zared sat on a chair near the window. I knelt beside him.

"I'm not really sure what it is she does," I admitted. "When I brought those fish back to life, I felt...under their skin."

I hadn't given it much thought until now. Too many other things had occupied my time and thoughts. Now I thought about it, I realised I could have sliced off a layer or two.

"I'll try to take a peek."

He nodded. "I said I trust you. I know you're not going to kill me. And if you do, you know how to bring me back to life, right?" He gave me a smile that was now tentative.

I almost backed away and told him no, I wouldn't even *try* to do anything to him.

I didn't because he wanted this, and because if I stepped away now, he'd ask Lyra to try instead. He'd risk everything to know the truth.

I took a deep breath and put a hand on his muscular bicep. His rock hard muscles gave me reassurance. If he trusted me, then I could trust myself.

I grabbed hold of what magic I could get. Now the mist was gone, I could access more than ever. Cavan surmised the mist was somehow created by me from my magic. It was a part of me. Now it was gone, I had less of a drain on the rest of me.

I delved into Zared, worming the magic under his skin.

He shivered lightly. "That tickles."

I smiled. "It's good to know I can tickle you from the inside and the outside. I know how much you love being tickled." About as much as I did. Not at all.

"Don't make me regret letting you do this," he said in a mock growl. Even speaking playfully like that, he got my pulse racing.

I never could resist his growls.

I delved in further, trying to discern what might make him Fae and what would clarify that he was all human. I looked for a hint of magic, but didn't find one. I didn't expect to. I wouldn't have found one in Tavian either, so that was far from an indication.

I pushed a little further, until I reached a place inside him that seemed familiar. Strangely so. I couldn't figure out what it was at first.

"What the fuck?" I whispered.

"No offence, but that's not what a man wants to hear when you're literally under his skin," Zared said softly. "I'd prefer something along the lines of, 'oh my gods, he's hot on the inside too.'" He grinned.

"Which is undeniably accurate." I hadn't known Ryze approached until I heard him speak near me. The rest of the pack was close now too.

"Definitely accurate," Tavian agreed.

"You two are out of your minds," Vayne told them. "I'm clearly the best looking under my skin."

"Says you," Tavian said.

I shook my head slightly at their banter. Only they would argue over who was the best looking on the *inside*.

Cavan crouched down beside me and brushed his fingers over the side of my neck. "What is it? Is he part Fae?"

"I..." I considered a response while I delved a little deeper. "I think he might be... But, I don't know, there's more to it than that."

Zared twitched. "What do you mean?" He sounded scared, but didn't pull away.

I looked over to Cavan. "When Dalyth put that block on his mind—"

"What did she do?" Zared sounded frantic now. His heart started to beat faster.

"Nothing," I said quickly. "This isn't about her. This is about the block. I thought it was something—I don't know—unnatural and intrusive."

"But now?" Cavan asked. "What do you think it was?"

"Now I think maybe she used..." I thought about it for a few moments longer.

"She used his body against him, I guess you could say. Like the alpha-order you put on me to ignore all other orders, and to put aside what...*he* did to me. The order acts on natural instincts. I needed to forget and move on, for my own sanity. Without that, I'd still be a mess. But the orders don't always follow what an omega really wants."

"He overrode what was best for you. His order forced your omega instincts to respond to him," Tavian said gently.

I tried not to shudder. "Something like that," I agreed. "When an omega goes into heat, those instincts take over. He used those against me."

"Are you saying I *wanted* to forget you?" Zared asked.

I glanced up his face. "No. You said yourself when you got here, you wanted to leave. You were under a lot of stress and pressure. She took that and used it against you."

"That makes sense, but what does that have to do with whatever you've found now?" Ryze asked.

My gaze went over to him. "All we want in life is to belong. We don't want to be the odd one out."

"I prefer to be the odd one *in*," Tavian said. "It's much more fun that way."

I smiled at him briefly. "Do you remember the border patrol?"

"The young Fae male with the human ears?" he asked. "I remember that. He definitely would have been an odd one out."

Of course, Ryze couldn't resist saying, "That's the Summer Court for you."

Cavan rolled his eyes.

"I think those of us who are part Fae have the same kind of block Dalyth put on Zared's mind. It keeps us from looking different to those around us. That particular Fae either had a smaller block or none at all." I was guessing here. Unless there were others like him, we'd never know.

Cavan nodded slowly. "You think when you went into heat, the block was destroyed? That's what made you transform."

"That makes sense," Tavian said. "It had to be something that was triggered off. A block is as good a word for it as any."

"Are you saying Zared has a block like that?" Vayne asked bluntly. Trust him to get right down to the point.

"That's what it feels like," I agreed. "It feels familiar because I had one the same."

"Wait a minute, are you saying that if you take the block away, I'll transform?" Zared asked. He looked hopeful. And terrified.

"I'm not sure," I admitted reluctantly. I didn't want to get his hopes up and then dash them again. He'd be devastated. "It might take something like a mating heat, or it might kill you."

Silence hung in the air, thick and heavy.

"I'm guessing a mating heat is out of the question," Tavian remarked.

"He's definitely a beta," Ryze said. "So yes, it is out of the question. Unfortunately. Three omegas would be even more fun."

Zared's face swivelled towards him, then back to me.

"This isn't something you have to decide right now," Ryze said. "That block has been there this long, it can stay for as long as you need, if not forever. Which, if Khala is right, is longer than we initially anticipated."

That was certainly something to thank the gods for.

"Have you ever heard of anything like this?" I asked Cavan.

"To be honest, I don't think anyone has thought to look," he admitted. "We knew to watch for alphas and omegas, but beyond that... No. Very few humans would have allowed themselves to be delved with magic like this. It's possible this is more common than we know."

I nodded slowly. He was right about humans not letting Fae in, in this way. I wouldn't have let anyone delve into me.

"Do it," Zared said softly. "I want you to try to take the block out now."

"Are you sure?" Tavian asked.

"I'm absolutely sure." Zared nodded firmly. "I want this. Do it."

I hesitated for longer than a few moments. I appreciated his faith in my abilities, but I was a little short on faith in myself.

"If this is what you really want..."

He twisted his upper body and took my hands in his. "This is what I want. I want to be one of us in every way that counts."

"You are one of us in every way that counts," I told him. "Just because you don't have pointed ears—"

"It makes me the odd one out," he said.

"You still belong," I argued.

"Do I? Didn't you just say we have a block to make sure we do belong? Mine was to make sure I belonged with other humans. That's not my life. I don't need it. I need *this*. I need *you*. I want you to do this for me. *Please*." He begged me with his eyes.

I exhaled softly. "All right, I'll try, but it may not work. It might just be a part of you. If it is, if nothing happens, I love you. No matter what you look like. No matter..."

I shook my head. "No matter what."

"I love you too," he replied. He sat back in the chair and put his head back. "I'm ready."

"Wait," Tavian said. He stepped over and kissed Zared on the mouth. "I love you."

"I love you too," Zared told him. He waited until Tavian stepped back and closed his eyes.

"I'm ready."

CHAPTER
EIGHTEEN
KHALA

I almost told Zared no, but the look on his face convinced me to close my own eyes and delve in deeper still. The block was different to the one in his mind. He was born with this one. It was as much a part of him as his eye colour or his stubbornness. I couldn't change either one of those even if I wanted to, which I didn't.

Fortunately, the block wasn't in his mind. His mind was a complicated place, I didn't want to touch that again if I didn't have to.

On the other hand, it was close to his heart. I'd have to go carefully.

"Tell me if this doesn't feel right," I said. "I'll stop straight away if it does."

He murmured his agreement and sat completely still. I suspected he was holding his breath.

Like I had with the one in his mind, I worked magic around the block, testing and teasing to see if it would come away.

The moment my magic touched it, it flinched. It leapt onto my magic, completely untangling itself from him.

"What the fuck?" I let out a short cry of surprise. The block was completely gone.

Zared's heart beat rapidly a few times, then stopped entirely.

"Fuck," I whispered.

Over the pounding in my ears, I heard Tavian frantically calling out Zared's name.

"He's not breathing." I couldn't tell who said that. I could hardly think past my own panic.

"Khala, take a breath," Cavan said. "Stay calm. You know what to do."

"Yes, you do," Ryze agreed. "Khala, you can do this. You have the magic of the gods inside you."

574

His words echoed around my mind.

The magic of the gods...

The magic of the...

The magic of...

The magic...

The...

I grabbed every bit of it I could and worked heat into Zared's heart. Not hot enough to burn, but hot enough to work its way inside and pump for him. Once. Twice.

I put air into his lungs to inflate them. In. Out.

Don't you dare die on me, I silently begged. *I need you.*

If I killed him, I'd never forgive myself. For the rest of my life, I'd wish I hadn't told him about the block. I should have kept my lips shut. I should have—

Zared gasped in a breath. His heart started to pound on its own.

A moment later, everything started to shift. His whole body started to change from the inside out.

I pulled my magic free of his body before it was consumed.

His back arched against the chair. Eyes shot open. He tilted his head back and cried out in pure agony.

His face became pale. His chin grew longer, more pointed. His ears lost their roundness. His eyes changed from human, to the Fae catlike shape. Even his hair seemed to grow longer. His body became slender and lithe, if just as muscular.

When I thought he couldn't take any more pain, he slumped down, covered in a sheen of sweat. He panted heavily out his nose and groaned.

He sat like that for a good few minutes, catching his breath. Eventually, he looked up, looked over at me.

"That sucked."

I smiled, relieved at hells to hear him speak. "How do you feel?" I asked.

That was shorter and less dramatic than when I transformed. Potentially because of the way it happened. It wasn't a spontaneous change. Or an unexpected one.

He shrugged and ran a hand up his face and over his ear. "I feel... The same. I guess I don't look the same?" He poked a finger at the tip of his ear.

"You look even more attractive than you already did," Tavian told him.

He grabbed Zared's hand and pulled him to his feet. He tugged him over to a mirror on the wall. "See for yourself."

Zared stared at himself for what seemed like a lifetime.

I was about to ask him if he regretted letting me remove the block, when he said, "Tavian is right, I do look even more handsome." He grinned at his reflection.

I socked him on the arm. "You're just as handsome as you were."

"Yeah, but—" He turned around to face me. "I'm taller than you again."

I looked up at him and grimaced. "I knew I should have left you the way you were. Maybe I could try to put you back."

"Not a chance," he said lightly. "I'm one of us now. Inside and out."

"Fucking hells," Vayne growled. "I'm never going to hear the end of this from Ryze."

Ryze looked at him innocently. "I have no idea what you mean."

"Bullshit," Vayne spat. "You're probably already planning to replace me with him." He jabbed a finger in Zared's direction.

"I wasn't," Ryze said slowly. "But now..."

Cavan clapped Vayne on the shoulder. "If he tries to do that, you can always come and command my army. I could use someone with your experience."

Ryze looked outraged. "You do not have my permission to poach my commander."

Cavan responded with a sly smile. "Fine, I'll poach Zared."

Ryze pretended to splutter, while Tavian laughed. "You two are adorable together."

Cavan and Ryze both looked at him and rolled their eyes.

I shook my head at the lot of them and grabbed Zared's wrist. "I'm sure you want to get changed before we go to Phikus," I said. "You seem to have outgrown your clothes."

He glanced down at his pants, which were now a hand span too short. "Well, fuck, you're right."

Did I imagine it, or was his voice deeper? Sultrier? Holy gods.

He looked back up. "Any way of knowing which court I might have come from?"

It was Ryze who responded. "Judging from your hair and eye colour, and your tendency to be as grumpy as shit, I'd say you're from the Winter Court."

A smile slowly grew on his lips. "Hells, for all I know you could be my son. Would that be funny?"

"No," Zared stated. "Not even a little bit." He shot Vayne a dirty look when the army commander chuckled. "Fuck off."

"That's fuck off, *sir*, to you," Vayne told him. "I'm still your commanding officer. More so, now no one will question your presence in my army."

"I'm thinking of poaching him to finish his assassin training," Tavian said thoughtfully.

"Don't you start," Vayne growled.

Tavian grinned. He didn't even look slightly apologetic.

I shook my head at them all and pulled Zared away to hunt down a new pair of pants for him.

"Are you sure you're all right?" I asked. "It takes time to get used to looking and feeling different."

"I feel fine," he said. "Better than fine. My vision is clearer. My hearing is stronger. I bet if you made a wall of ice across the river, I could run as fast as any of you. Faster. I'll be quicker with a sword too. But—"

I wasn't surprised to hear him add that on. Of course there had to be a but somewhere in there.

"What is it?" I asked gently.

He pulled me into his room and closed the door behind us.

"Aren't you curious to know if my cock is as big as theirs now?"

I should have known that was the first thing he'd think of it. That might have been his motivation for wanting to change in the first place.

Men.

"Now you mention it, I might be a little curious," I said, giving him a sideways, cagey look.

"Good. Get on your knees and take him out." He crossed his arms over his chest and arched an eyebrow at me.

I smiled and lowered myself down onto the rug that lay on the floor. My eyes on his, I undid the front of his pants and eased them down.

I lowered my gaze and blinked a couple of times.

"Holy gods." He was longer and thicker than he was before. As I expected, he had no knot, but what he had was impressive as fuck.

"Suck me," he ordered. "I want to know how I feel in your mouth."

"Yes, sir." I gripped his length in my fingers and teased his thick tip with my tongue. I traced circles all the way around and tasted the pre-cum that leaked from his slit. I fastened my mouth around him and started to suck lightly.

He quivered. "This feels different too. More...sensitive. More... I don't know, just more. Gods, it feels so fucking good."

He tangled his fingers in my hair and drove me harder on and off his cock. His hips moved in rhythm with my sucks.

Eventually, he pulled me off him and drew me to my feet. "On my bed, now. I need to be inside you."

My whole body was throbbing with need. I scrambled onto the bed, shedding clothes as I went. By the time I lay back on the mattress, I was naked and dripping wet.

He was just as gloriously naked as he stepped up to the side of the bed. He grabbed my ankles and dragged me down to him until I lay with my ass right on the edge. He locked my legs around his waist and impaled me on his heavy cock.

His lips dropped apart. "Gods, I didn't think it could feel better than you did before, but this is something else. So tight. So fucking good."

He stayed like that for a while before slowly thrusting into me, his eyes half closed as he took his time. He reached in between us to run his fingers over and around my clit.

"Do I feel good to you?" he asked. "Do I feel better to you than I ever did before?"

I groaned softly. "You feel incredible. You fill me so much. So fucking much." I rocked my hips gently, sliding myself across his fingers and letting my muscles milk his cock.

"I'm going to fill you even more," he said. "I'm going to fill you to the brim with my cum. That is going to be even better too. So much it's going to fill you until you overflow."

"Gods, yes please," I said breathlessly. "I'm going to come."

"Yes, you are. Come on my cock." He rubbed more deliberately now, slender fingers feeling even more incredible than they used to. Expertly bringing me to the edge and holding me there before I tipped all the way over into sweet oblivion. The world shattered into a million tiny lights before coming back together again.

He came a moment later, thrusting, driving hard into me, his teeth gritted. "Fucking hells, yes." He grunted and panted several times, groaning and grinding, drawing out every delicious drop.

Finally, he gasped and sagged, panting heavily before he caught his breath. "So fucking good," he whispered. "Fucking incredible."

He slowly slid out of me and gripped my knees. He held me like that, my legs spread wide, watching as his cum trickled out of my pussy. Letting go of one knee, he pressed his finger into the entrance to my pussy.

"Don't want it to dribble out too quickly."

He stayed like that for a few minutes before sliding his finger out and pressing it between my lips. "Suck."

I opened my mouth and sucked his finger, tasting the combination of him and myself. Delicious.

"We're going to go to Phikus with the others. I'm going to enjoy knowing you're going to be sticky with my cum the entire time." He turned me slightly to the side and slapped my ass before stepping away. "We should hurry or they'll leave without us."

"They better not," I growled. But I jumped up and started to pull my clothes back on.

NINETEEN

VAYNE

Zared looked like the cat that got the fucking cream when he and Khala finally reappeared. She was still combing her fingers through her hair and patting it down into place.

Ryze grinned. "It's about time you two reappeared." No doubt, like the rest of us, he'd felt them screwing down the bond. "We were about to leave without you."

"No, you weren't," Zared said.

It would take some time to get used to the way he looked now. The asshole was taller than me, and wider too.

Luckily I had looks, brains and personality.

"Figures the first thing you'd do when you looked like the rest of us was fuck Khala," I told him.

"Because it's exactly what you'd do?" Tavian asked. He was busy checking all his knives were in place all over his body. If you didn't know him, you wouldn't think he had any, but he seemed to have found a way to carry ten of them. I got the impression his life's ambition was to see how many he could carry without looking armed. As life ambitions went, it wasn't a bad one, I supposed.

"Damn right it is," I agreed. I adjusted my sheath on my shoulder, making sure my sword was sitting right. Earlier in the day we had a conversation about whether we should go to Phikus unarmed, or at least without visible weapons.

I'd argued it was a quick way to end up dead. Fortunately, Ryze agreed. He wore his bow and quiver on his back, although Phikus was nestled beside a lake that meant Ryze's magic would probably do.

I suspected he was slightly jealous of Khala's apparent ability to use her magic anywhere. Only slightly jealous though. Ryze didn't really do feelings like that too often. Even Fae life was too short for that kind of shit.

I caught Cavan looking at Zared, in the corner of my eye. I turned towards him the same time Zared noticed his expression.

"What?" Zared asked.

Cavan inclined his head slightly. "I was thinking this might be easier if you still looked human."

"Too late for that," I pointed out. "If you thought it would be a problem, you should have said so before Khala did the thing she did." I wasn't going to pretend to understand how any of that worked.

"Do you think that would have changed anything?" He seemed genuinely curious.

"Not one thing," I said. "Once they were set on doing what they did, that's what they were going to do. Nothing you or I could do about that."

"Would you have tried to stop them?" Ryze asked him.

Cavan considered the question for a moment. "I'd be a hypocrite if I said I'd try to stop someone from transitioning, but it does raise some issues. How many are there like him who don't know it? Would they want to know? And how many Fae could change to look human? If they could, would they?"

"For the record, I don't want to know," I said. "And if I did, the answer is no. I like me just the way I am."

Khala stepped over to me and pressed the back of her knuckles against my cheek. "We like you just the way you are too. I love you just the way you are."

"Me too," Tavian said.

"Yes, yes, we all love Vayne as he is," Ryze said. "I think we should keep this to ourselves for now. It raises far too many questions we don't have time to answer. Same with Khala's ability to bring people back to life. I'd hate to be cynical and suggest people might want to abuse such an ability, but they might."

"They very much would," Cavan agreed. "Not to mention the fact if the humans knew the Court of Shadows had an ability like that, there's no chance they'd agree to share their land."

"I hope you have a backup plan," I said. "Because there's no chance they're going to agree to this."

"Maybe not," Ryze said, "but we have to try, if only so we can go back to Vernissa and say we did." Judging by the look on his face, there was no backup plan.

I sighed softly to myself. So far, the inevitable all-out war hadn't happened yet. Even with the griffins, the Court of Dreams didn't have the resources for it.

The Court Of Shadows, on the other hand, had a lot more people. They were also a lot more desperate. They wanted out of those caverns and I had a feeling there was nothing they wouldn't do to achieve that.

They also had the ability to encase people in fucking stone. I shuddered at the memory.

Ryze nodded to Cavan. "You're more familiar with the land around Phikus than I am. You might as well make the portal."

For once, no one turned it into a sexual innuendo. If that didn't speak volumes about the tension, nothing would.

Cavan checked his weapons, then opened a portal in front of us.

His portals were freaky as fuck, I have to admit. I felt like I was about to step through the flames into the depths of one of the seven hells.

Before anyone else could, I took Khala's hand and we stepped through together. I kept her a little behind me, in case we encountered something nasty on the other end.

As commander of the army, it was my job to make sure the other side was safe. As a member of her pack, I wanted to keep her close.

We stepped out on grassland that reminded me of the Court of Dreams, but without the castle. Although, since the court didn't have a castle anymore either, I looked around carefully, just in case.

No, this definitely wasn't the same place. For one thing, there was no hill. Nothing but flat farmland, with trees dotted here and there.

"It's pretty," she remarked. We moved aside to let the others step out.

"If dirt and cows are your thing," I remarked. "No running hot water. No decent taverns anywhere close." Nothing but wheat and corn as far as the eye could see.

"You prefer the city?" she guessed.

"Definitely," I agreed. "Don't get me wrong, this is nice, but it's...boring. I'd go as crazy as Tavian in half a day."

"Some would say you're already almost there." Ryze stepped out behind us.

I smirked at him.

"There's nothing wrong with being crazy," Tavian was on Ryze's heels. "Some people would say sanity is overrated."

"Are you those people?" Cavan asked. He closed the portal behind us.

Tavian grinned. "I'm certainly *one* of those people. If you all look deep inside yourselves, you'll find out you are too."

I grunted softly. "Speak for yourself. In fact, don't. Let's get to Phikus and get this over with." I wasn't big on talking at the best of times. Ryze and Tavian would talk anyone's ear off if they got the chance. Mostly I tuned them out unless they had something interesting to say.

"How far is it?" Khala asked. She scanned the skyline and obviously came to the same conclusion I did. It must be a long way, because the land was so flat we'd see it if it wasn't.

"A few kilometres," Cavan said. "In that direction." He nodded. "Once we get to the road, we'll see humans. Especially ones with horses. By the time we arrive in Phikus, they'll know we're coming."

"We may not be welcome," I pointed out.

"It's very likely we won't be," Zared agreed. He seemed disconcerted to realise he really was one of us. He couldn't march into the city and have a pleasant chat with the king.

Granted, that was unlikely anyway. Kings and High Lords didn't seem to like it when people just turned up unannounced, expecting to see them. How they'd take it when a group of Fae turned up was anyone's guess. Hence that we were armed.

At uneasy times like this, I was glad people around me could use magic. Three of them could open a portal and get us the fuck out of here at a moment's notice.

Although, fighting people who lived in a place like this wouldn't be an even match anyway. They were farmers and shopkeepers. Regular humans, not soldiers. No doubt the king had guards around here somewhere, but they wouldn't be at the level of skill of the rest of us. Not to mention the speed and agility that came with being Fae.

"We'll deal with that when we arrive," Ryze said easily. He didn't seem even slightly concerned we'd be turned away. Then again, it was Ryze. He'd charm his way in.

I glanced over to Khala and shrugged. Keeping close by her side, I started walking.

"PHIKUS LOOKS like a bigger version of Ebonfalls," Khala remarked. She appeared underwhelmed, to say the least. I wasn't sure what she was expecting, but it clearly wasn't this.

Personally, I wasn't surprised. Human cities seemed more focused on function than form. The buildings were timber and stone cubes, with windows in the side. Some had balconies, but most didn't. All of them were built three or four steps off the ground, with a small set of stairs leading up to a door.

Some of the buildings were painted white or green, but the paint was peeling off in chunks. In spite of that, they looked structurally sound. None of the fascia was cracked, or the corbels broken. Most of the windows were clean, including a couple of high transoms.

If nothing here looked like flowers, or leaves, or ice, at least they were well taken care of.

The largest building in the city was a castle nestled in the centre. It was smaller and less grand than the one in the Court of Dreams, but was otherwise strikingly similar. In spite of its simple design, it was clearly Fae built, and old. One of many abandoned by the Court of Shadows when they went into hiding.

Chin raised, I walked through the streets with the others, ignoring the plentiful stares of humans as we went past. Mutters followed us as we went, but no one tried to approach us.

None of them dared.

Tave, being Tave, smiled and spoke to several of them as he went past.

"Lovely day," he called out to one of them. "Nice flowers. I might have to come back and buy some." Pleasant greetings from a man who would cut their throats in a moment if he needed to. Of course, he'd also buy flowers from them.

I had a feeling he'd get much more enjoyment out of them if the petals were sprinkled with droplets of blood. No one ever said he wasn't fucked up.

Although, I was having these thoughts about him, so maybe we were as bad as each other.

The closer to the castle we went, the more the rumblings increased. In volume, in intensity and in barely suppressed aggression.

I kept my whole body tense and ready. I locked eyes with a few humans before walking past. If they thought about attacking us, they might think again. Sometimes, a little bit of fear went a long way.

"I have a bad feeling about this," Khala said. "Something isn't right."

"Something is definitely off," I agreed. "It's probably just that they don't like Fae here. They wouldn't see any of us very often." Unless one of the other courts visited more frequently than we did. The gods only knew what Harel used to get up to. Thiron either, for that matter.

"That could be it," she said slowly. "But I don't think—"

She was interrupted by the opening of the wide gate that led from the castle.

A contingent of Fae stepped out towards us.

At the front of them walked Wornar.

TWENTY

KHALA

I froze completely. I couldn't have run if I wanted to, which I didn't.

I didn't know what I wanted to do more, punch him in the face or knee him in the cock. Maybe slice off his balls with a blunt knife and feed them to him.

The list was long and without any firm answers. Maybe I could start at the top and work my way down slowly.

"Well, well, well," Wornar drawled.

"One of my favourite sources of water," Ryze drawled. His eyes glinted dangerously. I suspected the only thing keeping him from killing Wornar was wondering why the hells he was here in the first place.

Wornar smirked. "Always with the ridiculous comments. So predictable."

"I won't say the same about you," Ryze said. "What the fuck are you doing here?"

Wornar raised his hand to admire his own fingernails. "One of my contacts told me those lost courts returned. It was a simple matter to realise, sooner or later, they'd come here, wanting their land back. I thought it prudent to come and warn King Mikohal of that possibility. My apologies, that *probability*," he corrected. "I didn't quite anticipate your involvement, but I should have. You can't help but stick your nose in places it doesn't belong."

Vayne gripped my hand and growled. "At least he doesn't stick his cock where it doesn't belong."

Wornar laughed. "Is that what she told you? That she didn't enjoy every moment of fucking me?" He took a step towards me. He locked his eyes on mine and continued.

"She loved every bit of it. She begged me to pound my cock into her pussy. She loved pleasing me. She loved the feeling of my cum between her legs."

My stomach turned and suddenly the feeling of Zared's cum on my thighs didn't feel so exciting.

"You know as well as I do all of that is a lie," I said coldly. "You violated me. You violated the alpha-omega connection. You used it for your own twisted enjoyment. I hated every single touch."

He stepped closer and I had to force myself not to flinch. He was so close I smelled the alpha scent all over him. Even now, some tiny amount of omega instinct wanted me to please him.

Fortunately, the amount was so tiny I could dismiss it, but not before that made my stomach turn too.

He raised one eyebrow and said, "I don't care. You're one insignificant, worthless, omega slut. Your opinion of me is entirely irrelevant. What matters right now is that you are aligned with the court that would make war on poor, innocent humans."

Only Vayne's hand in mine kept me from blasting him to oblivion. Forget the seven hells, he wouldn't even be in enough pieces to go there.

"What have you done with the King?" Cavan asked.

Wornar's gaze slid off me like a snake. "I have done nothing but warn him of the enemy on his doorstep. I have assured him the Spring Court will come to his assistance if you should try to press the matter."

Tavian started to laugh. "That's the funniest thing I've heard in a long time. Even funnier than Ryze's daddy jokes." His smile faded to a brutal, calculating fury. "You realise you would stand against the combined forces of the Winter, Summer and Autumn Courts as well as the courts of Shadow and Dreams."

Wornar tilted his head to the side. "You'd go to war for humans? Have you become that bored?"

"You tell us," Ryze said. "You're also here, provoking conflict. Thiron wouldn't have wanted this."

"Thiron was a fool," Wornar said scathingly. "He would have let you walk all over him. Or better yet, he would have bent over and let you fuck his ass."

"You say ass fucking like it's a bad thing," Tavian remarked. He still had the dangerous look on his face. His hands were at his sides, but I doubted anyone was fooled. He'd have a couple of blades in his hand, and then embedded in Wornar before anyone could blink.

"We'd like to speak to King Mikohal ourselves," Cavan said. "Unless you're declaring war right now, step aside and let us pass." His voice was ice cold fury.

For the first time, Wornar looked uncertain, but that didn't last more than half a heartbeat. It was immediately replaced with his usual slick smile.

"Of course, I don't think you'll be welcome. In fact, I should escort you. Humans are known for acting rashly. I wouldn't want any of you to die the moment you step through the door."

The expression on his face said otherwise. His gaze scanned us and settled on Zared. He briefly looked confused, but shook his head and looked away. He must have recognised Zared, but didn't understand how he was now Fae.

I sure as fuck wasn't going to explain it to him.

He turned on his booted heel and gestured for the Fae who accompanied him to proceed us all back into the castle.

"Keep your eyes out for an ambush," Vayne whispered, his mouth next to my ear.

He didn't need to tell me that, all my senses were on alert for anything Wornar might try to pull. I trusted him as far as I could spit him.

Not, I thought, grimacing to myself, that I'd want him anywhere near my mouth.

"Can I just kill him?" Tavian asked Ryze.

"Not yet," Ryze said regretfully.

"What about me?" Zared asked. "Can I kill him?"

"Not you either," Ryze said wearily. "We need to find out what's really going on here. We can't do that if he's dead."

"Listen to Ryzellius," Wornar said over his shoulder. "You'll never understand the situation if you kill me. Not to mention the fact that the king would definitely not speak to you if you commit an act of aggression in his castle."

"Wouldn't want to leave a puddle of blood on his pretty tiles," Vayne said sarcastically. "Fuck that, yes I would."

Wornar clicked his tongue. "So bloodthirsty. Ryze, it's past time you had your subordinates under control. Perhaps you should surround yourself with more omegas and order them to protect and respect you."

Only my hand on Vayne's stopped him from lunging at Wornar and driving his sword through his chest. I didn't know why I stopped myself. If it wasn't for Ryze telling the others not to kill Wornar, I might not have bothered.

"I don't need to order people to respect and protect me," Ryze said to Wornar. "They do it willingly. It's you they don't respect, because you're a shithead. Does King Mikohal know you're a rapist?"

I thought Wornar might get angry and give us an excuse to kill him, but instead he laughed.

"That's such a harsh word for someone who always takes what he wants too," Wornar said lightly.

"Did you give Khala a choice of which alpha she spent her first heat with? Don't answer that, I know you didn't. The only option you presented her with was yourself. You as good as forced yourself on her. And you didn't even tell her she might be part Fae. No, she had to find that out for herself. I gather it was extremely unpleasant for her. You consider yourself so much better than me, In the end, you and I are very much alike."

I felt Ryze's fury through the bond and his struggle to keep from planting his fist in Wornar's face.

In addition to that, I felt a surge of remorse. As ugly as Wornar's words were, they were also painfully accurate. Ryze did do all those things, but not out of malice or the need to control me. He did it because he didn't want me to get hurt. There was a world of difference between that and what Wornar did to me.

Wornar was wrong, they were nothing alike.

We passed through doors big enough to fit a carriage and a couple of horses, and into the castle itself.

Humans who were occupied with their daily tasks stopped to stare at us. One woman almost lost hold of a basketful of laundry. She caught it at the last minute before hurrying away.

Several children stopped to stare, eyes wide, mouths opened. I offered them a smile, but none smiled back. They didn't look scared, just overwhelmed.

"The throne room is through here." Wornar led the way as if he thought he owned the place.

The further we went, the more uneasy I felt. It wasn't just being in Wornar's company, it was something more than that. He was definitely up to something, I just didn't know what.

I found myself walking with Cavan on one side of me and Ryze on the other. Tavian and Zared walked ahead and Vayne behind. The message was clear. If anyone touched me, they would be dealt with.

If they managed to get close enough.

We stepped into the throne room. It was sparsely decorated, like the rest of Phikus. Function instead of form.

One wall was lined with narrow windows, wide enough for an archer to fire through. Not big enough for a person to climb in or out.

The other wall was covered in tapestries depicting past kings and queens. They all seemed to have a fondness for black horses.

The ceiling was lined with beams of dark wood that looked like they'd hung there for hundreds of years. The stone floor was worn smooth from thousands and thousands of passing feet.

A long, woollen carpet led the way from the door to the foot of a throne made of the same heavy wood as the ceiling beams. The throne itself was covered with no carvings, no decorations, no gems inset in the surface. The only remotely ornate aspect of it was a padded cushion on the seat. Even that was relatively simple.

Unlike Fae, it was easier to discern the ages of humans. King Mikohal was in his middle fifties, lines on his face, grey heavily sprinkled through his hair. His brown eyes were bright and clear, He looked weary. And wary.

He seemed as cautious of Wornar as he was of the rest of us. He was dressed in simple leather pants, and a cotton shirt laced at the chest. His feet were covered in boots that reached to just under his knees.

If he wasn't seated on a throne, I would have taken him for a huntsman, or maybe a soldier.

When I was human, I would have found him attractive. On some level, I still did, but the glance he gave me said it wouldn't be reciprocated because of how I now looked, and the company I kept.

Honestly, I wasn't too impressed with the company he kept, either.

"Your Highness," Wornar said smoothly, with a hint of sarcasm. "As I told you, Fae have come to take your kingdom from you. I told them you wouldn't allow it, but they insisted upon speaking to you. They are most insistent these lands don't belong to you."

Mikohal regarded us with a steady look. He was careful, but not afraid.

"Your Highness." Ryze gave him a bow. "Allow me to introduce myself. I'm High Lord Ryzellius of the Winter Court. Wornar here is mistaken about our intentions." He jerked his thumb towards Wornar.

His lack of title didn't go unnoticed by Wornar, who looked irritated.

Mikohal stood slowly. "Are you suggesting you haven't come on behalf of the Court of Shadows to ask for Fraxius to be returned to them? Or that at the very least, you expect us to reside with them and be subservient to them as we once were?"

"No one said you had to be subservient," Ryze said.

"But you do not deny the rest?" Mikohal asked.

"I cannot deny that we have come on their behalf to ask," Ryze admitted. "But—"

Mikohal nodded at Wornar just as I realised what was off about the atmosphere in the room.

"Kill them," Wornar ordered.

"They're all omegas!" I shouted as a dozen Fae closed in on us.

CHAPTER
TWENTY-ONE
KHALA

I shuddered under the pressure of Wornar's order. I didn't feel the need to obey, but it still weighed down heavily on me.

Was this how Zared and Vayne felt when they were encased in stone? I gritted my teeth and shook it off.

The pack had swords and knives in their hands, or magic ready, but none moved to use them. Not yet. Instead, they arrayed themselves around me, facing outward. All five of them felt confident, but waiting. Biding their time. Not one would make a rash move. If they did, it might cost them their lives. No, they needed clear heads and they knew it.

The Spring Court omegas moved in closer, wary. Some looked eager to kill us, many didn't. It was the latter which made up my mind.

I thought taking a life might be difficult.

Especially when it wasn't in self-defence. When no one was wielding a sword, about to remove my head from my shoulders. Or had an arrow aimed at my heart.

Wornar wielded no weapon of his own. No knife. No magic as far as I could tell. He stood off to the side, watching, expecting his weapons to do his work for him.

In the end, it was easy to slide magic under his skin. Through his chest and into his heart. It was a simple matter of curling magic around the organ and making it stop.

The widening of his eyes was the only indication that he understood what was happening. An accusing glance in my direction. His whole body froze. He toppled to the ground.

The reluctant omegas froze. Several took hurried steps back, hastily lowering weapons. A couple looked around in confusion, as if they had no idea where they were or how they got there.

The remaining four shook their heads, undecided, until one lept at Ryze.

She got a blade through her forehead from Tavian for her trouble. The other three separated and lunged at Vayne, Cavan and Zared.

Vayne made quick work of his opponent with a couple of parries and slashes with his sword.

Cavan incinerated the third without raising a sweat. A pile of ashes lay on the floor at his feet, still smoldering for a long while.

We all turned to Zared as he parried with his new sword. He never told me where he got that from. It was a much better sword than the one he used to carry. And he was better with it than the last time I saw him use one. Then, Ryze intervened, firing an arrow into the forehead of Zared's opponent.

Now, Zared held his own, pushing the Fae back further and further before he got the chance to run his blade through the man's chest. He gave Ryze a look when the High Lord started to applaud.

"You really do know how to use a sword," Ryze teased, but his expression was approving.

"I can practice on you if you'd like," Zared said dryly.

Ryze grinned in response and crouched down beside Wornar. "That was almost anticlimactic."

He pressed his fingers to Wornar's neck. "He's definitely dead. It seems like he just...dropped down dead. Perhaps his heart gave out under the pressure of his new duties." He clicked his tongue. "I did tell him being High Lord was a lot of work and stress. He should have listened."

He glanced up at me and smiled. He clearly knew what I did, but this way there would be no retribution for assassinating Wornar. It was nothing more than a sad tragedy.

In reality, it was bittersweet. Vengeance didn't feel as good as I thought it would. Whatever I was expecting, it wasn't the hollow feeling inside. Maybe later, the full extent of what I did would sink in.

Either way, Wornar was dead and the omegas acting under his orders were free from him.

Mikohal flopped back down on his throne and shook his head. "What in the name of the gods?"

"Wornar was controlling their minds," Ryze told him. "When he died so suddenly, it broke the connection. They are free to return to the Spring Court."

He gave them a meaningful look. Something along the lines of, 'get the hells out of here before I change my mind.'

They scattered like petals in the breeze, hurrying out the door without looking back.

Mikohal rubbed a hand over his forehead and eyes. "I didn't realise Fae had such an ability." For the first time, he looked slightly scared.

"We don't," Ryze said. "Only certain Fae and only over other certain Fae. We couldn't do that to you." He didn't elaborate any further.

"You won't force me to surrender my land?" Mikohal asked carefully.

"I can't and I won't," Ryze assured him. "All I want is to work out some compromise that suits everyone. That may prove difficult, if not impossible. The Court of Shadows currently resides in caves. I'm sure you'd agree that's no way to live."

"Neither is constant suspicion of one's neighbours," Mikohal said. "I fear that's what will result from letting them return here. However..." He looked thoughtful, if somewhat reluctant. "There is a place, if they're willing to work at clearing the land and building their homes from scratch."

"What place?" Cavan asked slowly.

"Allow me to show you." Mikohal rose. "If you'll please come this way." He gestured towards the door, indicating that we should follow him out.

He led the way to a small library. All right, a large library, but small compared to the one in the Winter Court.

Along one wall hung a map. It showed all four of the seasonal courts, their names written in a flowing script. Beside them were the three human lands, Fraxius, Freid and Gerian. The map also showed an island far out to sea. On that island was a small image of a griffin. The only thing missing was Nallis, as far as I could tell.

"Here," Mikohal pointed to a jut of land to the south of Fraxius. "Myself and the King of Gerian have spoken many times as to who owns this land. Both countries claim it as their own. We often have border skirmishes over that land. Most of our wars have been fought over it. Perhaps giving that piece of land to the Court Of Shadows would be a compromise that may satisfy both countries."

"You think the King of Gerian will give up any claim he has over it?" Cavan asked.

"Not easily," Mikohal conceded. "But faced with the possible alternative of handing over land we already occupy to the Fae, then perhaps he will understand it may result in fewer conflicts."

"Or more conflicts," Tavian said softly.

"Potentially," Mikohal agreed. "I won't claim it's an easy compromise. My own people may strenuously object, but I see no clear alternative."

"Neither do I," Ryze said. "Now would be a good time to establish the council Cavan would like us to have. In my experience, open communication is the best way to prevent further misunderstanding."

Cavan raised an eyebrow at him.

Ryze smiled. "It took me a while, but I got there."

Cavan shook his head, but smiled back. "A Council of High Lords, High Ladies and Kings might be the quickest way to reach an agreement."

"And Queens," Mikohal said. "Freid has a queen now." For some reason, he looked amused at that.

I wasn't sure if it was because he thought women shouldn't rule, or if there was more to it.

"Ah, and Queens," Ryze said. "I'm more than happy to host such an auspicious gathering."

Cavan looked like he might object, but he gestured his agreement after a few moments. "I'll send word to Hycanthe, Illaria, Vernissa and whoever will take over from Wornar."

"No assholes," Tavian said.

"No assholes," Cavan agreed. "I gather Wornar has a younger brother who is much less ambitious than he was. With any luck, we can convince the Spring Court to accept him as High Lord."

While they talked amongst themselves, I looked more closely at the map.

"What is it?" Zared placed a hand on my shoulder and leaned in to look too.

"That has to be where the Court of Dreams ended up." I pointed at the island. "It was right here all along and we didn't know."

"It was also right there in the room you slept for ten years," he said. "This might have been another clue for us to find if we came here instead of doing all the things we did. Or it might be a coincidence. Someone went there at some point and saw they were griffins, so they added it to the map. They might have had no clue there were Fae there too."

"You're right," I conceded. "I just wonder what else there is out there we didn't find."

"Like an island full of dragons?" Tavian stepped over to the other side of me and laughed softly. He had that glow about him that he always had after he killed someone.

"Maybe," I said, giving a laugh of my own. "What would you do if there was an island on this map and it had a dragon on it?"

"That's easy, I'd tell Ryze. He'd organise the ship and we'd sail there to take a look. He wouldn't be able to resist the lure of an adventure like that."

"Going to a place that might have dragons would probably not end very fucking well," Vayne said over my shoulder. "With my luck, I'd get eaten. Not in the good way." His lips brushed the side of my neck.

"But you'd go anyway," I said.

"Someone has to keep Ryze and Tavian out of trouble," Vayne replied. "Besides, if they go, you'd go, and wherever you go, I go. So yes, I'd go."

"So would I," Zared said. "Wherever you go, I go. You can't even send me back to Havenmoor any more."

"Are you all right with that?" I asked him gently. "Neither of us can go back there again."

"I don't want to go back," he said steadily. "I want to move forward. With you and our pack."

I smiled and lightly kissed his mouth. "Good, because that's what I want too."

The past was the past and I didn't want to think about it anymore. I made a note to mention to Ryze and Cavan that the council should discuss the Silent Maidens, and what was best for them, now and in the future. They deserved to understand what was happening to them and why. We needed to find a better way to ascertain who was an omega long before they went into heat.

I might even be able to tell who would transition and who wouldn't. That would change a lot of things.

"Although, I wouldn't mind having a bit of peace and quiet after this," I added. "Now the lost courts aren't lost anymore and Wornar is dead, maybe we can relax. I can't remember the last time I sat down and read a good book."

"Neither can I," Tavian said. "I can recommend one about a Fae with wings who goes into this weird human world. It even has a talking cat in it."

Vayne snorted. "How do people think up these things?" He rolled his eyes toward the ceiling.

"It's called having an imagination," Tavian told him. "Maybe you should try it sometime."

"I have a very good imagination." Vayne sniffed. "Right now, I'm imagining Khala naked, her mouth around my cock."

"Funny, I imagine that quite often," Tavian said.

"Me too," Zared said. "I also imagine Tavian's mouth around my cock. I guess that means I'm more imaginative than Vayne."

Vayne shook his head. "No, I could imagine that too, I just don't want to."

"Sure," Tavian drew out the word. "I bet you imagine it all the time, and that's all right. If you imagine it often enough, it might even happen." He wiggled his eyebrows at Vayne, who simply muttered something under his breath in response.

CHAPTER
TWENTY-TWO
CAVAN

"Wornar's brother seems heartbroken at his loss," Ryze said sarcastically.

I snorted softly. "I'd noticed that. It would seem Rian recently discovered Wornar was responsible for Thiron's death. I would assume from that, his days were numbered. His sudden death in such a tragic manner took care of the problem for the Spring Court."

My only regret was not incinerating Wornar myself, but Khala killing him the way she did made things easier for everyone. Except perhaps for her. She seemed conflicted about what she'd done. I understood that.

Taking a life wasn't something anyone should do lightly, no matter what they did to deserve it. I would have been surprised if she enjoyed it as much as Tavian seemed to. She wasn't the bloodthirsty type. She was practical and did what needed to be done.

I glanced over the wide table and watched Rian as he spoke to Illaria. He looked very much like his brother, but without the predatory glint in his eyes.

"I heard a rumour," Ryze started.

I turned to him and grimaced. "I don't think I should listen to any sentence that starts with that. Especially after the last twenty years. Rumours have a way of sometimes being partly true, and sometimes not."

I'd likely always be curious as to why the stories of the two lost courts got so mixed up. I don't suppose it mattered much, but I was naturally curious and liked nothing more than learning and understanding new things.

No, that's not accurate, I loved nothing more than Khala, but learning new things was high on my list.

Ryze grinned. "You'll like this one."

I sighed. "Fine. Are you going to make me ask or are you going to tell me?"

Trust him to find yet another way to taunt me. He seemed to have made it his life's work over the last couple of weeks. Naturally, I gave it back, and then some.

I couldn't let someone like him get the better of me. In addition, a little healthy competition never hurt anyone. It kept things interesting between us. Or maybe it was just our way of skirting around whatever might be forming between Ryze and I.

I didn't know what that was yet, and I didn't think he did either. I doubted we'd ever have the kind of relationship with each other that we had with Khala, or that Tavian and Zared had, but he was slightly more tolerable than I'd spent the last couple of hundred years thinking he was.

I might not admit it to myself, but he could kiss.

"I think I should make you ask." The asshole smiled more broadly.

I shook my head. "You're such a prick."

He laughed. "So I've been told." He picked up a piece of cheese from the platter in front of him and popped it into his mouth. "I heard a rumour that Rian and at least two other Fae men are in a relationship with a human woman. Apparently, she lives in the Spring Court with them."

My eyebrows rose. "That is interesting. Most human women would run from an arrangement like that. She must be very impressive." After I lost Alivia to Terald, I was bitter towards humans for a long time.

Now I'd come to realise the only important thing in life was love. I thought about taking Khala back home to see her parents, but I suspected she wasn't ready for that yet. Some day she would be. And if she wasn't, I wouldn't press the issue. That was her choice to make.

"Any woman who would put up with one man, much less several, might be considered impressive," Ryze said. "Some of us can be a pain in the ass at times." He quirked an eyebrow at me.

"I see you're referring to yourself," I said dryly. I watched vaguely as Khala and Zared led the two human kings and the human queen into the conference room. They looked anxious to be surrounded by so many Fae, but they took their seats with their backs straight, chins raised.

I hoped this meeting would dispel some myths about Fae for them. And vice versa. It was past time for some serious change and today was the start of that.

"Not one asshole present," Ryze observed. "Apparently Illaria quietly... 'took care' of Harel. No more Wornar. Even you and I get along."

"Will wonders never cease?" I asked.

"Hopefully not," he said. "Life would be boring without any wonders in it."

"The gods forbid you'd get bored," I said drolly. "I can only imagine the things you'd get up to to keep yourself amused."

"You're starting to sound like Vayne." Ryze took a sip of water from his clay cup.

"I didn't realise Vayne was so wise." I took a sip of my own water. I would have preferred wine, but we agreed we should start the meeting with clear heads. Wine would have to wait until later.

"Of course he is. He wouldn't be the commander of my army if he wasn't wise." He eyed me like I planned to poach Vayne after all.

I thought about it, but the pack spent so much time between the Winter Court and the Summer Court that I saw Vayne almost daily. Having him work for me would be potentially awkward. Better to leave that to Ryze.

Khala stepped around the table and leaned down between us. Gods, she always smelled so good. Even better now she was close to her heat again. So was Tavian. I fully intended to make sure I was present for both of them. If they went together...all the better.

"Everyone's here," she said. "Will you start the meeting?"

Although the meeting was taking place in the Winter Court, they all agreed I should speak first.

"This was your idea," Tavian had pointed out. "You've been trying to unite us all for twenty years. It seems appropriate to me." He shrugged.

No one argued with him, not even Ryze.

"THAT WENT WELL, for the most part." I took a long sip of wine.

As we had anticipated, the King of Gerian wasn't impressed with the proposal to give land to the Court of Shadows.

He was even less impressed at the suggestion he could give up the part of the country he actually *could* claim. Of course, he argued that Fae should live on Fae land. We'd gone around and around on the subject for a couple of hours before coming to a tentative agreement.

The Court of Shadows would occupy the land for the time being and we would see how things went.

Meanwhile, the Court of Dreams would return to the island and make their life there. From what Hycanthe said, none of the griffin riders objected to that arrangement. All they wanted to do was live their lives with their beasts and not put them at risk again. Since no one wanted the giant creatures in their cities, no one argued that decision. Hycanthe's well practised glare helped in that regard.

To my surprise, the humans actually asked about running hot water. The easiest part of the meeting was offering to show them how to install and use it. That had helped sway the King of Gerian to our way of thinking about that contested piece of land. That was understandable; a hot bath was a lot better than conflict any day.

We were almost finished, when Khala asked to address Vernissa.

"Since you have land out in the sun, I'd like to suggest you discontinue the practice of culling older Fae."

The room fell silent in shock, before people started to mutter. The humans in particular. They seemed very surprised Fae would undertake such a barbaric practice.

"If we no longer have to limit our numbers, then we can certainly reconsider the practice," Vernissa replied, not meeting anyone's eye.

"I don't see any reason why you have to limit yourselves," Khala told her. She looked around the table. "Does anyone?"

Most of us shook our heads, but the King of Gerian looked like he might disagree.

"If your numbers grow, you may need more land," he said finally.

"It would take several generations for that possibility," I told him. "Fae generations. Hundreds of years. I promise you, it will be no concern of yours or many many of your descendants."

Eventually it might be a problem, but not in the near enough future to matter to any of us. That would be an issue when and if it became one.

He seemed mollified at that. "Then I don't suppose it matters what I think. I would prefer the murder of people just because they're older to not catch on." His tone was gruff, but his bearded face curled up in a smile. Given he was at least in his late sixties, that was a sensible standpoint.

Vernissa was visibly unimpressed at hearing it referred to that way, but she got the biggest concession for her and her court. They would live their lives in the sun, like they wanted to.

I wondered if any of them would stay underground, in spite of saying they'd follow her wherever she led. That was a matter for them.

"In the end, that was much more civilised than when we met up at Nallis," Ryze said. "Although, in the past, it was more likely someone would turn up with an army, not for a friendly conversation."

"Are you referring to yourself again?" I asked. I couldn't resist needling him. That was something I didn't think we'd ever stop doing to each other. It was certainly a lot better than trading insults with actual bad intentions behind them.

"Probably." He grinned. He swirled his whiskey around in his glass and took a sip. "We've all come a long way since then."

"Especially you two," Tavian remarked. He sat on the couch beside Khala, her feet in his lap. "Which I have to admit I'm conflicted about." He pulled off her socks and started to rub her feet.

We all turned to him and waited for him to elaborate.

"On one hand, seeing you kiss was one of the hottest things I've ever seen in my life. On the other hand, if you two get along with each other, we won't have to sneak into the Summer Court ever again."

He sighed exaggeratedly. "I enjoyed doing that. I've been thinking, I might take on a few jobs as an assassin again. I miss sneaking and killing."

"Whatever makes you happy," Ryze told him.

"As long as you don't assassinate me," Vayne said with a grunt.

"I'll only assassinate you if someone pays me a lot of money to do it," Tavian said. He smiled lopsidedly.

Khala socked him on the arm. "No assassinating Vayne," she scolded. "No matter how much money someone offers you to do it."

Tavian pouted playfully. "Fine, just for you, I promise not to assassinate Vayne."

She gave him a steady look.

"Or anyone else in the pack," he added. "The only thing I'll stick inside any of them is my cock."

She nodded, satisfied. "That goes for all of you. No killing each other."

"You're a hard woman," Ryze joked. "What if we want you to kill us so you can bring us back to life? I've always been curious about what that would be like."

She and Tavian exchanged a look and started laughing.

He raised his hand in question, but shook his head when he got no answer from them. "Young Fae these days." He smiled indulgently.

"Finally," Vayne said. "Ryze admits he's old."

Ryze stuck his middle finger up at him. "I am not fucking old, they're just young.

From the chair in the corner, Zared groaned. "I just realised I have hundreds of years to spend with all of you."

"Fuck, me too," Vayne said.

That only made Tavian and Khala laugh harder.

I couldn't help smiling at all of them.

CHAPTER
TWENTY-THREE

KHALA

T trailed my fingers across the surface of the conference table. If I wasn't there myself, I might not believe so many important people sat around it only hours earlier.

Honestly, I was surprised they all turned up. The three human leaders in particular. They were all both willing and curious. More open-minded than Harel had been. More receptive to change than I think any of us expected.

When I thought back to how scared I used to be of the Fae, I felt somewhat silly. What I was afraid of, was the unknown. Now I knew Fae in general weren't scary, any more than humans were. There were bad Fae, just as they were bad humans, but bylarge most were reasonably harmless.

And those who weren't, fate caught up with them sooner or later.

"This is where you got to," Ryze said softly. He stepped into the room, followed by Cavan. "We were starting to worry."

"I wasn't worried," Cavan said. "But I was curious. You seemed...contemplative."

"Yes, that's exactly it," Ryze agreed. "It was a lot of deep thought for this place." He smiled.

"I'm sure deep thought happens a lot here." I let him wrap his large hands around my hips and lift me until I was sitting on the conference table, between his legs.

"A lot of deep something," he agreed. He leaned in and kissed me lightly.

Cavan regarded us both for a moment or two. He stepped back over to the door.

I thought he was about to leave, but instead he turned the lock until it clicked into place.

That small act made my blood heat and race through my veins. I'd been with all of the guys in different combinations, but never just the two High Lords. The idea made me hot and wet between the thighs.

All right, when was I not hot and wet between my thighs these days?

Ryze eased me down so I lay on my back in front of them both. He ran his hands up and down my body before undoing the front of my pants and sliding them down my hips.

Cavan stepped around to the side of the table and undid the buttons of my shirt, one by one. He peeled the sides away, exposing my breasts.

"I have never seen anyone more beautiful," he said softly. He leaned down to press feather light kisses on my nipples.

"Thank you," Ryze said, as though Cavan was speaking to him. He pulled the gusset of my panties aside and kissed the inside of my thigh and up to my pussy.

Cavan snorted softly without stopping as he delivered a circle of tiny kisses around my breast. Every so often, he'd graze the tip of his nose, or his cheek, against my nipple. The slightest touch sent white hot heat through me, making me shiver with anticipation.

Ryze teased all around my clit and entrance, barely touching, taunting.

"Please," I said breathlessly.

"Please, what?" Ryze asked.

"Please, sir." They were going to drive me wild with their gentle touches and brushes. "Sirs," I corrected.

"I think she's asking to be our dirty little slut." Cavan kissed the underside of my breast.

Ryze's eyebrows rose in a combination of surprise and curiosity. "Is that right?" He cocked his head at me. "Are you begging to be our dirty slut?"

"Yes, sir," I replied. I swallowed hard. "I'm yours to fuck." If they didn't soon, I was going to go out of my mind. My hand drifted down to my pussy and over my clit, before Ryze gripped my wrists and pressed both of them against the tabletop above my head.

"That's our job," he scolded lightly. "We're the ones who are going to make you come, not yourself. Right, Cav?"

"Correct," Cavan agreed. "We'll make her scream."

"I like the sound of that." Ryze leaned down further and ran his tongue from my rear hole, all the way up to my clit. "Mmmm, delicious. Hands down the tastiest meal ever to be eaten at this table."

I moaned at the jolt of lightning that shot all the way through me, from my toes, to the top of my head. He'd barely touched me, but I knew what he'd feel when he slipped the tip of his finger inside my pussy.

"She's so wet. I think you're right about her wanting to be our slut." He slid his finger in and out of me a few times before adding a second one.

"I don't think she's ever been so wet in her life. I could make several portals just out of her pussy." He was clearly impressed.

"Of course she is, because she's a good girl," Cavan said. "She's the best girl."

I couldn't decide what I liked better, being called a good girl, or the dirty talk. In the end, I decided I liked all of it.

Especially when Ryze said, "She's a good little slut."

He licked me again, more firmly this time, while gently but smoothly fucking me with his fingers.

Cavan fastened his mouth around my nipple and began to suck, just as gentle and teasing as Ryze. After a minute or two, he switched to the other nipple, tasting me lightly with his tongue before drawing my tender flesh between his lips and sucking more firmly.

Through the bond, I saw myself how they saw me. They loved the way I moaned and writhed, and shivered at their touch. I saw their excitement at driving me closer and closer to the edge. I felt it build as their touch became firmer. All of their attention was on me and wanting me to come.

I pressed my palms against the cool top of the conference table as I shattered into too many pieces to count. Probably something beyond infinity. I was overwhelmed with the feeling of bliss and their arousal at my sounds and movement. So overwhelmed, I plunged over the edge into an even deeper abyss. One I would have happily stayed in with them forever.

Ryze lifted his shining face and carefully swivelled me around to face Cavan as the other High Lord unfastened the front of his pants and freed his erection.

Cavan gripped my hips and pulled me onto his cock. With almost painful slowness, he impaled me all the way to his knot.

He waited for me to get used to him, before pushing inside a little further. Bit by bit, my muscles stretched to take in his knot.

I didn't think it was possible, until he was fully seated inside me. I was stretched almost all the way to the limit, and it felt utterly incredible. He was touching me everywhere inside and out in exactly the right place and precisely the right way.

"Gods," I breathed. "That feels incredible."

"You feel incredible," he said. He ran his hands up and down my sides, his hips still until finally he started to move slowly. He slid all the way out of me, before impaling me to his knot again.

Ryze pushed his own pants down to the top of his thighs and gripped my chin between his thumb and forefinger. He turned my face towards him and pressed his cock against my lips. "Open up, there's a good slut."

I smiled at him with my eyes and opened my mouth to take in his thick length almost to the back of my throat. His cock was so warm and hard, yet smooth against my lips. I'd always enjoyed sucking cocks, but these five guys had the best that ever passed my lips. So firm, throbbing and giving. Everything a girl could want in a cock.

I kept my gaze on Ryze while he rolled his hips, sliding himself in and out of my mouth.

"So fucking good," he said breathlessly.

"So very good," Cavan agreed. He thrust faster, then slower, then faster again, always careful with his knot. He wanted to wreck my pussy, not break her.

They found a rhythm and started to build towards their own orgasms.

I let them feel how they felt, moving in and out of my body with even, deliberate strokes. I showed them how good it was to have two, incredible men fucking me at the same time. And how much I loved both of them.

I felt love back from them, in a wave of devoted adoration. I'd never felt as loved in my life as I did then. That increased by three, when the other men sent their own warmth and love down the bond.

Along with some envy on the part of Vayne that it wasn't his cock down my throat. I told him he could get a turn later. That seemed to mollify him.

Between all of that and the way Cavan's knot brushed over my clit with each thrust, I tumbled over the edge for a third time.

I arched my back and screamed toward the ceiling, the sound muffled by Ryze's cock and his cum as he spilled himself into my mouth. I swallowed down every drop quickly, before I choked on the delicious mouthful.

Cavan came at the same time, stilling and grunting as his hot cum rushed out of his tip and into my body.

As one, we all sagged, panting and waiting for our blood to cool.

"That was even better than deep thought," Ryze said.

I slipped my mouth off his cock and laughed softly. "There's a time and place for everything."

"It's always a good time and place for showing you how we feel about you," he said. He pulled his pants up and leaned over to kiss my mouth. "I love you."

"I love you too," I told him. "If you're not careful, I'll get used to all this love."

"We'll make sure you get used to it." Cavan eased his cock out of me and did up his own pants. "Because none of us is going anywhere without you."

"You better not," I said in a mock growl. "I might decide not to be a good girl after all.

"If you aren't a good girl, then I'm going to have to spank your ass," Cavan said in a mock growl of his own.

I grinned. "In that case, I'm going to be very, very bad."

CHAPTER
TWENTY-FOUR
KHALA

Wind whipped hair across my face. I brushed it off and stepped over closer to the rubble. What was once a proud castle, was now nothing more than a pile of stones, splintered wood and shards of glass. Anyone who moved around here, had to tread carefully to keep from stepping on anything sharp or dangerous.

"We were fucking lucky we got out in time," Vayne remarked. He stood with his arms crossed, taking in the sight with an unusually sombre expression. Even for him. We'd come close to dying, but we hadn't. We were two of the lucky ones. Two of all too few.

"Did they find Dennin and Ramela?" He tore his eyes away from the ruins long enough to glance at Hycanthe.

"It took five days of searching, but they did." It was Jezalyn who answered. "They seemed very determined to find them."

"They wanted to know for sure they were dead," Hycanthe said flatly.

She'd gone into heat two days ago. As a result, she seemed more relaxed than she had before. She appeared very much like she found her place in the world. A challenging one, to be sure, but something she could be a part of and be proud of.

I was happy for her. For both of them. As happy as anyone could be while standing amongst a place that held the memory of so much death.

I remembered the children who ran around kicking the ball. Some of them got out in time, but many didn't. It was always the innocent who got caught up in situations made by others for reasons that had nothing to do with them. The fact it was children, compounded the heartbreak for all of us.

"They actually found six people still alive." Jezalyn smiled, clearly thinking back on the last few days. "Five of them children. A couple were badly injured, but Hycanthe healed them. She's become like a hero to the court." She turned fond eyes on her lover.

"Jezalyn might be exaggerating slightly," Hycanthe said. "I did what I had to do, that was all." A blush crept up her cheeks.

"And they love you for it," Jezalyn told her. "Almost as much as I do." She kissed Hycanthe's cheek.

"There's nothing wrong with owning what you can do," I said. I sent a quick thanks to any of the gods who might be listening for sparing those five young lives. They were lucky to have not only made it through the collapse of the castle, but to have her there to heal their bodies. No doubt it would take longer to heal their minds.

"You're going to rebuild the castle?"

"Down off the hill." Hycanthe seemed pleased with the change of subject. "The griffins are good at picking up the blocks of stone and moving them. They're carrying them down there one by one for the builders. There was talk about leaving the ruins as they are, but everyone agreed they didn't want a reminder of the past. They're looking to the future. The new Court Of Dreams is going to be built on a brand-new foundation. We're all excited about what we're making here."

"We really are," Jezalyn agreed. "We're a community." Her eyes shone with pride and unshed tears. "Everyone has been amazing and willing to pitch in whenever they're needed. We have griffin riders cooking and doing laundry, and farmers helping to take care of the griffins. For a while there, I was worried they wouldn't accept us. None of them knew us. Why should they follow people they don't know? But everyone has been wonderful. All anyone wants is a fresh start. And to be able to travel to Jorius, and go into heat as the gods intended."

Hycanthe rubbed a hand over the back of her neck. "We need some more alphas, if the other courts can spare them. At the moment, we have only two, and four omegas. And I'm not sharing Jezalyn with anyone." She glanced at me and Tavian as though either of us might possibly try to poach her lover.

I resisted the urge to roll my eyes and nodded instead. "I'll put the word out. I'm sure there are plenty of alphas and omegas who'd welcome the chance to be part of a court that's building itself the way you're doing here. One of the things Cavan wanted was to encourage Fae and humans to move between any courts and countries without sneaking around." Many Fae didn't stay put in the court they were born in, but most did. He wanted them to go where they fit in and were content. That may be a more challenging dream to achieve than it sounded, but we could encourage people. Whatever came from that would come.

I suspected it might cause some tension with Vernissa, if her people decided to leave, but if any court needed fresh blood, it was hers. No doubt she'd welcome new arrivals if that was a choice some wanted to make.

"I think a lot of Fae would love the chance to ride a griffin," I added. No one could deny they were magnificent beasts. I'd never seen anything like them in my life, not even in books.

Vayne grunted. "Only if they're out of their minds."

"I want to ride a griffin," Tavian said from where he crouched beside the rubble.

"I rest my case," Vayne said. He dusted his hands on each other as though wiping the matter away.

Tavian grinned and rose to his feet. "Scared?"

"Yes," Vayne replied. "Yes, I fucking am. It's a long way down off the back of one of those beasts. But if you want to get on one, be my guest." He waved towards a pair who approached, wings outstretched until they landed beside the ruined castle.

They fastened their massive talons around blocks and heaved them up. With what looked like little strain at all, they lifted them several metres off the ground and flew away slowly with them held carefully in front of them.

"They are very useful." Ryze shielded his eyes from the sun with his hand. "I wonder how hard it would be to convince a couple of them to move to the Winter Court."

"What for?" Zared asked.

Ryze considered the question for a moment, but shrugged. "I'm sure I'd think of something."

"I think you want a couple of griffins for the sake of having a couple of griffins," Vayne said. He scowled at Ryze.

"What would be wrong with that?" Ryze asked.

"Griffins eat a lot," Cavan said. "I doubt the Winter Court would want to feed them if they're not productive."

Ryze shrugged. "I'll think of something."

I shook my head at him but smiled. Sometimes the High Lord was more like a young child than a man a few hundred years old. Always looking out for something new and exciting to do or see. So far, I'd managed to talk him out of dying, just so he knew how it felt to be brought back to life. The gods only knew how long that would last. His insatiable curiosity had no bounds.

I wouldn't have him any other way.

A couple more griffins flew in. One went to work picking up a block. The other landed near us.

Vayne took a couple of steps back from the beast, as though concerned she might eat him.

I admit to being slightly nervous in their presence myself. After the attacks, and the battle, they didn't exactly evoke the *best* memories. That was one of the reasons I was here. Partly to check on Hycanthe and Jezalyn to see if they needed any help, and partly to face my fearfulness of the beasts.

I was done living my life in fear. I wanted to face this one head on. The sooner I did that, the sooner I could put it behind me.

"Gavil wanted to talk to you when you came in to check on our progress," Jezalyn told me.

Hycanthe gave him the side eye, but Jezalyn squeezed her hand reassuringly.

I doubted Hycanthe had anything to worry about when it came to any other omega. Jezalyn was a one woman alpha.

I smiled at Gavil as he approached and slipped his helmet off.

"You're looking well," I told him. He looked slightly less anxious than the last time I saw him. Although, he still wore the misplaced guilt of taking part in the attack on his face.

"I'm feeling well," he replied. "I wanted to thank you for everything you did. Since you came here...everything has changed. Everything is better. Without Patric, Ramela and Dennin we are free. High Lady Hycanthe has already done so much for us. The Court of Dreams may yet live up to its name." He dashed a tear off his cheek.

I might have blinked back a few of my own. It was difficult not to be choked with emotion when I realised what impact I and my pack had on people like him. People who had terrible things done to them, none of which they deserved. He should have spent his life unscarred, going into heat when his body was ready.

Why no one founded an order of Silent Boys, I had no idea. Tavian was lucky to have avoided enduring either.

In the corner of my eye, I caught Jezalyn giving Hycanthe a look that clearly conveyed both pride and a healthy dose of, 'I told you so.'

Hycanthe shrugged and smiled slightly. "I'm just doing what any reasonable person would do."

"Because you're not an asshole," Tavian told her. "That part makes all the difference. Right, Ryze?"

"Right," Ryze replied. "It does, and that in turn helps us to make a real difference. I haven't had to kill anyone from the Summer Court in quite some time. It's remarkably refreshing."

"I hope it's something you'll continue to refrain from doing," Cavan said dryly. "I prefer my people not dead."

"Unless they deserve it," Hycanthe said. She raised her eyebrows at him.

Zared and I may have forgiven and forgotten, but she clearly hadn't. She didn't make trouble over it either though. She had enough on her proverbial plate without picking a fight with Cavan every chance she got.

"Part of our rebuild is going to be a place for Silent Maidens," Hycanthe said. "The omegas here know how it feels to be suppressed. We believe they're best equipped to help those omegas and alphas to deal with their first heat and the choice to suppress themselves if they prefer. Not all omegas want to go through heat. We intend to find a way to do that without suppressing everyone or their ability to speak. It may take some time, but we have plenty of that."

That was an admirable idea. She was right, this was the perfect place for it.

I wondered what my life would have been like with a sanctuary like this. Certainly very different to the way it actually went.

"If you need any help, you only have to ask. I'll do whatever I can." I turned back to Gavil and spontaneously gave him a hug. "You're more than welcome. I wish I could have done something sooner, but..."

"The time wasn't right," Cavan said. "You needed to become who you are before you could help everyone else. And you did. All three of you former Silent Maidens did. You've done so much to change...basically the whole world as I know it. Personally, I couldn't be more pleased."

I let him pull me into his arms and kiss me, not caring if we had an audience. Let them watch, it didn't bother me one little bit.

"There's one more matter," Ryze said when we came up for air. "If you'll excuse Khala and I for a few minutes." He offered his hand.

I took it and we walked side by side down the hill. Neither of us said anything until we reached the place where the castle was being rebuilt. Right now, it was nothing more than a patch of cleared land with a pile of blocks beside it. It would take months to build, but no doubt it would be impressive when it was finished.

"Cavan is right," Ryze said finally. "Since meeting you, everything has changed. Well, almost everything. Vayne is still grumpy as fuck. And Tavian still likes killing people for fun. And I still..."

He shook his head. "Some things are the same but most things have changed and they're wonderful. The last few months have been an adventure like nothing else I've ever experienced before. The best thing I ever did in my life was help you get away from that caravan in the rain. You and Zared."

He turned to me and cupped my cheek with his hands. "I love you."

"I love you too," I said softly. "Going with you three that day was the best choice I ever made. At the time, I had no doubt it was the right thing to do, even when I had no idea why or who any of you were. Hells, I didn't even know who *I* was. I don't know if the gods put you in my path, or if it was part of the Court of Dreams' plan. Whatever it was, I'm glad it happened."

He kissed me then, softly at first and then with increasing heat. His hands slid up the back of my shirt and skated over my skin.

"I'll never get enough of you," he said between kisses. "You and the rest of our pack. You're everything."

I couldn't argue with that. Not just because my mouth was busy, but because he was right. Our pack *was* everything.

I hesitated, mid-kiss as a surge came down the bond. Immediately, my whole body was throbbing and I was wet between my thighs.

"I know I'm a good kisser, but that's not what this is, is it?" Ryze asked.

I shook my head. "No. Tavian is going into heat."

TWENTY-FIVE

KHALA

Ryze threw open a portal to the hill beside the ruin. We leapt through just as Cavan opened one to the Winter Court.

We gathered around Tavian, who was already drenched in sweat, his eyes wide. He was pressed hard against Zared. When he saw Ryze, he grabbed his jacket, dragged him forward and kissed him.

"Let's get back home before this gets messy." Vayne all but shoved us into the portal and out the other side.

The moment Cavan closed the portal behind us, Tavian grabbed him and kissed him.

"I need all of you," he said, his voice hoarse.

"Whatever the omega wants." Ryze manoeuvred all of us towards Tavian's room.

By the time we got there, Tavian was already naked and all but purring between Cavan, Ryze and Zared.

I hesitated at the doorway. Tavian took part in my heat, but he may not want me here at his. It was his choice. He may choose to keep the alphas, or at least one of them, to himself the way Hycanthe would.

I'd understand if that was what he wanted, what he needed. He was the important one right now. Before I could step away, he grabbed my hand and pulled me down on the nest with the rest of them.

"I need you too," he said breathlessly. "Please stay." He pleaded with me with his eyes.

"Of course I'll stay," I said. "I wouldn't want to be anywhere else." Especially with my whole body responding to him the way it was. I was close to my own heat, but not close enough for him to set me off. Not this time anyway.

"Do we need—" Zared gestured over to the table to the side of the room where a half-full bottle of lubricating oil sat.

"No, during heat he makes his own," Ryze said. He was busy shedding his clothes and carelessly tossing them aside.

Vayne tugged me down to the end of the bed and started helping me out of mine.

Zared watched us for a moment with uncertainty, before he stepped over. He grabbed my foot and pulled my pants over it before dropping them on the floor.

Both of them grabbed the side of my panties and tore them right down the middle. Once I was naked, I returned the favour, helping them pull off shirts and slide off pants, and leaving them discarded where they fell. In moments, the floor was covered in a pile of leather, cotton and wool.

I found myself surrounded by five extremely attractive men with very erect cocks.

Fortunately, Tavian's nest was more than big enough to accommodate Ryze and Cavan lavishing attention on him, while I lay between Vayne and Zared. One omega and his alphas and another omega with her two betas. There was more than enough love and cocks to go around.

Tavian was already on all fours, Ryze kneeling beside him. The heat must have made Tavian ready quickly, because Ryze slid his cock straight inside him. He reached around to grip Tavian's cock in firm fingers.

Cavan stroked himself while he watched them fuck.

"You like how that looks?" Zared asked me. "Up on all fours then."

I scrambled up and looked over my shoulder at Zared, who slid his hands up and down my thighs and up to my pussy. He ghosted his fingers over my flesh so lightly I thought I might go crazy. Between that and the heat coursing through the bond, I might come with the slightest touch.

Vayne reached under me to run his hands over my breasts and pinch my nipples. He did that for a while before kneeling beside me and pressing his cock between my lips.

Just as he did that, Tavian came for the first time, and the second, squirting hot cum over Ryze's fingers.

Ryze came a moment later, once, twice. Panting, he moved aside to make room for Cavan. He leaned against one of the posts as the other alpha slipped into Tavian's ass.

Zared started to work me more firmly, fingers sliding in and out. "I think we need that oil after all," he said to Vayne.

Vayne nodded and slipped his cock out of my mouth to get it.

He handed it to Zared who opened it, dipped his fingers inside and worked them into my ass. Stretching me and making me ready with his warm, slippery fingers.

"Please," I pleaded. I needed to feel more inside me. Much more.

Zared slapped my ass once, twice, then slid his hand out of me and positioned his cock there instead. He gripped my hips and slipped his cock inside. He thrust into my ass a few times, then said something to Vayne.

I couldn't make out what it was past the pounding of blood through my ears. It didn't matter. All that mattered was how good he felt inside my body.

Vayne lay down on his back. He looked up at me and smiled. Actually smiled. His expression made my heart flip upside down and inside out. He should smile more often. But if he didn't, that would be all right too. It would make each smile that much more special.

Zared positioned me carefully before he lowered me onto Vayne's cock. He leaned me forward and pressed back into me.

I shivered with the deliciousness of being filled by both of them. I wanted to close my eyes and savour it, but I couldn't tear my gaze away from Cavan who was pumping heavily into Tavian.

Between the sight, the bond and the heat radiating off the other omega, I was absolutely gone. All I wanted was to get lost in this moment forever.

We all moved in rhythm to Cavan thrusts. All of our eyes on him and Tavian.

When Tavian came again, so did I. And again. And again.

My back arched. I drove myself harder onto Vayne's cock. I was so aroused I might almost have been on heat myself.

I cried out as I drenched Vayne's cock.

"Fuck yeah," Vayne muttered. "Gods, you will never *not* feel good."

"I'm going to come again," I panted. "Come with me. Both of you. All of you."

Tavian gripped Ryze's cock in his hand and worked at him while he rocked back onto Cavan.

"You heard her," he said breathlessly. "We can do this."

We thrust and rocked in near perfect unison before tipping over the edge into a shared oblivion.

We all cried out and panted as the bond was filled with a sensation of complete and utter bliss. The world could have ended then and there and none of us would have known or cared.

Luckily, it didn't end, but eventually I came down from my rush and lay tangled and panting with Vayne and Zared. For the longest time, we lay and watched Ryze and Cavan swap back and forth, making Tavian feel unbelievably good over and over again.

Eventually, Tavian grew exhausted. He came one more time before flopping down, taking Cavan with him.

"Oh my gods," he panted. "Best heat ever. I thought one alpha was amazing, but two..."

He sighed heavily. "I think I've died and gone somewhere incredible. Definitely no kind of hell. I need a bath, but I want to lie here for a while first."

He smelled of sex and cum, and satisfaction.

He snuggled up in the middle of all of us and nestled down.

"I love all of you," he said sleepily.

"We love you too," I told him.

"We all love you as well." Zared brushed hair off my sweaty face.

"I'm the luckiest Fae woman in the entire world," I whispered. The most loved, the most blessed.

The happiest.

THANK you so much for reading. If you'd love a steamy bonus scene, you cab grab yours here.

My next book is Heartless, Brutal Academy book 1

ABOUT THE AUTHOR

Maggie Alabaster writes reverse harem and, paranormal, sci-fi and fantasy romance.

She lives in NSW, Australia with one spouse, two daughters, one dog, and countless birds.

Sign up for Maggie's newsletter! Sign Up!

Join Maggie's reader group! Join here!

Follow Maggie on Bookbub! Click here to follow me!

Check out Maggie's website- www.maggiealabaster.com

ALSO BY MAGGIE ALABASTER

Ruthless Claws
Book 1 Ivory
Book 2 Crimson
Book 3 Elodie

Harmony's Magic
Book 1 Summoned by Fire
Book 2 Summoned by Fate
Book 3 Summoned by Desire

My Alien Mates
Book 1 Star Warriors
Book 2 Star Defenders
Book 3 Star Protectors

Academy of Modern Magic
Book 1 Digital Magic
Book 2 Virtual Magic
Book 3 Logical Magic
Complete Collection

Short reads
Taken by the Snowmen
Jingle All the Way

Also by Maggie Alabaster and Erin Yoshikawa
Caught by the Tide
Book 1–Pursued by Shadows
Book 2 Pursued by Darkness
Book 3 Pursued by Monsters

Printed in the USA
CPSIA information can be obtained
at www.ICGtesting.com
LVHW040341140924
790893LV00001B/11